About the Author

Jeffery Deaver is the bestselling author of a number of powerful suspense novels. He was a lawyer before quitting work to become a full-time writer. He divides his time between Washington, DC and California. *The Bone Collector* is now a major film starring Denzel Washington and Angelina Jolie.

Also by Jeffery Deaver

The Empty Chair
The Devil's Teardrop
Speaking in Tongues
A Maiden's Grave
Praying for Sleep
The Lesson of her Death
Mistress of Justice
Manhattan is My Beat
Death of a Blue Movie Star
Hard News
Shallow Graves
Bloody River Blues
Hell's Kitchen
The Blue Nowhere

The Bone Collector

and

The Coffin Dancer

Jeffery Deaver

First published in Great Britain in 2001 for WHSmith PLC
by Hodder and Stoughton
A division of Hodder Headline

A Coronet paperback

2 4 6 8 10 9 7 5 3 1

Hodder and Stoughton
A division of Hodder Headline
338 Euston Road
London NW1 3BH

A CIP catalogue record for this title
is available from the British Library.

ISBN 0 340 82325 9

Printed and bound in Great Britain by
Clays Ltd, St Ives plc

WHSmith PLC
Greenbridge Road
Swindon SN3 3LD
www.whsmith.co.uk

The Bone Collector

Jeffery Deaver

For my family, Dee, Danny, Julie, Ethel
and Nelson . . . Apples don't fall far.

And for Diana too.

Contents

1	King for a Day	1
2	Locard's Principle	101
3	The Portable's Daughter	203
4	Down to the Bone	309
5	When You Move They Can't Getcha	389

Appendix:

Extracts from Rhyme, *Physical Evidence*, 4th Ed. 401

1

KING FOR A DAY

"The present in New York is so powerful
that the past is lost."

John Jay Chapman

Friday, 10:30 P.M., to Saturday, 3:30 P.M.

ONE

She wanted only to sleep.

The plane had touched down two hours late and there'd been a marathon wait for the luggage. And *then* the car service had messed up; the limo'd left an hour ago. So now they were waiting for a cab.

She stood in the line of passengers, her lean body listing against the weight of her laptop computer. John rattled on about interest rates and new ways of restructuring the deal but all she could think was: Friday night, 10:30. I wanna pull on my sweats and hit the hay.

Gazing at the endless stream of Yellow Cabs. Something about the color and the similarity of the cars reminded her of insects. And she shivered with the creepy-crawly feeling she remembered from her childhood in the mountains when she and her brother'd find a gut-killed badger or kick over a red-ant nest and gaze at the wet mass of squirming bodies and legs.

T.J. Colfax shuffled forward as the cab pulled up and squealed to a stop.

The cabbie popped the trunk but stayed in the car. They had to load their own luggage, which ticked John off. He was used to people doing things for him. Tammie Jean didn't care; she was still occasionally surprised to find that she had a secretary to type and file for her. She tossed her suitcase in, closed the trunk and climbed inside.

John got in after her, slammed the door and mopped his pudgy face and balding scalp as if the effort of pitching his suitbag in the trunk had exhausted him.

"First stop East Seventy-second," John muttered through the divider.

"Then the Upper West Side," T.J. added. The Plexiglas between the front and back seats was badly scuffed and she could hardly see the driver.

The cab shot away from the curb and was soon cruising down the expressway toward Manhattan.

"Look," John said, "that's why all the crowds."

He was pointing at a billboard welcoming delegates to the UN peace conference, which was starting on Monday. There were going to be ten thousand visitors in town. T.J. gazed up at the bill-board—blacks and whites and Asians, waving and smiling. There was something wrong about the artwork, though. The proportions and the colors were off. And the faces all seemed pasty.

T.J. muttered, "Body snatchers."

They sped along the broad expressway, which glared an uneasy yellow under the highway lights. Past the old Navy Yard, past the Brooklyn piers.

John finally stopped talking and pulled out his Texas Instruments, started crunching some numbers. T.J. sat back in the seat, looking at the steamy sidewalks and sullen faces of people sitting on the brownstone stoops overlooking the highway. They seemed half-comatose in the heat.

It was hot in the cab too and T.J. reached for the button to lower the window. She wasn't surprised to find that it didn't work. She reached across John. His was broken too. It was then that she noticed that the door locks were missing.

The door handles too.

Her hand slid over the door, feeling for the nub of the handle. Nothing—it was as if someone had cut it off with a hacksaw.

"What?" John asked.

"Well, the doors . . . How do we open them?"

John was looking from one to the other when the sign for the Midtown Tunnel came and went.

"Hey!" John rapped on the divider. "You missed the turn. Where're you going?"

"Maybe he's going to take the Queensboro," T.J. suggested. The bridge meant a longer route but avoided the tunnel's toll. She sat forward and tapped on the Plexiglas, using her ring.

"Are you taking the bridge?"

He ignored them.

"Hey!"

And a moment later they sped past the Queensboro turnoff.

"Shit," John cried. "Where're you taking us? Harlem. I'll bet he's taking us to Harlem."

T.J. looked out the window. A car was moving parallel to them, passing slowly. She banged on the window hard.

"Help!" she shouted. "Please . . ."

The car's driver glanced at her once, then again, frowning. He slowed and pulled behind them but with a hard jolt the cab skidded down an exit ramp into Queens, turned into an alley and sped through a deserted warehouse district. They must've been going sixty miles an hour.

"What're you *doing*?"

T.J. banged on the divider. "Slow down. Where are?—

"Oh, God, no," John muttered. "Look."

The driver had pulled on a ski mask.

"What do you want?" T.J. shouted.

"Money? We'll give you money."

Still, silence from the front of the cab.

T.J. ripped open her Targus bag and pulled out her black laptop. She reared back and slammed the corner of the computer into the window. The glass held though the sound of the bang seemed to scare the hell out of the driver. The cab swerved and nearly hit the brick wall of the building they were speeding past.

"Money! How much? I can give you a lot of money!" John sputtered, tears dripping down his fat cheeks.

T.J. rammed the window again with the laptop. The screen flew off under the force of the blow but the window remained intact.

She tried once more and the body of the computer split open and fell from her hands.

"Oh, shit . . ."

They both pitched forward violently as the cab skidded to a stop in a dingy, unlit cul-de-sac.

The driver climbed out of the cab, a small pistol in his hand.

"Please, no," she pleaded.

He walked to the back of the cab and leaned down, peering into the greasy glass. He stood there for a long time, as she and John scooted backwards, against the opposite door, their sweating bodies pressed together.

The driver cupped his hands against the glare from the streetlights and looked at them closely.

A sudden crack resonated through the air, and T.J. flinched. John gave a short scream.

In the distance, behind the driver, the sky filled with red and blue fiery streaks. More pops and whistles. He turned and gazed up as a huge, orange spider spread over the city.

Fireworks, T.J. recalled reading in the *Times*. A present from the mayor and the UN secretary-general for the conference delegates, welcoming them to the greatest city on earth.

The driver turned back to the cab. With a loud snap he pulled up on the latch and slowly opened the door.

The call was anonymous. As usual.

So there was no way of checking back to see *which* vacant lot the RP meant. Central had radioed, "*He said Thirty-seven near Eleven. That's all.*"

Reporting parties weren't known for Triple A directions to crime scenes.

Already sweating though it was just nine in the morning, Amelia Sachs pushed through a stand of tall grass. She was walking the strip search—what the Crime Scene people called it—an S-shaped pattern. Nothing. She bent her head to the speaker/mike pinned to her navy-blue uniform blouse.

"Portable 5885. Can't find anything, Central. You have a further-to?"

Through crisp static the dispatcher replied, "Nothing more on location, 5885. But one thing . . . the RP said he hoped the vic was dead. K."

"Say again, Central."

"The RP said he hoped the victim was dead. For his sake. K."

"K."

Hoped the vic was dead?

Sachs struggled over a wilted chain-link and searched another empty lot. Nothing.

She wanted to quit. Call in a 10-90, unfounded report, and go back to the Deuce, which was her regular beat. Her knees hurt and she was hot as stew in this lousy August weather. She wanted to slip into the Port Authority, hang with the kids and have a tall can of Arizona iced tea. Then, at 11:30—just a couple of hours away—she'd clean out her locker at Midtown South and head downtown for the training session.

But she didn't—couldn't—blow off the call. She kept going: along the hot sidewalk, through the gap between two abandoned tenements, through another vegetation-filled field.

Her long index finger pushed into her flattop uniform cap, through the layers of long red hair piled high on her head. She scratched compulsively then reached up underneath the cap and scratched some more. Sweat ran down her forehead and tickled and she dug into her eyebrow too.

Thinking: My last two hours on the street. I can live with it.

As Sachs stepped farther into the brush she felt the first uneasiness of the morning.

Somebody's watching me.

The hot wind rustled the dry brush and cars and trucks sped noisily to and from the Lincoln Tunnel. She thought what Patrol officers often did: This city is so damn loud somebody could come up right behind me, knife-range away, and I'd never know it.

Or line up iron sights on my back . . .

She spun around quickly.

Nothing but leaves and rusting machinery and trash.

Climbing a pile of stones, wincing. Amelia Sachs, thirty-one—a *mere* thirty-one, her mother would say—was plagued by arthritis. Inherited from her grandfather as clearly as she'd received her mother's willowy build and her father's good looks and career (the red hair was anybody's guess). Another jolt of pain as she eased through a tall curtain of dying bushes. She was fortunate to stop herself one pace from a sheer thirty-foot drop.

Below her was a gloomy canyon—cut deep into the bedrock of the West Side. Through it ran the Amtrak roadbed for trains bound north.

She squinted, looking at the floor of the canyon, not far from the railroad bed.

What *is* that?

A circle of overturned earth, a small tree branch sticking out of the top? It looked like—

Oh, my good Lord . . .

She shivered at the sight. Felt the nausea rise, prickling her skin like a wave of flame. She managed to step on that tiny part inside her that wanted to turn away and pretend she hadn't seen this.

He hoped the victim was dead. For his sake.

She ran toward an iron ladder that led down from the sidewalk to the roadbed. She reached for the railing but stopped just in time. Shit. The perp might've escaped, this way. If she touched it she might screw up any prints he'd left. Okay, we do it the hard way. Breathing deeply to dull the pain in her joints, she began climbing down the rock face itself, slipping her issue shoes—polished like silver for the first day of her new assignment—into crevices cut in the stone. She jumped the last four feet to the roadbed and ran to the grave.

"Oh, man . . ."

It wasn't a branch sticking out of the ground; it was a hand. The body'd been buried vertical and the dirt piled on until just the forearm, wrist and hand protruded. She stared at the ring finger; all the flesh had been whittled away and a woman's diamond cocktail ring had been replaced on the bloody, stripped bone.

Sachs dropped to her knees and began to dig.

Dirt flying under her dog-paddling hands, she noticed that the uncut fingers were splayed, stretched beyond where they could normally bend. Which told her that the vic had been alive when the last shovelful of dirt was spooned onto the face.

And maybe still was.

Sachs dug furiously into the loosely packed earth, cutting her hand on a bottle shard, her dark blood mixing into the darker earth. And then she came to the hair and a forehead below it, a cyanotic bluish-gray from the lack of oxygen. Digging further until she could see the dull eyes and the mouth, which had twisted into a horrible grin as the vic had tried in the last few seconds to stay above the rising tide of black earth.

It wasn't a woman. Despite the ring. He was a heavyset man in his fifties. As dead as the soil he floated in.

Backing away, she couldn't take her eyes off his and nearly stumbled over a railroad track. She could think of absolutely nothing for a full minute. Except what it must've been like to die that way.

Then: Come *on*, honey. You got yourself a homicide crime scene and you're first officer.

You know what to do.

ADAPT

A is for Arrest a known perp.

D is for Detain material witnesses and suspects.

A is for Assess the crime scene.

P is for . . .

What was *P* again?

She lowered her head to the mike. "Portable 5885 to Central. Further-to. I've got a 10-29 by the train tracks at Three-eight and Eleven. Homicide, K. Need detectives, CS, bus and tour doctor. K."

"Roger, 5885. Perp in custody, K?"

"No perp."

"Five-eight-eight-five, K."

Sachs stared at the finger, the one whittled down to the bone. The incongruous ring. The eyes. And the grin . . . oh, that fucking grin. A shudder ripped through her body. Amelia Sachs had swum among snakes in summer-camp rivers and had boasted truthfully she'd have no problem bungee-jumping from a hundred-foot bridge. But let her think of confinement . . . think of being trapped, immobile, and the panic attack'd grab her like an electric shock. Which was why Sachs walked fast when she walked and why she drove cars like light itself.

When you move they can't getcha . . .

She heard a sound and cocked her head.

A rumble, deep, getting louder.

Scraps of paper blowing along the roadbed of the tracks. Dust dervishes swirling about her like angry ghosts.

Then a low wail . . .

Five-foot-nine Patrol Officer Amelia Sachs found herself facing down a thirty-ton Amtrak locomotive, the red, white and blue slab of steel approaching at a determined ten miles an hour.

"Hold up, there!" she shouted.

The engineer ignored her.

Sachs jogged onto the roadbed and planted herself right in the middle of the track, spread her stance and waved her arms, signaling him to stop. The locomotive squealed to a halt. The engineer stuck his head out the window.

"You can't go through here," she told him.

He asked her what she meant. She thought he looked woefully young to be driving such a big train.

"It's a crime scene. Please shut off the engine."

"Lady, I don't see any crimes."

But Sachs wasn't listening. She was looking up at a gap in the chain-link on the west side of the train viaduct, at the top, near Eleventh Avenue.

That would have been one way to get the body here without being seen—parking on Eleventh and dragging the body through the narrow alley to the cliff. On Thirty-seventh, the cross street, he could be spotted from two dozen apartment windows.

"That train, sir. Just leave it right there."

"I can't leave it here."

"Please shut off the engine."

"We don't shut off the engines of trains like this. They run all the time."

"And call the dispatcher. Or somebody. Have them stop the southbound trains too."

"We can't do that."

"Now, sir. I've got the number of that vehicle of yours."

"Vehicle?"

"I'd suggest you do it immediately," Sachs barked.

"What're you going to do, lady? Gimme a ticket?"

But Amelia Sachs was once again climbing back up the stone walls, her poor joints creaking, her lips tasting limestone dust, clay and her own sweat. She jogged to the alley she'd noticed from the roadbed and then turned around, studying Eleventh Avenue and the Javits Center across it. The hall was bustling with crowds—spectators and press. A huge banner proclaimed, *Welcome UN Delegates!* But earlier this morning, when the street was deserted, the perp could easily have found a parking space along here and carried the body to the tracks undetected. Sachs strode to Eleventh, surveyed the six-lane avenue, which was jammed with traffic.

Let's do it.

She waded into the sea of cars and trucks and stopped the north-bound lanes cold. Several drivers tried end runs and she had to issue two citations and finally drag trash cans out into the middle of the street as a barricade to make sure the good residents did their civic duty.

Sachs had finally remembered the next of the first officer's ADAPT rules.

P is for Protect the crime scene.

The sound of angry horns began to fill the hazy morning sky, soon supplemented by the drivers' angrier shouts. A short time later she heard the sirens join the cacophony as the first of the emergency vehicles arrived.

Forty minutes later, the scene was swarming with uniforms and investigators, dozens of them—a lot more than a hit in Hell's Kitchen, however gruesome the cause of death, seemed to warrant. But, Sachs learned from another cop, this was a hot case, a media groper—the vic was one of two passengers who'd arrived at JFK last night, gotten into a cab and headed for the city. They'd never arrived at their homes.

"CNN's watching," the uniform whispered.

So Amelia Sachs wasn't surprised to see blond Vince Peretti, chief of the Central Investigation and Resource Division, which oversaw the crime scene unit, climb over the top of the embankment and pause as he brushed dust from his thousand-dollar suit.

She was, however, surprised to see him notice her and gesture her over, a faint smile on his clean-cut face. It occurred to her she was about to receive a nod of gratitude for her *Cliffhanger* routine. Saved the fingerprints on *that* ladder, boys. Maybe even a commendation. In the last hour of the last day of Patrol. Going out in a blaze of glory.

He looked her up and down. "Patrolwoman, you're no rookie, are you? I'm safe in making that assumption."

"I'm sorry, sir?"

"You're not a rookie, I assume."

She wasn't, not technically, though she had only three years' service under her belt, unlike most of the other Patrol officers her age; they had nine or ten years in. Sachs had foundered for a few years before attending the academy. "I'm not sure what you're asking."

He looked exasperated and the smile vanished. "You were first officer?"

"Yessir."

"Why'd you close down Eleventh Avenue? What were you *thinking* of?"

She looked along the broad street, which was still blocked by her trash-can barricade. She'd gotten used to the honking but realized now it was really quite loud; the line of cars extended for miles.

"Sir, the first officer's job is to arrest a perp, detain any witnesses, protect—"

"I know the ADAPT rule, officer. You closed the street to protect the crime scene?"

"Yessir. I didn't think the perp would park on the cross street. He could be seen too easily from those apartments. See, there? Eleventh seemed like a better choice."

"Well, it was a wrong choice. There were no footprints on *that* side of the tracks, and two sets going to the ladder that leads up to Thirty-seven."

"I closed Thirty-seven too."

"That's my point. That's all that needed to be closed. And the train?" he asked. "Why'd you stop that?"

"Well, sir. I thought that a train going through the scene might disturb evidence. Or something."

"Or *something*, officer?"

"I didn't express myself very well, sir. I meant—"

"What about Newark Airport?"

"Yessir." She looked around for help. There were officers nearby but they were busily ignoring the dressing-down. "What exactly about Newark?"

"Why didn't you shut that down too?"

Oh, wonderful. A schoolmarm. Her Julia Roberts lips grew taut but she said reasonably, “Sir, in my judgment, it seemed likely that—”

“The New York Thruway would’ve been a good choice too. And the Jersey Pike and Long Island Expressway. I-70, all the way to St Louis. Those are likely means of escape.”

She lowered her head slightly and stared back at Peretti. The two of them were exactly the same height, though his heels were higher.

“I’ve gotten calls from the commissioner,” he continued, “the head of the Port Authority, the UN secretary-general’s office, the head of that expo—” He nodded toward the Javits Center. “We’ve fucked up the conference schedule, a U.S. senator’s speech and traffic on the entire West Side. The train tracks were fifty feet from the vic and the street you closed was a good two-hundred feet away and thirty above. I mean, even Hurricane Eva didn’t fuck up Amtrak’s Northeast Corridor like this.”

“I just thought—”

Peretti smiled. Because Sachs was a beautiful woman—her “foundering” before attending the academy had involved steady assignments for the Chantelle Modeling Agency on Madison Avenue—the cop chose to forgive her.

“Patrolwoman Sachs”—he glanced at the name tag on her chest, flattened chastely by the American Body Armor vest—“an object lesson. Crime scene work is a balance. It’d be nice if we could cordon off the whole city after every homicide and detain about three million people. But we can’t do that. I say this constructively. For your edification.”

“Actually, sir,” she said brusquely, “I’m transferring out of Patrol. Effective as of noon today.”

He nodded, smiled cheerfully. “Then, enough said. But for the record, it *was* your decision to stop the train and close the street.”

“Yessir, it was,” she said smartly. “No mistake about that.”

He jotted this into a black watch book with slashing strokes of his sweaty pen.

Oh, please . . .

“Now, remove those garbage cans. You direct traffic until the street’s clear again. You hear me?”

Without a yessir or nosir or any other acknowledgment she wandered to Eleventh Avenue and slowly began removing the garbage cans. Every single driver who passed her scowled or muttered something. Sachs glanced at her watch.

An hour to go.

I can live with it.

TWO

With a terse flutter of wings the peregrine dropped onto the window ledge. The light outside, midmorning, was brilliant and the air looked fiercely hot.

"There you are," the man whispered. Then cocked his head at the sound of the buzzer of the door downstairs.

"Is that him?" he shouted toward the stairs. "Is it?"

Lincoln Rhyme heard nothing in response and turned back to the window. The bird's head swiveled, a fast, jerky movement that the falcon nevertheless made elegant. Rhyme observed that its talons were bloody. A piece of yellow flesh dangled from the black nutshell beak. It extended a short neck and eased to the nest in movements reminiscent not of a bird's but a snake's. The falcon dropped the meat into the upturned mouth of the fuzzy blue hatchling. I'm looking, Rhyme thought, at the only living creature in New York City with no predator. Except maybe God Himself.

He heard the footsteps come up the stairs slowly.

"Was that him?" he asked Thom.

The young man answered, "No."

"Who was it? The doorbell rang, didn't it?"

Thom's eyes went to the window. "The bird's back. Look, bloodstains on your windowsill. Can you see them?"

The female falcon inched into view. Blue-gray like a fish, iridescent. Her head scanned the sky.

"They're always together. Do they mate for life?" Thom wondered aloud. "Like geese?"

Rhyme's eyes returned to Thom, who was bent forward at

his trim, youthful waist, gazing at the nest through the spattered window.

"Who was it?" Rhyme repeated. The young man was stalling now and it irritated Rhyme.

"A visitor."

"A visitor? Ha." Rhyme snorted. He tried to recall when his last *visitor* had been here. It must have been three months ago. Who'd it been? That reporter maybe or some distant cousin. Well, Peter Taylor, one of Rhyme's spinal cord specialists. And Blaine had been here several times. But she of course was not a *vis-i-tor*.

"It's freezing," Thom complained. His reaction was to open the window. Immediate gratification. Youth.

"Don't open the window," Rhyme ordered. "And tell me who the hell's here."

"It's freezing."

"You'll disturb the bird. You can turn the air conditioner down. *I'll* turn it down."

"We were here first," Thom said, further lifting the huge pane of window. "The birds moved in with full knowledge of you." The falcons glanced toward the noise, glaring. But then they always glared. They remained on the ledge, lording over their domain of anemic ginkgo trees and alternate-side-of-the-street parkers.

Rhyme repeated. "Who *is* it?"

"Lon Sellitto."

"Lon?"

What was he doing here?

Thom examined the room. "The place is a mess."

Rhyme didn't like the fuss of cleaning. He didn't like the bustle, the noise of the vacuum—which he found particularly irritating. He was content here, as it was. This room, which he called his office, was on the second floor of his Gothic townhouse on the Upper West Side of the city, overlooking Central Park. The room was large, twenty-by-twenty, and virtually every one of those feet was occupied. Sometimes he closed his eyes, playing a game, and tried to detect the smell of the different objects in the room here. The thousands of books and magazines, the Tower of Pisa stacks of photocopies, the hot transistors of the TV, the dust-frosted lightbulbs, the cork bulletin boards. Vinyl, peroxide, latex, upholstery.

Three different kinds of single-malt Scotch.

Falcon shit.

"I don't want to see him. Tell him I'm busy."

"And a young cop. Ernie Banks. No, he was a baseball player, right? You really should let me clean. You never notice how filthy someplace is till people come to call."

"Come to call? My, that sounds quaint. Victorian. How does *this* sound? Tell 'em to get the hell out. How's that for fin-desiècle etiquette?"

A mess . . .

Thom was speaking of the room but Rhyme supposed he meant his boss too.

Rhyme's hair was black and thick as a twenty-year-old's—though he was twice that age—but the strands were wild and bushy, desperately in need of a wash and cut. His face sprouted a dirty-looking three days' growth of black beard and he'd wakened with an incessant tickle in his ear, which meant that those hairs needed trimming as well. Rhyme's nails were long, finger and toe, and he'd been wearing the same clothes for a week—polka-dotted pajamas, god-awful ugly. His eyes were narrow, deep brown, and set in a face that Blaine had told him on a number of occasions, passionate and otherwise, was handsome.

"They want to talk to you," Thom continued. "They say it's very important."

"Well, bully for them."

"You haven't seen Lon for nearly a year."

"Why does that mean I want to see him now? Have you scared off the bird? I'll be pissed if you have."

"It's important, Lincoln."

"*Very* important, I recall you saying. Where's that doctor? He might've called. I was dozing earlier. And you were out."

"You've been awake since six A.M."

"No." He paused. "I woke up, yes. But then I dozed off. I was sound asleep. Did you check messages?"

Thom said, "Yes. Nothing from him."

"He said he'd be here midmorning."

"And it's just past eleven. Maybe we'll hold off notifying air-sea rescue. What do you say?"

"Have you been on the phone?" Rhyme asked abruptly. "Maybe he tried to call while you were on."

"I was talking to—"

"Did I say anything?" Rhyme asked. "Now you're angry. I didn't say you shouldn't be making phone calls. You can do that. You've always been able to do that. My point is just that he might've called while you were on the line."

"No, your point this morning is to be a shit."

"There you go. You know, they have this thing—call waiting. You can get two calls at once. I wish we had that. What does my old friend Lon want? And *his* friend the baseball player?"

"Ask them."

"I'm asking *you*."

"They want to see you. That's all I know."

"About something vay-ree im-por-tant."

"Lincoln." Thom sighed. The good-looking young man ran his hand through his blond hair. He wore tan slacks and a white shirt, with a blue floral tie, immaculately knotted. When he'd hired Thom a year ago Rhyme had said he could wear jeans and T-shirts if he wanted. But he'd been dressed impeccably every day since. Rhyme didn't know why it contributed to the decision to keep the young man on, but it had. None of Thom's predecessors had lasted more than six weeks. The number of those who quit was exactly equal to the firees.

"All right, what did you tell them?"

"I told them to give me a few minutes to make sure you were decent then they could come up. Briefly."

"You did that. Without asking me. Thank you very much."

Thom retreated a few steps and called down the narrow stairway to the first floor, "Come on, gentlemen."

"They told you something, didn't they?" Rhyme said. "You're holding out on me."

Thom didn't answer and Rhyme watched the two men approach. As they entered the room Rhyme spoke first. He said to Thom, "Close the curtain. You've already upset the birds way too much."

Which really meant only that he'd had enough of the sputtering sunlight.

Mute.

With the foul, sticky tape on her mouth she couldn't speak a word and that made her feel more helpless than the metal handcuffs tight on her wrists. Than the grip of his short, strong fingers on her biceps.

The taxi driver, still in his ski mask, led her down the grimy, wet corridor, past rows of ducts and piping. They were in the basement of an office building. She had no idea where.

If I could talk to him . . .

T.J. Colfax was a player, the bitch of Morgan Stanley's third floor. A negotiator.

Money? You want money? I'll get you money, lots of it, boy. Bushels. She thought this a dozen times, trying to catch his eye, as if she could actually force the words into his thoughts.

Pleeeeeeeease, she begged silently, and began thinking about the mechanics of cashing in her 401(k) and giving him her retirement fund. *Oh, please . . .*

She remembered last night: The man turning back from the fireworks, dragging them from the cab, handcuffing them. He'd thrown them into the trunk and they'd begun driving again. First over rough cobblestones and broken asphalt then smooth roads then rough again. She heard the whir of wheels on a bridge. More turns, more rough roads. Finally, the cab stopped and the driver got out and seemed to open a gate or some doors. He drove into a garage, she thought. All the sounds of the city were cut off and the car's bubbling exhaust rose in volume, reverberating off close walls.

Then the cab trunk opened and the man pulled her out. He yanked the diamond ring off her finger and pocketed it. Then he led her past walls of spooky faces, faded paintings of blank eyes staring at her, a butcher, a devil, three sorrowful children—painted on the crumbling plaster. Dragged her down into a moldy basement and dumped her on the floor. He clopped upstairs, leaving her in the dark, surrounded by a sickening smell—rotting flesh, garbage. There she'd lain for hours, sleeping a little, crying a lot. She'd wakened abruptly at a loud sound. A sharp explosion. Nearby. Then more troubled sleep.

A half hour ago he'd come for her again. Led her to the trunk and they'd driven for another twenty minutes. Here. Wherever *here* was.

They now walked into a dim basement room. In the center was a thick black pipe; he handcuffed her to it then gripped her feet and pulled them out straight in front of her, propping her in a sitting position. He crouched and tied her legs together with thin rope—it took several minutes; he was wearing leather gloves. Then he rose and gazed at her for a long moment, bent down and tore her blouse open. He walked around behind her and she gasped, feeling his hands on her shoulder, probing, squeezing her shoulder blades.

Crying, pleading through the tape.

Knowing what was coming.

The hands moved down, along her arms, and then under them and around the front of her body. But he didn't touch her breasts. No, as the hands spidered across her skin they seemed to be searching for her ribs. He prodded them and stroked. T.J. shivered and tried to pull away. He gripped her tight and caressed some more, pressing hard, feeling the give of the bone.

He stood. She heard receding footsteps. For a long moment there was silence except for the groans of air conditioners and elevators. Then she barked a frightened grunt at a sound right behind her. A repetitive noise. *Wsssh. Wsssh.* Very familiar but something she couldn't place. She tried to turn to see what he was doing but couldn't. What was it? Listening to the rhythmic sound, over and over and over. It took her right back to her mother's house.

Wsssh. Wsssh.

Saturday morning in the small bungalow in Bedford, Tennessee. It was the only day her mother didn't work and she devoted most of it to housecleaning. T.J. would wake up to a hot sun and stumble downstairs to help her. *Wsssh.* As she cried at this memory she listened to the sound and wondered why on earth he was sweeping the floor and with such careful, precise strokes of the broom.

He saw surprise and discomfort on their faces.

Something you don't find very often with New York City homicide cops.

Lon Sellitto and young Banks (Jerry, not Ernie) sat where Rhyme gestured with his bush-crowned head: twin dusty, uncomfortable rattan chairs.

Rhyme had changed considerably since Sellitto had last been here and the detective didn't hide his shock very well. Banks had no benchmark against which to judge what he was seeing but he was shocked nonetheless. The sloppy room, the vagrant gazing at them suspiciously. The smell too certainly—the visceral aroma surrounding the creature Lincoln Rhyme now was.

He immensely regretted letting them up.

"Why didn't you call first, Lon?"

"You would've told us not to come."

True.

Thom crested the stairs and Rhyme preempted him. "No, Thom, we won't be needing you." He'd remembered that the young man always asked guests if they wanted something to drink or eat.

Such a goddamn Martha Stewart.

Silence for a moment. Large, rumpled Sellitto—a twenty-year vet—glanced down into a box beside the bed and started to speak. Whatever he'd been about to say was cut off by the sight of disposable adult diapers.

Jerry Banks said, "I read your book, sir." The young cop had a bad hand when it came to shaving, lots of nicks. And what a charming cowlick in his hair! My good Lord, he can't be more than twelve. The more worn the world gets, Rhyme reflected, the younger its inhabitants seem to be.

"Which one?"

"Well, your crime scene manual, of course. But I meant the picture book. The one a couple years ago."

"There were words too. It was *mostly* words, in fact. Did you read them?"

"Oh, well, sure," Banks said quickly.

A huge stack of remaindered volumes of *The Scenes of the Crime* sat against one wall of his room.

"I didn't know you and Lon were friends," Banks added.

"Ah, Lon didn't trot out the yearbook? Show you the pictures? Strip his sleeve and show his scars and say these wounds I had with Lincoln Rhyme?"

Sellitto wasn't smiling. Well, I can give him even less to smile about if he likes. The senior detective was digging through his attaché case. And what does he have in *there*?

"How long were you partnered?" Banks asked, making conversation.

"There's a verb for you," Rhyme said. And looked at the clock.

"We weren't partners," Sellitto said. "I was Homicide, he was head of IRD."

"Oh," Banks said, even more impressed. Running the Central Investigation and Resource Division was one of the most prestigious jobs in the department.

"Yeah," Rhyme said, looking out the window, as if his doctor might be arriving via falcon. "The two musketeers."

In a patient voice, which infuriated Rhyme, Sellitto said, "Seven years, off and on, we worked together."

"And good years they were," Rhyme intoned.

Thom scowled but Sellitto missed the irony. Or more likely ignored it. He said, "We have a problem, Lincoln. We need some help."

Snap. The stack of papers landed on the bedside table.

"Some help?" The laugh exploded from the narrow nose Blaine had always suspected was the product of a surgeon's vision though it was not. She also thought his lips were too perfect (Add a scar, she'd once joked and during one of their fights she nearly had). And why, he wondered, does her voluptuous apparition keep rising today? He'd wakened thinking about his ex and had felt compelled to write her a letter, which was on the computer screen at that moment. He now saved the document on the disk. Silence filled the room as he entered the commands with a single finger.

"Lincoln?" Sellitto asked.

"Yessir. Some help. From me. I heard."

Banks kept an inappropriate smile on his face while he shuffled his butt uneasily in the chair.

"I've got an appointment in, well, any minute now," Rhyme said.

"An appointment."

"A doctor."

"Really?" Banks asked, probably to murder the silence that loomed again.

Sellitto, not sure where the conversation was going, asked, "And how've you been?"

Banks and Sellitto hadn't asked about his health when they'd arrived. It was a question people tended to avoid when they saw Lincoln Rhyme. The answer risked being a very complicated, and almost certainly an unpleasant, one.

He said simply, "I've been fine, thanks. And you? Betty?"

"We're divorced," Sellitto said quickly.

"Really?"

"She got the house and I got half a kid." The chunky cop said this with forced cheer, as if he'd used the line before, and Rhyme supposed there was a painful story behind the breakup. One he had no desire to hear. Still, he wasn't surprised that the marriage had tanked. Sellitto was a workhorse. He was one of the hundred or so first-grade detectives on the force and had been for years—he got the grade when they were handed out for merit not just time served. He'd worked close to eighty hours a week. Rhyme hadn't even known he was married for the first few months they'd worked together.

"Where you living now?" Rhyme asked, hoping a nice social conversation would tucker them out and send them on their way.

"Brooklyn. The Heights. I walk to work sometimes. You know those diets I was always on? The trick's not dieting. It's exercise."

He didn't look any fatter or thinner than the Lon Sellitto of three and a half years ago. Or the Sellitto of fifteen years ago for that matter.

"So," collegiate Banks said, "a doctor, you were saying. For a . . ."

"A new form of treatment?" Rhyme finished the dwindling question. "Exactly."

"Good luck."

"Thank you *so* much."

It was 11:36 A.M. Well past midmorning. Tardiness is inexcusable in a man of medicine.

He watched Bank's eyes twice scan his legs. He caught the pimply boy a second time and wasn't surprised to see the detective blush.

"So," Rhyme said. "I'm afraid I don't really have time to help you."

"But he's not here yet, right, the doctor?" asked Lon Sellitto in the same bulletproof tone he'd used to puncture homicide suspects' cover stories.

Thom appeared at the doorway with a coffeepot.

Prick, Rhyme mouthed.

"Lincoln forgot to offer you gentlemen something."

"Thom treats me like a child."

"If the bootie fits," the aide retorted.

"All right," Rhyme snapped. "Have some coffee. I'll have some mother's milk."

"Too early," Thom said. "The bar isn't open." And weathered Rhyme's glowering face quite well.

Again Bank's eyes browsed Rhyme's body. Maybe he'd been expecting just skin and bones. But the atrophying had stopped not long after the accident and his first physical therapists had exhausted him with exercise. Thom too, who may have been a prick at times and an old mother hen at others, was a damn good PT. He put Rhyme through passive ROM exercises every day. Taking meticulous notes on the goniometry—measurements of the range of motion that he applied to each joint in Rhyme's body. Carefully checking the spasticity as he kept the arms and legs in a constant cycle of abduction and adduction. ROM work wasn't a miracle but it built up some tone, cut down on debilitating contractures and kept the blood flowing. For someone whose muscular activities had been limited to his shoulders, head and left ring finger for three and a half years, Lincoln Rhyme wasn't in such bad shape.

The young detective looked away from the complicated black ECU control sitting by Rhyme's finger, hardwired to another controller, sprouting conduit and cables, which ran to the computer and a wall panel.

A quad's life is wires, a therapist had told Rhyme a long time ago. The rich ones, at least. The lucky ones.

Sellitto said, "There was a murder early this morning on the West Side."

"We've had reports of some homeless men and women disappearing over the past month," Banks said. "At first we thought it might be one of them. But it wasn't," he added dramatically. "The vic was one of those people last night."

Rhyme trained a blank expression on the young man with the dotted face. "Those *people*?"

"He doesn't watch the news," Thom said. "If you're talking about the kidnapping he hasn't heard."

"You don't watch the news?" Sellitto laughed. "You're the SOB read four papers a day and recorded the local news to watch when he got home. Blaine told me you called her Katie Couric one night when you were making love."

"I only read literature now," Rhyme said pompously, and falsely.

Thom added, "'Literature is news that stays news.'"

Rhyme ignored him.

Sellitto said, "Man and woman coming back from business on the Coast. Got into a Yellow Cab at JFK. Never made it home."

"There was a report about eleven-thirty. This cab was driving down the BQE in Queens. White male and female passenger in the back seat. Looked like they were trying to break a window out. Pounding on the glass. Nobody got tags or medallion."

"This witness—who saw the cab. Any look at the driver?"

"No."

"The woman passenger?"

"No sign of her."

Eleven forty-one. Rhyme was furious with Dr William Berger. "Nasty business," he muttered absently.

Sellitto exhaled long and loud.

"Go on, go on," Rhyme said.

"He was wearing her ring," Banks said.

"*Who* was wearing *what*?"

"The vic. They found this morning. He was wearing the woman's ring. The other passenger's."

"You're sure it was hers?"

"Had her initials inside."

"So you've got an unsub," Rhyme continued, "who wants you to know he's got the woman and she's still alive."

"What's an unsub?" Thom asked.

When Rhyme ignored him Sellitto said, "Unknown subject."

"But you know how he got it to fit?" Banks asked, a little wide-eyed for Rhyme's taste. "Her ring?"

"I give up."

"Cut the skin off the guy's finger. All of it. Down to the bone."

Rhyme gave a faint smile. "Ah, he's a smart one, isn't he?"

"Why's that smart?"

"To make sure nobody came by and took the ring. It was bloody, right?"

"A mess."

"Hard to see the ring in the first place. Then AIDS, hepatitis. Even if somebody noticed, a lot of folks'd take a pass on that trophy. What's her name, Lon?"

The older detective nodded to his partner, who flipped open his watchbook.

"Tammie Jean Colfax. She goes by T.J. Twenty-eight. Works for Morgan Stanley."

Rhyme observed that Banks too wore a ring. A school ring of some sort. The boy was too polished to be just a high-school and academy grad. No whiff of army about him. Wouldn't be surprised if the jewelry bore the name Yale. A homicide detective? What was the world coming to?

The young cop cupped his coffee in hands that shook sporadically. With a minuscule gesture of his own ring finger on the Everest & Jennings ECU panel, to which his left hand was strapped, Rhyme clicked through several settings, turning the AC down. He tended not to waste controls on things like heating and air conditioning; he reserved it for necessities like lights, the computer and his page-turning frame. But when the room got too cold his nose ran. And *that's* fucking torture for a quad.

"No ransom note?" Rhyme asked.

"Nothing."

"You're the case officer?" Rhyme asked Sellitto.

"Under Jim Polling. Yeah. And we want you to review the CS report."

Another laugh. "Me? I haven't looked at a crime scene report in three years. What could I possibly tell you?"

"You could tell us tons, Linc."

"Who's head of IRD now?"

"Vince Peretti."

"The congressman's boy," Rhyme recalled. "Have him review it."

A moment's hesitation. "We'd rather have you."

"Who's we?"

"The chief. Yours truly."

"And how," Rhyme asked, smiling like a schoolgirl, "does Captain Peretti feel about this vote of no confidence?"

Sellitto stood and paced through the room, glancing down at the stacks of magazines. *Forensic Science Review*. Harding & Boyle Scientific Equipment Company catalog. *The New Scotland Yard Forensic Investigation Annual. American College of Forensic Examiners Journal. Report of the American Society of Crime Lab Directors*. CRC Press *Forensics. Journal of the International Institute of Forensic Science*.

"Look at them," Rhyme said. "The subscriptions lapsed ages ago. And they're all dusty."

"*Everything* in here's fucking dusty, Linc. Why don't you get off your lazy ass and clean this pigsty up?"

Banks looked horrified. Rhyme squelched the burst of laughter that felt alien inside him. His guard had slipped and irritation had dissolved into amusement. He momentarily regretted that he and Sellitto had drifted apart. Then he shot the feeling dead. He grumbled, "I can't help you. Sorry."

"We've got the peace conference starting on Monday. We—"

"What conference?"

"At the UN. Ambassadors, heads of state. There'll be ten thousand dignitaries in town. You heard about that thing in London two days ago?"

"*Thing?*" Rhyme repeated caustically.

"Somebody tried to bomb the hotel where UNESCO was meeting. The mayor's scared shitless somebody's going to move on the conference here. He doesn't want ugly *Post* headlines."

"There's also the little problem," Rhyme said astringently,

"that Miss Tammie Jean might not be enjoying her trip home either."

"Jerry, tell him some details. Whet his appetite."

Banks turned his attention from Rhyme's legs to his bed, which was—Rhyme readily admitted—by far the more interesting of the two. Especially the control panel. It looked like something off the space shuttle and cost just about as much. "Ten hours after they're snatched we find the male passenger—John Ulbrecht—shot and buried alive in the Amtrak roadbed near Thirty-seventh and Eleventh. Well, we find him dead. He'd *been* buried alive. Bullet was a .32." Banks looked up and added, "The Honda Accord of slugs."

Meaning there'd be no wily deductions about the unsub from exotic weaponry. This Banks seems smart, Rhyme thought, and all he suffers from is youth, which he might or might not outgrow. Lincoln Rhyme believed he himself had never been young.

"Rifling on the slug?" Rhyme asked.

"Six lands and grooves, left twist."

"So he's got himself a Colt," Rhyme said and glanced over the crime scene diagram again.

"You said 'he,'" the young detective continued. "Actually it's 'they.'"

"What?"

"Unsubs. There're two of them. There were two sets of footprints between the grave and the base of an iron ladder leading up to the street," Banks said, pointing to the CS diagram.

"Any prints on the ladder?"

"None. It was wiped. Did a good job of it. The footprints go to the grave and back to the ladder. Anyway, there *had* to be two of 'em to schlepp the vic. He weighed over two hundred pounds. One man couldn't've done it."

"Keep going."

"They got him to the grave, dropped him in, shot him and buried him, went back to the ladder, climbed it and vanished."

"Shot him in the grave?" Rhyme inquired.

"Yep. There was no blood trail anywhere around the ladder or the path to the grave."

Rhyme found himself mildly interested. But he said, "What do you need me for?"

Sellitto grinned ragged yellow teeth. "We got ourselves a mystery, Linc. A buncha PE that doesn't make any fucking sense at all."

"So?" It was a rare crime scene when every bit of physical evidence made sense.

"Naw, this is real weird. Read the report. Please. I'll put it here. How's this thing work?" Sellitto looked at Thom, who fitted the report in the page-turning frame.

"I don't have time, Lon," Rhyme protested.

"That's quite a contraption," Banks offered, looking at the frame. Rhyme didn't respond. He glanced at the first page then read it carefully. Moved his ring finger a precise millimeter to the left. A rubber wand turned the page.

Reading. Thinking: Well, this *is* odd.

"Who was in charge of the scene?"

"Peretti himself. When he heard the vic was one of the taxi people he came down and took over."

Rhyme continued to read. For a minute the unimaginative words of cop writing held his interest. Then the doorbell rang and his heart galloped with a great shudder. His eyes slipped to Thom. They were cold and made clear that the time for banter was over. Thom nodded and went downstairs immediately.

All thoughts of cabdrivers and PE and kidnapped bankers vanished from the sweeping mind of Lincoln Rhyme.

"It's Dr Berger," Thom announced over the intercom.

At last. At long last.

"Well, I'm sorry, Lon. I'll have to ask you to leave. It was good seeing you again." A smile. "Interesting case, this one is."

Sellitto hesitated then rose. "But will you read through the report, Lincoln? Tell us what you think?"

Rhyme said, "You bet," then leaned his head back against the pillow. Quads like Rhyme, who had full head-and-neck movement, could activate a dozen controls just by three-dimensional movements of the head. But Rhyme shunned headrests. There were so few sensuous pleasures left to him that he was unwilling to abdicate the comfort of nestling his head against his two-hundred-dollar down pillow. The visitors had tired him out. Not even noon, and all he wanted to do was sleep. His neck muscles throbbed in agony.

When Sellitto and Banks were at the door Rhyme said, "Lon, wait."

The detective turned.

"One thing you should know. You've only found half the crime scene. The important one is the other one—the primary scene. His house. That's where he'll be. And it'll be hard as hell to find."

"Why do you think there's another scene?"

"Because he didn't shoot the vic at the grave. He shot him there—at the primary scene. And that's probably where he's got the woman. It'll be underground or in a very deserted part of city. Or both . . . Because, Banks"—Rhyme preempted the young detective's question—"he wouldn't risk shooting someone and holding a captive there unless it was quiet and private."

"Maybe he used a silencer."

"No traces of rubber or cotton baffling on the slug," Rhyme snapped.

"But how could the man've been shot there?" Banks countered. "I mean, there wasn't any blood spatter at the scene."

"I assume the victim was shot in the face," Rhyme announced.

"Well, yes," Banks answered, putting a stupid smile on his own. "How'd you know?"

"Very painful, very incapacitating, very little blood with a .32. Rarely lethal if you miss the brain. With the vic in that shape the unsub could lead him around wherever he wanted. I say unsub singular because there's only one of them."

A pause. "But . . . there were two sets of prints," Banks nearly whispered, as if he were defusing a land mine.

Rhyme sighed. "The soles're identical. They were left by the same man making the trip twice. To fool us. And the prints going north are the same depth as the prints going south. So he wasn't carrying a two-hundred-pound load one way and not the other. Was the vic barefoot?"

Banks flipped through his notes. "Socks."

"Okay, then the perp was wearing the vic's shoes for his clever little stroll to the ladder and back."

"If he didn't come down the ladder how *did* he get to the grave?"

"He led the man along the train tracks themselves. Probably from the north."

"There're no other ladders to the roadbed for blocks in either direction."

"But there *are* tunnels running parallel to the tracks," Rhyme continued. "They hook up with the basements of some of the old warehouses along Eleventh Avenue. A gangster during Prohibition—Owney Madden—had them dug so he could slip shipments of bootleg whisky onto New York Central trains going up to Albany and Bridgeport."

"But why not just bury the vic near the tunnel? Why risk being seen schlepping the guy all the way to the overpass?"

Impatient now. "You *do* get what he's telling us, don't you?"

Banks started to speak then shook his head.

"He *had* to put the body where it'd be seen," Rhyme said. "He needed someone to find it. That's why he left the hand in the air. He's *waving* at us. To get our attention. Sorry, you may have only one unsub but he's plenty smart enough for two. There's an access door to a tunnel somewhere nearby. Get down there and dust it for prints. There won't be any. But you'll have to do it just the same. The press, you know. When the story starts coming out . . . Well, good luck, gentlemen. Now, you'll have to excuse me. Lon?"

"Yes?"

"Don't forget about the primary crime scene. Whatever happens, you'll have to find it. And fast."

"Thanks, Linc. Just read the report."

Rhyme said of course he would and observed that they believed the lie. Completely.

THREE

He had the best bedside manner Rhyme had ever encountered. And if anyone had had experience with bedside manners it was Lincoln Rhyme. He'd once calculated he'd seen seventy-eight degreed, card-carrying doctors in the past three and a half years.

"Nice view," Berger said, gazing out the window.

"Isn't it? Beautiful."

Though because of the height of the bed Rhyme could see nothing except a hazy sky sizzling over Central Park. That—and the birds—had been the essence of his view since he'd moved here from his last rehab hospital two and half years ago. He kept the shades drawn most of the time.

Thom was busy rolling his boss—the maneuver helped keep his lungs clear—and then catheterizing Rhyme's bladder, which had to be done every five or six hours. After spinal cord trauma, sphincters can be stuck open or they can be stuck closed. Rhyme was fortunate that his got jammed closed—fortunate, that is, provided someone was around to open up the uncooperative little tube with a catheter and K-Y jelly four times a day.

Dr Berger observed this procedure clinically and Rhyme paid no heed to the lack of privacy. One of the first things crips get over is modesty. While there's sometimes a halfhearted effort at draping—shrouding the body when cleaning, evacuating and examining—serious crips, real crips, *macho* crips don't care. At Rhyme's first rehab center, after a patient had gone to a party or been on a date the night before, all the wardmates would wheel over to his bed to check the patient's urine output, which was the barometer of how successful the outing had been. One time Rhyme earned his fellow crips' undying admiration by registering a staggering 1430 cc's.

He said to Berger, "Check out the ledge, doctor. I have my own guardian angels."

"Well. Hawks?"

"Peregrine falcons. Usually they nest higher. I don't know why they picked me to live with."

Berger glanced at the birds then turned away from the window, let the curtain fall back. The aviary didn't interest him. He wasn't a large man but he looked fit, a runner, Rhyme guessed. He seemed to be in his late forties but the black hair didn't have a trace of gray in it and he was as good-looking as any news anchor.

"That's quite a bed."

"You like it?"

The bed was a Clinitron, a huge rectangular slab. It was an air-fluidized support bed and contained nearly a ton of silicone-coated glass beads. Pressurized air flowed through the beads, which supported Rhyme's body. If he had been able to feel, it would have felt as if he was floating.

Berger was sipping the coffee that Rhyme had ordered Thom to fetch and that the young man had brought, rolling his eyes, whispering, "Aren't we suddenly social?" before retreating.

The doctor asked Rhyme, "You were a policeman, you were telling me."

"Yes. I was head of forensics for the NYPD."

"Were you shot?"

"Nope. Searching a crime scene. Some workmen'd found a body at a subway-stop construction site. It was a young patrolman who'd disappeared six months before—we had a serial killer shooting cops. I got a request to work the case personally and when I was searching it a beam collapsed. I was buried for about four hours."

"Someone was actually going around murdering policemen?"

"Killed three and wounded another one. The perp was a cop himself. Dan Shepherd. A sergeant working Patrol."

Berger glanced at the pink scar on Rhyme's neck. The

telltale insignia of quadriplegia—the entrance wound for the ventilator tube that remains embedded in the throat for months after the accident. Sometimes for years, sometimes forever. But Rhyme had—thanks to his own mulish nature and his therapists' herculean efforts—weaned himself off the ventilator. He now had a pair of lungs on him that he bet could keep him underwater for five minutes.

"So, a cervical trauma."

"C4."

"Ah, yes."

C4 is the demilitarized zone of spinal cord injuries. An SCI above the fourth cervical vertebra might very well have killed him. Below C4 he would have regained some use of his arms and hands, if not his legs. But trauma to the infamous fourth kept him alive though virtually a total quadriplegic. He'd lost the use of his legs and arms. His abdominal and intercostal muscles were mostly gone and he was breathing primarily from his diaphragm. He could move his head and neck, his shoulders slightly. The only fluke was that the crushing oak beam had spared a single, minuscule strand of motor neuron. Which allowed him to move his left ring finger.

Rhyme spared the doctor the soap opera of the year following the accident. The month of skull traction: tongs gripping holes drilled into his head and pulling his spine straight. Twelve weeks of the halo device—the plastic bib and steel scaffolding around his head to keep the neck immobile. To keep his lungs pumping, a large ventilator for a year then a phrenic nerve stimulator. The catheters. The surgery. The paralytic ileus, the stress ulcers, hypotension and bradycardia, bedsores turning into decubitus ulcers, contractures as the muscle tissue began to shrink and threatened to steal away the precious mobility of his finger, the infuriating phantom pain—burns and aches in extremities that could feel no sensation.

He did, however, tell Berger about the latest wrinkle. "Autonomic dysreflexia."

The problem had been occurring more often recently. Pounding heartbeat, off-the-charts blood pressure, raging headaches. It could be brought on by something as simple as constipation. He explained that nothing could be done to prevent it except avoiding stress and physical constriction.

Rhyme's SCI specialist, Dr Peter Taylor, had become concerned with the frequency of the attacks. The last one—a month ago—was so severe that Taylor'd given Thom instructions in how to treat the condition without waiting for medical help and insisted that the aide program the doctor's number into the phone's speed dialer. Taylor had warned that a severe enough bout could lead to a heart attack or stroke.

Berger took in the facts with some sympathy then said, "Before I got into my present line I specialized in geriatric orthopedics. Mostly hip and joint replacements. I don't know much neurology. What about chances for recovery?"

"None, the condition's permanent," Rhyme said, perhaps a little too quickly. He added, "You understand my problem, don't you, doctor?"

"I think so. But I'd like to hear it in your words."

Shaking his head to clear a renegade strand of hair, Rhyme said, "Everyone has the right to kill himself."

Berger said, "I think I'd disagree with that. In most societies you may have the power but *not* the right. There's a difference."

Rhyme exhaled a bitter laugh. "I'm not much of a philosopher. But I don't even have the power. That's why I need you."

Lincoln Rhyme had asked four doctors to kill him. They'd all refused. He'd said, okay, he'd do it himself and simply stopped eating. But the process of wasting himself to death became pure torture. It left him violently stomach-sick and racked with unbearable headaches. He couldn't sleep. So he'd given up on that and, during the course of a hugely awkward conversation, asked Thom to kill him. The young man had grown tearful—the only time he'd shown that much emotion—and said he wished he could. He'd sit by and watch Rhyme die, he'd refuse to revive him. But he wouldn't actually kill him.

Then, a miracle. If you could call it that.

After *The Scenes of the Crime* had come out, reporters had appeared to interview him. One article—in *The New York Times*—contained this stark quotation from author Rhyme:

"No, I'm not planning any more books. The fact is, my next big project is killing myself. It's quite a challenge.

I've been looking for someone to help me for the past six months."

That screeching-stop line got the attention of the NYPD counseling service and several people from Rhyme's past, most notably Blaine (who told him he was nuts to consider it, he had to quit thinking only about himself—just like when they'd been together—and, now that she was here, she thought she should mention that she was remarrying).

The quotation also caught the attention of William Berger, who'd called unexpectedly one night from Seattle. After a few moments of pleasant conversation Berger explained that he'd read the article about Rhyme. Then a hollow pause and he'd asked, "Ever hear of the Lethe Society?"

Rhyme had. It was a pro-euthanasia group he'd been trying to track down for months. It was far more aggressive than Safe Passage or the Hemlock Society. "Our volunteers are wanted for questioning in dozens of assisted suicides throughout the country," Berger explained. "We have to keep a low profile."

He said he wanted to follow up on Rhyme's request. Berger refused to act quickly and they'd had several conversations over the past seven or eight months. Today was their first meeting.

"There's no way you can pass, by yourself?"

Pass . . .

"Short of Gene Harrod's approach, no. And even that's a little iffy."

Harrod was young man in Boston, a quad, who decided he wanted to kill himself. Unable to find anyone to help him he finally committed suicide the only way he was able to. With the little control he had he set a fire in his apartment and when it was blazing drove his wheelchair into it, setting himself aflame. He died of third-degree burns.

The case often raised by right-to-deathers as an example of the tragedy that anti-euthanasia laws can cause.

Berger was familiar with the case and shook his head sympathetically. "No, that's no way for anyone to die." He assayed Rhyme's body, the wires, the control panels. "What are your mechanical skills?"

Rhyme explained about the ECUs—the E&J controller that

his ring finger operated, the sip-and-puff control for his mouth, the chin joysticks, and the computer dictation unit that could type out words on the screen as he spoke them.

"But everything has to be set up by someone else?" Berger asked. "For instance, someone would have to go to the store, buy a gun, mount it, rig the trigger and hook it up to your controller?"

"Yes."

Making that person guilty of a conspiracy to commit murder, as well as manslaughter.

"What about your equipment?" Rhyme asked. "It's effective?"

"Equipment?"

"What you use? To, uhm, do the deed?"

"It's very effective. I've never had a patient complain."

Rhyme blinked and Berger laughed. Rhyme joined him. If you can't laugh about death what can you laugh about?

"Take a look."

"You have it with you?" Hope blossomed in Rhyme's heart. It was the first time he'd felt that warm sensation in years.

The doctor opened his attaché case and—rather ceremonially, Rhyme thought—set out a bottle of brandy. A small bottle of pills. A plastic bag and a rubber band.

"What's the drug?"

"Seconal. Nobody prescribes it anymore. In the old days suicide was a lot easier. These babies'd do the trick, no question. Now, it's almost impossible to kill yourself with modern tranquilizers. Halcion, Librium, Dalmane, Xanax . . . You may sleep for a long time but you're going to wake up eventually."

"And the bag?"

"Ah, the bag." Berger picked it up. "That's the emblem of the Lethe Society. Unofficially, of course—it's not like we have a logo. If the pills and the brandy aren't enough then we use the bag. Over the head, with a rubber band around the neck. We add a little ice inside because it gets pretty hot after a few minutes."

Rhyme couldn't take his eyes off the trio of implements. The bag, thick plastic, like a painter's drop cloth. The brandy was cheap, he observed, and the drugs generic.

"This's a nice house," Berger said, looking around. "Central Park West . . . Do you live on disability?"

"Some. I've also done consulting for the police and the FBI. After the accident . . . the construction company that was doing the excavating settled for three million. They swore there was no liability but there's apparently a rule of law that a quadriplegic automatically wins any lawsuits against construction companies, no matter who was at fault. At least if the plaintiff comes to court and drools."

"And you wrote that book, right?"

"I get some money from that. Not a lot. It was a 'better-seller.' Not a best-seller."

Berger picked up a copy of *The Scenes of the Crime*, flipped through it. "Famous crime scenes. Look at all this." He laughed. "There are, what, forty, fifty scenes?"

"Fifty-one."

Rhyme had revisited—in his mind and imagination, since he'd written it after the accident—as many old crime scenes in New York City as he could recall. Some solved, some not. He'd written about the Old Brewery, the notorious tenement in Five Points, where thirteen unrelated murders were recorded on a single night in 1839. About Charles Aubridge Deacon, who murdered his mother on July 13, 1863, during the Civil War draft riots, claiming former slaves had killed her and fueling the rampage against blacks. About architect Stanford White's love-triangle murder atop the original Madison Square Garden and about Judge Crater's disappearance. About George Metesky, the mad bomber of the '50s, and Murph the Surf, who boosted the Star of India diamond.

"Nineteenth-century building supplies, underground streams, butler's schools," Berger recited, flipping through the book, "gay baths, Chinatown whorehouses, Russian Orthodox churches . . . How d'you learn all this about the city?"

Rhyme shrugged. In his years as head of IRD he'd studied as much about the city as he had about forensics. Its history, politics, geology, sociology, infrastructure. He said, "Criminalistics doesn't exist in a vacuum. The more you know about your environment, the better you can apply—"

Just as he heard the enthusiasm creep into his voice he stopped abruptly.

Furious with himself that he'd been foxed so easily.

"Nice try, Dr Berger," Rhyme said stiffly.

"Ah, come on. Call me Bill. Please."

Rhyme wasn't going to be derailed. "I've heard it before. Take a big, clean, smooth piece of paper and write down all the reasons why I should kill myself. And then take another big, clean smooth piece of paper and write all the reasons why I shouldn't. Words like *productive, useful, interesting, challenging* come to mind. Big words. Ten-dollar words. They don't mean shit to me. Besides, I couldn't pick up a fucking pencil to save my soul."

"Lincoln," Berger continued kindly, "I have to make sure you're the appropriate candidate for the program."

"'Candidate'? 'Program'? Ah, the tyranny of euphemism," Rhyme said bitterly. "Doctor, I've made up my mind. I'd like to do it today. Now, as a matter of fact."

"Why today?"

Rhyme's eyes had returned to the bottles and the bag. He whispered, "Why not? What's today? August twenty-third? That's as good a day to die as any."

The doctor tapped his narrow lips. "I *have* to spend some time talking to you, Lincoln. If I'm convinced that you really want to go ahead—"

"I do," Rhyme said, noting as he often did how weak our words sound without the body gestures to accompany them. He wanted desperately to lay his hand on Berger's arm or lift his palms beseechingly.

Without asking if he could, Berger pulled out a packet of Marlboros and lit a cigarette. He took a folding metal ashtray from his pocket and opened it up. Crossed his thin legs. He looked like a foppish frat boy at an Ivy League smoker. "Lincoln, you understand the problem here, don't you?"

Sure, he understood. It was the very reason why Berger was here and why one of Rhyme's own doctors hadn't "done the deed." Hastening an inevitable death was one thing; nearly one-third of practicing doctors who treated terminal patients had prescribed or administered fatal doses of drugs. Most prosecutors turned a blind eye toward them unless a doctor flaunted it—like Kevorkian.

But a quad? A hemi? A para? A crip? Oh, that was different.

Lincoln Rhyme was forty years old. He'd been weaned off the ventilator. Barring some insidious gene in the Rhyme stock, there was no medical reason why he couldn't live to eighty.

Berger added, "Let me be blunt, Lincoln. I also have to be sure this isn't a setup."

"Setup?"

"Prosecutors. I've been entrapped before."

Rhyme laughed. "The New York attorney general's a busy man. He's not going to wire a crip to bag himself a euthanasist."

Glancing absently at the crime scene report.

> *. . . ten feet southwest of victim, found in a cluster on a small pile of white sand: a ball of fiber, approximately six centimeters in diameter, off-white in color. The fiber was sampled in the energy-dispersive X-ray unit and found to consist of* $A_2\,B_5\,(Si,\,A_8\,O_{22}\,(OH)_2$. *No source was indicated and the fibers could not be individuated. Sample sent to FBI PERT office for analysis.*

"I just have to be careful," Berger continued. "This is my whole professional life now. I gave up orthopedics completely. Anyway, it's more than a job. I've decided to devote my life to helping others end theirs."

> *Adjacent to this fiber, approximately three inches away were found two scraps of paper. One was common newsprint, with the words "three P.M." printed in Times Roman type, in ink consistent with that used in commercial newspapers. The other scrap appeared to be the corner of a page from a book with the page number "823" printed on it. The typeface was Garamond and the paper was calendared. ALS and subsequent ninhydrin analysis reveal no latent friction-ridge prints on either . . . Individuation was not possible.*

Several things nagged Rhyme. The fiber, for one. Why hadn't Peretti caught on as to what it was? It was so obvious.

And why was this PE—the newspaper scraps and the fiber—all clustered together? Something was wrong here.

"Lincoln?"

"Sorry."

"I was saying . . . You're not a burn victim in unbearable pain. You're not homeless. You've got money, you've got talent. Your police consulting . . . that helps a lot of people. If you want one, you could have a, yes, *productive* life ahead of you. A long life."

"Long, yes. That's the problem. A long life." He was tired of being on good behavior. He snapped, "But I don't *want* a long life. It's as simple as that."

Berger said slowly, "If there's the slightest chance you might've regretted your decision, well, see, *I'm* the one who'd have to live with it. Not you."

"Who's ever certain about something like this?"

Eyes slipping back to the report.

> *An iron bolt was found on top of the scraps of paper. It was a hex bolt, bead-stamped with the letters "CE". Two inches long, clock-wise twist, 15/16" in diameter.*

"I've got a busy schedule for the next few days," Berger said, looking at his watch. It was a Rolex; well, death has always been lucrative. "Let's take an hour or so now. Talk for a while, then have a cooling-off day and I'll come back."

Something was nagging at Rhyme. An infuriating itch—the curse of all quads—though in this case it was an intellectual itch. The kind that had plagued Rhyme all his life.

"Say, doctor, I wonder if you could do me a favor. That report there. Could you flip through it? See if you could find a picture of a bolt."

Berger hesitated. "A picture?"

"A Polaroid. It'll be glued in somewhere toward the back. The turning frame takes too long."

Berger lifted the report out of the frame and turned the pages for Rhyme.

"There. Stop."

As he gazed at the photo a twinge of urgency pricked at him. Oh, not here, not now. *Please, no.*

"I'm sorry, could you flip back to the page where we were?"

Berger did.

Rhyme said nothing and read carefully.

The paper scraps . . .

Three P.M. . . . page 823.

Rhyme's heart was pounding, sweat popped out on his head. He heard a frantic buzzing in his ears.

Here's a headline for the tabloids. MAN DIES DURING TALK WITH DEATH DOC . . .

Berger blinked. "Lincoln? Are you all right?" The man's canny eyes examined Rhyme carefully.

As casually as he could, Rhyme said, "You know, doctor, I'm sorry. But there's something I've got to take care of."

Berger nodded slowly, uncertainly. "Affairs aren't in order after all?"

Smiling. Nonchalant. "I'm just wondering if I could ask you to come back in a few hours."

Careful here. If he senses *purpose* he'll mark you down non-suicidal, take his bottles and his plastic bag and fly back to Starbucks land.

Opening a date book, Berger said, "The rest of the day isn't good. Then tomorrow . . . No. I'm afraid Monday's the earliest. Day after tomorrow."

Rhyme hesitated. Lord . . . His soul's desire was finally within his grasp, what he'd dreamed of every day for the past year. Yes or no?

Decide.

Finally, Rhyme heard himself say, "All right. Monday." Plastering a hopeless smile on his face.

"What exactly's the problem?"

"A man I used to work with. He asked for some advice. I wasn't paying as much attention to it as I should have. I have to call him."

No, it wasn't dysreflexia at all—or an anxiety attack.

Lincoln Rhyme was feeling something he hadn't felt in years. He was in one big fucking hurry.

"Could I ask you to send Thom up here? I think he's downstairs in the kitchen."

"Yes, of course. I'd be happy to."

Rhyme could see something odd in Berger's eyes. What was it? Caution? Maybe. It almost seemed like disappointment. But there was no time to think about it now. As the doctor's footsteps receded down the stairs Rhyme shouted in a booming baritone, "Thom? Thom!"

"What?" the young man's voice called.

"Call Lon. Get him back here. Now!"

Rhyme glanced at the clock. It was after noon. They had less than three hours.

FOUR

The crime scene was staged," Lincoln Rhyme said.

Lon Sellitto had tossed his jacket off, revealing a savagely wrinkled shirt. He now leaned back, arms crossed, against a table strewn with papers and books.

Jerry Banks was back too and his pale-blue eyes were on Rhyme's; the bed and its control panel no longer interested him.

Sellitto frowned. "But what story's the unsub tryin' to sell us?"

At crime scenes, especially homicides, perps often monkeyed with PE to lead investigators astray. Some were clever about it but most weren't. Like the husband who beat his wife to death then tried to make it look like a robbery—though he only thought to steal *her* jewelry, leaving his gold bracelets and diamond pinkie ring on his dresser.

"That's what's so interesting," Rhyme continued. "It's not about what happened, Lon. It's what's *going to* happen."

Sellitto the skeptic asked, "What makes you think so?"

"The scraps of paper. They mean three o'clock today."

"Today?"

"Look!" Nodding toward the report, an impatient jerk of his head.

"That one scrap says three P.P.," Banks pointed out. "But the other's a page number. Why do you think it means today?"

"It's *not* a page number." Rhyme lifted an eyebrow. They still didn't get it. "Logic! The only reason to leave clues was to tell us something. If that's the case then 823 has to be something more than just a page number because there's no clue as to what book it's from. Well, if it's not a page number what is it?"

Silence.

Exasperated, Rhyme snapped, "It's a *date*! Eight twenty-three. August twenty-third. Something's going to happen at three P.M. today. Now, the ball of fiber? It's asbestos."

"Asbestos?" Sellitto asked.

"In the report? The formula? It's hornblende. Silicon dioxide. That *is* asbestos. Why Peretti sent it to the FBI is beyond me. So. We have asbestos on a railbed where there shouldn't be any. And we've got an iron bolt with decaying oxidation on the head but none on the threads. That means it's been bolted someplace for a long time and just recently removed."

"Maybe it was overturned in the dirt," Banks offered. "When he was digging the grave?"

Rhyme said, "No. In Midtown the bedrock's close to the surface, which means so are the aquifers. All the soil from Thirty-fourth Street up to Harlem contains enough moisture to oxidize iron within a few days. It'd be completely rusted, not just the head, if it'd been buried. No, it was unbolted from someplace, carried to the scene and left there. And that sand . . . Come on, what's white sand doing on a train roadbed in Midtown Manhattan? The soil composition there is loam, silt, granite, hardpan and soft clay."

Banks started to speak but Rhyme cut him off abruptly. "And what were these things doing all clustered together? Oh, he's telling us something, our unsub. You bet he is. Banks, what about the access door?"

"You were right," the young man said. "They found one about a hundred feet north of the grave. Broken open from the inside. You were also right about the prints. Zip. And no tire tracks or trace evidence either."

A lock of dirty asbestos, a bolt, a torn newspaper . . .

"The scene?" Rhyme asked. "Intact?"

"Released."

Lincoln Rhyme, the crip with the killer lungs, exhaled a loud hiss of air, disgusted. "Who made *that* mistake?"

"I don't know," Sellitto said lamely. "Watch commander probably."

It was Peretti, Rhyme understood. "Then you're stuck with what you've got."

Whatever clues as to who the kidnapper was and what he had in mind were either in the report or gone forever, trampled under the feet of cops and spectators and railroad workers. Spadework—canvassing the neighborhood around the scene, interviewing witnesses, cultivating leads, traditional *detective* work—was done leisurely. But crime scenes themselves had to be worked "like mad lightning," Rhyme would command his officers in IRD. And he'd fired more than a few CSU techs who hadn't moved fast enough for his taste.

"Peretti ran the scene himself?" he asked.

"Peretti and a full complement."

"Full complement?" Rhyme asked wryly. "What's a *full complement*?"

Sellitto looked at Banks, who said, "Four techs from Photo, four from Latents. Eight searchers. ME tour doctor."

"*Eight* crime scene searchers?"

There's a bell curve in processing a crime scene. Two officers are considered the most efficient for a single homicide. By yourself you can miss things; three and up you tend to miss more things. Lincoln Rhyme had always searched scenes alone. He let the Latents people do the print work and Photo do the snap-shooting and videoing. But he always walked the grid by himself.

Peretti. Rhyme had hired the young man, son of a wealthy politico, six, seven years ago and he'd proved a good, by-the-book CS detective. Crime Scene is considered a plum and there's always a long waiting list to get into the unit. Rhyme took perverse pleasure in thinning the ranks of applicants by offering them a look at the family album—a collection of particularly gruesome crime-scene photos. Some officers would blanch, some would snicker. Some handed the book back, eyebrows raised, as if asking, So what? And those were the ones that Lincoln Rhyme would hire. Peretti'd been one of them.

Sellitto had asked a question. Rhyme found the detective looking at him. He repeated, "You'll work with us on this, won't you, Lincoln?"

"Work with you?" He coughed a laugh. "I can't, Lon. No.

I'm just spitting out a few ideas for you. You've got it. Run with it. Thom, get me Berger." He was now regretting the decision to postpone his tête-à-tête with the death doctor. Maybe it wasn't too late. He couldn't bear the thought of waiting another day or two of his *passing*. And Monday . . . He didn't want to die on Monday. It seemed common.

"Say please."

"Thom!"

"All right," the young aide said, hands raised in surrender.

Rhyme glanced at the spot on his bedside table where the bottle, the pills and the plastic bag had sat—so very close, but like everything else in this life wholly out of Lincoln Rhyme's reach.

Sellitto made a phone call, cocked his head as the call was answered. He identified himself. The clock on the wall clicked to twelve-thirty.

"Yessir." The detective's voice sank into a respectful whisper. The mayor, Rhyme guessed. "About the kidnapping at Kennedy. I've been talking to Lincoln Rhyme . . . Yessir, he has some thoughts on it." The detective wandered to the window, staring blankly at the falcon and trying to explain the inexplicable to the man running the most mysterious city on earth. He hung up and turned to Rhyme.

"He and the chief both want you, Linc. They asked specifically. Wilson himself."

Rhyme laughed. "Lon, look around the room. Look at *me*! Does it seem like I could run a case?"

"Not a normal case, no. But this isn't a very normal one now, is it?"

"I'm sorry. I just don't have time. That doctor. The treatment. Thom, did you call him?"

"Haven't yet. Will in just a minute."

"Now! Do it now!"

Thom looked at Sellitto. Walked to the door, stepped outside. Rhyme knew he wasn't going to call. Bugger the world.

Banks touched a dot of razor scar and blurted, "Just give us some thoughts. Please. This unsub, you said he—"

Sellitto waved him silent. He kept his eyes on Rhyme.

Oh, you prick, Rhyme thought. The old silence. How we

hate it and hurry to fill it. How many witnesses and suspects had caved under hot, thick silences just like this. Well, he and Sellitto *had* been a good team. Rhyme knew evidence and Lon Sellitto knew people.

The two musketeers. And if there was a third it was the purity of unsmiling science.

The detective's eyes dipped to the crime scene report. "Lincoln. What do you think's going to happen today at three?"

"I don't have any idea," Rhyme pronounced.

"Don'tcha?"

Cheap, Lon. I'll get you for that.

Finally, Rhyme said. "He's going to kill her—the woman in the taxi. And in some real bad way, I guarantee you. Something that'll rival getting buried alive."

"Jesus," Thom whispered from the doorway.

Why couldn't they just leave him alone? Would it do any good to tell them about the agony he felt in his neck and shoulders? Or about the phantom pain—far weaker and far eerier—roaming through his alien body? About the exhaustion he felt from the daily struggle to do, well, everything? About the most overwhelming fatigue of all—from having to rely on someone else?

Maybe he could tell them about the mosquito that'd gotten into the room last night and strafed his head for an hour; Rhyme grew dizzy with fatigue nodding it away until the insect finally landed on his ear, where Rhyme let it stab him—since that was a place he could rub against the pillow for relief from the itch.

Sellitto lifted an eyebrow.

"Today," Rhyme sighed. "One day. That's it."

"Thanks, Linc. We owe you." Sellitto pulled up a chair next to the bed. Nodded Banks to do the same. "Now. Gimme your thoughts. What's this asshole's game?"

Rhyme said, "Not so fast. I don't work alone."

"Fair enough. Who d'you want on board?"

"A tech from IRD. Whoever's the best in the lab. I want him here with the basic equipment. And we better get some tactical boys. Emergency Services. Oh, and I want some phones," Rhyme instructed, glancing at the Scotch on his dresser. He remembered the brandy Berger had in his kit. No way was he going out on cheap crap like that. His *Final Exit* number would be courtesy of either sixteen-year-old Lagavulin or opulent Macallan aged for decades. Or—why not?—both.

Banks pulled out his own cellular phone. "What kind of lines? Just—"

"Landlines."

"In here?"

"Of course not," Rhyme barked.

Sellitto said, "He means he wants people to make calls. From the Big Building."

"Oh."

"Call downtown," Sellitto ordered. "Have 'em give us three or four dispatchers."

"Lon," Rhyme asked, "who's doing the spadework on the death this morning?"

Banks stifled a laugh. "The Hardy Boys."

A glare from Rhyme took the smile off his face. "Detectives Bedding and Saul, sir," the boy added quickly.

But then Sellitto grinned too. "The Hardy Boys. Everybody calls 'em that. You don't know 'em, Linc. They're from the Homicide Task Force downtown."

"They look kind of alike is the thing," Banks explained. "And, well, their delivery is a little funny."

"I don't want comedians."

"No, they're good," Sellitto said. "The best canvassers we got. You know that beast 'napped that eight-year-old girl in Queens last year? Bedding and Saul did the canvass. Interviewed the entire 'hood—took twenty-two *hundred* statements. It was 'causa them we saved her. When we heard the vic this morning was the passenger from JFK, Chief Wilson himself put 'em on board."

"What're they doing now?"

"Witnesses mostly. Around the train tracks. And sniffing around about the driver and the cab."

Rhyme yelled to Thom in the hallway, "Did you call Berger? No, of course you didn't. The word 'insubordination' mean anything to you? At least make yourself useful. Bring that crime scene report closer and start turning the pages." He nodded toward the turning frame. "That damn thing's an Edsel."

"Aren't we in a sunny mood today?" the aide spat back.

"Hold it up *higher*. I'm getting glare."

He read for a minute. Then looked up.

Sellitto was on the phone but Rhyme interrupted him. "Whatever happens at three today, if we can find where he's talking about, it's going to be a crime scene. I'll need someone to work it."

"Good," Sellitto said. "I'll call Peretti. Toss him a bone. I know his nose'll be out of joint 'cause we're tiptoeing around him."

Rhyme grunted. "Did I ask for Peretti?"

"But he's the IRD golden boy," Banks said.

"I don't want him," Rhyme muttered. "There's somebody else I want."

Sellitto and Banks exchanged glances. The older detective smiled, brushing pointlessly at his wrinkled shirt. "Whoever you want, Linc, you got him. Remember, you're king for a day."

Staring at the dim eye.

T.J. Colfax, dark-haired refugee from the hills of Eastern Tennessee, NYU Business School grad, quick-as-a-whip currency trader, had just swum out of a deep dream. Her tangled hair stuck to her cheeks, sweat crawling in veins down her face and neck and chest.

She found herself looking into the black eye—a hole in a rusty pipe, about six inches across, from which a small access plate had been removed.

She sucked mildewy air through her nose—her mouth was still taped shut. Tasting plastic, the hot adhesive. Bitter.

And John? she wondered. Where was he? Refusing to think about the loud crack she'd heard last night in the basement. She'd grown up in Eastern Tennessee and knew what gunshots sounded like.

Please, she prayed for her boss. Let him be all right.

Stay calm, she raged to herself. You fucking start to cry again, you remember what happened. In the basement, after the gunshot, she'd lost it completely, breaking down, sobbing in panic, and had nearly suffocated.

Right. Calm.

Look at the black eye in the pipe. Pretend it's winking at you. The eye of your guardian angel.

T.J. sat on the floor, surrounded by a hundred pipes and ducts and snakes of conduit and wires. Hotter than her brother's diner, hotter than the back seat of Jule Whelan's Nova ten years ago. Water dripped, stalactites drooped from the ancient girders above her head. A half-dozen tiny yellow bulbs were the only illumination. Above her head—directly above—was a sign. She couldn't read it clearly, though she caught the red border. At the end of whatever the message might have been was a fat exclamation point.

She struggled once more but the cuffs held her tight, pinching against the bone. From her throat rose a desperate cry, an animal's cry. But the thick tape on her mouth and the insistent churning of machinery swallowed up the sound; no one could've heard her.

The black eye continued to stare. You'll save me, won't you? she thought.

Suddenly the silence was broken by a clanging slam, an iron bell, far away. Like a ship's door slamming shut. The noise came from the hole in the pipe. From her friendly eye.

She jerked the cuffs against the pipe and tried to stand. But she couldn't move more than a few inches.

Okay, don't panic. Just relax. You'll be all right.

It was then that she happened to see the sign above her head. In her jockeying for slack she'd straightened up slightly and moved her head to the side. This gave her an oblique view of the words.

Oh, no. Oh, Jesus in my heart . . .

The tears began again.

She imagined her mother, her hair pulled back from her round face, wearing her cornflower-blue housedress, whispering, "Be all raht, honey love. Doan' you worry."

But she didn't believe the words.

She believed what the sign said.

> *Extreme Danger! Superheated steam under High Pressure. Do not remove plate from pipe. Call Consolidated Edison for access. Extreme danger!*

The black eye gaped at her, the eye that opened into the heart of the steam pipe. It stared directly at the pink flesh of her chest. From somewhere deep inside the pipe came another clink of metal on metal, workers hammering, tightening old joints.

As Tammie Jean Colfax cried and cried she heard another clink. Then a distant groan, very faint. And it seemed to her, through her tears, that the black eye finally winked.

FIVE

Here's the situation," Lincoln Rhyme announced. "We've got a kidnap victim and a three P.M. deadline."

"No ransom demands"—Sellitto supplemented Rhyme's synopsis, then turned aside to answer his chirping phone.

"Jerry," Rhyme said to Banks, "brief them about the scene this morning."

There were more people hovering in Lincoln Rhyme's dark room than in recent memory. Oh, after the accident friends had sometimes stopped by unannounced (the odds were pretty good that Rhyme'd be home of course) but he'd discouraged that. And he'd stopped returning phone calls too, growing more and more reclusive, drifting into solitude. He'd spend his hours writing his book and, when he was uninspired to write another one, reading. And when that grew tedious there were rental movies and pay-per-view and music. And then he'd given up TV and the stereo and spent hours staring at the art prints the aide had dutifully taped up on the wall opposite the bed. Finally they too had come down.

Solitude.

It was all he craved, and oh how he missed it now.

Pacing, looking tense, was compact Jim Polling. Lon Sellitto was the case officer but an incident like this needed a captain on board and Polling had volunteered for the job. The case was a time bomb and could nuke careers in a heartbeat so the chief and the dep coms were happy to have him intercept the flak. They'd be practicing the fine art of distancing and when the Betacams rolled their press conferences would be peppered with words like *delegated* and *assigned* and *taking the advice of* and they'd be fast to glance at Polling when it came time to field the hardball questions. Rhyme couldn't imagine why any cop in the world would volunteer to head up a case like this one.

But Polling was an odd one. The little man had pummeled his way through Midtown North Precinct as one of the city's most successful, and notorious, homicide detectives. Known for his bad temper, he'd gotten into serious trouble when he'd killed an unarmed suspect. But he'd managed, amazingly, to pull his career together by getting a conviction in the Shepherd case—the cop-serial-killer case, the one in which Rhyme'd been injured. Promoted to captain after that very public collar, Polling went through one of those embarrassing midlife changes—giving up blue jeans and Sears suits for Brooks Brothers (today he wore navy-blue Calvin Klein casual) and began his dogged climb toward a plush corner office high in One Police Plaza.

Another officer leaned against a nearby table. Crew-cut, rangy Bo Haumann was a captain and head of the Emergency Services Unit. NYPD's SWAT team.

Banks finished his synopsis just as Sellitto pushed disconnect and folded his phone. "The Hardy Boys."

"Anything more on the cab?" Polling asked.

"Nothing. They're still beating bushes."

"Any sign she was fucking somebody she shouldn't've been?" Polling asked. "Maybe a psycho boyfriend?"

"Naw, no boyfriends. Just dated a few guys casually. No stalkers, it looks like."

"And still no ransom calls?" Rhyme asked.

"No."

The doorbell rang. Thom went to answer it.

Rhyme looked toward the approaching voices.

A moment later the aide escorted a uniformed police officer up the stairs. She appeared very young from a distance but as she drew closer he could see she was probably thirty or so. She was tall and had that sullen, equine beauty of women gazing out from the pages of fashion magazines.

We see others as we see ourselves and since the accident Lincoln Rhyme rarely thought of people in terms of their bodies. He observed her height, trim hips, fiery red hair.

Somebody else'd weigh those features and say, What a knockout. But for Rhyme that thought didn't occur to him. What did register was the look in her eyes.

Not the surprise—obviously, nobody'd warned he was a crip—but something else. An expression he'd never seen before. It was as if his condition was putting her at ease. The exact opposite of how most people reacted. As she walked into the room she was relaxing.

"Officer Sachs?" Rhyme asked.

"Yessir," she said, catching herself just as she was about to extend a hand. "Detective Rhyme."

Sellitto introudced her to Polling and Haumann. She'd know about the latter two, by reputation if nothing else, and now her eyes grew cautious once more.

She took in the room, the dust, the gloominess. Glanced at one of the art posters. It was partially unrolled, lying under a table. *Nighthawks*, by Edward Hopper. The lonely people in a diner late at night. That one had been the last to come down.

Rhyme briefly explained about the 3:00 P.M. deadline. Sachs nodded calmly but Rhyme could see the flicker of what?—fear? disgust?—in her eyes.

Jerry Banks, fingers encumbered by a class ring but not a wedding band, was attracted immediately by the lamp of her beauty and offered her a particular smile. But Sachs's single glance in response made clear that no matches were being made here. And probably never would be.

Polling said, "Maybe it's a trap. We find the place he's leading us to, walk in and there's a bomb."

"I doubt it," Sellitto said, shrugging. "Why go to all this trouble? If you want to kill cops all you gotta do is find one and fucking shoot him."

Awkward silence for a moment as Polling looked quickly from Sellitto to Rhyme. The collective thought registered that it was on the Shepherd case that Rhyme had been injured.

But faux pas meant nothing to Lincoln Rhyme. He continued, "I agree with Lon. But I'd tell any Search and Surveillance or HRT teams to keep an eye out for ambush. Our boy seems to be writing his own rules."

Sachs looked again at the poster of the Hopper painting. Rhyme followed her gaze. Maybe the people in the diner really weren't lonely, he reflected. Come to think of it, they all looked pretty damn content.

"We've got two types of physical evidence here," Rhyme continued. "Standard PE. What the unsub didn't mean to leave behind. Hair, fibers, fingerprints, maybe blood, shoeprints. If we can find enough of it—and if we're lucky—that'll lead us to the primary crime scene. That's where he lives."

"Or his hidey-hole," Sellitto offered. "Something temporary."

"A safe house?" Rhyme mused, nodding. "Bet you're right, Lon. He needs someplace to operate out of." He continued, "Then there's the planted evidence. Apart from the scraps of paper—which tell us the time and date—we've got the bolt, the wad of asbestos and the sand."

"A fucking scavenger hunt," Haumann growled and ran a hand through his slick buzz cut. He looked just like the drill sergeant Rhyme recalled he'd been.

"So I can tell the brass there's a chance of getting the vic in time?" Polling asked.

"I think so, yes."

The captain made a call and wandered to the corner of the room as he talked. When he hung up he grunted, "The mayor. The chief's with 'im. There's gonna to be a press conference in an hour and I gotta be there to make sure their dicks're in their pants and their flies're zipped. Anything more I can tell the big boys?"

Sellitto glanced at Rhyme, who shook his head.

"Not yet," the detective said.

Polling gave Sellitto his cellular phone number and left, literally jogging out the door.

A moment later a skinny, balding man in his thirties ambled up the stairs. Mel Cooper was as goofy-looking as ever, the nerdy neighbor in a sitcom. He was followed by two younger cops carrying a steamer trunk and two suitcases that seemed to weigh a thousand pounds each. The officers deposited their heavy loads and left.

"Mel."

"Detective." Cooper walked up to Rhyme and gripped his useless right hand. The only physical contact today with any of his guests, Rhyme noted. He and Cooper had worked together for years. With degrees in organic chemistry, math and physics, Cooper was an expert both in identification—friction-ridge prints, DNA and forensic reconstruction—and in PE analysis.

"How's the world's foremost criminalist?" Cooper asked him.

Rhyme scoffed good-naturedly. The title had been bestowed on him by the press some years ago, after the surprising news that the FBI had selected him—a city cop—as adviser in putting together PERT, their Physical Evidence Response Team. Not satisfied with "forensic scientist" or "forensic specialist," reporters dubbed Rhyme a "criminalist."

The word had actually been around for years, first applied in the United States to the legendary Paul Leland Kirk, who ran the UC Berkeley School of Criminology. The school, the first in the country, had been founded by the even more legendary Chief August Vollmer. The handle had recently become chic, and when techs around the country sidled up to blondes at cocktail parties now they described themselves as criminalists, not forensic scientists.

"Everybody's nightmare," Cooper said, "you get into a cab and turns out there's a psycho behind the wheel. And the whole world's watching the Big Apple 'causa that conference. Wondered if they might not bring you out of retirement for this one."

"How's your mother?" Rhyme asked.

"Still complaining about every ache and pain. Still healthier than me."

Cooper lived with the elderly woman in the Queens bungalow where he'd been born. His passion was ballroom dancing—the tango his speciality. Cop gossip being what it is, there'd been speculation around IRD as to the man's sexual preference. Rhyme had had no interest in his employees' personal lives but had been as surprised as everyone else to finally meet Greta, Cooper's steady girlfriend, a stunning Scandinavian who taught advanced mathematics at Columbia.

Cooper opened the large trunk, which was padded with velvet. He lifted out parts for three large microscopes and began assembling them.

"Oh, house current." He glanced at the outlets, disappointed. He pushed his metal-rimmed glasses up on his nose.

"That's because it's a house, Mel."

"I assumed you lived in a lab. Wouldn't have been surprised."

Rhyme stared at the instruments, gray and black, battered. Similar to the ones he'd lived with for over fifteen years. A standard compound microscope, a phase-contrast 'scope, and a polarized-light model. Cooper opened the suitcases, which contained a Mr Wizard assortment of bottles and jars and scientific instruments. In a flash, words came back to Rhyme, words that had once been part of his daily vocabulary. EDTA vacuum blood-collection tubes, acetic acid, orthotolidine, luminol reagent, Magna-Brush, Ruhemann's purple phenomenon . . .

The skinny man looked around the room. "Looks just like your office used to, Lincoln. How do you *find* anything? Say, I need some room here."

"Thom." Rhyme moved his head toward the least cluttered table. They moved aside magazines and papers and books, revealing a tabletop Rhyme had not seen in a year.

Sellitto gazed at the crime scene report. "Whatta we call the unsub? We don't have a case number yet."

Rhyme glanced at Banks. "Pick a number. Any number."

Banks suggested, "The page number. Well, the date, I mean."

"Unsub 823. Good as any."

Sellitto jotted this on the report.

"Uhm, excuse me? Detective Rhyme?"

It was the patrolwoman who'd spoken. Rhyme turned to her.

"I was supposed to be at the Big Building at noon." Coptalk for One Police Plaza.

"Officer Sachs . . ." He'd forgotten about her momentarily. "You were first officer this morning? At that homicide by the railroad tracks."

"That's right, I took the call." When she spoke, she spoke to Thom.

"I'm *here*, officer," Rhyme reminded sternly, barely controlling his temper. "Over here." It infuriated him when people talked to him through others, through *healthy* people.

Her head swiveled quickly and he saw the lesson had been learned. "Yessir," she said, a soft tone in her voice but ice in her eyes.

"I'm decommissioned. Just call me Lincoln."

"Would you just get it over with, please?"

"How's that?" he asked.

"The reason why you brought me here. I'm sorry. I wasn't thinking. If you want a written apology I'll do it. Only, I'm late for my new assignment and I haven't had a chance to call my commander."

"Apology?" Rhyme asked.

"The thing is, I didn't have any real crime scene experience. I was sort of flying by the seat of my pants."

"What are you talking about?"

"Stopping the trains and closing Eleventh Avenue. It was *my* fault the senator missed his speech in New Jersey and that some of the senior UN people didn't make it in from Newark Airport in time for their meetings."

Rhyme was chuckling. "Do you know who I am?"

"Well, I've heard of you of course. I thought you . . ."

"Were dead?" Rhyme asked.

"No. I didn't mean that." Though she had. She continued quickly, "We all used your book in the academy. But we don't hear about you. Personally, I mean . . ." She looked up at the wall and said stiffly, "In my judgment, as first officer, I thought it was best to stop the train and close the street to protect the scene. And that's what I did. Sir."

"Call me Lincoln. And you're . . ."

"I—"

"Your first name?"

"Amelia."

"Amelia. After the aviatrix?"

"Nosir. A family name."

"Amelia, I don't want an apology. You were right and Vince Peretti was wrong."

Sellitto stirred at this indiscretion but Lincoln Rhyme didn't care. He was, after all, one of the few people in the world who could stay flat on his ass when the president of the United States himself walked into the room. He continued, "Peretti worked the scene like the mayor was looking over his shoulder and that's the A-number-one way to screw it up. He had too many people, he was dead wrong to let the trains and traffic move and he should never have released the scene as early as he did. If we'd kept the tracks secure, who knows, we might've just found a credit card receipt with a name on it. Or a big beautiful thumbprint."

"That may be," Sellitto said delicately. "But let's just keep it to ourselves." Giving silent orders, his eyes swiveling toward Sachs and Cooper and young Jerry Banks.

Rhyme snorted an irreverent laugh. Then turned back to Sachs, whom he caught, like Banks that morning, staring at his legs and body under the apricot-colored blanket. He said to her, "I asked you here to work the next crime scene for us."

"What?" No speaking through interpreters this time.

"Work for us," he said shortly. "The next crime scene."

"But"—she laughed—"I'm not IRD. I'm Patrol. I've never done CS work."

"This is an unusual case. As Detective Sellitto himself'll tell you. It's real *weird*. Right, Lon? True, if it was a classic scene, I wouldn't want you. But we need a fresh pair of eyes on this one."

She glanced at Sellitto, who said nothing. "I just . . . I'd be no good at it. I'm sure."

"All right," Rhyme said patiently. "The truth?"

She nodded.

"I need somebody who's got the balls to stop a train in its tracks to protect a scene and to put up with the heat afterwards."

"Thank you for the opportunity, sir. Lincoln. But—"

Rhyme said shortly, "Lon."

"Officer," the detective grunted to Sachs, "you're not being given any options here. You've been assigned to this case to assist at the crime scene."

"Sir, I have to protest. I'm transferring out of Patrol. Today. I've got a medical transfer. Effective an hour ago."

"Medical?" Rhyme inquired.

She hesitated, glancing unwilling at his legs again. "I have arthritis."

"Do you?" Rhyme asked.

"Chronic arthritis."

"I'm sorry to hear that."

She continued quickly, "I only took that call this morning because someone was home sick. I didn't plan on it."

"Yes, well, I had other plans too," Lincoln Rhyme said. "Now, let's look at some evidence."

SIX

The bolt."

Remembering the classic crime scene rule: Analyze the most unusual evidence first.

Thom turned the plastic bag over and over in his hands as Rhyme studied the metal rod, half rusted, half not. Dull. Worn.

"You're sure about the prints? You tried small-particle reagent? That's the best for PE exposed to the elements."

"Yup," Mel Cooper confirmed.

"Thom," Rhyme ordered, "get this hair out of my eyes! Comb it back. I told you to comb it back this morning."

The aide sighed and brushed at the tangled black strands. "Watch it," he whispered ominously to his boss and Rhyme jerked his head dismissively, mussing his hair further. Amelia Sachs sat sullenly in the corner. Her legs rested under the chair in a sprinter's starting position and, sure enough, she looked like she was just waiting for the gun.

Rhyme turned back to the bolt.

When he headed IRD, Rhyme had started assembling databases. Like the federal auto-paint-chip index or the BATF's tobacco files. He'd set up a bullet-standards file, fibers, cloth, tires, shoes, tools, motor oil, transmission fluid. He'd spent hundreds of hours compiling lists, indexed and cross-referenced.

Even during Rhyme's obsessive tenure, though, IRD had never gotten around to cataloging hardware. He wondered why not and he was angry at himself for not taking the time to do it and angrier still at Vince Peretti for not thinking of it either.

"We need to call every bolt manufacturer and jobber in the Northeast. No, in the *country*. Ask if they make a model like this and who they sell to. Fax a description and picture of the bolt to our dispatchers at Communications."

"Hell, there could be a million of them," Banks said. "Every Ace Hardware and Sears in the country."

"I don't think so," Rhyme responded. "It's got to be a viable clue. He wouldn't have left it if it was useless. There's a limited source of these bolts. I bet you."

Sellitto made a call and looked up a few minutes later. "I've got you dispatchers, Lincoln. Four of them. Where do we get a list of manufacturers?"

"Get a patrolman down to Forty-second Street," Rhyme replied. "Public Library. They have corporate directories there. Until we get one, have the dispatchers start working through the Business-to-Business Yellow Pages."

Sellitto repeated this into the phone.

Rhyme glanced at the clock. It was one-thirty.

"Now, the asbestos."

For an instant, the word glowed in his mind. He felt a jolt—in places where no jolts could be felt. What was familiar about asbestos? Something he'd read or heard about—recently, it seemed, though Lincoln Rhyme no longer trusted his sense of time. When you lie on your back frozen in place month after month after month, time slows to near-death. He might be thinking of something he'd read two years ago.

"What do we know about asbestos?" he mused. No one answered but that didn't matter; he answered himself. As he preferred to do anyway. Asbestos was a complex molecule, silicate polymer. It doesn't burn because, like glass, it's already oxidized.

When he'd run crime scenes of old murders—working with forensic anthropologists and odontologists—Rhyme often found himself in asbestos-insulated buildings. He remembered the peculiar taste of the face masks they'd had to wear during the excavation. In fact, he now recalled, it'd been during an asbestos-removal cleanup at the City Hall subway stop three and a half years ago that crews found the body of one of the policemen murdered by Dan Shepherd dumped in a generator room. As Rhyme had bent down over it slowly to lift a fiber from the officer's light-blue blouse, he'd heard the crack and groan of the oak beam. The mask had probably saved him from choking to death on the dust and dirt that caved in around him.

"Maybe he's got her at a cleanup site," Sellitto said.

"Could be," Rhyme agreed.

Sellitto ordered his young assistant, "Call EPA and city Environmental. Find out if there're any sites where cleanup's going on right now."

The detective made the call.

"Bo," Rhyme asked Haumann, "you have teams to deploy?"

"Ready to roll," the ESU commander confirmed. "Though I gotta tell you, we've got over half the force tied up with this UN thing. They're on loan to the Secret Service and UN security."

"Got some EPA info here." Banks gestured to Haumann and they retired to a corner of the room. They moved aside several stacks of books. As Haumann unfurled one of ESU's tactical maps of New York something clattered to the floor.

Banks jumped. "Jesus."

From the angle where he lay, Rhyme couldn't see what had fallen. Haumann hesitated then bent down and retrieved the bleached piece of spinal column and replaced it on the table.

Rhyme felt several pairs of eyes on him but he said nothing about the bone. Haumann leaned over the map, as Banks, on the phone, fed him information about asbestos-cleanup sites. The commander marked them in grease pencil. There appeared to be a lot of them, scattered all over the five boroughs of the city. It was discouraging.

"We have to narrow it down more. Let's see, the sand," Rhyme said to Cooper. "'Scope it. Tell me what you think."

Sellitto handed the evidence envelope to the tech, who poured the contents out onto an enamel examination tray. The glistening powder left a small cloud of dust. There was also a stone, worn smooth, which slid into the center of the pile.

Lincoln Rhyme's throat caught. Not at what he saw—he didn't yet know *what* he was looking at—but at the flawed nerve impulse that shot from his brain and died halfway to his useless right arm, urging it to grab a pencil and to probe. The first time in a year or so he'd felt that urge. It nearly brought tears into his eyes and his only solace was the memory of the tiny bottle of Seconal and the plastic bag that Dr Berger carried with him—images that hovered like a saving angel over the room.

He cleared his throat. "Print it!"

"What?" Cooper asked.

"The stone."

Sellitto looked at him inquiringly.

"The rock doesn't belong there," Rhyme said. "Apples and oranges. I want to know why. Print it."

Using porcelain-tipped forceps, Cooper picked up the stone and examined it. He slipped on goggles and hit the rock with a beam from a PoliLight—a power pack the size of a car battery with a light wand attached.

"Nothing," Cooper said.

"VMD?"

Vacuum metal deposition is the Cadillac of techniques for raising latent prints on nonporous surfaces. It evaporates gold or zinc in a vacuum chamber containing the object to be tested; the metal coats the latent print, making the whorls and peaks very visible.

But Cooper didn't have a VMD with him.

"What *do* you have?" asked Rhyme, not pleased.

"Sudan black, stabilized physical developer, iodine, amido black, DFO and gentian violet, Magna-Brush."

He'd also brought ninhydrin for raising prints on porous surfaces and a Super Glue frame for smooth surfaces. Rhyme recalled the stunning news that had swept the forensic community some years ago: A technician working in a U.S. Army forensic lab in Japan had used Super Glue to fix a broken camera and found to his amazement that the fumes from the adhesive raised latent fingerprints better than most chemicals made for that purpose.

This was the method Cooper now used. With forceps he set the rock in a small glass box and put a dab of glue on the hot plate inside. A few minutes later he lifted the rock out.

"We've got something," he said. He dusted it with long-wavelength UV powder and hit it with the beam from the

PoliLight wand. A print was clearly visible. Dead center. Cooper photographed it with Polaroid CU-5, a 1:1 camera. He showed the picture to Rhyme.

"Hold it closer." Rhyme squinted as he examined it. "Yes! He rolled it."

Rolling prints—rocking a finger onto a surface—produced an impression different from one made by picking up an object. It was a subtle difference—in the width of the friction ridges at various points on the pattern—but one that Rhyme now recognized clearly.

"And look, what's that?" he mused. "That line." There was a faint crescent mark above the print itself.

"It looks almost like—"

"Yep," Rhyme said, "her fingernail. You wouldn't normally get that. But I'll bet he tipped the stone just to make sure it got picked up. It left an oil impression. Like a friction ridge."

"Why would he do that?" Sachs asked.

Once more miffed that nobody seemed to be picking up these points as fast as he was, Rhyme explained tersely, "He's telling us two things. First, he's making sure we know the victim's a woman. In case we didn't make the connection between her and the body this morning."

"Why do that?" Banks asked.

"To up the ante," Rhyme said. "Make us sweat more. He's let us know there's a woman at risk. He's valuated the victims—just like we all do—even though we claim we don't." Rhyme happened to glance at Sachs's hands. He was surprised to see that, for such a beautiful woman, *her* fingers were a mess. Four ended in fleshy Band-Aids and several others were chewed to the quick. The cuticle of one was caked with brown blood. He noticed too the red inflammation of the skin beneath her eyebrows, from plucking them, he assumed. And a scratch mark beside her ear. All self-destructive habits. There're a million ways to do yourself in besides pills and Armagnac.

Rhyme announced, "The other thing he's telling us I already warned you about. He knows evidence. He's saying, Don't bother with regular forensic PE. I won't be leaving any. That's what *he* thinks of course. But we'll find something. You bet we will." Suddenly Rhyme frowned. "The map! We need the map. Thom!"

The aide blurted, "What map?"

"You *know* what map I mean."

Thom sighed. "Not a clue, Lincoln."

Glancing out the window and speaking half to himself, Rhyme mused, "The railroad underpass, the bootleg tunnels and access doors, the asbestos—those're all old. He likes *historical* New York. I want the Randel map."

"Which is where?"

"The research files for my book. Where else?"

Thom dug through folders and pulled out a photocopy of a long, horizontal map of Manhattan. "This?"

"*That, yes!*"

It was the Randel Survey, drawn in 1811 for the commissioners of the city to plan out the grid of streets in Manhattan. The map had been printed horizontally, with Battery Park, south, to the left and Harlem, north, to the right. Laid out this way, the island resembled the body of a dog leaping, its narrow head lifted for an attack.

"Pin it up there. Good."

As the aide did, Rhyme blurted, "Thom, we're going to deputize you. Give him a shiny badge or something, Lon."

"Lincoln," he muttered.

"We need you. Come on. Haven't you always wanted to be Sam Spade or Kojak?"

"Only Judy Garland," the aide replied.

"Jessica Fletcher then! You'll be writing the profile. Come on now, get out that Mont Blanc you're always letting stick vainly out of your shirt pocket."

The young man rolled his eyes as he lifted his Parker pen and took a dusty yellow pad from a stack under one of the tables.

"No, I've got a better idea," Rhyme announced. "Put up one of those posters. Those art posters. Tape it up backwards and write on the back in marker. Write big now. So I can see it."

Thom selected a Monet lily pads and mounted it to the wall.

"On the top," the criminalist ordered, "write 'Unsub

823.' Then four columns. 'Appearance. Residence. Vehicle. Other.' Beautiful. Now, let's start. What do we know about him?"

Sellitto said, "Vehicle . . . He's got a Yellow Cab."

"Right. And under 'Other' add that he knows CS—crime scene—procedures."

"Which," Sellitto added, "maybe means he's had his turn in the barrel."

"How's that?" Thom asked.

"He might have a record," the detective explained.

Banks said, "Should we add that he's armed with a .32 Colt?"

"Fuck yes," his boss confirmed.

Rhyme contributed, "And he knows FRs. . . ."

"What?" Thom asked.

"Friction ridges—fingerprints. That's what they are, you know, ridges on our hands and feet to give us traction. And put down that he's probably working out of a safe house. Good job, Thom. Look at him. He's a born law enforcer."

Thom glowered and stepped away from the wall, brushing at his shirt, which had picked up a stringy cobweb from the wall.

"There we go, folks," Sellitto said. "Our first look at Mr 823."

Rhyme turned to Mel Cooper. "Now, the sand. What can we tell about it?"

Cooper lifted the goggles onto his pale forehead. He poured a sample onto a slide and slipped it under the polarized-light 'scope. He adjusted dials.

"Hmm. This is curious. No birefringence."

Polarizing microscopes show birefringence—the double refraction of crystals and fibers and some other materials. Seashore sand birefringes dramatically.

"So it isn't sand," Rhyme muttered. "It's something ground up. . . .Can you individuate it?"

Individuation . . . The goal of the criminalist. Most physical evidence can be *identified.* But even if you know what it is there are usually hundreds or thousands of sources it might have come from. *Individuated* evidence is something that could have come from only one source or a very limited number of sources. A fingerprint, a DNA profile, a paint chip that fits into a missing spot on the perp's car like a jigsaw-puzzle piece.

"Maybe," the tech responded, "if I can figure out *what* it is."

"Ground glass?" Rhyme suggested.

Glass is essentially melted sand but the glassmaking process alters the crystalline structure. You don't get birefringence with ground glass. Cooper examined the sample closely.

"No, I don't think it's glass. I don't know what it is. I wish I had an EDX here."

A popular crime lab tool was a scanning electron microscope married to an energy-dispersive X-ray unit; it determined what elements were in trace samples found at crime scenes.

"Get him one," Rhyme ordered Sellitto, then looked around the room. "We need more equipment. I want a vacuum metal fingerprint unit too. And a GC-MS." A gas chromatograph broke down substances into their component elements, and mass photospectrometry used light to identify each one of them. These instruments let criminalists test an unknown sample as small as one millionth of a gram and compare it against a database of a hundred thousand known substances, cataloged by identity *and* name brand.

Sellitto phoned the wish list in to the CSU lab.

"But we can't wait for the fancy toys, Mel. You'll have to do it the old-fashioned way. Tell me more about our phony sand."

"It's mixed with a little dirt. There's loam, flecks of quartz, feldspar and mica. But minimal leaf and decomposed-plant fragments. Flecks here of what could be bentonite."

"Bentonite." Rhyme was pleased. "That's a volcanic ash that builders use in slurry when they're digging foundations in watery areas of the city where the bedrock's deep. It prevents cave-ins. So we're looking for a developed area that's on or near the water, probably south of Thirty-fourth Street. North of that the bed-rock's much closer to the surface and they don't need slurry."

Cooper moved the slide. "If I had to guess, I'd say this is mostly calcium. Wait, something fibrous here."

The knob turned and Rhyme would've paid anything to be looking through that eyepiece. Flashed back to all the evenings he'd spent with his face pressed against the gray sponge rubber, watching fibers or flecks of humus or blood cells or metal shavings swim into and out of focus.

"Here's something else. A larger granule. Three layers. One similar to horn, then two layers of calcium. Slightly different colors. The other one's translucent."

"Three layers?" Rhyme spat out angrily. "Hell, it's a seashell!" He felt furious with himself. He should have thought of that.

"Yep, that's it." Cooper was nodding. "Oyster, I think."

The oyster beds around the city were mostly off the coasts of Long Island and New Jersey. Rhyme had hoped that the unsub would limit the geographic area of the search to Manhattan—where the victim that morning was found. He muttered, "If he's opening up the whole metro area the search'll be hopeless."

Cooper said, "I'm looking at something else. I think it's lime. But very old. Granular."

"Concrete maybe?" Rhyme suggested.

"Possibly. Yes. I don't get the shells then," Cooper added reflectively. "Around New York the oyster beds're full of vegetation and mud. This is mixed with concrete and there's virtually no vegetable matter at all."

Rhyme barked suddenly. "Edges! What are the edges of the shell like, Mel?"

The tech gazed into the eyepiece. "Fractured, not worn. This's been pulverized by dry pressure. Not eroded by water."

Rhyme's eyes slipped over the Randel map, scanning right and left. Focusing on the leaping dog's rump.

"Got it!" he cried.

In 1913 F. W. Woolworth built the sixty-story structure that still bears his name, terracotta-clad, covered with gargoyles and Gothic sculpture. For sixteen years it was the world's tallest building. Because the bedrock in that part of Manhattan was more than a hundred feet below Broadway, workmen had to dig deep shafts to anchor the building. It wasn't long after the groundbreaking that workmen discovered the remains of Manhattan industrialist Talbott Soames, who'd been kidnapped in 1906. The man's body was found buried in a thick bed of what looked like white sand but was really ground oyster shells, a fact the tabloids had a hey-day with, noting the obese tycoon's obsession with rich food. The shells were so common along the lower eastern tip of Manhattan they'd been used for landfill. They were what had given Pearl Street its name.

"She's downtown somewhere," Rhyme announced. "Probably the east side. And maybe near Pearl. She'll be underground, about five to fifteen feet down. Maybe a construction site, maybe a basement. An old building or tunnel."

"Cross-check the EPA diagram, Jerry," Sellitto instructed. "Where they're doing asbestos cleanup."

"Along Pearl? Nothing." The young officer held up the map he and Haumann were working from. "There're three-dozen cleanup sites—in Midtown, Harlem and the Bronx. But nothing downtown."

Asbestos . . . asbestos . . ." Rhyme mused again. *What* was so familiar about it?

It was 2:05 P.M.

"Bo, we've got to move. Get your people down there and start a search. All the buildings along Pearl Street. Water Street too."

"Man," the cop sighed, "that's beaucoup buildings." He started for the door.

Rhyme said to Sellitto, "Lon, you better go too. This's going to be a photo finish. They'll need all the searchers they can get. Amelia, I want you down there too."

"Look, I've been thinking—"

"Officer," Sellitto snapped, "you got your orders."

A faint glower crossed her beautiful face.

Rhyme said to Cooper, "Mel, you drive over here in a bus?"

"An RRV," he answered.

The city's big crime scene buses were large vans—filled

with instruments and evidence-collection supplies, better equipped than the entire labs of many small towns. But when Rhyme was running IRD he'd ordered smaller crime scene vehicles—station wagons basically—containing the essential collection-and-analysis equipment. The Rapid Response Vehicles looked placid but Rhyme had bullied Transportation into getting them fitted with turbocharged Police Interceptor engines. They often beat Patrol's squad cars to the scene; on more than one occasion the first officer was a seasoned crime scene tech. Which is every prosecutor's dream.

"Give Amelia the keys."

Cooper handed them to Sachs, who stared briefly at Rhyme then wheeled and hurried down the stairs. Even her footsteps sounded angry.

"All right, Lon. What's on your mind?"

Sellitto glanced at the empty hallway and walked up close to Rhyme. "You really want P.D. for this?"

"P.D.?"

"I mean her. Sachs. P.D.'s a nickname."

"For what?"

"Don't say it around her. Ticks her off. Her dad was a beat cop for forty years. So they call her the Portable's Daughter."

"You don't think I should've picked her?"

"Naw, I don't. Why d'you want her?"

"Because she climbed down a thirty-foot embankment so she wouldn't contaminate the scene. She closed a major avenue and an Amtrak line. That's initiative."

"Come on, Linc. I know a dozen CS cops'd do something like that."

"Well, she's the one I wanted." And Rhyme gave Sellitto a grave look, reminding him, subtly but without debate, what the terms of this bargain had been.

"All I'll say is," the detective muttered, "I just talked to Polling. Peretti's fucking outa joint about being flanked and if—no, I'll say *when*—the brass finds out somebody from Patrol's walking the grid at the scene, there'll be fucking trouble."

"Probably," Rhyme said softly, gazing at the profile poster, "but I have a feeling that's going to be the least of our trouble today."

And let his weary head ease back into the thick down pillow.

SEVEN

The station wagon raced toward the dark, sooty canyons of Wall Street, downtown New York.

Amelia Sachs's fingers danced lightly on the steering wheel as she tried to imagine where T.J. Colfax might be held captive. Finding her seemed hopeless. The approaching financial district had never looked so enormous, so full of alleys, so filled with manholes and doorways and buildings peppered with black windows.

So many places to hide a hostage.

In her mind she saw the hand sticking out of the grave beside the railroad tracks. The diamond ring sitting on the bloody bone of a finger. Sachs recognized the type of jewelry. She called them consolation rings—the sort lonely rich girls bought themselves. The sort she'd be wearing if she were rich.

Speeding south, dodging bicycle messengers and cabs.

Even on this glaring afternoon, under a choked sun, this was a spooky part of town. The buildings cast grim shadows and were coated with grime dark as dried blood.

Sachs took a turn at forty, skidding on the spongy asphalt, and punched the pedal to bring the station wagon back up to sixty.

Excellent engine, she thought. And decided to see how well the wagon handled at seventy.

Years before, while her old man slept—he worked the three-to-eleven watch usually—teenage Amie Sachs would palm the keys to his Camaro and tell her mother Rose she was going shopping, did she want anything from the Fort Hamilton pork store? And before her mother could say, "No, but you take

UNSUB 823			
Appearance	Residence	Vehicle	Other
	• Prob. has safe house	• Yellow Cab	• knows CS proc. • possibly has record • knows FR prints • gun = .32 Colt

the train, you're not driving," the girl would disappear out the door, fire up the car and race west.

Coming home three hours later, pork-less, Amie would sneak up the stairs to be confronted by a mother frantic and angry, who—to her daughter's amusement—would lecture her about the risks of getting pregnant and how that would ruin her chances to use her beautiful face to make a million dollars at modeling. And when finally the woman learned that her daughter wasn't sleeping around but was merely driving a hundred m.p.h. on Long Island highways, she grew frantic and angry and would lecture the girl about smashing up her beautiful face and ruining her chances to make a million dollars at modeling.

Things grew even worse when she got her driver's license.

Sachs now sliced between two double-parked trucks, hoping that neither a passenger nor a driver would open his door. In a Doppler whisper she was past them.

When you move they can't getcha. . . .

Lon Sellitto kneaded his rotund face with blunt fingertips and paid no attention to the Indy 500 driving. He talked with his partner about the case like an accountant discussing a balance sheet. As for Banks, though, he was no longer stealing infatuated glances at Sachs's eyes and lips and had taken to checking the speedometer every minute or so.

They skidded in a frantic turn past the Brooklyn Bridge. She thought again of the woman captive, picturing T.J.'s long, elegant nails, while she tapped her own picked fingers on the wheel. She saw again in her mind the image that refused to go away: the white birch branch of a hand, sticking up out of the moist grave. The single bloody bone.

"He's kind of loony," she blurted suddenly, to change the direction of her thoughts.

"Who?" Sellitto asked.

"Rhyme."

Banks added, "Ask me, he looks like Howard Hughes's kid brother."

"Yeah, well, that surprised me," the older detective admitted. "Wasn't looking too good. Used to be a handsome guy. But, well, you know. After what he's been through. How come if you drive like this, Sachs, you're a portable?"

"Where I got assigned. They didn't ask, they *told* me." Just like you did, she reflected. "Was he really as good as that?"

"Rhyme? Better. Most CSU guys in New York handle two hundred bodies a year. Tops. Rhyme did double that. Even when he was running IRD. Take Peretti, he's a good man but he gets out once every two weeks or so and only on media cases. You're not hearing this from me, officer."

"Nosir."

"But Rhyme'd run the scenes himself. And when he wasn't running scenes he'd be out walking around."

"Doing what?"

"Just walking around. Looking at stuff. He walked miles. All over the city. Buying things, picking up things, *collecting* things."

"What kinds of things?"

"Evidence standards. Dirt, food, magazines, hubcaps, shoes, medical books, drugs, plants . . . You name it, he'd find it and catalog it. You know—so when some PE came in he'd have a better idea where the perp might've been or what he'd been doing. You'd page him and he'd be in Harlem or the Lower East Side or Hell's Kitchen."

"Police in his blood?"

"Naw. Father was some kind of scientist at a national laboratory or something."

"Is that what Rhyme studied? Science?"

"Yeah. Went to school at Champaign-Urbana, got a coupla fancy degrees. Chemistry and history. Which I have no idea why. His folks're gone since I knew him. That'd be, hell, coming on fifteen years now. And he doesn't have any brothers or sisters. He grew up in Illinois. That's why the name, Lincoln."

She wanted to ask if he was, or had been, married but didn't. She settled for: "Is he really that much of a . . ."

"You can say it, officer."

"A shit?"

Banks laughed.

Sellitto said, "My ma had this expression. She said somebody was 'of a mind.' Well, that describes Rhyme. He's of a mind. One time this dumb-ass tech sprayed luminol—that's a blood reagent—on a fingerprint, instead of ninhydrin. Ruined the print. Rhyme fired him on the spot. Another time a cop took a leak at a scene and flushed the toilet. Man, Rhyme went ballistic, told him to get his ass down to the basement and bring back whatever was in the sewer trap." Sellitto laughed. "The cop, he had rank, he said, 'I'm not doing that, I'm a lieutenant." And Rhyme said, 'Got news, You're a plumber now.' I could go on and on. Fuck, officer, you doing eighty?"

They streaked past the Big Building and she thought, achingly, That's where I oughta be right now. Meeting fellow information officers, sitting through the training session, soaking up the air conditioning.

She steered expertly around a taxi that was oozing through a red light.

Jesus, this is hot. Dust hot, stink hot, gas hot. The ugly hours of the city. Tempers spurted like gray water shooting from hydrants up in Harlem. Two Christmases ago, she and her boyfriend had an abbreviated holiday celebration—from 11:00 P.M. to midnight, the only mutual free time their watches allowed—in the four-degree night. She and Nick, sitting at Rockefeller Center, outside, near the skating rink, drinking coffee and brandy. They'd agreed they'd rather have a week of cold than a single hot August day.

Finally, streaking down Pearl she spotted Haumann's command post. Leaving eight-foot skid marks, Sachs put the RRV into a slot between his car and an EMS bus.

"Damn, you drive good." Sellitto climbed out. For some reason Sachs was delighted to notice Jerry Banks's sweaty fingerprints remained prominently on the window when he pushed the rear door open.

EMS officers and Patrol uniforms were everywhere, fifty or sixty of them. And more were on their way. It seemed as if the entire attention of Police Plaza was focused on downtown New York. Sachs found herself thinking idly that if anybody wanted to try an assassination or to take over Gracie Mansion or a consulate, this'd be the time to do it.

Haumann trotted up to the station wagon. He said to Sellitto, "We're doing door-to-door, seeing about construction along Pearl. Nobody knows anything about asbestos work and nobody's heard any calls for help."

Sachs started to climb out but Haumann said, "No, officer. Your orders're to stay here with the CS vehicle."

She got out anyway.

"Yessir. Who exactly said that?"

"Detective Rhyme. I just talked to him. You're supposed to call in to Central when you're at the CP."

Haumann was walking away. Sellitto and Banks hurried toward the command post.

"Detective Sellitto," Sachs called.

He turned. She said, "Excuse me, detective. The thing is, who's my watch commander? Who'm I reporting to?"

He said shortly, "You're reporting to Rhyme."

She laughed. "But I can't be *reporting* to him."

Sellitto gazed at her blankly.

"I mean, aren't there liability issues or something? Jurisdiction? He's a *civilian*. I need somebody, a shield, to report to."

Sellitto said evenly, "Officer, listen up. We're *all* reporting to Lincoln Rhyme. I don't care whether he's a civilian or he's the chief or he's the fucking Caped Crusader. Got that?"

"But—"

"You wanna complain, do it in writing and do it tomorrow."

And he was gone. Sachs stared after him for a moment then returned to the front seat of the wagon and called in to Central that she was 10–84 at the scene. Awaiting instructions.

She laughed grimly as the woman reported, "Ten-four, Portable 5885. Be advised. Detective Rhyme will be in touch shortly, K."

Detective Rhyme.

"Ten-four, K," Sachs responded and looked in the back of the wagon, wondering idly what was in the black suitcases.

Two-forty P.M.

The phone rang in Rhyme's townhouse. Thom answered. "It's a dispatcher from headquarters."

"Put 'em through."

The speakerphone burst to life. "Detective Rhyme, you don't remember me but I worked at IRD when you were there. Civilian. Did phone detail then. Emma Rollins."

"Of course. How're the youngsters, Emma?" Rhyme had a memory of a large, cheerful black woman, supporting five children with two jobs. He recalled her blunt finger stabbing buttons so hard she once actually broke one of the government-issue phones.

"Jeremy's starting college in a couple weeks and Dora's still acting, or she thinks she is. The little ones're doing just fine."

"Lon Sellitto recruited you, did he?"

"Nosir. I heard you were working on the case and I booted some child back to 911. Emma's taking this job, I told her."

"What've you got for us?"

"We're working out of a directory of companies making bolts. And a book that lists places wholesaling them. Here's what we found. It was the letters did it. The ones stamped on the bolt. The *CE*. They're made special for Con Ed."

Hell. Of course.

"They're marked that way because they're a different size than most bolts this company sells—fifteen-sixteenths of an inch, and a lot more threads than most other bolts. That'd be Michigan Tool and Die in Detroit. They use 'em in old pipes only in New York. Ones made sixty, seventy years ago. The way the parts of the pipe fit together they have to be real close seals. Fit closer'n a bride and groom on their wedding night's what the man told me. Trying to make me blush."

"Emma, I love you. You stay on call, will you?"

"You bet I will."

"Thom!" Rhyme shouted. "This phone isn't going to work. I need to make calls myself. That voice-activation thing in the computer. Can I use it?"

"You never ordered it."

"I didn't?"

"No."

"Well, I need it."

"Well, we don't have it."

"Do *something*. I want to be able to make calls."

"I think there's a manual ECU somewhere." Thom dug through a box against the wall. He found a small electronic console and plugged one end into the phone and the other into a stalk control that mounted next to Rhyme's cheek.

"That's too awkward!"

"Well, it's all we've got. If we'd hooked up the infrared above your eyebrow like I suggested, you could've been making phone-sex calls for the past two years."

"Too many fucking wires," Rhyme spat out.

His neck spasmed suddenly and knocked the controller out of reach. "Fuck."

Suddenly this minute task—not to mention their mission—seemed impossible to Lincoln Rhyme. He was exhausted, his neck hurt, his head. His eyes particularly. They stung and—this was *more* painful to him—he felt a chip of urge to rub the backs of his fingers across his closed lids. A tiny gesture of relief, something the rest of the world did every day.

Thom replaced the joystick. Rhyme summoned patience from somewhere and asked his aide, "How does it work?"

"There's the screen. See it on the controller? Just move the stick till it's on a number, wait one second and it's programmed in. Then do the next number the same way. When you've got all seven, push the stick here to dial."

He snapped, "It's not working."

"Just practice."

"We don't have time!"

Thom snarled, "I've been answering the phone for you way too long."

"All right," Rhyme said, lowering his voice—his way of apology. "I'll practice later. Could you please get me Con Ed? And I need to speak to a supervisor."

The rope hurt and the cuffs hurt but it was the noise that scared her the most.

Tammie Jean Colfax felt all the sweat in her body run down her face and chest and arms as she struggled to saw the handcuff links back and forth on the rusty bolt. Her wrists were numb but it seemed to her that she was wearing through some of the chain.

She paused, exhausted, and twitched her arms this way and that to keep a cramp at bay. She listened again. It was, she thought, the sound of workmen tightening bolts and hammering parts into place. Final taps of hammers. She imagined they were just finishing up their job on the pipe and thinking of going home.

Don't go, she cried to herself. Don't leave me. As long as the men were there, working, she was safe.

A final bang, then ringing silence.

Git on outa thayr, girl. G'on.

Mamma . . .

T.J. cried for several minutes, thinking of her family back in Eastern Tennessee. Her nostrils clogged but as she began to choke she blew her nose violently, felt an explosion of tears and mucus. Then she was breathing again. It gave her confidence. Strength. She began to saw once more.

"I appreciate the urgency, detective. But I don't know how I can help you. We use bolts all over the city. Oil lines, gas lines . . ."

"All right," Rhyme said tersely and asked the Con Ed supervisor at the company's headquarters on Fourteenth Street, "Do you insulate wiring with asbestos?"

A hesitation.

"We've cleaned up ninety percent of that," the woman said defensively. "Ninety-*five*."

People could be so irritating. "I understand that. I just need to know if there's still any asbestos used for insulation."

"No," she said adamantly. "Well, never for electricity. Just the steam and that's the smallest percentage of our service."

Steam!

It was the least-known and the scariest of the city's utilities. Con Ed heated water to 1,000 degrees then shot it through a hundred-mile network of pipes running under Manhattan. The blistering steam itself was superheated—about 380 degrees—and rocketed through the city at seventy-five miles an hour.

Rhyme now recalled an article in the paper. "Didn't you have a break in the line last week?"

"Yessir. But there was no asbestos leak. That site had been cleaned years ago."

"But there *is* asbestos around some of your pipes in the system downtown?"

She hesitated. "Well . . ."

"Where was the break?" Rhyme continued quickly.

"Broadway. A block north of Chambers."

"Wasn't there an article in the *Times* about it?"

"I don't know. Maybe. Yes."

"And did the article mention asbestos?"

"It did," she admitted, "but it just said that in the past asbestos contamination'd been a problem."

"The pipe that broke, was it . . . does it cross Pearl Street farther south?"

"Well, let me see. Yes, it does. At Hanover Street. On the north side."

He pictured T.J. Colfax, the woman with the thin fingers and long nails, about to die.

"And the steam's going back on at three?"

"That's right. Any minute now."

"It can't!" Rhyme shouted. "Somebody's tampered with the line. You can't turn that steam back on!"

Cooper looked up uneasily from his microscope.

The supervisor said, "Well, I don't know . . ."

Rhyme barked to Thom, "Call Lon, tell him she's in a basement at Hanover and Pearl. The north side." He told him about the steam. "Get the fire department there too. Heat-protective outfits."

Rhyme shouted into the speakerphone. "Call the work crews! Now! They can't turn that steam back on. They *can't*!" He repeated the words absently, detesting his exquisite imagination, which showed, in an endless loop, the woman's flesh growing pink then red then splitting apart under the fierce clouds of sputtering white steam.

In the station wagon the radio crackled. It was three minutes to three by Sachs's watch. She answered the call.

"Portable 5885, K—"

"Forget the officialese, Amelia," Rhyme said. "We don't have time."

"I—"

"We think we know where she is. Hanover and Pearl."

She glanced over her shoulder and saw dozens of ESU officers running flat-out toward an old building.

"Do you want me to—"

"They'll look for her. You have to get ready to work the scene."

"But I can help—"

"No. I want you to go to the back of the station wagon. There's a suitcase in it labeled zero two. Take it with you. And in a small black case there's a PoliLight. You saw one in my room. Mel was using it. Take that too. In the suitcase marked zero three you'll find a headset and stalk mike. Plug it into your Motorola and get over to the building where the officers are. Call me back when you're rigged. Channel thirty-seven. I'll be on a landline but you'll be patched through to me."

Channel thirty-seven. The special ops citywide frequency. The priority frequency.

"What?—" she asked. But the dead radio did not respond.

She had a long black halogen flashlight on her utility belt so she left the bulky twelve-volter in the back of the wagon and grabbed the PoliLight and the heavy suitcase. It must have weighed fifty pounds. Just what my damn joints need. She adjusted her grip and, teeth clamped together against the pain, hurried toward the intersection.

Sellitto, breathless, ran to the building. Banks joined them.

"You hear?" the older detective asked. Sachs nodded.

"This is it?" she asked.

Sellitto nodded toward the alley. "He had to take her in this way, The lobby's got a guard station." They now trotted down the shadowy, cobblestoned canyon, steaming hot, smelling of piss and garbage. Battered blue Dumpsters sat nearby.

"There," Sellitto shouted. "Those doors."

The cops fanned out, running. Three of the four doors were locked tight from the inside.

The fourth had been jimmied open and was now chained shut. The chain and lock were new.

"This's it!" Sellitto reached for the door, hesitated. Thinking probably about fingerprints. Then he grabbed the handle and yanked. It opened a few inches but the chain held tight. He sent three of the uniforms around to the front to get into the basement from the inside. One cop worked a cobblestone loose from the alley floor and began pounding on the door handle. A half-dozen blows, a dozen. He winced as his hand struck the door; blood gushed from a torn finger.

A fireman ran up with a Halligan tool—a combination pickax and crowbar. He rammed the end into the chain and ripped the padlock open. Sellitto looked at Sachs expectantly. She gazed back.

"Well, go, officer!" he barked.

"What?"

"Didn't he tell you?"

"Who?"

"Rhyme."

Hell, she'd forgotten to plug in the headset. She fumbled it, finally got it plugged in. Heard: "Amelia, where—"

"I'm here."

"Are you at the building?"

"Yes."

"Go inside. They shut the steam off but I don't know if it was in time. Take a medic and one ESU trooper. Go to the boiler room. You'll probably see her right away, the Colfax woman. Walk to her but not directly, not in a straight line from the door to her. I don't want you to disturb any footprints he might've left. Understand?"

"Yes." She nodded emphatically, not thinking that he couldn't see her. Gesturing the medic and an Emergency Services trooper after her, Sachs stepped forward into the murky corridor, shadows everywhere, the groan of machinery, dripping water.

"Amelia," Rhyme said.

"Yes."

"We were talking about ambush before. From what I know about him now I don't think that's the case. He's not there, Amelia. That would be illogical. But keep your shooting hand free."

Illogical.

"Okay."

"Now go! Fast."

EIGHT

A murky cavern. Hot, black, damp.

The three of them moved quickly down the filthy hallway toward the only doorway Sachs could see. A sign said BOILER ROOM. She was behind the ESU officer, who wore full body armor and helmet. The medic was in the rear.

Her right knuckles and shoulder throbbed from the weight of the suitcase. She shifted it to her left hand, nearly dropped it and readjusted her grip. They continued to the door.

There, the SWAT officer pushed inside and swung his machine gun around the dimly lit room. A flashlight was attached to the barrel and it cast a line of pale light in the shreds of steam. Sachs smelled moisture, mold. And another scent, loathsome.

Click. "Amelia?" The staticky burst of Rhyme's voice scared the absolute hell out of her. "Where are you, Amelia?"

With a shaking hand she turned down the volume.

"Inside," she gasped.

"Is she alive?"

Sachs rocked on her feet, staring at the sight. She squinted, not sure at first what she was seeing. Then she understood.

"Oh, no." Whispering. Feeling the nausea.

The sickening boiled-meat smell wafted around her. But that wasn't the worst of it. Neither was the sight of the woman's skin, bright red, almost orange, peeling off in huge scales. The face completely stripped of skin. No, what brought the dread home was the angle of T.J. Colfax's body, the impossible twisting of her limbs and torso as she'd tried to get away from the spray of ravaging heat.

He hoped the vic was dead. For his sake. . . .

"Is she alive?" Rhyme repeated.

"No," Sachs whispered. "I don't see how . . . No."

"Is the room secure?"

Sachs glanced at the officer, who'd heard the transmission and nodded.

"Scene secure."

Rhyme told her, "I want the ESU trooper out then you and the medic go check on her."

Sachs gagged once on the smell and forced herself to control the reflex. She and the medic walked in an oblique path to the pipe. He bent unemotionally forward and felt the woman's neck. He shook his head.

"Amelia?" Rhyme asked.

Her second body in the line of duty. Both in one day.

The medic said, "DCDS."

Sachs nodded, said formally into the mike, "We have a deceased, confirmed dead at the scene."

"Scalded to death?" Rhyme asked.

"Looks like it."

"Tied to the wall?"

"A pipe. Handcuffed, hands behind. Feet tied with clothes-line. Duct-tape gag. He opened the steam pipe. She was only a couple of feet from it. God."

Rhyme continued, "Back the medic out the way you came. To the door. Watch where you put your feet."

She did this, staring at the body. How could the skin be so red? Like a boiled crab shell.

"All right, Amelia. You're going to work the scene. Open the suitcase."

She said nothing. Kept staring.

"Amelia, are you at the door? . . . Amelia?"

"*What?*" she shouted.

"Are you at the door?"

His voice was so fucking calm. So different from the snide, demanding voice of the man she remembered in the bedroom. Calm . . . and something else. She didn't know what.

"Yes, I'm at the door. You know, this is crazy."

"Utterly insane," Rhyme agreed, almost cheerfully. "Is the suitcase open?"

She flipped up the lid and glanced inside. Pliers and forceps, a flex mirror on a handle, cotton balls, eyedroppers, pinking sheers, pipettes, spatulas, scalpels . . .

What *is* all this?

. . . a Dustbuster, cheesecloth, envelopes, sifting screens, brushes, scissors, plastic and paper bags, metal cans, bottles—5 percent nitric acid, ninhydrin, silicone, iodide, friction-ridge-printing supplies.

Impossible. Into the mike she said, "I don't think you believed me, detective. I really *don't* know anything about CS work."

Eyes on the woman's ruined body. Water dripped off her peeled nose. A bit of white—bone—showed through the cheek. And her face was drawn into a anguished grin. Just like the vic that morning.

"I believed you, Amelia," he said dismissively. "Now, the case is open?" He was calm and he sounded . . . what? Yes, *that* was the tone. Seductive. He sounds like a lover.

I hate him, she thought. It's wrong to hate a cripple. But I fucking hate him.

"You're in the basement, right?"

"Yessir."

"Listen, you've got to call me Lincoln. We're going to know each other very well by the time this is over."

Which is gonna be about sixty minutes, tops.

"You'll find some rubber bands in the suitcase, if I'm not mistaken."

"I see some."

"Put them around your shoes. Where the ball of your foot is. If there's any confusion as to footprints you'll know which ones are yours."

"Okay, done."

"Take some evidence bags and envelopes. Put a dozen of each in your pocket. Can you use chopsticks?"

"What did you say?"

"You live in the city, right? You ever go to Mott Street? For General Tsao's chicken? Cold noddles with sesame paste?"

Her gorge rose at the talk of food. She refused to glance at the woman dangling in front of her.

"I can use chopsticks," she said icily.

"Look in the suitcase. I'm not sure you'll find them. They kept them there when I was running scenes."

"I don't see any."

"Well, you'll find some pencils. Put those in your pocket. Now you're going to walk a grid. Cover every inch. Are you ready?"

"Yes."

"First tell me what you see."

"One big room. Maybe twenty by thirty. Full of rusted pipes. Cracked concrete floor. Walls're brick. Mold."

"Any boxes? Anything on the floor?"

"No, it's empty. Except for the pipes, oil tanks, the boiler. There's the sand—the shells, a pile of it spilling out of a crack in the wall. And there's some gray stuff too—"

"'Stuff'?" he jumped. "I don't recognize that word. What's '*stuff*'?"

A burst of anger tore through her. She calmed and said, "It's the asbestos but not wadded up like this morning. It's in crumbling sheets."

"Good. Now, the first sweep. You're looking for footprints and any staged clues that he's left for us."

"You think he left more?"

"Oh, I'll betcha," Rhyme said. "Put on the goggles and use the PoliLight. Keep it low. Grid the room. Every inch. Get going. You know how to walk a grid?"

"Yes."

"How?"

She bristled. "I don't need to be tested."

"Ah, humor me. How?"

"Back and forth in one direction, then back and forth in the perpendicular direction."

"Each step, no more than one foot in length."

She hadn't known that. "I know," she said.

"Go ahead."

The PoliLight flashed on with an eerie, otherworldy glow. She knew it was something called an ALS—alternative light source—and that it made fingerprints and semen and blood and some shoeprints fluoresce. The brilliant bile-green light made shadows dance and jump and more than once she nearly drew down on a dark form that turned out to be a mere phantom of darkness.

"Amelia?" Rhyme's voice was sharp. She jumped again.

"Yes? What?"

"Do you see any footprints?"

She continued to stare at the floor. "I, uh, no. I see streaks in the dust. Or something." She cringed at the careless word. But Rhyme, unlike Peretti that morning, paid no attention. He said, "So. He swept up afterwards."

She was surprised. "Yeah, that's it! Broom marks. How'd you know?"

Rhyme laughed—a jarring sound to Sachs in this rank tomb—and he said, "He was smart enough to cover his tracks this morning; no reason to stop now. Oh, he's good, this boy is. But we're good too. Keep going."

Sachs bent over, her joints on fire, and began the search. She covered every square foot of the floor. "Nothing here. Nothing at all."

He picked up on the note of finality in her voice. "You've only just started, Amelia. Crime scenes are three-dimensional. Remember that. What you mean is there's nothing on the floor. Now search the walls. Start with the spot farthest away from the steam and cover every inch."

She slowly circled the horrible marionette in the center of the room. She thought of a Maypole game she'd played at some Brooklyn street feast when she was six or seven, as her father proudly took home movies. Circling slowly. It was an empty room and yet there were a thousand different places to search.

Hopeless . . . Impossible.

But it wasn't. On a ledge, about six feet above the floor, she found the next set of clues. She barked a fast laugh. "Got something here."

"In a cluster?"

"Yes. A big splinter of dark wood."

"Chopsticks."

"What?" she asked.

"The pencils. Use them to pick it up. Is it wet?"

"Everything in here's wet."

"Sure, it would be. The steam. Put it in a paper evidence bag.

Plastic keeps the moisture in and in this heat bacteria'll destroy the trace evidence. What else is there?" he asked eagerly.

"It's, I don't know, hairs, I think. Short, trimmed. A little pile of them."

"Loose or attached to skin?"

"Loose."

"There's a role of two-inch tape in the suitcase. 3M. Pick them up with that."

Sachs lifted most of the hairs, placed them in a paper envelope. She studied the ledge around the hairs. "I see some stains. Looks like rust or blood." She thought to hit the spot with the PoliLight. "They're fluorescing."

"Can you do a presumptive blood test?"

"No."

"Let's just assume it's blood. Could it be the victim's?"

"Doesn't seem to be. It's too far away and there's no trail to her body."

"Does it lead anywhere?"

"Looks like it. To a brick in the wall. It's loose. No prints on it. I'm going to move it aside. I—oh, Jesus!" Sachs gasped and stumbled back a foot or two, nearly fell.

"What?" Rhyme asked.

She eased forward, staring in disbelief.

"Amelia. Talk to me."

"It's a bone. A bloody bone."

"Human?"

"I don't know," she answered. "How would I . . . ? I don't know."

"Recent kill?"

"Looks like it. About two inches long and two in diameter. There's blood and flesh on it. It's been sawn off. Jesus. Who the fuck'd do something—"

"Don't get rattled."

"What if he got it from another victim?"

"Then we better find 'im pretty damn soon, Amelia. Bag it. Plastic for the bone."

As she did this, he asked, "Any other staged clues?" He sounded concerned.

"No."

"That's all? Hairs, a bone and a splinter of wood. He's not making it very easy, is he?"

"Should I bring it back to your . . . office?"

Rhyme was laughing. "He'd like us to call it quits. But no. We're not through yet. Let's find out a little more about Unsub 823."

"But there's nothing here."

"Oh, yes there is, Amelia. There's his address and his phone number and his description and his hopes and aspirations. They're all around you."

She was furious at his professor's tone and remained silent.

"You have the flashlight?"

"I've got my issue halogen—"

"No," he grumbled. "Issue lights are too narrow. You need the twelve-volt broad beam."

"Well, I didn't bring it," she snapped. "Should I go back and get it?"

"No time. Check out the pipes."

She searched for ten minutes, climbing up to the ceiling, and with the powerful light she illuminated spots that perhaps hadn't been lit in fifty years. "No, I don't see a thing."

"Go back to the door. Hurry."

She hesitated and returned.

"Okay, I'm here."

"Now. Close your eyes. What do you smell?"

"Smell? Did you say smell?" Was he crazy?

"Always smell the air at a crime scene. It can tell you a hundred things."

She kept her eyes wide and breathed in. She said, "Well, I don't *know* what I smell."

"That's not an acceptable answer."

She exhaled in exasperation and hoped the hiss was coming through his telephone loud and clear. She jammed her lids closed, inhaled, fought the nausea again. "Mold, mustiness. The smell of hot water from the steam."

"You don't know where it's from. Just describe it."

"Hot water. The woman's perfume."

"Are you sure it's hers?"

"Well, no."

"Are you wearing any?"

"No."

"How 'bout aftershave? The medic? The ESU officer?"

"I don't think so. No."

"Describe it."

"Dry. Like gin."

"Take a guess, man's aftershave or woman's perfume."

What had Nick worn? Arrid Extra Dry.

"I don't know," she said. "Man's."

"Walk to the body."

She glanced once at the pipe then down to the floor.

"I—"

"Do it," Lincoln Rhyme said.

She did. The peeling skin was like black-and-red birch.

"Smell her neck."

"It's all . . . I mean, there isn't much skin left."

"I'm sorry, Amelia, but you have to do it. We have to see if it's her perfume."

She did, inhaled. Gagged, nearly vomited.

I'm going to puke, she thought. Just like Nick and me that night at Pancho's, done in by those damn frozen daiquiris. Two hard-ass cops, swigging down sissy drinks with blue plastic swordfish swimming in them.

"Do you smell the perfume?"

Here it comes . . . Gagging again.

No. No! She closed her eyes, concentrated on her aching joints. The most painful one—her knee. And, miraculously, the wave of nausea passed. "It's not her perfume."

"Good. So maybe our boy's vain enough to wear a lot of aftershave. That could be a social-class indicator. Or maybe he wants to cover up some of the smell he might've left. Garlic, cigars, fish, whisky. We'll have to see. Now, Amelia, listen carefully."

"What?"

"I want you to be him."

Oh. Psychoshit. Just what I need.

"I really don't think we have time for this."

"There's never enough time in crime scene work," Rhyme continued soothingly. "But that doesn't stop us. Just get into his head. You've been thinking the way we think. I want you to think the way he does."

"Well, how do I do that?"

"Use your imagination. That's why God gave us one. Now, you're him. You've got her cuffed and gagged. You take her into the room there. You cuff her to the pipe. You scare her. You're enjoying this."

"How do you know he's enjoying it?"

"*You're* enjoying it. Not *him*. How do I know? Because nobody goes to this much trouble to do something they don't enjoy. Now, you know your way around. You've been here before."

"Why d'you think that?"

"You had to check it out earlier—to find a deserted place with a feeder pipe from the steam system. And to get the clues he left by the train tracks."

Sachs was mesmerized by his fluid, low voice. She forgot completely that his body was destroyed. "Oh. Right."

"You take the steam-pipe cover off. What are you thinking?"

"I don't know. That I want to get it over with. Get out."

But the words were hardly out of her mouth before she thought: Wrong. And she wasn't surprised when she heard Rhyme's tongue click in her headset. "Do you really?" he asked.

"No. I want to make it last."

"Yes! I think that's exactly what you want. You're thinking about what the steam will do to her. What else do you feel?"

"I . . ."

A thought formed in her mind, vague. She saw the woman screaming, crying, calling for help. Saw something else . . . some*one* else. Him, she thought. Unsub 823. But what about him? She was close to understanding. What . . . *what*? But suddenly the thought vanished. Gone.

"I don't know," she whispered.

"Do you feel any urgency? Or are you pretty cool about what you're doing?"

"I'm in a hurry. I have to leave. The cops could be here at any minute. But I still . . ."

"What?"

"Shhhh," she ordered, and scanned the room again, looking for whatever had put the seed of the vanished thought in her mind.

The room was swimming, a black, starry night. Swirls of darkness and distant, jaundiced lights. Lord, don't let me faint!

Maybe he—

There! That's it. Sachs's eyes were following the steam pipe. She was looking at another access plate in a shadowy alcove of the room. It would have been a better hiding place for the girl—you couldn't see it from the doorway if you were walking past—and the second plate had only four bolts on it, not eight, like the one he chose.

Why not that pipe?

Then she understood.

"He doesn't want . . . *I* don't want to leave just yet because I want to keep an eye on her."

"Why do you think that?" he inquired, echoing her own words just moments before.

"There's another pipe I could've chained her to but I picked the one that was in the open."

"So you could see her?"

"I think so."

"Why?"

"Maybe to make sure she can't get away. Maybe to make sure the gag's tight . . . I don't know."

"Good, Amelia. But what does it *mean*? How can we *use* that fact?"

Sachs looked around the room for the place where he'd have the best view of the girl without being seen. It turned out to be a shadowy spot between two large heating-oil tanks.

"Yes!" she said excitedly, looking at the floor. "He was here." Forgetting the role-playing. "He swept up."

She scanned the area with the bile glow of the PoliLight wand.

"No footprints," she said, disappointed. But as she lifted the light to shut it off, a smudge glowed on one of the tanks.

"I've got a print!" she announced.

"A print?"

"You get a better view of the girl if you lean forward and support yourself on a tank. That's what he did, I'm sure. Only, it's weird, Lincoln. It's . . . deformed. His hand." She shivered looking at the monstrous palm.

"In the suitcase there's an aerosol bottle labeled DFO. It's a fluorescent stain. Spray that on the print, hit the PoliLight and shoot the image with the one-to-one Polaroid."

She told him when she'd finished this and he said, "Now Dustbust the floor between the tanks. If we're lucky he scratched off a hair or chewed a fingernail."

My habits, Sachs thought. It was one of the things that had finally ruined her modeling career—the bloody nail, the worried eyebrow. She'd tried and tried and tried to stop. Finally gave up, discouraged, bewildered that a tiny habit could change the direction of your life so dramatically.

"Bag the vacuum filter."

"In paper?"

"Yes, paper. Now, the body, Amelia."

"What?"

"Well, you've *got* to process the body."

Her heart sank. Somebody else, please. Have somebody else do it. She said, "Not until the ME's finished. That's the rule."

"No rules today, Amelia. We're making up our own. The medical examiner'll get her after us."

Sachs approached the woman.

"You know the routine?"

"Yes." She stepped close to the destroyed body.

Then froze. Hands inches from the victim's skin.

I can't do it. She shuddered. Told herself to keep going. But she couldn't; the muscles weren't responding.

"Sachs? You there?"

She couldn't answer.

I can't do this . . . It was as simple as that. Impossible. I *can't*.

"Sachs?"

And then she looked into herself and, somehow, saw her father, in uniform, stooping low on the hot, pitted sidewalk of West Forty-second Street, sliding his arm around a scabby drunk to help him home. Then was seeing her Nick as he laughed and drank beer in a Bronx tavern with a hijacker who'd kill him in a second if he knew the young cop was working undercover. The two men in her life, doing what they had to do.

"Amelia?"

These two images bobbed in her thoughts, and why they calmed her, or where that calm came from, she couldn't begin to guess. "I'm here," she said to Lincoln Rhyme and went about her business as she'd been taught. Taking the nail scrapings, combing the hair—pubic and head. Telling Rhyme what she did as she did it.

Ignoring the dull orbs of eyes . . .

Ignoring the crimson flesh.

Trying to ignore the smell.

"Get her clothing," Rhyme said. "Cut off everything. Put a sheet of newsprint under them first to pick up any trace that falls off."

"Should I check the pockets?"

"No, we'll do that here. Wrap them up in the paper."

Sachs cut the blouse and skirt off, the panties. She reached out for what she thought was the woman's bra, dangling from her chest. It felt curious, disintegrating in her fingers. Then, like a slap she realized what she held and she gave a short scream. It wasn't cloth, it was skin.

"Amelia? Are you all right?"

"Yes!" she gasped. "I'm fine."

"Describe the restraints."

"Duct tape for the gag, two inches wide. Standard-issue cuffs for hands, clothesline for the feet."

"PoliLight her body. He might've touched her with his bare hands. Look for prints."

She did. "Nothing."

"Okay. Now cut the clothesline—but not through the knot. Bag it. In plastic."

Sachs did. Then Rhyme said, "We need the cuffs."

"Okay. I've got a cuff key."

"No, Amelia. Don't open them."

"What?"

"The cuff lock mechanism is one of the best ways to pick up trace from the perp."

"Well, how'm I supposed to get them off without a key?" She laughed.

"There's a razor saw in the suitcase."

"You want me to cut off the cuffs?"

There was a pause. Rhyme said, "No, not the cuffs, Amelia."

"Well, what *do* you want me to . . . Oh, you can't be serious. Her *hands*?"

"You have to." He was irritated at her reluctance.

Okay, that's it. Sellitto and Polling've picked a nutcase for a partner. Maybe *their* careers're tanking but I'm not going down with them.

"Forget it."

"Amelia, it's just another way to collect evidence."

Why did he sound so reasonable? She thought desperately for excuses. "They'll get blood all over them if I cut—"

"Her heart's not beating. Besides," he added like a TV chef, "the blood'll be cooked into a solid."

The gorge rising again.

"Go on, Amelia. Go to the suitcase. Get the saw. In the lid." He added a frosty, "Please."

"Why'd you have me scrape under her nails? I could've just brought you back her hands!"

"Amelia, we need the cuffs. We have to open them here and we can't wait for the ME. It has to be done."

She walked back to the doorway. Unsnapped the thongs, lifted the wicked-looking saw from the case. She stared at the woman, frozen in her tortured pose in the center of the vile room.

"Amelia? *Amelia*?"

Outside, they sky was still clogged with stagnant, yellow air and the buildings nearby were covered with soot like charred bones. But Sachs had never been so glad to be out in the city air as now. The CU suitcase in one hand, the razor saw in the other; the headset dangling dead around her neck. Sachs ignored the huge crowd of cops and spectators staring at her and walked straight toward the station wagon.

As she passed Sellitto she handed him the saw without pausing, practically tossed it to him. "If he wants it done that badly tell him he can damn well walk down here and do it himself."

2
LOCARD'S PRINCIPLE

In real life, you only get one shot at the homicide crime scene.

Vernon J. Geberth,
Lieutenant Commander (Ret.)
New York Police Department

Saturday, 4:00 P.M., to Saturday, 10:15 P.M.

NINE

I've got myself into a situation here, sir."

The man across the desk looked like a TV show's idea of a big-city deputy police commissioner. Which happened to be his rank. White hair, a temperate jowl, gold-rimmed glasses, posture to die for.

"Now what's the problem, officer?"

Dep. Com. Randolph C. Eckert looked down his long nose with a gaze that Sachs recognized immediately; his nod to equality was to be as stern with the female officers as with the male ones.

"I've got a complaint, sir," she said stiffly. "You heard about that taxi kidnapping case?"

He nodded. "Ah, has *that* got the city in double dutch."

She believed that was a schoolchild's game of jump rope but wouldn't presume to correct a deputy commissioner.

"That damn UN conference," he continued, "and the whole world's watching. It's unfair. People don't talk about crime in Washington. Or Detroit. Well, Detroit they do. Say, Chicago. Never. No, it's New York that people thump on. Richmond, Virginia, had more murders per capital than we did last year. I looked it up. And I'd rather parachute unarmed into Central Harlem than drive windows-up through South East D.C. any day."

"Yessir."

"Understand they found that girl dead. It was on all the news. Those reporters."

"Downtown. Just now."

"Now that's a pity."

"Yessir."

"They just killed her? Like that? No ransom demand or anything?"

"I didn't hear about any ransom."

"What's this complaint?"

"I was first officer in a related homicide this morning."

"You're Patrol?" Eckert asked.

"I *was* Patrol. I was supposed to be transferring to Public Affairs today at noon. For a training session." She lifted her hands, tipped with flesh-colored Band-Aids, and dropped them in her lap. "But they shanghaied me."

"Who?"

"Detective Lon Sellitto, sir. And Captain Haumann. And Lincoln Rhyme."

"Rhyme?"

"Yessir."

"Not the fellow was in charge of IRD a few years ago?"

"Yessir. That's him."

"I thought he was dead."

Egos like that will never die.

"Very much alive, sir."

The dep com was looking out his window. "He's not on the force anymore. What's he doing involved in this?"

"Consultant, I guess. It's Lon Sellitto's case. Captain Polling's overseeing it. I've been waiting for this reassignment for eight months. But they've got me working crime scene. I've never *done* crime scene. It doesn't make any sense and frankly I resent being assigned to a job I've had no training for."

"Crime scene?"

"Rhyme ordered me to run the whole scene. By myself."

Eckert didn't understand this. The words weren't registering. "Why is a civilian ordering uniformed officers to do *anything*?"

"My point, sir." She set the hook. "I mean, I'll help up to a point. But I'm just not prepared to dismember victims . . ."

"What?"

She blinked as if surprised he hadn't heard. She explained about the handcuffs.

"Lord in heaven, what the hell're they thinking of? Pardon my French. Don't they know the whole country's watching.

It's been on CNN all day, this kidnapping. Cutting off her hands? Say, you're Herman Sachs's daughter."

"That's right."

"Good officer. *Excellent* officer. I gave him one of his commendations. The man was what a beat cop ought to be. Midtown South, right?"

"Hell's Kitchen. My beat."

My *former* beat.

"Herman Sachs probably prevented more crime than the entire detective division solves in a year. Just calming everything down, you know."

"That was Pop. Sure."

"Her hands?" Eckert snorted. "The girl's family'll sue us. As soon as they find out about it. They sue us for everything. There's a rapist suing us now 'cause he got shot in the leg coming at an officer with a knife. His lawyer's got this theory he's calling the 'least deadly alternative.' Instead of shooting, we're supposed to taze them or use Mace. Or ask them politely, I don't know. I better give the chief and the mayor a heads-up on this one. I'll make some calls, officer." He looked at a wall clock. It was a little after four. "Your watch over for the day?"

"I have to report back to Lincoln Rhyme's house. That's where we're working out of." She thought of the hacksaw. She said coolly, "His bedroom really. That's our CP."

"A civilian's bedroom is your command post?"

"I'd appreciate anything you can do, sir. I've waited a long time for that transfer."

"Cut her hands off. My good Lord."

She stood and walked to the door and out into one of the corridors that would soon be her new assignment. The feeling of relief took only a little longer to arrive than she'd expected.

He stood at the bottle-glass window, watching a pack of wild dogs prowl though the lot across the street.

He was on the first floor of this old building, a marble-clad Federal dating to the early 1800s. Surrounded by vacant lots and tenements—some abandoned, some occupied by paying tenants though most by squatters—this old mansion had been empty for years.

The bone collector took the piece of emery paper in his hand once more and continued to rub. He looked down at his handiwork. Then out the window again.

His hands, in their circular motion, precise. The tiny scrap of sandpaper whispering, *shhhhh, shhhhh* . . . Like a mother hushing her child.

A decade ago, the days of promise in New York, some crazy artist had moved in here. He'd filled the dank, two-storey place with broken and rusting antiques. Wrought-iron grilles, hunks of crown molding and framed squares of spidered stained glass, scabby columns. Some of the artist's work remained on the walls. Frescoes on the old plaster: murals, never completed, of workers, children, angst-ridden lovers. Round, emotionless faces—the man's motif—stared blankly, as if the souls had been nipped out of their smooth bodies.

The painter was never very successful, even after the most ironclad of marketing ideas—his own suicide—and the bank foreclosed on the building several years ago.

Shhhhh . . .

The bone collector had stumbled across the place last year and he'd known immediately that this was home. The desolation of the neighborhood was certainly important to him—it was obviously practical. But there was another appeal, more personal: the lot across the street. During some excavation several years ago a backhoe had unearthed a load of human bones. It turned out this had been one of the city's old cemeteries. Newspaper articles about it suggested the graves might contain the remains not only of Federal and Colonial New Yorkers but Manate and Lenape Indians as well.

He now set aside what he'd been smoothing with the emery paper—a carpal, the delicate palm bone—and picked up the wrist, which he'd carefully detached from the radius and ulna last night just before leaving for Kennedy Airport to collect the first victims. It had been drying for over a week and most of the flesh was gone but it still took some effort to separate the elaborate cluster of bones. They snapped apart with faint plops, like fish breaking the surface of a lake.

Oh, the constables, they were a lot better than he'd anticipated. He'd been watching them search along Pearl Street, wondering if they'd ever figure out where he'd left the woman from the airport. Astonished when they suddenly ran toward the right building. He'd guessed it would take two or three victims until they got a feel for the clues. They hadn't saved her of course. But they might have. A minute or two earlier would have made all the difference.

As with so much in life.

The navicular, the lunate, the hamate, the capitate . . . the bones, intertwined like a Greek puzzle ring, came apart under his strong fingers. He picked bits of flesh and tendon off them. He selected the greater multangulum—at the base of where the thumb had once been—and began to sand once more.

Shhhhh, shhhhhhh.

The bone collector squinted as he looked outside and imagined he saw a man standing beside one of the old graves. It *must* have been his imagination because the man wore a bowler hat and was dressed in mustard-colored gabardine. He rested some dark roses beside the tombstone and then turned away from it, dodging the horses and carriages on his way to the elegantly arched bridge over the Collect Pond outlet at Canal Street. Who'd he been visiting? Parents? A brother? Family who'd died of consumption or in one of the terrible influenza epidemics that'd been ravaging the city recently—

Recently?

No, not recently of course. A hundred years ago—*that's* what he meant.

He squinted and looked again. No sign of the carriages or the horses. Or the man with the bowler hat. Though they'd seemed as real as flesh and blood.

However real *they* are.

Shhhhh, shhhhhh.

It was intruding again, the past. He was seeing things that'd happened *before*, that had happened *then*, as if they were now. He could control it. He *knew* he could.

But as he gazed out the window he realized that of course there was no before or after. Not for him. He drifted back and forth through time, a day, five years, a hundred years or two, like a dried leaf on a windy day.

He looked at his watch. It was time to leave.

Setting the bone on the mantel, he washed his hands carefully—like a surgeon. Then for five minutes he ran a pet-hair roller over his clothes to pick up any bone dust or dirt or body hairs that might lead the constables to him.

He walked into the carriage house past the half-finished painting of a moon-faced butcher in a bloody white apron. The bone collector started to get into the taxi but then changed his mind. Unpredictability is the best defense. This time he'd take the carriage . . . the *sedan*, the Ford. He started it, he drove into the street, closed and locked the garage door behind him.

No before or after . . .

As he passed the cemetery the pack of dogs glanced up at the Ford then returned to scuffling through the brush, looking for rats and nosing madly for water in the unbearable heat.

No then or now . . .

He took the ski mask and gloves from his pocket, set them on the seat beside him as he sped out of the old neighborhood. The bone collector was going hunting.

TEN

Something had changed about the room but she couldn't quite decide what.

Lincoln Rhyme saw it in her eyes.

"We missed you, Amelia," he said coyly. "Errands?"

She looked away from him. "Apparently nobody'd told my new commander I wouldn't be showing up for work today. I thought somebody ought to."

"Ah, yes."

She was gazing at the wall, slowly figuring it out. In addition to the basic instruments that Mel Cooper had brought with him, there was now a scanning electron microscope fitted with the X-ray unit, flotation and hot-stage 'scope setups for testing glass, a comparison microscope, a density-gradient tube for soil testing and a hundred beakers, jars and bottles of chemicals.

And in the middle of the room, Cooper's pride—the computerized gas chromatograph and mass spectrometer. Along with another computer, on-line with Cooper's own terminal at the IRD lab.

Sachs stepped over the thick cables snaking downstairs—house current worked, yes, but the amperage was too taxed for the bedroom outlets alone. And in that slight sidestep, an elegant, practiced maneuver, Rhyme observed how truly beautiful she was. Certainly the most beautiful woman he'd ever seen in the police department ranks.

For a brief instant he found her immeasurably appealing. People said that sex was all in the mind and Rhyme knew that this was true. Cutting the cord didn't stop the urge. He remembered, still with a faint crunch of horror, a night six months after the accident. He and Blaine had tried. Just to see what happened, they'd disclaimed, trying to be casual. No big deal.

But it *had* been a big deal. Sex is a messy business to start with and when you add catheters and bags to the equation you need a lot of stamina and humor and a better foundation than they'd had. Mostly, though, what killed the moment, and killed it fast, was her face. He saw in Blaine Chapman Rhyme's tough, game smile that she was doing it from pity and that stabbed him in the heart. He filed for divorce two weeks later. Blaine had protested but she signed the papers on the first go-round.

Sellitto and Banks had returned and were organizing the evidence Sachs had collected. She looked on, mildly interested.

Rhyme said to her, "The Latents Unit only found eight other recent partials and they belong to the two maintenance men in the building."

"Oh."

He nodded broadly. "Only *eight*!"

"He's complimenting you," Thom explained. "Enjoy it. That's the most you'll ever get out of him."

"No translations needed, please and thank you, Thom."

She responded, "I'm happy I could help." Pleasant as could be.

Well, what was *this*? Rhyme had fully expected her to storm into his room and fling the evidence bags onto his bed. Maybe the saw itself or even the plastic bag containing the vic's severed hands. He'd been looking forward to a real knock-down, drag-out; people rarely take the gloves off when they fight with a crip. He'd been thinking of that look in her eyes when she'd met him, perhaps evidence of some ambiguous kinship between them.

But no, he saw now he was wrong. Amelia Sachs was like everybody else—patting him on the head and looking for the nearest exit.

With a snap, his heart turned to ice. When he spoke it was to a cobweb high on the far wall. "We've been talking about the deadline for the next victim, officer. There doesn't seem to be specific time."

"What we think," Sellitto continued, "whatever this prick's got planned for the next one is something ongoing. He doesn't know exactly when the time of death will be. Lincoln thought maybe he's buried some poor SOB someplace where there's not much air."

Sachs's eye narrowed slightly at this. Rhyme noticed it. Burial alive. If you've got to have a phobia, that's as good as any.

They were interrupted by two men in gray suits who climbed the stairs and walked into the bedroom as if they lived here.

"We knocked," one of them said.

"We rang the bell," said the other.

"No answer."

They were in their forties, one taller than the other but both with the same sandy-colored hair. They bore identical smiles and before the Brooklyn drawl destroyed the image Rhyme had thought: Hayseed farm boys. One had an honest-to-God dusting of freckles along the bridge of his pale nose.

"Gentlemen."

Sellitto introduced the Hardy Boys: Detectives Bedding and Saul, the spadework team. Their skill was canvassing—interviewing people who live near a crime scene for wits and leads. It was a fine art but one that Rhyme had never learned, had no desire to. He was content to unearth hard facts and hand them off to officers like these, who, armed with the data, became living lie detectors who could shred perps' best cover stories. Neither of them seemed to think it was the least bit weird to be reporting to a bedridden civilian.

Saul, the taller of them, the frecklee, said, "We've found thirty-six—"

"-eight, if you count a couple of crack-heads. Which he doesn't. I do."

"—subjects. Interviewed all of them. Haven't had much luck."

"Most of 'em blind, deaf, amnesiacs. You know, the usual."

"No sign of the taxi. Combed the West Side. Zero. Zip."

Bedding: "But tell them the good news."

"We found a wit."

"A witness?" Banks asked eagerly. "Fan-tastic."

Rhyme, considerably less enthusiastic, said, "Go on."

"'Round the TOD this morning at the train tracks."

"He saw a man walk down Eleventh Avenue, turn—"

"'Suddenly,' he said," added no-freckle Bedding.

"—And go through an alley that led to the train underpass. He just stood there for a while—"

"Looking down."

Rhyme was troubled by this. "That doesn't sound like our boy. He's too smart to risk being seen like that."

"But—" Saul continued, raising a finger and glancing at his partner.

"There was only one window in the whole 'hood you could see the place from."

"Which is where our wit happened to be standing."

"Up early, bless his heart."

Before he remembered he was angry with her Rhyme asked, "Well, Amelia, how's it feel?"

"I'm sorry?" Her attention returned from the window.

"To be right," Rhyme said. "You pegged Eleventh Avenue. Not Thirty-seventh."

She didn't know how to respond but Rhyme turned immediately back to the twins. "Description?"

"Our wit couldn't say much."

"Was on the sauce. Already."

"He said it was a smallish guy. No hair color. Race—"

"Probably white."

"Wearing?" Rhyme asked.

"Something dark. Best he could say."

"And doing what?" Sellitto asked.

"I quote. 'He just like stood there, looking down. I thought he gonna jump. You know, in front of a train. Looked at his watch a couple times.'"

"And then finally left. Said he kept looking around. Like he didn't want to be seen."

What had he been doing? Rhyme wondered. Watching the victim die? Or was this before he planted the body, checking to see if the roadbed was deserted?

Sellitto asked, "Walked or drove?"

"Walked. We checked every parking lot—"

"And garage."

"—in the neighborhood. But that's near the convention center so you got parking coming out your ears. There're so many lots the attendants stand in the street with orange flags and wave cars in."

"And 'causa the expo half of them were full by seven. We got a list of about nine hundred tags."

Sellitto shook his head. "Follow up on it—"

"It's delegated," said Bedding.

"—but I betcha this's one unsub who ain't putting cars in lots," the detective continued. "Or getting parking tickets."

Rhyme nodded his agreement and asked, "The building at Pearl Street?"

One, or both, of the twins said, "That's next on our list. We're on our way."

Rhyme caught Sachs checking her watch, which sat on her white wrist near her ruddy fingers. He instructed Thom to add these new characteristics of the unsub to the profile chart.

"You want to interview that guy?" Banks asked. "The one by the railroad?"

"No. I don't trust witnesses," Rhyme said bombastically. "I want to get back to work." He glanced at Mel Cooper. "Hairs, blood, bone, and a sliver of wood. The bone first," Rhyme instructed.

Morgen . . .

Young Monelle Gerger opened her eyes and slowly sat up in the sagging bed. In her two years in east Greenwich Village she'd never gotten used to morning.

Her round, twenty-one-year-old body eased forward and she got a blast of unrelenting August sunlight in her bleary eyes. "*Mein Gott* . . ."

She'd left the club at five, home at six, made love with Brian until seven . . .

What time was it now?

Early morning, she was sure.

She squinted at the clock. Oh. Four-thirty in the afternoon. Not so *früh morgens* after all.

Coffee or laundry?

It was around this time of day that she'd wander over to

Dojo's for a veggie-burger breakfast and three cups of their tough coffee. There she'd meet people she knew, clubbies like herself—downtown people.

But she'd let a lot of things go lately, the domestic things. And so now she pulled on two baggy T-shirts to hide her chubby figure and jeans, hung five or six chains around her neck and grabbed the laundry basket, tossed the Wisk onto it.

Monelle undid the three dead bolts barring the door. She hefted the laundry basket and walked down the dark staircase of the residence hall. At the basement level she paused.

Irgendwas stimmt hier nicht.

Feeling uneasy, Monelle looked around the deserted stairway, the murky corridors.

What's different?

The light, that's it! The bulbs in the hall're burned out. No—she looked closely—they were *missing*. Fucking kids'll steal anything. She'd moved in here, the Deutsche Haus—because it was supposedly a haven for German artists and musicians. It turned out to be just another filthy, way-overpriced East Village walk-up, like all the other tenements around here. The only difference was that she could bitch to the manager in her native tongue.

She continued through the basement door into the incinerator room, which was so dark she had to grope her way along the wall to make sure she didn't trip over the junk on the floor.

Pushing open the door, she stepped into the corridor that led to the laundry room.

A shuffling. A skitter.

She turned quickly and saw nothing but motionless shadows. All she heard was the sound of traffic, the groans of an old, old building.

Through the dimness. Past stacks of boxes and discarded chairs and tables. Under wires caked with greasy dust. Monelle continued toward the laundry room. No bulbs here either. She was uneasy, recalling something that hadn't occurred to her for years. Walking with her father down a narrow alley off Lange Strasse, near the Obermain Brücke, on their way to the zoo. She must have been five or six. Her father had suddenly gripped her by the shoulder and pointed to the bridge and told her matter-of-factly that a hungry troll lived underneath it. When they crossed it on their way home, he warned, they'd have to walk quickly. She now felt a ripple of panic rise up her spine to her crew-cut blonde hair.

Stupid. Trolls . . .

She continued down the dank corridor, listening to the humming of some electrical equipment. Far off she heard a song by the feuding brothers in Oasis.

The laundry room was dark.

Well, if *those* bulbs were gone, that was it. She'd go upstairs, and pound on Herr Neischen's door until he came running. She'd given him hell for the broken latches on the front and back doors and for the beer-guzzling kids he never kicked off the front stoop. She'd give him hell for the missing bulbs too.

She reached inside and flicked the switch.

Brilliant white light. Three large bulbs glowed like suns, revealing a room that was filthy but empty. Monelle strode up to the bank of four machines and dumped the whites in one, the colors in the next. She counted out quarters, dropped them into slots and shoved the levers forward.

Nothing.

Monelle jiggled the lever. Then hit the machine itself. No response.

"Shit. This *gottverdammte* building."

Then she saw the power cord. Some idiot had unplugged the machines. She knew who. Neischen had a twelve-year-old son who was responsible for most of the carnage around the building. When she'd complained about something last year the little shit'd tried to kick her.

She picked up the cord and crouched, reaching behind the machine to find the outlet. She plugged it in.

And felt the man's breath on her neck.

Nein!

He was sandwiched between the wall and the back of the washer. Barking a fast scream, she caught a glimpse of ski mask and dark clothes then his hand clamped down on her arm like an animal's jaw. She was off balance and he easily jerked her forward. She tumbled to the floor, hitting her face on the rough concrete, and swallowed the scream forming in her throat.

He was on her in an instant, pinning her arms to the concrete, slapping a piece of thick gray tape over her mouth.

Hilfe!

Nein, bitte nicht.

Bitte nicht.

He wasn't large but he was strong. He easily rolled her over onto her stomach and she heard the ratcheting of the handcuffs closing on her wrists.

Then he stood up. For a long moment, no sound but the drip of water, the rasp of Monelle's breath, the click of a small motor somewhere in the basement.

Waiting for the hands to touch her body, to tear off her clothes. She heard him walk to the doorway to make sure they were alone.

Oh, he had complete privacy, she knew, furious with herself; she was one of the few residents who used the laundry room. Most of them avoided it because it was so deserted, so close to the back doors and windows, so far away from help.

He returned and rolled her over onto her back. Whispered something she couldn't make out. Then: "Hanna."

Hanna? It's a mistake! He thinks I'm somebody else. She shook her head broadly, trying to make him understand this.

But then, looking at his eyes, she stopped. Even though he wore a ski mask, it was clear that something was wrong. He was upset. He scanned her body, shaking his head. He closed his gloved fingers around her big arms. Squeezed her thick shoulders, grabbed a pinch of fat. She shivered in pain.

That's what she saw: disappointment. He'd caught her and now he wasn't sure he wanted her after all.

He reached into his pocket and slowly withdrew his hand. The click of the knife opening was like an electric shock. It started a jag of sobbing.

Nein, nein, nein!

A hiss of breath escaped from his teeth like wind through winter trees. He crouched over her, debating.

"Hanna," he whispered. "What am I going to do?"

Then, suddenly, he made a decision. He put the knife away and yanked her to her feet then led her out to the corridor and through the rear door—the one with the broken lock she'd been hounding Herr Neischen for weeks to fix.

ELEVEN

A criminalist is a renaissance man.

He's got to know botany, geology, ballistics, medicine, chemistry, literature, engineering. If he knows facts—that ash with a high strontium content probably came from a highway flare, that *faca* is Portuguese for "knife," that Ethiopian diners use no utensils and eat with their right hands exclusively, that a slug with five land-and-groove rifling marks, right twist, could not have been fired by a Colt pistol—if he knows these things he may just make the connection that places an unsub at the crime scene.

One subject all criminalists know is anatomy. And this was certainly a specialty of Lincoln Rhyme's, for he had spent the past three and a half years enmeshed in the quirky logic of bone and nerve.

He now glanced at the evidence bag from the steam room, dangling in Jerry Bank's hand, and announced, "Leg bone. Not human. So it's not from the next vic."

It was a ring of bone about two inches around, sawn through evenly. There was blood in the tracks left by the saw blade.

"A medium-sized animal," Rhyme continued. "Large dog, sheep, goat. It'd support, I'd guess, a hundred to a hundred fifty pounds of weight. Let's make sure the blood's from an animal though. Still could be the vic's."

Perps had been known to beat or stab people to death with bones. Rhyme himself had had three such cases; the weapons had been a beef knuckle bone, a deer's leg bone, and in one disturbing case the victim's own ulna.

Mel Cooper ran a gel-diffusion test for blood origin.

UNSUB 823			
Appearance	Residence	Vehicle	Other
• Caucasian male, slight build • Dark clothing	• Prob. has safe house	• Yellow Cab	• knows CS proc. • possibly has record • knows FR prints • gun = .32 Colt

"We'll have to wait a bit for the results," Cooper explained apologetically.

"Amelia," Rhyme said, "maybe you could help us here. Use the eye loupe and look the bone over carefully. Tell us what you see."

"Not the microscope?" she asked. He thought she'd protest but she stepped forward to the bone, peered at it with curiosity.

"Too much magnification," Rhyme explained.

She put on the goggles and bent over the white enamel tray. Cooper turned on a gooseneck lamp.

"The cutting marks," Rhyme said. "Is it hacked up or are they even?"

"They're pretty even."

"A power saw."

Rhyme wondered if the animal had been alive when he'd done this.

"See anything unusual?"

She pored over the bone for a moment, muttered, "I don't know. I don't think so. It just looks like a hunk of bone."

It was then that Thom walked past and glanced at the tray. "That's your clue? That's funny."

"Funny," Rhyme said. "*Funny*?"

Sellitto asked, "You got a theory?"

"No theory." He bent down and smelled it. "It's osso bucco."

"What?"

"Veal shank. I made it for you once, Lincoln. Osso bucco. Braised veal shank." He looked at Sachs and grimaced. "He said it needed more salt."

"Goddamn!" Sellitto cried. "He bought it at a grocery store!"

"If we're lucky," Rhyme said, "he bought it at *his* grocery store."

Cooper confirmed that the precipitin test showed negative for human blood on the samples Sachs had collected. "Probably bovine," he said.

"But what's he trying to tell us?" Banks asked.

Rhyme had no idea. "Let's keep going. Oh, anything on the chain and padlock?"

Cooper glanced at the hardware in a crisp plastic bag. "Nobody name-stamps chain anymore. So we're out of luck there. The lock's a Secure-Pro middle-of-the-line model. It isn't very secure and definitely not professional. How long d'it take to break it?"

"Three whole seconds," Sellitto said.

"See. No serial numbers and it's sold in every hardware and variety store in the country."

"Key or combination?" Rhyme asked.

"Combination."

"Call the manufacturer. Ask them if we take it apart and reconstruct the combination from the tumblers, will that tell us which shipment it was in and where it went to?"

Banks whistled. "Man, that's a long shot."

Rhyme's glare sent a ferocious blush across his face. "And the enthusiasm in your voice, detective, tells me you're just the one to handle the job."

"Yessir"—the young man held up his cellular phone defensively—"I'm on it."

Rhyme asked, "Is that blood on the chain?"

Sellitto said, "One of our boys. Cut himself pretty bad trying to break the lock off."

"So it's contaminated." Rhyme scowled.

"He was trying to save her," Sachs said to him.

"I understand. That was good of him. It's still contaminated." Rhyme glanced back at the table beside Cooper. "Prints?"

Cooper said he'd checked it and found only Sellitto's on the links.

"All right, the splinter of wood Amelia found. Check for prints."

"I did," Sachs said quickly. "At the scene."

P.D., Rhyme reflected. She didn't seem to be the nickname sort. Beautiful people rarely were.

"Let's try the heavy guns, just to be sure," Rhyme said and instructed Cooper, "Use DFO or ninhydrin. Then hit it with the nit-yag."

"The what?" Banks asked.

"A neodymium:yttrium aluminum garnet laser."

The tech spritzed the splinter with liquid from a plastic spray bottle and trained the laser beam on the wood. He slipped on tinted goggles and examined it carefully. "Nothing."

He shut off the light and examined the splinter closely. It was about six inches long, dark wood. There were black smears on it, like tar, and it was impregnated with dirt. He held it with forceps.

"I know Lincoln likes the chopstick approach," Cooper said, "but I always ask for a fork when I go to Ming Wa's."

"You could be crushing the cells," the criminalist grumbled.

"I *could* be but I'm not," Cooper responded.

"What kind of wood?" Rhyme wondered. "Want to run an spodogram?"

"No, it's oak. No question."

"Saw or plane marks?" Rhyme leaned forward. Suddenly his neck spasmed and the cramp that bolted through the muscles was unbearable. He gasped, closed his eyes and twisted his neck, stretching. He felt Thom's strong hands massaging the muscles. The pain finally faded.

"Lincoln?" Sellitto asked. "You okay?"

Rhyme breathed deeply. "Fine. It's nothing."

"Here." Cooper brought the piece of wood over to the bed, lowered the magnifying goggles over Rhyme's eyes.

Rhyme examined the specimen. "Cut in the direction of the grain with a frame saw. There're big variations in the cuts. So I'd guess it was a post or beam milled over a hundred years ago. Steam saw probably. Hold it closer, Mel. I want to smell it."

He held the splinter under Rhyme's nose.

"Creosote—coal-tar distillation. Used for weather-proofing wood before lumber companies started pressure-treating. Piers, docks, railroad ties."

"Maybe we've got a train buff here," Sellitto said. "Remember the tracks this morning."

"Could be." Rhyme ordered, "Check for cellular compression, Mel."

The tech examined the splinter under the compound microscope. "It's compressed all right. But *with* the grain. Not against it. Not a railroad tie. This is from a post or column. Weight-bearing."

A bone . . . an old wooden post . . .

"I see dirt embedded in the wood. That tell us anything?"

Cooper set a large pad of newsprint on the table, tore the cover off. He held the splinter over the pad and brushed some dirt from cracks in the wood. He examined the speckles lying on the white paper—a reverse constellation.

"You have enough for a density-gradient test?" Rhyme asked.

In a D-G test, dirt is poured into a tube containing liquids of different specific gravities. The soil separates and each particle hangs suspended according to its own gravity. Rhyme had established a very extensive library of density-gradient profiles for dirt from all over the five boroughs. Unfortunately the test only worked with a fair amount of soil; Cooper didn't think they had enough. "We could try it but we'd have to use the entire sample. And if it didn't work we wouldn't have anything left for other tests."

Rhyme instructed him to do a visual then analyze it in the GC-MS—the chromatograph-spectrometer.

The technician brushed some dirt onto a slide. He gazed at it for a few minutes under the compound microscope. "This is strange, Lincoln. It's topsoil. With an unusually high level of vegetation in it. But it's in a curious form. Very deteriorated, very decomposed." He looked up and Rhyme noticed the dark lines under his eyes from the eyepieces. He remembered that after hours of lab work the marks were quite pronounced and that occasionally a forensic tech would emerge from the IRD lab only to be greeted by a chorus of *Rocky Raccoon.*

"Burn it," Rhyme ordered.

Cooper mounted a sample in the GC-MS unit. The machine rumbled to life and there was a hiss. "A minute or two."

"While we're waiting," Rhyme said, "the bone . . . I keep wondering about the bone. 'Scope it, Mel."

Cooper carefully set the bone onto the examination stage of the compound microscope. He went over it carefully. "Whoa, got something here."

"What?"

"Very small. Transparent. Hand me the hemostat," Cooper said to Sachs, nodding at a pair of gripper tweezers. She handed them to him and he carefully probed in the marrow of the bone. He lifted something out.

"A tiny piece of regenerated cellulose," Cooper announced.

"Cellophane," Rhyme said. "Tell me more."

"Stretch and pinch marks. I'd say he didn't leave it intentionally; there are no cut edges. It's not inconsistent with heavy-duty cello," Cooper said.

"'Not inconsistent.'" Rhyme scowled. "I don't like his hedges."

"We *have* to hedge, Lincoln," Cooper said, cheerfully.

"'Associate with.' 'Suggest.' I particularly hate 'not inconsistent.'"

"Very versatile," Cooper said. "The boldest I'll be is that it's probably commerical butcher or grocery store cellophane. Not Saran Wrap. Definitely not generic-brand wrap."

Jerry Banks walked inside from the hallway. "Bad news. The Secure-Pro company doesn't keep any records on combinations. A machine sets them at random."

"Ah."

"But interesting . . . they said they get calls from the police all the time about their products and you're the first one who's ever thought of tracing a lock through the combination."

"How 'interesting' can it be if it's a dead end?" Rhyme grumbled and turned to Mel Cooper, who was shaking his head as he stared at the GC-MS computer. "What?"

"Got that soil sample result. But I'm afraid the machine might be on the fritz. The nitrogen's off the charts. We should run it again, use more sample this time."

Rhyme instructed him to go ahead. His eyes turned back to the bone. "Mel, how recent was the kill?"

He examined some scrapings under the electron microscope.

"Minimal bacteria clusters. Bambi here was recently deceased, looks like. Or just out of the fridge about eight hours."

"So our perp just bought it," Rhyme said.

"Or a month ago and froze it," Sellitto suggested.

"No," Cooper said. "It hasn't been frozen. There's no evidence of tissue damage from ice crystals. And it hasn't been refrigerated that long. It's not desiccated; modern refrigerators dehydrate food."

"It's a good lead," Rhyme said. "Let's get to work on it."

"'Get to work'?" Sachs laughed. "Are you saying we call

up all the grocery stores in the city and find out who sold veal bones yesterday?"

"No," Rhyme countered. "In the past *two* days."

"You want the Hardy Boys?"

"Let them keep doing what they're doing. Call Emma, down-town, if she's still working. And if she isn't get her back to the office with the other dispatchers and put them on overtime. Get her a list of every grocery chain in town. I'll bet our boy isn't buying groceries for a family of four so have Emma limit the list to customers buying five items or less."

"Warrants?" Banks asked.

"Anybody balks, we'll get a warrant," Sellitto said. "But let's try without. Who knows? Some citizens might actually cooperate. I'm told it happens."

"But how are the stores going to know who bought veal shanks?" Sachs asked. She was no longer as aloof as she had been. There was an edge in her voice. Rhyme wondered if her frustration might be a sympton of what he himself had often felt—the burdensome weight of the evidence. The essential problem for the criminalist is not that there's too little evidence but that there's too much.

"Checkout scanners," Rhyme said. "They record purchases on computer. For inventory and restocking. Go ahead, Banks. I see something just crossed your mind. Speak up. I won't send you to Siberia this time."

"Well, only the chains have scanners, sir," the young detective offered. "There're hundreds of independents and butcher shops that don't."

"Good point. But I think he wouldn't go to a small shop. Anonymity's important to him. He'll be doing his buying at big stores. Impersonal."

Sellitto called Communications and explained to Emma what they needed.

"Let's get a polarized shot of the cellophane," Rhyme said to Cooper.

The technician put the minuscule fragment in a polarizing 'scope, then fitted the Polaroid camera to the eyepiece and took a shot. It was a colorful picture, a rainbow with gray streaks through it. Rhyme examined it. This pattern told them nothing by itself but it could be compared with other cello samples to see if they came from a common source.

Rhyme had a thought. "Lon, get a dozen Emergency Service officers over here. On the double."

"Here?" Sellitto asked.

"We're going to put an operation together."

"You're sure about that?" the detective asked.

"Yes! I want them now."

"All right." He nodded to Banks, who made the call to Haumann.

"Now, what about the other planted clue—those hairs Amelia found?"

Cooper poked through them with a probe then mounted several in the phase-contrast microscope. This instrument shot two light sources at a single subject, the second beam delayed slightly—out of phase—so the sample was both illuminated and set off by shadow.

"It's not human," Cooper said. "I'll tell you that right now. And they're guard hairs, not down."

Hairs from the animal's coat, he meant.

"What kind? Dog?"

"Veal calf?" Banks suggested, once again youthfully enthusiastic.

"Check the scales," Rhyme ordered. Meaning the microscopic flakes that make up the outer sheath of a strand of hair.

Cooper typed on his computer keyboard and a few seconds later thumbnail images of scaly rods popped onto the screen. "This is thanks to you, Lincoln. Remember the database?"

At IRD Rhyme had compiled a huge collection of micrographs of different types of hair. "I do, yes, Mel. But they were in three-ring binders when I saw 'em last. How'd you get them on the computer?"

"ScanMaster of course. JPEG compressed."

Jay-peg? What was that? In a few years technology had soared beyond Rhyme. Amazing . . .

And as Cooper examined the images, Lincoln Rhyme wondered again what he'd been wondering all day—the question that kept floating to the surface: Why the clues? The human creature is so astonishing but count on it before anything else to be just that—a creature. A laughing animal, a dangerous one, a clever one, a scared one, but always acting for a *reason*—a motive that will move the beast toward its desires. Scientist Lincoln Rhyme didn't believe in chance, or randomness, or frivolity. Even psychopaths had their own logic, twisted though it may have been, and he knew there was a reason Unsub 823 spoke to them only in this cryptic way.

Cooper called, "Got it. Rodent. Probably a rat. And the hairs were shaved off."

"That's a hell of a clue," Banks said. "There's a million rats in the city. That doesn't pin down anyplace. What's the point of telling us that?"

Sellitto closed his eyes momentarily and muttered something under his breath. Sachs didn't notice the look. She glanced at Rhyme curiously. He was surprised that she hadn't figured out what the kidnapper's message was but he said nothing. He saw no reason to share this horrifying bit of knowledge with anyone else for the time being.

James Schneider's seventh victim, or eighth, should you choose to number poor, angelic little Maggie O'Connor among them, was the wife of a hardworking immigrant, who had established the family's modest habitation near Hester Street on the Lower East Side of the City.

It was thanks to the courage of this unfortunate woman that the constables and the police discovered the identity of the criminal. Hanna Goldschmidt was of German–Jewish extraction and was held in high esteem by the close-knit community in which she, her husband and their six children (one had died at birth) lived.

The bone collector drove through the streets slowly, careful to remain under the speed limit though he knew perfectly well that the traffic cops in New York wouldn't stop you for something as minor as speeding.

He paused at a light and glanced up at another UN billboard. His eyes took in the bland, smiling faces—like the eerie faces painted on the walls of the mansion—and then looked beyond it, at the city around him. He was, occasionally, surprised to look up and find the buildings so massive, the stone cornices so high aloft, the glass so smooth, the cars so sleek, the people so scrubbed. The city he knew was dark, low, smoky, smelling of sweat and mud. Horses would trample you, roving gangs of hoodlums—some as young as ten or eleven—would knock you on the head with a shillelagh or sap and make off with your pocket watch and billfold . . . *This* was the bone collector's city.

Sometimes, though, he found himself just like this—driving a spiffy silver Taurus XL along a smooth asphalt road, listening to WNYC and irritated, like all New Yorkers, when he missed a green light, wondering why the hell didn't the city let you make right turns on red.

He cocked his head, heard several thumps from the trunk of the car. But there was so much ambient noise that no one would hear Hanna's protests.

The light changed.

It is, of course, exceptional even in these enlightened times for a woman to venture forth into the city streets in the evening, unaccompanied by a gentlemen; and in those days it was more exceptional still. Yet on this unfortunate night Hanna had no choice but to quit her abode for a brief time. Her youngest had a fever, and, with her husband praying devoutly at a nearby synagogue, she issued forth into the night to secure a poultice for the child's fiery forehead. As she closed the door she said to her eldest daughter,—

"Lock tight the bolt behind me. I shall return soon."

But, alas, she would not be true to those words. For only moments later she chanced to encounter James Schneider.

The bone collector looked around at the shabby streets here. This area—near where he'd buried the first victim—was Hell's Kitchen, on the West Side of the city, once the bastion of Irish gangs, now populated more and more with young professionals, ad agencies, photo studios and stylish restaurants.

He smelled manure and wasn't the least surprised when suddenly a horse reared in front of him.

Then he noticed that the animal wasn't an apparition from the 1800s but was being hitched to one of the hansom cabs that cruised Central Park charging very twentieth-century fees. Their stables were located here.

He laughed to himself. Though it was a hollow sound.

One can only speculate as to what occurred, for there were no witnesses. But we can picture the horror all too clearly. The villain drew the struggling woman into an alley and stabbed her with a dagger, his cruel intent not to kill but to subdue, as was his wont. But such was the strength in good Mrs Goldschmidt's soul, thinking as she surely was of her fledglings back in the nest, that she surprised the monster by assaulting him ferociously:—she struck him repeatedly about the face and ripped hair from his head.

She freed herself momentarily and from her mouth issued an horrendous scream. The cowardly Schneider struck her several times more and fled.

The brave woman staggered to the sidewalk and collapsed, where she died in the arms of a constable who had responded to the alarm neighbors had raised.

This story appeared in a book, which was with the bone collector now, resting in his hip pocket. *Crime in Old New York*. He couldn't explain his overwhelming attraction to the slim volume. If he had to describe his relation to this book he would have to say he was addicted to it. Seventy-five years old and still in remarkable shape, a bookbinding jewel. It was his good-luck charm and his talisman. He'd found it at a small branch of the public library and committed one of the few larcenies of his life by slipping it into his raincoat one day and strolling out of the building.

He'd read the chapter on Schneider a hundred times and virtually had it memorized.

Driving slowly. They were almost there.

When Hanna's poor, weeping husband huddled over her lifeless body, he looked upon her face:—one last time before she was taken to the funeral home (for in the Jewish faith it is dictated that the dead must be interred as quickly as possible). And he noticed upon her porcelain cheek a bruise in the shape of a curious emblem. It was a round symbol and appeared to be a crescent moon and a cluster of what might be taken to be stars hovering over the same.

The constable exclaimed that this must have been an imprint made by the ring of the heinous butcher himself when he struck the poor victim. Detectives enlisted the aid of an artist and he sketched a picture of the impression. (The good reader is referred to plate XXII.) Rounds were made of jewelers in the city, and several names and addresses were secured of men who had bought such rings in the recent past. Two of the gentlemen purchasing these rings were beyond suspicion, being as they were a deacon of a church and another a learned professor at a fine university. Yet the third was a man of whom the constables had long harbored suspicion of nefarious activity. To wit:—one James Schneider.

This gentleman had at one time been influential in several benevolent organizations in the city of Manhattan: the Consumptives' Assistance League and the Pensioners' Welfare Society, most notably. He had come under the eye of the constabulary when several elderly charges from said groups vanished not long after Schneider paid them calls. He was never charged with any offense but soon after the investigations, he dropped from sight.

In the aftermath of Hanna Goldschmidt's heinous murder, a still search of the dubious haunts of the city revealed no abode where Schneider might be found. The constables posted broadsides throughout the down-town and River-front areas, setting forth the description of the villain, but he could not be apprehended;—a true tragedy, to be sure, in light of the carnage that was soon to befall the city at his vile hands.

The streets were clear. The bone collector drove into the alley. He opened the warehouse door and drove down a wooden ramp into a long tunnel.

After making sure the place was deserted, he walked to the back of the car. He opened the trunk and pulled Hanna out. She was fleshy, fat, like a bag of limp mulch. He grew angry again and he carried her roughly down another wide tunnel. Traffic from the West Side Highway sped over them. He listened to her wheezing and was just reaching out to loosen the gag when he felt her shudder and go completely limp. Gasping for breath with the effort of carrying her, he rested her on the floor of the tunnel and eased the tape off her mouth. Air dribbled in weakly. Had she just fainted? He listened to her heart. It seemed to be beating fine.

He cut the clothesline binding her ankles, leaned forward

and whispered, "Hanna, *kommen Sie mit mir mit*, Hanna Goldschmidt . . ."

"*Nein*," she muttered, her voice trailing to silence.

He leaned closer, lightly slapped her face. "Hanna, you must come with me."

And she screamed: "*Mein Name ist nicht Hanna!*" Then kicked him square in the jaw.

A burst of yellow light flashed through his head and he leapt sideways two or three feet, trying to keep his balance. Hanna sprang up, raced blindly down a dark corridor. But he was after her fast. He tackled her before she'd gotten ten yards away. She fell hard; he did too, grunting as he lost his breath.

He lay on his side for a minute, consumed with pain, struggling to breathe, gripping her T-shirts as she thrashed. Lying on her back, hands still cuffed, the girl used the only weapon she had—one of her feet, which she lifted in the air and brought down hard onto his hand. A spike of pain shot through him and his glove flew off. She lifted her strong leg again and only her bad aim saved him from her heel, which slammed so hard into the ground it would've broken bones if she'd connected.

"*So nicht!*" he growled madly and grabbed her by the throat with his bare hand and squeezed until she squirmed and whined and then stopped squirming and whining. She trembled several times and went still.

When he listened to her heart the beating was very faint. No tricks this time. He snatched up his glove, pulled it on and dragged her back through the tunnel to the post. Bound her feet once more and put a new piece of tape on her mouth. As she came to, his hand was straying over her body. She gasped at first and shrank away as he caressed the flesh behind her ear. Her elbow, her jaw. There weren't many other places he wanted to touch her. She was so *padded* . . . it disgusted him.

Yet *beneath* the skin . . . He gripped her leg firmly. Her wide eyes stared as he fumbled in his pocket and the knife appeared. Without a moment's hesitation he cut through her skin down to the yellow-white bone. She screamed through the tape, a manic wail, and kicked hard but he held her tight. Enjoying this, Hanna? The girl sobbed and groaned loudly. So he had to lower his ear to her leg to hear the delicious sound of the tip of the blade scraping back and forth on the bone. *Skrisssss.*

Then he took her arm.

They locked eyes for a moment and as she shook her head pathetically, begging in silence. His gaze dropped to her pudgy forearm and again the cut was deep. Her whole body went rigid with the pain. Another wild, muted scream. Again he lowered his head like a musician, listening to the sound of the blade scraping the ulna. Back and forth. *Skrissss, skrisssss* . . . It was some moments later that he realized she'd fainted.

Finally he pried himself away and returned to the car. He planted the next clues then took the broom from the trunk and carefully swept over their footsteps. He drove up the ramp, parked, left the engine running and climbed out once more, carefully sweeping away the tire tracks.

He paused and looked back down the tunnel. Staring at her, just staring. Suddenly a rare smile crossed the bone collector's lips. He was surprised that the first of the guests had already shown up. A dozen pairs of tiny red eyes, two dozen, then three . . . It seemed they were gazing at Hanna's bloody flesh with curiosity . . . and what might have been hunger. Though that could have been his imagination; Lord knew, it was vivid enough.

TWELVE

"Mel, go through the Colfax woman's clothes. Amelia, would you help him?"

She offered him another pleasant nod, the sort meant for polite society. Rhyme realized he was really quite angry with her.

At the tech's direction she pulled on latex gloves, gently opened the clothing and ran a horsehair brush through the garments, above large sheets of clean newsprint. Tiny flecks fell out. Cooper picked them up on tape and examined them through the compound 'scope.

"Not much," he reported. "The steam took care of most of the trace. I see a little soil. Not enough to D-G. Wait . . . Excellent. I've got a couple of fibers. Look at these. . . ."

Well, I can't, Rhyme thought angrily.

"Navy blue, acrylic-and-wool blend, I'd guess. It isn't coarse enough to be carpet and it's not lobed. So it's clothing."

"In this heat he's not going to be wearing thick socks or a sweater. Ski mask?"

"That'd be my bet," Cooper said.

Rhyme reflected, "So he's serious about giving us a chance to save them. If he was bent on killing, it wouldn't matter if they saw him or not."

Silletto added, "Also means the asshole thinks he can get away. Doesn't have suicide on his mind. Might just give us some bargaining power if he's got hostages when we nail him."

"I like that optimism of yours, Lon," Rhyme said.

Thom answered the buzzer and a moment later Jim Polling climbed the stairs, looking disheveled and harried. Well, shuttling between press conferences, the mayor's office and the federal building would do that to you.

"Too bad about the trout," Sellitto called to him. Then explained to Rhyme, "Jimmy here's one of those *real* fishermen. Ties his own flies and everything. Me, I go out on a party boat with a six-pack and I'm happy."

"We'll nail this fucker then worry about the fish," Polling said, helping himself to the coffee Thom had left by the window. He looked outside and blinked in surprise to find two large birds staring at him. He turned back to Rhyme and explained that because of the kidnapping he'd had to postpone a fishing trip to Vermont. Rhyme had never fished—never had the time or inclination for any hobbies—but he found he envied Polling. The serenity of fishing appealed to him. It was a sport you could practice in solitude. Crip sports tended to be in-your-face athletics. Competitive. Proving things to the world . . . and to yourself. Wheelchair basketball, tennis, marathons. Rhyme decided if he had to have a sport it'd be fishing. Though casting a line with a single finger was probably beyond modern technology.

Polling said, "The press is calling him a serial kidnapper."

If the bootie fits, Rhyme reflected.

"And the mayor's going nuts. Wants to call in the feds. I talked the chief into sitting tight on that one. But we can't lose another vic."

"We'll do our best," Rhyme said caustically.

Polling sipped the black coffee and stepped close to the bed. "You okay, Lincoln?"

Rhyme said, "Fine."

Polling appraised him for a moment longer then nodded to Sellitto. "Brief me. We got another press conference in a half hour. You see the last one? Hear what that reporter asked? What did we think the vic's family felt about her being scalded to death?"

Banks shook his head. "Man."

"I nearly decked the fucker," Polling said.

Three and a half years ago, Rhyme recalled, during the cop-killer investigation, the captain had smashed a news crew's videocam when the reporter wondered if Polling was being too aggressive in his investigations just because the suspect, Dan Shepherd, was a member of the force.

Polling and Sellitto retired to a corner of Rhyme's room and the detective filled him in. When the captain descended the stairs this time, Rhyme noticed, he wasn't half as buoyant as he had been.

"Okay," Cooper announced. "We've got a hair. It was in her pocket."

"The whole shaft?" Rhyme asked, without much hope, and was not surprised when Cooper sighed. "Sorry. No bulb."

Without a bulb attached, hair isn't individuated evidence; it's merely class evidence. You can't run a DNA test and link it to a specific person. Still, it has good probative value. The famous Canadian Mounties study a few years ago concluded that if a hair found at the scene matches a suspect's hair the odds are around 4,500 to 1 that he's the one who left it. The problem with hair, though, is that you can't deduce much about the person it belonged to. Sex is almost impossible to determine, and race can't be reliably established. Age can be estimated only with infant hair. Color is deceptive because of wide pigmentation variations and cosmetic dyes, and since everybody loses dozens of hairs every day you can't even tell if the suspect is going bald.

"Check it against the vic's. Do a scale count and medulla pigmentation comparison," Rhyme ordered.

A moment later Cooper looked up from the 'scope. "It's not hers, the Colfax woman's."

"Description?" asked Rhyme.

"Light brown. No kink so I'd say not Negroid. Pigmentation suggests it's not Mongoloid."

"So Caucasian," Rhyme said, nodding at the chart on the wall. "Confirms what the wit said. Head or body hair?"

"There's little diameter variation and a uniform pigment distribution. It's head hair."

"Length?"

"Three centimeters."

Thom asked if he should add to the profile that the kidnapper had brown hair.

Rhyme said no. "We'll wait for some corroboration. Just

write down that we know he wears a ski mask, navy blue. Fingernail scrapings, Mel?"

Cooper examined the trace but found nothing useful.

"The print you found. The one on the wall. Let's take a look at it. Could you show it to me, Amelia?"

Sachs hesitated then carried the Polaroid over to him.

"Your monster," Rhyme said. It was a large deformed palm, indeed grotesque, not with the elegant swirls and bifurcations of friction ridges but a mottled pattern of tiny lines.

"It's a wonderful picture—you're a virtual Edward Weston, Amelia. But unfortunately it's not a hand. Those aren't ridges. It's a glove. Leather. Old. Right, Mel?"

The technician nodded.

"Thom, write down that he has an old pair of gloves." Rhyme said to the others, "We're starting to get some ideas about him. He's not leaving *his* FR prints at the scene. But he is leaving glove prints. If we find the glove in his possession we can still place him at the scene. He's smart. But not brilliant."

Sachs asked, "And what do brilliant criminals wear?"

"Cotton-lined suede," Rhyme said. Then asked, "Where's the filter? From the vacuum?"

The technician emptied the cone filter—like one from a coffee-maker—onto a sheet of white paper.

Trace evidence . . .

DAs and reporters and juries loved obvious clues. Bloody gloves, knives, recently fired guns, love letters, semen and fingerprints. But Lincoln Rhyme's favorite evidence was trace—the dust and effluence at crime scenes, so easily overlooked by perps.

But the vacuum had captured nothing helpful.

"All right," Rhyme said, "let's move on. Let's look at the handcuffs."

Sachs stiffened as Cooper opened the plastic bag and slid the cuffs out onto a sheet of newsprint. There was, as Rhyme had predicted, minimal blood. The tour doctor from the medical examiner's office had done the honors with the razor saw, after an NYPD lawyer had faxed a release to the ME.

Cooper examined the cuffs carefully. "Boyd & Keller. Bottom of the line. No serial number." He sprayed the chrome with DFO and hit the PoliLight. "No prints, just a smudge from the glove."

"Let's open them up."

Cooper used a generic cuff key to click them open. With a lens-cleaning air puffer he blew into the mechanism.

"You're still mad at me, Amelia," Rhyme said. "About the hands."

The question caught her off guard. "I wasn't mad," she said after a moment. "I thought it was unprofessional. What you were suggesting."

"Do you know who Edmond Locard was?"

She shook her head.

"A Frenchman. Born in 1877. He founded the University of Lyons' Institute of Criminalistics. He came up with the one rule I lived by when I ran IRD. Locard's Exchange Principle. He thought that whenever two human beings come into contact, something from one is exchanged to the other, and vice versa. Maybe dust, blood, skin cells, dirt, fibers, metallic residue. It might be tough to find exactly what's been exchanged, and even harder to figure out what it means. But an exchange *does* occur—and because of that we can catch our unsubs."

This bit of history didn't interest her in the least.

"You're lucky," Mel Cooper said to Sachs, not looking up. "He was going to have you and the medic do a spot autopsy and examine the contents of her stomach."

"It would've been helpful," Rhyme said, avoiding her eyes.

"I talked him out of it," Cooper said.

"Autopsy," Sachs said, sighing, as if nothing about Rhyme could surprise her.

Why, she isn't even *here*, he thought angrily. Her mind's a thousand miles away.

"Ah," Cooper said. "Found something. I think it's a bit of the glove."

Cooper mounted a fleck on the compound microscope. Examined it.

"Leather. Reddish-colored. Polished on one side."

"Red, that's good," Sellitto said. To Sachs he explained, "The wilder their clothes, the easier it is to find the perp. They don't teach you that at the academy, bet. Sometime

I'll tell you 'bout the time we collared Jimmy Plaid, from the Gambino crew. You remember that, Jerry?"

"You could spot those pants a mile away," the young detective said.

Cooper continued, "The leather's desiccated. Not much oil in the grain. You were right too about them being old."

"What kind of animal?"

"I'd say kidskin. High quality."

"If they were new it might mean he was rich," Rhyme grumbled. "But since they're old he might've found them on the street or bought them secondhand. No snappy deductions from 823's accessorizing, looks like. Okay. Thom, just add to the profile that the gloves are reddish kidskin. What else do we have?"

"He wears aftershave," Sachs reminded him.

"Forgot that. Good. Maybe to cover up another scent. Unsubs do that sometimes. Write it down, Thom. What did it smell like again, Amelia? You described it."

"Dry. Like gin."

"What about the clothesline?" Rhyme asked.

Cooper examined it. "I've seen this before. Plastic. Several dozen interior filaments composed of six to ten different plastic types and one—no, two—metallic filaments."

"I want a manufacturer and source."

Cooper shook his head. "Impossible. Too generic."

"Damn," Rhyme muttered. "And the knot?"

"Now *that's* unusual. Very efficient. See how it loops around twice? PVC is the hardest cord to tie and this knot ain't going anywhere."

"They have a knot file downtown?"

"No."

Inexcusable, he thought.

"Sir?"

Rhyme turned to Banks.

"I do some sailing . . ."

"Out of Westport," Rhyme said.

"Well, as a matter of fact, yeah. How'd you know?"

If there were a forensic test for location of origin Jerry Banks would turn up positive for Connecticut. "Lucky guess."

"It isn't nautical. I don't recognize it."

"That's good to know. Hang it up there." Rhyme nodded toward the wall, next to the Polaroid of the cellophane and the Monet poster. "We'll get to it later."

The doorbell rang and Thom disappeared to answer it. Rhyme had a bad moment thinking that perhaps it was Dr Berger returning to tell him he was no longer interested in helping him with their "project."

But the heavy thud of boots told Rhyme who had come a-calling.

The Emergency Services officers, all large, all somber, dressed in combat gear, entered the room politely and nodded to Sellitto and Banks. They were men of action and Rhyme bet that behind the twenty still eyes were ten very bad reactions to the sight of a man laid up forever on his back.

"Gentlemen, you've heard about the kidnapping last night and the death of the victim this afternoon." He continued through the affirmative muttering, "Our unsub has another victim. We have a lead in the case and I need you to hit locations around the city and secure evidence. Immediately and simultaneously. One man, one location."

"You mean," one mustachioed officer asked uncertainly, "no backup."

"You won't need it."

"All due respect, sir, I'm not inclined to go into any tactical situation without backup. A partner at least."

"I don't think there'll be any firefights. The targets are the major chain grocery stores in town."

"Grocery stores?"

"Not every store. Just one of every chain. J&G's, ShopRite, Food Warehouse . . ."

"What exactly are we going to do?"

"Buy veal shanks."

"What?"

"One package at each store. I'm afraid I'll have to ask you to pay from your own pocket, gentlemen. But the city'll reimburse you. Oh, and we need them ASAP."

She lay on her side, immobile.

Her eyes had grown accustomed to the dimness of the old

tunnel and she could see the little fuckers moving closer. One in particular she kept her eyes on.

Monelle's leg stung like a bitch but most of the pain was in her arm, from where he'd cut deep into her skin. Because it was cuffed behind her she couldn't see the wound, didn't know how much she'd bled. But it must have been a lot; she was very faint and could feel the sticky ooze all over her arms and side.

The sound of scratching—needlish claws on concrete. The gray-brown lumps rustling in the shadows. The rats continued to twitch their way toward her. There must have been a hundred of them.

She forced herself to stay completely still and kept her eyes on the big black one. Schwarzie, she called him. He was in the front, moving back and forth, studying her.

Monelle Gerger had been around the world twice by the time she was nineteen. She'd hitched through Sri Lanka and Cambodia and Pakistan. Through Nebraska, where women stared at her eyebrow rings and braless boobs with contempt. Through Iran, where men stared at her bare arms like dogs in heat. She'd slept in city parks in Guatemala City and spent three days with rebel forces in Nicaragua after getting lost on the way to a wildlife refuge.

But she'd never been so scared as now.

Mein Gott.

And what scared her the most was what she was about to do to herself.

One rat ran close, a small one, its brown body zipping forward, backing up, moving forward again a few inches. Rats were scary, she decided, because they were more like reptiles than rodents. A snaky nose and snaky tail. And those fucking red eyes.

Behind him was Schwarzie, the size of a small cat. He rose up on his haunches and stared at what fascinated him. Watching. Waiting.

Then the little one attacked. Scurrying on his four needlish feet, ignoring her muffled scream, he darted fast and straight. Quick as a roach he tore a bite from her cut leg. The wound stung like fire. Monelle squealed—in pain, yes, but from anger too. I don't fucking want *you*! She slammed her heel into his back with a dull crunch. He quivered once and lay still.

Another one raced up to her neck, ripped away a bite then leapt back, staring at her, twitching his nose as if he were running his tongue around his little rat mouth, savoring her flavor.

Dieser Schmerz . . .

She shivered as the searing burn radiated from the bite. *Dieser Schmerz!* The pain! Monelle forced herself to lie still again.

The tiny attacker poised for another run but suddenly he twitched and turned away. Monelle saw why. Schwarzie was finally easing to the front of the pack. He was coming after what he wanted.

Good, good.

He was the one she'd been waiting for. Because he hadn't seemed interested in the blood or her flesh; he'd padded up close twenty minutes before, fascinated by the silver tape across her mouth.

The smaller rat scurried back into the swarming bodies as Schwarzie eased forward, on his obscenely tiny feet. Paused. Then advanced again. Six feet, five.

Then three.

She remained completely still. Breathing as shallowly as she dared, afraid the inhalation would scare him off.

Schwarzie paused. Padded forward again. Then stopped. Two feet away from her head.

Don't move a muscle.

His back was humped high and his lips kept retracting over his brown and yellow teeth. He moved another foot closer and stopped, eyes darting. Sat up, rubbed his clawed paws together, eased forward again.

Monelle Gerger played dead.

Another six inches. *Vorwärts!*

Come on!

Then he was at her face. She smelled garbage and oil on his body, feces, rotten meat. He sniffed and she felt the unbearable tickle of whiskers on her nose as his tiny teeth emerged from his mouth and began to chew the tape.

For five minutes he gnawed around her mouth. Once another

rat scooted in, sank his teeth into her ankle. She closed her eyes to the pain and tried to ignore it. Schwarzie chased him away then stood in the shadows studying her.

Vorwärts, Schwarzie! Come on!

Slowly he padded back to her. Tears running down her cheek, Monelle reluctantly lowered her mouth to him.

Chewing, chewing . . .

Come on!

She felt his vile, hot breath in her mouth as he broke through the tape and began to rip off larger chunks of the shiny plastic. He pulled the pieces from his mouth and squeezed them greedily in his front claws.

Big enough now? she wondered.

It would have to be. She couldn't take any more.

Slowly she lifted her head up, one millimeter at a time. Schwarzie blinked and leaned forward, curiously.

Monelle spread her jaws and heard the wonderful sound of the ripping tape. She sucked air deep into her lungs. She could breathe again!

And she could shout for help.

"*Bitte, helfen Sie mir!*" Please help me.

Schwarzie backed away, startled by her ragged howl, dropping his precious silver tape. But he didn't go very far. He stopped and turned back, rose on his pudgy haunches.

Ignoring his black, humped body she kicked the post she was tied to. Dust and dirt floated down like gray snow but the wood didn't give a bit. She screamed until her throat burned.

"*Bitte.* Help me!"

The sticky rush of traffic swallowed the sound.

Stillness for a moment. Then Schwarzie started toward her again. He wasn't alone this time. The slimy pack followed his lead. Twitching, nervous. But drawn steadily by the tempting smell of her blood.

Bone and wood, wood and bone.

"Mel, what do you have there?" Rhyme was nodding toward the computer attached to the chromatograph-spectrometer. Cooper had once more retested the dirt they'd found in the splinter of wood.

"It's still nitrogen-rich. Off the charts."

Three separate tests, the results all the same. A diagnostic check of the unit showed it was working fine. Cooper reflected and said, "That much nitrogen—maybe a firearms or ammunition manufacturer."

"That'd be Connecticut, not Manhattan." Rhyme looked at the clock. 6:30. How fast time had raced past today. How slowly it had moved for the past three and a half years. He felt as if he'd been awake for days and days.

The young detective pored over the map of Manhattan, moving aside the pale vertebra that had fallen to the floor earlier.

The disk had been left here by Rhyme's SCI specialist, Peter Taylor. An early appointment with the man. The doctor had examined him expertly then sat back in the rustling rattan chair and pulled something out of his pocket.

"Show-and-tell time," the doctor had said.

Rhyme had glanced at Taylor's open hand.

"This's a fourth cervical vertebra. Just like the one in your neck. The one that broke. See the little tails on the end?" The doctor turned it over and over for a moment then asked, "What do you think of when you see it?"

Rhyme respected Taylor—who didn't treat him like a child or a moron or a major inconvenience—but that day he hadn't been in the mood to play the inspiration game. He hadn't answered.

Taylor continued anyway, "Some of my patients think it looks like a stingray. Some say it's a spaceship. Or an airplane. Or a truck. Whenever I ask that question people usually compare it to something big. Nobody ever says, 'Oh, a hunk of calcium and magnesium.' See, they don't like the idea that something so insignificant has made their lives pure hell."

Rhyme had glanced back at the doctor skeptically but the placid, gray-haired medico was an old hand at SCI patients and he said kindly, "Don't tune me out, Lincoln."

Taylor had held the disk up close to Rhyme's face. "You're thinking it's unfair this little thing causing you so much grief. But forget that. *Forget* it. I want you to remember what it was like before the accident. The good and bad in your life. Happiness, sadness . . . You can feel that again." The doctor's face had grown still. "But frankly all I see now is somebody who's given up."

Taylor had left the vertebra on the bedside table. Accidentally, it seemed. But then Rhyme realized the act was calculated. Over the past months while Rhyme was trying to decide whether or not to kill himself he'd stared at the tiny disk. It became an blem for Taylor's argument—the pro-living argument. But in the end that side lost; the doctor's words, as valid as they might be, couldn't overcome the burden of pain and heartache and exhaustion Lincoln Rhyme felt day after day after day.

He now looked away from the disk—to Amelia Sachs—and said, "I want you to think about the scene again."

"I told you everything I saw."

"Not *saw*, I want to know what you felt."

Rhyme remembered the thousands of times he'd run crime scenes. Sometimes a miracle would happen. He'd be looking around and somehow ideas about the unsub would come to him. He couldn't explain how. The behaviorists talked about profiling as if they'd invented it. But criminalists had been profiling for hundreds of years. Walk the grid, walk where *he's* walked, find what *he's* left behind, figure out what *he's* taken with him—and you'll come away from the scene with a profile as clear as a portrait.

"Tell me," he prodded. "What did you feel?"

"Uneasy. Tense. Hot." She shrugged. "I don't know. I really don't. Sorry."

If he'd been mobile Rhyme would have leapt from the bed, grabbed her shoulders and shaken her. Shouted: *But you know what I'm talking about! I know you do. Why won't you work with me? . . . Why are you ignoring me?*

Then he understood something. . . .That she *was* there, in the steamy basement. Hovering over T.J.'s ruined body. Smelling the vile smell. He saw it in the way her thumb flicked a bloody cuticle, he saw it in the way she maintained the no-man's-land of politeness between the two of them. She detested being in that vile basement, and she hated him for reminding her that part of her was still there.

"You're walking through the room," he said.

"I really don't think I can be any more help."

"Play along," he said, forcing his temper down. He smiled. "Tell me what you thought."

Her face went still and she said, "It's . . . just thoughts. Impressions everybody'd have."

"But *you* were there. *Everybody* wasn't. Tell us."

"It was scary or something . . ." She seemed to regret the clumsy word.

Unprofessional

"I felt—"

"Somebody watching you?" he asked.

This surprised her. "Yes. That's exactly it."

Rhyme had felt it himself. Many times. He'd felt it three and a half years ago, bending down over the decomposing body of the young policeman, picking a fiber off the uniform. He'd been *positive* that someone was nearby. But there was no one—just a large oak beam that chose that moment to groan and splinter and come crashing down on the fulcrum of Lincoln Rhyme's fourth cervical vertebra with the weight of the earth.

"What else did you think, Amelia?"

She wasn't resisting anymore. Her lips were relaxed, her eyes drifting over the curled *Nighthawks* poster—the diners, lonely or contentedly alone. She said, "Well, I remember saying to myself, 'Man, this place is old.' It was like those pictures you see of turn-of-the-century factories and things. And I—"

"Wait," Rhyme barked. "Let's think about that. Old . . ."

His eyes strayed to the Randel Survey map. He'd commented before on the unsub's interest in historical New York. The building where T.J. Colfax had died was old too. And so was the tunnel for the railroad where they'd found the first body. The New York Central trains used to run aboveground. There'd been so many crossing fatalities that Eleventh Avenue had earned the name Death Avenue and the railroad had finally been forced to move the tracks belowground.

"And Pearl Street," he mused to himself, "was a major byway in early New York. Why's he so interested in old things?" He asked Sellitto, "Is Terry Dobyns still with us?"

"Oh, the shrink? Yeah. We worked a case last year. Come

to think of it, he asked about you. Said he called you a couple times and you never—"

"Right, right, right," Rhyme said. "Get him over here. I want his thoughts on 823's patterns. Now, Amelia, what else did you think?"

She shrugged but far too nonchalantly. "Nothing."

"No?"

And where *did* she keep her feelings? he wondered, recalling something Blaine had said once, seeing a gorgeous woman walking down Fifth Avenue: *The more beautiful the package, the harder it is to unwrap.*

"I don't know . . . All right, I remember one thing I thought. But it doesn't mean anything. It's not, like a professional observation."

Professional . . .

It's a bitch when you set your own standards, ain't it, Amelia?

"Let's hear it," he said to her.

"When you were having me pretend to be him? And I found where he stood to look back at her?"

"Keep going."

"Well, I thought . . ." For a moment it seemed that tears threatened to fill her beautiful eyes. They were iridescent blue, he noticed. Instantly she controlled herself. "I wondered, did she have a dog. The Colfax woman."

"A dog? Why'd you wonder that?"

She hesitated a moment then said, "This friend of mine . . . a few years ago. We were talking about getting a dog when, well, if we moved in together. I always wanted one. A collie. It was funny. That was the kind my friend wanted too. Even before we knew each other."

"A dog." Rhyme's heart popped like beetles on a summer screen door. "And?"

"I thought that woman—"

"T.J.," Rhyme said.

"T.J.," Sachs continued. "I just thought how sad it was—if she had any pets she wouldn't be coming home to them and playing with them anymore. I didn't think about her boyfriends or husbands. I thought about pets."

"But why *that* thought? Dogs, pets. Why?"

"I don't know why."

Silence.

Finally she said, "I suppose seeing her tied up there . . . And I was thinking how he stood to the side to watch her. Just standing between the oil tanks. It was like he was watching an animal in a pen."

Rhyme glanced at the sine waves on the GC-MS computer screen.

Animals . . .

Nitrogen . . .

"Shit!" Rhyme blurted.

Heads turned toward him.

"It's shit." Staring at the screen.

"Yes, of course!" Cooper said, replastering his strands of hair. "All the nitrogen. It's manure. And it's old manure at that."

Suddenly Lincoln Rhyme had one of those moments he'd reflected on earlier. The thought just burst into his mind. The image was of lambs.

Sellitto asked, "Lincoln, you okay?"

A lamb, sauntering down the street.

It was like he was watching an animal . . .

"Thom," Sellitto was saying, "is he all right?"

. . . in a pen.

Rhyme could picture the carefree animal. A bell around its neck, a dozen others behind.

"Lincoln," Thom said urgently. "You're sweating. Are you all right?"

"Shhhhh," the criminalist ordered.

He felt the tickle running down his face. Inspiration and heart failure; the symptoms are oddly similar. Think, think . . .

Bones, wooden posts and manure . . .

"Yes!" he whispered. A Judas lamb, leading the flock to slaughter.

"Stockyards," Rhyme announced to the room. "She's being held in a stockyard."

THIRTEEN

There are no stockyards in Manhattan."

"The *past*, Lon," Rhyme reminded him. "Old things turn on him. Get his juices flowing. We should think of *old* stockyards. The older the better."

In researching his book, Rhyme had read about a murder that gentleman mobster Owney Madden was accused of committing: gunning down a rival bootlegger outside his Hell's Kitchen townhouse. Madden was never convicted—not for this particular murder, at any rate. He took the stand and, in his melodious British-accented voice, lectured the courtroom about betrayal. "This entire case has been trumped up by my rivals, who are speaking lies about me. Your honor, do you know what they remind me of? In my neighborhood, in Hell's Kitchen, the flocks of lambs were led through the streets from the stockyards to the slaughterhouses on Forty-second Street. And you know who led them? Not a dog, not a man. But one of theirs. A Judas lamb with a bell around its neck. He'd lead the flock up that ramp. But then he'd stop and the rest of them would go on inside. I'm an innocent lamb and those witnesses against me, they're the Judases."

Rhyme continued. "Call the library, Banks. They must have a historian."

The young detective flipped open his cellular phone and called. His voice dropped a tone or two as he spoke. After he explained what they needed he stopped speaking and gazed at the map of the city.

"Well?" Rhyme asked.

"They're finding someone. They've got—" He lowered his

UNSUB 823			
Appearance	Residence	Vehicle	Other
• Caucasian male, slight build • Dark clothing • Old gloves, reddish kidskin • Aftershave; to cover up other scent? • Ski mask? Navy blue?	• Prob. has safe house	• Yellow Cab	• knows CS proc. • possibly has record • knows FR prints • gun = .32 Colt • Ties vics w/ unusual knots • "Old" appeals to him

head as someone answered and the young man repeated his request. He started nodding and announced to the room, "I've got two locations . . . no, three."

"Who is it?" Rhyme barked. "Who're you talking to?"

"The curator of the city archives . . . He says there've been three major stockyard areas in Manhattan. One on the West Side, around Sixtieth Street . . . One in Harlem in the 1930s or '40s. And on the Lower East Side during the Revolution."

"We need addresses, Banks. Addresses!"

Listening.

"He's not sure."

"Why can't he look it up? Tell him to look it up!"

Banks responded, "He heard you, sir . . . He says, in what? Look them up in what? They didn't have Yellow Pages back then. He's looking at old—"

"Demographic maps of commercial neighborhoods without street names," Rhyme groused. "Obviously. Have him *guess*."

"That's what he's doing. He's guessing."

Rhyme called, "Well, we need him to guess *fast*."

Banks listened, nodding.

"What, what, what, *what*?"

"Around Sixtieth Street and Tenth," the young officer said. A moment later: "Lexington near the Harlem River . . . And then . . . where the Delancey farm was. Is that near Delancey Street?—"

"Of *course* it is. From Little Italy all the way to the East River. Lots of territory. *Miles*. Can't he narrow it down?"

"Around Catherine Street. Lafayette . . . Walker. He's not sure."

"Near the courthouses," Sellitto said and told Banks, "Get Haumann's teams moving. Divide 'em up. Hit all three neighborhoods."

The young detective made the call, then looked up. "What now?"

"We wait," Rhyme said.

Sellitto muttered, "I fucking hate waiting."

Sachs asked Rhyme, "Can I use your phone."

Rhyme nodded toward the one on his bedside table.

She hesitated. "You have one in there?" She pointed to the hallway.

Rhyme nodded.

With perfect posture she walked out of the bedroom. In the hallway mirror he could see her, solemn, making the precious phone call. Who? he wondered. Boyfriend, husband? Day-care center? Why had she hesitated before mentioning her "friend" when she told them about the collie? There was a story behind that, Rhyme bet.

Whomever she was calling wasn't there. He noticed her eyes turn to dark-blue pebbles when there was no answer. She looked up and caught Rhyme gazing at her in the dusty glass. She turned her back. The phone slipped to the cradle and she returned to his room.

There was silence for a full five minutes. Rhyme lacked the mechanism most people have for bleeding off tension. He'd been a manic pacer when he was mobile, drove the officers in IRD crazy. Now, his eyes energetically scanned the Randel map of the city as Sachs dug beneath her Patrol cap and scratched at her scalp. Invisible Mel Cooper cataloged evidence, calm as a surgeon.

All but one of the people in the room jumped inordinately when Sellitto's phone brayed. He listened; his face broke into a grin.

"Got it!" One of Haumann's squads is at Eleventh and Sixtieth. They can hear a woman's screams coming from somewhere around there. They dunno where for sure. They're doing a door-to-door."

"Get your running shoes on," Rhyme ordered Sachs.

He saw her face sag. She glanced at Rhyme's phone, as if it might be ringing with a reprieve call from the governor at any minute. Then a look at Sellitto, who was poring over the ESU tactical map of the West Side.

"Amelia," Rhyme said, "we lost one. That's too bad. But we don't have to lose any more."

"If you saw her," she whispered. "If you only saw what he did to her—"

"Oh, but I have, Amelia," he said evenly, his eyes relentless and challenging. "I've seen what happened to T.J. I've seen what happens to bodies left in hot trunks for a month. I've seen what a pound of C4 does to arms and legs and faces. I worked the Happy Land social club fire. Over eighty people burned to death. We took Polaroids of the vics' faces, or what was left of them, for their families to identify—because there's no way in hell a human being could walk past those rows of bodies and stay sane. Except us. We didn't have any choice." He inhaled against the excruciating pain that swept through his neck. "See, if you're going to get by in this business, Amelia . . . If you're going to get by in *life*, you're going to have to learn to give up the dead."

One by one the others in the room had stopped what they were doing and were looking at the two of them.

No pleasantries now from Amelia Sachs. No polite smiles. She tried for a moment to make her gaze cryptic. But it was transparent as glass. Her fury at him—out of proportion to his comment—roiled through her, her long face folded under the dark energy. She swept aside a lock of lazy red hair and snatched the headset from the table. At the top of the stairs she paused and looked at him with a withering glance, reminding Rhyme that there was nothing colder than a beautiful woman's cold smile.

And for some reason he found himself thinking: Welcome back, Amelia.

"Whatcha got? You got goodies, you got a story, you got pictures?"

The Scruff sat in a bar on the East Side of Manhattan, Third Avenue—which is to the city what strip malls are to the 'burbs. This was a dingy tavern, soon to be rockin' with Yuppies on the make. But now it was the refuge of badly dressed locals, eating suppers of questionable fish and limp salads.

The lean man, skin like knotty ebony, wore a very white shirt and a very green suit. He leaned closer to the Scruff. "You got news, you got secret codes, you got letters? You got shit?"

"Man. Ha."

"You're not laughing when you say ha," said Fred Dellray, really D'Ellret but that had been generations ago. He was six foot four, rarely smiled despite the Jabberwocky banter, and was a star special agent in the Manhattan office of the FBI.

"No, man. I'm not laughing."

"So what've you *got*?" Dellray squeezed the end of a cigarette, which perched over his left ear.

"It takes time, man." The Scruff, a short man, scratched his greasy hair.

"But you ain't got time. Time is precious, time is fleeing, and time is one thing you. Ain't. Got."

Dellray put his huge hand under the table, on which sat two coffees, and squeezed the Scruff's thigh until he whined.

Six months ago the skinny little guy had been caught trying to sell automatic M-16s to a couple of right-wing crazies, who—whether they actually were or not—also happened to be under-cover BATF agents.

The feds hadn't wanted the Scruff himself of course, the greasy little wild-eyed *thing*. They wanted whoever was supplying the guns. ATF swam upstream a ways but no great busts were forthcoming and so they gave him to Dellray, the Bureau's Número Uno snitch handler, to see if he might be some use. So far, though, he'd proved to be just an irritating, mousy little skel who didn't, apparently, have news, secret codes or even shit for the feds.

"The only way we're dropping down a charge, any charge, is you give us something beautiful and sticky. Are we all together on that?"

"I don't have nothing for youse guys right *now* is what I'm saying. Just *now*."

"Not true, not true. You gotchaself somethin'. I can see it in your face. You're knowing something, mon."

A bus pulled up outside, with a hiss of brake air. A crowd of Pakistanis climbed from the open door.

"Man, that fucking UN conference," the Scruff muttered. "What the fuck they coming here for? This city's too crowded already. All them foreigners."

"'Fucking conference.' You little skel, you little turd," Dellray snapped. "Whatcha got against world peace?"

"Nothin'."

"Now, tell me something good."

"I don't know nothin' good."

"Who you talking to here?" Dellray grinning devilishly. "I'm the Chameleon. I can smile'n be happy or I can frown and play squeezie."

"No, man, no," the Scruff squealed. "Shit, that hurts. Cut it out."

The bartender looked over at them and a short glance from Dellray sent him back to polishing polished glasses.

"All right, maybe I know one thing. But I need help. I need—"

"Squeezie time again."

"Fuck you, man. Just fuck you!"

"Oh, that's mighty smart dialogue," Dellray shot back. "You sound like in those bad movies, you know, the bad guy and the good guy finally meet. Like Stallone and somebody. And all they can say to each other is, 'Fuck you, man.' 'No, fuck you.' 'No, fuck *you*.' Now, you're gonna tell me something useful. Are we all together on that?"

And just stared at the Scruff until he gave up.

"Okay, here's what it is. I'm trusting you, man. I'm—"

"Yeah, yeah, yeah. Whatcha got?"

"I was talking to Jackie, you know Jackie?"

"I know Jackie."

"An' he was telling me."

"What was he telling you?"

"He was telling me he heard anything anybody got coming in or going out this week, don't do it the airports."

"So what was coming in or going out? More 16s?"

"I told you, man, there wasn't nothing *I* had. I'm telling you what Jackie—"

"Told you."

"Right, man. Just in general, you know?" The Scruff turned big brown eyes on Dellray. "Would I lie to you?"

"Don't ever lose your dignity," the agent warned solemnly, pointing a stern finger at the Scruff's chest. "Now what's this about airports. Which one? Kennedy, La Guardia?"

"I don't know. All I know is word's up that somebody was gonna be at a airport here. Somebody who was pretty bad."

"Gimme a name."

"Don't got a name."

"Where's Jackie?"

"Dunno. South Africa, I think. Maybe Liberia."

"What's all this *mean*?" Dellray squeezed his cigarette again.

"I guess just there was a chance something was going down, you know, so nobody should be having shipments coming in then."

"You guess." The Scruff cringed but Dellray wasn't thinking about tormenting the little man any longer. He was hearing alarm bells: Jackie—an arms broker both Bureaus had known about for a year—might have heard something from one of his clients, soldiers in Africa and Central Europe and militia cells in America, about some terrorist hit at the airports. Dellray normally wouldn't've thought anything about this, except for that kidnapping at JFK last night. He hadn't paid much attention to it—it was NYPD's case. But now he was also thinking about that botched fragging at the UNESCO meeting in London the other day.

"Yo boy dint tell you anything more?"

"No, man. Nothing more. Hey, I'm hungry. Can we eat somethin'?"

"Remember what I told you about dignity? Quit moaning." Dellray stood up. "I gotta make a call."

The RRV skidded to a stop on Sixtieth Street.

Sachs snagged the crime-scene suitcase, the PoliLight and the big twelve-volt flashlight.

"Did you get her in time?" Sachs called to an ESU trooper. "Is she all right?"

No one answered at first. Then she heard the screams.

"What's going on?" she muttered, running breathless up to the large door, which had been battered in by Emergency Services. It opened onto a wide driveway that descended underneath an abandoned brick building. "She's still *there*?"

"That's right."

"Why?" demanded a shocked Amelia Sachs.

"They told us not to go in."

"Not to go in? She's screaming. Can't you hear her?"

An ESU cop said, "They told us to wait for you."

They. No, not *they* at all. Lincoln Rhyme. That son of a bitch.

"We were supposed to find her," the officer said. "*You're* supposed to go in."

She clicked the headset on. "Rhyme!" she barked. "Are you there?"

No answer . . . You goddamn coward.

Give up the dead . . . Sonofabitch! As furious as she'd been storming down the stairs in his townhouse a few minutes ago, she was twice as angry now.

Sachs glanced behind her and noticed a medic standing beside an EMS bus.

"You, come with me."

He took a step forward and saw her draw her weapon. He stopped.

"Whoa, time out," the medic said. "I don't have to go in until the area's secure."

"Now! Move!" She spun around and he must have seen more muzzle than he wanted. He grimaced and hurried after her.

From underground they heard: "Aiiiii! *Hilfe!*" Then sobbing.

Jesus. Sachs started to run toward the looming doorway, twelve feet high, smoky blackness inside.

She heard in her head: *You're him, Amelia. What are you thinking?*

Go away, she said silently.

But Lincoln Rhyme didn't go away.

You're a killer and a kidnapper, Amelia. Where would you walk, what would you touch?

Forget it! I'm going to save her. Hell with the crime scene . . .

"*Mein Gott!* Pleece! Some-von, Pleece help!"

Go, Sachs shouted to herself. Sprint! He's not in here. You're safe. Get her, go . . .

She picked up the pace, her utility belt clanking as she ran. Then, twenty feet down the tunnel, she pulled up. Debating. She didn't like which side won.

"Oh, fuck," she spat out. She set down the suitcase and opened it up. She blurted to the medic, "You, what's your name?"

The uneasy young man answered, "Tad Walsh. I mean, what's going on?" He glanced down into the murk.

"Oh . . . *Bitte, helfen Sie mir!*"

"Cover me," Sachs whispered.

"Cover you? Wait a minute, I don't do that."

"Take the gun, all right?"

"What'm I supposed to cover you *from*?"

Thrusting the automatic into his hand, she dropped to her knees. "Safety's off. Be careful."

She grabbed two rubber bands and slipped them over her shoes. Taking the pistol back she ordered him to do the same.

With unsteady hands he slipped the bands on.

"I'm just thinking—"

"Quiet. He could still be here."

"Wait a minute now, ma'am," the medic whispered. "This ain't in my job description."

"It's not in mine either. Hold the light." She handed him the flashlight.

"But if he's here he's probably gonna shoot at the light. I mean, that's what *I'd* shoot at."

"Then hold it up high. Over my shoulder. I'll go in front. If anybody gets shot it'll be me."

"Then whatta I do?" Tad sounded like a teenager.

"I myself'd run like hell," Sachs muttered. "Now follow me. And keep that beam steady."

Lugging the black CS suitcase in her left hand, holding her weapon in front of her, she gazed at the floor as they moved into the darkness. She saw the familiar broom marks again, just like at the other scene.

"*Bitte nicht, bitte nicht, bitte* . . ." There was a brief scream, then silence.

"What the hell's going on down there?" Tad whispered.

"Shhhh," Sachs hissed.

They walked slowly. Sachs blew on her fingers gripping the Glock—to dry the slick sweat—and carefully eyed the random targets of wooden pillars, shadows and discarded machinery picked out by the flashlight held unsteadily in Tad's hand.

She found no footprints.

Of course not. He's smart.

But we're smart too, she heard Lincoln Rhyme say in her thoughts. And she told him to shut up.

Slower now.

Five more feet. A pause. Then moving slowly forward. Trying to ignore the girl's moans. She felt it again—that sensation of being watched, the slippery crawl of the iron sights tracking you. The body armor, she reflected, wouldn't stop a full-metal jacket. Half the bad guys used Black Talons anyway—so a leg or arm shot would kill you just as efficiently as a chest hit. And a lot more painfully. Nick had told her how one of those bullets could open up a human body; one of his partners, hit by two of the vicious slugs, had died in his arms.

Above and behind . . .

Thinking of him, she remembered one night, lying against Nick's solid chest, gazing at the silhouette of his handsome Italian face on her pillow as he told her about hostage-rescue entry—"Somebody inside wants to nail you when you go in they'll do it from above and behind . . ."

"Shit." She dropped to a crouch, spinning around and aiming the Glock toward the ceiling, ready to empty the entire clip.

"What?" Tad whispered, cowering. "*What*?"

The emptiness gaped at her.

"Nothing." And breathed deeply, stood up.

"Don't *do* that."

There was a gurgling noise ahead of them.

"Jesus," came Tad's high voice again. "I hate this."

This guy's a pussy, she thought. I know that 'cause he's saying everything *I* want to.

She stopped. "Shine the light up there. Ahead."

"Oh, my everloving . . ."

Sachs finally understood the hairs she'd found at the last scene. She remembered the look that had passed between Sellitto and Rhyme. He'd known then what the unsub had planned. He'd known this was what was happening to her—and *still* he'd told ESU to wait. She hated him that much more.

In front of them a pudgy girl lolled on the floor, in a pool of blood. She glanced toward the light with glazed eyes and passed out. Just as a huge black rat—big as a housecat—crawled up onto her belly and moved toward the girl's fleshy throat. He bared its dingy teeth to take a bite from the girl's chin.

Sachs smoothly lifted the chunky black Glock, her left palm circling under the butt for support. She aimed carefully.

Shooting is breathing.

Inhale, out. Squeeze.

Sachs fired her weapon for the first time in the line of duty. Four shots. The huge black rat standing on the girl's chest exploded. She hit one more on the floor behind and another one that, panicking, raced toward Sachs and the medic. The others vanished silently, fast as water on sand.

"Jesus," the medic said. "You could've hit the girl."

"From thirty feet?" Sachs snorted. "Not hardly."

The radio burst to life and Haumann asked if they were under fire.

"Negative," Sachs replied. "Just shooing a few rats."

"Roger, K."

She took the flashlight from the medic and shining it low, started forward.

"It's all right, miss," Sachs called. "You'll be all right."

The girl's eyes opened, head flipping from side to side.

"*Bitte, bitte* . . ."

She was very pale. Her blue eyes clung to Sachs, as if she was afraid to look away. "*Bitte, bitte* . . . Pleece . . ." Her voice rose to a wild keening and she began to sob and thrash in terror as the medic pressed bandages on her wounds.

Sachs cradled her bloody blond head, whispering, "You'll be all right, honey, you'll be all right, you'll be all right. . . ."

FOURTEEN

The office, high above downtown Manhattan, looked out over Jersey. The crap in the air made the sunset absolutely beautiful.

"We gotta."

"We can't."

"Gotta," Fred Dellray repeated and sipped his coffee—even worse than in the restaurant where the Scruff and he'd been sitting not long before. "Take it away from 'em. They'll live with it."

"It's a local case," responded the FBI's assistant special agent in charge of the Manhattan office. The ASAC was a meticulous man who could never work undercover—because when you saw him you thought, Oh, look, an FBI agent.

"It's not local. They're *treating* it local. But it's a big case."

"We're down eighty men because of the UN thing."

"And this's related to it," Dellray said. "I'm positive."

"Then we'll tell UN Security. Let everybody . . . Oh, don't give me that look."

"UN Security? UN *Security*? Say, you ever heara the words oxy-moron? . . . Billy, you see that picture? Of the scene this morning? The hand comin' outa the dirt, and all the skin cut offa that finger? That's a sick fuck out there."

"NYPD's keeping us informed," the ASAC said smartly. "We've got Behavioral on call if they want."

"Oh, Jesus Christ on the merry cross. 'Behavioral on call'? We gotta catch this ripper, Billy. *Catch* him. Not figger out his tick-tocky workings."

"Tell me what your snitch said again."

Dellray knew a crack in a rock when he saw one. Wasn't going to let it seal up again. Rapid fire now: about the Scruff and Jackie in Johannesburg or Monrovia and the hushed word throughout the illicit arms trade that something was going down at a New York airport this week so stay clear. "It's *him*," Dellray said. "Gotta be."

"NYPD's got a task force together."

"Not Anti-Terror. I made calls. Nobody at A-T there knows zippo about it. To NYPD it's 'dead tourists equal bad public relations.' I want this case, Billy." And Fred Dellray said the one word he'd never uttered in his eight years of undercover work. "Please."

"What grounds're you talking?"

"Oh-oh, bullshit question," Dellray said, stroking his index finger like a scolding teacher. "Lessee. We got ourselves that spiffy new anti-terrorism bill. But that's not enough for you, you want jurisdiction? I'll give you jurisdiction. A Port Authority felony. Kidnapping. I can fucking argue that this prick's driving a taxi so he's affecting interstate commerce. We don't want to play *those* games, do we, Billy?"

"You're not listening, Dellray. I can recite the U.S. Code in my sleep, thank you. I want to know if we're going to take over, what we tell people and make *everybody* happy. 'Cause remember, after this unsub's bagged and tagged we're going to have to keep working with NYPD. I'm not going to send my big brother to beat up their big brother even though I can. Anytime I want. Lon Sellitto's running the case and he's a good man."

"A lieutenant?" Dellray snorted. He tugged the cigarette out from behind his ear and held it under his nostrils for a moment.

"Jim Polling's in charge."

Dellray reared back with mock horror. "Polling? Little Adolph? The 'You-have-the-right-to-remain-silent-'cause-I'ma-hit-you-upside-the-motherfuckin'-head' Polling? *Him*?"

The ASAC had no response for that. He said, "Sellitto's good. A real workhorse. I've been with him on two OC task forces."

"That unsub's grabbing bodies right and left and this here boy's betting he's going to work his way up."

"Meaning?"

"We got senators in town. We got congressmen, we got heads of state. I think these folk he's grabbing now're just for practice."

"*You* been talking to Behavioral and not telling me?"

"It's what I smell." Dellray couldn't resist touching his lean nose.

The ASAC blew air from his clean-shaven-federal-agent cheeks. "Who's the CI?"

Dellray had trouble thinking of the Scruff as a confidential informant, which sounded like something out of a Dashiell Hammett novel. Most *CI*s were skels, short for skeletons, meaning scrawny, disgusting little hustlers. Which fit the Scruff to a T.

"He's a tick," Dellray admitted. "But Jackie, this guy he heard it from's solid."

"I know you want it, Fred. I understand." The ASAC said this with some sympathy. Because he knew exactly what was behind Dellray's request.

Even as a boy in Brooklyn, Dellray had wanted to be a cop. It hadn't mattered much to him what kind of cop as long as he could spent twenty-four hours a day doing it. But soon after joining the Bureau he found his calling—undercover work.

Teamed with his straight man and guardian angel Toby Dolittle, Dellray was responsible for sending a large number of perps away for a very long time—the sentences totaled close to a thousand years. ("They kin call us the Millennium Team, Toby-o," he declared to his partner once.) The clue to Dellray's success was his nickname: "the Chameleon." Bestowed after—in the space of twenty-four hours—he played a brain-dead cluckhead in a Harlem crack house and a Haitian dignitary at a dinner in the Panamanian consulate, complete with diagonal red ribbon on his chest and impenetrable accent. The two of them were regularly loaned out to ATF or DEA and, occasionally, city police departments. Drugs and guns were their specialty though they had a minor in 'jacked merchandise.

The irony of undercover work is that the better you are, the earlier the retirement. Word gets around and the big boys, the perps worth going after, become harder to fox. Dolittle and Dellray found themselves working less in the field and more as handlers of informants and other undercover agents. And while it wasn't Dellray's first choice—nothing excited him like the street—it still got him out of the office more often than most SAs in the Bureau. It had never occurred to him to request a transfer.

Until two years ago—a warm April morning in New York. Dellray was just about to leave the office to catch a plane at La Guardia when he got a phone call from the assistant director of the Bureau in Washington. The FBI is a nest of hierarchy and Dellray couldn't imagine why the big man himself was calling. Until he heard the AD's somber voice break the news that Toby Dolittle, along with an assistant U.S. attorney from Manhattan, had been on the ground floor of the Oklahoma City federal building that morning, preparing for the deposition session that Dellray himself was just about to depart for.

Their bodies were being flown back to New York the next day.

Which was the same day that Dellray put in the first of his RFT-2230 forms, requesting a transfer to the Bureau's Anti-Terror Division.

The bombing had been the crime of crimes to Fred Dellray, who, when no one was looking, devoured books on politics and philosophy. He believed there was nothing essentially unAmerican about greed or lust—hey, those qualities were encouraged everywhere from Wall Street to Capitol Hill. And if people stepped over the border of legality, Dellray was pleased to track them down—but he never did so with personal animosity. But to murder people for their beliefs—hell, to murder children before they even knew *what* they believed—my God, that was a stab at the heart of the country. Sitting in his two-room, sparsely furnished Brooklyn apartment after Toby's funeral, Dellray decided that this was the kind of crime he wanted a crack at.

But unfortunately the Chameleon's reputation preceded him. The Bureau's best undercover agent was now their best handler, running agents and CIs throughout the East Coast. His bosses simply couldn't afford to let him go to one of the more quiescent departments of the FBI. Dellray was a minor legend, personally responsible for some of the Bureau's greatest recent successes. So it was with considerable regret that his persistent requests were turned down.

The ASAC was well aware of this history and he now added a sincere, "I wish I could help out, Fred. I'm sorry."

But all Dellray heard in these words was the rock cracking a little further. And so the Chameleon pulled a persona off the rack and stared down his boss. He wished he still had his fake gold tooth. Street man Dellray was a tough hombre with one mother-fucker of a mean stare. And in that look was the unmistakable message anybody on the street would know instinctively: I done for you, now you do for me.

Finally the smarmy ASAC said lamely, "It's just that we need *something*."

"Somethin'?"

"A hook," the ASAC said. "We don't have a hook."

A reason to take the case away from NYPD, he meant.

Politics, politics, polifuckingtics.

Dellray lowered his head but the eyes, brown as polish, didn't waver a millimeter from the ASAC. "He cut the skin off that vic's finger this morning, Billy. Clean down to the bone. Then buried him alive."

Two scrubbed, federal-agent hands met beneath a crisp jaw. The ASAC said slowly, "Here's a thought. There's a deputy commissioner at NYPD. Name's Eckert. You know him? He's a friend of mine."

The girl lay on her back on a stretcher, eyes closed, conscious but groggy. Still pale. An IV of glucose ran into her arm. Now that she'd been rehydrated she was coherent and surprisingly calm, all things considered.

Sachs walked back to the gates of hell and stood looking down into the black doorway. She clicked on the radio and called Lincoln Rhyme. This time he answered.

"How's the scene look?" Rhyme asked casually.

Her answer was a curt: "We got her out. If you're interested."

"Ah, good. How is she?"

"Not good."

"But alive, right."

"Barely."

"You're upset because of the rats, aren't you, Amelia?"

She didn't answer.

"Because I didn't let Bo's men get her right away. Are you there, Amelia?"

"I'm here."

"There are five contaminants of crime scenes," Rhyme explained. She noticed he'd gone into his low, seductive tone again. "The weather, the victim's family, the suspect, souvenir hunters. The last is the worst. Guess what it is?"

"You tell me."

"Other cops. If I'd let ESU in they could've destroyed all the trace. You know how to handle a scene now. And I'll bet you preserved everything just fine."

Sachs needed to say, "I don't think she'll ever be the same after this. The rats were all over her."

"Yes, I imagine they were. That's their nature."

Their nature . . .

"But five minutes or ten wasn't going to make any difference. She—"

Click.

She shut off the radio and walked to Walsh, the medic.

"I want to interview her. Is she too groggy?"

"Not yet. We gave her locals—to stitch the lacerations and the bites. She'll want some Demerol in a half hour or so."

Sachs smiled and crouched down beside her. "Hi, how you doing?"

The girl, fat but very pretty, nodded.

"Can I ask you some questions?"

"Yes, pleece. I want you get him."

Sellitto arrived and ambled up to them. He smiled down at the girl, who gazed at him blankly. He proffered a badge she had no interest in and identified himself.

"You all right, miss?"

The girl shrugged.

Sweating fiercely in the muggy heat, Sellitto nodded Sachs aside. "Polling been here?"

"Haven't seen him. Maybe he's at Lincoln's."

"No, I just called there. He's gotta get to City Hall pronto."

"What's the problem?"

Sellitto lowered his voice, his doughy face twisted up. "A fuckup—our transmissions're supposed to be secure. But those fucking reporters, somebody's got an unscrambler or something. They heard we didn't go in right away to get her." He nodded toward the girl.

"Well, we *didn't*," Sachs said harshly. "Rhyme told ESU to wait until I got here."

The detective winced. "Man, I hope they don't have *that* on tape. We need Polling for damage control." He nodded to the girl. "Interviewed her yet?"

"No. Just about to." With some regret Sachs clicked on the radio and heard Rhyme's urgent voice.

". . . you there? This goddamn thing doesn't—"

"I'm here," Sachs said coolly.

"What happened?"

"Interference, I guess. I'm with the vic."

The girl blinked at the exchange and Sachs smiled. "I'm not talking to myself." Gestured toward the mike. "Police headquarters. What's your name?"

"Monelle. Monelle Gerger." She looked at her bitten arm, pulled up a dressing and examined a wound.

"Interview her fast," Rhyme instructed, "then work the scene."

Hand covering the microphone stalk, Sachs whispered fiercely to Sellitto, "This man is a pain in the ass to work for. Sir."

"Humor him, officer."

"Amelia!" Rhyme barked. "Answer me!"

"We're interviewing her, all right?" she snapped.

Sellitto asked, "Can you tell us what happened?"

Monelle began to talk, a disjointed story about being in the laundry room of a residence hall in the East Village. He'd been hiding, waiting for her.

"What residence hall?" Sellitto asked.

"The Deutsche Haus. It's, you know, mostly German expatriates and students."

"What happened then?" Sellitto continued. Sachs noted that

although the big detective appeared gruffer, more ornery than Rhyme, he was really the more compassionate of the two.

"He threwed me in the trunk of car and drove here."

"Did you get a look at him?"

The woman closed her eyes. Sachs repeated the question and Monelle said she hadn't; he was, as Rhyme had guessed, wearing a navy-blue ski mask.

"*Und* gloves."

"Describe them."

They were dark. She didn't remember what color.

"Any unusual characteristics? The kidnapper?"

"No. He was white. I could tell that."

"Did you see the license plate of the taxi?" Sellitto asked.

"*Was?*" the girl asked, drifting into her native tongue.

"Did you see—"

Sachs jumped as Rhyme interrupted: "*Das Nummernschild.*"

Thinking: How the hell does he *know* all this? She repeated the word and the girl shook her head no then squinted. "What you mean, taxi?"

"Wasn't he driving a Yellow Cab?"

"Taxicab? *Nein*. No. It was regular car."

"Hear that, Lincoln?"

"Yup. Our boy's got another set of wheels. And he put her in the trunk so it's not a station wagon or hatchback."

Sachs repeated this. The girl nodded. "Like a sedan."

"Any idea of the make or color?" Sellitto continued.

Monelle answered, "Light, I think. Maybe silver or gray. Or that, you know, what is it? Light brown."

"Beige?"

She nodded.

"Maybe beige," Sachs added for Rhyme's benefit.

Sellitto asked, "Was there anything in the trunk? Anything at all? Tools, clothes, suitcases?"

Monelle said there wasn't. It was empty.

Rhyme had a question. "What did it smell like? The trunk."

Sachs relayed the query.

"I don't know."

"Oil and grease?"

"No. It smelled . . . clean."

"So maybe a new car," Rhyme reflected.

Monelle dissolved into tears for a moment. Then shook her head. Sachs took her hand and, finally, she continued. "We drove for long time. *Seemed* like long time."

"You're doing fine, honey," Sachs said.

Rhyme's voice interrupted. "Tell her to strip."

"What?"

"Take her clothes off."

"I will not."

"Have the medics give her a robe. We need her clothes, Amelia."

"But," Sachs whispered, "she's crying."

"Please," Rhyme said urgently. "It's important."

Sellitto nodded and Sachs, tight-lipped, explained to the girl about the clothes and was surprised when Monelle nodded. She was, it turned out, eager to get out of the bloody garments anyway. Giving her privacy, Sellitto walked away, to confer with Bo Haumann. Monelle put on a gown the medic offered her and one of the plain-clothes detectives covered her with his sportscoat. Sachs bagged the jeans and T-shirts.

"Got them," Sachs said into the radio.

"Now she's got to walk the scene with you," Rhyme said.

"What?"

"But make sure she's behind you. So she doesn't contaminate any PE."

Sachs looked at the young woman, huddling on a gurney beside the two EMS buses.

"She's in no shape to do that. He cut her. All the way to the bone. So she'd bleed and the rats'd get her."

"Is she mobile?"

"Probably. But you know what she's just been through?"

"She can give you the route they walked. She can tell you where he stood."

"She's going to the ER. She lost a lot of blood."

A hesitation. He said pleasantly, "Just ask her."

But his joviality was fake and Sachs heard just impatience. She could tell that Rhyme was a man who wasn't used to coddling people, who didn't *have* to. He was someone used to having his own way.

He persisted, "Just once around the grid."

You can go fuck yourself, Lincoln Rhyme.

"It's—"

"Important. I know."

Nothing from the other end of the line.

She was looking at Monelle. Then she heard a voice, no, *her* voice say to the girl, "I'm going down there to look for evidence. Will you come with me?"

The girl's eyes nailed Sachs deep in her heart. Tears burst. "No, no, no. I am not doing that. *Bitte nicht, oh, bitte nicht* . . ."

Sachs nodded, squeezed the woman's arm. She began to speak into the mike, steeling herself for his reaction, but Rhyme surprised her by saying, "All right, Amelia. Let it go. Just ask her what happened when they arrived."

The girl explained how she'd kicked him and escaped into an adjoining tunnel.

"I kick him again," she said with some satisfaction. "Knock off his glove. Then he get all pissed and strangle me. He—"

"Without the glove on?" Rhyme blurted.

Sachs repeated the question and Monelle said, "Yes."

"Prints, excellent!" Rhyme shouted, his voice distorting in the mike. "When did it happen? How long ago?"

Monelle guessed about an hour and a half.

"Hell," Rhyme muttered. "Prints on skin last an hour, ninety minutes, tops. Can you print skin, Amelia?"

"I never have before."

"Well, you're about to. But fast. In the CS suitcase there'll be a packet labeled Kromekote. Pull out a card."

She found a stack of glossy five-by-seven cards, similar to photographic paper.

"Got it. Do I dust her neck?"

"No. Press the card, glossy side down, against her skin where she thinks he touched her. Press for about three seconds."

Sachs did this, as Monelle stoically gazed at the sky. Then, as Rhyme instructed, she dusted the card with metallic powder, using a puffy Magna-Brush.

"Well?" Rhyme asked eagerly.

"It's no good. A shape of a finger. But no visible ridges. Should I pitch it?"

"Never throw away *anything* at a crime scene, Sachs," he lectured sternly. "Bring it back. I want to see it anyway."

"One thing, I am thinking I forget," said Monelle. "He touch me."

"You mean he molested you?" Sachs asked gently. "Rape?"

"No, no. Not in a sex way. He touch my shoulder, face, behind my ear. Elbow. He squeezed me. I don't know why."

"You hear that, Lincoln? He touched her. But it didn't seem like he was getting off on it."

"Yes."

"*Und* . . . And one thing I am forgetting," Monelle said. "He spoke German. Not good. Like he only study it in school. And he call me Hanna."

"Called her what?"

"Hanna," Sachs repeated into the mike. "Do you know why?" she asked the girl.

"No. But that's all he call me. He seemed to like saying the name."

"Did you get that, Lincoln."

"Yes, I did. Now do the scene. Time's awasting."

As Sachs stood, Monelle suddenly reached up and gripped her wrist.

"Miss . . . Sachs. You are German?"

She smiled and answered, "A long time ago. A couple generations."

Monelle nodded. She pressed Sachs's palm to her cheek. "*Vielen Dank*. Thank you, Miss Sachs. *Danke schön*."

FIFTEEN

The three ESU halogens clicked to light, bringing an eerie tide of white glare to the grim tunnel.

Alone now at the scene Sachs gazed at the floor for a moment. Something had changed. What?

She drew her weapon again, dropped into a crouch. "He's here," she whispered, stepping behind one of the posts.

"What?" Rhyme asked.

"He's come back. There were some dead rats here. They're gone."

She heard Rhyme's laughter.

"What's so funny?"

"No, Amelia. Their friends took the bodies away."

"Their friends?"

"Had a case up in Harlem once. Dismembered, decomposed body. A lot of the bones were hidden in a big circle around the torso. The skull was in an oil drum, toes underneath piles of leaves . . . Had the borough in an uproar. The press was talking about Satanists, serial killers. Guess who the perp turned out to be?"

"No idea," she said stiffly.

"The vic himself. It was a suicide. Raccoons, rats and squirrels made off with the remains. Like trophies. Nobody knows why but they love their souvenirs. Now, where are you?"

"At the foot of the ramp."

"What do you see?"

"A wide tunnel. Two side tunnels, narrower. Flat ceiling, supported by wooden posts. The posts're all battered and nicked. The floor's old concrete, covered with dirt."

UNSUB 823

Appearance	Residence	Vehicle	Other
• Caucasian male, slight build • Dark clothing • Old gloves, reddish kidskin • Aftershave; to cover up other scent? • Ski mask? Navy blue? • Gloves are dark	• Prob. has safe house	• Yellow Cab • Recent model sedan • Lt. gray, silver, biege	• knows CS proc. • possibly has record • knows FR prints • gun = .32 Colt • Ties vics w/ unusual knots • "Old" appeals to him • Called one vic "Hanna" • Knows basic German

"And manure?"

"Looks like it. In the center, right in front of me's the post she was tied to."

"Windows?"

"None. No doors either." She looked over the wide tunnel, the floor disappearing into a black universe a thousand miles away. She felt the crawl of hopelessness. "It's too big! There's too much space to cover."

"Amelia, relax."

"I'll never find *anything* here."

"I know it seems overwhelming. But just keep in mind that there're only three types of PE that we're concerned about. Objects, body materials and impressions. That's all. It's less daunting if you think of it that way.

Easy for you to say.

"And the scene isn't as big as it looks. Just concentrate on the places they walked. Go to the post."

Sachs walked the path. Staring down.

The ESU lights were brilliant but they also made the shadows starker, revealing a dozen places the kidnapper could hide. A chill trickled down her spine. Stay close, Lincoln, she thought reluctantly. I'm pissed, sure, but I wanna hear you. Breathe or something.

She paused, shone the PoliLight over the ground.

"Is it all swept?" he asked.

"Yes. Just like before."

The body armor chafed her breasts despite the sports bra and undershirt and as hot as it was outside it was unbearable down here. Her skin prickled and she felt a ravenous desire to scratch under her vest.

"I'm at the post."

"Vacuum the area for trace."

Sachs ran the Dustbuster. Hating the noise. It covered up any sound of approaching footsteps, guns cocking, knives being drawn. Involuntarily she looked behind her once, twice. Nearly dropped the vacuum as her hand strayed to her gun.

Sachs looked at the impression in the dust of where Monelle's body had lain. *I'm him. I'm dragging her along. She kicks me. I stumble . . .*

Monelle could have kicked in only one direction, away from

the ramp. The unsub didn't fall, she'd said. Which meant he must've landed on his feet. Sachs walked a yard or two into the gloom.

"Bingo!" Sachs shouted.

"What? Tell me?"

"Footprints. He missed a spot sweeping up."

"Not hers?"

"No. She was wearing running shoes. These are smooth soles. Like dress shoes. Two good prints. We'll know what size feet he's got."

"No, they won't tell us that. Soles can be larger or smaller than the uppers. But it may tell us something. In the CS bag there's an electrostatic printer. It's a small box with a wand on it. There'll be some sheets of acetate next to it. Separate the paper, lay the acetate on the print and run the wand over it."

She found the device and made two images of the prints. Carefully slipped them into a paper envelope.

Sachs returned to the post. "And here's a bit of straw from the broom."

"From?—"

"Sorry," Sachs said quickly. "We don't know where it's from. A bit of straw. I'm picking it up and bagging it."

Getting good with these pencils. Hey, Lincoln, you son of a bitch, know what I'm doing to celebrate my permanent retirement from crime scene detail? I'm going out for Chinese.

The ESU halogens didn't reach into the side tunnel where Monelle had run. Sachs paused at the day-night line then plunged forward into the shadows. The flashlight beam swept the floor in front of her.

"Talk to me, Amelia."

"There isn't much to see. He swept up here too. Jesus, he thinks of everything."

"What *do* you see?"

"Just marks in the dust."

I tackle her, I bring her down. I'm mad. Furious. I try to strangle her.

Sachs stared at the ground.

"Here's something—knee prints! When he was strangling her he must have straddled her waist. He left knee prints and he missed them when he swept."

"Electrostatic them."

She did, quicker this time. Getting the hang of the equipment. She was slipping the print into the envelope when something caught her eye. Another mark in the dust.

What is that?

"Lincoln . . . I'm looking at the spot where . . . it looks like the glove fell here. When they were struggling."

She clicked on the PoliLight. And couldn't believe what she saw.

"A print. I've got a fingerprint!"

"What?" Rhyme asked, incredulous. "It's not hers?"

"Nope, couldn't be. I can see the dust where she was lying. Her hands were cuffed the whole time. It's where he picked up the glove. He probably thought he'd swept here but missed it. It's a big, fat beautiful one!"

"Stain it, light it and shoot the son of a bitch on the one-to-one."

It took her only two tries to get a crisp Polaroid. She felt like she'd found a hundred-dollar bill in the street.

"Vacuum the area and then go back to the post. Walk the grid," he told her.

She slowly walked the floor, back and forth. One foot at a time.

"Don't forget to look up," he reminded her. "I once caught an unsub because of a single hair on the ceiling. He'd loaded a .357 round in a true .38 and the blowback pasted a hair from his hand on the crown molding."

"I'm looking. It's a tile ceiling. Dirty. Nothing else. Nowhere to stash anything. No ledges or doorways."

"Where're the staged clues?" he asked.

"I don't see anything."

Back and forth. Five minutes passed. Six, seven.

"Maybe he didn't leave any this time," Sachs suggested. "Maybe Monelle's the last."

"No," Rhyme said with certainty.

Then behind one of the wooden pillars a flash caught her eye.

"Here's something in the corner . . . Yep. Here they are."

"Shoot it 'fore you touch it."

She took a photograph and then picked up a wad of white cloth with the pencils. "Women's underwear. Wet."

"Semen?"

"I don't know," she said. Wondering if he was going to ask her to smell it.

Rhyme ordered, "Try the PoliLight. Proteins will fluoresce."

She fetched the light, turned it on. It illuminated the cloth but the liquid didn't glow. "No."

"Bag it. In plastic. What else?" he asked eagerly.

"A leaf. Long, thin, pointed at one end."

It had been cut sometime ago and was dry and turning brown.

She heard Rhyme sigh in frustration. "There're about eight thousand varieties of deciduous vegetation in Manhattan," he explained. "Not very helpful. What's underneath the leaf?"

Why does he think there's anything there?

But there was. A scrap of newsprint. Blank on one side, the other was printed with a drawing of the phases of the moon.

"The moon?" Rhyme mused. "Any prints? Spray it with ninhydrin and scan it fast with the light."

A blast of the PoliLight revealed nothing.

"That's all."

Silence for a moment. "What're the clues sitting on?"

"Oh, I don't know."

"You *have* to know."

"Well, the ground," she answered testily. "Dirt." What else would they be sitting on?

"Is it like all the rest of the dirt around there?"

"Yes." Then she looked closely. Hell, it was different. "Well, not exactly. It's a different color."

Was he *always* right?

Rhyme instructed, "Bag it. In paper."

As she scooped up the grains he said, "Amelia?"

"Yeah?"

"He's not there," Rhyme said reassuringly.

"I guess."

"I heard something in your voice."

"I'm fine," she said shortly. "I'm smelling the air. I smell blood. Mold and mildew. And the aftershave again."

"The same as before?"

"Yes."

"Where's it coming from?"

Sniffing the air, Sachs walked in a spiral, the Maypole again, until she came to another wooden post.

"Here. It's strongest right here."

"What's 'here,' Amelia? You're my legs *and* my eyes, remember."

"One of these wooden columns. Like the kind she was tied to. About fifteen feet away."

"So he might have rested against it. Any prints?"

She sprayed it with ninhydrin and shone the light on it.

"No. But the smell's very strong."

"Sample a portion of the post where it's the strongest. There's a Moto Tool in the case. Black. A portable drill. Take a sampling bit—it's like a hollow drill bit—and mount it in the tool. There's something called a chuck. It's a—"

"I own a drill press," she said tersely.

"Oh," Rhyme said.

She drilled a piece of the post out, then flicked sweat from her forehead. "Bag it in plastic?" she asked. He told her yes. She felt faint, lowered her head and caught her breath. No fucking air in here.

"Anything else?" Rhyme asked.

"Nothing that I can see."

"I'm proud of you, Amelia. Come on back and bring your treasures with you."

SIXTEEN

"Careful," Rhyme barked.
"I'm an expert at this."
"Is it new or old?"
"Shhh," Thom said.
"Oh, for Christ's sake. The blade, is it old or new?"
"Don't breathe . . . Ah, there we go. Smooth as a baby's butt."
The procedure was not forensic but cosmetic.
Thom was giving Rhyme his first shave in a week. He had also washed his hair and combed it straight back.
A half hour before, waiting for Sachs and the evidence to arrive, Rhyme had sent Cooper out of the room while Thom slicked up a catheter with K-Y and wielded the tube. After that business had been completed Thom had looked at him and said, "You look like shit. You realize that?"
"I don't care. Why would I care?"
Realizing suddenly that he did.
"How 'bout a shave?" the young man had asked.
"We don't have time."
Rhyme's real concern was that if Dr Berger saw him groomed he'd be less inclined to go ahead with the suicide. A disheveled patient is a despondent patient.
"And a wash."
"No."
"We've got company now, Lincoln."
Finally Rhyme had grumbled, "All right."
"And let's lose those pajamas, what do you say?"
"There's nothing wrong with them."

But that meant all right too.

Now, scrubbed and shaved, dressed in jeans and a white shirt, Rhyme ignored the mirror his aide held in front of him.

"Take that away."

"Remarkable improvement."

Lincoln Rhyme snorted derisively. "I'm going for a walk until they get back," he announced and settled his head back into the pillow. Mel Cooper turned to him with a perplexed expression.

"In his head," Thom explained.

"Your head?"

"I imagine it," Rhyme continued.

"That's quite a trick," Cooper said.

"I can walk through any neighborhood I want and never get mugged. Hike in the mountains and never get tired. *Climb* a mountain if I want. Go window-shopping on Fifth Avenue. Of course the things I see aren't necessarily there. But so what? Neither are the stars."

"How's that?" Cooper asked.

"The starlight we see is thousands or millions of years old. By the time it gets to Earth the stars themselves've moved. They're not where we see them." Rhyme sighed as the exhaustion flooded over him. "I suppose some of them have already burned out and disappeared." He closed his eyes.

"He's making it harder."

"Not necessarily," Rhyme answered Lon Sellitto.

Sellitto, Banks and Sachs had just returned from the stockyard scene.

"Underwear, the moon and a plant," cheerfully pessimistic Jerry Banks said. "That's not exactly a road map."

"Dirt too," Rhyme reminded, ever appreciative of soil.

"Have any idea what they mean?" Sellitto asked.

"Not yet," Rhyme said.

"Where's Polling?" Sellitto muttered. "He *still* hasn't answered his page."

"Haven't seen him," Rhyme said.

A figure appeared in the doorway.

"As I live and breathe," rumbled the stranger's smooth baritone.

Rhyme nodded the lanky man inside. He was somber-looking but his lean face suddenly cracked into a warm smile, as it tended to do at odd moments. Terry Dobyns was the sum total of the NYPD's behavioral science department. He'd studied with the FBI behaviorists down at Quantico and had degrees in forensic science and psychology.

The psychologist loved opera and touch football and when Lincoln Rhyme had awakened in the hospital after the accident three years ago Dobyns had been sitting beside him listening to *Aïda* on a Walkman. He'd then spent the next three hours conducting what turned out to be the first of many counseling sessions about Rhyme's injury.

"Now what's this I recall the textbooks sayin' 'bout people who don't return phone calls?"

"Analyze me later, Terry. You hear about our unsub?"

"A bit," Dobyns said, looking Rhyme over. He wasn't an M.D. but he knew physiology. "You all right, Lincoln? Looking a little peaked."

"I'm getting a bit of a workout today," Rhyme admitted. "And I could use a nap. You know what a lazy SOB I am."

"Yeah, right. You're the man'd call me at three in the morning with some question about a perp and couldn't understand why I was in the sack. So what's up? You fishin' for a profile?"

"Whatever you can tell us'll help."

Sellitto briefed Dobyns, who—as Rhyme recalled from the days they worked together—never took notes but managed to retain everything he heard inside a head crowned with dark-red hair.

The psychologist paced in front of the wall chart, glancing up at it occasionally as he listened to the detective's rumbling voice.

He held up a finger, interrupting Sellitto. "The victims, the victims . . . They've all been found underground. Buried, in a basement, in the stockyard tunnel."

"Right," Rhyme confirmed.

"Go on."

Sellitto continued, explaining about the rescue of Monelle Gerger.

"Fine, all right," Dobyns said absently. Then braked to a halt and turned to the wall again. He spread his legs and, hands on hips, gazed at the sparse facts about Unsub 823. "Tell me more about this idea of yours, Lincoln. That he likes old things."

"I don't know what to make of it. So far his clues have something to do with historical New York. Building materials from the turn of the century, the stockyards, the steam system."

Dobyns stepped forward suddenly and tapped the profile. "Hanna. Tell me about Hanna."

"Amelia?" Rhyme asked.

She told Dobyns how the unsub had referred to Monelle Gerger as Hanna for no apparent reason. "She said he seemed to like saying the name. And speaking to her in German."

"And he took a bit of a chance to 'nap her, didn't he?" Dobyns noted. "The cab, at the airport—that was safe for him. But hiding in a laundry room . . . He must've been real motivated to snatch somebody German."

Dobyns twined some ruddy hair around a lengthy finger and flopped down in one of the squeaky rattan chairs, stretched his feet out in front of him.

"Okay, try this on for size. The underground . . . that's the key. It tells me he's somebody who's hiding something and when I hear that I start thinking hysteria."

"He's not acting hysterical," Sellitto said. "He's pretty damn calm and calculating."

"Not hysteria in that sense. It's a category of mental disorders. The condition manifests when something traumatic happens in a patient's life and the subconscious *converts* that trauma into something else. It's an attempt to protect the patient. With traditional conversion hysteria you see physical symptoms—nausea, pain, paralysis. But I think here we're dealing with a related problem. Dissociation—that's what we call it when the reaction to the trauma affects the mind, not the physical body. Hysterical amnesia, fugue states. And multiple personalities."

"Jekyll and Hyde?" Mel Cooper played straight man this time, beating Banks to the punch.

"Well, I don't think he's got true multiple personalities," Dobyns continued. "That's a very rare diagnosis and the classic mult pers is young and has a lower IQ than your boy." He nodded at the profile chart. "He's slick and he's smart. Clearly an organized offender." Dobyns stared out the window for a moment. "This is interesting, Lincoln. I think your unsub pulls on his other personality when it suits him—when he wants to kill—and that's important."

"Why?"

"Two reasons. First, it tells us something about his main personality. He's someone who's been trained—maybe at his job, maybe his upbringing—to help people, not hurt them. A priest, a counselor, politician, social worker. And, two, I think it means he's found himself a blueprint. If you can find out what it is, maybe you can get a lead to him."

"What kind of blueprint?"

"He may have wanted to kill for a long time. But he didn't act until he found himself a role model. Maybe from a book or movie. Or somebody he actually knows. It's someone he can identify with, someone whose own crimes in effect give him permission to kill. Now, I'm going out on a limb here—"

"Climb," Rhyme said. "Climb."

"His obsession with history tells me that his personality is a character from the past."

"Real life?"

"That I couldn't say. Maybe fictional, maybe not. Hanna, whoever she is, figures in the story somewhere. Germany too. Or German Americans."

"Any idea what might've set him off?"

"Freud felt it was caused by—what else?—sexual conflict at the Oedipal stage. Nowadays, the consensus is that developmental glitches're only one cause—any trauma can trigger it. And it doesn't have to be a single event. It could be a personality flaw, a long series of personal or professional disappointments. Hard to say." His eyes glowed as they gazed at the profile. "But I sure hope you bag him alive, Lincoln. I'd love the chance to get him on the couch for a few hours."

"Thom, are you writing this down?"

"Yes, bwana."

"But one question," Rhyme began.

Dobyns whirled around. "I'd say it's *the* question, Lincoln: Why is he leaving the clues? Right?"

"Yep. Why the clues?"

"Think about what he's done . . . He's talking to you. Not rambling incoherently like Son of Sam or the Zodiac killer. He's not schizophrenic. He's communicating—in *your* language. The language of forensics. Why?" More pacing, eyes flipping over the chart. "All I can think of is that he wants to share the guilt. See, it's hard for him to kill. It becomes easier if he makes us accomplices. If we don't save the vics in time their deaths are partly *our* fault."

"But that's good, isn't it?" Rhyme asked. "It means he'll keep giving us clues that are solvable. Otherwise, if the puzzle's too hard, he's not sharing the burden."

"Well, that's true," Dobyns said, smiling no longer. "But there's another factor at work too."

Sellitto supplied the answer. "Serial activity escalates."

"Right," Dobyns confirmed.

"How can he strike more often?" Banks muttered. "Every three hours isn't fast enough?"

"Oh, he'll find a way," the psychologist continued. "Most likely, he'll probably start targeting multiple victims." The psychologist's eyes narrowed. "Say, you all right, Lincoln?"

There were beads of sweat on the criminalist's forehead and he'd been squinting his eyes hard. "Just tired. A lot of excitement for an old crip."

"One last thing. The profile of the victims's vital in serial crimes. But here we've got different sexes, ages and economic classes. All white but he's been preying in a predominantly white pool so that's not statistically significant. With what we know so far we can't figure out why he's taken these particular people. If you can, you might just get ahead of him."

"Thanks, Terry," Rhyme said. "Stick around for a while."

"Sure, Lincoln. If you'd like."

Rhyme ordered, "Let's look at the PE from the stockyard scene. What've we got? The underwear?"

Mel Cooper assembled the bags that Sachs had brought back from the scene. He glanced at the one containing the underwear. "Katrina Fashion's D'Amore line," he announced. "One hundred percent cotton, elastic band. Cloth made in the U.S. They were cut and sewn in Taiwan."

"You can tell that just by looking at them?" Sachs asked, incredulous.

"Naw, I was reading," he answered, pointing at the label.

"Oh."

The cops laughed.

"He's telling us he's got another woman then?" Sachs asked.

"Probably," Rhyme said.

Cooper opened the bag. "Don't know what the liquid is. I'll do a chromatograph."

Rhyme asked Thom to hold up the scrap of paper with the phases of the moon on it. He studied it closely. A scrap like this was wonderful individuated evidence. You could fit it to the sheet it'd been torn from and link the two as closely as fingerprints. The problem here of course was that they had no original piece of paper. He wondered if they'd ever find it. The unsub might have destroyed it once he'd torn this bit out. Yet Lincoln Rhyme preferred to think not. He liked to picture it somewhere. Just waiting to be found. The way he always pictured source evidence: the automobile the paint chip had scraped off of, the finger that had lost the nail, the gun barrel that had discharged the rifled slug found in the victim's body. These sources—always close to the unsub—took on personalities of their own in Rhyme's mind. They could be imperious or cruel.

Or mysterious.

Phases of the moon.

Rhyme asked Dobyns if their unsub could be driven to act cyclically.

"No. The moon isn't in a major phase right now. We're four days past new."

"So the moons mean something else."

"If they're even moons in the first place," Sachs said. Pleased with herself, and rightly so, Rhyme thought. He said, "Good point, Amelia. Maybe he's talking about circles. About ink. About paper. About geometry. The planetarium . . ."

Rhyme realized that she was staring at him. Maybe just realizing now that he'd shaved and his hair was combed, his clothes changed.

And what was her mood now? he wondered. Angry at him, or disengaged? He couldn't tell. At the moment Amelia Sachs was as cryptic as Unsub 823.

The beeping of the fax machine sounded in the hallway. Thom went to get it and returned a moment later with two sheets of paper.

"It's from Emma Rollins," he announced. He held the sheets up for Rhyme to see.

"Our grocery scanner survey. Eleven stores in Manhattan sold veal shanks to customers buying fewer than five items in the last two days." He started to write on the poster then glanced at Rhyme. "The names of the stores?"

"Of course. We'll need them for cross-referencing later."

Thom wrote them down on the profile chart.

B'way & 82nd,
  ShopRite
B'way & 96th,
  Anderson Foods
Greenwich & Bank,
  ShopRite
2nd Ave., 72nd-73rd,
  Grocery World
Battery Park City,
  J&G's Emporium
1709 2nd Ave.,
  Anderson Foods
34th & Lex.,
  Food Warehouse
8th Ave. & 24th,
  ShopRite
Houston & Lafayette,
  ShopRite
6th Ave. & Houston,
  J&G's Emporium
Greenwich & Franklin,
  Grocery World

"That narrows it down," Sachs said, "to the entire city."

"Patience," said restless Lincoln Rhyme.

Mel Cooper was examining the straw that Sachs had found. "Nothing unique here." He tossed it aside.

"Is it new?" Rhyme asked. If it was they might cross-reference stores that had sold brooms and veal shanks on the same day.

But Cooper said, "Thought of that. It's six months old or older." He began shaking the trace evidence in the German girl's clothing out over a piece of newsprint.

"Several things here," he said, poring over the sheet. "Dirt."

"Enough for a density-gradient?"

"Nope. Just dust really. Probably from the scene."

Cooper looked over the rest of the effluence he'd brushed off the bloodstained clothing.

"Brick dust. Why's there so much brick?"

"From the rats I shot. The wall was brick."

"You shot them? At the scene?" Rhyme winced.

Sachs said defensively, "Well, yes. They were all over her."

He was angry but he let it go. Adding just, "All *kinds* of contaminants from gunfire. Lead, arsenic, carbon, silver."

"And here . . . another bit of reddish leather. From the glove. And . . . We've got another fiber. A different one."

Criminalists love fibers. This was a tiny gray tuft barely visible to the naked eye.

"Excellent," Rhyme announced. "And what else?"

"And here's the photo of the scene," Sachs said, "and the fingerprints. The one from her throat and from where he picked up the glove." She held them up.

"Good," Rhyme said, looking them over carefully.

There was a sheen of reluctant triumph on her face—the rush of winning, which is the flip side of hating yourself for being unprofessional.

Rhyme was studying the Polaroids of the prints when he heard footsteps on the stairs and Jim Polling arrived. He entered the room, did a double-take at the spiffed-up Lincoln Rhyme and strode to Sellitto.

"I was just at the scene," he said. "You saved the vic. Great job, guys." He nodded toward Sachs to show the noun included her too. "But the prick's 'napped another one?"

"Or's about to," Rhyme muttered, gazing at the prints.

"We're working on the clues right now," Banks said.

"Jim, I've been trying to track you down," Sellitto said. "I tried the mayor's office."

"I was with the chief. He had to fucking beg for some extra searchers. Got another fifty men pulled off UN security detail."

"Captain, there's something we got to talk about. We gotta problem. Something happened at the last scene . . ."

A voice as yet unheard from boomed through the room, "Problem? Who got a *problem*? We don't got no problems here, do we? None ay-tall."

Rhyme looked up at the tall, thin man in the doorway. He was jet black and wore a ridiculous green suit and shoes that shone like brown mirrors. Rhyme's heart plummeted. "Dellray."

"Lincoln Rhyme. New York's own Ironside. Hey, Lon. And Jim Polling, how's it hangin', buddy?"

Behind Dellray were a half-dozen other men and a woman. Rhyme knew in a heartbeat why the federal agents were here. Dellray scanned the officers in the room, his attention alighting momentarily on Sachs then flying away.

"What do you want?" Polling asked.

Dellray said, "Haven't you guessed, gemmuns. You're outa business. We closin' you up. Yessir. Just like a bookie."

SEVENTEEN

One of us.

That's how Dellray was looking at Lincoln Rhyme as he walked around the bed. Some people did this. Paralysis was a club and they crashed the party with jokes, nods, winks. You know I love you, man, 'cause I'm makin' funna you.

Lincoln Rhyme had learned that this attitude got tiring very, very quickly.

"Lookit that," Dellray said, poking at the Clinitron. "That's something outa *Star Trek*. Commander Riker, get your ass in the shuttle."

"Go away, Dellray," Polling said. "It's our case."

"And how's dis here patient doing, Dr Crusher?"

The captain was stepping forward, a rooster the lanky FBI agent towered over. "Dellray, you listening? Go away."

"Man, I'ma get me one of those, Rhyme. Lay my ass down in it, watcha game. Seriously, Lincoln, how you doin'? Been a few years."

"Did they knock?" Rhyme asked Thom.

"No, they didn't knock."

"You didn't knock," Rhyme said. "So may I suggest that you leave?"

"Gotta warrant," Dellray murmured, flicking papers in his breast pocket.

Amelia Sachs's right index fingernail worried her thumb, which was on the verge of bleeding.

Dellray looked around the room. He was clearly impressed at their impromptu lab but strangled the feeling fast. "We're taking over. Sorry."

UNSUB 823

Appearance	Residence	Vehicle	Other
• Caucasian male, slight build • Dark clothing • Old gloves, reddish kidskin • Aftershave; to cover up other scent? • Ski mask? Navy blue? • Gloves are dark	• Prob. has safe house • Located near; B'way & 82nd, ShopRite B'way & 96th Anderson Foods Greenwich & Bank ShopRite 2nd Ave., 72nd-73rd, Grocery World Battery Park City, J&G's Emporium 1709 2nd Ave., Anderson Foods 34th & Lex., Food Warehouse 8th Ave. & 24th, ShopRite Houston & Lafayette, ShopRite 6th Ave. & Houston, J&G's Emporium Greenwich & Franklin, Grocery World	• Yellow Cab • Recent model sedan • Lt. gray, silver, biege	• knows CS proc. • possibly has record • knows FR prints • gun = .32 Colt • Ties vics w/ unusual knots • "Old" appeals to him • Called one vic "Hanna" • Knows basic German • Underground appeals to him • Dual personalities • Maybe priest, soc. worker, counselor

In twenty years of policing, Rhyme had never seen a peremptory takeover like this.

"Fuck this, Dellray," Sellitto began, "you passed on the case."

The agent swiveled his glossy black face around until he was looking down at the detective.

"Passed? Passed? I never got no ring-a-ling about it. D'jou call me?"

"No."

"Then who dropped the dime?"

"Well . . ." Sellitto, surprised, glanced at Polling, who said, "You got an advisory. That's all we've gotta send you." On the defensive now too.

"An advisory. Yeah. And, hey, how 'xactly was that delivered? Would that have been by Pony *Ex*-press? Book-rate mail? Tell me, Jim, what's the good of an overnight advisory when there's an ongoing operation?"

Polling said, "We didn't see the need."

"We?" Dellray asked quickly. Like a surgeon spotting a microscopic tumor.

"*I* didn't see the need," Polling snapped. "I told the mayor to keep it a local operation. We've got it under control. Now fuck off, Dellray."

"And you thought you could wrap it up in time for the eleven o'clock news."

Rhyme was startled when Polling shouted, "What we thought was none of your goddamn business. It's our fucking case." He knew about the captain's legendary temper but he'd never seen it in action.

"Ac-tu-ally, it's ou-ur fuck-ing case now." Dellray strolled past the table that held Cooper's equipment.

Rhyme said, "Don't do this, Fred. We're getting a handle on this guy. Work with us but don't take it away. This unsub isn't like anything you've ever seen."

Dellray smiled. "Let's see, what's the latest I hear about this 'fuck-ing' case? That you've got a civvy doin' the 'rensics." The agent forewent a glance at the Clinitron bed. "You got a portable doing crime scene. You got soldiers out buying groceries."

"Evidence standards, Frederick," Rhyme reminded stridently. "That's SOP."

Dellray looked disappointed. "But ESU, Lincoln? All those taxpayer dollars. Then there's cutting up people like *Texas Chainsaw* . . ."

How had *that* news got out? Everyone was sworn to secrecy on the dismemberment issue.

"And whatsis I hear 'bout Haumann's boys found the vic but dint go in and save her right away? Channel Five had a Big Ear mike on it. Got her screaming for a good five minutes 'fore you sent somebody in." He glanced at Sellitto with a wry grin. "Lon, my man, would that've been the *problem* you were just talking about?"

They'd come so far, Rhyme was thinking. They *were* getting a feel for him, starting to learn the unsub's language. Starting to see him. With a burst of surprise he understood that he was once again doing what he loved. After all these years. And now somebody was going to take it away from him. Anger rippled inside him.

"Take the case, Fred," Rhyme grumbled. "But don't cut us out. Don't do it."

"You lost two vics," Dellray reminded.

"We lost *one*," Sellitto corrected, looking uneasily at Polling, who was still fuming. "Nothing we coulda done about the first. He was a calling card."

Dobyns, arms crossed, merely observed the argument. But Jerry Banks leapt in. "We've got his routine down now. We aren't going to lose any more."

"You are if ESU's gonna sit around listenin' to vics scream their heads off."

Sellitto said, "It was my—"

"*My* decision," Rhyme sang out. "Mine."

"But you're civvy, Lincoln. So it couldn't have been your decision. It mighta been your *suggestion*. It mighta been your *recommendation*. But I don't think it was your decision."

Dellray's attention had turned to Sachs again. His eyes on her, he said to Rhyme, "You told Peretti not to run the scene? That's mighty curious, Lincoln. Why'd you go and do something like that?"

Rhyme said, "I'm better than he is."

"Peretti's not a happy boy scout. Nosir. He and I had a chin wag with Eckert."

Eckert? The dep com? How was he involved?

And with one glance at Sachs, at the evasive blue eyes, framed by strands of mussed red hair, he knew how.

Rhyme nailed her with a look, which she promptly avoided, and he said to Dellray, "Let's see . . . Peretti? Wasn't he the one opened up traffic on the spot where the unsub'd stood to watch the first vic? Wasn't he the one released the scene before we'd had a chance to pick up any serious trace? The scene my own Sachs here had the foresight to seal off. *My* Sachs had it right and Vince Peretti and everybody *else* had it wrong. Yes, she did."

She was gazing at her thumb, a look that bespoke seeing a familiar sight, and slipped a Kleenex from her pocket, wrapped it around the bloody digit.

Dellray summarized, "You shoulda called us at the beginning."

"Just get out," Polling muttered. Something snapped in his eyes and his voice rose. "Get the hell out!" he screamed.

Even cool Dellray blinked and eased back as the spittle flew from the captain's mouth.

Rhyme frowned at Polling. There was a chance they might salvage something of the case but not if Polling had a tantrum. "Jim . . ."

The captain ignored him. "Out!" he shouted again. "You are not taking over our case!" And startling everyone in the room, Polling leapt forward, grabbed the agent by his green lapels and shoved him against the wall. After a moment of stunned silence Dellray simply pushed the captain back with his fingertips and took out a cellular phone. He offered it to Polling.

"Call the mayor. Or Chief Wilson."

Polling eased instinctively away from Dellray—a short man putting some distance between himself and a tall one. "You want the case, you fucking got it." The captain strode to the stairs and then down them. The front door slammed.

"Jesus, Fred," Sellitto said, "work with us. We can nail this scumbag."

"We need the Bureau's A-T," said Dellray, now sounding like reason itself. "You're not set up for the terrorist angle."

"What terrorist angle?" Rhyme asked.

"The UN peace conference. Snitch o' mine said word was up that something was gonna go down at the airport. Where he snatched the vics."

"I wouldn't profile him as a terrorist," Dobyns said. "Whatever's going on inside him's psychologically motivated. It's not ideological."

"Well, fact is, Quantico and us're pegging him one way. 'Preciate that you feel different. But this's how we're handling it."

Rhyme gave up. Fatigue was spiriting him away. He wished Sellitto and his scar-faced assistant had never shown up this morning. He wished he'd never met Amelia Sachs. Wished he wasn't wearing the ridiculous crisp white shirt, which felt stiff at his neck and felt like nothing below it.

He realized that Dellray was speaking to him.

"I'm sorry?" Rhyme cocked a muscular eyebrow.

Dellray asked, "I mean, *couldn't* politics be a motive too?"

"Motive doesn't interest me," Rhyme said. "Evidence interests me."

Dellray glanced again at Cooper's table. "So. The case's ours. We all together on that?"

"What're our options?" Sellitto asked.

"You back us up with searchers. Or you can drop out altogether. That's about all that's left. We'll take the PE now, you don't mind."

Banks hesitated.

"Give 'em it," Sellitto ordered.

The young cop picked up the evidence bags from the most recent scene, slipped them into a large plastic bag. Dellray held his hands out. Banks glanced at the lean fingers and tossed the bag onto the table, walking back to the far side of the room—the cop side. Lincoln Rhyme was a demilitarized zone between them and Amelia Sachs stood riveted at the foot of Rhyme's bed.

Dellray said to her, "Officer Sachs?"

After a pause, her eyes on Rhyme, she responded, "Yes?"

"Commissioner Eckert wants ya t'come with us for debriefing 'bout the crime scenes. He said something about starting your new assignment on Monday."

She nodded.

Dellray turned to Rhyme and said sincerely, "Don'tcha worry, Lincoln. We're gonna git him. Next you hear, his head gonna be on a stake at the gates to the city."

He nodded to his fellow agents, who packed up the evidence and headed downstairs. From the hallway Dellray called to Sachs, "You coming, officer?"

She stood with her hands together, like a schoolgirl at a party she regretted she'd come to.

"In a minute."

Dellray vanished down the stairs.

"Those pricks," Banks muttered, flinging his watchbook onto the table. "Can you believe that?"

Sachs rocked on her heels.

"Better get going, Amelia," Rhyme said. "Your carriage awaits."

"Lincoln." Walking closer to the bed.

"It's all right," he said. "You did what you had to do."

"I have no business doing CS work," she blurted. "I never wanted to."

"And you won't be doing it anymore. That works out well, doesn't it?"

She started to walk to the door then turned and blurted, "You don't care about anything but the evidence, do you?"

Sellitto and Banks stirred but she ignored them.

"Say, Thom, could you show Amelia out?"

Sachs continued, "This is all just a game to you, isn't it? Monelle—"

"Who?"

Her eyes flared, "There! See? You don't even remember her name. Monelle Gerger. The girl in the tunnel . . . she was just a part of the puzzle to you. There were rats crawling all over her and you said, 'That's their nature'? That's their *nature*? She's never going to be the same again and all you cared about was your precious evidence."

"In living victims," he droned, lecturing, "rodent wounds are always superficial. As soon as the first li'l critter drooled on her she needed rabies vaccine. What did a few more bites matter?"

"Why don't we ask her opinion?" Sachs's smile was different now. It had turned pernicious, like those of the nurses and therapy aides who hated crips. They walked around rehab wards with smiles like this. Well, he hadn't been happy with the polite Amelia Sachs; he'd wanted the feisty one . . .

"Answer me something, Rhyme. Why did you really want me?"

"Thom, our guest has overstayed her welcome. Would you—?"

"Lincoln," the aide began.

"Thom," Rhyme snapped, "believe I asked you to do something."

"Because I don't know shit," Sachs blurted. "That's why! You didn't want a real CS tech because then you wouldn't be in charge. But me . . . you can send me here, send me there. I'll do exactly what you want, and I won't bitch and moan."

"Ah, the troops mutiny . . ." Rhyme said, lifting his eyes to the ceiling.

"But I'm not one of the troops. I never wanted this in the first place."

"I didn't want it either. But here we are. In bed together. Well, one of us." And he knew his cold smile was far, far icier than any she could muster.

"Why, you're just a spoiled brat, Rhyme."

"Hey, officer, time out here," Sellitto barked.

But she kept going. "You can't walk your crime scenes anymore and I'm sorry about that. But you're risking an investigation just to massage your ego and I say fuck that." She grabbed her Patrol hat and stormed out of the room.

He expected to hear a slamming door from downstairs, maybe breaking glass. But there was a faint click and then silence.

As Jerry Banks retrieved his watchbook and thumbed through it with more concentration than was needed, Sellitto said, "Lincoln, I'm sorry. I—"

"Nothing to it," Rhyme said, yawning excessively in the false hope that it would calm his stinging heart. "Nothing at all."

The cops stood beside the half-empty table for a few moments, difficult silence, then Cooper said, "Better get packed up." He hefted a black 'scope case onto the table and began to unscrew an eyepiece with the loving care of a musician disassembling his saxophone.

"Well, Thom," Rhyme said, "it's after sunset. You know what that tells me? Bar's open."

Their war room was impressive. It beat Lincoln Rhyme's bedroom hands down.

Half a floor at the federal building, three dozen agents, computers and electronic panels out of some Tom Clancy movie. The agents looked like lawyers or investment bankers. White shirts, ties. *Crisp* was the word that came to mind. And Amelia Sachs in the center, conspicuous in her navy-blue uniform, soiled with rat blood, dust and grainy shit from cattle dead a hundred years.

She was no longer shaking from her blowup with Rhyme and though her mind kept reeling with a hundred things she wanted to say, wished she *had* said, she forced herself to concentrate on what was happening around her.

A tall agent in an immaculate gray suit was conferring with Dellray—two large men, heads down, solemn. She believed he was the special agent in charge of the Manhattan office, Thomas Perkins, but she didn't know for certain; a Patrol officer has as much contact with the FBI as a dry cleaner or insurance salesman does. He seemed humorless, efficient, and kept glancing at a large map of Manhattan pinned to the wall. Perkins nodded several times as Dellray briefed him then he stepped up to a fiber-board table filled with manila folders, looked over the agents and began to speak.

"If I could have your attention . . . I've just been in communication with the director and the AG in Washington. You've all heard about the Kennedy Airport unsub by now. It's an unusual profile. Kidnapping, absent a sexual element, is rarely the basis for serial activity. In fact this's the first unsub of the sort we've had in the Southern District. In light of the possible connection with the events at the UN this week we're coordinating with headquarters, Quantico and the secretary-general's office. We've been told to be completely proactive on this case. It's getting prioritization at the highest level."

The SAC glanced at Dellray, who said, "We've taken over the case from the NYPD but we'll be using them for backup and personpower. We have the crime scene officer here to brief us on the scenes." Dellray sounded completely different here. Not a shred of Superfly.

"Have you vouchered the PE?" Perkins asked Sachs.

Sachs admitted that she hadn't. "We were working on saving the vics."

The SAC was troubled by this. At trial, otherwise solid cases tanked regularly because of slipups in recording the chain of custody of the physical evidence. It was the first thing the perps' defense lawyers wailed on.

"Make sure you do that before you leave."

"Yessir."

What a look on Rhyme's face when he guessed I bitched to Eckert and got them shut down. What a look . . .

My Sachs figured it out, my Sachs preserved the scene.

She worried a nail again. Stop it, she told herself, as she always did, and continued to dig into the flesh. The pain felt good. That's what the therapists never understood.

The SAC said, "Agent Dellray? Could you brief the room as regards the approach we'll be taking."

Dellray looked from the SAC to the other agents and continued, "At this moment we have field agents hitting every major terrorist cell in the city and pursuing whatever leads we can find that'll get us to the unsub's residence. *All* CIs, *all* undercover agents. It'll mean compromising some existing operations but we've decided it's worth the risk.

"Our job here is to be rapid response. You'll break out into groups of six agents each and be ready to move on any lead. You'll have complete hostage-rescue and barricade-entry support."

"Sir," Sachs said.

Perkins looked up, frowning. Apparently one didn't interrupt briefings until the approved Q&A break. "Yes, what is it, officer?"

"Well, I'm just wondering, sir. What about the victim?"

"Who, that German girl? You think we should interview her again?"

"No, sir. I meant the *next* victim."

Perkins responded, "Oh, we'll certainly stay cognizant of the fact that there may be other targets."

Sachs continued, "He's got one now."

"He does?" The SAC glanced at Dellray, who shrugged. Perkins asked Sachs, "How do you know?"

"Well, I don't exactly know, sir. But he left clues at the last scene and he wouldn't've done that if he didn't have another vic. Or was just about to snatch one."

"Noted, officer," the SAC continued. "We're going to mobilize as fast as we can to make sure nothing happens to them."

Dellray said to her, "We think it's best to focus on the beast himself."

"Detective Sachs—" Perkins began.

"I'm not a detective, sir. I'm assigned to Patrol."

"Yes, well," the SAC continued, looking at the stacks of files. "If you could just give us some of your bullet points, that would be helpful."

Thirty agents watching her. Two women among them.

"Just tell us whatcha saw," Dellray said, gripping an unlit cigarette between prominent teeth.

She gave them a synopsis of her searches of the crime scenes and the conclusions Rhyme and Terry Dobyns had come to. Most of the agents were troubled by the unsub's curious MO.

"Like a goddamn game," an agent muttered.

One asked if the clues had any political messages they could decipher.

"Well, sir, we really don't think he's a terrorist," Sachs persisted.

Perkins turned his high-powered attention toward her. "Let me ask you, officer, you concede he's smart, this unsub?"

"Very smart."

"Couldn't he be double-bluffing?"

"How do you mean?"

"You . . . I should say the NYPD's thinking is that he's just a nutcase. I mean, a criminal personality. But isn't it possible he's smart enough to make you *think* that. When something else's going on."

"Like what?"

"Take those clues he left. Couldn't they be diversions?"

"No, sir, they're directions," Sachs said. "Leading us to the vics."

"I understand that," quick Thomas Perkins said. "But by doing that he's also leading us *away* from other targets, right?"

She hadn't considered that. "I suppose it's possible."

"And Chief Wilson's been pulling men off UN security detail right and left to work the kidnapping. This unsub might be keeping everyone distracted, which leaves him free for his real mission."

Sachs remembered that she'd had a similar thought herself earlier in the day, watching all the searchers along Pearl Street. "And that'd be the UN?"

"We think so," Dellray said. "The perps behind the UNESCO bombing attempt in London might want to try again."

Meaning Rhyme was going off in the completely wrong direction. It eased the weight of her guilt somewhat.

"Now, officer, could you itemize the evidence for us?" Perkins asked.

Dellray gave her an inventory sheet of everything she'd found and she went through it item by item. As she spoke Sachs was aware of bustling activity around her—some agents taking calls, some standing and whispering to other agents, some taking notes. But when, glancing down at the sheet, she added, "Then I picked up this fingerprint of his at the last scene," she realized that the room had fallen utterly silent. She looked up. Every face in the office was staring at her in what could pass for shock—if federal agents were capable of that.

She glanced helplessly at Dellray, who cocked his head, "You saying you gotchaself a print?"

"Well, yes. His glove fell off in a struggle with the last vic and when he picked it up he brushed against the floor."

"Where is it?" Dellray asked quickly.

"Jesus," one agent called. "Why didn't you *say* anything?"

"Well, I—"

"Find it, find it!" somebody else called.

A murmur ran through the room.

Her hands shaking, Sachs dug through the evidence bags

and handed Dellray the Polaroid of the fingerprint. He held it up, looked carefully. Showed it to someone who, she guessed, was a friction-ridge expert. "Good," the agent offered. "It's definitely A-grade."

Sachs knew that prints were rated A, B and C, the lower category being unacceptable to most law enforcement agencies. But whatever pride she felt in her evidence-gathering skills was crushed by their collective dismay that she hadn't mentioned it before this.

Then everything started to happen at once. Dellray handed off to an agent who jogged to an elaborate computer in the corner of the office and rested the Polaroid on a large, curved bed of something called an Opti-Scan. Another agent turned on the computer and started typing in commands as Dellray snatched up the phone. He tapped his foot impatiently and then lowered his head as, somewhere, the call was answered.

"Ginnie, S'Dellray. This's gonna be a true-blue pain but I needya to shut down all AFIS Northeast Region requests and give the one I'm sending priority . . . I got Perkins here. He'll okay it and if that ain't enough I'll call the man in Washington himself. . . . It's the UN thing."

Sachs knew the Bureau's Automated Fingerprint Identification System was used by police departments throughout the country. That's what Dellray would be braking to a halt at the moment.

The agent at the computer said, "It's scanned. We're transmitting now."

"How long's it gonna take?"

"Ten, fifteen minutes."

Dellray pressed his dusty fingers together. "Please, please, please."

All around her was a cyclone of activity. Sachs heard voices talking about weapons, helicopters, vehicles, anti-terror negotiators. Phone calls, clattering keyboards, maps unrolling, pistols being checked.

Perkins was on the phone, talking to the hostage-rescue people, or the director, or the mayor. Maybe the president. Who knew? Sachs said to Dellray, "I didn't know the print was that big a deal."

"S'always a big deal. Least, with AFIS now it is. Used to

be you dusted for prints mostly for show. Let the vics and the press know you were doing *something*."

"You're kidding."

"Naw, not a bit. Take New York City. You do a cold search—that's when you don't have any suspects—you do a cold search manually, it'd take a tech fifty years to go through all the print cards. No foolin'. An automated search? Fifteen minutes. Used to be you'd ID a suspect maybe two, three percent of the time. Now we're running close to twenty, twenty-two percent. Oh, yup, prints're golden. Dincha tell Rhyme about it?"

"He knew, sure."

"And he didn't get all hands on board? My oh my, the man's slipping."

"Say, officer," SAC Perkins called, holding his hand over the phone, "I'll ask you to complete those chain-of-custody cards now. I want to get the PE off to PERT."

The Physical Evidence Response Team. Sachs remembered that Lincoln Rhyme had been the one the feds hired to help put it together.

"I'll do that. Sure."

"Mallory, Kemple, take that PE to an office and get our guest some COC cards. You have a pen, officer?"

"Yes, I do."

She followed the two men into a small office, clicking her ballpoint nervously while they hunted down and returned with a pack of federal-issue chain-of-custody cards. She sat down and broke the package open.

The voice behind her was the hip Dellray, the persona that seemed the eagerest to break out. In the car on the way here someone had referred to him as the Chameleon and she was beginning to see why.

"We call Perkins the Big Dict. Nyup—not 'dick' like you're thinking. 'Dict' like *dictionary*. But don' worry over him. He's smarter'n an agent sandwich. And better'n that he's pulled strings all the way to D.C., which is where strings gotta be pulled in cases like this." Dellray ran his cigarette beneath his nose as if it were a fine cigar. "You know, officer, you're foxy smart doing whatch're doing."

"Which is?"

"Getting out of Major Crimes. You don't want it." The lean black face, glossy and wrinkled only about the eyes, seemed sincere for the first time since she'd met him. "Best thing you ever did, going into Public Affairs. You'll do some good there and it won't turn you to dust. That's what happens, you bet. This job turns you to dust."

One of the last victims of James Schneider's mad compulsion, a young man named Ortega, had come to Manhattan from Mexico City, where political unrest (the much-heralded populist uprising, which had begun the year before) had made commerce difficult at best. Yet the ambitious entrepreneur had been in the city no more than one week when be vanished from sight. It was learned that he was last seen in front of a West Side tavern and authorities immediately suspected that be was yet another victim of Schneider's. Sadly, this was discovered to be the case.

The bone collector cruised the streets for fifteen minutes around NYU, Washington Square. Plenty of people hanging out. But kids mostly. Students in summer school. Skateboarders. It was festive, weird. Singers, jugglers, acrobats. It reminded him of the "museums," down on the Bowery, popular in the 1800s. They weren't museums at all of course but arcades, teeming with burlesque shows, exhibits of freaks and daredevils, and vendors selling everything from French postcards to splinters of the True Cross.

He slowed once or twice but nobody wanted a cab, or could afford one. He turned south.

Schneider tied bricks to Señor Ortega's feet and rolled him under a pier into the Hudson River so the foul water and the fish might reduce his body to mere bone. The corpse was found two weeks after he had vanished and so it was never known whether or not the unfortunate victim was alive or had full use of his senses when he was thrown into the drink. Yet it is suspected that this was so. For Schneider cruelly shortened the rope so that Señor Ortega's face was inches below the surface of Davy Jones's locker;—his hands undoubtedly thrashed madly about as he gazed upward at the air that would have been his salvation.

The bone collector saw a sickly young man standing by the curb. AIDS, he thought. But your bones are healthy—and *so* prominent. Your bones'll last forever. . . . The man didn't want a cab and the taxi cruised past, the bone collector hungrily gazing at his thin frame in the rearview mirror.

He looked back to the street just in time to swerve around an elderly man who'd stepped off the curb, his thin arm raised to flag down the cab. The man leapt back, as best he could, and the cab skidded to a stop just past him.

The man opened the back door and leaned inside. "You should look where you're going." He said this instructionally. Not with anger.

"Sorry," the bone collector muttered contritely.

The elderly man hesitated for a moment, looked up the street but saw no other taxis. He climbed in.

The door slammed shut.

Thinking: Old and thin. The skin would ride on his bones like silk.

"So, where to?" he called.

"East Side."

"You got it," he said as he pulled on the ski mask and spun the wheel sharply right. The cab sped west.

3

THE PORTABLE'S DAUGHTER

Overturn, overturn, overturn! is the maxim of New York. . . . The very bones of our ancestors are not permitted to lie quiet a quarter of a century, and one generation of men seem studious to remove all relics of those which preceded them.

Philip Hone, Mayor of New York, Diary, 1845

Saturday, 10:15 P.M., to Sunday, 5:30 A.M.

EIGHTEEN

"Hit me again, Lon."

Rhyme drank through a straw, Sellitto from a glass. Both took the smoky liquor neat. The detective sank down in the squeaky rattan chair and Rhyme decided he looked a little like Peter Lorre in *Casablanca*.

Terry Dobyns was gone—after offering some acerbic psychological insights about narcissism and those employed by the federal government. Jerry Banks had left too. Mel Cooper continued to painstakingly disassemble and pack up his equipment.

"This is good, Lincoln." Sellitto sipped his Scotch. "Goddamn. I can't afford this shit. How old's it?"

"I think that one's twenty."

The detective eyed the tawny liquor. "Hell, this was a woman, she'd be legal and then some."

"Tell me something, Lon: Polling? That little tantrum of his. What was that all about?"

"Little Jimmy?" Sellitto laughed. "He's in trouble now. He's the one ran interference to take Peretti off the case and keep it out of the feds' hands. Really went out on a limb. Asking for you too, that took some doing. There were noses outa joint over that. I don't mean you personally. Just a civilian in on a hot case like this."

"Polling asked for me? I thought it was the chief."

"Yeah, but it was Polling put the bug in his ear in the first place. He called soon as he heard there'd been a taking and there was some bogus PE on the scene."

And wanted me? Rhyme wondered. This was curious.

Rhyme hadn't had any contact with Polling over the past few years—not since the cop-killer case in which Rhyme had been hurt. It had been Polling who'd run the case and eventually collared Dan Shepherd.

"You seem surprised," Sellitto said.

"That he asked for me? I am. We weren't on the best of terms. Didn't used to be anyway."

"Why's that?"

"I 14-43'd him."

An NYPD complaint form.

"Five, six years ago, when he was a lieutenant, I found him interrogating a suspect right in the middle of a secure scene. Contaminated it. I blew my stack. Put in a report and it got cited at one of his IA reviews—the one where he popped the unarmed suspect."

"Well, I guess all's forgiven, 'cause he wanted you bad."

"Lon, make a phone call for me, would you?"

"Sure."

"No," Thom said, lifting the phone out of the detective's hand. "Make him do it himself."

"I didn't have time to learn how it works," Rhyme said, nodding toward the dialing ECU Thom had hooked up earlier.

"You didn't *spend* the time. Big difference. Who're you calling?"

"Berger."

"No, you're not," Thom said. "It's late."

"I've been reading clocks for a while now," Rhyme replied coolly. "Call him. He's staying at the Plaza."

"No."

"I asked you to call him."

"Here." The aide slapped a slip of paper down on the far edge of the table but Rhyme read it easily. God may have taken much from Lincoln Rhyme but He'd given him the eyesight of a young man. He went through the process of dialing with his cheek on the control stalk. It was easier than he'd thought but he purposely took a long time and muttered as he did it. Infuriatingly, Thom ignored him and went downstairs.

Berger wasn't in his hotel room. Rhyme disconnected, mad that he wasn't able to slam the phone down.

"Problem?" Sellitto asked.

"No," Rhyme grumbled.

Where is he? Rhyme thought testily. It *was* late. Berger ought to be at his hotel room by now. Rhyme was stabbed with an odd feeling—jealousy that *his* death doctor was out helping someone else die.

Sellitto suddenly chuckled softly. Rhyme looked up. The cop was eating a candy bar. He'd forgotten that junk food'd been the staple of the big man's diet when they were working together. "I was thinking. Remember Bennie Ponzo?"

"The OC Task Force ten, twelve years ago?"

"Yeah."

Rhyme had enjoyed organized-crime work. The perps were pros. The crime scenes challenging. And the vics were rarely innocent.

"Who was that?" Mel Cooper asked.

"Hitman outa Bay Ridge," Sellitto said. "Remember after we booked him, the candy sandwich?"

Rhyme laughed, nodding.

"What's the story?" Cooper asked.

Sellitto said, "Okay, we're down at Central Booking, Lincoln and me and a couple other guys. And Bennie, remember, he was a big guy, he was sitting all hunched over, feeling his stomach. All of a sudden he goes, 'Yo, I'm hungry, I wanna candy sandwich.' And we're like looking at each other and I go, 'What's a candy sandwich?" And he looks at me like I'm from Mars and goes, 'What the fuck you think it is? Ya take a Hershey bar, ya put it between two slices of bread and ya eat it. That's a fucking candy sandwich.'"

They laughed. Sellitto held out the bar to Cooper, who shook his head, then to Rhyme, who felt a sudden impulse to take a bite. It'd been over a year since he'd had chocolate. He avoided food like that—sugar, candy. Troublesome food. The little things about life were the biggest burdens, the ones that saddened and exhausted you the most. Okay, you'll never scuba-dive or hike the Alps. So what? A lot of people don't. But everybody brushes their teeth. And goes to the dentist, gets a filling, takes the train home. Everybody picks a hunk of peanut from out behind a molar when nobody's looking.

Everybody except Lincoln Rhyme.

He shook his head to Sellitto and drank a long swallow of

Scotch. His eyes slid back to the computer screen, recalling the goodbye letter to Blaine he'd been composing when Sellitto and Banks had interrupted him that morning. There were some other letters he wanted to write as well.

The one he was putting off writing was to Pete Taylor, the spinal cord trauma specialist. Most of the time Taylor and Rhyme had talked not about the patient's condition but about death. The doctor was an ardent opponent of euthanasia. Rhyme felt he owed him a letter to explain why he'd decided to go ahead with the suicide.

And Amelia Sachs?

The Portable's Daughter would get a note too, he decided.

Crips are generous, crips are kind, crips are iron . . .

Crips are nothing if not forgiving.

> *Dear Amelia:*
> *My Dear Amelia:*
> *Amelia:*
> *Dear Officer Sachs:*
>
> *Inasmuch as we have had the pleasure of working together, I would like to take this opportunity to state that although I consider you a betraying judas, I've forgiven you. Furthermore I wish you well in your future career as a kisser of the media's ass. . . .*

"What's her story, Lon? Sachs."

"Aside from the fact she's got a ball-buster temper I didn't know about?"

"She married?"

"Naw. A face and bod like that, you'da thought some good-lookin' hunk woulda snagged her by now. But she doesn't even date. We heard she was going with somebody a few years ago but she never talks about it." He lowered his voice. "Lipstick lesbos's what the rumor is. But I don't know from that—*my* social life's picking up women at the laundromat on Saturday night. Hey, it works. What can I say?"

You'll have to learn to give up the dead. . . .

Rhyme was thinking about the look in her face when he'd said that to her. What was that all about? Then he grew angry with himself for spending any time thinking about her. And took a good slug of Scotch.

The doorbell rang, then footsteps on the stairs. Rhyme and Sellitto glanced toward the doorway. The sound was from the boots of a tall man, wearing city-issue jodhpurs and a blue helmet. One of NYPD's elite mounted police. He handed a bulky envelope to Sellitto and returned down the stairs.

The detective opened it. "Lookit what we got here." He poured the contents onto the table. Rhyme glanced up with irritation. Three or four dozen plastic evidence bags, all labeled. Each contained a patch of cellophane from the packages of veal shanks they'd sent ESU to buy.

"A note from Haumann." He read: "'To: L. Rhyme. L. Sellitto. From: B. Haumann, TSRF.'"

"What's 'at?" Cooper asked. The police department is a nest of initials and acronyms. RMP—remote mobile patrol—is a squad car. IED—improvised explosive device—is a bomb. But TSRF was a new one. Rhyme shrugged.

Sellitto continued to read, chuckling. "'Tactical Supermarket Response Force. Re: Veal shanks. Citywide search discovered forty-six subjects, all of which were apprehended and neutralized with minimal force. We read them their rights and have transported same to detention facility in the kitchen of Officer T. P. Giancarlo's mother. Upon completion of interrogation, a half-dozen suspects will be transferred to your custody. Heat at 350 for thirty minutes.'"

Rhyme laughed. Then sipped more Scotch, savoring the flavor. This was one thing he'd miss, the smoky breath of the liquor. (Though in the peace of senseless sleep, how could you miss anything? Just like evidence, take away the baseline standard and you have nothing to judge the loss against; you're safe for all eternity.)

Cooper fanned out some of the samples. "Forty-six samples of the cello. One from each chain and the major independents."

Rhyme gazed at the samples: The odds were good for class identification. Individuation of cellophane'd be a bitch—the scrap found on the veal bone clue wouldn't of course exactly match one of these. But, because parent companies buy identical supplies for all their stores, you might learn in which *chain* 823 bought the veal and narrow down the neighborhoods he might live in. Maybe he should call the Bureau's physical-evidence team and—

No, no. Remember: it's their *fuck-ing* case now.

Rhyme commanded Cooper, "Bundle them up and ship them to our federal brethren."

Rhyme tried shutting down his computer and hit the wrong button with his sometimes ornery ring finger. The speakerphone came on with a loud wail of squelch.

"Shit," Rhyme muttered darkly. "Fucking machinery."

Uneasy with Rhyme's sudden anger, Sellitto glanced at his glass and joked, "Hell, Linc, Scotch this good's supposed to make you mellow."

"Got news," Thom replied sourly. "He *is* mellow."

He parked close to the huge drainpipe.

Climbing from the cab he could smell the fetid water, slimy and ripe. They were in a cul-de-sac leading to the wide runoff pipe that ran from the West Side Highway down to the Hudson River. No one could see them here.

The bone collector walked to the back of the cab, enjoying the sight of his elderly captive. Just like he'd enjoyed staring at the girl he'd tied in front of the steam pipe. And the wiggling hand by the railroad tracks early this morning.

Gazing at the frightened eyes. The man was thinner than he'd thought. Grayer. Hair disheveled.

Old in the flesh but young in the bone . . .

The man cowered away from him, arms folded defensively across his narrow chest.

Opening the door, the bone collector pressed his pistol against the man's breastbone.

"Please," his captive whispered, his voice quavering. "I don't have much money but you can have it all. We can go to an ATM. I'll—"

"Get out."

"Please don't hurt me."

The bone collector gestured with his head. The frail man looked around miserably then scooted forward. He stood beside the car, cowering, his arms still crossed, shivering despite the relentless heat.

"Why are you doing this?"

The bone collector stepped back and fished the cuffs from his pocket. Because he wore the thick gloves it took a few seconds to find the chrome links. As he dug them out he thought he saw a four-rigger tacking up the Hudson. The opposing current here wasn't as strong as in the East River, where sailing ships had a hell of a time making their way from the East, Montgomery and Out Ward wharves north. He squinted. No, wait—it wasn't a sailboat, it was just a cabin cruiser, Yuppies lounging on the long front deck.

As he reached forward with the cuffs, the man grabbed his captor's shirt, gripped it hard. "Please. I was going to the hospital. That's why I flagged you down. I've been having chest pains."

"Shut up."

And the man suddenly reached for the bone collector's face, the liver-spotted hands gripping his neck and shoulder and squeezing hard. A jolt of pain radiated from the spot where the yellow nails dug into him. With a burst of temper, he pulled his victim's hands off and cuffed him roughly.

Slapping a piece of tape on the man's mouth, the bone collector dragged him down the gravel embankment toward the mouth of the pipe, four feet in diameter. He stopped, examined the old man.

It'd be so easy to take you down to the bone.

The bone . . . Touching it. Hearing it.

He lifted the man's hand. The terrified eyes gazed back, his lips trembling. The bone collector caressed the man's fingers, squeezed the phalanges between his own (wished he could take his glove off but didn't dare). Then he lifted the man's palm and pressed it hard against his own ear.

"What?—"

His left hand curled around his mystified captive's little finger and slowly pulled until he heard the deep *thonk* of brittle bone snapping. A satisfying sound. The man screamed, a muted cry stuttering through the tape. And slumped to the ground.

The bone collector pulled him upright and led the stumbling

man into the mouth of the pipe. He prodded the man forward.

They emerged underneath the old, rotting pier. It was a disgusting place, strewn with the decomposed bodies of animals and fish, trash on the wet rocks, a gray-green sludge of kelp. A mound of seaweed rose and fell in the water, humping like a fat lover. Despite the evening heat in the rest of the city, down here it was cold as a March day.

Señor Ortega . . .

He lowered the man into the river, cuffed him to a pier post, ratcheting the bracelet tight around his wrist again. The captive's grayish face was about three feet above the surface of the water. The bone collector walked carefully over the slick rocks to the drainpipe. He turned and paused for a moment, watching, watching. He hadn't cared much whether the constables found the others or not. Hanna, the woman in the taxi. But this one . . . The bone collector hoped they didn't find him in time. Indeed, that they didn't find him at all. So he could come back in a month or two and see if the clever river had scrubbed the skeleton clean.

Back on the gravel drive he pulled the mask off and left the clues to the next scene not far from where he'd parked. He was angry, furious at the constables, and so this time he hid the clues. And he also included a special surprise. Something he'd been saving for them. The bone collector returned to the taxi.

The breeze was gentle, carrying the fragrance of the sour river with it. And the rustle of grass and, as always in the city, the *shushhhh* of traffic.

Like emery paper on bone.

He stopped and listened to this sound, head cocked as he looked out over the billion lights of the buildings, stretching to the north like an oblong galaxy. It was then that a woman, running fast, emerged on a jogging path beside the drainpipe and nearly collided with him.

In purple shorts and top, the thin brunette danced out of his way. Gasping, she stopped, flicked sweat from her face. In good shape—taut muscles—but not pretty. A hook of a nose, broad lips, blotchy skin.

But beneath that . . .

"You're not supposed . . . You shouldn't park here. This's a jogging path . . ."

Her words fading and fear rising into her eyes, which flicked from his face to the taxi to the wad of ski mask in his hand.

She knew who he was. He smiled, noting her remarkably pronounced clavicle.

Her right ankle shifted slightly, ready to take her weight when she sprinted away. But he got her first. He ducked low, to tackle her, and when she gave a fast scream and dropped her arms to block him the bone collector straightened up fast from his feint and swung his elbow into her temple. There was a crack like a snapping belt.

She went down on the gravel, hard, and lay still. Horrified, the bone collector dropped to his knees and cradled her head. He moaned, "No, no, no . . ." Furious with himself for striking so hard, sick at heart that he might've broken what seemed to be a perfect skull beneath the tentacles of stringy hair and the unremarkable face.

Amelia Sachs finished another COC card and took a break. She paused, found a vending machine and bought a paper cup of vile coffee. She returned to the windowless office, looked over the evidence she'd gathered.

She felt a curious fondness for the macabre collection. Maybe because of what she'd gone through to collect it—her fiery joints ached and she still shuddered when she thought of the buried body at the first scene this morning, the bloody branch of a hand, and of T.J. Colfax's dangling flesh. Until today physical evidence hadn't meant anything to her. PE was boring lectures on drowsy spring afternoons at the academy. PE was math, it was charts and graphs, it was science. It was dead.

No, Amie Sachs was going to be a people cop. Walking beats, dissing back the dissers, outing druggies. Spreading respect for the law—like her father. Or pounding it into them. Like handsome Nick Carelli, a five-year vet, the star of Street Crimes, grinning at the world with his *yo-you-gotta-problem?* smile.

That's just who *she* was going to be.

She looked at the crisp brown leaf she'd found in the stockyard tunnel. One of the clues 823 had left for them. And here was the underwear too. She remembered that the feebies had snagged the PE before Cooper'd finished the test on the . . . what was that machine? The chromatograph? She wondered what the liquid soaking the cotton was.

But these thoughts led to Lincoln Rhyme and he was the one person she didn't want to think about just now.

She began to voucher the rest of the PE. Each COC card had a series of blank lines that would list the custodians of the evidence, in sequence, from the initial discovery at the scene all the way to trial. Sachs had transported evidence several times and her name had appeared on COC cards. But this was the first time *A. Sachs, NYPD 5885* had occupied the first slot.

Once again she lifted the plastic bag containing the leaf.

He'd actually touched it. *Him*. The man who'd killed T. J. Colfax. Who'd held Monelle Gerger's pudgy arm and cut deep into it. Who was out searching for another vic right now—if he hadn't already snatched one.

Who'd buried that poor man this morning, waving for mercy he never got.

She thought of Locard's Exchange Principle. People coming into contact, each transferring something to the other. Something big, something small. Most likely they didn't even know what.

Had something of 823 come off on this leaf? A cell of skin? A dot of sweat? It was a stunning thought. She felt a thrill of excitement, of fear as if the killer were right here, in this tiny airless room with her.

Back to the COC cards. For ten minutes she filled them out and was just finishing the last one when the door burst open, startling her. She spun around.

Fred Dellray stood in the doorway, his green jacket abandoned, his starched shirt rumpled. Fingers pinching the cigarette behind his ear. "Step inside a minute'r two, officer. It's payoff time. Thought you might wanna be there."

Sachs followed him down the short corridor, two steps behind his lope.

"The AFIS results're comin' in," Dellray said.

The war room was even busier than before. Jacketless agents

hovered over desks. They were armed with their on-duty weapons—the big Sig-Sauer and Smith & Wesson automatics, 10mm and .45s. A half-dozen agents were clustered around the computer terminal beside the Opti-Scan.

Sachs hadn't liked the way Dellray'd taken the case away from them, but she had to admit that beneath the slick-talking hipster Dellray was one hell of a good cop. Agents—young and old—would come up to him with questions and he'd patiently answer them. He'd yank a phone from the cradle and cajole or berate whoever was on the other end to get him what he needed. Sometimes, he'd look up across the bustling room and roar, "We gonna nail this prick-dick? Yep, you betcha we are." And the straight-arrows'd look at him uneasily but with the obvious thought in mind that if anybody could nail him it'd be Dellray.

"Here, it's coming in now," an agent called.

Dellray barked, "I want open lines to New York, Jersey and Connecticut DMVs. And Corrections and Parole. INS too. Tell 'em to stand by for an incoming ID request. Put everything else on hold."

Agents peeled off and began making phone calls.

The computer screen filled.

She couldn't believe that Dellray actually crossed his stickish fingers.

Utter silence throughout the room.

"Got him!" the agent at the keyboard shouted.

"Ain't no unsub anymore," Dellray sang melodically, bending over the screen. "Listen up, people. We gotta name: Victor Pietrs. Born here, 1948. His parents were from Belgrade. So, we got a Serbian connection. ID brought to us courtesy of New York D of C. Convictions for drugs, assault, one with a deadly. Two sentences served. Okay, listen to this—psychiatric history, committed three times on involuntary orders. Intake at Bellevue and Manhattan Psychiatric. Last release date three years ago. LKA Washington Heights."

He looked up. "Who's got the phone companies?"

Several agents raised their hands.

"Make the calls," Dellray ordered.

An interminable five minutes.

"Not there. No current New York Telephone listing."

"Nothing in Jersey," another agent echoed.

"Negative, Connecticut."

"Fuck-all," Dellray muttered. "Mix the names up. Try variations. An' lookit phone-service accounts canceled in the past year for nonpayment."

For several minutes voices rose and fell like the tide.

Dellray paced manically and Sachs understood why his frame was so scrawny.

Suddenly an agent shouted, "Found him!"

Everyone turned to look.

"I'm on with NY DMV," another agent called. "They've got him. It's coming through now. . . . He's a cabbie. Got a hack license."

"Why don' that s'prise me," Dellray muttered. "Shoulda thoughta that. Where's home sweet home?"

"Morningside Heights. A block from the river." The agent wrote down the address and held it aloft as Dellray swept past and took it. "Know the neighborhood. Pretty deserted. Lotta druggies."

Another agent typed the address into his computer terminal. "Okay, checking deeds . . . Property's an old house. A bank's got title. He must be renting."

"You want HRT?" one agent called across the bustling room. "I got Quantico on the line."

"No time," Dellray announced. "Use the field office SWAT. Get 'em suited up."

Sachs asked, "And what about the next victim?"

"What next victim?"

"He's already taken somebody. He knows we've had the clues for an hour or two. He'd've planted the vic awhile ago. He had to."

"No reports of anybody missing," the agent said. "And if he did snatch 'em they're probably at his house."

"No, they wouldn't be."

"Why not?"

"They'd pick up too much PE," she said. "Lincoln Rhyme said he has a safe house."

"Well, then we'll get him to tell us where they are."

Another agent said, "We can be real persuasive."

"Let's move it," Dellray called. "Yo, ever'body, let's thank

Officer Amelia Sachs here. She's the one found that print and lifted it."

She was blushing. Could feel it, hated it. But she couldn't help herself. As she glanced down she noticed strange lines on her shoes. Squinting, she realized she was still wearing the rubber bands.

When she looked up she saw a room full of unsmiling federal agents checking weapons and heading for the door as they glanced at her. The same way, she thought, lumberjacks look at logs.

NINETEEN

In 1911 a tragedy of massive dimension befell our fair city. On March 25, hundreds of industrious young women were hard at work in a garment factory, one of the many, known notoriously as "sweat-shops," in Greenwich Village in down-town Manhattan.

So enamored of profits were the owners of this company that they denied the poor girls in their employ even the rudimentary facilities that slaves might enjoy. They believed the laborers could not be trusted to make expeditious visits to the rest-room facilities and so kept the doors to the cutting and sewing rooms under lock and key.

The bone collector was driving back to his building. He passed a squad car but he kept his eyes forward and the constables never noticed him.

On the day in question a fire started on the eighth floor of the building and within minutes swept through the factory, from which the young employees tried to flee. They were unable to escape, however, owing to the chained state of the door. Many died on the spot and many more, some horribly afire, leapt into the air a hundred feet above the cobblestones and died from the collision with unyielding Mother Earth.

There numbered 146 victims of the Triangle Shirtwaist fire. The police, however, were confounded by the inability to locate one of the victims, a young woman, Esther Weinraub, whom several witnesses had seen leap in desperation from the eighth floor window. None of the other girls who similarly leapt survived the fall. Was it possible that she, miraculously, had? For when the bodies were laid out in the street for bereaved family members to identify, poor Miss Weinraub's was not to be found.

Reports began to circulate of a ghoul, a man seen carting off a large bundle from the scene of the fire. So incensed were the constables that someone might violate the sacred remains of an innocent young woman that they put on a still search for the man.

After several weeks, their diligent efforts bore fruit. Two residents of Greenwich Village reported seeing a man leaving the scene of the fire and carrying a heavy bundle "like a carpet" over his shoulder. The constables picked up his trail and tracked him to the West Side of the city, where they interviewed neighbors and learned that the man fit the description of James Schneider, who was still at large.

They narrowed their search to a decrepit abode in an alley in Hell's Kitchen, not far from the 60th Street stock-yards. As they entered the alleyway they were greeted with a revolting stench . . .

He was now driving past the very site of the Triangle fire itself—maybe he'd even been subconsciously prompted to come here. The Asch Building—the ironic name of the structure that had housed the doomed factory—was gone and the site was now a part of NYU. *Then and now . . .* The bone collector would not have been surprised to see white-bloused working girls, trailing sparks and faint smoke, tumbling gracefully to their deaths, falling around him like snow.

Upon breaking into Schneider's habitation, the authorities found a sight that sent even the most seasoned of them reeling with horror. The body of wretched Esther Weinraub—(or what remained of it)—was found in the basement. Schneider was bent on completing the work of the tragic fire and was slowly removing the woman's flesh through means too shocking to recount here.

A search of this loathsome place revealed a secret room, off the basement, filled with bones that had been stripped clean of flesh.

Beneath Schneider's bed, a constable found a diary, in which the madman chronicled his history of evil. "Bone"—(Schneider wrote)—"is the ultimate core of a human being. It alters not, deceives not, yields not. Once the facade of our intemperate ways of the flesh, the flaws of the lesser Races, and the weaker gender, are burnt or boiled away, we are—all of us—noble bone. Bone does not lie. It is immortal."

The lunatic writings set forth a chronicle of gruesome experimentation as he sought to ascertain the most effective way of cleansing his victims of their flesh. He tried boiling the bodies, burning them, rendering with lye, staking them out for animals, and immersing them in water.

But one method above all he favored for this macabre sport. "It is best, I have concluded"—(his diary continues)—"simply to bury the body in rich earth and let Nature do the tedious work. This is the most time-consuming method but the least likely to arouse suspicion as the odors are kept to a minimum. I prefer to inter the individuals while still alive, though why that might be I cannot say with any certainty."

In his heretofore secret room three more bodies were discovered in this very condition. The splayed hands and agog faces of the poor victims attest that they were indeed alive when Schneider piled the last shovelful of dirt upon their tormented crowns.

It was these dark designs that prompted the journalists of the day to christen Schneider with the name by which be was forever after known:—"The Bone Collector."

He drove on, his mind returning to the woman in the trunk, Esther Weinraub. Her thin elbow, her collarbone delicate as a bird's wing. He sped the cab forward, even risked running two red lights. He couldn't wait much longer.

"I'm not tired," Rhyme snapped.

"Tired or not, you need to rest."

"No, I need another drink."

Black suitcases lined the wall, awaiting the help of officers from the Twentieth Precinct to transport them back to the IRD lab. Mel Cooper was carting a microscope case downstairs. Lon Sellitto was still sitting in the rattan chair but he wasn't saying much. Just coming to the obvious conclusion that Lincoln Rhyme was not a mellow drunk at all.

Thom said, "I'm sure your blood pressure's up. You need rest."

"I need a drink."

Goddamn you, Amelia Sachs, Rhyme thought. And didn't know why.

"You should give it up. Drinking's never been any good for you."

Well, I'm *am* giving it up, Rhyme responded silently. For good. Monday. And no twelve-step plan for me; it's a one-stepper.

"Pour me another drink," he ordered.

Not really wanting one.

"No."

"Pour me a drink *now*!" Rhyme snapped.

"No way."

"Lon, would you please pour me another drink?"

"I—"

Thom said, "He doesn't get any more. When he's in a mood like this he's insufferable and we're not going to put up with him."

"You're going to withhold something from me? I could fire you."

"Fire away."

"Crip abuse! I'll get you indicted. Arrest him, Lon."

"Lincoln," Sellitto said placatingly.

"Arrest him!"

The detective was taken aback by the viciousness of Rhyme's words.

"Hey, buddy, maybe you should go a little light," Sellitto said.

"Oh, Christ," Rhyme groaned. He started to moan loudly.

Sellitto blurted, "What is it?" Thom was silent, looking on cautiously.

"My liver." Rhyme's face broke into a cruel grin. "Cirrhosis probably."

Thom swung around, furious. "I will *not* put up with this crap. Okay?"

"No, It's not oh-kay—"

A woman's voice, from the doorway: "We don't have much time."

"—at all."

Amelia Sachs walked into the room, glanced at the empty

tables. Rhyme felt spittle on his lip. He was overwhelmed with fury. Because she saw the drool. Because he wore a crisp white shirt he'd changed into just for her. And because he wanted desperately to be alone, forever, alone in the dark of motionless peace—where he was king. Not king for a day. But king for eternity.

The spit tickled. He cramped his already sore neck muscles trying to wipe his lip dry. Thom deftly swiped a Kleenex from a box and dried his boss's mouth and chin.

"Officer Sachs," Thom said. "Welcome. A shining example of maturity. We aren't seeing much of *that* right at the moment."

She wasn't wearing her hat and her navy blouse was open at the collar. Her long red hair tumbled to her shoulders. Nobody'd have any trouble differentiating *that* hair under a comparison 'scope.

"Mel let me in," she said, nodding toward the stairs.

"Isn't it past your bedtime, Sachs?"

Thom tapped a shoulder. *Behave yourself*, the gesture meant.

"I was just at the federal building," she said to Sellitto.

"How are our tax dollars doing?"

"They've caught him."

"*What?*" Sellitto asked. "Just like that? Jesus. They know about it downtown?"

"Perkins called the mayor. The guy's a cabbie. He was born here but his father's Serbian. So they're thinking he's trying to get even with the UN, or something. Got a yellow sheet. Oh, and a history of mental problems too. Dellray and feebie SWAT're on their way there right now."

"How'd they do it?" Rhyme asked. "Betcha it was the fingerprint."

She nodded.

"I suspected that would figure prominently. And, tell me, how concerned were they about the next victim?"

"They're concerned," she said evenly. "But mostly they want to nail the unsub."

"Well, that's *their* nature. And let me guess. They're figuring they'll sweat the location of the vic out of him after they take him down."

"You got it."

"That may take some doing," Rhyme said. "I'll venture that opinion without the benefit of our Dr Dobyns and the Behavioral mavens. So, a change of heart, Amelia? Why'd you come back?"

"Because whether Dellray collars him or not I don't think we have time to wait. To save the next vic, I mean."

"Oh, but we're dismantled, haven't you heard? Shut down, done gone outa business." Rhyme was looking in the dark computer screen, trying to see if his hair had stayed combed.

"You giving up?" she asked.

"Officer," Sellitto began, "even if we wanted to do somethin' we don't have any of the PE. That's the only link—"

"I've got it."

"What?"

"All of it. It's downstairs in the RRV."

The detective glanced out the window.

Sachs continued, "From last scene. From all the scenes."

"You have it?" Rhyme asked. "How?"

But Sellitto was laughing. "She 'jacked it, Lincoln. Gawdamn!"

"Dellray doesn't need it," Sachs pointed out. "Except for the trial. They've got the unsub, we'll save the victim. Works out nice, hm?"

"But Mel Cooper just left."

"Naw, he's downstairs. I asked him to wait." Sachs crossed her arms. She glanced at the clock. After eleven. "We don't have much time," she repeated.

His eyes too were on the clock. Lord, he was tired. Thom was right; he'd been awake longer than in years. But, he was surprised—no, *shocked*—to find, that, while he might have been furious or embarrassed or stabbed with heartless frustration today, the passing minutes had not lain like hot, unbearable weights on his soul. As they had for the past three and a half years.

"Well, church mice in heaven." Rhyme barked a laugh. "Thom? *Thom!* We need coffee. On the double. Sachs, get those cello samples to the lab along with the Polaroid of the bit Mel lifted from the veal bone. I want a polarization-comparison report in an hour. And none of this 'most probably' crap. I want an answer—*which* grocery chain did our unsub buy the veal bone at. And get that little shadow of yours back here, Lon. The one named after the baseball player."

The black vans sped through side streets.

This was a more circuitous route to the perp's location but Dellray knew what he was doing; anti-terror operations were supposed to avoid major city streets, which were often monitored by accomplices. Dellray, in the back of the lead van, tightened the Velcro strap on the body armor. They were less than ten minutes away.

He looked at the failing apartments, the trash-filled lots as they sped along. The last time he'd been in this decrepit neighborhood he'd been Rastafarian Peter Haile Thomas from Queens. He'd bought 137 pounds of cocaine from a shriveled little Puerto Rican, who decided at the last minute to 'jack his buyer. He took Dellray's buy-and-bust money and aimed a gun at Dellray's groin, pulling the trigger as calmly as if he were picking vegetables at the A&P. Click, click, click. Misfire. Toby Dolittle and the backup team took the fucker and his minders down before the scumbag found his other piece, leaving one shook-up Dellray to reflect on the irony of nearly getting killed because the perp truly bought the agent's performance—that he was a dealer not a cop.

"ETA, four minutes," the driver called.

For some reason Dellray's thoughts flipped to Lincoln Rhyme. He regretted he'd been such a shit when he took over the case. But there hadn't been much choice. Sellitto was a bulldog and Polling was a psycho—though Dellray could handle them. Rhyme was the one who made him uneasy. Sharp as a razor (hell, it *had* been his team that found Pietrs's print, even if they didn't jump on it as fast as they should've). In the old days, before his accident, you couldn't beat Rhyme if he didn't want to get beat. And you couldn't fool him either.

Now, Rhyme was a busted toy. It was a sad thing what could happen to a man, how you could die and still be alive. Dellray had walked into his room—his *bedroom*, no less—and hit him hard. Harder than he needed to.

Maybe he'd call. He could—

"Show time," the driver called, and Dellray forgot all about Lincoln Rhyme.

The vans turned onto the street where Pietrs lived. Most of the other streets they'd passed had been filled with sweating residents, clutching beer bottles and cigarettes, hoping for a breath or two of cool air. But this one was dark, empty.

The vans cruised slowly to a stop. Two dozen agents climbed out, in black tactical outfits, carrying their H&Ks equipped with muzzle lights and laser sights. Two homeless men stared at them; one quickly hid his bottle of Colt 44 malt liquor under his shirt.

Dellray gazed at a window in Pietrs's building; it gave off a faint yellow glow.

The driver backed the first van into a shadowy parking space and whispered to Dellray, "It's Perkins." Tapping his headset. "He's got the director on the horn. They want to know who's leading the assault."

"I am," snapped the Chameleon. He turned to his team. "I want surveillance across the street and in the alleys. Snipers, there, there and there. An' I want ever'body in place fi' minutes ago. Are we all together on that?"

Down the stairs, the old wood creaking.

His arm around her, he guided the woman, half-conscious from the blow to her head, into the basement. At the foot of the stairs, he shoved her to the dirt floor and gazed down at her.

Esther . . .

Her eyes rose to meet his. Hopeless, begging. He didn't notice. All he saw was her body. He began to remove her clothing, the purple jogging outfit. It was unthinkable that a woman would actually go outside in this day and age wearing what was no more than, well, undergarments. He hadn't thought that Esther Weinraub was a whore. She'd been a working girl, stitching shirts, five for a penny.

The bone collector observed how her collarbone showed at her throat. And where some other man might glance over her breasts and dark areolae *he* stared at the indentation at the manubrium and the ribs blossoming from it like spider's legs.

"What're you doing?" she asked, groggy from the blow to her head.

The bone collector looked her over carefully but what he saw wasn't a young, anorectic woman, nose too broad, lips too full, with skin like dirty sand. He saw beneath those imperfections the perfect beauty of her *structure*.

He caressed her temple, stroked it gently. Don't let it be cracked, please. . . .

She coughed and her nostrils flared—the fumes *were* very strong down here though he hardly noticed them anymore.

"Don't hurt me again," she whispered, her head lolling. "Just don't hurt me. Please."

He took the knife from his pocket and bent down, cut her underwear off. She looked down at her naked body.

"You want that?" she said breathlessly. "Okay, you can fuck me. Okay."

The pleasure of the flesh, he thought . . . it just doesn't come close.

He pulled her to her feet and madly she pushed away from him and began stumbling toward a small doorway in the corner of the basement. Not running, not really trying to escape. Just sobbing, reaching out a hand, weaving toward the door.

The bone collector watched her, entranced by her slow, pathetic gait.

The doorway, which had once opened onto a coal chute, now led to a narrow tunnel that connected to the basement of the abandoned building next door.

Esther struggled to the metal door and pulled it open. She climbed inside.

It was no more than a minute later that he heard the wailing scream. Followed by a breathless, wrenching, "God, no, no, no . . ." Other words too, lost in her boiling howls of terror.

Then she was coming back through the tunnel, moving faster now, whipping her hands around her, as if she was trying to shake off what she'd just seen.

Come to me, Esther.

Stumbling over the dirt floor, sobbing.

Come to me.

Running straight into his patient, waiting arms, which

wrapped around her. He squeezed the woman tight as a lover, felt that marvelous collarbone beneath his fingers, and slowly dragged the frantic woman back toward the tunnel doorway.

TWENTY

The phases of the moon, the leaf, the damp underwear, dirt. Their team was back in Rhyme's bedroom—all except Polling and Haumann; it was straining NYPD loyalty to bring captains in on what was, no two ways about it, an unauthorized operation.

"You G-C'd the liquid in the underwear, right, Mel?"

"Have to do it again. They shut us down before we got the results."

He blotted out a sample and injected it into the chromatograph. As he ran the machine Sachs jockeyed to look at the peaks and valleys of the profile appearing on the screen. Like a stock index. Rhyme realized she was standing close to him, as if she'd edged near when he wasn't looking. She spoke in a low voice. "I was . . ."

"Yes?"

"I was blunter than I meant to be. Before, I mean. I have a temper. I don't know where I got it from. But I have it."

"You were right," Rhyme said.

They easily held each other's eyes and Rhyme thought of the times he and Blaine had had serious discussions. As they talked they always focused on an object between them—one of the ceramic horses she collected, a book, a nearly empty bottle of Merlot or Chardonnay.

He said, "I work scenes differently than most criminalists. I needed somebody without any preconceived ideas. But I also needed somebody with a mind of her own."

The contradictory qualities we seek in that elusive perfect lover. Strength and vulnerability, in equal measures.

"When I talked to Commissioner Eckert," she said, "it was just to get my transfer through. That's all I wanted. It never occurred to me that word'd get back to the feds and they'd take the case away."

"I know that."

"I still let my temper go. I'm sorry for that."

"Don't backpedal, Sachs. I need somebody to tell me I'm a jerk when I act like one. Thom does. That's why I love him."

"Don't get sentimental on me, Lincoln," Thom called from across the room.

Rhyme continued, "Nobody else ever tells me to go to hell. They're always walking on eggshells. I hate it."

"It doesn't seem like there've been many people around here to say much of anything to you lately."

After a moment he said, "That's true."

On the screen of the chromatograph-spectrometer the peaks and valleys stopped moving and became one of nature's infinite signatures. *Mel* Cooper tapped on the computer keys and read the results. "Water, diesel oil, phosphate, sodium, trace minerals . . . No idea what it means."

What, Rhyme wondered, was the message? The underwear itself? The liquid? He said, "Let's move on. I want to see the dirt."

Sachs brought him the bag. It contained pinkish sand, laced with chunks of clay and pebbles.

"Bull's liver," he announced. "Rock-and-sand mixture. Found just above the bedrock in Manhattan. Sodium silicate mixed in?"

Cooper ran the chromatograph. "Yep. Plenty of it."

"Then we're looking for a downtown location within fifty yards of the water—" Rhyme laughed at the astonished gaze on Sachs's face. "It's not magic, Sachs. I've just done my homework, that's all. Contractors mix sodium silicate with bull's liver to stabilize the earth when they dig foundations in deep-bedrock areas near the water. That means it's got to be downtown. Now, let's take a look at the leaf."

She held up the bag.

"No clue what it is," Rhyme said. "I don't think I've ever seen one like that. Not in Manhattan."

"I've got a list of horticulture web sites," Cooper said, staring at his computer screen. "I'll do some surfing."

Rhyme himself had spent some time on-line, cruising the Internet. As it had with books, movies and posters, his interest in the cyberworld had eventually paled. Perhaps because so much of his own world was virtual, the net was, in the end, a forlorn place for Lincoln Rhyme.

Cooper's screen flicked and danced as he clicked on hyperlinks and disappeared deeper into the web. "I'm downloading some files. Should take ten, twenty minutes."

Rhyme said, "All right. The rest of the clues Sachs found . . . Not the planted ones. The others. They might tell us about where he's been. Let's look at our secret weapon, Mel."

"Secret weapon?" Sachs asked.

"The trace evidence."

Special Agent Fred Dellray had put together a ten-man entry operation. Two teams plus search and surveillance. The flak-jacketed agents stood in the bushes, sweating madly. Across the street, upstairs in an abandoned brownstone, the S&S team had their Big Ears and video infrareds trained on the perp's house.

The three snipers, with their big Remingtons strapped, loaded and locked, lay prone on rooftops. Their binoculared spotters crouched beside them like Lamaze coaches.

Dellray—wearing an FBI windbreaker and jeans instead of his Leprechaun-green outfit—listened through his clip-on ear-phone.

"Surveillance to Command. We've got infrared on the basement. Somebody moving down there."

"What'sa view like?" Dellray asked.

"No view. Windows're too dirty."

"He all by his humble self? Maybe got a vic with him?" Knowing somehow that Officer Sachs was probably right; that he'd already 'napped somebody else now.

"Can't tell. We've just got motion and heat."

Dellray had sent other officers around to the sides of the house. They reported in. "No sign of anyone on the first or second floor. Garage is locked."

"Snipers?" Dellray asked. "Report."

"Shooter One to Command. I've acquired on front door. Over."

The others were covering the hallway and a room on the first floor. "Loaded and locked," they radioed in.

Dellray drew his large automatic.

"Okay, we got paper," Dellray said. Meaning a warrant. They wouldn't have to knock. "Lessgo! Teams one and two, deploy, deploy, deploy."

The first team took out the front door with a battering ram while the second used the slightly more civilized approach of breaking in the back-door window and unlocking the dead bolt. They streamed inside, Dellray following the last of Team One's officers into the old, filthy house. The smell of rotting flesh was overwhelming and Dellray, no stranger to crime scenes, swallowed hard, struggling to keep from vomiting.

The second team secured the ground floor and then charged up the stairs toward the bedroom while the first sped down the basement stairs, boots thumping loudly on the old wood.

Dellray raced down into the foul-smelling basement. He heard a door being kicked in somewhere below and the shout of, "Don't move! Federal agents. Freeze, freeze, freeze!"

But when he reached the basement doorway he heard the same agent blurt in very different tone, "What the hell's this? Oh, Jesus."

"Fuck," another one called. "That's gross."

"Shit in a flaming pile," Dellray spat out, choking, as he stepped inside. Swallowing hard at the vile smell.

The man's body lay on the floor, leaching black fluid. Throat cut. His dead, glazed eyes stared at the ceiling but his torso seemed to be moving—swelling and shifting. Dellray shuddered; he'd never developed much immunity to the sight of insect infestation. The number of bugs and worms suggested the vic'd been dead for at least three days.

"Why'd we get positive on the infrared?" one agent asked.

Dellray pointed out the rat and mouse teeth marks along the vic's bloated leg and side. "They're around here someplace. We interrupted dinner hour."

"So what happened? One of the vics get *him*?"

"Watcha talkin' about?" Dellray snapped.

"Isn't that him?"

"No, it's not *him*," Dellray exploded, gazing at one particular wound on the corpse.

One of the team was frowning. "Naw, Dellray. This's the guy. We got mug shots. That's Pietrs."

"Of course it's fucking Pietrs. But he ain't the unsub. Don'tcha get it?"

"No? What do you mean?"

It was all clear to him now. "Sumvabitch."

Dellray's phone chirped and made him jump. He flipped it open, listened for a minute. "She did *what*? Oh, like I really need this too. . . . No, we don't have the fucking perp in fucking custody."

He jammed the OFF button, pointed an angry finger at two SWAT agents. "You're coming with me."

"What's up, Dellray?"

"We gonna pay ourselves a visit. And what ain't we gonna be when we do it?" The agents looked at each other, frowning. But Dellray supplied the answer. "We ain't gonna be very nice at all."

Mel Cooper shook contents of the envelopes out onto print. Examined the dust with an eye loupe. "Well, there's the brick dust. And some other kind of stone. Marble, I think."

He put a sample on the slide and examined it under the compound 'scope. "Yep, marble. Rose-colored."

"Was there any marble at the stockyard tunnel? Where you found the German girl?"

"None," Sachs responded.

Cooper suggested it might have come from Monelle's residence hall when Unsub 823 grabbed her.

"No, I know the block the Deutsche Haus is in. It's just a converted East Village tenement. The best stone you'd find there'd be polished granite. Maybe, just maybe, it's a fleck of his hidey-hole. Anything notable about it?"

"Chisel marks," Cooper said, bending over the 'scope.

"Ah, good. How clean?"

"Not very. Ragged."

"So an old steam stonecutter?"

"Yes, I'd guess."

"Write, Thom," Rhyme instructed, nodding at the poster. "There's marble in his safe house. And it's old."

"But why do we care about his safe house?" Banks asked, looking at his watch. "The feds'll be there by now."

"You can never have too much information, Banks. Remember that. Now, what else've we got?"

"Another bit of the glove. That red leather. And what's this?" he asked Sachs, holding up a plastic bag containing a plug of wood.

"The sample of the aftershave. Where he brushed up against a post."

"Should I run an olfactory profile?" Cooper wondered.

"Let me smell it first," Rhyme said.

Sachs brought the bag over to him. Inside was a tiny disk of wood. She opened it up and he inhaled the air.

"Brut. How could you miss it? Thom, add that our man uses drugstore cologne."

Cooper announced, "Here's that other hair." The technician mounted it in a comparison 'scope. "Very similar to the one we found earlier. Probably the same source. Oh, hell, Lincoln, for you, I'll say it *is* the same. Brown."

"Are the ends cut or fractured naturally?"

"Cut."

"Good, we're closing in on hair color," Rhyme said.

Thom wrote *brown* just as Sellitto said, "Don't write that!"

"What?"

"Obviously it's not brown," Rhyme continued.

"I thought—"

"It's anything *but* brown. Blond, sandy, black, red . . ."

The detective explained, "'S'an old trick. You go into an alley behind a barbershop, cop some hairs from the garbage. Drop 'em around the scene."

"Oh." Banks filed this somewhere in his enthusiastic brain.

Rhyme said, "Okay. The fiber."

Cooper mounted it in the polarizing 'scope. As he adjusted knobs he said, "Birefringence of .053."

Rhyme blurted, "Nylon 6. What's it look like, Mel?"

"Very coarse. Lobed cross-section. Light gray."

"Carpet."

"Right. I'll check the database." A moment later he looked up from the computer. "It's a Hampstead Textile 118B fiber."

Rhyme exhaled a disgusted sigh.

"What?" Sachs asked.

"The most common trunk liner used by U.S. automakers. Found in over two hundred different makes going back fifteen years. Hopeless . . . Mel, is there anything *on* the fiber? Use the SEM."

The tech cranked up the scanning electron microscope. The screen burst to life with an eerie blue-green glow. The strand of fiber looked like a huge rope.

"Got something here. Crystals. A lot of 'em. They use titanium dioxide to deluster shiny carpet. That might be it."

"Gas it. It's important."

"There's not enough here, Lincoln. I'd have to burn the whole fiber."

"So, burn it."

Sellitto said delicately, "Borrowing federal evidence is one thing. Destroying it? I don't know 'bout that, Lincoln. If there's a trial . . ."

"We have to."

"Oh, man," Banks said.

Sellitto nodded reluctantly and Cooper mounted the sample. The machine hissed. A moment later the screen flickered and columns appeared. "There, that's the long-chained polymer molecule. The nylon. But that small wave, that's something else. Chlorine, detergent . . . It's cleanser."

"Remember," Rhyme said, "the German girl said the car smelled clean. Find out what kind it is."

Cooper ran the information through a brand-name database. "Pfizer Chemicals makes it. It's sold under the name Tidi-Kleen by Baer Automotive Products in Teterboro."

"Perfect!" cried Lincoln Rhyme. "I know the company. They sell in bulk to fleets. Mostly rental-car companies. Our unsub's driving a rental."

"He wouldn't be crazy enough to drive a rental car to crime scenes, would he?" Banks asked.

"It's stolen," Rhyme muttered, as if the young man had asked what was two plus two. "And it'll have stolen tags on it. Is Emma still with us?"

"She's probably home by now."

"Wake her up and have her start canvassing Hertz, Avis, National, Budget for thefts."

"Will do," Sellitto said, though uneasily, perhaps smelling the faint stench of burned federal evidence wafting through the air.

"The footprints?" Sachs asked.

Rhyme looked over the electrostatic impressions she'd lifted.

"Unusual wear on the soles. See the rubbed-down portion on the outsides of each shoe at the ball of the foot?"

"Pigeon-toed?" Thom wondered aloud.

"Possibly but there's no corresponding heel wear, which you'd expect to see." Rhyme studied the prints. "What I think is, he's a reader."

"A reader?"

"Sit in a chair there," Rhyme said to Sachs. "And hunch over the table, pretend you're reading."

She sat, then looked up. "And?"

"Pretend you're turning pages."

She did, several times. Looked up again

"Keep going. You're reading *War and Peace*."

The pages kept turning, her head was bowed. After a moment, without thinking, she crossed her ankles. The outside edges of her shoes were the only part that met the floor.

Rhyme pointed this out. "Put *that* in the profile, Thom. But add a question mark. Now let's look at the friction ridges."

Sachs said she didn't have the good fingerprint, the one they'd ID'd the unsub with. "It's still at the federal building."

But Rhyme wasn't interested in that print. It was the other one, the Kromekote Sachs had lifted from the German girl's skin, he wanted to look at.

"Not scannable," Cooper announced. "Isn't even C grade. I wouldn't give an opinion about this if I had to."

Rhyme said, "I'm not interested in identity. I'm interested

in that line there." It was crescent-shaped and sat right in the middle of the pad of the finger.

"What is it?" Sachs asked.

"A scar, I think," Cooper said. "From an old cut. A bad one. Looks like it went all the way to the bone."

Rhyme thought back to other markings and defects he'd seen on skin over the years. In the days before jobs became mostly paper shuffling and computer keyboarding it was far easier to tell people's jobs by examining their hands: distorted finger pads from manual typewriters, punctures from sewing machines and cobbler's needles, indentations and ink stains from stenographers' and accountants' pens, paper cuts from printing presses, scars from die cutters, distinctive calluses from various types of manual labor. . . .

But a scar like this told them nothing.

Not yet at any rate. Not until they had a suspect whose hands they might examine.

"What else? The knee print. This is good. Give us an idea of what he's wearing. Hold it up, Sachs. Higher! Baggy slacks. It retained that deep crease there so it's natural fiber. In this weather, I'll bet cotton. Not wool. You don't see silk slacks much nowadays."

"Lightweight, not denim," Cooper said.

"Sports clothes," Rhyme concluded. "Add that to our profile, Thom."

Cooper looked back at the computer screen and typed some more. "No luck with the leaf. Doesn't match anything at the Smithsonian."

Rhyme stretched back into his pillow. How much time would they have? An hour? Two?

The moon. Dirt. Brine . . .

He glanced at Sachs who was standing by herself in the corner. Her head was down and her long red hair fell dramatically toward the floor. She was looking into an evidence bag, a frown on her face, lost in concentration. How many times had Rhyme himself stood in the same pose, trying to—

"A newspaper!" she cried, looking up. "Where's a newspaper?" Her eyes were frantic as she looked from table to table. "Today's paper?"

"What is it, Sachs?" Rhyme asked.

She grabbed *The New York Times* from Jerry Banks and leafed quickly through it.

"That liquid . . . in the underwear," she said to Rhyme. "Could it be salt water?"

"Salt water?" Cooper pored over the GC-MS chart. "Of course! Water and sodium and other minerals. And the oil, phosphates. It's polluted seawater."

Her eyes met Rhyme's and they said simultaneously, "High tide!"

She held up the paper, open to the weather map. It contained a phases-of-the-moon diagram identical to the one found at the scene. Below it was a tidal chart. "High tide's in forty minutes."

Rhyme's face curled in disgust. He was never angrier than when he was angry with himself. "He's going to drown the vic. They're under a pier downtown." He looked hopelessly at the map of Manhattan, with its miles of shoreline. "Sachs, time to play race-car driver again. You and Banks go west. Lon, why don't you take the East Side? Around the South Street Seaport. And Mel, figure out what the hell that leaf is!"

A fluke of wave slapped his sagging head.

William Everett opened his eyes and snorted the shivery water from his nose. It was icy cold and he felt his questionable heart stutter as it struggled to send warming blood through his body.

He almost fainted again, like when the son of a bitch'd broken his finger, he floated back to waking, his thoughts. Then on his late wife—and for some reason, on their travels. They'd been to Giza. And to Guatemala. Nepal. Teheran (one week before the embassy takeover).

Their Southeast China Airlines plane had lost one of two engines an hour out of Beijing and Evelyn had lowered her head, the crash position, preparing to die and staring at an article in the in-flight magazine. It warned that drinking hot tea right after a meal was dangerous for you. She told him about it afterwards, at the Raffles bar in Singapore, and they'd laughed hysterically until tears came to their eyes.

Thinking of the kidnapper's cold eyes. His teeth, the bulky gloves.

Now, in this horrid wet tomb the unbearable pain rolled up his arm and into his jaw.

Broken finger or heart attack? he wondered.

Maybe a little of both.

Everett closed his eyes until the pain subsided. He looked around him. The chamber where he was handcuffed was beneath a rotting pier. A lip of wood dipped from the edge toward the churning water, which was about six inches below the bottom of the rim. Lights from boats on the river and the industrial sites of Jersey reflected through the narrow slit. The water was up to his neck now and although the roof of the pier was several feet above his head the cuffs were extended as far as they'd go.

The pain swept up from his finger again and Everett's head roared with the agony and dipped toward the water as he passed out. A noseful of water and the racking cough that followed revived him.

Then the moon tugged the plane of water slightly higher and with a sodden gulp the chamber was sealed off from the river outside. The room went dark. He was aware of the sounds of groaning waves and his own moaning from the pain.

He knew he was dead, knew he couldn't keep his head above the greasy surface for more than a few minutes. He closed his eyes, pressed his face against the slick, black column.

TWENTY-ONE

All the way downtown, Sachs," Rhyme's voice clattered from the radio.

She punched the accelerator of the RRV, red lights flashing, as they screamed downtown along the West Side Highway. Ice-cool, she goosed the wagon up to eighty.

"Okay, whoa," said Jerry Banks.

Counting down. Twenty-third Street, Twentieth, the skidding jog at the Fourteenth Street garbage-barge dock. As they roared through the Village, the meatpacking district, a semi pulled out of a side street directly into her path. Instead of braking she nudged the wagon over the center curb like a steeple-chaser, drawing breathless oaths from Banks and a wail from the air horn of the big White, which jackknifed spectacularly.

"Oops," said Amelia Sachs and swung back into the southbound lane. To Rhyme she added, "Say again. Missed that."

Rhyme's tinny voice popped through her earphones. "Downtown is all I can tell you. Until we figure out what the leaf means."

"We're coming up on Battery Park City."

"Twenty-five minutes to high tide," Banks called.

Maybe Dellray's team could get the exact location out of him. They could drag Mr 823 into an alley somewhere with a bag of apples. Nick had told her that was the way they talked perps into "cooperating." Whack 'em in the gut with a bag of fruit. Really painful. No marks. When she was growing up she wouldn't have thought cops did that. Now she knew different.

Banks tapped her shoulder. "There. A bunch of old piers."

UNSUB 823			
Appearance	Residence	Vehicle	Other
• Caucasian male, slight build • Dark clothing • Old gloves, reddish kidskin • Aftershave; to cover up other scent? • Ski mask? Navy blue? • Gloves are dark • Aftershave = Brut • Hair color not brown • Deep scar, index finger • Casual clothes	• Prob. has safe house • Located near; B'way & 82nd, ShopRite B'way & 96th Anderson Foods Greenwich & Bank ShopRite 2nd Ave., 72nd-73rd, Grocery World Battery Park City, J&G's Emporium 1709 2nd Ave., Anderson Foods 34th & Lex., Food Warehouse 8th Ave. & 24th, ShopRite Houston & Lafayette, ShopRite 6th Ave. & Houston, J&G's Emporium Greenwich & Franklin, Grocery World • Old building, pink marble	• Yellow Cab • Recent model sedan • Lt. gray, silver, biege	• knows CS proc. • possibly has record • knows FR prints • gun = .32 Colt • Ties vics w/ unusual knots • "Old" appeals to him • Called one vic "Hanna" • Knows basic German • Underground appeals to him • Dual personalities • Maybe priest, soc. worker, counselor • Unusual wear on shoes, reads a lot?

Rotten wood, filthy. Spooky places.

They skidded to a stop and climbed out, running toward the water.

"You there, Rhyme?"

"Talk to me, Sachs. Where are you?"

"A pier just north of Battery Park City."

"I just heard from Lon, on the East Side. He hasn't found anything."

"It's hopeless," she said. "There're a dozen piers. Then the whole promenade . . . And the fireboat house and ferry docks and the pier at Battery Park . . . We need ESU."

"We don't *have* ESU, Sachs. They're not on our side anymore."

Twenty minutes to high tide.

Her eyes darted along the waterfront. Her shoulders sagged with helplessness. Hand on her weapon, she sprinted to the river, Jerry Banks not far behind.

"Get me *something* on that leaf, Mel. A guess, anything. Wing it."

Fidgeting, Cooper looked from the microscope to the computer screen.

Eight thousand varieties of leafy plants in Manhattan.

"It doesn't fit the cell structure of *anything*."

"It's old," Rhyme said. "How old?"

Cooper looked at the leaf again. "Mummified. I'd put it at a hundred years, little less maybe."

"What's gone extinct in the last hundred years?"

"Plants don't go extinct in an ecosystem like Manhattan. They always show up again."

A ping in Rhyme's mind. He was close to remembering something. He both loved and hated this feeling. He might grab the thought like a slow pop-up fly. Or it might vanish completely, leaving him with only the sting of lost inspiration.

Sixteen minutes to high tide.

What *was* the thought? He grappled with it, closed his eyes . . .

Pier, he was thinking. The vic's under a pier.

What about it? *Think*!

Pier . . . ships . . . unloading . . . cargo.

Unloading cargo!

His eyes snapped open. "Mel, is it a crop?"

"Oh, hell. I've been looking at general-horticulture pages, not cultivated crops." He typed for what seemed like hours.

"Well?"

"Hold on, hold on . . . Here's a list of the encoded binaries." He scanned it. "Alfalfa, barley, beets, corn, oats, tobacco . . ."

"Tobacco! Try that."

Cooper double clicked his mouse and the image slowly unfurled on the screen.

"That's it!"

"The World Trade Towers," Rhyme announced. "The land from there north used to be tobacco plantations. Thom, the research for my book—I want the map from the 1740s. And that modern map Bo Haumann was using for the asbestos-cleanup sites. Put them up there on the wall, next to each other."

The aide found the old map in Rhyme's files. He taped them both onto the wall near his bed. Crudely drawn, the older map showed the northern part of the settled city—a cluster on the lower portion of the isle—covered with plantations. There were three commercial wharves along the river, which was then called not the Hudson but the West River. Rhyme glanced at the recent map of the city. The farmland was gone of course, as were the original wharves, but the contemporary map showed an abandoned wharf in the exact location of one of the tobacco exporter's old piers.

Rhyme strained forward, struggling to see the street name it was near. He was about to shout for Thom to come hold the map closer when, from downstairs, he heard a loud snap and the door crashed inward. Glass shattered.

Thom started down the stairs.

"I want to see him." The terse voice filled the hallway.

"Just a—" the aide began.

"No. Not inaminute, not in a hour. But right. Fucking. Now."

"Mel," Rhyme whispered, "ditch the evidence, shut the systems down."

"But—"

"Do it!"

Rhyme shook his head violently, dislodging the headset microphone. It fell onto the side of the Clinitron. Footsteps pounded up the stairs.

Thom did the best he could to stall but the visitors were three federal agents and two of the three were holding large guns. Slowly they backed him up the stairs.

Bless him, Mel Cooper pulled apart a compound microscope in five seconds flat and was calmly replacing the components with meticulous care as the FBI crested the stairs and stormed into Rhyme's room. The evidence bags were stuffed under a table and covered with *National Geographics*.

"Ah, Dellray," Rhyme asked. "Find our unsub, did you?"

"Why didn't you tell us?"

"Tell you what?"

"That the fingerprint was bogus."

"No one asked me."

"Bogus?" Cooper asked, mystified.

"Well, it was a real print," Rhyme said, as if it were obvious. "But it wasn't the unsub's. Our boy needed a taxi to catch his fish with. So he met—what *was* his name?"

"Victor Pietrs," Dellray muttered and gave the cabbie's history.

"Nice touch," Rhyme said with some genuine admiration. "Picked a Serb with a rap sheet and mental problems. Wonder how long he looked for a candidate. Anyway, 823 killed poor Mr Pietrs and stole his cab. Cut off his finger. He kept it and figured if we were getting too close he'd leave a nice obvious print at a scene to throw us off. I guess it worked."

Rhyme glanced at the clock. Fourteen minutes left.

"How'd you know?" Dellray glanced at the maps on Rhyme's wall but, thank God, wasn't interested in them.

"The print showed signs of dehydration and shriveling. Bet the body was a mess. And you found it in the basement? Am I right? Where our boy likes to stow his victims."

Dellray ignored him and nosed around the room like a giant terrier.

"Where you hidin' our evidence?"

"Evidence? I don't know what you're talking about. Say, did

you break my door? Last time you walked in without knocking. Now you just kicked it in."

"You know, Lincoln, I was thinking of apologizing to you for before—"

"That's big of you, Fred."

"But now I'm a inch away from collaring your ass."

Rhyme glanced down at the microphone headset, dangling on the floor. He imagined Sachs's voice bleating from the earphones.

"Gimme that evidence, Rhyme. You don't realize what kind of pissy-bad trouble you're in."

"Thom," Rhyme asked slowly, "Agent Dellray startled me and I dropped my Walkman headset. Could you hook it on the bedframe?"

The aide didn't miss a beat. He rested the mike next to Rhyme's head, out of Dellray's sight.

"Thank you," Rhyme said to Thom. Then added, "You know, I haven't had my bath yet. I think it's about time, wouldn't you say?"

"I've been wondering when you were going to ask," said Thom, with the ability of a natural-born actor.

"Come in, Rhyme. For Christ's sake. Where are you?"

Then she heard a voice in her headset. Thom's. It sounded stilted, exaggerated. Something was wrong.

"I've got the new sponge," the voice said.

"Looks like a good one," Rhyme answered.

"Rhyme?" Sachs blurted. "What the hell's going on?"

"Cost seventeen dollars. It ought to be good. I'm going to turn you over."

More voices sounded through the earphone but she couldn't make them out.

Sachs and Banks were jogging along the waterfront, peering over the wharves into the gray-brown water of the Hudson. She motioned to Banks to stop, leaned away from the cramp below her breastbone, spit into the river. Tried to catch her breath.

Through the headset she heard: ". . . won't take long. You'll have to excuse us, gentlemen."

". . . we'll just wait, you don't mind."

"I do mind," Rhyme said. "Can't I get a little privacy here?"

"Rhyme, can you hear me?" Sachs called desperately. What the hell was he doing?

"Nup. No privacy for them that steal evidence."

Dellray! He was in Rhyme's room. Well, that's the end of it. The vic's as good as dead.

"I want that evidence," the agent barked.

"Well, what you're going to *get* is a panoramic view of a man taking a sponge bath, Dellray."

Banks started to speak but she waved him quiet.

Some muttered words she couldn't hear.

The agent's angry shout.

Then Rhyme's calm voice again. ". . . You know, Dellray, I used to be a swimmer. Swam every day."

"We've got less than ten minutes," Sachs whispered. The water lapped calmly. Two placid boats cruised past.

Dellray muttered something.

"I'd go down to the Hudson River and swim. It was a lot cleaner then. The water, I mean."

A garbled transmission. He was breaking up.

". . . old pier. My favorite one's gone now. Used to be the home of the Hudson Dusters. That gang, you ever hear of them? In the 1890s. North of where Battery Park City is now. You look bored. Tired of looking at a crip's flabby ass? No? Suit yourself. That pier was between North Moore and Chambers. I'd dive in, swim around the piers . . ."

"North Moore and Chambers!" Sachs shouted. Spinning around. They'd missed it because they'd gone too far south. It was a quarter mile from where they were. She could see the brown scabby wood, a large drainpipe backing up with tidal water. How much time was left? Hardly any. There was no way they could save him.

She ripped the headset off and started sprinting to the car, Banks close behind.

"Can you swim?" she asked.

"Me? A lap or two at the Health and Racquet Club."

They'd never make it.

Sachs stopped suddenly, spun around in a fast circle, gazing at the deserted streets.

The water was nearly to his nose.

A small wave washed over William Everett's face just as he inhaled and the foul, salty liquid streamed into his throat. He began to choke, a deep, horrible sound. Racking. The water filled his lungs. He lost his grip on the pier piling and sank under the surface, stiffened and rose once more, then sank again.

No, Lord, no . . . please don't let—

He shook the cuffs, kicked hard, trying to get some play. As if some miracle might happen and his puny muscles could bend the huge bolt he was cuffed to.

Snorting water from his nose, swiping his head back and forth in panic. He cleared his lungs momentarily. Neck muscles on fire—as painful as his shattered finger—from bending his head back to find the faint layer of air just above his face.

He had a moment's respite.

Then another wave, slightly higher.

And that was it.

He couldn't fight anymore. Surrender. Join Evelyn, say good-bye . . .

And William Everett let go. He floated beneath the surface into the drecky water, full of junk and tendrils of seaweed.

Then jerked back in horror. No, no . . .

He was here. The kidnapper! He'd come back.

Everett kicked to the surface, sneezing more water, trying desperately to get away. The man shone a brilliant light into Everett's eyes and reached toward him with a knife.

No, no . . .

It wasn't enough to drown him, he had to slash him to death. Without thinking Everett kicked out toward him. But the kidnapper vanished under the water . . . and then, *snap*, Everett's hands were free.

The old man forgot his placid goodbyes and kicked like hell to the surface, sucking sour air through his nose and ripping the tape from his mouth. Gasping, spitting the foul water. His head banged solidly into the underside of the oak pier and he laughed out loud. "Oh, God, God, God . . ."

Then another face appeared . . . Also hooded, with another

blindingly bright lamp attached, and Everett could just make out the NYFD emblem on the man's wetsuit. They weren't knives the men held but metal cutters. One of them thrust a bitter rubber mouthpiece between Everett's lips and he inhaled a dazzling breath of oxygen.

The diver slipped his arm around him and together they swam to the lip of the pier.

"Take a deep breath, we'll be out in a minute."

He filled his narrow lungs to bursting and, eyes closed, sailed with the diver deep into the water, lit eerily by the man's yellow light. It was a short but harrowing trip, straight down then up again through cloudy, flecked water. Once he slipped out of the diver's hands and they separated momentarily. But William Everett took the glitch in stride. After this evening, a solo swim in the choppy Hudson River was a piece of cake.

She hadn't planned on taking a cab. The airport bus would've been fine.

But Pammy was wired from too little sleep—they'd both been up since five that morning—and she was getting restless. The little girl needed to be in bed soon, tucked away with her blanket and her bottle of Hawaiian Punch. Besides, Carole herself couldn't wait to get to Manhattan—she was just a skinny Midwest gal who'd never been farther east than Ohio in all her forty-one years, and she was dying for her first look at the Big Apple.

Carole collected her luggage and they started toward the exit. She checked to make sure she had everything they'd left Kate and Eddie's house with that afternoon.

Pammy, Pooh, purse, blanket, suitcase, yellow knapsack.

Everything accounted for.

Her friends had warned her about the city. "They'll hustle you," Eddie'd said. "Purse snatchers, pickpockets."

"And don't play those card games on the street," maternal Kate had added.

"I don't play cards in my *living* room," Carole reminded her, laughing. "Why'm I going to start playing on the streets of Manhattan?"

But she appreciated their concern. After all, here she was,

a widow with a three-year-old, heading to the toughest city on earth for the UN conference—more foreigners, hell, more *people* than she'd ever seen at one time.

Carole found a pay phone and called the residence hotel to check on their reservations. The night manager said the room was ready and waiting for them. He'd see them in forty-five minutes or so.

They walked through automatic doors and were socked breathless by the scalding summer air. Carole paused, looking around. Gripping Pammy firmly with one hand, the handle of the battered suitcase with the other. The heavy yellow knapsack was snug on her shoulder.

They joined the line of passengers waiting at the taxi starter's booth.

Carole glanced at a huge billboard across the highway. *Welcome U.N. Delegates!* it announced. The artwork was terrible, but she stared at it for a long moment; one of the men on the board looked like Ronnie.

For a time, after he died, two years ago, virtually everything reminded her of her handsome, crew-cut husband. She'd drive past McDonald's and remember that he liked Big Macs. Actors in movies who didn't look a thing like him might cock their heads the way he used to. She'd see a flyer for a lawn-mower sale and remember how much he loved to cut their tiny square of grass in Arlington Heights.

Then the tears would come. And she'd go back on Prozac or imipramine. She'd spend a week in bed. Reluctantly acquiesce in Kate's offer that she stay with her and Eddie for a night. Or a week. Or a month.

But no tears anymore. She was here to jump-start her life. The sorrow was behind her now.

Tossing her mass of dark-blond hair off her sweaty shoulders, Carole ushered Pammy forward and kicked the luggage ahead of them as the taxi queue moved up several places. She looked all around, trying to catch a glimpse of Manhattan. But she could see nothing except traffic and the tails of airplanes and a sea of people and cabs and cars. Steam rose like frantic ghosts from manholes and the night sky was black and yellow and hazy.

Well, she'd see the city soon enough, she guessed. She

hoped that Pammy was old enough to keep her first memory of the sight.

"How do you like our adventure so far, honey?"

"Adventure. I like adventures. I want some 'Waiin Punch. Can I please have some?"

Please . . . That was new. The three-year-old was learning all the keys and buttons. Carole laughed. "We'll get you some soon."

Finally they got their cab. The trunk popped open and Carole dumped the luggage inside, slammed the lid. They climbed into the back seat and closed the door.

Pammy, Pooh, purse . . .

The driver asked, "Where to?" And Carole gave him the address of the Midtown Residence Hotel, shouting through the Plexiglas divider.

The driver pulled into traffic. Carole sat back and settled Pammy on her lap.

"Will we go past the UN?" she called.

But the man was concentrating on changing lanes and didn't hear her.

"I'm here for the conference," she explained. "The UN conference."

Still no answer.

She wondered if he had trouble with English. Kate had warned her that the taxi drivers in New York were all foreigners. ("Taking American jobs," Eddie grumbled. "But don't get me started on *that*.") She couldn't see him clearly through the scuffed divider.

Maybe he just doesn't want to talk.

They swung onto another highway—and, suddenly, there it was in front of her, the jagged skyline of the city. Brilliant. Like the crystals that Kate and Eddie collected. A huge cluster of blue and gold and silver buildings in the middle of the island and another cluster way to the left. It was bigger than anything Carole had ever seen in her life and for a moment the island seemed like a massive ship.

"Look, Pammy, that's where we're going. Is that beeaaauti-ful or what?"

A moment later, though, the view was cut off as the driver turned off the expressway and made a fast turn at the bottom of the ramp. Then they were moving through hot, deserted streets, lined with dark brick buildings.

Carole leaned forward. "Is this the right way to the city?"

Again, no answer.

She rapped hard on the Plexiglas. "Are you going the right way? Answer me. *Answer me*!"

"Mommy, what's wrong?" Pammy said and started to cry.

"Where are you going?" Carole shouted.

But the man just kept driving—leisurely, stopping at all the red lights, never going over the speed limit. And when he pulled into the deserted parking lot behind a dark, abandoned factory he made sure he signaled properly.

Oh no . . . no!

He pulled on a ski mask and climbed from the cab. Walking to the back, he reached for the door. But he hesitated and his hand dropped. He leaned forward, face against the window, and tapped on the glass. Once, twice, three times. Getting the attention of lizards in the reptile room at a zoo. He stared at the mother and daughter for a long moment before he opened the door.

TWENTY-TWO

"How'd you do it, Sachs?"

Standing beside the pungent Hudson River, she spoke into her stalk mike. "I remembered seeing the fireboat station at Battery Park. They scrambled a couple divers and were at the pier in about three minutes. Man, you should've seen that boat move! I want to try one of those someday."

Rhyme explained to her about the fingerless cabbie.

"Son of a bitch!" she said, clicking her tongue in disgust. "The weasel tricked us all."

"Not all of us," Rhyme reminded her coyly.

"So Dellray knows I boosted the evidence. Is he looking for me?"

"He said he was heading back to the federal building. Probably to decide which one of us to collar first. How's the scene there, Sachs?"

"Pretty bad," she reported. "He parked on gravel—"

"So no footprints."

"But it's worse than that. The tide backed out of this big drainpipe and where he parked's underwater."

"Hell," Rhyme muttered. "No trace, no prints, no nothing. How's the vic?"

"Not so good. Exposure, broken finger. He's had heart problems. They're going to keep him in the hospital for a day or two."

"Can he tell us anything?"

Sachs walked over to Banks, who was interviewing William Everett.

"He wasn't big," the man said matter-of-factly, carefully

examining the splint the medic was putting on his hand. "And he wasn't really strong, not a muscle man. But he was stronger'n me. I grabbed him and he just pulled my hands away."

"Description?" Banks asked.

Everett recounted the dark clothes and ski mask. That was all he could remember.

"One thing I should tell you," Everett held up his bandaged hand. "He's got a mean streak. I grabbed him, like I said. I wasn't thinking—I just panicked. But he got real mad. That's when he busted my finger."

"Retaliation, hm?" Banks asked.

"I guess. But that's not the strange part."

"No?"

"The strange part is he listened to it."

The young detective had stopped writing. Looked at Sachs.

"He held my hand against his ear, real tight, and bent the finger until it broke. Like he was listening. And liking it."

"Did you hear that, Rhyme?"

"Yes. Thom's added it to our profile. I don't know what it means, though. We'll have to think about it."

"Any sign of the planted PE?"

"Not yet."

"Grid it, Sachs. Oh, and get the vic's—"

"Clothes? I've already asked him. I—Rhyme, you all right?" She heard a fit of coughing.

The transmission was shut off momentarily. He came back on a moment later. "You there, Rhyme? Everything okay?"

"Fine," he said quickly. "Get going. Walk the grid."

She surveyed the scene, lit starkly by the ESU halogens. It was so frustrating. He'd *been* here. He'd walked on the gravel just a few feet away. But whatever PE he'd inadvertently left behind was lying inches below the surface of the dim water. She covered the ground slowly. Back and forth.

"I can't see *anything*. The clues might've been washed away."

"No, he's too smart not to've taken the tide into account. They'll be on dry land somewhere."

"I've got an idea," she said suddenly. "Come on down here."

"What?"

"Work the scene with me, Rhyme."

Silence.

"Rhyme, did you hear me?"

"Are you talking to me?" he asked.

"You *look* like De Niro. You can't act as good as De Niro. You know? That scene from *Taxi Driver*?"

Rhyme didn't laugh. He said, "The line's 'Are you looking at me?' Not 'talking to me.'"

Sachs continued, unfazed, "Come on down. Work the scene with me."

"I'll spread my wings. No, better yet, I'll project myself there. Telepathy, you know."

"Quit joking. I'm serious."

"I—"

"We need you. I can't find the planted clues."

"But they'll be there. You just have to try a little harder."

"I've walked the entire grid twice."

"Then you've defined the perimeter too narrowly. Add another few feet and keep going. Eight twenty-three's not finished yet, not by a long shot."

"You're changing the subject. Come on down and help me."

"How?" Rhyme asked. "How'm I supposed to do that?"

"I had a friend who was challenged," she began. "And he—"

"You mean he was a *crip*," Rhyme corrected. Softly but firmly.

She continued, "His aide'd put him into this fancy wheelchair every morning and he drove himself all over the place. To the movies, to—"

"Those chairs . . ." Rhyme's voice sounded hollow. "They don't work for me."

She stopped speaking.

He continued, "The problem's how I was injured. It'd be dangerous for me to be in a wheelchair. It could"—he hesitated—"make things worse."

"I'm sorry. I didn't know."

After a moment he said, "Of course you didn't."

Blew that one. Oh, boy. Brother . . .

But Rhyme didn't seem any the worse for her faux pas. His

voice was smooth, unemotional. "Listen, you've got to get on with the search. Our unsub's making it trickier. But it won't be impossible . . . Here's an idea. He's the underground man, right? Maybe he buried them."

She looked over the scene.

Maybe there . . . She saw a mound of earth and leaves in a patch of tall grass near the gravel. It didn't look right; the mound seemed too assembled.

Sachs crouched beside it, lowered her head and, using the pencils, began to clear away leaves.

She turned her face slightly to the left and found she was staring at a rearing head, bared fangs . . .

"Jesus Lord," she shouted, stumbling backwards, falling hard on her butt, scrambling to draw her weapon.

No . . .

Rhyme shouted, "You all right?"

Sachs drew a target and tried to steady the gun with very unsteady hands. Jerry Banks came running up, his own Glock drawn. He stopped. Sachs climbed to her feet, looking at what was in front of them.

"Man," Banks whispered.

"It's a snake—well, a snake's skeleton," Sachs told Rhyme. "A rattlesnake. Fuck." Holstered the Glock. "It's mounted on a board."

"A snake? Interesting." Rhyme sounded intrigued.

"Yeah, real interesting," she muttered. She pulled on latex gloves and lifted the coiled bones. She turned it over. "'Metamorphosis.'"

"What?"

"A label on the bottom. The name of the store it came from, I'd guess. 604 Broadway."

Rhyme said, "I'll have the Hardy Boys check it out. What've we got? Tell me the clues."

They were underneath the snake. In a Baggie. Her heart pounded as she crouched down over the bag.

"A book of matches," she said.

"Okay, maybe he's thinking arson. Anything printed on them?"

"Nope. But there's a smear of something. Like Vaseline. Only stinky."

"Good, Sachs—always smell evidence you're not sure about. Only be more precise."

She bent close. "Yuck."

"That's not precise."

"Sulfur maybe."

"Could be nitrate-based. Explosive. Tovex. Is it blue?"

"No, it's milky clear."

"Even if it could go bang I imagine it's a secondary explosive. They're the stable ones. Anything else?"

"Another scrap of paper. Something on it."

"What, Sachs? His name, his address, e-mail handle?"

"Looks like it's from a magazine. I can see a small black-and-white photo. Looks like part of a building but you can't see which one. And underneath that, all you can read is a date. May 20, 1906."

"Five, twenty, oh-six. I wonder if it's a code. Or an address. I'll have to think about it. Anything else?"

"Nope."

She heard him sigh. "All right, come on back, Sachs. What time is it? My God, almost one A.M. I haven't been up this late in years. Come on back and let's see what we have."

Of all the neighborhoods in Manhattan, the Lower East Side has remained the most unchanged over the course of the city's history.

Much of it's gone of course: The rolling pastoral fields. The solid mansions of John Hancock and early government luminaries. Der Kolek, the large freshwater lake (its Dutch name eventually corrupted to "The Collect," which more accurately described the grossly polluted pond). The notorious Five Points neighborhood—in the early 1800s the most dangerous square mile on earth—where a single tenement, like the decrepit Gates of Hell, might be the site of two or three hundred murders every year.

But thousands of the old buildings remained—tenements from the nineteenth century and Colonial frame houses and Federal brick townhomes from the prior, baroque meeting halls, several of the Egyptian-style public buildings constructed by order of the regally corrupt Congressman Fernando

Wood. Some were abandoned, their facades overgrown with weeds and floors cracked by persistent saplings. But many were still in use; this had been the land of Tammany Hall iniquity, of pushcarts and sweatshops, of the Henry Street Settlement house, Minsky's burlesque and the notorious Yiddish Gomorra—the Jewish Mafia. A neighborhood that gives birth to institutions like these does not die easily.

It was toward this neighborhood that the bone collector now piloted the taxi containing the thin woman and her young daughter.

Observing that the constabulary was on to him, James Schneider went once again to ground like the serpent that he was, seeking accommodations—it is speculated—in the cellars of the city's many tenant-houses (which the reader may perchance recognize as the still-prevalent "tenements"). And so he remained, quiescent for some months.

As he drove home, the bone collector saw around him not the Manhattan of the 1990s—the Korean delis, the dank bagel shops, the X-rated-video stores, the empty clothing boutiques—but a dreamy world of bowler-clad men, women in rustling crinoline, hems and cuffs filthy with street refuse. Hordes of buggies and wagons, the air filled with the sometimes pleasant, sometimes repulsive scent of methane.

But such was the foul, indefatigable drive within him to start his collection anew that he was soon forced from his lair to waylay yet another good citizen;—this, a young man newly arrived in town to attend university.

Driving through the notorious Eighteenth Ward, once the home of nearly fifty thousand people crammed into a thousand decrepit tenements. When most people thought of the nineteenth century they thought in sepia—because of old photographs. But this was wrong. Old Manhattan was the color of stone. With choking industrial smoke, paint prohibitively expensive and dim lighting, the city was many shades of gray and yellow.

Schneider snuck up behind the fellow and was about to strike when Fortune's conscience, at last, cried out. Two constables chanced upon the assault. They recognized Schneider and gave chase. The killer fled east, across that engineering marvel, the Manhattan Bridge, completed in 1909, two years before these events. But he stopped halfway across, seeing that three constables were approaching from Brooklyn, having heard the alarm raised by the whistles and pistol reports of their confederates from Manhattan.

Schneider, unarmed, as chance would have it, climbed onto the railing of the bridge as he was surrounded by the law. He shouted maniacal diatribes against the constables, condemning them for having ruined his life. His words grew ever madder. As the constabulary moved closer, he leapt from the rail into the River. A week later a pilot discovered his body on the shore of Welfare Island, near Hell Gate. There was little left, for the crabs and turtles had been diligently working to reduce Schneider to the very bone which he, in his madness, cherished.

He turned the taxi onto his deserted cobblestoned street, East Van Brevoort, and paused in front of the building. He checked the two filthy strings he'd run low across the doors to make certain that no one had entered. A sudden motion startled him and he heard the guttural snarling of the dogs again, their eyes yellow, teeth brown, bodies dotted with scars and sores. His hand strayed to his pistol but they suddenly turned and, yelping, charged after a cat or rat in the alley.

He saw no one on the hot sidewalks and opened the padlock securing the carriage-house door then climbed back inside the car and drove into the garage, parked beside his Taurus.

After the villain's death his effects were secured and perused by detectives. His diary showed that he had murdered eight good citizens of the city. Nor was he above grave robbery, for it was ascertained from his pages (if his claims be true) that he had violated several holy resting places in cemeteries around the city. None of his victims had accorded him the least affront;—nay, most were upstanding citizens, industrious and innocent. And yet he felt not a modicum of guilt. Indeed, he seems to have labored under the mad delusion that he was doing his victims a favor.

He paused, wiped sweat from his mouth. The ski mask itched. He dragged the woman and her daughter out of the trunk and through the garage. She was strong and fought hard. At last he managed to get the cuffs on them.

"You prick!" she howled. "Don't you dare touch my daughter. You touch her and I'll kill you."

He gripped her hard around the chest and taped her mouth. Then he did the little girl's too.

"Flesh withers and can be weak,"—(the villain wrote in his ruthless yet steady hand)—"Bone is the strongest aspect of the body. As old as we may be in the flesh, we are always young in the bone. It is a noble goal I had, and it is beyond me why any-one might quarrel with it. I did a kindness to them all. They are immortal now. I freed them. I took them down to the bone."

He dragged them into the basement and pushed the woman down hard on the floor, her daughter beside her. Tied their cuffs to the wall with clothesline. Then returned upstairs.

He lifted her yellow knapsack from the back of the cab, the suitcases from the trunk, and pushed through a bolt-studded wooden door into the main room of the building. He was about to toss them into a corner but found that, for some reason, he was curious about these particular captives. He sat down in front of one of the murals—a painting of a butcher, placidly holding a knife in one hand, a slab of beef in the other.

He examined the luggage tag. Carole Ganz. Carole with an *E*. Why the extra letter? he wondered. The suitcase contained nothing but clothes. He started through the knapsack. He found the cash right away. There must have been four or five thousand. He put it back in the zippered compartment.

There were a dozen child's toys: a doll, a tin of watercolors, a package of modeling clay, a Mr Potato Head kit. There were also an expensive Discman, a half-dozen CDs and a Sony travel clock radio.

He looked through some pictures. Photos of Carole and her girl. In most of the pictures the woman seemed very somber. In a few others, she seemed happier. There were no photos of Carole and her husband even though she wore a wedding ring. Many were of the mother and daughter with a couple—a heavyset woman wearing one of those old granny dresses and a bearded, balding man in a flannel shirt.

For a long time the bone collector gazed at a portrait of the little girl.

The fate of poor Maggie O'Connor, the young slip of a

girl, merely eight years of age, was particularly sad. It was her misfortune, the police speculate, that she stumbled across the path of James Schneider as he was disposing of one of his victims.

The girl, a resident of notorious "Hell's Kitchen," had come out to pluck horsehairs from one of the many dead animals found in that impoverished part of the city. It was the custom of youngsters to wind tail-hairs into bracelets and rings—the only trinkets such urchins might have to adorn themselves with.

Skin and bone, skin and bone.

He propped the photo on the mantelpiece, beside the small pile of bones he'd been working on that morning and some that he'd stolen from the store where he'd found the snake.

It is surmised that Schneider found young Maggie near his lair, witnessing the macabre spectacle of his murdering one of his victims. Whether he dispatched her quickly or slowly we cannot guess. But unlike his other victims, whose remains were ultimately discovered,—of frail, becurled Maggie O'Connor, nought was ever found.

The bone collector walked downstairs.

He ripped the tape off the mother's mouth and the woman gasped for air, eyed him with cold fury. "What do you want?" she rasped. "*What*?"

She wasn't as thin as Esther but, thank God, she was nothing at all like fat Hanna Goldschmidt. He could see so *much* of her soul. The narrow mandible, the clavicle. And, through the thin blue skirt, the hint of the innominate bone—a fusion of the ilium, the ischium, the pubis. Names like Roman gods.

The little girl squirmed. He leaned forward and placed his hand on her head. Skulls don't grow from a single piece of bone but from eight separate ones, and the crown rises up like the triangular slabs of the Astrodome roof. He touched the girl's occipital bone, the parietal bones of the cap of the skull. And two of his favorites, the sensuous bones around the eye sockets—the sphenoid and the ethmoid.

"Stop it!" Carole shook her head, furious. "Keep away from her."

"Shhhh," he said, holding his gloved finger to his lips. He

looked at the little girl, who cried and pressed close to her mother.

"Maggie O'Connor," he cooed, looking at the shape of the girl's face. "My little Maggie."

The woman glared at him.

"You were in the wrong place at the wrong time, child. What did you see me do?"

Young in the bone.

"What are you talking about?" Carole whispered.

He turned his attention to her.

The bone collector had always wondered about Maggie O'Connor's mother.

"Where's your husband?"

"He's dead," she spat out. Then glanced at the little girl and said more softly, "He was killed two years ago. Look, just let my daughter go. She can't tell them anything about you. Are you . . . listening to me? What are you doing?"

He gripped Carole's hands and lifted them.

He fondled the metacarpals of the wrists. The phalanges—the tiny fingers. Squeezing the bones.

"No, don't do that. I don't like that. Please!" Her voice crackled with panic.

He felt out of control and didn't like the sensation one bit. If he was going to succeed here, with the victims, with his plans, he had to fight down the encroaching lust—the madness was driving him further and further into the past, confusing the now with the then.

Before and after . . .

He needed all of his intelligence and craftiness to finish what he'd started.

And yet . . . yet . . .

She was *so* thin, she was so taut. He closed his eyes and imagined how a knife blade scraping over her tibia would sing like the bowing of an old violin.

His breathing was fast, he was sweating rivers.

When finally he opened his eyes he found he was looking at her sandals. He didn't have many foot bones in good condition. The homeless people he'd been preying on in the past months . . . well, they'd suffered from rickets and osteoporosis, their toes were impacted by badly fitting shoes.

"I'll make a deal with you," he heard himself saying.

She looked down at her daughter. Wriggled closer to her.

"I'll make a deal. I'll let you go if you let me do something."

"What?" Carole whispered.

"Let me take your skin off."

She blinked.

He whispered, "Let me. Please? A foot. Just one of your feet. If you do that I'll let you go."

"What . . . ?"

"Down to the bone."

She gazed at him with horror. Swallowed.

What would it matter? he thought. She was so nearly there anyway, so thin, so angular. Yes, there was something different about her—different from the other victims.

He put the pistol away and took the knife out of his pocket. Opened it with a startling click.

She didn't move, her eyes slid to the little girl. Back to him.

"You'll let us go?"

He nodded. "You haven't seen my face. You don't know where this place is."

A long moment. She stared around her at the basement. She muttered a word. A name, he thought. Ron or Rob.

And with her eyes firmly on his, she extended her legs and pushed her feet toward him. He slipped her shoe off the right foot.

He took her toes. Kneaded the fragile twigs.

She leaned back, the cables of her tendons rising beautifully from her neck. Her eyes squeezed shut. He caressed her skin with the blade.

A firm grip on the knife.

She closed her eyes, inhaled and gave a faint whimper. "Go ahead," she whispered. And turned the girl's face away. Hugged her tightly.

The bone collector imagined her in a Victorian outfit, crinoline and black lace. He saw the three of them, sitting together at Delmonico's or strolling down Fifth Avenue. He saw little Maggie with them, dressed in frothy lace, rolling a hoop with a stick as they walked over the Canal bridge.

Then and now . . .

He nestled the stained blade in the arch of her foot.

"Mommy!" the girl screamed.

Something popped within him. For a moment he was overwhelmed with revulsion at what he was doing. At himself.

No! He couldn't do it. Not to *her*. Esther or Hanna, yes. Or the next one. But not her.

The bone collector shook his head sadly and touched her cheekbone with the back of his hand. He slapped the tape over Carole's mouth again and cut the cord binding her feet.

"Come on," he muttered.

She struggled fiercely but he gripped her head hard and pinched her nostrils till she passed out. Then he hefted her over his shoulder and started up the stairs, carefully lifting the bag that sat nearby. Very carefully. It was not the sort of thing he wanted to drop. Up the stairs. Pausing only once, to look at young, curly-haired Maggie O'Connor, sitting in the dirt, looking hopelessly up at him.

TWENTY-THREE

He snagged them both in front of Rhyme's townhouse. Quick as the coiled snake that Jerry Banks was carrying at his side like a souvenir from Santa Fe.

Dellray and two agents stepped from an alley. He announced casually, "Got some news, honey dear. You're under arrest for the theft of evidence under custodial care of the U.S. government."

Lincoln Rhyme had been wrong. Dellray hadn't made it to the federal building after all. He'd been staking out Rhyme's digs.

Banks rolled his eyes. "Chill out, Dellray. We saved the vic."

"And a mighty good thing you did, sonny. If you hadn't we were gonna bring you up on homicide."

"But *we* saved 'im," Sachs said. "And you didn't."

"Thanks for that snappy recap, officer. Hold your wrists out."

"This is bullshit."

"Cuff this young lady," the Chameleon said dramatically to a burly agent beside him.

She began, "We found more clues, Agent Dellray. He's got another one. And I don't know how much time we have."

"Oh, and invite that thayre boy to ouah party too." Dellray nodded to Banks, who turned to the woman FBI agent approaching him and seemed to be thinking of decking her.

Dellray said a cheerful, "No, no, no. You don' wanna."

UNSUB 823			
Appearance	Residence	Vehicle	Other
• Caucasian male, slight build • Dark clothing • Old gloves, reddish kidskin • Aftershave; to cover up other scent? • Ski mask? Navy blue? • Gloves are dark • Aftershave = Brut • Hair color not brown • Deep scar, index finger • Casual clothes	• Prob. has safe house • Located near; B'way & 82nd, ShopRite B'way & 96th Anderson Foods Greenwich & Bank ShopRite 2nd Ave., 72nd-73rd, Grocery World Battery Park City, J&G's Emporium 1709 2nd Ave., Anderson Foods 34th & Lex., Food Warehouse 8th Ave. & 24th, ShopRite Houston & Lafayette, ShopRite 6th Ave. & Houston, J&G's Emporium Greenwich & Franklin, Grocery World • Old building, pink marble	• Yellow Cab • Recent model sedan • Lt. gray, silver, biege • Rental car; prob. stolen	• knows CS proc. • possibly has record • knows FR prints • gun = .32 Colt • Ties vics w/ unusual knots • "Old" appeals to him • Called one vic "Hanna" • Knows basic German • Underground appeals to him • Dual personalities • Maybe priest, soc. worker, counselor • Unusual wear on shoes, reads a lot? • Listened as he broke vic's finger

Banks reluctantly held out his hands.

Sachs, angry, offered the agent a cold smile. "How was your trip to Morningside Heights?"

"He still killed that cabbie. Our PERT boys're crawling over that house now like beetles on dung."

"And that's all they're going to find," Sachs said. "This unsub knows crime scenes better than you and I do."

"Downtown," Dellray announced, nodding at Sachs, who winced as the cuffs ratcheted tight around her wrists.

"We can save the next one too. If you—"

"You know what you got, Officer Sachs? Take a guess. You gotchaself the right to *re*-main silent. You got—"

"All right," the voice called from behind them. Sachs looked around and saw Jim Polling striding along the sidewalk. His slacks and dark sports shirt were rumpled. It looked as if he'd napped in them, though his bleary face suggested he hadn't slept in days. You could see a day's growth of beard and his sandy hair was an unruly mess.

Dellray blinked uneasily though it wasn't the cop he was troubled by but the tall physique of the U.S. attorney for the Southern District behind Polling. And bringing up the rear, SAC Perkins.

"Okay, Fred. Let 'em go." From the U.S. attorney.

In the modulated baritone of an FM disk jockey the Chameleon said, "She stole evidence, sir. She—"

"I just expedited some forensic analysis," Sachs said.

"Listen—" Dellray began.

"Nope," Polling said, completely in control now. No temper tantrums. "No, we're *not* listening." He turned to Sachs and barked, "But don't you try to be funny."

"Nosir. Sorry, sir."

The U.S. attorney said to Dellray. "Fred, you made a judgment call and it went south. Facts of life."

"It was a good lead," Dellray said.

"Well, we're changing the direction of the investigation," the U.S. attorney continued.

SAC Perkins said, "We've been conferencing with the director and with Behavioral. We've decided that Detectives Rhyme and Sellitto's positioning is the approach to pursue."

"But my snitch was clear that *something* was going down at the airport. That's not the sorta thing he'd be wishy about."

"It comes down to this, Fred," the U.S. attorney said bluntly. "*Whatever* the fucker's up to, it was Rhyme's team that saved the vics."

Dellray's lengthy fingers folded into an uncertain fist, opened again. "I appreciate that fact, sir. But—"

"Agent Dellray, this's a decision that has already been made."

The glossy black face—so energized at the federal building when he was marshaling his troops—was now somber, reserved. For the moment, the hipster was gone. "Yessir."

"This most recent hostage would've died if Detective Sachs here hadn't intervened," the U.S. attorney said.

"That'd be *Officer* Sachs," she corrected. "And it was mostly Lincoln Rhyme. I was his legman. So to speak."

"The case is going back to the city," the U.S. attorney announced. "The Bureau's A-T is to continue to handle terrorist-informant liaison but with reduced manpower. Anything they learn should be conveyed to Detectives Sellitto and Rhyme. Dellray, you're gonna put bodies at their disposal for any search-and-surveillance or hostage-rescue effort. Or anything else they might need. Got that?"

"Yessir."

"Good. You want to remove those handcuffs from these officers now?"

Dellray placidly unlocked the cuffs and slipped them into his pocket. He walked to a large van parked nearby. As Sachs picked up the evidence bag she saw him standing by himself at the edge of a pool of streetlight, his index finger lifted, stroking the cigarette behind his ear. She wasted a moment's sympathy on the fee-bie then turned and ran up the stairs, two at a time, after Jerry Banks and his rattlesnake.

"I have it figured out. Well, almost."

Sachs had just walked into Rhyme's room when he made this pronouncement. He was quite pleased with himself.

"Everything except the rattler and the glop."

She delivered the new evidence to Mel Cooper. The room

had been transformed yet again and the tables were covered with new vials and beakers and pillboxes and lab equipment and boxes. It wasn't much compared to the feds' headquarters but, to Amelia Sachs, it felt oddly like home.

"Tell me," she said.

"Tomorrow's Sunday . . . pardon me—today's Sunday. He's going to burn down a church."

"How do you figure?"

"The date."

"On the scrap of paper? What's it mean?"

"You ever hear of the anarchists?"

"Little Russians in trench coats carrying around those bombs that look like bowling balls?" Banks said.

"From the man who reads picture books," Rhyme commented dryly. "Your Saturday-morning-cartoon roots are showing, Banks. Anarchism was an old social movement calling for the abolition of government. One anarchist, Enrico Malatesta—his shtick was 'propaganda by deed.' Translated that means murder and mayhem. One of his followers, an American named Eugene Lockworthy, lived in New York. One Sunday morning he bolted the doors of a church on the Upper East Side just after the service began and set the place on fire. Killed eighteen parishioners."

"And that happened on May 20, 1906?" Sachs asked.

"Yep."

"I'm not going to ask how you figured that out."

Rhyme shrugged. "Obvious. Our unsub likes history, right? He gave us some matches so he's telling us he's planning arson. I just thought back to the city's famous fires—the Triangle Shirt-waist, Crystal Palace, the *General Slocum* excursion boat . . . I checked the dates—May twentieth was the First Methodist Church fire."

Sachs asked, "But where? Same location as that church?"

"Doubt it," Sellitto said. "There's a commercial high-rise there now. Eight twenty-three doesn't like new places. I've got a couple men on it just in case but we're sure he's going for a church."

"And we think," Rhyme added, "that he's going to wait till a service starts."

"Why?"

"For one thing, that's what Lockworthy did," Sellitto continued. "Also, we were thinking 'bout what Terry Dobyns was telling us—upping the ante. Going for multiple vics."

"So we've got a little more time. Until the service starts."

Rhyme looked up at the ceiling. "Now, how many churches are there in Manhattan?"

"Hundreds."

"That was rhetorical, Banks. I mean—let's keep looking over the clues. He'll have to narrow it down some."

Footsteps on the stair.

It was the twins once again.

"We passed Fred Dellray outside."

"He wasn't the least bit cordial."

"Or happy."

"Whoa, look at that." Saul—Rhyme believed it was Saul; he'd forgotten who had the freckles—nodded at the snake. "I've seen more of those in one night than I ever want to again."

"Snakes?" Rhyme asked.

"We were at Metamorphosis. It's a—"

"—very spooky place. Met the owner there. Weird guy. As you may've guessed."

"Long, long beard. Wish we hadn't gone at night," Bedding continued.

"They sell taxidermied bats and insects. You wouldn't believe some of the insects—"

"Five inches long."

"—and critters like that one." Saul nodded at the snake.

"Scorpions, a lot of scorpions."

"Anyway, they had a break-in a month ago and guess what got took? A rattler's skeleton."

"Reported?" Rhyme asked.

"Yep."

"But total value of the perped merch was only a hundred bucks or so. So Larceny wasn't like all-hands-on-board, you know."

"But tell them."

Saul nodded. "The snake wasn't the only thing missing. Whoever broke in took a couple dozen bones."

"Human bones?" Rhyme asked.

"Yep. That's what the owner thought was funny. Some of those insects—"

"Forget five inches, some of 'em were eight. Easy."

"—are worth three or four hundred. But all the perp boosted was the snake and some bones."

"Any particular ones?" Rhyme asked.

"An assortment. Like your Whitman's Sampler."

"His words, not ours."

"Mostly little ones. Hand and foot. And a rib, maybe two."

"The guy wasn't sure."

"Any CS report?"

"For 'jacked bones? Noooope."

The Hardy Boys departed once more, heading downtown to the last scene to start canvassing the neighborhood.

Rhyme wondered about the snake. Was it giving them a location? Did it relate to the First Methodist fire? If rattlers had been indigenous to Manhattan, urban development had long ago played Saint Patrick and purged the island of them. Was he making a play on the word *snake* or *rattler*?

Then Rhyme suddenly believed he understood. "The snake's for us."

"Us?" Banks laughed.

"It's a slap in the face."

"Whose face?"

"Everybody who's looking for him. I think it's a practical joke."

"I wasn't laughing very hard," Sachs said.

"Your expression *was* pretty funny." Banks grinned.

"I think we're better than he expected and he's not happy about it. He's mad and he's taking it out on us. Thom, add that to our profile, if you would. He's mocking us."

Sellitto's phone rang. He opened it and answered. "Emma darlin'. Whatcha got?" He nodded as he jotted notes. Then looked up and announced, "Rental-car thefts. Two Avises disappeared from their location in the Bronx in the past week, one in Midtown. They're out 'cause the colors're wrong: red, green and white. No Nationals. Four Hertz were 'jacked. Three in Manhattan—one from their downtown East Side location, from Midtown and from the Upper West Side. There were two green and—this could be it—one tan. But a silver Ford got boosted from White Plains. That's my vote."

"Agree," Rhyme announced. "White Plains."

"How do you know?" Sachs asked. "Monelle said it could've been either beige or silver."

"Because our boy's in the city," Rhyme explained, "and if he's going to boost something as obvious as a car he'll do it as far away from his safe house as he can. It's a Ford, you said?"

Sellitto asked Emma the question, then looked up. "Taurus. This year's model. Dark-gray interior. Tag's irrelevant."

Rhyme nodded. "The first thing he changed, the plates. Thank her and tell her to get some sleep. But not to wander too far from the phone."

"Got something here, Lincoln," Mel Cooper called.

"What's that?"

"The glop. I'm running it through the database of brand names now." He stared at the screen. "Cross-referencing . . . Let's see, the most likely match is Kink-Away. It's a retail hair straightener."

"Politically incorrect but helpful. That puts us up in Harlem, wouldn't you think? Narrows down the churches considerably."

Banks was looking through the religious-service directories of all three metro newspapers. "I count twenty-two."

"When's the earliest service?"

"Three have services at eight. Six at nine. One at nine-thirty. The rest at ten or eleven."

"He'll go for one of the first services. He's already giving us hours to find the place."

Sellitto said, "I've got Haumann getting the ESU boys together again."

"How 'bout Dellray?" Sachs said. She pictured the forlorn agent by himself on the street corner outside.

"What about him?" Sellitto muttered.

"Aw, let's cut him in. He wants a piece of this guy bad."

"Perkins said he was supposed to help," Banks offered.

"You really want him?" Sellitto asked, frowning.

Sachs was nodding. "Sure."

Rhyme agreed. "Okay, he can run the fed S&S teams. I

want a team on each church right away. All entrances. But they should stay way back. I don't want to spook him. Maybe we can nail him in the act."

Sellitto took a phone call. He looked up, eyes closed. "Jesus."

"Oh, no," Rhyme muttered.

The detective wiped his sweating face and nodded. "Central got a 9–1–1 from the night manager at this place? The Midtown Residence Hotel? Woman and her little girl called him from La Guardia, said they were just about to get a cab. That was a while ago; they never showed up. With all the news about the 'nappings he thought he should call. Her name's Carole Ganz. From Chicago."

"Hell," Banks muttered. "A little girl too? Oughta just pull all the cabs off the streets till we nail his butt."

Rhyme was drenched with weariness. His head raged. He remembered working a crime scene at a bomb factory. Nitroglycerin had bled out of some dynamite and seeped into an armchair Rhyme had to search for trace. Nitro gave you blinding headaches.

The screen of Cooper's computer flickered. "E-mail," he announced and called up the message. He read the fine type.

"They've polarized all the samples of cello that ESU collected. They think the scrap we found in the bone at the Pearl Street scene was from a ShopRite grocery store. It's closest to the cello they use."

"Good," Rhyme called. He nodded at the poster. "Cross off all the grocery stores but the ShopRites. What locations do we have?"

He watched Thom ink through the stores, leaving Four.

B'way & 82nd
Greenwich & Bank
8th Ave. & 24th
Houston & Lafayette

"That leaves us with the Upper West Side, West Village, Chelsea and the Lower East Side."

"But he could have gone anywhere to buy them."

"Oh, sure he could've, Sachs. He could've bought them in

White Plains when he was stealing the car. Or in Cleveland visiting his mother. But see, there's a point when unsubs feel comfortable in their deception and they stop bothering to cover their tracks. The stupid—or lazy—ones toss the smoking gun in the Dumpster behind their building and go on their merry way. The smarter ones drop it in a bucket of Spackle and pitch it into Hell Gate. The brilliant ones sneak into a refinery and vaporize it in a five-thousand-degree-centigrade furnace. Our unsub's smart, sure. But he's like every other perp in the history of the world. He's got limits. I'm betting he thinks we won't have the time or inclination to look for him or his safe house because we'll be concentrating on the planted clues. And of course he's dead wrong. This is *exactly* how we'll find him. Now, let's see if we can't get a little closer to his lair. Mel, anything in the vic's clothes from the last scene?"

But the tidal water had washed away virtually everything from William Everett's clothing.

"You say they fought, Sachs? The unsub and this Everett?"

"Wasn't much of a fight. Everett grabbed his shirt."

Rhyme clicked his tongue. "I must be getting tired. If I'd thought about it I would have had you scrape under his nails. Even if he was underwater that's one place—"

"Here you go," she said, holding up two small plastic bags.

"You scraped?"

She nodded.

"But why're there two bags?"

Holding up one bag then the other she said, "Left hand, right hand."

Mel Cooper broke into a laugh. "Even *you* never thought about separate bags for scraping, Lincoln. It's a great idea."

Rhyme grunted. "Differentiating the hands *might* have some marginal forensic value."

"Whoa," Cooper said, laughing still. "That means he thinks it's a brilliant idea and he's sorry he didn't think of it first."

The tech examined the scrapings. "Got some brick here."

"There was no brick anywhere around the drainpipe or the field," Sachs said.

"It's fragments. But there's something attached to it. I can't tell what."

Banks asked, "Could it've come from the stockyard tunnel? There was a lotta brick there, right?"

"All *that* came from Annie Oakley here," Rhyme said, nodding ruefully at Sachs. "No, remember, the unsub'd left before she pulled out her six-gun." Then he frowned, found himself straining forward. "Mel, I want to see that brick. In the 'scope. Is there any way?"

Cooper looked over Rhyme's computer. "I think we can rig something up." He ran a cable from the video-output port on the compound 'scope to his own computer and then dug into a large suitcase. He pulled out a long, thick gray wire. "This's a serial cable." He connected the two computers and transferred some software to Rhyme's Compaq. In five minutes, Rhyme, delighted, was seeing exactly what Cooper was looking at through the eyepiece.

The criminalist's eyes scanned the chunk of brick—hugely magnified. He laughed out loud. "He outfoxed himself. See those white blobs attached to the brick?"

"What are they?" Sellitto asked.

"Looks like glue," Cooper offered.

"Exactly. From a pet-hair roller. Perps who're real cautious use them to clean trace off themselves. But it backfired. Some bits of adhesive must've come off the roller and stuck to his clothes. So we *know* it's from his safe house. Held the brick in place until Everett picked it up under his fingernails."

"Does the brick tell us anything?" Sachs asked.

"It's old. And it's expensive—cheap brick was very porous because they mixed in filler. I'd guess his place is either institutional or built by someone wealthy. At least a hundred years old. Maybe older."

"Ah, here we go," Cooper said. "Another bit of glove, it looks like. If the damn things keep disintegrating we'll be down to his friction ridges before too long."

Rhyme's screen flashed and a moment later what he recognized as a tiny fleck of leather came on the screen. "Something's funny here," Cooper said.

"It's not red," Rhyme observed. "Like the other particle. This fleck's black. Run it through the microspectrophotometer."

Cooper ran the test and then tapped his computer screen.

"It's leather. But the dye is different. Maybe it's stained or faded."

Rhyme was leaning forward, straining, looking closely at the fleck on the screen when he realized he was in trouble. Serious trouble.

"Hey, you okay?" It was Sachs who'd spoken.

Rhyme didn't answer. His neck and jaw began to shiver violently. A feeling like panic rose from the crest of his shattered spine and moved up into his scalp. Then, as if a thermostat had clicked on, the chills and goose bumps vanished and he began to sweat. Perspiration poured from his face and tickled frantically.

"Thom!" he whispered. "Thom, it's happening."

Then he gasped as the headache seared through his face and spread along the walls of his skull. He jammed his teeth together, swayed his head, anything to stop the unbearable agony. But nothing worked. The light in the room flickered. The pain was so bad his reaction was to flee from it, to run flat-out on legs that hadn't moved in years.

"Lincoln!" Sellitto was shouting.

"His face," Sachs gasped, "it's bright red."

And his hands were pale as ivory. All of his body below the magic latitude at C4 was turning white. Rhyme's blood, on its phony, desperate mission to get to where it thought it was needed, surged into the tiny capillaries of his brain, expanding them, threatening to burst the delicate filaments.

As the attack grew worse Rhyme was aware of Thom over him, ripping the blankets off the Clinitron. He was aware of Sachs stepping forward, her radiant blue eyes narrowed in concern. The last thing he saw before the blackness was the falcon pushing off the ledge on his huge wings, startled by the sudden flurry of activity in the room, seeking easy oblivion in the hot air over the empty streets of the city.

TWENTY-FOUR

When Rhyme passed out, Sellitto got to the phone first. "Call 911 for EMS," Thom instructed. "Then hit that number there. Speed dial. It's Pete Taylor, our spinal cord specialist."

Sellitto made the calls.

Thom was shouting, "I'll need some help here. Somebody!"

Sachs was closest. She nodded, stepped up to Rhyme. The aide had grabbed the unconscious man under the arms and pulled him higher up in bed. He ripped open the shirt and prodded the pale chest, saying, "Everybody else, if you could just leave us."

Sellitto, Banks and Cooper hesitated for a moment then stepped through the doorway. Sellitto closed the door behind them.

A beige box appeared in the aide's hands. It had switches and dials on the top and sprouted a wire ending in a flat disk, which he placed over Rhyme's chest and taped down.

"Phrenic nerve stimulator. It'll keep him breathing." He clicked on the machine.

As Thom slipped a blood-pressure cuff onto Rhyme's alabaster-white arm, Sachs realized with a start that his body was virtually wrinkle-free. He was in his forties but his body was that of a twenty-five-year-old.

"Why's his face so red? It looks like he's going to explode."

"He is," Thom said matter-of-factly, yanking a doctor's kit from underneath the bedside table. He opened it then he continued to take the pressure. "Dysreflexia . . . All the stress today. Mental *and* physical. He's not used to it."

"He kept saying he was tired."

"I know. And I wasn't paying careful enough attention. Shhhh. I have to listen." He plugged the stethoscope into his ears, inflated the cuff and let the air out slowly. Staring at his watch. His hands were rock-steady. "Shit. Diastolic's one twenty-five. Shit."

Father in heaven, Sachs thought. He's going to stroke out.

Thom nodded at the black bag. "Find the bottle of nifedipine. And open up one of those syringes." As she searched, Thom yanked down Rhyme's pajamas and grabbed a catheter from beside the bed, tore open its plastic wrapper too. He smeared the end with K-Y jelly and lifted Rhyme's pale penis, inserting the catheter gently but quickly into the tip.

"This's part of the problem. Bowel and urinary pressure can trigger an attack. He's been drinking way more than he should today."

She opened the hypodermic but said, "I don't know how to do the needle."

"I'll do it." He looked up at her. "Could I ask . . . would you mind doing this? I don't want the tube to get a kink in it."

"Okay. Sure."

"You want gloves?"

She pulled on a pair and carefully took Rhyme's penis in her left hand. She held the tube in her right. It had been a long, long time since she'd held a man here. The skin was soft and she thought how strange it was that this center of a man's being is, most of the time, as delicate as silk.

Thom expertly injected the drug.

"Come on, Lincoln . . ."

A siren sounded in the distance.

"They're almost here," she said glancing out the window.

"If we don't bring him back now there's nothing they can do."

"How long does it take the drug to work?"

Thom stared at the unresponsive Rhyme, said, "It should've by now. But too high a dose and he goes into shock." The aide bent down and lifted an eyelid. The blue pupil was glazed, unfocused.

"This isn't good." He took the pressure again. "One fifty. Christ."

"It'll kill him," she said.

"Oh. That's not the problem."

"What?" a shocked Amelia Sachs whispered.

"He doesn't mind dying." He looked at her briefly as if surprised she hadn't figured this out. "He just doesn't want to be any more paralyzed than he already is." He prepared another injection. "He may already've had one. A stroke, I mean. *That's* what terrifies him."

Thom leaned forward and injected more of the drug.

The siren was closer now. Honking too. Cars would be blocking the ambulance's way, in no hurry to pull aside—one of the things that infuriated Sachs about the city.

"You can take the catheter out now."

She carefully extracted the tube. "Should I . . ." Nodding toward the urine bag.

Thom managed a weak smile. "That's my job."

Several minutes passed. The ambulance seemed to make no progress then a voice crackled over a speaker and gradually the siren grew closer.

Suddenly Rhyme stirred. His head shook slightly. Then it lolled back and forth, pressed into the pillow. His skin lost some of its florid tone.

"Lincoln, can you hear me?"

He moaned, "Thom . . ."

Rhyme was shivering violently. Thom covered him with a sheet.

Sachs found herself smoothing Rhyme's mussed hair. She took a tissue and wiped his forehead.

Footsteps pounded on the stairs and two burly EMS medics appeared, radios crackling. They hurried into the room, took Rhyme's blood pressure and checked the nerve stimulator. A moment later Dr Peter Taylor burst into the room.

"Peter," Thom said. "Dysreflexia."

"Pressure?"

"It's down. But it was bad. Crested at one fifty."

The doctor winced.

Thom introduced Taylor to the EMS techs. They seemed pleased an expert was there and stepped back as Taylor walked over to the bedside.

"Doctor," Rhyme said groggily.

"Let's look at those eyes." Taylor shone a light into Rhyme's pupils. Sachs scanned the doctor's face for a reaction and was troubled by his frown.

"Don't need the nerve stimulator," Rhyme whispered.

"You and your lungs, right?" the doctor asked wryly. "Well, let's keep it going for a little while, why don't we? Just till we see what exactly's going on here." He glanced at Sachs. "Maybe you could wait downstairs."

Taylor leaned close and Rhyme noticed the beads of sweat dotting the doctor's scalp under his thin hair.

The man's deft hands lifted a lid and gazed again into one pupil, then the next. He rigged up the sphygmomanometer and took Rhyme's blood pressure, his eyes distant with that concentration of medicos lost in their minute, vital tasks.

"Approaching normal," he announced. "How's the urine?"

"Eleven hundred cc's," Thom said.

Taylor glowered. "Been neglecting things? Or just drinking to excess?"

Rhyme glowered right back. "We were distracted, doctor. It's been a busy night."

Taylor followed Rhyme's nod and glanced around the room, surprised, as if someone had just sneaked the equipment in when he wasn't looking. "What's all this?"

"They hauled me out of retirement."

Taylor's perplexed frown grew into a smile. "About time. I've been after you for months to do something with your life. Now, what's the bowel situation?"

Thom said, "Probably twelve hours, fourteen."

"Careless of you," Taylor chided.

"It wasn't *his* fault," Rhyme snapped. "I've had a roomful of people here all day."

"I don't want to hear excuses," the doctor shot back. This was Pete Taylor, who never spoke *through* anyone when he talked to Rhyme and never let his bullying patient bully him.

"We better take care of things." He pulled on surgical gloves, leaned over Rhyme's torso. His fingers began manipulating the abdomen to trick the numb intestines into doing their work. Thom lifted the blankets and got the disposable diapers.

A moment later the job was done and Thom cleaned his boss.

Taylor said suddenly, "So you've given up that nonsense, I hope?" Studying Rhyme closely.

That nonsense . . .

He'd meant the suicide. With a glance at Thom, Rhyme said, "Haven't thought about that for a while."

"Good." Taylor looked over the instruments on the table. "This is what you ought to be doing. Maybe the department'll put you back on the payroll."

"Don't think I could pass the physical."

"How's the head?"

"'A dozen sledgehammers' comes close to describing it. My neck too. Had two bad cramps so far today."

Taylor walked behind the Clinitron, pressed his fingers on either side of Rhyme's spine, where—Rhyme supposed, though he'd never seen the spot of course—there were prominent incision scars from the operations he'd had over the years. Taylor gave Rhyme an expert massage, digging deep into the taut straps of muscle in his shoulders and neck. The pain slowly vanished.

He felt the doctor's thumbs pause at what he guessed was the shattered vertebra.

The spaceship, the stingray . . .

"Someday they'll fix this," Taylor said. "Someday, it'll be no worse than breaking your leg. You listen to me. I predict it."

Fifteen minutes later Peter Taylor came down the stairs and joined the cops on the sidewalk.

"Is he all right?" Amelia Sachs asked anxiously.

"The pressure's down. He needs rest mostly."

The doctor, a plain-looking man, suddenly realized he was talking to a very beautiful woman. He smoothed his thinning gray hair and cast a discreet glance at her willowy figure. His eyes then went to the squad cars in front of the townhouse and he asked, "What's the case he's helping you with?"

Sellitto demurred, as all detectives will in the face of that question from civilians. But Sachs had guessed Taylor and Rhyme were close so she said, "The kidnappings? Have you heard about them?"

"The taxi-driver case? It's on all the news. Good for him. Work is the best thing that could happen to him. He needs friends and he needs purpose."

Thom appeared at the top of the stairs. "He said thanks, Pete. Well, he didn't actually say thanks. But he meant it. You know how he is."

"Level with me," Taylor asked, voice lower now, conspiratorial. "Is he still planning on talking to them?"

And when Thom said, "No, he's not," something in his tone told Sachs that he was lying. She didn't know about what or what significance it might have. But it rankled.

Planning on talking to them?

In any case Taylor seemed not to pick up on the aide's deceit. He said, "I'll come back tomorrow, see how he's doing."

Thom said he'd appreciate it and Taylor slung his bag over his shoulder and started up the sidewalk. The aide gestured to Sellitto. "He'd like to talk to you for a minute." The detective climbed the stairs quickly. He disappeared into the room and a few minutes later he and Thom walked outside. Sellitto, solemn himself now, glanced at her. "Your turn." And nodded toward the stairs.

Rhyme lay in the massive bed, hair mussed, face no longer red, hands no longer ivory. The room smelled ripe, visceral. There were clean sheets on the bed and his clothes had been changed again. This time the pajamas were as green as Dellray's suit.

"Those are the ugliest PJs I've ever seen," she said. "Your ex gave them to you, didn't she?"

"How'd you guess? An anniversary present . . . Sorry for the scare," he said, looking away from her. He seemed suddenly timid and that upset her. She thought of her father in the pre-op room at Sloan-Kettering before they took him down to the exploratory surgery he never awoke from. Weakness can be more frightening than threat.

"Sorry?" she asked ominously. "No more of that shit, Rhyme."

He appraised her for a minute then said, "You two'll do fine."

"We two?"

"You and Lon. Mel too of course. And Jim Polling."

"What do you mean?"

"I'm retiring."

"You're *what?*"

"Too taxing for the old system, I'm afraid."

"But you can't quit." She waved at the Monet poster. "Look at everything we've found about 823. We're so close."

"So you don't need me. All you need is a little luck."

"Luck? It took years to get Bundy. And what about the Zodiac killer? And the Werewolf?"

"We've got good information here. Hard information. You'll come up with some good leads. You'll nail him, Sachs. Your swan song before they lap you up into Public Affairs. I've got a feeling Unsub 823's getting cocky; they might even collar him at the church."

"You look fine," she said after a moment. Though he didn't.

Rhyme laughed. Then the smile faded. "I'm very tired. And I hurt. Hell, I think I hurt in places the docs'll say I *can't* hurt."

"Do what I do. Take a nap."

He tried to snort a derisive laugh but he sounded weak. She hated seeing him this way. He coughed briefly, glanced down at the nerve stimulator, and grimaced, as if he was embarrassed that he depended on the machine. "Sachs . . . I don't suppose we'll be working together again. I just wanted to say that you've got a good career ahead of you, you make the right choices."

"Well, I'll come back and see you after we snag his bad ass."

"I'd like that. I'm glad you were first officer yesterday morning. There's nobody else I'd rather've walked the grid with."

"I—"

"Lincoln," a voice said. She turned to see a man in the doorway. He looked around the room curiously, taking in all the equipment.

"Been some excitement around here, looks like."

"Doctor," Rhyme said. His face blossoming into a smile. "Please come in."

He stepped into the room. "I got Thom's message. Emergency, he said?"

"Dr William Berger, this is Amelia Sachs."

But Sachs could see she'd already ceased to exist in Lincoln Rhyme's universe. Whatever else was left to be said—and she felt there were some things, maybe many things—would have to wait. She walked through the door. Thom, who stood in the large hallway outside, closed the door behind her and, ever proper, paused, nodding for her to precede him.

As Sachs walked out into the steamy night she heard a voice from nearby. "Excuse me."

She turned and found Dr Peter Taylor standing by himself under a ginkgo tree. "Can I talk to you for a minute?"

Sachs followed Taylor up the sidewalk a few doors.

"Yes?" she asked. He leaned against a stone wall and gave another self-conscious swipe at his hair. Sachs recalled how many times she'd intimidated men with a single word or glance. She thought, as she often did: What a useless power beauty is.

"You're his friend, right?" the doctor asked her. "I mean, you work with him but you're a friend too."

"Sure. I guess I am."

"That man who just went inside. Do you know who he is?"

"Berger, I think. He's a doctor."

"Did he say where he was from?"

"No."

Taylor looked up at Rhyme's bedroom window for a moment. He asked, "You know the Lethe Society?"

"No, oh, wait . . . It's a euthanasia group, right?"

Taylor nodded. "I know all of Lincoln's doctors. And I've never heard of Berger. I was just thinking maybe he's with them."

"What?"

Is he still talking to them . . .

So *that's* what the conversation was about.

She felt weightless from the shock. "Has he . . . has he seriously talked about this before?"

"Oh, yes." Taylor sighed, gazed into the smoky night sky. "Oh, yes." Then glanced at her name badge. "Officer Sachs, I've spent hours trying to talk him out of it. Days. But I've also worked with quads for years and I know how stubborn they are. Maybe he'd listen to you. Just a few words. I was thinking . . . Could you?—"

"Oh, goddamn it, Rhyme," she muttered and started down the sidewalk at a run, leaving the doctor in midsentence.

She got to the front door of the townhouse just as Thom was closing it. She pushed past him. "Forgot my watchbook."

"Your?—"

"Be right back."

"You can't go up there. He's with his doctor."

"I'll just be a second."

She was at the landing before Thom started after her.

He must have known it was a scam because he took the stairs two at a time. But she had a good lead and had shoved open Rhyme's door before the aide got to the top of the stairs.

She pushed in, startling both Rhyme and the doctor, who was leaning against the table, arms crossed. She closed the door and locked it. Thom began pounding. Berger turned toward her with a frown of curiosity on his face.

"Sachs," Rhyme blurted.

"I have to talk to you."

"What about?"

"About you."

"Later."

"How much later, Rhyme?" she asked sarcastically. "Tomorrow? Next week?"

"What do you mean?"

"You want me to schedule a meeting for, maybe, a week from Wednesday? Will you be able to make it then? Will you be *around?*"

"Sachs—"

"I want to talk to you. Alone."

"No."

"Then we'll do it the hard way." She stepped up to Berger. "You're under arrest. The charge is attempted assisted suicide." And the handcuffs flashed, click, click, snapping onto his wrists in a silver blur.

She guessed the building was a church.

Carole Ganz lay in the basement, on the floor. A single shaft of cold, oblique light fell on the wall, illuminating a shabby picture of Jesus and a stack of mildewy Golden Book Bible stories. A half-dozen tiny chairs—for Sunday-school students, she guessed—were nested in the middle of the room.

The cuffs were still on and so was the gag. He'd also tied her to a pipe near the wall with a four-foot-long piece of clothesline.

On a tall table nearby she could see the top of a large glass jug.

If she could knock it off she might use a piece of glass to cut the clothesline. The table seemed out of reach but she rolled over onto her side and started to squirm, like a caterpillar, toward it.

This reminded her of Pammy when she was an infant, rolling on the bed between herself and Ron; she thought of her baby, alone in that horrible basement, and started to cry.

Pammy, Pooh, purse.

For a moment, for a brief moment, she weakened. Wished she'd never left Chicago.

No, stop thinking that way! Quit feeling sorry for yourself! This was the absolute right thing to do. You did it for Ron. And for yourself too. He'd be proud of you. Kate had told her that a thousand times, and she believed it.

Struggling once more. She moved a foot closer to the table.

Groggy, couldn't think straight.

Her throat stung from the terrible thirst. And the mold and mildew in the air.

She crawled a little farther then lay on her side, catching her breath, staring up at the table. It seemed hopeless. What's the use? she thought.

Wondering what was going through Pammy's mind.

You fucker! thought Carole. I'll *kill* you for this!

She squirmed, trying to move farther along the floor. But instead, she lost her balance and rolled onto her back. She gasped, knowing what was coming. No! With a loud pop, her wrist snapped. She screamed through the gag. Blacked out. When she came to a moment later she was overwhelmed with nausea.

No, no, no . . . If she vomited she'd die. With the gag on, that would be it.

Fight it down! Fight it. Come on. You can do it. Here I go . . . She retched once. Then again.

No! Control it.

Rising in her throat.

Control . . .

Control it. . . .

And she did. Breathing through her nose, concentrating on Kate and Eddie and Pammy, on the yellow knapsack containing all her precious possessions. Seeing it, picturing it from every angle. Her whole life was in there. Her *new* life.

Ron, I don't want to blow it. I came here for you, honey . . .

She closed her eyes. Thought: Breathe deep. In, out.

Finally, the nausea subsided. And a moment later she was feeling better and, though she was crying in pain from the snapped wrist, she managed to continue to caterpillar her way toward the table, one foot. Two.

She felt a thump as her head collided with the table leg. She'd just managed to connect with it and couldn't move any farther. She swung her head back and forth and jostled the table hard. She heard the bottle slosh as it shifted on the tabletop. She looked up.

A bit of the jug was showing beyond the edge of the table. Carole drew back her head and hit the table leg one last time.

No! She'd knocked the leg out of reach. The jug teetered for a moment but stayed upright. Carole strained to get more slack from the clothesline but couldn't.

Damn. Oh, damn! As she gazed hopelessly up at the filthy bottle she realized it was filled with a liquid and something floated inside. What *is* that?

She scrunched her way back toward the wall a foot or two and looked up.

It seemed like a lightbulb inside. No, not a whole bulb, just the filament and the base, screwed into a socket. A wire ran from the socket out of the jug to one of those timers that turn the lights on and off when you're away on vacation. It looked like—

A bomb! Now she recognized the faintest whiff of gasoline.

No, no . . .

Carole began to squirm away from the table as fast as she could, sobbing in desperation. There was a filing cabinet by the wall. It'd give her some protection. She drew her legs up then felt a chill of panic and unwound them furiously. The motion knocked her off balance. She realized, to her horror, that she was rolling onto her back once more. Oh, stop. Don't . . . She stayed poised, perfectly still, for a long moment, quivering as she tried to shift her weight forward. But then she continued to roll, collapsing onto her cuffed hand, her shattered wrist taking the weight of her body. There was a moment of incredible pain and, mercifully, she fainted once more.

TWENTY-FIVE

"No way, Rhyme. You can't do it."

Berger looked on uneasily. Rhyme supposed that in this line of work he'd seen all sorts of hysterical scenarios played out at moments like this. The biggest problem Berger'd have wasn't those wanting to die but those who wanted everyone else to live.

Thom pounded on the door.

"Thom," Rhyme called. "It's all right. You can leave us." Then to Sachs: "We've said our farewells. You and me. It's bad form to ruin a perfect exit."

"You can't do this."

Who'd blown the whistle? Pete Taylor maybe. The doctor must've guessed that he and Thom were lying.

Rhyme saw her eyes slip to the three items on the table. The gifts of the Magi. The brandy, the pills and the plastic bag. Also a rubber band, similar to the ones Sachs still wore on her shoes. (How many times had he come home from a crime scene to find Blaine staring at the bands on his shoes, horrified? "Everybody'll think my husband can't afford new shoes. He's keeping the soles on with rubber bands. *Honestly*, Lincoln!")

"Sachs, take the cuffs off the good doctor here. I'll have to ask you to leave one last time."

She barked a fast laugh. "Excuse me. This's a crime in New York. The DA could bootstrap it into murder, he wanted to."

Berger said, "I'm just having a conversation with a patient."

"That's why the charge's only attempt. So far. Maybe we

should run your name and prints through NCIC. See what we come up with."

"Lincoln," Berger said quickly, alarmed. "I can't—"

"We'll get it worked out," Rhyme said. "Sachs, please."

Feet apart, hands on trim hips, her gorgeous face imperious. "Let's go," she barked to the doctor.

"Sachs, you have no idea how important this is."

"I won't let you kill yourself."

"Let me?" Rhyme snapped. "*Let* me? And why exactly do I need your permission?"

Berger said, "Miss . . . Officer Sachs, it's his decision and it's completely consensual. Lincoln's more informed than most of the patients I deal with."

"Patients? Victims, you mean."

"Sachs!" Rhyme blurted, trying to keep the desperation from his voice. "It's taken me a year to find someone to help me."

"Maybe because it's wrong. Ever consider that? Why now, Rhyme? Right in the middle of the case?"

"If I have another attack and a stroke, I might lose all ability to communicate. I could be conscious for forty years and completely unable to move. And if I'm not brain-dead, nobody in the universe is going to pull the plug. At least now I'm still able to communicate my decisions."

"But why?" she blurted.

"Why not?" Rhyme answered. "Tell me. Why not?"

"Well . . ." It seemed as if the arguments against suicide were so obvious she was having trouble articulating them. "Because . . ."

"Because *why*, Sachs?"

"For one thing, it's cowardly."

Rhyme laughed. "Do you want to debate it, Sachs? *Do* you? Fair enough. 'Cowardly,' you say. That leads us to Sir Thomas Browne: 'When life is more terrible than death, it's the truest valor to live.' Courage in the face of insurmountable adversity . . . A classic argument in favor of living. But if that's true then why anesthetize patients before surgery? Why sell aspirin? Why fix broken arms? Why is Prozac the most prescribed medicine in America? Sorry, but there's nothing intrinsically good about pain."

"But you're not in pain."

"And how do you define pain, Sachs? Maybe the absence of all feeling can be pain too."

"You can contribute so much. Look at all you know. All the forensics, all the history."

"The social-contribution argument. That's a popular one." He glanced at Berger but the medico remained silent. Rhyme saw his interest dip to the bone sitting on the table—the pale disk of spinal column. He picked it up, kneaded it in his cuffed hands. He was a former orthopedics man, Rhyme recalled.

He continued to Sachs, "But who says we should contribute anything to life? Besides, the corollary is I might contribute something bad. I might cause some harm too. To myself or someone else."

"That's what life is."

Rhyme smiled. "But I'm choosing death, not life."

Sachs looked uneasy as she thought hard. "It's just . . . death isn't natural. Life is."

"No? Freud'd disagree with you. He gave up on the pleasure principle and came to feel that there was another force—a nonerotic primary aggression, he called it. Working to unbind the connections we build in life. Our own destruction's a perfectly natural force. Everything dies; what's more natural than that?"

Again she worried a portion of her scalp.

"All right," she said. "Life's more of a challenge to you than most people. But I thought . . . everything I've seen about you tells me you're somebody who likes challenges."

"Challenges? Let me tell you about challenges. I was on a ventilator for a year. See the tracheostomy scar on my neck? Well, through positive-pressure breathing exercises—and the greatest willpower I could muster—I managed to get off the machine. In fact I've got lungs like nobody's business. They're as strong as yours. In a C4 quad that's one for the books, Sachs. It consumed my life for eight months. Do you understand what I'm saying? Eight months just to handle a basic animal function. I'm not talking about painting the Sistine Chapel or playing the violin. I'm talking about fucking *breathing*."

"But you could get better. Next year, they might find a cure."

"No. Not next year. Not in ten years."

"You don't know that. They must be doing research—"

"Sure they are. Want to know what? I'm an expert. Transplanting embryonic nerve tissue onto damaged tissue to promote axonal regeneration." These words tripped easily from his handsome lips. "No significant effect. Some doctors are chemically treating the affected areas to create an environment where cells can regenerate. No significant effect—not in advanced species. Lower forms of life show pretty good success. If I were a frog I'd be walking again. Well, hopping."

"So there *are* people working on it?" Sachs asked.

"Sure. But no one expects any breakthroughs for twenty, thirty years."

"If they were expected," she shot back, "then they wouldn't be breakthroughs, now would they?"

Rhyme laughed. She was good.

Sachs tossed the veil of red hair from her eyes and said, "Your career was law enforcement, remember. Suicide's illegal."

"It's a sin too," he responded. "The Dakota Indians believed that the ghosts of those who committed suicide had to drag around the tree they'd hanged themselves from for all eternity. Did that stop suicide? Nope. They just used small trees."

"Tell you what, Rhyme. Here's my last argument." She nodded at Berger, grabbed the cuff chain. "I'm taking him in and booking him. Refute *that* one."

"Lincoln," Berger said uneasily, panic in his eyes.

Sachs took the doctor by the shoulder and led him to the door. "No," he said. "Please. Don't do this."

As Sachs opened the door Rhyme called out, "Sachs, before you do that answer me something."

She paused. One hand on the knob.

"One question."

She looked back.

"Have you ever wanted to? Kill yourself?"

She unlocked the door with a loud snap.

He said, "Answer me!"

Sachs didn't open the door. She stood with her back to him. "No. Never."

"Are you happy with your life?"

"As much as anybody."

"You're never depressed?"

"I didn't say that. I said I've never wanted to kill myself."

"You like to drive, you were telling me. People who like to drive like to drive fast. You do, don't you?"

"Yes. Sometimes."

"What's the fastest you've done?"

"I don't know."

"Over eighty?"

A dismissing smile. "Yes."

"Over a hundred?"

She gestured upward with her thumb.

"One ten? One twenty?" he asked, smiling in astonishment.

"Clocked at 168."

"My, Sachs, you *are* impressive. Well, driving that fast, didn't you think that maybe, just maybe, something might happen. A rod or axle or something would break, a tire would blow, a spot of oil on the road?"

"It was pretty safe. I'm not crazy."

"*Pretty* safe. But driving as fast as a small plane, well, that's not *completely* safe, now, is it?"

"You're leading the witness."

"No, I'm not. Stay with me. You drive that fast, you have to accept that you could have an accident and die, right?"

"Maybe," she conceded.

Berger, cuffed hands in front of him, looked on nervously, as he kneaded the pale yellow disk of spinal column.

"So you've moved close to that line, right? Ah, you know what I'm talking about. I know you do—the line between the *risk* of dying and the *certainty* of dying. See, Sachs, if you carry the dead around with you it's a very short step over that line. A short step to joining them."

She lowered her head and her face went completely still, as the curtain of hair obscured her eyes.

"Giving up the dead," he whispered, praying she wouldn't leave with Berger, knowing he was so very close to pushing her over the edge. "I touched a nerve there. How much of you wants to follow the dead? More than a little, Sachs. Oh, much more than a little."

She was hesitating. He knew he was near her heart.

She turned angrily to Berger, gripped him by the cuffs. "Come on." Pushed through the door.

Rhyme called, "You know what I'm saying, don't you?"

Again she stopped.

"Sometimes . . . things happen, Sachs. Sometimes you just can't be what you ought to be, you can't have what you ought to have. And life changes. Maybe just a little, maybe a lot. And at some point it just isn't worth the fight to try to fix what went wrong."

He watched them standing, motionless, in the doorway. The room was utterly silent. She turned and looked back at him.

"Death cures loneliness," Rhyme continued. "It cures tension. It cures the itch." Just like she'd glanced at his legs earlier he now gave a fast look at her torn fingers.

She released Berger's cuffs and walked to the window. Tears glistened on her cheeks in the yellow radiance from the street-lights outside.

"Sachs, I'm tired," he said earnestly. "I can't tell you how tired I am. You know how hard life is to start with. Pile on a whole mountainful of . . . burdens. Washing, eating, crapping, making phone calls, buttoning shirts, scratching your nose . . . Then pile on a thousand more. And more after that."

He fell silent. After a long moment she said, "I'll make a deal with you."

"What's that?"

She nodded toward the poster. "Eight twenty-three's got that mother and her little girl . . . Help us save them. Just them. If you do that I'll give him an hour alone with you." She glanced at Berger. "Provided he gets the hell out of town afterwards."

Rhyme shook his head. "Sachs, if I have a stroke, if I can't communicate . . ."

"If that happens," she said evenly, "even if you can't say a word, the deal still holds. I'll make sure you have one hour together." She crossed her arms, spread her feet again, in what was now Rhyme's favorite image of Amelia Sachs. He wished he could've seen her on the railroad tracks that morning, stopping the train. She said, "That's the best I'll do."

A moment passed. Rhyme nodded. "Okay. It's a deal." To Berger he said, "Monday?"

"Okay, Lincoln. Fair enough." Berger, still shaken, watched Sachs cautiously as she unlocked the cuffs. Afraid, it seemed, that she might change her mind. When he was free he walked quickly to the door. He realized he was still holding the vertebra and returned, set it—almost reverently—next to Rhyme on the crime scene report for the first murder that morning.

"Happier'n hogs in red Virginia mud," Sachs remarked, slouching in the squeaky rattan chair. Meaning Sellitto and Polling, after she'd told them that Rhyme had agreed to remain on the case for another day.

"Polling particularly," she said. "I thought the little guy was going to hug me. Don't tell him I called him that. How are you feeling? You look better." She sipped some Scotch and set the glass back on the bedside table, beside Rhyme's tumbler.

"Not bad."

Thom was changing the bedclothes. "You were sweating like a fountain," he said.

"But only above my neck," Rhyme pointed out. "Sweating, I mean."

"That right?" Sachs asked.

"Yep. That's how it works. Thermostat's busted below that. I never need any axial deodorant."

"Axial?"

"Pit," Rhyme snorted. "*Armpit*. My first aide never said armpit. He'd say, 'I'm going to elevate you by your axials, Lincoln.' Oh, and: 'If you feel like regurgitating go right ahead, Lincoln.' He called himself a 'caregiver.' The word was actually on his résumé. I have no idea why I hired him. We're very superstitious, Sachs. We think calling something by a different name is going to change it. Unsub. Perpetrator. But that aide, he was just a nurse who was up to his own armpits in piss 'n' puke. Right, Thom? Nothing to be ashamed of. It's an honorable profession. Messy but honorable."

"I thrive on mess. That's why I work for you."

"What're you, Thom? An aide or a caregiver?"

"I'm a saint."

"Ha, fast with the comebacks. And fast with the needle too. He brought me back from the dead. Done it more than once."

Rhyme was suddenly pierced with a fear that Sachs had seen him naked. Eyes fixed firmly on the unsub profile, he asked, 'Say, do I owe you some thanks too, Sachs? Did you play Clara Barton here?" He uneasily waited for her answer, didn't know how he could look at her again if she had.

"Nup," Thom answered. "Saved you all by my lonesome. Didn't want any of these sensitive souls repulsed by the sight of your baggy rear end."

Thank you, Thom, he thought. Then barked, "Now go away. We have to talk about the case. Sachs and me."

"You need some sleep."

"Of course I do. But we still need to talk about the case. Good night, good night."

After Thom left, Sachs poured some Macallan in a glass. She lowered her head and inhaled the smoky vapors.

"Who snitched?" Rhyme asked. "Pete?"

"Who?" she asked.

"Dr Taylor, the SCI man."

She hesitated long enough for him to know that Taylor was the one. She said finally, "He cares about you."

"Of course he does. That's the problem—I want him to care a little *less*. Does he know about Berger?"

"He suspects."

Rhyme grimaced. "Look, tell him that Berger's just an old friend. He . . . what?"

Sachs exhaled slowly, as if shooting cigarette smoke through her pursed lips. "You not only want me to let you kill yourself you want me to lie to the one person who could talk you out of it."

"He couldn't talk me out of it," Rhyme responded.

"Then why do you want me to lie?"

He laughed. "Let's just keep Dr Taylor in the dark for a few more days."

"All right," she said. "Jesus, you're a tough person to deal with."

He examined her closely. "Why don't you tell me about it."

"About what?"

"Who's the dead? That you haven't given up?"

"There's plenty of them."

"Such as?"

"Read the newspaper."

"Come on, Sachs."

She shook her head, stared down at her Scotch with a faint smile on her lips. "No, I don't think so."

He put her silence down to reluctance about having an intimate conversation with someone she'd known only for one day. Which seemed ironic, considering she sat next to a dozen catheters, a tube of K-Y jelly and a box of Depends. Still he wasn't going to push it and said nothing more. So he was surprised when she suddenly looked up and blurted, "It's just . . . It's just . . . Oh, *hell.*" And as the sobbing began she lifted her hands to her face, spilling a good two inches of Scotland's best all over the parquet.

TWENTY-SIX

"I can't believe I'm telling you this." She sat huddled in the deep chair, legs drawn up, issue shoes kicked off. The tears were gone though her face was as ruddy as her hair.

"Go on," he encouraged.

"That guy I told you about? We were going to get an apartment together."

"Oh, with the collie. You didn't say it was a guy. Your boyfriend?"

The secret lover? Rhyme wondered.

"He *was* my boyfriend."

"I was thinking maybe it was your father you'd lost."

"Naw. Pop did pass away—three years ago. Cancer. But we knew it was coming. If that prepares you for it I guess we were prepared. But Nick . . ."

"He was killed?" Rhyme asked softly.

But she didn't answer. "Nick Carelli. One of us. A cop. Detective, third. Worked Street Crimes."

The name was familiar. Rhyme said nothing and let her continue.

"We lived together for a while. Talked about getting married." She paused, seemed to be lining up her thoughts like targets at a shooting range. "He worked undercover. So we were pretty secret about our relationship. He couldn't let word get around on the street that his gal was a cop." She cleared her throat. "It's hard to explain. See, we had this . . . thing between us. It was . . . it hasn't happened for me very often. Hell, it *never* happened before Nick. We clicked in some really deep way. He knew I had to be a cop and that wasn't a problem for him. Same with me and his working undercover. That kind of . . . wave-length. You know, where you just completely understand someone? You ever felt what I'm talking about? With your wife?"

Rhyme smiled faintly. "I did. Yes. But not with Blaine, my wife." And that was all he wanted to say on the subject. "How'd you meet?" he asked.

"The assignments lectures at the academy. Where somebody gets up and they tell you a little about what their division does. Nick was lecturing on undercover work. He asked me out on the spot. Our first date was at Rodman's Neck."

"The gun range?"

She nodded, sniffing. "Afterwards, we went to his mom's in Brooklyn and had pasta and a bottle of Chianti. She pinched me hard and said I was too skinny to have babies. Made me eat two cannoli. We went back to my place and he stayed over that night. Quite a first date, huh? From then on we saw each other all the time. It was gonna work, Rhyme. I felt it. It was gonna work just fine."

Rhyme said, "What happened?"

"He was . . ."

Another bolstering hit of old liquor. "He was on the take is what happened. The whole time I knew him."

"He was?"

"Crooked. Oh, way crooked. I never had a clue. Not a single goddamn clue. He socked it away in banks around the city. He dusted close to two hundred thousand."

Lincoln was silent a moment. "I'm sorry, Sachs. Drugs?"

"No. Merch, mostly. Appliances, TVs. 'Jackings. They called it the Brooklyn Connection. The papers did."

Rhyme was nodding. "That's why I remember it. There were a dozen of them in the ring, right? All cops?"

"Mostly. A few ICC people too."

"What happened to him? Nick?"

"You know what happens when cops bust cops. They beat the crap out of him. Said he resisted but I know he didn't. Broke three ribs, a couple fingers, smashed his face all up. Pleaded guilty but he still got twenty to thirty."

"For hijacking?" Rhyme was astonished.

"He worked a couple of the jobs himself. Pistol-whipped

one driver, took a shot at another one. Just to scare him. I *know* it was just to scare him. But the judge threw him away." She closed her eyes, pressed her lips together hard.

"When he got collared, Internal Affairs went after him like they were in heat. They checked pen registers. We were real careful about calling each other. He said perps sometimes tapped his line. But there were some calls to my place. IA came after me too. So Nick just cut me off. I mean, he *had* to. Otherwise I would've gone down with him. You know IA—it's always a goddamn witch-hunt."

"What happened?"

"To convince them that I wasn't anything to him . . . Well, he said some things about me." She swallowed, her eyes fixed on the floor. "At the IA inquest they wanted to know about me. Nick said, 'Oh, P.D. Sachs? I just fucked her a few times. Turned out she was lousy. So I dumped her.'" She tilted her head back and mopped tears with her sleeve. "The nickname? P.D."

"Lon told me."

She frowned. "Did he tell you what it means?"

"The Portable's Daughter. After your father."

She smiled wanly. "That's how it started. But that's not how it ended up. At the inquest Nick said I was such a lousy fuck it really stood for 'Pussy Diver' 'cause I probably liked girls better. Guess how fast *that* went through the department."

"It's a low common denominator out there, Sachs."

She took a deep breath. "I saw him in court toward the end of the inquest. He looked at me once and . . . I can't even describe what was in his eyes. Just pure heartbreak. Oh, he did it to protect me. But still . . . You were right, you know. About the lonely stuff."

"I didn't mean—"

"No," she said, unsmiling. "I hit you, you hit me. That was fair. And you were right. I hate being alone. I *want* to go out, I *want* to meet somebody. But after Nick I lost my taste for sex." Sachs gave a sour laugh. "Everybody thinks looking like me's wonderful. I could have my pick of guys, right? Bullshit. The only ones with the balls to ask me out're the ones who want to screw all the time. So I just gave up. It's easier by myself. I hate it, but it's easier."

At last Rhyme understood her reaction at seeing him for the first time. She was at ease with him because here was a man who was no threat to her. No sexual come-ons. Someone she wouldn't have to fend off. And perhaps a certain camaraderie too—as if they were both missing the same, crucial gene.

"You know," he joked, "you and me, we ought to get together and *not* have an affair."

She laughed. "So tell me about your wife. How long were you married?"

"Seven years. Six before the accident, one after."

"And she left you?"

"Nope. I left her. I didn't want her to feel guilty about it."

"Good of you."

"I'd have driven her out eventually. I'm a prick. You've only seen my good side." After a moment he asked, "This thing with Nick . . . it have anything to do with why you're leaving Patrol?"

"No. Well, yes."

"Gunshy?"

Finally she nodded. "Life on the street's different now. That's what did it to Nick, you know. What turned him. It's not like it was when Pop was walking his beat. Things were better then."

"You mean it's not like the *stories* your dad told you."

"Maybe," she conceded. Sachs slumped the chair. "The arthritis? That's true but it's not as serious as I pretend it is."

"I know," Rhyme said.

"You know? How?"

"I just looked at the evidence and drew some conclusions."

"Is that why you've been on my case all day? You knew I was faking?"

"I've been on your case," he said, "because you're better than you think you are."

She gave him a screwy look.

"Ah, Sachs, you remind me of me."

"I do?"

"Let me tell you a story. I'd been on crime scene detail maybe a year when we got a call from Homicide there was a guy found dead in an alley in Greenwich Village. All the sergeants were out and so I got elected to run the scene. I was twenty-six years old, remember. I go up there and check it out and it turns out the dead guy's the head of the City Health and Human Services. Now, what's he got all around him but a load of Polaroids? You should've seen some of those snaps—he'd been to one of those S&M clubs off Washington Street. Oh, and I forgot to mention, when they found him he was dressed in a stunning little black minidress and fishnet stockings.

"So, I secure the scene. All of a sudden a captain shows up and starts to cross the tape. I know he's planning to have those pictures disappear on the way to the evidence room but I was so naive I didn't care much about the pictures—I was just worried about somebody walking through the scene."

"P is for Protect the crime scene."

Rhyme chuckled. "So I didn't let him in. While he was standing at the tape screaming at me a dep com tried an end run. I told him no. *He* started screaming at me. The scene stays virgin till IRD's through with it, I told them. Guess who finally showed up?"

"The mayor?"

"Well, deputy mayor."

"And you held 'em all off?"

"Nobody got into that scene except Latents and Photography. Of course my payback was spending six months printing floaters. But we nailed the perp with some trace and a print off one of those Polaroids—happened to be the same snap the *Post* used on page one, as a matter of fact. Just like what you did yesterday morning, Sachs. Closing off the tracks and Eleventh Avenue."

"I didn't think about it," she said. "I just did it. Why're you looking at me that way?"

"Come on, Sachs. You *know* where you ought to be. On the street. Patrol, Major Crimes, IRD, doesn't matter . . . But Public Affairs? You'll rot there. It's a good job for some people but not you. Don't give up so fast."

"Oh, and you're *not* giving up? What about Berger?"

"Things're a little different with me."

Her glance questioned, They are? And she went prowling for a Kleenex. When she returned to the chair she asked, "You don't carry any corpses around with you?"

"I have in my day. They're all buried now."

"Tell me."

"Really, there's nothing—"

"Not true. I can tell. Come on—I showed you mine."

He felt an odd chill. He knew it wasn't dysreflexia. His smile faded.

"Rhyme, go on," she persisted. "I'd like to hear."

"Well, there was a case a few years ago," he said, "I made a mistake. A bad mistake."

"Tell me." She poured them each another finger of the Scotch.

"It was a domestic murder-suicide call. Husband and wife in a Chinatown apartment. He shot her, killed himself. I didn't have much time for the scene; I worked it fast. And I committed a classic error—I'd made up my mind about what I was going to find before I started looking. I found some fibers that I couldn't place but I assumed that the husband and wife'd tracked them in. I found the bullet fragments but didn't check them against the gun we found at the scene. I noticed the blowback pattern but didn't grid it to double-check the exact position of the gun. I did the search, signed off and went back to the office."

"What happened?"

"The scene had been staged. It was really a burglary-murder. And the perp had never left the apartment."

"What? He was still there?"

"After I left he crawled out from under the bed and started shooting. He killed one forensic tech and wounded an assistant ME. He got out on the street and there was a shootout with a couple of portables who'd heard the 10–13. The perp was shot up—he died later—but he killed one of the cops and wounded the other. He also shot up a family that'd just come out of a Chinese restaurant across the street. Used one of the kids as a shield."

"Oh, my God."

"Colin Stanton was the father's name. He wasn't hurt at all and he'd been an army medic—EMS said he probably could've saved his wife or one or both of the kids if he'd tried to stop the bleeding but he panicked and froze. He just stood there, watching them all die in front of him."

"Jesus, Rhyme. But it wasn't your fault. You—"

"Let me finish. That wasn't the end of it."

"No?"

"The husband went back home—upstate New York. Had a breakdown and went into a mental hospital for a while. He tried to kill himself. They put him under a suicide watch. First he tried to cut his wrist with a piece of paper—a magazine cover. Then he sneaked into the library and found a water glass in the librarian's bathroom, shattered it and slashed his wrists. They stitched him up okay and kept him in the mental hospital for another year or so. Finally they released him. A month or so after he was out he tried again. Used a knife." Rhyme added coolly, "That time it worked."

He'd learned about Stanton's death in an obituary faxed from the Albany County coroner to NYPD Public Affairs. Someone there had sent it to Rhyme via interoffice mail with a Post-It attached: *FYI—thought you'd be interested*, the officer had written.

"There was an IA investigation. Professional incompetence. They slapped my wrist. I think they should've fired me."

She sighed and closed her eyes for a moment. "And you're telling me you don't feel guilty about that?"

"Not anymore."

"I don't believe you."

"I served my time, Sachs. I lived with those bodies for a while. But I gave 'em up. If I hadn't, how could I have kept on working?"

After a long moment she said, "When I was eighteen I got a ticket. Speeding. I was doing ninety in a forty zone."

"Well."

"Dad said he'd front me the money for the fine but I'd have to pay him back. With interest. But you know what else he told me? He said he would've tanned my hide for running a red light or reckless driving. But going fast he understood. He told me, 'I know how you feel, honey. When you move they can't getcha.'" Sachs said to Rhyme, "If I couldn't drive, if I couldn't move, then maybe I'd do it too. Kill myself."

"I used to walk everywhere," Rhyme said. "I never did drive much. Haven't owned a car in twenty years. What kind do you have?"

"Nothing a snooty Manhattanite like you'd drive. A Chevy. Camaro. It was my father's."

"Who gave you the drill press. For working on cars, I assume?"

She nodded. "And a torque wrench. And spark-gap set. And my first set of ratcheting sockets—my thirteenth-birthday present." Laughing softly. "That Chevy, it's a wobbly-knob car. You know what that is? An American car. The radio and vents and light switches are all loose and cheesy. But the suspension's like a rock, it's light as an egg crate and I'll take on a BMW any day."

"And I'll be you have."

"Once or twice."

"Cars are status in the crip world," Rhyme explained. "We'd sit—or lie—around the ward in rehab and talk about what we could get out of our insurance companies. Wheelchair vans were the top of the heap. Next are hand-control cars. Which wouldn't do me any good of course." He squinted, testing his supple memory. "I haven't been in a car in years. I can't remember the last time."

"Got an idea," Sachs said suddenly. "Before your friend—Dr Berger—comes back, let me take you for a ride. Or is that a problem? Sitting up? You were saying that wheelchairs don't work for you."

"Well, no, wheelchairs're a problem. But a car? I think that'd be okay." He laughed. "A hundred and sixty-eight? Miles per hour?"

"That was a special day," Sachs said, nodding at the memory. "Good conditions. And no highway patrol."

The phone buzzed and Rhyme answered it himself. It was Lon Sellitto.

"We got S&S on all the target churches in Harlem. Dellray's in charge of that—man's become a true believer, Lincoln. You wouldn't recognize him. Oh, and I've got thirty portables and a ton of UN security cruising for any other churches we might've missed. If he doesn't show up, we're going to do a sweep of all of them at seven-thirty. Just in case he snuck in without us seeing him. I think we're going to nail him, Linc," the detective said, suspiciously enthusiastic for a New York City homicide cop.

"Okay, Lon, I'll send Amelia up to your CP around eight."

They hung up.

Thom knocked on the door before coming into the room.

As if he'd catch us in a compromising position, Rhyme laughed to himself.

"No more excuses," he said testily. "Bed. Now."

It was after 3:00 A.M. and Rhyme had left exhaustion far behind long ago. He was floating somewhere else. Above his body. He wondered if he'd start to hallucinate.

"Yes, mother," he said. "Officer Sachs's staying over, Thom. Could you get her a blanket, please?"

"What did you say?" Thom turned to face him.

"A blanket."

"No, after that," the aide said. "That word?"

"I don't know. 'Please'?"

Thom's eyes went wide with alarm. "Are you all right? You want me to get Pete Taylor back here? The head of Columbia-Presbyterian? The surgeon general?"

"See how this son of a bitch torments me?" Rhyme said to Sachs. "He never knows how close he comes to getting fired."

"A wake-up call for when?"

"Six-thirty should be fine," Rhyme said.

When he was gone, Rhyme asked, "Hey, Sachs, you like music?"

"Love it."

"What kind?"

"Oldies, doo-wop, Motown . . . How 'bout you? You seem like a classical kind of guy."

"See that closet there?"

"This one?"

"No, no, the other one. To the right. Open it up."

She did and gasped in amazement. The closet was a small room filled with close to a thousand CDs.

"It's like Tower Records."

"That stereo, see it on the shelf?"

She ran her hand over the dusty black Harmon Kardon.

"It cost more than my first car," Rhyme said. "I don't use it anymore."

"Why not?"

He didn't answer but said instead, "Put something on. Is it plugged in? It is? Good. Pick something."

A moment later she stepped out of the closet and walked over to the couch as Levi Stubbs and the Four Tops started singing about love.

It had been a year since there'd been a note of music in this room, Rhyme estimated. Silently he tried to answer Sachs's question about why he'd stopped listening. He couldn't.

Sachs lifted files and books off the couch. Lay back on it and thumbed through a copy of *Scenes of the Crime*.

"Can I have one?" she asked.

"Take ten."

"Will you . . ." Her voice braked to a halt.

"Sign it for you?" He laughed. She joined him. "How 'bout if I put my thumbprint on it? Graphoanalysts'll never give you more than an eighty-five percent probability of a handwriting match. But a thumbprint? Any friction-ridge expert'll certify it's mine."

He watched her read the first chapter. Her eyes drooped. She closed the book.

"Will you do something for me?" she asked.

"What?"

"Read to me. Something from the book. When Nick and I were together . . ." Her voice faded.

"What?"

"When we were together, a lot of times Nick'd read out loud before we went to sleep. Books, the paper, magazines . . . It's one of the things I miss the most."

"I'm a terrible reader," Rhyme confessed. "I sound like I'm reciting crime scene reports. But I've got this memory . . . It's pretty good. How 'bout if I just tell you about some scenes?"

"Would you?" She turned her back, pulled her navy blouse off and unstrapped the thin American Body Armor vest, tossed it aside. Beneath it she wore a mesh T-shirt and under that a sports bra. She pulled the blouse back on and lay on the couch, pulling the blanket over her, and curled up on her side, closed her eyes.

With the environmental-control unit Rhyme dimmed the lights.

"I always found the sites of death fascinating," he began. "They're like shrines. We're a lot more interested in where people bought the big one than where they were born. Take John Kennedy. A thousand people a day visit the Texas Book Depository in Dallas. How many you think make pilgrimages to some obstetrics ward in Boston?"

Rhyme nestled his head in the luxurious softness of the pillow. "Is this boring you?"

"No," she said. "Please don't stop."

"You know what I've always wondered about, Sachs?"

"Tell me."

"It's fascinated me for years—Calvary. Two thousand years ago. Now, *there's* a crime scene I'd like to've worked. I know what you're going to say: But we know the perps. Well, do we? All we really know is what the witnesses tell us. Remember what I say—never trust a wit. Maybe those Bible accounts aren't what happened at all. Where's the *proof*? The PE. The nails, blood, sweat, the spear, the cross, the vinegar. Sandal prints and friction ridges."

Rhyme turned his head slightly to the left and he continued to talk about crime scenes and evidence until Sachs's chest rose and fell steadily and faint strands of her fiery red hair blew back and forth under her shallow breath. With his left index finger he flipped through the ESU control and shut off the light. He too was soon asleep.

A faint light of dawn was in the sky.

Awakening, Carole Ganz could see it through the chicken-wire-impregnated glass above her head. Pammy. Oh, baby . . . Then she thought of Ron. And all her possessions sitting in that terrible basement. The money, the yellow knapsack . . .

Mostly, though, she was thinking about Pammy.

Something had wakened her from a light, troubled sleep. What was it?

The pain from her wrist? It throbbed horribly. She adjusted herself slightly. She—

The tubular howl of a pipe organ and a rising chorus of voices filled the room again.

That's what had wakened her. Music. A crashing wave

of music. The church wasn't abandoned. There were people around! She laughed to herself. Somebody would—

And that was when she remembered the bomb.

Carole peered around the filing cabinet. It was still there, teetering on the edge of the table. It had the crude look of real bombs and murder weapons—not the slick, shiny gadgets you see in movies. Sloppy tape, badly stripped wires, dirty gasoline . . . Maybe it's a dud, she thought. In the daylight it didn't look so dangerous.

Another burst of music. It came from directly over her head. Accompanied by a shuffling of footsteps. A door closed. Creaks and groans as people moved around the old, dry wood floors. Plumes of dust fell from the joists.

The soaring voices were cut off in mid-passage. A moment later they started singing again.

Carole banged with her feet but the floor was concrete, the walls brick. She tried to scream but the sound was swallowed by the gag. The rehearsal continued, the solemn, vigorous music rattling through the basement.

After ten minutes Carole collapsed on the floor in exhaustion. Her eyes were drawn back to the bomb again. Now the light was better and she could see the timer clearly.

Carole squinted. The timer!

It wasn't a dud at all. The arrow was set for 6:15 A.M. The dial showed the time was now 5:30.

Squirming her way farther behind the filing cabinet, Carole began to kick the metal sides with her knee. But whatever faint noises the blows made immediately vanished in the booming, mournful rendition of "Swing Low, Sweet Chariot" filling the church basement from above.

4

DOWN TO THE BONE

"This only is denied the Gods: the power to remake the past."

Aristotle

Sunday, 5:45 A.M., to Monday, 7:00 P.M.

TWENTY-SEVEN

He awoke to a scent. As he often did.

And—as on many mornings—he didn't at first open his eyes but just remained in his half-seated position, trying to figure out what the unfamiliar smell might be:

The gassy scent of dawn air? The dew on the oil-slick streets? Damp plaster? He tried to detect the scent of Amelia Sachs but could not.

His thoughts skipped over her and continued. What *was* it?

Cleanser? No.

A chemical from Cooper's impromptu lab?

No, he recognized all of those.

It was . . . Ah, yes . . . marking pen.

Now he could open his eyes and—after a glance at sleeping Sachs to make certain she hadn't deserted him—found himself gazing at the Monet poster on the wall. That's where the smell was coming from. The hot, humid air of this August morning had wilted the paper and brought the scent out.

- knows CS proc.
- possibly has record
- knows FR prints
- gun = .32 Colt
- Ties vics w/ unusual knots
- "Old" appeals to him
- Called one vic "Hanna"
- Knows basic German
- Underground appeals to him

UNSUB 823			
Appearance	Residence	Vehicle	Other
• Caucasian male, slight build • Dark clothing • Old gloves, reddish kidskin • Aftershave; to cover up other scent? • Ski mask? Navy blue? • Gloves are dark • Aftershave = Brut • Hair color not brown • Deep scar, index finger • Casual clothes • Gloves faded? Stained?	• Prob. has safe house • Located near; B'way & 82nd, ShopRite Greenwich & Bank, ShopRite 8th Ave. & 24th ShopRite Houston & Lafayette, ShopRite • Old building, pink marble • At least 100 years old, prob. mansion or institutional	• Yellow Cab • Recent model sedan • Lt. gray, silver, biege • Rental car; prob. stolen • Hertz, silver Taurus, this year's model	• knows CS proc. • possibly has record • knows FR prints • gun = .32 Colt • Ties vics w/ unusual knots • "Old" appeals to him • Called one vic "Hanna" • Knows basic German • Underground appeals to him • Dual personalities • Maybe priest, soc. worker, counselor • Unusual wear on shoes, reads a lot? • Listened as he broke vic's finger • Left snake as slap at investigators

The wall clock's pale numbers glowed: 5:45 A.M. His eyes returned to the poster. He couldn't see it clearly, just a ghostly pattern of pure white against a lesser white. But there was enough light from the dawn sky to make out most of the words.

- Dual personalities
- Maybe priest, soc. worker, counselor
- Unusual wear on shoes, reads a lot?
- Listened as he broke vic's finger
- Left snake as slap at investigators

The falcons were waking. He was aware of a flutter at the window. Rhyme's eyes skipped over the chart again. In his office at IRD he'd nailed up a dozen erasable marker boards and on them he'd keep a tally of the characteristics of the unsubs in major cases. He remembered: pacing, staring at them, wondering about the people they described.

Molecules of paint, mud, pollen, leaf . . .

- Old building, pink marble

Thinking about a clever jewel thief he and Lon had collared ten years ago. At Central Booking the perp had coyly said they'd never find the loot from the prior jobs but if they'd consider a plea he'd tell them where he'd hidden it. Rhyme had responded, "Well, we *have* been having some trouble figuring out where it is."

"I'm sure you have," the snide crook said.

"See," Rhyme continued, "we've narrowed it down to the stone wall in the coal bin of a Colonial farmhouse on the Connecticut River. About five miles north of Long Island Sound. I just can't tell whether the house is on the east bank or the west bank of the river."

When the story made the rounds the phrase everybody used to describe the expression on the perp's face was: You had to fucking be there.

Maybe it *is* magic, Sachs, he thought.

- At least 100 years old,
  prob. mansion or
  institutional

He scanned the poster once again and closed his eyes, leaning back into his glorious pillow. It was then that he felt the jolt. Almost like a slap on his face. The shock rose to his scalp like spreading fire. Eyes wide, locked onto the poster.

- "Old" appeals to him

"Sachs!" he cried. "Wake up!"

She stirred and sat up. "What? What's . . . ?"

Old, old, old . . .

"I made a mistake," he said tersely. "There's a problem."

She thought at first it was something medical and she leapt from the couch, reaching for Thom's medical bag.

"No, the clues, Sachs, the *clues* . . . I got it wrong." His breathing was rapid and he ground his teeth together as he thought.

She pulled her clothes on, sat back, her fingers disappearing automatically into her scalp, scratching. "What, Rhyme? What is it?"

"The church. It might not be in Harlem." He repeated, "I made a mistake."

Just like with the perp who killed Colin Stanton's family. In criminalistics you can nail down a hundred clues perfectly and it's the one you miss that gets people killed.

"What time is it?" she asked.

"Quarter to six, a little after. Get the newspaper. The church-services schedule."

Sachs found the paper, thumbed through it. Then looked up. "What're you thinking?"

"Eight twenty-three's obsessed with what's old. If he's after an old black church then he might not mean uptown. Philip Payton started the Afro-American Realty Company in Harlem in 1900. There were two other black settlements in the city. Downtown where the courthouses are now and San Juan Hill.

They're mostly white now but . . . Oh, what the hell was I thinking of?"

"Where's San Juan Hill?"

"Just north of Hell's Kitchen. On the West Side. It was named in honor of all the black soldiers who fought in the Spanish–American War."

She read through the paper.

"Downtown churches," she said. "Well, in Battery Park there's the Seamen's Institute. A chapel there. They have services. Trinity. Saint Paul's."

"That wasn't the black area. Farther north and east."

"A Presbyterian church in Chinatown."

"Any Baptist. Evangelical?"

"No, nothing in that area at all. There's—Oh, hell." With resignation in her eyes she sighed. "Oh, no."

Rhyme understood. "Sunrise service!"

She was nodding. "Holy Tabernacle Baptist . . . Oh, Rhyme, there's a gospel service starting at six. Fifty-ninth and Eleventh Avenue."

"That's San Juan Hill! Call them!"

She grabbed the phone and dialed the number. She stood, head down, fiercely plucking an eyebrow and shaking her head. "Answer, answer . . . Hell. It's a recording. The minister must be out of his office." She said into the receiver, "This is the New York Police Department. We have reason to believe there's a firebomb in your church. Evacuate as fast as possible." She hung up, pulled her shoes on.

"Go, Sachs. You've got to get there. Now!"

"Me?"

"We're closer than the nearest precinct. You can be there in ten minutes."

She jogged toward the door, slinging her utility belt around her waist.

"I'll call the precinct," he yelled as she leapt down the stairs, hair a red cloud around her head. "And Sachs, if you ever wanted to drive fast, do it now."

The RRV wagon skidded into 81st Street, speeding west.

Sachs burst into the intersection at Broadway, skidded hard

and whacked a *New York Post* vending machine, sending it through Zabar's window before she brought the wagon under control. She remembered all the crime scene equipment in the back. Rear-heavy vehicle, she thought; don't corner at fifty.

Then down Broadway. Brake at the intersections. Check left. Check right. Clear. Punch it!

She peeled off on Ninth Avenue at Lincoln Center and headed south. I'm only—

Oh, hell!

A mad stop on screaming tires.

The street was closed.

A row of blue sawhorses blocked Ninth for a street fair later that morning. A banner proclaimed, *Crafts and Delicacies of all Nations. Hand in hand, we are all one.*

Gaw . . . *damn* UN! She backed up a half block and got the wagon up to fifty before she slammed into the first sawhorse. Spreading portable aluminum tables and wooden display racks in her wake, she tore a swath through the deserted fair. Two blocks later the wagon broke through the southern barricade and she skidded west on Fifty-ninth, using far more of the sidewalk than she meant to.

There was the church, a hundred yards away.

Parishioners on the steps—parents, little girls in frilly white and pink dresses, young boys in dark suits and white shirts, their hair in gangsta knobs or fades.

And from a basement window, a small puff of gray smoke.

Sachs slammed the accelerator to the floor, the engine roaring.

Grabbing the radio. "RRV Two to Central, K?"

And in the instant it took her to glance down at the Motorola to make sure the volume was up, a big Mercedes slipped out of the alley directly into her path.

A fast glimpse of the family inside, eyes wide in horror, as the father slammed on the brakes.

Sachs instinctively spun the wheel hard to the left, putting the wagon into controlled skid. Come on, she was begging the tires, grip, grip, grip! But the oily asphalt was loose from the heat of the past few days and covered with dew. The wagon danced over the road like a hydrofoil.

The rear end met the Merc's front flat-on at fifty miles an hour. With an explosive boom the 560 sheared off the rear right side of the wagon. The black CS suitcases flew into the air, breaking open and strewing their contents along the street. Church-goers dove for cover from the splinters of glass and plastic and sheet metal.

The air bag popped and deflated, stunning Sachs. She covered her face as the wagon tumbled over a row of cars and through a newsstand then skidded to a stop upside down. Newspapers and plastic evidence bags floated to the ground like tiny paratroopers.

Held upside down by the harness, blinded by her hair, Sachs wiped blood from her torn forehead and lip and tried to pop the belt release. It held tight. Hot gasoline flowed into the car and trickled along her arm. She pulled a switchblade from her back pocket, flicked the knife open and cut the seat belt. Falling, she nearly skewered herself on the knife and lay, gasping, choking on the gas fumes.

Come on, girl, get out. Out!

The doors were jammed closed and there was no escape through the crushed rear end of the wagon. Sachs began kicking the windows. The glass wouldn't break. She drew her foot back and slammed it hard into the cracked windshield. No effect, except that she nearly sprained her ankle.

Her gun!

She slapped her hip; the gun had been torn from the holster and tossed somewhere inside the car. Feeling the hot drizzle of gasoline on her arm and shoulder, she searched frantically through the papers and CS equipment littering the ceiling of the station wagon.

Then she saw the clunky Glock near the dome light. She swept it up and aimed at the side window.

Go ahead. Backdrop's clear, no spectators yet.

Then she hesitated. Would the muzzle flash ignite the gas?

She held the gun as far away from her soaked uniform blouse as she could, debating. Then squeezed the trigger.

TWENTY-EIGHT

Five shots, a star pattern, and even then the honest General Motors glass held firm.

Three more blasts, deafening her in the confines of the wagon. But at least the gas didn't explode.

She began to kick again. Finally the window burst outward in a cascade of blue-green ice. Just as she rolled out the interior of the wagon exploded with a breathless *woosh*.

Stripping down to her T-shirt, she flung away her gas-soaked uniform blouse and bulletproof vest and tossed aside the head-set mike. Felt her ankle wobble but sprinted to the front door of the church, past the fleeing churchgoers and choir. The ground floor was filled with bubbling smoke. Nearby, a section of the floor rippled and steamed and then burst into flames.

The minister appeared suddenly, choking, tears streaming down his face. He was dragging an unconscious woman behind him. Sachs helped him get her to the door.

"Where's the basement?" she asked.

He coughed hard, shook his head.

"Where?" she cried, thinking of Carole Ganz and her little daughter. "The *basement*?"

"There. But . . ."

On the other side of the patch of burning floor.

Sachs could barely see it, the smoke was so thick. A wall collapsed in front of them, the old joists and posts behind it snapping and firing sparks and jets of hot gas, which hissed into the cloudy room. She hesitated, then started for the basement door.

The minister took her arm. "Wait." He opened a closet

and grabbed a fire extinguisher, yanked the arming pin. "Let's go."

Sachs shook her head. "Not you. Keep checking up here. Tell the fire department there's a police officer and another victim in the basement."

Sachs was sprinting now.

When you move . . .

She jumped over the fiery patch of floor. But because of the smoke she misjudged the distance to the wall; it was closer than she'd thought and she slammed into the wood paneling then fell backwards, rolling as her hair brushed the fire, some strands igniting. Gagging on the stink, she crushed the flames out and started to push herself to her feet. The floor, weakened by the flames beneath, broke under her weight and her face crashed into the oak. She felt the blaze in the basement lick her hands and arms as she yanked her hands back.

Rolling away from the edge she climbed to her feet and reached for the knob to the basement door. She stopped suddenly.

Come on, girl, think better! Feel a door before opening it. If it's too hot and you let oxygen into a superheated room it'll ignite and the backdraft'll fry your ass good. She touched the wood. It was scorching hot.

Then thought: But what the hell else can I do?

Spitting on her hand, she gripped the knob fast, twisting it open and releasing it just before the burn seared her palm.

The door burst open and a cloud of smoke and sparks shot outward.

"Anybody down there?" she called and started down.

The lower stairs were burning. She blasted them with a short burst of carbon dioxide and leapt into the murky basement. She broke through the second-to-last step, pitching forward. The extinguisher clattered to the floor as she grabbed the railing just in time to save her leg from snapping.

Pulling herself out of the broken step, Sachs squinted through the haze. The smoke wasn't as bad down here—it was rising—but the flames were raging all around her. The extinguisher had rolled under a burning table. Forget it! She ran through the smoke.

"Hello?" she shouted.

No answer.

Then remembered that Unsub 823 used duct tape; he liked his vics silent.

She kicked in a small doorway and looked inside the boiler room. There was a door leading outside but burning debris blocked it completely. Beside it stood the fuel tank, which was now surrounded by flames.

It won't explode, Sachs remembered from the academy—the lecture on arson. Fuel oil doesn't explode. Kick aside the debris and push the door open. Clear your escape route. *Then* go look for the woman and the girl.

She hesitated, watching the flames roll over the side of the oil tank.

It won't explode, it won't explode.

She started forward, edging toward the door.

It won't—

The tank suddenly puffed out like a heated soda can and split down the middle. The oil squirted into the air, igniting in a huge orange spume. A fiery pool formed on the floor and flowed toward Sachs.

Won't explode. Okay. But it burns pretty fucking well. She leapt back through the door, slammed it shut. So much for her escape route.

Backing toward the stairs, choking now, keeping low, looking for any signs of Carole and Maggie. Could 823 have changed the rules? Could he have given up on basements and put these vics in the church attic?

Crack.

A fast look upward. She saw a large oak beam, rippling with flames, start to fall.

With a scream Sachs leapt aside, but tripped and landed hard on her back, staring at the huge falling bar of wood streaking directly at her face and chest. Instinctively she held her hands up.

A huge bang as the beam landed on a child's Sunday-school chair. It stopped inches from Sachs's head. She crawled out from underneath and rolled to her feet.

Looking around the room, peering through the darkening smoke.

Hell no, she thought suddenly. I'm not losing another one.

Choking, Sachs turned back to the fire and staggered toward the one corner she hadn't checked.

As she jogged forward a leg shot out from behind a file cabinet and tripped her.

Hands flying outward, Sachs landed face down inches from a pool of burning oil. She rolled to her side, drawing her weapon and swinging it into the panicked face of a blond woman struggling to sit up.

Sachs pulled the gag off her mouth and the woman spit black mucus. She gagged for a moment, a deep, dying sound.

"Carole Ganz?"

She nodded.

"Your daughter?" Sachs cried.

"Not . . . here. My hands! The cuffs."

"No time. Come on." Sachs cut Carole's ankles free with her switchblade.

It was then that she saw, against the wall by the window, a melting plastic bag.

The planted clues! The ones that told where the little girl would be. She stepped toward it. But with a deafening bang the door to the boiler room cracked in half, spewing a six-inch tidal wave of burning oil over the floor, surrounding the bag, which disintegrated instantly.

Sachs stared for a moment and then heard the woman's scream. All the stairs were blazing now. Sachs knocked the fire extinguisher out from under the smoldering table. The handle and nozzle had melted away and the metal canister was too hot to grasp. With her knife she cut a patch off her uniform blouse and lifted the crackling extinguisher by its neck, flung it to the top of the burning stairs. It staggered for a moment, like an uncertain bowling pin, and then started down.

Sachs drew her Glock and when the red cylinder was halfway down, fired one round.

The extinguisher erupted in a huge booming explosion; pieces of red shrapnel from the casing hissed over their heads. The mushroom cloud of carbon dioxide and powder settled over the stairs and momentarily dampened most of the flames.

"Now, move!" Sachs shouted.

Together they took the steps two at a time, Sachs carrying

her own weight and half the woman's, and pushed through the doorway into the inferno on the first floor. They hugged the wall as they stumbled toward the exit, while above them stained-glass windows burst and rained hot shards—the colorful bodies of Jesus and matthew and Mary and God Himself—down upon the bent backs of the escaping women.

TWENTY-NINE

Forty minutes later, Sachs had been salved and bandaged and stitched and had sucked so much pure oxygen she felt like she was tripping. She sat beside Carole Ganz. They stared at what was left of the church. Which was virtually nothing.

Only two walls remained and, curiously, a portion of the third floor, jutting into space above a lunar landscape of ash and debris piled in the basement.

"Pammy, Pammy . . ." Carole moaned, then retched and spit. She took her own oxygen mask to her face, leaned back, weary and in pain.

Sachs examined another alcohol-soaked rag with which she was wiping the blood from her face. The rags had started out brown and were now merely pink. The wounds weren't serious—a cut on her forehead, swatches of second-degree burns on her arm and hand. Her lips were no longer flawless, however; the lower one had been cut deeply in the crash, the tear requiring three stitches.

Carole was suffering from smoke inhalation and a broken wrist. An impromptu cast covered her left wrist and she cradled it, head down, speaking through clenched teeth. Every breath was an alarming wheeze. "That son of a bitch." Coughing. "Why . . . Pammy? Why on earth? A three-year-old child!" She wiped angry tears with the back of her uninjured arm.

"Maybe he doesn't want to hurt her. So he just brought you to the church."

"No," she spat out angrily. "He doesn't care about her. He's sick! I saw the way he looked at her. I'm going to kill him. I'm going to fucking kill him." The harsh words dissolved into a harsher bout of coughing.

Sachs winced in pain. She'd unconsciously dug a nail into a burned fingertip. She pulled out her watchbook. "Can you tell me what happened?"

Between bouts of sobbing and throaty coughs, Carole told her the story of the kidnapping.

"You want me to call anybody?" Sachs asked. "Your husband?"

Carole didn't answer. She drew her knees up to her chin, hugged herself, wheezing roughly.

With her scalded right hand Sachs squeezed the woman's biceps and repeated the question.

"My husband . . ." She stared at Sachs with an eerie look. "My husband's dead."

"Oh, I'm sorry."

Carole grew groggy from the sedative and a woman medic helped her into the ambulance to get some rest. Sachs looked up and saw Lon Sellitto and Jerry Banks running toward her from the burned-out church.

"Jesus, officer." Sellitto was surveying the carnage in the street. "What about the girl?"

Sachs nodded. "He's still got her."

Banks said, "You okay?"

"Nothing serious." Sachs glanced toward the ambulance. "The vic, Carole, she doesn't have any money, no place to stay. She's in town to work for the UN. Think you could make some calls, detective? See if they could set her up for a while?"

"Sure," Sellitto said.

"And the planted clues?" Banks asked. He winced as he touched a bandage over his right eyebrow.

"Gone," Sachs said. "I saw them. In the basement. Couldn't get to them in time. Burned up and buried."

"Oh, man," Banks muttered. "What's going to happen to the little girl?"

What does he *think's* going to happen to her?

She walked back toward the wreck of the IRD wagon, found the headset. She pulled it on and was about to call in a patch request to Rhyme but hesitated then lifted off the mike. What could he tell her anyway? She looked at the church. How can you work a crime scene when there *is* no scene?

She was standing with her hands on her hips, staring out onto the smoldering hulk of the building, when she heard a sound she couldn't place. A whining, mechanical sound. She paid no attention to it until she was aware of Lon Sellitto pausing as he dusted ash off his wrinkled shirt. He said, "I don't believe it."

She turned toward the street.

A large black van was parked a block away. A hydraulic ramp was protruding off the side and something sat on it. She squinted. One of those bomb squad robots, it seemed. The ramp lowered to the sidewalk and the robot rolled off.

Then she laughed out loud.

The contraption turned toward them and started to move. The wheelchair reminded her of a Pontiac Firebird, candy-apple red. It was one of those electric models, small rear wheels, a large battery and motor mounted underneath.

Thom walked along beside it but Lincoln Rhyme himself was driving—in control, she observed wryly—via a straw that he held in his mouth. His movements were oddly graceful. Rhyme pulled up to her and stopped.

"All right, I lied," he said abruptly.

She exhaled a sigh. "About your back? When you said you couldn't use a wheelchair."

"I'm confessing I lied. You're going to be mad, Amelia. So be mad and get it over with."

"You ever notice when you're in a good mood you call me Sachs, when you're in a bad mood, you call me Amelia?"

"I'm not in a bad mood," he snapped.

"He really isn't," Thom agreed. "He just hates to get caught at anything." The aide nodded toward the impressive wheelchair. She glanced at the side. It was made by the Action Company, a Storm Arrow model. "He had this in the closet downstairs all the while he spun his pathetic little tale of woe. Oh, I let him have it for that."

"No annotations, Thom, thank you. I'm apologizing, all right? I. Am. Sorry."

"He's had it for years," Thom continued. "Learned the sip-'n'-puff cold. That's the straw control. He's really very good at it. By the way, he always calls *me* Thom. I *never* get preferential last-name treatment."

"I got tired of being stared at," Rhyme said matter-of-factly. "So I stopped going for joyrides." Then glanced at her torn lip. "Hurt?"

She touched her mouth, which was bent into a grin. "Stings like hell."

Rhyme glanced sideways. "And what happened to you, Banks? Shaving your forehead now?"

"Walked into a fire truck." The young man grinned and touched the bandage again.

"Rhyme," Sachs began, smiling no longer. "There's nothing here. He's got the little girl and I couldn't get to the planted PE in time."

"Ah, Sachs, there's always *something*. Have faith in the teachings of Monsieur Locard."

"I saw them burn up, the clues. And if there was anything left at all, it's all buried under tons of debris."

"Then we'll look for the clues he didn't mean to leave. We'll do this scene together, Sachs. You and me. Come on."

He gave two short breaths into the straw and started forward. They'd got ten feet nearer the church when she said suddenly, "Wait."

He braked to a stop.

"You're getting careless, Rhyme. Get some rubber bands on those wheels. Wouldn't want to confuse your prints with the unsub's."

"Where do we start?"

"We need a sample of the ash," Rhyme said. "There were some clean paint cans in the back of the wagon. See if you can find one."

She collected a can from the remains of the RRV.

"You know where the fire started?" Rhyme asked.

"Pretty much."

"Take a sample of ash—a pint or two—as close to the point of origin as you can get."

"Right," she said, climbing up on a five-foot-high wall of

brick—all that remained of the north side of the church. She peered down into the smoky pit at her feet.

A fire marshal called, "Hey, officer, we haven't secured the area yet. It's dangerous."

"Not as dangerous as the last time I was there," she answered. And holding the handle of the can in her teeth started down the wall.

Lincoln Rhyme watched her but he was really seeing himself, three and a half years ago, pull his suit jacket off and climb down into the construction site at the subway entrance near City Hall. "Sachs," Rhyme called. She turned. "Be careful. I saw what was left of the RRV. I don't want to lose you twice in one day."

She nodded and then disappeared over the edge of the wall.

After a few minutes Rhyme barked to Banks, "Where is she?"

"I don't know."

"What I'm saying is, could you go check on her?"

"Oh, sure." He walked to the wall, looked over.

"Well?" Rhyme asked.

"It's a mess."

"Of *course* it's a mess. Do you see her?"

"No."

"Sachs?" Rhyme shouted.

There was a long groan of wood then a crash. Dust rose.

"Sachs? Amelia?"

No answer.

Just as he was about to send ESU in after her they heard her voice. "Incoming."

"Jerry?" Rhyme called.

"Ready," the young detective called.

The can came flying up out of the basement. Banks caught it one-handed. Sachs climbed out of the basement, wiping her hands on her slacks, wincing.

"Okay?"

She nodded.

"Now, let's work the alley," Rhyme ordered. "There's traffic at all hours around here so he'd want the car off the street while he got her inside. That's where he parked. Used that door right there."

"How do you know?"

"There're two ways to open locked doors—without explosives, that is. Locks and hinges. This one'd be dead-bolted from the inside so he took the pins out of the hinges. See, he didn't bother to put them in very far again when he left."

They started at the door and worked their way to the back of the grim canyon, the smoldering building on their right. They moved a foot at a time, Sachs training the PoliLight on the cobblestones. "I want tire treads," Rhyme announced. "I want to know where his trunk was."

"Here," she said, examining the ground. "Treads. But I don't know whether these're the front or the rear tires. He might've backed in."

"Are they clear or fuzzy? The treadmarks?"

"A little fuzzy."

"Then those're the front." He laughed at her bewildered expression. "You're the automotive expert, Sachs. Next time you get in a car and start it see if you don't spin the wheel a little before you start moving. To see if the tires are pointed straight. The front treads're always fuzzier than the rear. Now, the stolen car was a '97 Ford Taurus. It measures 197.5 stem to stern, wheelbase 108.5. Approximately 45 inches from the center of the rear tire to the trunk. Measure that and vacuum."

"Come on, Rhyme. How'd you know that?"

"Looked it up this morning. You do the vic's clothing?"

"Yep. Nails and hair too. And, Rhyme, get this: the little girl's name is Pam but he called her Maggie. Just like he did with the German girl—he called her Hanna, remember?"

"You mean his other persona did," Rhyme said. "I wonder who the characters are in his little play."

"I'm going to vacuum around the door too," she announced. Rhyme watched her—face cut and hair uneven, singed short in spots. She vacuumed the base of the door and just as he was about to remind her that crime scenes were three-dimensional she ran the vacuum up and around the jamb.

"He probably looked inside before he took her in," she said and began vacuuming the windowsills too.

Which would have been Rhyme's next order.

He listened to the whine of the Dustbuster. But second by second he was fading away. Into the past, some hours before.

"I'm—" Sachs began.

"Shhh," he said.

Like the walks he now took, like the concerts he now attended, like so many of the conversations he had, Rhyme was slipping deeper and deeper into his consciousness. And when he got to a particular place—even he had no idea where—he found he wasn't alone. He was picturing a short man wearing gloves, dark sports clothes, a ski mask. Climbing out of the silver Ford Taurus sedan, which smelled of cleanser and new car. The woman—Carole Ganz—was in the trunk, her child captive in an old building made of pink marble and expensive brick. He saw the man dragging the woman from the car.

Almost a memory, it was that clear.

Popping the hinges, pulling open the door, dragging her inside, tying her up. He started to leave but paused. He walked to a place where he could look back and see Carole clearly. Just like he'd stared down at the man he'd buried at the railroad tracks yesterday morning.

Just like he'd chained Tammie Jean Colfax to the pipe in the center of the room. So he could get a good look at her.

But why? Rhyme wondered. Why does he look? To make sure the vic can't escape? To make sure he hasn't left anything behind? To—

His eyes sprang open; the indistinct apparition of Unsub 823 vanished. "Sachs! Remember the Colfax scene? When you found the glove print?"

"Sure."

"You said he was watching her, that's the reason he chained her out in the open. But you didn't know why. Well, I figured it out. He watches the vics because he *has to*."

Because it's his nature.

"What do you mean?"

"Come on!"

Rhyme sipped twice into the straw control, which turned the Arrow wheelchair around. Then puffed hard and he started forward.

He wheeled to the sidewalk, sipped hard into the straw to stop. He squinted as he looked all around him. "He wants to see his victims. And I'm betting he wanted to see the parishioners too. From someplace he thought was safe. Where he didn't bother to sweep up afterwards."

He was gazing across the street at the only secluded vantage point on the block: the outdoor patio of a restaurant opposite the church.

"There! Sweep it clean, Sachs."

She nodded, slipped a new clip into her Glock, grabbed evidence bags, a pair of pencils and the Dustbuster. He saw her run across the street and work her way up the steps carefully, examining them. "He was here," she shouted. "There's a glove print. And the shoeprint—it's worn just like the other ones."

Yes! Rhyme thought. Oh, this felt good. The warm sun, the air, the spectators. And the excitement of the chase.

When you move they can't getcha.

Well, if *we* move faster, maybe we can.

Rhyme happened to glance at the crowd and saw that some people were staring at him. But far more were watching Amelia Sachs.

For fifteen minutes she pored over the scene and when she returned she held up a small evidence bag.

"What did you find, Sachs? His driver's license? His birth certificate?"

"Gold," she said, smiling. "I found some gold."

THIRTY

"Come on, people," Rhyme called. "We've got to move on this one. Before he gets the girl to the next scene. I mean *move*!"

Thom did a sitting transfer to get Rhyme from the Storm Arrow back into bed, perching him momentarily on a sliding board and then easing him back into the Clinitron. Sachs glanced at the wheelchair elevator that had been built into one of the bedroom closets—it was the one he hadn't wanted her to open when he was directing her to the stereo and CDs.

Rhyme lay still for a moment, breathing deeply from the exertion.

"The clues're gone," he reminded them. "There's no way we can figure out where the next scene is. So we're going for the big one—his safe house."

"You think you can find it?" Sellitto asked.

Do we have a choice? Rhyme thought, and said nothing.

Banks hurried up the stairs. He hadn't even stepped into the bedroom before Rhyme blurted, "What did they say? Tell me. *Tell* me."

Rhyme knew that the tiny fleck of gold that Sachs had found was beyond the capabilities of Mel Cooper's impromptu lab. He'd asked the young detective to speed it down to the FBI's regional PERT office and have it analyzed.

"They'll call us in the next half hour."

"Half *hour*?" Rhyme muttered. "Didn't they give it priority?"

"You bet they did. Dellray was there. You should've seen him. He ordered every other case put on hold and said if the metallurgy report wasn't in your hands ASAP there'd be one mean mother—you get the picture—reaming their—you get the rest of the picture."

"Rhyme," Sachs said, "there's something else the Ganz woman said that might be important. He told her he'd let her go if she agreed to let him flail her foot."

"Flail?"

"Cut the skin off it."

"*Flay*," Rhyme corrected.

"Oh. Anyway, he didn't do anything. She said it was—in the end—like he couldn't bring himself to cut her."

"Just like the first scene—the man by the railroad tracks," Sellitto offered.

"Interesting. . . ." Rhyme reflected, "I thought he'd cut the vic's finger to discourage anybody from stealing the ring. But maybe not. Look at his behavior: Cutting the finger off the cabbie and carrying it around. Cutting the German girl's arm and leg. Stealing the bones and the snake skeleton. Listening while he broke Everett's finger . . . There's something about the way he sees his victims. Something . . ."

"Anatomical?"

"Exactly, Sachs."

"Except the Ganz woman," Sellitto said.

"My point," Rhyme said. "He could've cut her and still kept her alive for us. But something stopped him. What?"

Sellitto said, "What's different about her? Can't be that she's a woman. Or she's from out of town. So was the German girl."

"Maybe he didn't want to hurt her in front of her daughter," Banks said.

"No," Rhyme said, laughing grimly, "compassion isn't his thing."

Sachs said suddenly, "But that *is* one thing different about her—she's a mother."

Rhyme considered this. "That could be it. Mother and daughter. It didn't carry enough weight for him to let them go. But it stopped him from torturing her. Thom, jot that down. With a question mark." He then asked Sachs, "Did she say anything else about the way he looked?"

Sachs flipped through her notebook.

"Same as before." She read. "Ski mask, slight build, black gloves, he—"

"*Black* gloves?" Rhyme looked at the chart on the wall. "Not red?"

"She said black. I asked her if she was sure."

"And that other bit of leather was black too, wasn't it, Mel? Maybe *that* was from the gloves. So what's the red leather from?"

Cooper shrugged. "I don't know but we found a couple pieces of it. So it's something close to him."

Rhyme looked over the evidence bags. "What else did we find?"

"The trace we vacuumed in the alley and by the doorway." Sachs tapped the filter over a sheet of newsprint and Cooper went over it with a loupe. "Plenty o' nothin'," he announced. "Mostly soil. Bits of minerals. Manhattan mica schist. Feldspar."

Which was found throughout the city.

"Keep going."

"Decomposed leaves. That's about it."

"How about the Ganz woman's clothes?"

Cooper and Sachs opened the newspaper and examined the trace.

"Mostly soil," Cooper said. "And a few bits of what look like stone."

"Where did he keep her at his safe house? Exactly?"

"On the floor in the basement. She said it was a dirt floor."

"Excellent!" Rhyme shouted. To Cooper: "Burn it. The soil."

Cooper placed a sample in the GC-MS. They waited impatiently for the results. Finally the computer screen blinked. The grid resembled a lunar landscape.

"All right, Lincoln. Interesting. I'm reading off-the-charts for tannin and—"

"Sodium carbonate?"

"Ain't he amazin'?" Cooper laughed. "How'd you know?"

"They were used in tanneries in the eighteenth and nineteenth centuries. The tannic acid cures the hide and the alkaline fixes it. So, his safe house is near the site of an old tannery."

He smiled. Couldn't help himself. He thought: You hear foot-steps, 823? That's us behind you.

His eyes slipped to the Randel Survey map. "Because of the smell no one wanted tanneries in their neighborhoods so the commissioners restricted them. I know there were some on the Lower East Side. And in West Greenwich Village—when it literally *was* a village, a suburb of the city. And then on the far West Side in the Fifties—near the stockyard tunnel where we found the German girl. Oh, and in Harlem in the early 1900s."

Rhyme glanced at the list of grocery stores—the locations of the ShopRites that sold veal shanks. "Chelsea's out. No tanning there. Harlem too—no *ShopRites* there. So, it's the West Village, Lower East Side or Midtown West Side—Hell's Kitchen again. Which he seems to like."

Only about ten square miles, Rhyme estimated cynically. He'd figured out on his first day on the job that it was easier to hide in Manhattan than in the North Woods.

"Let's keep going. What about the stone in Carole's clothes?"

Cooper was bent over the microscope. "Okay. Got it."

"Patch it in to me, Mel."

Rhyme's computer screen burst to life and he watched the flecks of stone and crystal, like brilliant asteroids.

"Move it around," Rhyme instructed. Three substances were bonded together.

"The one on the left is marble, pinkish," Cooper said. "Like what we found before. And in between, that gray stuff . . ."

"It's mortar. And the other is brownstone." Rhyme announced. "It's from a Federal-style building, like the 1812 City Hall. Only the front facade was marble; the rest was brownstone. They did it to save money. Well, they *did* it so the money appropriated for marble could find its way into various pockets. Now, what else do we have? The ash. Let's find the arson accelerant."

Cooper ran the ash sample through the GC-MS. He stared at the curve that appeared on the screen.

Newly refined gasoline, containing its manufacturer's dyes and additives, was unique and could be traced back to a single source, as long as different batches of gas weren't mixed together at the service station where the perp bought it. Cooper announced that the gasoline matched perfectly the brand sold by the Gas Exchange service stations.

Banks grabbed the Yellow Pages and flipped them open. "We've got six stations in Manhattan. Three downtown. One at Sixth Avenue and Houston. One on Delancey, 503 East. And one at Nineteenth and Eighth."

"Nineteenth's too far north," Rhyme said. He stared at the profile chart. "East Side or West. Which is it?"

Grocery stores, gasoline . . .

A lanky figure suddenly filled the doorway.

"I still invited to this here party?" Frederick Dellray asked.

"Depends," Rhyme countered. "You bearing gifts?"

"Ah got presents galore," the agent said, waving a folder emblazoned with the familiar disk of the FBI emblem.

"You *ever* knock, Dellray?" Sellitto asked.

"Got outa the habit, you know."

"Come on in," Rhyme said. "What've you got?"

"Dunno for sure. Doesn't make any sense to this boy. But then, whatta I know?"

Dellray read from the report for a moment then said, "We had Tony Farco at PERT—said 'Hey' to you by the way, Lincoln—analyze that bit of PE you found. Turns out it's gold leaf. Probably sixty to eighty years old. He found a few cellulose fibers attached so he thinks it's from a book."

"Of *course*! Gold topstain from a page," Rhyme said.

"Now he also found some particles of ink on it. He said, I'm quotin' the boy now: 'It's not inconsistent with the type of ink the New York Public Library uses to stamp the ends of their books.' Don't he talk funny?"

"A library book," Rhyme mused.

Amelia Sachs said, "A *red-leather-bound* library book."

Rhyme stared at her. "Right!" he shouted. "*That's* what the bits of red leather're from. Not the glove. It's a book he carries around with him. Could be his bible."

"Bible?" Dellray asked. "You thinkin' he's some kinda religious nutzo?"

"Not *the* Bible, Fred. Call the library again, Banks. Maybe that's how he wore down his shoes—in the reading room. I know, it's a long shot. But we don't have a lot of options here.

I want a list of all the antiquarian books stolen from Manhattan locations in the past year."

"Will do." The young man rubbed a shaving scar as he called the mayor at home and bluntly asked hizzoner to contact the director of the public library and tell them what they needed.

A half hour later the fax machine buzzed and spewed out two pages. Thom ripped the transmission out of the machine. "Whoa, readers sure have sticky fingers in this city," he said as he brought it to Rhyme.

Eighty-four books fifty years old or older had disappeared from the public library branches in the past twelve months, thirty-five of them in Manhattan.

Rhyme scanned the list. Dickens, Austen, Hemingway, Dreiser . . . Books about music, philosophy, wine, literary criticism, fairy tales. Their value was surprisingly low. Twenty, thirty dollars. He supposed that none of them were first editions but perhaps the thieves hadn't known that.

He continued to scan the list.

Nothing, nothing. Maybe—

And then he saw it.

Crime in Old New York, by Richard Wille Stephans, published by Bountiful Press in 1919. Its value was listed at sixty-five dollars, and it had been stolen from the Delancey Street branch of the New York Public Library nine months earlier. It was described as five by seven inches in size, bound in red kidskin, with marbleized endpapers, gilded edges.

"I want a copy of it. I don't care how. Get somebody to the Library of Congress if you have to."

Dellray said, "I'll take care of that one."

Grocery stores, gasoline, the library . . .

Rhyme had to make a decision. There were three hundred searchers available—cops and state troopers and federal agents—but they'd be spread microscopically thin if they had to search both the West and East sides of downtown New York.

Gazing at the profile chart.

Is your house in the West Village? Rhyme silently asked 823. Did you buy the gas and steal the book on the East Side to fox us? Or is that your real neighborhood? How clever are you? No, no, the question's not how clever you are but how clever you *think* you are. How confident were you that we'd never find those minuscule bits of yourself that M. Locard assures us you'd leave behind?

Finally Rhyme ordered, "Go with the Lower East. Forget the Village. Get everybody down there. All of Bo's troops, all of yours, Fred. Here's what you're looking for: A large Federal-style building, close to two hundred years old, rose-colored marble front, brownstone sides and back. May have been a mansion or a public building at one time. With a garage or carriage house attached. A Taurus sedan and a Yellow Cab coming and going for the past few weeks. More often in the last few days."

Rhyme glanced at Sachs.

Giving up the dead . . .

Sellitto and Dellray made their calls.

Sachs said to Rhyme, "I'm going too."

"I hadn't expected anything else."

When the door had closed downstairs he whispered, "God-speed, Sachs. Godspeed."

THIRTY-ONE

Three squad cars cruised slowly through the streets of the Lower East Side. Two constables in each. Eyes searching.

And a moment later two black broughams appeared . . . two *sedans*, he meant. Unmarked, but their telltale searchlights next to the left side-view mirrors left no doubt who they were.

He'd known they were narrowing the search, of course, and that it was only a matter of time until they found his house. But he was shocked that they were this close. And he was particularly upset to see the cops get out and examine a silver Taurus parked on Canal Street.

How the hell had they found out about his carriage? He'd known that stealing a car was a huge risk but he thought it would take Hertz days to notice the missing vehicle. And even if they did he was sure the constables would never connect him with the theft. Oh, they were good.

One of the mean-eyed cops happened to glance at his cab.

Staring forward, the bone collector turned slowly onto Houston Street, lost himself in a crowd of other cabs. A half hour later, he'd ditched the taxi and the Hertz Taurus and had returned on foot to the mansion.

Young Maggie looked up at him.

She was scared, yes, but she'd stopped crying. He wondered if he should just keep her. Take himself a daughter. Raise her. The idea glowed within him for a moment or two then it faded.

UNSUB 823

Appearance	Residence	Vehicle	Other
• Caucasian male, slight build • Dark clothing • Old gloves, reddish kidskin • Aftershave; to cover up other scent? • Ski mask? Navy blue? • Gloves are dark • Aftershave = Brut • Hair color not brown • Deep scar, index finger • Casual clothes • Gloves are black	• Prob. has safe house • Located near; B'way & 82nd, ShopRite Greenwich & Bank, ShopRite 8th Ave. & 24th ShopRite Houston & Lafayette, ShopRite • Old building, pink marble • At least 100 years old, prob. mansion or institutional • Federal-style building, Lower East Side	• Yellow Cab • Recent model sedan • Lt. gray, silver, biege • Rental car; prob. stolen • Hertz, silver Taurus, this year's model	• knows CS proc. • possibly has record • knows FR prints • gun = .32 Colt • Ties vics w/ unusual knots • "Old" appeals to him • Called one vic "Hanna" • Knows basic German • Underground appeals to him • Dual personalities • Maybe priest, soc. worker, counselor • Unusual wear on shoes, reads a lot? • Listened as he broke vic's finger • Left snake as slap at investigators • Wanted to flay vic's foot • Called one vic "Maggie" • Mother & child, special meaning to him? • Book "Crime in Old NY," his model?

No, there'd be too many questions. Also, there was something eerie about the way the girl was looking at him. She seemed older than her years. She'd always remember what he'd done. Oh, for a while she might think it had been a dream. But then someday the truth would come out. It always did. Repress what you will, someday the truth comes out.

No, he couldn't trust her any more than he trusted anyone else. Every human soul would let you down in the end. You could trust hate. You could trust bone. Everything else was betrayal.

He crouched beside Maggie and eased the tape off her mouth.

"Mommy!" she howled. "I want my mommy!"

He said nothing, just stood and looked down at her. At her delicate skull. At her twigs of arms.

She screamed like a siren.

He took off his glove. His fingers hovered over her for a moment. Then he caressed the soft hair on her head. *("Fingerprints can be lifted from flesh, if taken within 90 minutes of contact [See KROMEKOTE], but no one has as yet successfully lifted and reconstructed friction-ridge prints from human hair."* Rhyme, *Physical Evidence*, 4th ed., Forensic Press, 1994.)

The bone collector slowly rose and walked upstairs, into the large living room of the building, past the paintings on the walls—the workers, the staring women and children. He cocked his head at a faint noise outside. Then louder—a clatter of metal. He grabbed his weapon and hurried to the back of the building. Unbolting the door he pushed it open suddenly, dropping into a two-handed shooting stance.

The pack of wild dogs glanced at him. They returned quickly to the trash can they'd knocked over. He slipped the gun into his pocket and returned to the living room.

He found himself next to the bottle-glass window again, looking out at the old graveyard. Oh, yes. There! There was the man again, wearing black, standing in the cemetery. In the distance the sky was spiked by the black masts of clipper ships and sloops docked in the East River along the Out Ward's shore.

The bone collector felt an overwhelming sense of sorrow.

He wondered if some tragedy had just occurred. Maybe the Great Fire of 1776 had just destroyed most of the buildings along Broadway. Or the yellow fever epidemic of 1795 had decimated the Irish community. Or the *General Slocum* excursion-boat fire in 1904 had killed killed over a thousand women and children, destroying the Lower East Side's German neighborhood.

Or maybe he was sensing tragedies soon to occur.

After a few minutes Maggie's screams grew quiet, replaced by the sounds of the old city, the roar of steam engines, the clang of bells, the pops of black-powder gunshots, the clop of hooves on resonant cobblestones.

He continued to stare, forgetting the constables who pursued him, forgetting Maggie, just watching the ghostly form stroll down the street.

Then and now.

His eyes remained focused out the window for a long moment, lost in a different time. And so he didn't notice the wild dogs, who'd pushed through the back door he'd left ajar. They looked at him through the doorway of the living room and paused only momentarily before turning around and loping quietly into the back of the building.

Noses lifted at the smells, ears pricked at the sounds of the strange place. Particularly the faint wailing that rose from somewhere beneath them.

It was a sign of their desperation that even the Hardy Boys split up.

Bedding was working a half-dozen blocks around Delancey, Saul was farther south. Sellitto and Banks each had their search areas, and the hundreds of other officers, FBI agents and troopers made the door-to-door rounds, asking about a slight man, a young child crying, a silver Ford Taurus, a deserted Federal-style building, fronted in rose marble, the rest of it dark brownstone.

Huh? What the hell you mean, Federal? . . . Seen a kid? You asking if I ever seen a kid on the Lower East? Yo, Jimmy, you ever see any kids 'round here? Like not in the last, what, sixty seconds?

Amelia Sachs was flexing her muscle. She insisted that she be on Sellitto's crew, the one hitting the ShopRite on East Houston that had sold Unsub 823 the veal chop. And the gas station that had sold him the gasoline. The library from which he'd stolen *Crime in Old New York*.

But they'd found no leads there and scattered like wolves smelling a dozen different scents. Each picked a chunk of neighborhood to call his or her own.

As Sachs gunned the engine of the new RRV and tried another block she felt the same frustration she'd known when working the crime scenes over the past several days: too damn much evidence, too much turf to cover. The hopelessness of it. Here, on the hot, damp streets, branching into a hundred other streets and alleys running past a thousand buildings—all old—finding the safe house seemed as impossible as finding that hair that Rhyme had told her about, pasted to the ceiling by the blowback from a .38 revolver.

She'd intended to hit every street but as time wore on and she thought of the child buried underground, near death, she began to search more quickly, speeding down streets, glancing right and left for the rosy-marble building. Doubt stabbed her. Had she missed the building in her haste? Or should she drive like lightning and cover more streets?

On and on. Another block, another. And still nothing.

> *After the villain's death his effects were secured and perused by detectives. His diary showed that he had murdered eight good citizens of the city. Nor was he above grave robbery, for it was ascertained from his pages (if his claims be true) that he had violated several holy resting places in cemeteries around the city. None of his victims had accorded him the least affront;—nay, most were upstanding citizens, industrious and innocent. And yet he felt not a modicum of guilt. Indeed, he seems to have labored under the mad delusion that he was doing his victims a favor.*

Lincoln Rhyme's left ring finger twitched slightly and the

frame turned the onion-skin page of *Crime in Old New York*, which had been delivered by two federal officers ten minutes earlier, service expedited thanks to Fred Dellray's inimitable style.

> *"Flesh withers and can be weak,"—(the villain wrote in his ruthless yet steady hand)—"Bone is the strongest aspect of the body. As old as we may be in the flesh, we are always young in the bone. It is a noble goal I had, and it is beyond me why any-one might quarrel with it. I did a kindness to them all. They are immortal now. I freed them. I took them down to the bone."*

Terry Dobyns had been right. Chapter 10, "James Schneider: the 'Bone Collector,'" was a virtual blueprint for Unsub 823's behavior. The MOs were the same—fire, animals, water, boiling alive. Eight twenty-three prowled the same haunts Schneider had. He'd confused a German tourist with Hanna Goldschmidt, a turn-of-the-century immigrant, and had been drawn to a German residence hall to find a victim. And he'd called little Pammy Ganz by a different name too—Maggie. Apparently thinking she was the young O'Connor girl, one of Schneider's victims.

A very bad etching in the book, covered by tissue, showed a demonic James Schneider, sitting in a basement, examining a leg bone.

Rhyme stared at the Randel Survey map of the city.

Bones . . .

Rhyme was recalling a crime scene he'd run once. He'd been called to a construction site in lower Manhattan where some excavators had discovered a skull a few feet below the surface of a vacant lot. Rhyme saw immediately that the skull was very old and brought a forensic anthropologist into the case. They continued to dig and discovered a number of bones and skeletons.

A little research revealed that in 1741 there'd been a slave rebellion in Manhattan and a number of slaves—and militant white abolitionists—had been hanged on a small island in the Collect. The island became a popular site for hangings and several informal cemeteries and potter's fields sprang up in the area.

Where had the Collect been? Rhyme tried to recall. Near where Chinatown and the Lower East Side meet. But it was hard to say for certain because the pond had been filled in so long ago. It had been—

Yes! he thought, his heart thudding: The Collect had been filled in because it had grown so polluted the city commissioners considered it a major health risk. And among the main polluters were the tanneries on the eastern shore!

Pretty good with the dialer now, Rhyme didn't flub a single number and got put through to the mayor in the first try. Hizzoner, though, the man's personal secretary said, was at a brunch at the UN. But when Rhyme identified himself the secretary said, "One minute, sir," and in much less time than that he found himself on the line with a man who said, through a mouthful of food, "Talk to me, detective. How the fuck're we doing?"

"Five-eight-eight-five, K," Amelia Sachs said, answering the radio. Rhyme heard the edginess in her voice.

"Sachs."

"This isn't good," she told him. "We're not having any luck."

"I think I've got him."

"*What?*"

"The six-hundred block, East Van Brevoort. Near Chinatown."

"How'd you know?"

"The mayor put me in touch with the head of the Historical Society. There's an archaeologic dig down there. An old graveyard. Across the street from where a big tannery used to be. And there were some big Federal mansions in the area at one time. I think he's nearby."

"I'm rolling."

Through the speakerphone he heard a squeal of tires, then the siren cut in.

"I've called Lon and Haumann," he added. "They're on their way over now."

"Rhyme," her urgent voice cracked. "I'll get her out."

Ah, you've got a cop's good heart, Amelia, a *professional* heart, Rhyme thought. But you're still just a rookie. "Sachs?" he said.

"Yes?"

"I've been reading this book. Eight twenty-three's picked a bad one for this role model of his. Really bad."

She said nothing.

"What I'm saying is," he continued, "whether the girl's there or not, if you find him and he so much as flinches, you nail him."

"But we get him alive, he can lead us to her. We can—"

"No, Sachs. Listen to me. You take him out. Any sign he's going for a weapon, anything . . . you take him out."

Static clattered. Then he heard her steady voice, "I'm at Van Brevoort, Rhyme. You were right. Looks like his place."

Eighteen unmarkeds, two ESU vans and Amelia Sachs's RRV were clustered near a short, deserted street on the Lower East Side.

East Van Brevoort looked like it was in Sarajevo. The buildings were abandoned—two of them burned to the ground. On the east side of the street was a dilapidated hospital of some kind, its roof caved in. Next to it was a large hole in the ground, roped off, with a No Trespassing sign emblazoned with the County Court seal—the archaeologic dig Rhyme had mentioned. A scrawny dog had died and lay in the gutter, its corpse picked over by rats.

In the middle of the other side of the street was a marble-fronted townhouse, faintly pink, with an attached carriage house, marginally nicer than the other decrepit tenements along Van Brevoort.

Sellitto, Banks and Haumann stood beside the ESU van, as a dozen officers suited up in Kevlar and racked their M-16s. Sachs joined them and, without asking, tucked her hair under a helmet and started to vest up.

Sellitto said, "Sachs, you're not tactical."

Slapping the Velcro strap down, she stared at the detective, eyebrow lifted high, until he relented and said, "Okay. But you're rear guard. That's an order."

Haumann said, "You'll be Team Two."

"Yessir. I can live with that."

One ESU cop offered her an MP-5 machine gun. She thought about Nick—their date on the range at Rodman's Neck. They'd spent two hours practicing with automatic weapons, firing Z-patterns through doors, flip-reloading with taped banana clips and field-stripping M-16s to clear the sand jams that plagued the Colts. Nick loved the staccato clutter but Sachs didn't much like the messy firepower of the big weapons. She'd suggested a match between them with Glocks and had whupped him three straight at fifty feet. He laughed and kissed her hard as the last of her empty casings spun, ringing, onto the firing range.

"I'll just use my sidearm," she told the ESU officer.

The Hardy Boys ran up, crouching as if they were mindful of snipers.

"Here's what we've got. There's nobody around. Block is—"

"Completely empty."

"The windows of his building're all barred. A back entrance—"

"Leading into the alley. The door's open."

"Open?" Haumann asked, glancing at several of his officers.

Saul confirmed, "Not just unlocked but open."

"Booby traps?"

"Not that we could see. Which isn't to say—"

"There aren't any."

Sellitto asked, "Any vehicles in the alley?"

"Nope."

"Two front entrances. Main front door—"

"Which looks painted shut. The second's the carriage-house doors. Double, wide enough for two vehicles. There's a padlock and chain."

"But they're lying on the ground."

Haumann nodded, "So maybe he's inside."

"Maybe," Saul said, then added, "And tell him what we think we heard."

"Very faint. Could have been crying."

"Could have been screaming."

Sachs asked, "The little girl?"

"Maybe. But then it just stopped. How'd Rhyme figure this place?"

"You tell *me* how his mind works," Sellitto said.

Haumann called one of his commanders and issued a series of orders. A moment later two ESU vans pulled into the intersection and blocked the other end of the street.

"Team One, front door. Blow it with cutting charges. It's wood and it's old so keep the plastic down, okay? Team Two, into the alley. On my three, you go. Got it? Neutralize but we're assuming the girl's in there so check your backdrops 'fore you squeeze. Officer Sachs, you're sure you want to do this?"

A firm nod.

"Okay, boys and girls. Go get him."

THIRTY-TWO

Sachs and the five other officers of Team Two ran into the torrid alley, which had been blocked off by ESU trucks. Renegade weeds grew profusely through the cobblestones and cracked foundations and the desolation reminded Sachs of the train-track grave yesterday morning.

He hoped the victim was dead. For his sake . . .

Haumann had ordered troopers onto the roofs of the surrounding buildings, and she saw the muzzles of their black Colts bristling like antennae.

The team paused at the rear doorway. Her fellow cops glanced at Sachs as she checked the rubber bands over her shoes. Heard one of them whisper to another something about superstition.

Then she heard through her earphone:

"Team One leader at front door, charge mounted and armed. We are clear, K."

"Roger, Team One leader. Team Two?"

"Team Two, in position, K."

"Roger, Team Two leader. Both teams, dynamic entry. On my three."

Checked her weapon one last time.

"One . . ."

Her tongue touched a dot of sweat hanging from the swollen wound on her lip.

"Two . . ."

Okay, Rhyme, here we go . . .

"Three!"

The explosion was very sedate, a distant pop, and then

the teams were moving. Fast. She sprinted along behind the ESU troopers as they slipped inside and scattered, their muzzle-mounted flashlights crisscrossing the shafts of brilliant sunlight that streamed through the windows. Sachs found herself alone as the rest of the team dispersed, checking out armoires and closets and the shadows behind the grotesque statues the place was filled with.

She turned the corner. A pale face loomed. A knife . . .

A thud in her heart. Combat stance, gun up. She laid five pounds of pressure on the slick trigger before she realized she was staring at a painting on the wall. An eerie, moon-faced butcher, holding a knife in one hand, a slab of meat in the other.

Brother . . .

He picked a great place for home.

The ESU troops clopped upstairs, searching the first and second floors.

But Sachs was looking for something else.

She found the door leading down to the basement. Partly open. Okay. Halogen off. You've got to take a look first. But she remembered what Nick had said: never look around corners at head or chest level—that's where he's expecting you. Down on one knee. A deep breath. Go!

Nothing. Blackness.

Back to cover.

Listen . . .

At first she heard nothing. Then there was a definite scratching. A clatter. The sound of a fast breath or grunt.

He's there and he's digging his way out!

Into her mike she said, "I've got activity in the basement. Backup."

"*Roger.*"

But she couldn't wait. She thought of the little girl down there with him. And she started down the stairs. Paused and listened again. Then she realized she was standing with her body fully exposed from the waist down. She practically leapt down to the floor, dropped into a crouch in the darkness.

Breathe deep.

Now, do it!

The halogen in her left hand stabbed a brilliant rod of light through the room. The muzzle of her weapon targeted the center of the white disk as it swung left to right. Keep the beam down. He'd be at crotch level too. Remembering what Nick had told her: Perps don't fly.

Nothing. No sign of him.

"Officer Sachs?"

An ESU trooper was at the top of the stairs.

"Oh, no," she muttered, as her beam fell on Pammy Ganz, frozen in the corner of the basement.

"Don't move," she called to the trooper.

Inches away from the girl stood the pack of emaciated wild dogs, sniffing at her face, her fingers, her legs. The girl's wide eyes darted from one animal to the other. Her tiny chest rose and fell and tears streamed down her face. Her mouth was open and the dot of her pink tongue seemed glued to the right arc of her lip.

"Stay up there," she said to the ESU trooper. "Don't spook 'em."

Sachs drew targets but didn't fire. She could kill two or three but the others might panic and grab the girl. One was big enough to snap her neck with a single flip of its scarred, mangy head.

"Is he down there?" the ESU cop asked.

"Don't know. Get a medic here. To the top of the stairs. Nobody come down."

"Roger."

Her weapon sights floating from one animal to another, Sachs slowly started forward. One by one the dogs became aware of her and turned away from Pammy. The little girl was merely food; Sachs was a predator. They growled and snarled, front legs quivering as their hindquarters tensed, ready to jump.

"I'm ascared," Pammy said shrilly, drawing their attention again.

"Shhhh, honey," Sachs cooed. "Don't say anything. Be quiet."

"Mommy. I want my *mommy*!" Her abrasive howl set the dogs off. They danced in place, and swung their battered noses from right to left, growling.

"Easy, easy . . ."

Sachs moved to the left. The dogs were facing her now, glancing from her eyes to her outstretched hand and the gun. They separated into two packs. One stayed close to Pammy. The other moved around Sachs, trying to flank her.

She eased between the little girl and the three dogs closest to her.

The Glock swinging back and forth, a pendulum. Their black eyes on the black gun.

One dog, with a scabby yellow coat, snarled and stepped forward on Sachs's right.

The little girl was whimpering, "Mommy . . ."

Sachs moved slowly. She leaned down, clamped her hand on the child's sweatshirt and dragged Pammy behind her. The yellow dog moved closer.

"Shoo," Sachs said.

Closer still.

"Go away!"

The dogs behind the yellow one tensed as he bared cracked brown teeth.

"Get the fuck outa here!" Sachs snarled and slammed the barrel of the Glock onto his nose. The dog blinked in dismay, yelped, skittered up the stairs.

Pammy screamed, sending the others into a frenzy. They started fighting among themselves, a whirlwind of snapping teeth and slaver. A scarred Rottweiler tossed a dustmop of a mutt to the floor in front of Sachs. She stamped her foot beside the scrawny brown thing and he skittered to his feet, raced up the stairs. The others chased him like greyhounds after a rabbit.

Pammy began to sob. Sachs crouched beside her and swept the basement again with her light. No sign of the unsub.

"It's okay, honey. We'll have you home soon. You'll be all right. That man here? You remember him?"

She nodded.

"Did he leave?"

"I don't know. I want my mommy."

She heard the other officers call in. The first and second floors were secure. "The car and taxi?" Sachs asked. "Any sign?"

A trooper transmitted, "They're gone. He's probably left."

He's not there, Amelia. That would be illogical.

From the top of the stairs an officer called, "Basement secure?"

She said, "I'm going to check. Hold on."

"We're coming down."

"Negative on that," she said. "We've got a pretty clean crime scene here and I want to keep it that way. Just get a medic down here to check out the little girl."

The young medic, a sandy-haired man, walked down the stairs and crouched beside Pammy.

It was then that Sachs saw the trail leading into the back of the basement—to a low, black-painted metal door. She walked to it, avoiding the path itself to save the prints, and crouched down. The door was partly open and there seemed to be a tunnel on the other side, dark but not completely black, leading to another building.

An escape route. The son of a bitch.

With the knuckles of her left hand she pushed the door open wider. It didn't squeak. She peered into the tunnel. Faint light, twenty, thirty feet away. No moving shadows.

If Sachs saw anything in the dimness it was T.J.'s contorted body dangling from the black pipe, Monelle Gerger's round, limp body as the black rat crawled toward her throat.

"Portable 5885 to CP," Sachs said into her mike.

"Go ahead, K," Haumann's terse voice responded.

"I've got a tunnel leading to the building south of the Unsub's. Have somebody cover the doors and windows."

"Will do, K."

"I'm going in," she told him.

"The tunnel? We'll get you some backup, Sachs."

"Negative. I don't want the scene contaminated. Just have somebody keep an eye on the girl."

"Say again."

"No. No backup."

She clicked the light out and started crawling.

There'd been no courses in tunnel-rat work at the academy of course. But the things Nick had told her about securing a unfriendly scene came back to her. Weapon close to the body, not extended too far, where it could be knocked aside. Three steps—well, shuffles—forward, pause. Listen.

Two more steps. Pause. Listen. Four steps next time. Don't do anything predictable.

Hell, it's dark.

And what's that *smell*? She shivered in disgust at the hot, foul stink.

The claustrophobia wrapped around her like a cloud of oil smoke and she had to stop for a moment, concentrating on anything but the closeness of the walls. The panic slipped away but the smell was worse. She gagged.

Quiet, girl. Quiet!

Sachs controlled the reflex and kept going.

And what's that noise? Something electrical. A buzzing. Rising and falling.

Ten feet from the end of the tunnel. Through the doorway she could see a second large basement. Murky though not quite as dark as the one Pammy had been in. Light leached in through a greasy window. She saw motes of dust pedaling through the gloom.

No, no, girl, the gun's too far in front of you. One kick and it's gone. Close to your face. Keep your weight low and back! Use your arms to aim, ass for support.

Then she was at the doorway.

She gagged again, tried to stifle the sound.

Is he waiting for me, or not?

Head out, a fast look. You've got a helmet. It'll deflect anything but a full-metal or Teflon and remember he's shooting a .32. A girl gun.

All right. Think. Look which way first?

The *Patrolman's Guide* wasn't any help and Nick wasn't offering any advice at the moment. Flip a coin.

Left.

She stuck her head out fast, glancing to the left. Back into the tunnel.

She'd seen nothing. A blank wall, shadows.

If he's the other way he's seen me and's got good target positioning.

Okay, fuck. Just go. Fast.

When you move . . .

Sachs leapt.

. . . they can't getcha.

She hit the ground hard, rolling. Twisting around.

The figure was hidden in shadows against the wall to the right, under the window. Drawing a target she started to fire. Then froze.

Amelia Sachs gasped.

Oh, my God . . .

Her eyes were inexorably drawn to the woman's body, propped up against the wall.

From the waist up she was thin, with dark-brown hair, a gaunt face, small breasts, bony arms. Her skin was covered with swarms of flies—the buzzing Sachs had heard.

From the waist down, she was . . . nothing. Bloody hip bones, femur, the whip of her spine, feet . . . All the flesh had been dissolved in the repulsive bath she rested next to—a horrible stew, deep brown, chunks of flesh floating in it. Lye or acid of some sort. The fumes stung Sachs's eyes, while horror—and fury too—boiled in her heart.

Oh, you poor thing . . .

Sachs waved pointlessly at the flies that strafed the new intruder.

The woman's hands were relaxed, palms upward as if she were meditating. Eyes closed. A purple jogging outfit sat by her side.

She wasn't the only victim.

Another skeleton—completely stripped—lay beside a similar vat, older, empty of the terrible acid but coated with a dark sludge of blood and melted muscle. Its forearm and hand were missing. And beyond that was another one—this victim picked apart, the bones carefully scrubbed of all the flesh, cleaned, resting carefully on the floor. A stack of triple-ought sandpaper rested beside the skull. The elegant curve of the head shone like a trophy.

And then she heard it behind her.

A breath. Faint but unmistakable. The snap of air deep in a throat.

She spun around, furious at herself for her carelessness.

But the emptiness of the basement gaped back at her. She swept the light over the floor, which was stone and didn't show footprints as clearly as the dirt floor in 823's building next door.

Another inhalation.

Where was he? *Where*?

Sachs crouched further, sending the light sideways, up and down. . . .Nothing.

Where the fuck is he? Another tunnel? An exit to the street?

Looking at the floor again she spotted what she thought was a faint trail, leading into the shadows of the room. She moved along beside it.

Pause. Listen.

Breathing?

Yes. No.

Stupidly she spun around and looked at the dead woman once more.

Come *on*!

Eyes back again.

Moving along the floor.

Nothing. How can I hear him and not see him?

The wall ahead of her was solid. No doors or windows. She backed up, toward the skeletons.

From somewhere, Lincoln Rhyme's words came back. "*Crime scenes're three-dimensional.*"

Sachs looked up suddenly, flashing the light in front of her. The huge Doberman's teeth shone back—dangling bits of gray flesh. Two feet away on a high ledge. He was waiting, like a wildcat, for her.

Neither of them moved for a moment. Absolutely frozen.

Then Sachs instinctively dropped her head and, before she could bring her weapon up, he launched himself toward her face. His teeth connected with the helmet. Gripping the strap in his mouth, he shook furiously, trying to break her neck as they fell backwards, onto the edge of an acid-filled pit. The pistol flew from her hand.

The dog kept his grip on her helmet while his hind legs galloped, his claws digging into her vest and belly and thighs. She hit him hard with her fists but it was like slugging wood; he didn't feel the blows at all.

Releasing the helmet, he reared back then lunged for her face. She flung her left arm over her eyes and, as he grabbed her forearm and she felt his teeth clamp down on her skin, she slipped the switchblade from her pocket and shoved the blade between his ribs. There was a yelp, a high sound, and he rolled off her, kept moving, speeding straight for the doorway.

Sachs snagged her pistol and was after him in an instant, scrabbling through the tunnel. She burst out to see the wounded animal sprinting straight toward Pammy and the medic, who stood frozen as the Doberman leapt into the air.

Sachs dropped into a crouch and squeezed off two rounds. One hit the back of the animal's head and the other streaked into the brick wall. The dog collapsed in a quivering pile at the medic's feet.

"Shots fired," she heard in her radio and a half-dozen troopers rushed down the stairs, pulled the dog away and deployed around the girl.

"It's all right!" Sachs shouted. "It was me!"

The team rose from their defensive positions.

Pammy was screaming, "Doggie dead . . . She made the doggie dead!"

Sachs holstered her weapon and hefted the girl onto her hip.

"Mommy!"

"You'll see your mommy soon," Sachs said. "We're going to call her right now."

Upstairs she set Pammy on the floor and turned to a young ESU officer standing nearby, "I lost my cuff key. Could you take those off her please? Open them over a piece of clean newspaper, wrap 'em up in the paper and put the whole thing in a plastic bag."

The officer rolled his eyes. "Listen, beautiful, go find yourself a rookie to order around." He started to walk away.

"Trooper," Bo Haumann barked, "you'll do what she says."

"Sir," he protested, "I'm ESU."

"Got news," Sachs muttered, "you're Crime Scene now."

Carole Ganz was lying on her back in a very beige bedroom, staring at the ceiling, thinking about the time a few weeks ago when she and Pammy and a bunch of friends were sitting around a campfire in Wisconsin at Kate and Eddie's place, talking, telling stories, singing songs.

Kate's voice wasn't so hot but Eddie could've been a pro. He could even play barre chords. He sang Carole King's "Tapestry" just for her and Carole sang along softly through her tears. Thinking that maybe, just maybe, she really was putting Ron's death behind her and getting on with her life.

She remembered Kate's voice from that night: "When you're angry, the only way to deal with it is to wrap up that anger and give it away. Give it to somebody else. Do you hear me? Don't keep it inside you. Give it away."

Well, she was angry now. Furious.

Some young kid—a mindless little shit—had taken her husband away, shot him in the back. And now some crazy man had taken her daughter. She wanted to explode. And it took all her willpower not to start flinging things against the wall and howling like a coyote.

She lay back on the bed and gingerly placed her shattered wrist on her belly. She'd taken a Demerol, which had eased the pain, but she hadn't been able to sleep. She'd done nothing but stay inside all day long, trying to get in touch with Kate and Eddie and waiting for news about Pammy.

She kept picturing Ron, kept picturing her anger, actually imagining herself packing it up in a box, wrapping it carefully, sealing it up . . .

And then the phone rang. She stared for a moment then yanked it off the cradle.

"Hello?"

Carole listened to the policewoman tell her that they'd found Pammy, that she was in the hospital but that she was okay. A moment later Pammy herself came on the phone and they were both crying and laughing at the same time.

Ten minutes later she was on her way to Manhattan Hospital, in the back seat of a black police sedan.

Carole practically sprinted down the corridor to Pammy's room and was surprised to be stopped by the police guard. So they hadn't caught the fucker yet? But was soon as she saw her daughter she forgot about him, forgot the terror in the taxi and the fiery basement. She threw her arms around her little girl.

"Oh, honey, I missed you! Are you okay? Really okay?"

"That lady, she killed a doggie—"

Carole turned and saw the tall, red-haired policewoman

standing nearby, the one who'd saved her from the church basement.

"—but it was all right because he was going to eat me."

Carole hugged Sachs. "I don't know what to say. . . .I just . . . Thank you, thank you."

"Pammy's fine," Sachs assured her. "Some scratches—nothing serious—and she's got a little cough."

"Mrs Ganz?" A young man walked into the room, carrying her suitcase and yellow knapsack. "I'm Detective Banks. We've got your things here."

"Oh, thank God."

"Is anything missing?" he asked her.

She looked through the knapsack carefully. It was all there. The money, Pammy's doll, the package of clay, the Mr Potato Head, the CDs, the clock radio . . . He hadn't taken anything. Wait. . . ."You know, I think there's a picture missing. I'm not sure. I thought I had more than these. But everything important's here."

The detective gave her a receipt to sign.

A young resident stepped into the room. He joked with Pammy about her Pooh bear as he took her blood pressure.

Carole asked him, "When can she leave?"

"Well, we'd like to keep her in for a few days. Just to make sure—"

"A few *days*? But she's fine."

"She's got a bit of bronchitis I want to keep an eye on. And . . ." He lowered his voice. "We're also going to bring in an abuse specialist. Just to make sure."

"But she was going to go with me tomorrow. To the UN ceremonies. I promised her."

The policewoman added, "It's easier to keep her guarded here. We don't know where the unsub—the kidnapper—is. We'll have an officer babysitting you too."

"Well, I guess. Can I stay with her for a while?"

"You bet," the resident said. "You can stay the night. We'll have a cot brought in."

Then Carole was alone with her daughter once more. She sat down on the bed and put her arm around the child's narrow shoulders. She had a bad moment remembering how *he*, that crazy man, had touched Pammy. How his eyes had looked when he'd asked if he could cut her own skin off . . . Carole shivered and began to cry.

It was Pammy who brought her back. "Mommy, tell me a story. . . . No, no, sing me something. Sing me the friend song. Pleeeeease?"

Calming down, Carole asked, "You want to hear that one, hm?"

"Yes!"

Carole hoisted the girl onto her lap and, in a reedy voice, started to sing "You've Got a Friend." Pammy sang snatches of it along with her.

It had been one of Ron's favorites and, in the past couple years, after he was gone, she hadn't been able to listen to more than a few bars without breaking into tears.

Today, she and Pammy finished it together, pretty much on key, dry-eyed and laughing.

THIRTY-THREE

Amelia Sachs finally made it home to her apartment in Carroll Gardens, Brooklyn.

Exactly six blocks from her parents' house, where her mother still lived. As soon as she walked in she hit the first speed-dial button on the kitchen phone.

"Mom. Me. I'm taking you to brunch at the Plaza. Wednesday. That's my day off."

"What for? To celebrate your new assignment? How *is* Public Affairs? You didn't call."

A fast laugh. Sachs realized her mother had no idea what she'd been doing for the past day and a half.

"You been following the news, Mom?"

"Me? I'm Brokaw's secret admirer, you know that."

"You hear about this kidnapper the last few days?"

"Who hasn't? . . . What're you telling me, honey?"

"I've got the inside scoop."

And she told her astonished mother the story—about saving the vics and about Lincoln Rhyme and, with some editing, about the crime scenes.

"Amie, your father'd be so proud."

"So, call in sick on Wednesday. The Plaza, OK?"

"Forget it, sweetheart. Save your money. I've got waffles and Bob Evans in the freezer. You can come here."

"It's not that expensive, Mom."

"Not that much? It's a *fortune*."

"Well, hey," Sachs said, trying to sound spontaneous, "you like the Pink Teacup, don't you?"

A little place in the West Village that served up platters

of the best pancakes and eggs on the East Coast for next to nothing.

A pause.

"That might be nice."

This was a strategy Sachs had used successfully over the years.

"I've gotta get some rest, Mom. I'll call tomorrow."

"You work too hard. Amie, this case of yours . . . it wasn't dangerous, was it?"

"I was just doing the technical stuff, Mom. Crime scene. It doesn't get any safer than that."

"And they asked for *you* especially!" the woman said. Then repeated, "Your father'd be so proud."

They hung up and Sachs wandered into the bedroom, flopped down on the bed.

After she'd left Pammy's room Sachs had paid visits to the other two surviving victims of Unsub 823. Monelle Gerger, dotted with bandages and pumped full of anti-rabies serum, had been released and was returning to her family in Frankfurt "but just for rest of summer," she explained adamantly. "Not, you know, for good." And she'd pointing to her stereo and CD collection in the decrepit apartment in the Deutsche Haus by way of proving that no New World psycho was driving her permanently out of town.

William Everett was still in the hospital. The shattered finger was not a serious problem of course but his heart had been acting up again. Sachs was astonished to find that he'd owned a shop in Hell's Kitchen years ago and thought he might have known her father. "I knew all the beat cops," he said. She showed him her wallet picture of the man in his dress uniform. "I think so. Not sure. But I think so."

The calls had been social but Sachs had gone armed with her watchbook. Neither of the vics, though, had been able to tell her anything more about Unsub 823.

In her apartment now Sachs glanced out her window. She saw the ginkgoes and maples shiver in the sharp wind. She stripped off her uniform, scratched under her boobs—where it always itched like mad from being squooshed under the body armor. She pulled on a bathrobe.

Unsub 823 hadn't had much warning but it had been

enough. The safe house on Van Brevoort had been hosed completely. Even though the landlord said he'd moved in a long time ago—last January (with a phony ID, no one was very surprised to learn)—823 had left with everything he'd brought, trash included. After Sachs had worked the scene, NYPD Latents had descended and was dusting every surface in the place. So far the preliminary reports weren't encouraging.

"Looks like he even wore gloves when he crapped," young Banks had reported to her.

A Mobile unit had found the taxi and the sedan. Unsub 823'd cleverly parked them near Avenue D and Ninth Street. Sellitto guessed it probably took a local gang seven or eight minutes to strip them down to their chassis. Any physical evidence the vehicles might've yielded was now in a dozen chop shops around the city.

Sachs turned on the tube and found the news. Nothing about the kidnappings. All the stories were about the opening ceremonies of the UN peace conference.

She stared at Bryant Gumbel, stared at the UN secretary-general, stared at some ambassador from the Middle East, stared far more intently than her interest warranted. She even studied the ads as if she were memorizing them.

Because there was something she definitely *didn't* want to think about: her bargain with Lincoln Rhyme.

The deal was clear. Now that the Carole and Pammy were safe, it was her turn to come through. To let him have his hour alone with Dr Berger.

Now *him*, Berger . . . She hadn't liked the look of the doctor at all. You could see one big fucking ego in his compact, athletic frame, his evasive eyes. His black hair perfectly combed. Expensive clothes. Why couldn't Rhyme have found someone like Kevorkian? He may have been quirky but at least seemed like a wise old grandfather?

Her lids closed.

Giving up the dead . . .

A bargain was a bargain. But goddammit, Rhyme . . .

Well, she couldn't let him go without one last try. He'd caught her off guard in his bedroom. She was flustered. Hadn't thought of any really good arguments. Monday. She had until tomorrow to try to convince him not to do it. Or at least to wait awhile. A month. Hell, a day.

What could she say to him? She'd jot down her arguments. Write a little speech.

Opening her eyes, she climbed out of bed to find a pen and some paper. I could—

Sachs froze, her breath whistling into her lungs like the wind outside.

He wore dark clothes, the ski mask and gloves black as oil.

Unsub 823 stood in the middle of her bedroom.

Her hand instinctively went toward the bedside table—her Glock and knife. But he was ready. The shovel swung fast and caught her on the side of her head. A yellow light exploded in her eyes.

She was on her hands and knees when the foot slammed into her rib cage and she collapsed to her stomach, struggling for breath. She felt her hands being cuffed behind her, a strip of duct tape slapped onto her mouth. Moving fast, efficiently. He rolled her onto her back; her robe fell open.

Kicking furiously, struggling madly to pull the cuffs apart.

Another blow to her stomach. She gagged and fell still as he reached for her. Gripped her at the armpits, dragged her out the back door and into the large private garden behind the apartment.

His eyes remained on her face, not even looking at her tits, her flat belly, her mound with its few red curls. She could easily have given that up to him if it would have saved her life.

But, no, Rhyme's diagnosis was right. It wasn't lust that drove 823. He had something else in mind. He dropped her willowy figure, face up, into a patch of black-eyed Susan and pachysandra, out of sight of the neighbors. He looked around, catching his breath. He picked up the shovel and plunged the blade into the dirt.

Amelia Sachs began to cry.

Rubbing the back of his head into the pillow.

Compulsive, a doctor had once told him after observing this behavior—an opinion Rhyme hadn't asked for. Or wanted.

His nestling, Rhyme reflected, was just a variation on Amelia Sachs's tearing her flesh with her own nails.

He stretched his neck muscles, rolling his head around, as he stared at the profile chart on the wall. Rhyme believed that the full story of the man's madness was here in front of him. In the black, swoopy handwriting—and the gaps between the words. But he couldn't see the story's ending. Not yet.

He looked over the clues again. There were only a few left unexplained.

The scar on the finger.

The knot.

The aftershave.

The scar was useless to them unless they had a suspect whose fingers they could examine. And there'd been no luck in identifying the knot—only preppy Banks's opinion that it wasn't nautical.

What about the cheap aftershave? Assuming that most unsubs wouldn't spritz themselves to go on a kidnapping spree, why had he worn it? Rhyme could only conclude again that he was trying to obscure another, a telltale scent. He ran through the possibilities: Food, liquor, chemicals, tobacco . . .

He felt eyes on him and looked to his right.

The black dots of the bony rattlesnake's eye sockets gazed toward the Clinitron. This was the one clue that was out of place. It had no purpose, except to taunt them.

Something occurred to him. Using the painstaking turning frame Rhyme slowly flipped back through *Crime in Old New York*. To the chapter on James Schneider. He found the paragraphs he'd remembered.

> *It has been suggested by a well-known physician of the mind (a practitioner of the discipline of "psyche-logy," which has been much in the news of late) that James Schneider's ultimate intent had little to do with harming his victims. Rather—this learnéd doctor has suggested—the villain was seeking revenge against those that did him what he perceived to be harm: the city's constabulary, if not Society as a whole.*
>
> *Who can say where the source of this hate lay? Perhaps, like the Nile of old, its wellsprings were*

hidden to the world—and possibly even to the villain himself. Yet one reason may be found in a little-known fact: Young James Schneider, at the tender age of ten, saw his father dragged away by constables only to die in prison for a robbery which, it was later ascertained, he did not commit. Following this unfortunate arrest, the boy's mother fell into life on the street and abandoned her son, who grew up a ward of the state.

Did the madman perchance commit these crimes to fling derision into the face of the very constabulary which had inadvertently destroyed his family?

We will undoubtedly never know.

Yet what does seem clear is that by mocking the ineffectualness of the protectors of its citizenry, James Schneider—the "bone collector"—was wreaking his vengeance upon the city itself as much as upon his innocent victims.

Lincoln Rhyme lay back in his pillow and looked at the profile chart again.

Dirt is heavier than anything.

It's the earth itself, the dust of an iron core, and it doesn't kill by strangling the air from the lungs but by compressing the cells until they die from the panic of immobility.

Sachs wished that she *had* died. She prayed that she would. Fast. From fear or a heart attack. Before the first shovelful hit her face. She prayed for this harder than Lincoln Rhyme had prayed for his pills and liquor.

Lying in the grave the unsub had dug in her own backyard Sachs felt the progress of the rich earth, dense and wormy, moving along her body.

Sadistically, he was burying her slowly, casting only a shallow scoop at a time, scattering it carefully around her. He'd started with her feet. He was now up to her chest, the dirt slipping into her robe and around her breasts like a lover's fingers.

Heavier and heavier, compressing, binding her lungs; she could suck only an ounce or two of air at a time. He paused once or twice to look at her then continued.

He likes to watch . . .

Hands beneath her, neck straining to keep her head above the tide.

Then her chest was buried completely. Her shoulders, her throat. The cold earth rose to the hot skin of her face, packing around her head so she couldn't move. Finally he bent down and ripped the tape off her mouth. As Sachs tried to scream he spilled a handful of dirt into her face. She shivered, choked on the black earth. Ears ringing, hearing for some reason an old song from her infancy—"The Green Leaves of Summer," a song her father played over and over again on the hi-fi. Sorrowful, haunting. She closed her eyes. Everything was going black. Opened her mouth once and got another cup's worth of soil.

Giving up the dead . . .

And then she was under.

Completely quiet. Not choking or gasping—the earth was a perfect seal. She had no air in her lungs, couldn't make any sounds. Silence, except for the haunting melody and the growing roar in her ears.

Then the pressure on her face ceased as her body went numb, as numb as Lincoln Rhyme's. Her mind began to shut down.

Blackness, blackness. No words from her father. Nothing from Nick . . . No dreams of downshifting from five to four to goose the speedometer into three digits.

Blackness.

Giving up the . . .

The mass sinking down onto her, pushing, pushing. Seeing only one image: The hand rising out of the grave yesterday morning, waving for mercy. When no mercy would be given.

Waving for her to follow.

Rhyme, I'll miss you.

Giving up . . .

THIRTY-FOUR

Something struck her forehead. Hard. She felt the thump but no pain.

What, what? His shovel? A brick? Maybe in an instant of compassion 823'd decided that this slow death was more than anyone could bear and was striking for her throat to sever her veins.

Another blow, and another. She couldn't open her eyes, but she was aware of light growing around her. Colors. And air. She forced the mass of dirt from her mouth and sucked in tiny breaths, all she could manage. Began coughing in a loud bray, retching, spitting.

Her lids sprang open and through tearing eyes she found herself looking up at the muddy vision of Lon Sellitto, kneeling over her, beside two EMS medics, one of whom dug into her mouth with latex-clad fingers and pulled out more gunk, while the other readied an oxygen mask and green tank.

Sellitto and Banks continued to uncover her body, shoving the dirt away with their muscular hands. They pulled her up, leaving the robe behind like a shed skin. Sellitto, old divorcé that he was, looked chastely away from her body as he put his jacket around her shoulders. Young Jerry Banks did look of course but she loved him anyway.

"Did . . . you . . . ?" she wheezed, then surrendered to a racking cough.

Sellitto glanced expectantly at Banks, who was the more breathless of the two. He must've done the most running after the unsub. The young detective shook his head. "Got away."

Sitting up, she inhaled oxygen for a moment.

"How?" she wheezed. "How'd you know?"

"Rhyme," he answered. "Don't ask me how. He called in 10–13's for everybody on the team. When he heard we were okay he sent us over here ASAP."

Then the numbness left, snap, in a flash. And for the first time she realized what had nearly happened. She dropped the oxygen mask, backed away in panic, tears streaming, her panicky keening growing louder and louder. "No, no, no . . ."

Slapping her arms and thighs, frantic, trying to shake off the horror clinging to her like a teeming swarm of bees.

"Oh God oh God . . . No . . ."

"Sachs?" Banks asked, alarmed. "Hey, Sachs?"

The older detective waved his partner away. "It's okay." He kept his arm around her shoulders as she dropped to all fours and vomited violently, sobbing, sobbing, gripping the dirt desperately between her fingers as if she wanted to strangle it.

Finally Sachs calmed and sat back on her naked haunches. She began laughing, softly at first then louder and louder, hysterical, astonished to find that the skies had opened and it had been raining—huge hot summer drops—and she hadn't even realized it.

Arm around his shoulders. Face pressed against his. They stayed that way for a long moment.

"Sachs . . . Oh, Sachs."

She stepped away from the Clinitron and scooted an old armchair from the corner of the room. Sachs—wearing navy sweat-pants and a Hunter College T-shirt—flopped down into the chair and dangled her exquisite legs over the arm like a schoolgirl.

"Why us, Rhyme? Why'd he come after us?" Her voice was a raspy whisper from the dirt she'd swallowed.

"Because the people he kidnapped aren't the real victims. We are."

"Who's *we*?" she asked.

"I'm not sure. Society maybe. Or the city. Or the UN. Cops. I went back and reread his bible—the chapter on James

Schneider. Remember Terry's theory about why the unsub'd been leaving the clues?"

Sellitto said, "Sort of making us accessories. To share the guilt. Make it easier for him to kill."

Rhyme nodded but said, "I don't think that's the reason though. I think the clues were a way to attack *us*. Every dead vic was a loss for us."

In her old clothes, hair pulled back in a ponytail, Sachs looked more beautiful than any time in the past two days. But her eyes were tin. She'd be reliving every shovelful of dirt, he supposed, and Rhyme found the thought of her living burial so disturbing he had to look away.

"What's he got against us?" she asked.

"I don't know. Schneider's father was arrested by mistake and died in prison. Our unsub? Who knows why? I only care about evidence—"

"—not motives." Amelia Sachs finished the sentence.

"Why'd he start going after us directly?" Banks asked, nodding at Sachs.

"We found his hidey-hole and saved the little girl. I don't think he expected us so soon. Maybe he just got pissed. Lon, we need twenty-four-hour babysitters for all of us. He could've just taken off after we saved the kid but he stuck around to do some damage. You and Jerry, me, Cooper, Haumann, Polling, we're all on his list, betcha. Meanwhile, get Peretti's boys over to Sachs's. I'm sure he kept it clean but there might be something there. He left a lot faster than he'd planned to."

"I better get over there," Sachs said.

"No," Rhyme said.

"I have to work the scene."

"You have to get some rest," he ordered. "*That*'s what you have to do, Sachs. You don't mind my saying, you look lousy."

"Yeah, officer," Sellitto said. "'S'an order. I told you to stand down for the rest of the day. We've got two hundred searchers looking for him. And Fred Dellray's got another hundred and twenty feebies."

"I got a crime scene in my own backyard and you're not gonna let me walk the grid?"

"That's it," Rhyme said, "in a nutshell."

Sellitto walked to the doorway. "Any problems with that, officer?"

"Nosir."

"Come on, Banks, we got work to do. You need a lift, Sachs? Or're they still trusting you with vehicles?"

"No thanks, got wheels downstairs," she said.

The two detectives left. Rhyme heard their voices echoing through the empty hall. Then the door closed and they were gone.

Rhyme realized the glaring overhead lights were on. He clicked through several commands and dimmed them.

Sachs stretched.

"Well," she said, just as Rhyme said, "So."

She glanced at the clock. "It's late."

"Sure is."

Rising, she walked to the table where her purse rested. She picked it up. Clicked it open, found her compact and examined her cut lip in the mirror.

"It doesn't look too bad," Rhyme said.

"Frankenstein," she said, prodding. "Why don't they use flesh-colored stitches?" She put the mirror away, slung the purse over her shoulder. "You moved the bed," she noticed. It was closer to the window.

"Thom did. I can look at the park. If I want to."

"Well, that's good."

She walked to the window. Looked down.

Oh, for Christ's sake, Rhyme thought to himself. Do it. What can happen? He blurted quickly, "You want to stay here? I mean, it's getting late. And Latents'll be dusting your place for hours."

He felt a mad bolt of anticipation deep within him. Well, kill *that*, he thought, furious with himself. Until her face blossomed into a smile. "I'd like that."

"Good." His jaw shivered from the adrenaline. "Wonderful. Thom!"

Listening to music, drinking some Scotch. Maybe he'd tell her more about famous crime scenes. The historian in him was also curious about her father, about police work in the '60s and '70s. About the infamous Midtown South Precinct in the old days.

Rhyme shouted, "Thom! Get some sheets. And a blanket. Thom! I don't know what the hell he's doing. *Thom*!"

Sachs started to say something but the aide appeared in the doorway and said testily, "One rude shout would've been enough, you know, Lincoln."

"Amelia's staying over again. Could you get some blankets and pillows for the couch?"

"No, not the couch again," she said. "It's like sleeping on rocks."

Rhyme was stabbed with a splinter of rejection. Thinking ruefully to himself: Been a few years since he'd felt *that* emotion. Resigned, he nonetheless smiled and said, "There's a bedroom downstairs. Thom can make it up for you."

But Sachs set down her purse. "That's okay, Thom. You don't have to."

"It's no bother."

"It's all right. Good night, Thom." She walked to the door.

"Well, I—"

She smiled.

"But—" he began, looking from her to Rhyme, who frowned, shook his head.

"Good *night*, Thom," she said firmly. "Watch your feet." And closed the door slowly, as he stepped back out of the way into the hall. It closed with a loud click.

Sachs kicked off her shoes, pulled off the sweats and T-shirt. She wore a lace bra and baggy cotton panties. She climbed into the Clinitron beside Rhyme, showing every bit of the authority beautiful women wield when it comes to climbing into bed with a man.

She wriggled down into the pellets and laughed. "This is one hell of a bed," she said, stretching like a cat. Eyes closed, Sachs asked, "You don't mind, do you?"

"I don't mind at all."

"Rhyme?"

"What?"

"Tell me more about your book, okay? Some more crime scenes?"

He started to describe a clever serial killer in Queens but in less than one minute she was asleep.

Rhyme glanced down and noted her breast against his chest, her knee resting on his thigh. A woman's hair was banked against his face for the first time in years. It tickled. He'd forgotten that this happened. For someone who lived so in the past, with such a good memory, he was surprised to find he couldn't exactly remember when he'd experienced this sensation last. What he could recall was an amalgam of evenings with Blaine, he supposed, before the accident. He *did* remember that he'd decided to endure the tickle, not push the strands away, so he wouldn't disturb his wife.

Now, of course, he couldn't brush away Sachs's hair if God Himself had asked. But he wouldn't think of moving it aside. Just the opposite; he wanted to prolong the sensation until the end of the universe.

THIRTY-FIVE

The next morning Lincoln Rhyme was alone again.

Thom had gone shopping and Mel Cooper was at the IRD lab downtown. Vince Peretti had completed the CS work at the mansion on Van Brevoort and at Sachs's. They'd found woefully few clues though Rhyme put the lack of PE down to the unsub's ingenuity, not Peretti's derivative talents.

Rhyme was awaiting the crime scene report. But both Dobyns and Sellitto believed that 823 had gone to ground—temporarily at least. There'd been no more attacks on the police and no other victims had been kidnapped in the past twelve hours.

Sachs's minder—a large Patrol officer from MTS—had accompanied her to an appointment with an ear, nose and throat man at a hospital in Brooklyn; the dirt had done quite a number on her throat. Rhyme himself had a bodyguard too—a uniform from the Twentieth Precinct, stationed in front of his townhouse—a friendly cop he'd known for years and with whom Rhyme enjoyed a running argument on the merits of Irish peat versus Scottish in the production of whisky.

Rhyme was in a great mood. He called downstairs on the intercom. "I'm expecting a doctor in a couple of hours. You can let him up."

The cop said he would.

Dr William Berger had assured Rhyme that today he'd be on time.

Rhyme leaned back in the pillow and realized he wasn't completely alone. On the windowsill, the falcons paced. Rarely skittish, they seemed uneasy. Another low front was

UNSUB 823

Appearance	Residence	Vehicle	Other
• Caucasian male, slight build • Dark clothing • Old gloves, reddish kidskin • Aftershave; to cover up other scent? • Ski mask? Navy blue? • Gloves are dark • Aftershave = Brut • Hair color not brown • Deep scar, index finger • Casual clothes • Gloves are black	• Prob. has safe house • Located near; Houston & Lafayette, ShopRite • Old building, pink marble • At least 100 years old, prob. mansion or institutional • Federal-style building, Lower East Side • Located near archaeologic dig	• Yellow Cab • Recent model sedan • Lt. gray, silver, biege • Rental car; prob. stolen • Hertz, silver Taurus, this year's model	• knows CS proc. • possibly has record • knows FR prints • gun = .32 Colt • Ties vics w/ unusual knots • "Old" appeals to him • Called one vic "Hanna" • Knows basic German • Underground appeals to him • Dual personalities • Maybe priest, soc. worker, counselor • Unusual wear on shoes, reads a lot? • Listened as he broke vic's finger • Left snake as slap at investigators • Wanted to flay vic's foot • Called one vic "Maggie" • Mother & child, special meaning to him? • Book "Crime in Old NY," his model? • Bases crimes on James Schneider, the "Bone Collector" • Has hatred of police

approaching. Rhyme's window revealed a calm sky but he trusted the birds; they were infallible barometers.

He glanced at the clock on the wall. It was 11:00 A.M. Here he was, just like two days ago, awaiting Berger's arrival. That's life, he thought: postponement upon postponement but ultimately, with some luck, we get to where we're meant to be.

He watched television for twenty minutes, trolling for stories about the kidnappings. But all the stations were doing specials on the opening day of the UN conference. Rhyme found it boring and turned to a rerun of *Matlock*, flipped back to a gorgeous CNN reporter standing outside UN headquarters and then shut the damn set off.

The telephone rang and he went through the complicated gestures of answering it. "Hello."

There was a pause before a man's voice said, "Lincoln?"

"Yes?"

"Jim Polling. How you doin'?"

Rhyme realized that he hadn't seen much of the captain since early yesterday, except for the news conference last night, where he'd whispered prompts to the mayor and Chief Wilson.

"Okay. Any word on our unsub?" Rhyme asked.

"Nothing yet. But we'll get him." Another pause. "Hey, you alone?"

"Yep."

A longer pause.

"Okay if I stop by?"

"Sure."

"A half hour?"

"I'll be here," Rhyme said jovially.

He rested his head in the thick pillow and his eyes slipped to the knotted clothesline hanging beside the profile poster. Still no answer about the knot. It was—he laughed aloud at the joke—a loose end. He hated the idea of leaving the case without finding out what kind of knot it was. Then he remembered that Polling was a fisherman. Maybe he'd recognize—

Polling, Rhyme reflected.

James Polling . . .

Funny how the captain had insisted Rhyme handle the case. How he'd fought to keep him on it, rather than Peretti—who was the better choice, politically, for Polling. Remembering too how he'd lost his temper at Dellray when the feebie tried to strong-arm the investigation away from the NYPD.

Now that he thought about it, Polling's whole involvement in the case was a mystery. Eight twenty-three wasn't the kind of perp you took on voluntarily—even if you were looking for juicy cases to hang on your collar record. Too many chances to lose vics, too many opportunities for the press—and the brass—to snipe at you for fucking up.

Polling . . . Recalling how he'd breeze into Rhyme's bedroom, check out their progress and leave.

Sure, he was reporting to the mayor and the chief. But—the thought slipped unexpectedly into Rhyme's mind—was there someone *else* Polling was reporting back to?

Someone who wanted to keep tabs on the investigation? The unsub himself?

But how on earth could Polling have any connection with 823? It seemed—

And then it struck him.

Could Polling *be* the unsub?

Of course not. It was ridiculous. Laughable. Even apart from motive and means, there was the question of opportunity. The captain had been here, in Rhyme's room, when some of the kidnappings had occurred. . . .

Or had he?

Rhyme looked up at the profile chart.

Dark clothing and wrinkled cotton slacks. Polling'd been wearing dark sports clothes over the past several days. But so what? So did a lot of—

Downstairs a door opened and closed.

"Thom?"

No answer. The aide wasn't due back for hours.

"Lincoln?"

Oh, no. Hell. He started to dial on the ECU.

9–1–

With his chin he bumped the cursor to 2.

Footsteps on the stairs.

He tried to redial but in his desperation he knocked the joystick out of reach.

And Jim Polling walked into the room. Rhyme had counted on the babysitter's calling upstairs first. But of course a beat cop would let a police captain inside without thinking twice.

Polling's dark jacket was unbuttoned and Rhyme got a look at the automatic on his hip. He couldn't see if it was his issue weapon. But he knew that .32 Colts were on the NYPD list of approved personal weapons.

"Lincoln," Polling said. He was clearly uneasy, cautious. His eyes fell to the bleached bit of spinal cord.

"How you doing, Jim?"

"Not bad."

Polling the outdoorsman. Had the scar on the fingerprint been left by years of casting a fishing line? Or an accident with hunting a knife? Rhyme tried to look but Polling kept his hands jammed into his pockets. Was he holding something in there? A knife?

Polling certainly knew forensics and crime scenes—he knew how *not* to leave evidence.

The ski mask? If Polling was the unsub he'd have to wear the mask of course—because one of the vics might see him later. And the aftershave . . . what if the unsub hadn't *worn* the scent at all but had just carried a bottle with him and sprayed some at the scenes to make them *believe* he wore Brut? So when Polling showed up here, not wearing any, no one would suspect him.

"You're alone?" Polling asked.

"My assistant—"

"The cop downstairs said he wouldn't be back for a while."

Rhyme hesitated. "That's right."

Polling was slight but strong, sandy-haired. Terry Dobyns's words came back: Someone helpful, upstanding. A social worker, counselor, politician. Somebody helping other people.

Like a cop.

Rhyme wondered now if he was about to die. And to his shock he realized that he didn't want to. Not this way, not on somebody else's terms.

Polling walked to the bed.

Yet there was nothing he could do. He was at this man's complete mercy.

"Lincoln," Polling repeated gravely.

Their eyes met and the feeling of electrical connection went through them. Dry sparks. The captain looked quickly out the window. "You've been wondering, haven't you?"

"Wondering?"

"Why I wanted you on the case."

"I figured it was my personality."

This drew no smile from the captain.

"Why *did* you want me, Jim?"

The captain's fingers knitted together. Thin but strong. The hands of a fisherman, a sport that, yes, may be genteel but whose purpose is nonetheless to wrench a poor beast from his home and slice through its smooth belly with a thin knife.

"Four years ago, the Shepherd case. We were on it together."

Rhyme nodded.

"The workers found the body of that cop in the subway stop."

A groan, Rhyme recalled, like the sound of the *Tatanic* sinking in *A Night to Remember*. Then an explosion loud as a gunshot as the beam came down on his hapless neck, and dirt packed around his body.

"And you ran the scene. You yourself, like you always did."

"I did, yes."

"Did you know how we convicted Shepherd? We had a wit."

A witness? Rhyme hadn't heard that. After the accident he'd lost all track of the case, except for learning that Shepherd had been convicted and, three months later, stabbed to death on Riker's Island by an assailant who was never captured.

"An eyewitness," Polling continued. "He could place Shepherd at one of the victim's homes with the murder weapon." The captain stepped closer to the bed, crossed his arms. "We had the wit a day *before* we found the last body—the one in the subway. Before I put in the request that you run the scene."

"What're you saying, Jim?"

The captain's eyes rooted themselves to the floor. "We didn't need you. We didn't *need* your report."

Rhyme said nothing.

Polling nodded. "You understand what I'm saying? I wanted to nail that fuck Shepherd so bad. . . . I wanted an airtight case. And you know what a Lincoln Rhyme crime scene report does to defense lawyers. It scares the everlovin' shit out of them."

"But Shepherd would've been convicted even without my report from the subway scene."

"That's right, Lincoln. But it's worse than that. See, I got word from MTA Engineering that the site wasn't safe."

"The subway site. And you had me work the scene before they shored it up?"

"Shepherd was a cop-killer." Polling's face twisted up in disgust. "I wanted him so bad. I woulda done anything to nail him. But . . ." He lowered his head to his hands.

Rhyme said nothing. He heard the groan of the beam, the explosion of the breaking wood. Then the rustle of the dirt nestling around him. A curious, warm peace in his body while his heart stuttered with terror.

"Jim—"

"That's why I wanted you on this case, Lincoln. You see?" A miserable look crossed the captain's tough face; he stared at the disk of spinal column on the table. "I kept hearing these stories that your life was crap. You were wasting away here. Talking about killing yourself. I felt so fucking guilty. I wanted to try to give you some of your life back."

Rhyme said, "And you've been living with this for the last three and a half years."

"You know about me, Lincoln. *Everybody* knows about me. I collar somebody, he gives me any shit, he goes *down*. I get a hardon for some perp, I don't stop till the prick's bagged and tagged. I can't control it. I know I've fucked over people sometimes. But they were perps—or suspects, at least. They weren't my own, they weren't cops. What happened to you . . . that was a sin. It was just fucking wrong."

"I wasn't a rookie," Rhyme said. "I didn't *have* to work a scene I thought wasn't safe."

"But—"

"Bad time?" another voice said from the doorway.

Rhyme glanced up, expecting to see Berger. But it was Peter Taylor who'd come up the stairs. Rhyme recalled that he was coming by today to check on his patient after the dysreflexia attack. He supposed too that the doctor was planning to give him hell about Berger and the Lethe Society. He wasn't in the mood for that; he wanted time alone—to digest Polling's confession. At the moment it just sat there, numb as Rhyme's thigh. But he said, "Come on in, Peter."

"You've got a very funny security system, Lincoln. The guard asked if I was a doctor and he let me up. What? Do lawyers and accountants get booted?"

Rhyme laughed. "I'll only be a second." Rhyme turned back to Polling. "Fate, Jim. That's what happened to me. I was in the wrong place at the wrong time. It happens."

"Thanks, Lincoln." Polling put his hand on Rhyme's right shoulder and squeezed it gently.

Rhyme nodded and, to deflect the uneasy gratitude, introduced the men. "Jim, this is Pete Taylor, one of my doctors. And this is Jim Polling, we used to work together."

"Nice to meet you," Taylor said, sticking out his right hand. It was a broad gesture and Rhyme's eyes followed it, noticing for some reason the deep crescent scar on Taylor's right index finger.

"No!" Rhyme shouted.

"So you're a cop too." Taylor gripped Polling's hand tightly as he slid the knife, held firmly in his left hand, in and out of the captain's chest three times, navigating around the ribs with the delicacy of a surgeon. Undoubtedly so he wouldn't nick the precious bone.

THIRTY-SIX

In two long steps Taylor was beside the bed. He grabbed the ECU controller from beneath Rhyme's finger, flung it across the room.

Rhyme took a breath to shout. But the doctor said, "He's dead too. The constable." Nodding toward the door, meaning the bodyguard downstairs. Taylor stared with fascination as Polling thrashed like a spine-cracked animal, spraying his blood on the floor and walls.

"Jim!" Rhyme cried. "No, oh, no . . ."

The captain's hands curled over his ruined chest. A repugnant gurgling from his throat filled the room, accompanied by the mad thudding of his shoes on the floor as he died. Finally he quivered once violently and lay still. His glazed eyes, dotted with blood, stared at the ceiling.

Turning to the bed he kept his eyes on Lincoln Rhyme as he walked around it. Slowly circling, the knife in his hand. His breathing was hard.

"Who *are* you?" Rhyme gasped.

Silently Taylor stepped forward, put his fingers around Rhyme's arm, squeezed the bone several times, perhaps hard, perhaps not. His hand strayed to Rhyme's left ring finger. He lifted it off the ECU and caressed it with the dripping blade of the knife. Slipped the sharp point up under the nail.

Rhyme felt faint pain, a queasy sensation. Then harder. He gasped.

Then Taylor noticed something and froze. He gasped. Leaned forward. Staring at the copy of *Crime in Old New York* on the turning frame.

"*That's* how . . . You actually found it. . . .Oh, the constables should be proud to have you in their ranks, Lincoln Rhyme. I thought it'd be days before you got to the house. I thought Maggie'd be stripped down by the dogs by then."

"Why're you doing this?" Rhyme asked.

But Taylor didn't answer; he was examining Rhyme carefully, muttering, half to himself, "You didn't used to be this good, you know. In the old days. You missed a lot back then, didn't you? In the old days."

The old days . . . What did he mean?

He shook his balding head, gray hair—not brown—and glanced at a copy of Rhyme's forensic textbook. There was recognition in his eyes and slowly Rhyme began to understand.

"You read my book," the criminalist said. "You studied it. At the library, right? The public library branch near you?"

Eight twenty-three was, after all, a reader.

So he knew Rhyme's CS procedures. That's why he'd swept up so carefully, why he'd worn gloves touching even surfaces most criminals wouldn't've thought would retain prints, why he'd sprayed the aftershave at the scene—he'd known exactly what Sachs would be looking for.

And of course the manual wasn't the only book he'd read.

Scenes of the Crime too. That's what had given him the idea for the planted clues—Old New York clues. Clues that only Lincoln Rhyme would be able to figure out.

Taylor picked up the disk of spinal column he'd given to Rhyme eight months ago. He kneaded it absently between his fingers. And Rhyme saw the gift, so touching back then, for the horrific preface that it was.

His eyes were unfocused, distant. Rhyme recalled he'd seen this before—when Taylor'd examined him over the past months. He'd put it down to a doctor's concentration but now knew it was madness. The control he'd been struggling to maintain was disappearing.

"Tell me," Rhyme asked. "Why?"

"Why?" Taylor whispered, moving his hand along Rhyme's leg, probing once more, knee, shin, ankle. "Because you were something remarkable, Rhyme. Unique. You were invulnerable."

"What do you mean?"

"How can you punish a man who wants to die? If you kill him you've done what he wants. So I had to make you want to live."

And the answer came to Rhyme finally.

The old days . . .

"It was fake, wasn't it?" he whispered. "That obituary from the Albany coroner. You wrote it yourself."

Colin Stanton. Dr Taylor was Colin Stanton.

The man whose family had been butchered in front of him on the streets of Chinatown. The man who stood paralyzed in front of the bodies of his wife and two children as they bled to death, and could not make the obscene choice about which of them to save.

You missed things. In the old days.

Now, too late, the final pieces fell into place.

His watching the victims: T.J. Colfax and Monelle and Carole Ganz. He'd risked capture to stand and stare at them—just as Stanton had stood over his family, watching as they died. He wanted revenge but he was a doctor, sworn never to take a life, and so in order to kill he had to become his spiritual ancestor—the bone collector, James Schneider, a nineteenth-century madman whose family had been destroyed by the police.

"After I got out of the mental hospital I came back to Manhattan. I read the inquest report about how you missed the killer at the crime scene, how he got out of the apartment. I knew I had to kill you. But I couldn't. I don't know why. . . .I kept waiting and waiting for something to happen. And then I found the book. James Schneider . . . He'd been through exactly what I had. He'd done it; I could too."

I took them down to the bone.

"The obituary," Rhyme said.

"Right. I wrote it myself on my computer. Faxed it to NYPD so they wouldn't suspect me. Then I became someone else. Dr Peter Taylor. I didn't realize until later why I picked that name. Can you figure it out?" Stanton's eyes strayed to the chart. "The answer's there."

Rhyme scanned the profile.

- Knows basic German.

"*Schneider*," Rhyme said, sighing. "It's German for 'tailor.'"

Stanton nodded. "I spent weeks at the library reading up on spinal cord trauma and then called you, claimed I'd been referred by Columbia SCI. I planned to kill you during the first appointment, cut your flesh off a strip at a time, let you bleed to death. It might've taken hours. Even days. But what happened?" His eyes grew wide. "I found out you wanted to kill *yourself*."

He leaned close to Rhyme. "Jesus, I still remember the first time I saw you. You son of a bitch. You *were* dead. And I knew what I had to do—I had to make you *want* to live. I had to give you purpose once more."

So it didn't matter whom he kidnapped. Anyone would do. "You didn't even care whether the victims lived or died."

"Of course not. All I wanted was to force *you* to try to save them."

"The knot," Rhyme asked, noticing the loop of clothesline hanging beside the poster. "It was a surgical suture?"

He nodded.

"Of course. And the scar on your finger?"

"My finger?" He frowned. "How did you . . . Her *neck*! You printed her neck, Hanna's. I *knew* that was possible. I didn't think about it." Angry with himself. "I broke a glass in the mental hospital library," Stanton continued. "To cut my wrist. I squeezed it till it broke." He madly traced the scar with his left index finger.

"The deaths," Rhyme said evenly, "your wife and children. It was an accident. A terrible accident, horrible. But it didn't happen on purpose. It was a mistake. I'm so sorry for you and for them."

In a sing-songy voice, Stanton chided, "Remember what you wrote? . . . in the preface of your textbook?" He recited perfectly, "'The criminalist knows that for every action there's a consequence. The presence of a perpetrator alters every crime scene, however subtly. It is because of this that we can identify and locate criminals and achieve justice.'" Stanton grabbed Rhyme's hair and tugged his head forward. They were inches apart. Rhyme could smell the madman's breath, see the lenses of sweat on the gray skin. "Well, I'm the consequence of *your* actions."

"What'll you accomplish? You kill me and I'm no worse off than I would've been."

"Oh, but I'm not going to kill you. Not yet."

Stanton released Rhyme's hair, backed away.

"You want to know what I'm going to do?" he whispered. "I'm going to kill your doctor, Berger. But not the way he's used to killing. Oh, no sleeping pills for him, no booze. We'll see how he likes death the old-fashioned way. Then your friend Sellitto. And Officer Sachs? Her too. She was lucky once. But I'll get her the next time. Another burial for her. And Thom too of course. He'll die right here in front of you. Work him down to the bone . . . Nice and slow." Stanton's breathing was fast. "Maybe we'll take care of him today. When's he due back?"

"*I* made the mistakes. It's my—" Rhyme suddenly coughed deeply. He cleared his throat, caught his breath. "It's *my* fault. Do whatever you want with me."

"No, it's all of you. It's—"

"Please. You can't—" Rhyme began to cough again. It turned into a violent racking. He managed to control it.

Stanton glanced at him.

"You *can't* hurt them. I'll do whatever—" Rhyme's voice seized. His head flew back, his eyes bulged.

And Lincoln Rhyme's breath stopped completely. His head thrashed, his shoulders shivered violently. The tendons in his neck tightened like steel cords.

"Rhyme!" Stanton cried.

Sputtering, saliva shooting from his lips, Rhyme trembled once, twice, an earthquake seemed to ripple through his entire limp body. His head fell back, blood trickled from the corner of his mouth.

"No!" Stanton shouted. Slamming his hands into Rhyme's chest. "You can't die!"

The doctor lifted Rhyme's lids, revealing only whites.

Stanton tore open Thom's medicine box and prepared a blood-pressure hypodermic, injected the drug. He yanked the pillow off the bed and pulled Rhyme flat. He tilted back Rhyme's lolling head, wiped the lips and placed his mouth on Rhyme's, breathing hard into the unresponsive lungs.

"No!" Stanton raged. "I won't let you die! You *can't*!"

No response.

Again. He checked the unmoving eyes.

"Come on! Come *on*!"

Another breath. Pounding on the still chest.

Then he backed up, frozen with panic and shock, staring, staring, watching the man die in front of him.

Finally he bent forward and one last time exhaled deeply into Rhyme's mouth.

And it was when Stanton turned his head and lowered his ear to listen for the faint sound of breath, any faint exhalation, that Rhyme's head shot forward like a striking snake. He closed his teeth on Stanton's neck, tearing through the carotid artery and gripping a portion of the man's own spine.

Down to . . .

Stanton screamed and scrabbled backwards, sliding Rhyme off the bed on top of him. Together they fell in a pile on the floor. The hot coppery blood gushed and gushed, filling Rhyme's mouth.

. . . the bone.

His lungs, his *killer* lungs, had already gone for a minute without air but he refused to loosen his grip now to gasp for breath, ignoring the searing pain from inside his cheek where he'd bit into the tender skin, bloodying it to give credence to his sham attack of dysreflexia. He growled in rage—seeing Amelia Sachs buried in dirt, seeing the steam spew over T.J. Colfax's body—and he shook his head, feeling the snap of bone and cartilage.

Pummeling Rhyme's chest, Stanton screamed again, kicking to get away from the monster that had socketed itself to him.

But Rhyme's grip was unbreakable. It was as if the spirits of all the dead muscles throughout his body had risen into his jaw.

Stanton clawed his way to the bedside table and managed to grab his knife. He jabbed it into Rhyme. Once, twice. But the only places he could reach were the criminalist's legs and arms. It's pain that incapacitates and pain was one thing to which Lincoln Rhyme was immune.

The vise of his jaws closed harder and Stanton's scream was cut off as his windpipe went. He plunged the knife deep into Rhyme's arm. It stopped when it hit bone. He started to draw it out to strike again but the madman's body froze then spasmed violently once, then again, and suddenly went completely limp.

Stanton collapsed to the floor, pulling Rhyme after him. The criminalist's head slammed onto the oak with a loud crack. Yet Rhyme wouldn't let go. He held tight and continued to crush the man's neck, shaking, tearing the flesh like a hungry lion crazed by blood and by the immeasurable satisfaction of a lust fulfilled.

5

WHEN YOU MOVE THEY CAN'T GETCHA

"A physician's duty is not just to extend life, it is to end suffering."

Dr Jack Kevorkian

Monday, 7:15 P.M., to Monday, 10:00 P.M.

THIRTY-SEVEN

It was nearly sunset when Amelia Sachs walked through his doorway.

She was no longer in sweats. Or uniform. She wore jeans and a forest-green blouse. Her beautiful face sported several scratches Rhyme didn't recognize, though given the events of the past three days he guessed the wounds weren't self-inflicted.

"Yuck," she said, walking around the portion of the floor where Stanton and Polling had died. It had been mopped with bleach—with the perp body-bagged, forensics became moot—but the pink island of stain was huge.

Rhyme watched Sachs pause and nod a cold greeting to Dr William Berger, who stood by the falcon window with his infamous briefcase at his side.

"So you got him, did you?" she asked, nodding at the bloodstain.

"Yeah," Rhyme said. "He's got."

"All by yourself?"

"It was hardly a fair fight," he offered. "I forced myself to hold back."

Outside, the liquid, ruddy light of the low sun ignited treetops and the marching line of elegant buildings along Fifth Avenue across the park.

Sachs glanced at Berger, who said, "Lincoln and I were just having a little talk."

"Were you?"

There was a long pause.

"Amelia," he began. "I'm going to go through with it. I've decided."

"I see." Her gorgeous lips, marred by the black lines of tiny stitches, tightened slightly. It was her only visible reaction. "You know, I hate it when you use my first name. I goddamn *hate* it."

How could he explain to her that *she* was largely the reason he was going ahead with his death? Waking that morning, with her beside him, he realized with a piquant sorrow that she would soon climb from the bed and dress and walk out the door—to her own life, to a *normal* life. Why, they were as doomed as lovers could be—if he dared even to think of them as lovers. It was only a matter of time until she met another Nick and fell in love. The 823 case was over, and without that binding them together, their lives would have to drift apart. Inevitable.

Oh, Stanton was smarter than he could've guessed. Rhyme *had* been drawn to the brink of the real world once again and, yes, he'd moved far over it.

Sachs, I lied: Sometimes you can't give up the dead. Sometimes you just have to go with them. . . .

Hands clenched, she walked to the window. "I tried to come up with a ballbuster of an argument to talk you out of it. You know, something real slick. But I couldn't. All I can say is, I just don't want you to do it."

"A deal's a deal, Sachs."

She looked at Berger. "Shit, Rhyme." Walking over to the bed, crouching down. She put her hand on his shoulder, brushed his hair off his forehead. "But will you do one thing for me?"

"What?"

"Give me a few hours."

"I'm not changing my mind."

"I understand. Just two hours. There's something you have to do first."

Rhyme looked at Berger, who said, "I can't stay much longer, Lincoln. My plane . . . If you want to wait a week I can come back. . . ."

"That's okay, doctor," Sachs said. "I'll help him do it."

"You?" the doctor asked cautiously.

Reluctantly she nodded. "Yes."

This wasn't *her* nature. Rhyme could see that clearly. But he glanced into her blue eyes, which though tearful were remarkably clear. He nodded. He said to Berger, "It's all right, doctor. Could you just leave the—what's the euphemism of the day?"

"How's 'paraphernalia'?" Berger suggested.

"Could you just leave them there, on the table?"

"You're sure?" he asked Sachs.

She nodded again.

The doctor set the pills, brandy and plastic bag on the bedside table. Then he rummaged through his briefcase. "I don't have any rubber bands, I'm afraid. For the bag."

"That's all right," Sachs said, glancing down at her shoes. "I've got some."

Then Berger stepped close to the bed, put his arm on Rhyme's shoulder. "I wish you a peaceful self-deliverance," he said.

"Self-deliverance," Rhyme said wryly as Berger left. Then, to Sachs: "Now. What's this I have to do?"

She took the turn at fifty, skidded hard, and slipped smoothly up into fourth gear.

The wind blasted through the open windows and tossed their hair behind them. The gusts were brutal but Amelia Sachs wouldn't hear of driving with the windows up.

"That'd be un-Amurican," she announced, and broke the 100-mph mark.

When you move . . .

Rhyme had suggested it might be wiser to take their spin on the NYPD training course but he wasn't surprised when Sachs declared that that was a pussy run; she'd disposed of it the first week at the academy. So they were out on Long Island, their cover stories for the Nassau County police ready, rehearsed and marginally credible.

"The thing above five-speeds is, top gear isn't the fastest. That's a mileage gear. I don't give a shit about mileage." Then she took his left hand and placed it on the round black knob, encircled it with hers, downshifted.

The engine screamed and they shot up to 120, as trees and houses streaked past and the uneasy horses grazing in the fields stared at the black streak of Chevrolet.

"Isn't this the *best*, Rhyme?" she shouted. "Man, better than sex. Better than anything."

"I can feel the vibrations," he said. "I think I can. In my finger."

She smiled and he believed she squeezed his hand beneath hers. Finally, they ran out of deserted road, population loomed, and Sachs reluctantly slowed, turned around and pointed the nose of the car toward the hazy crescent of moon as it rose above the distant city, nearly invisible in the stew of hot August air.

"Let's try for one-fifty," she proposed. Lincoln Rhyme closed his eyes and lost himself in the sensation of wind and the perfume of freshly cut grass and the speed.

The night was the hottest of the month.

From Lincoln's Rhyme's new vantage point he could look down into the park and see the weirdos on the benches, the exhausted joggers, the families reclining around the smoke of dwindling barbecue fires like the survivors of a medieval battle. A few dog walkers unable to wait for the night's fever to break made their obligatory rounds, Baggies in hand.

Thom had put on a CD—Samuel Barber's elegiac Adagio for Strings. But Rhyme had snorted a derisive laugh, declared it a sorry cliché and ordered him to replace it with Gershwin.

Amelia Sachs climbed the stairs and walked into his bedroom, noticed him looking outside. "What do you see?" she asked.

"Hot people."

"And the birds? The falcons?"

"Ah, yes, they're there."

"Hot too?"

He examined the male. "I don't think so. Somehow, they seem above that sort of thing."

She set the bag on the foot of the bed and lifted out the contents, a bottle of expensive brandy. He'd reminded her of the Scotch but Sachs said she'd contribute the liquor. She set it next to the pills and the plastic bag. Looking like a breezy professional wife, home from Balducci's with piles of vegetables and seafood and too little time to whip them into dinner.

She'd also bought some ice, at Rhyme's request. He'd remembered what Berger had explained about the heat in the bag. She lifted the cap off the Courvoisier and poured herself a glass and filled his tumbler, arranged the straw toward his mouth.

"Where's Thom?" she asked him.

"Out."

"Does he know?"

"Yes."

They sipped the brandy.

"Do you want me to say anything to your wife?"

Rhyme considered it for a long moment, thinking: We have years to converse with someone, to blurt and rant, to explain our desires and anger and regrets—and oh how we squander those moments. Here he'd known Amelia Sachs all of three days and they'd bared their hearts far more than he and Blaine had done in nearly a decade.

"No," he said. "I've e-mailed her." A chuckle. "That's a comment on our times, I'd say."

More brandy, the astringent bite on his palate was dissipating. Growing smoother, duller, lighter.

Sachs leaned over the bed and tapped her glass to his.

"I have some money," Rhyme began. "I'm giving a lot of it to Blaine and to Thom. I—"

But she shushed him with a kiss to the forehead and shook her head.

A soft clatter of pebbles as she spilled the tiny Seconals into her hand.

Rhyme instinctively thought: The Dillie-Koppanyi color test reagent. Add 1 percent cobalt acetate in methanol to the suspect material followed by 5 percent isopropylamine in methanol. If the substance is a barbiturate the reagent turns a beautiful violet-blue color.

"How should we do it?" she asked, gazing at the pills. "I really don't know."

"Mix them in the booze," he suggested.

She dropped them in his tumbler. They dissolved quickly.

How fragile they were. Like the dreams they induce.

She stirred the mixture with the straw. He glanced at her wounded nails but even that he couldn't be sorrowful for. This was *his* night and it was a night of joy.

Lincoln Rhyme had a sudden recollection of childhood in suburban Illinois. He never drank his milk and to get him to do so his mother bought straws coated on the inside with flavoring. Strawberry, chocolate. He hadn't thought about them until just this moment. It was a great invention, he remembered. He always looked forward to his afternoon milk.

Sachs pushed the straw close to his mouth. He took it between his lips. She put her hand on his arm.

Light or dark, music or silence, dreams or the meditation of dreamless sleep? What will I find?

He began to sip. The taste was really no different from straight liquor. A little more bitter maybe. It was like—

From downstairs came a huge pounding on the door. Hands and feet both, it seemed. Voices shouting too.

He lifted his lips away from the straw. Glanced into the dim stairwell.

She looked at him, frowning.

"Go see," he said to her.

She disappeared down the stairs and a moment later returned, looking unhappy. Lon Sellitto and Jerry Banks followed. Rhyme noticed that the young detective had done another butcher job on his face with a razor. He'd really have to get that under control.

Sellitto glanced at the bottle and the bag. His eyes swayed toward Sachs but she crossed her arms and held her own, silently ordering him to leave. This was not an issue of rank, the look told the detective, and what was happening here was none of his business. Sellitto's eyes acknowledged the message but he wasn't about to go anywhere just yet.

"Lincoln, I need to talk to you."

"Talk. But talk fast, Lon. We're busy."

The detective sat heavily in the noisy rattan chair. "An hour ago a bomb went off at the United Nations. Right next to the banquet hall. During the welcome dinner for the peace conference delegates."

"Six dead, fifty-four hurt," Banks added. "Twenty of them serious."

"My God," Sachs whispered.

"Tell him," Sellitto muttered.

Banks continued, "For the conference, the UN hired a bunch of temps. The perp was one of them—a receptionist. A half-dozen people saw her carrying a knapsack to work and putting it in a storeroom near the banquet hall. She left just before the bang. The bomb squad estimates we're looking at about two pounds of C4 or Semtex."

Sellitto said, "Linc, the bomb, it was a yellow knapsack, the wits said."

"Yellow?" Why was that familiar?

"UN human resources ID'd the receptionist as Carole Ganz."

"The mother," Rhyme and Sachs said simultaneously.

"Yeah. The woman you saved in the church. Only Ganz's an alias. Her real name's Charlotte Willoughby. She was married to a Ron Willoughby. Ring a bell?"

Rhyme said it didn't.

"It was in the news a couple years ago. He was an Army sergeant assigned to a UN peacekeeping force in Burma."

"Keep going," the criminalist said.

"Willoughby didn't want to go—thought an American soldier shouldn't be wearing a UN uniform and taking orders from anybody except the U.S. Army. It's a big right-wing issue nowadays. But he went anyway. Wasn't there a week before he's blown away by some little punk in Rangoon. Got shot in the back. Became a conservative martyr. Anti-Terror says his widow got recruited by an extremist group out in the Chicago burbs. Some U of C grads gone underground. Edward and Katherine Stone."

Banks took over the narrative. "The explosive was in a package of kid's modeling clay, along with some other toys. We think she was going to take the little girl with her so security at the banquet-hall entrance wouldn't think anything of the clay. But with Pammy in the hospital she didn't have her cover story so she gave up on the hall and just planted it in the storeroom. Did enough damage as it was."

"Rabitted?"

"Yep. Not a trace."

"What about the little girl," Sachs asked, "Pammy?"

"Gone. The woman checked her out of the hospital around the time of the bang. No sign of either of them."

Rhyme asked, "The cell?"

"The group in Chicago? They're gone too. Had a safe house in Wisconsin but it's been hosed. We don't know where they are."

"So *that* was the rumor Dellray's snitch heard." Rhyme laughed. "*Carole* was the one coming into the airport. Had nothing to do with Unsub 823."

He found Banks and Sellitto staring at him.

Oh, the old silent trick again.

"Forget it, Lon." Rhyme said, all too aware of the glass sitting inches from him, radiating a welcoming heat. "Impossible."

The older detective plucked his sweaty shirt away from his body, cringing. "God*damn* cold in here, Lincoln. Jesus. Look, just think about it. What'sa harm?"

"I can't help you."

Sellitto said, "There was a note. Carole wrote it and sent it to the secretary-general by interoffice envelope. Harping on world government, taking away American liberties. Some shit like that. Claimed credit for the UNESCO bombing in London too and said there'd be more. We've gotta get 'em, Linc."

Feeling his oats, scarface Banks said, "The secretary-general and the mayor both've asked for you. SAC Perkins too. And there'll be a call from the White House, you need any more persuading. We sure hope you don't, detective."

Rhyme didn't comment on the error regarding his rank.

"They've got the Bureau's PERT team ready to go. Fred Dellray's running the case and he asked—*respectfully*, yeah, he used that very word—he asked respectfully if you'd do the forensic work. And it's a virgin scene, except for getting the bodies and the wounded out."

"Then it's *not* virgin," Rhyme snapped. "It's extremely contaminated."

"All the more reason we need you," Banks ventured, adding "sir" to defuse Rhyme's glare.

Rhyme sighed, looked at the glass and the straw. Peace was so close to him just now. And pain too. Infinite sums of both.

He closed his eyes. Not a sound in the room.

Sellitto added, "It was just the woman herself, hey, wouldn't be that big a deal. But she's got her daughter with her, Lincoln. Underground, with a little girl? You know what that kid's life's going to be like?"

I'll get you for that too, Lon.

Rhyme nestled his head into the opulent pillow. Finally his eyes sprang open. He said, "There'd be some conditions."

"Name it, Linc."

"First of all," he said, "I don't work alone."

Rhyme looked toward Amelia Sachs.

She hesitated for a moment then smiled and stood, lifted the glass of tainted brandy out from under the straw. She opened the window wide and flung the tawny liquid into the ripe, hot air above the alley next to the townhouse, while, just feet away, the falcon looked up, glaring angrily at the motion of her arm, cocked his gray head, then turned back to feed his hungry youngster.

APPENDIX

Excerpts from: Glossary of Terms, Lincoln Rhyme, *Physical Evidence,* 4th ed., (New York, Forensic Press, 1994). Reprinted with permission.

Alternative light source (ALS): Any of several types of high-intensity lamps of varying wavelength and light color, used to visualize latent friction-ridge prints, and certain types of trace and biological evidence.

Automated Fingerprint Identification System (AFIS): One of several computerized systems for the scanning and storage of friction ridge prints.

Birefringence: The difference between two measures of refraction displayed by certain crystalline substances. Useful in identifying sand, fibers, and dirt.

Chain of custody (COC): A record of every person who has had possession of a piece of evidence from the moment of its collection at a crime scene to its introduction at trial.

COD: Cause of death.

Control samples: Physical evidence collected at a crime scene from known sources, used for comparison with evidence from an unknown source. For example, the victim's own blood and hair constitutes a control sample.

DCDS: Deceased, confirmed dead at scene.

Density-gradient testing (D-G): A technique for comparing soil samples to determine if they come from the same location. The test involves suspending dirt samples in tubes filled with liquids that have different density values.

DNA typing: Analyzing and charting the genetic structure within the cells of certain types of biological evidence (for example, blood, semen, hair) for the purpose of comparison with control samples from a known suspect. The process involves the isolation and comparison of fragments of DNA —deoxyribonucleic acid—the basic building block of the chromosome. Some types of DNA typing produce a mere likelihood that the evidence came from a suspect; other types are virtually conclusive, with the odds in the hundreds of millions that the evidence was from a particular individual. Also called "genetic typing," or—erroneously—"DNA fingerprinting" or "genetic fingerprinting."

Forensic anthropologist: A skeletal-remains expert, who aids crime scene investigators in evaluating and identifying remains and excavating grave sites.

Forensic odontologist: A dental expert also aids crime scene investigators in identifying victims through examination of dental remains and analysis of bite-mark evidence.

Friction ridges: The raised lines of skin on fingers, palms and the soles of feet, whose patterns are unique to each individual. Prints of friction ridges at crime scenes can be classified as 1) plastic (left in an impressionable substance such as putty); 2) evident (left by skin coated with a foreign substance like dust or blood), 3) latent (left by skin contaminated with bodily secretions such as grease or sweat and largely invisible).

Gas chromatograph/mass spectrometer (GC-MS): Two instruments used in forensic analysis to identify unknown substances such as drugs and trace evidence. They are often linked together. The gas chromatograph separates components in a substance and sends them to the mass spectrometer, which definitively identifies each of those components.

Grid: A common approach to searching for evidence whereby the searcher covers a crime scene back and forth in one direction (say, north–south) then covers the same scene in the perpendicular direction (east–west).

Gunshot residue (GSR): The material deposited on the hands and clothing of a person shooting a firearm, particularly barium and antimony. GSR remains on human skin for up to six hours if not removed intentionally by washing or inadvertently by excessive contact when a suspect is arrested and handcuffed (particularly if hands are cuffed behind back).

Identification of physical evidence: Determining the category or class of material that an item of evidence falls into. This is distinguishable from "individuation," which is determining the single source the item came from. For instance, a torn piece of paper can be *identified* as coated 40-lb. stock of the type often used in magazine printing. It can be *individuated* if the tear exactly matches a torn page in the July issue of *Vogue* found in the suspect's possession. Individuation, of course, has far more probative value than does identification.

Individuation of physical evidence: See "Identification of physical evidence."

Lividity: The purplish discoloring of portions of the skin of a deceased owing to the darkening and settling of the blood after death.

Locard's Exchange Principle: Formulated by Edmond Locard, a French criminalist, this theory holds that there is always an exchange of physical evidence between the perpetrator and the crime scene or his victim, however minute or difficult to detect that evidence might be.

Mass spectrometer: See "Gas chromatograph."

Ninhydrin: A chemical that visualizes latent friction-ridge prints on porous surfaces such as paper, cardboard, and wood.

Physical evidence (PE): In criminal law, PE refers to items or substances presented at trial to support the assertion by the defendant or the prosecution that a particular proposition is true. Physical evidence may comprise inanimate objects, body materials, or impressions.

Presumptive blood test: Any of a number of chemical techniques for determining if blood residue is present at a crime scene, even if it is not evident. Most common are tests using luminol and orthotolidine.

Scanning electron microscope (SEM): An instrument that fires electrons onto a specimen of evidence to be examined and projects the resulting image on a computer monitor. Magnification of 100,000X is possible with SEMs, compared with about 500X in the case of most optical microscopes. The SEM is often combined with an energy-dispersive X-ray unit (EDX), which can identify the elements in a sample at the same time the technician is viewing it.

Staging: A perpetrator's efforts to rearrange, add or remove evidence from a crime scene to make it appear that the crime he or she has committed did not occur or was committed by someone else.

Trace evidence: Bits of tiny, sometimes microscopic, substances such as dust, dirt, cellular material, and fibers.

Unsub: Unknown subject, that is, an unidentified suspect.

Vacuum-metal deposition (VMD): The most effective means for visualizing latent friction-ridge prints on smooth surfaces. Gold or zinc evaporated in a vacuum chamber, coats the object to be examined with a thin layer of metal, thereby making a print visible.

AUTHOR'S NOTE

I'm indebted to Peter A. Micheels, author of *The Detectives*, and E. W. Count, author of *Cop Talk*, whose books were not only wonderfully helpful in researching this one but great reads as well. Thanks to Pam Dorman, whose deft editorial touch is evident everywhere in this story. And of course thanks to my agent, Deborah Schneider . . . what would I do without ya? I'm grateful too to Nina Salter at Calmann-Lévy for her perceptive comments on an earlier draft of the book and to Karolyn Hutchinson at REP in Alexandria, Virginia, for invaluable help with wheelchairs and other equipment available for quadriplegics. And to Teddy Rosenbaum—a detective in her own right—for her fine copyediting job. Students of law enforcement may wonder about the structure of the NYPD and FBI as presented here; tweaking the organizational charts was my doing exclusively. Oh, yes—anyone interested in reading a copy of *Crime in Old New York* may have a little trouble finding one. The official story is that the book is a fictional creation, though I've also heard the rumor that the one copy in existence was recently stolen from the New York Public Library—by a person or persons unknown.

J.W.D.

The Coffin Dancer

Jeffery Deaver

To the memory of my grandmother Ethel May Rider

Author's note

All writers know that their books are only partly products of their own efforts. Novels are molded by our loved ones and friends, sometimes directly, sometimes in more subtle but no less important ways. I'd like to say thanks to some of the people who've helped me with this book: To Madelyn Warcholik for keeping my characters true to themselves, for making sure my plots don't move so recklessly they get pulled over for speeding, and for being an unlimited source of inspiration. To editors David Rosenthal, Marysue Rucci, and Carolyn Mays for brilliantly and unflinchingly doing all the hard work. To agent Deborah Scheider for being the best in the business. And to my sister and fellow author, Julie Reece Deaver, for being there throughout it all.

I

TOO MANY WAYS TO DIE

No hawk can be a pet. There is no sentimentality. In a way, it is the psychiatrist's art. One is matching one's mind against another mind with deadly reason and interest.

The Goshawk, T H. White

1

When Edward Carney said good-bye to his wife, Percey, he never thought it would be the last time he'd see her.

He climbed into his car, which was parked in a precious space on East Eighty-first Street in Manhattan, and pulled into traffic. Carney, an observant man by nature, noticed a black van parked near their town house. A van with mud-flecked, mirrored windows. He glanced at the battered vehicle and recognized the West Virginia plates, realizing he'd seen the van on the street several times in the past few days. But then the traffic in front of him sped up. He caught the end of the yellow light and forgot the van completely. He was soon on the FDR Drive, cruising north.

Twenty minutes later he juggled the car phone and called his wife. He was troubled when she didn't answer. Percey'd been scheduled to make the flight with him – they'd flipped a coin last night for the left-hand seat and she'd won, then given him one of her trademark victory grins. But then she'd wakened at 3 A.M. with a blinding migraine, which had stayed with her all day. After a few phone calls they'd found a substitute copilot and Percey'd taken a Fiorinal and gone back to bed.

A migraine was the only malady that would ground her.

Lanky Edward Carney, forty-five years old and still wearing a military hairstyle, cocked his head as he listened to the phone ringing miles away. Their answering machine clicked on and he returned the phone to the cradle, mildly concerned.

He kept the car at exactly sixty miles per hour, centered perfectly in the right lane; like most pilots he was conservative behind the wheel. He trusted other airmen but thought most drivers were crazy.

In the office of Hudson Air Charters, on the grounds of Mamaroneck Regional Airport, in Westchester, a cake awaited. Prim and assembled Sally Anne, smelling like the perfume department at Macy's, had baked it herself to commemorate the company's new contract. Wearing the ugly rhinestone biplane brooch her grandchildren had given her last Christmas, she scanned the room to make sure each of the dozen or so employees had a piece of devil's food sized just right for them. Ed Carney ate a few bites of cake and talked about tonight's flight with Ron Talbot, whose massive belly suggested he loved cake, though he survived mostly on cigarettes and coffee. Talbot wore the dual hats of operations and business manager and he worried out loud if the shipment would be on time, if the fuel usage for the flight had been calculated correctly, if they'd priced the job right. Carney handed him the remains of his cake and told him to relax.

He thought again about Percey and stepped away into his office, picked up the phone.

Still no answer at their town house.

Now concern became worry. People with children and people with their own business always pick up a ringing phone. He slapped the receiver down, thought about calling a neighbor to check up on her. But then the large white truck pulled up in front of the hangar next to the office and it was time to go to work.

Talbot gave Carney a dozen documents to sign just as young Tim Randolph arrived, wearing a dark suit, white shirt, and narrow black tie. Tim referred to himself as a "copilot" and Carney liked that. "First officers" were company people, airline creations, and while Carney respected any man who was competent in the right-hand seat, pretension put him off.

Tall, brunette Lauren, Talbot's assistant, had worn her lucky dress, whose blue color matched the hue of the Hudson Air logo – a silhouette of a falcon flying over a gridded globe. She leaned close to Carney and whispered, "It's going to be okay now, won't it?"

"It'll be fine," he assured her. They embraced for a moment. Sally Anne hugged him too and offered him some cake for the flight. He demurred. Ed Carney wanted to be gone. Away from the sentiment, away from the festivities. Away from the ground.

And soon he was. Sailing three miles above the earth, piloting a Lear 35A, the finest private jet ever made, clear of markings or insignia except for its *N* registration number, polished silver, sleek as a pike.

They flew toward a stunning sunset – a perfect orange disk easing into big, rambunctious clouds, pink and purple, leaking bolts of sunlight.

Only dawn was as beautiful. And only thunderstorms more spectacular.

It was 723 miles to O'Hare and they covered that distance in less than two hours. Air Traffic Control's Chicago Center politely asked them to descend to fourteen thousand feet, then handed them off to Chicago Approach Control.

Tim made the call. "Chicago Approach. Lear Four Niner *Charlie Juliet* with you at one four thousand."

"Evening, Niner *Charlie Juliet,*" said yet another placid air traffic controller. "Descend and maintain eight thousand. Chicago altimeter thirty point one one. Expect vectors to twenty-seven L."

"Roger, Chicago. Niner *Charlie Juliet* out of fourteen for eight."

O'Hare is the busiest airport in the world and ATC put them in a holding pattern out over the western suburbs of the city, where they'd circle, awaiting their turn to land.

Ten minutes later the pleasant, staticky voice requested, "Niner *Charlie Juliet,* heading zero nine zero over the numbers downwind for twenty-seven L."

"Zero nine zero. Nine *Charlie Juliet,*" Tim responded.

Carney glanced up at the bright points of constellations in the stunning gunmetal sky and thought, Look, Percey, it's all the stars of evening . . .

And with that he had what was the only unprofessional urge of perhaps his entire career. His concern for Percey arose like a fever. He needed desperately to speak to her.

"Take the aircraft," he said to Tim.

"Roger," the young man responded, hands going unquestioningly to the yoke.

Air Traffic Control crackled, "Niner *Charlie Juliet,* descend to four thousand. Maintain heading."

"Roger, Chicago," Tim said. "Niner *Charlie Juliet* out of eight for four."

Carney changed the frequency of his radio to make a unicom call. Tim glanced at him. "Calling the Company," Carney explained. When he got Talbot he asked to be patched through the telephone to his home.

As he waited, Carney and Tim went through the litany of the pre-landing check.

"Flaps approach . . . twenty degrees."

"Twenty, twenty, green," Carney responded.

"Speed check."

"One hundred eighty knots."

As Tim spoke into his mike – "Chicago, Niner *Charlie Juliet,* crossing the numbers; through five for four" – Carney heard the phone start to ring in their Manhattan town house seven hundred miles away.

Come on, Percey. Pick up! Where *are* you?

Please . . .

ATC said, "Niner *Charlie Juliet,* reduce speed to one eight zero. Contact tower. Good evening."

"Roger, Chicago. One eight zero knots. Evening."

Three rings.

Where the hell is she? What's wrong?

The knot in his gut grew tighter.

The turbofan sang, a grinding sound. Hydraulics moaned. Static crackled in Carney's headset.

Tim sang out, "Flaps thirty. Gear down."

"Flaps, thirty, thirty, green. Gear down. Three green."

And then, at last – in his earphone – a sharp click.

His wife's voice saying, "Hello?"

He laughed out loud in relief.

Carney started to speak but, before he could, the aircraft gave a huge jolt – so vicious that in a fraction of a second the force of the explosion ripped the bulky headset from his ears and the men were flung forward into the control panel. Shrapnel and sparks exploded around them.

Stunned, Carney instinctively grabbed the unresponsive yoke with his left hand; he no longer had a right one. He turned toward Tim just as the man's bloody, rag-doll body disappeared out of the gaping hole in the side of the fuselage.

"Oh, God. No, no . . ."

Then the entire cockpit broke away from the disintegrating plane and rose into the air, leaving the fuselage and wings and engines of the Lear behind, engulfed in a ball of gassy fire.

"Oh, Percey," he whispered, "Percey . . ." Though there was no longer a microphone to speak into.

2

Big as asteroids, bone yellow.

The grains of sand glowed on the computer screen. The man was sitting forward, neck aching, eyes in a hard squint – from concentration, not from any flaw in vision.

In the distance, thunder. The early morning sky was yellow and green and a storm was due at any moment. This had been the wettest spring on record.

Grains of sand . . .

"Enlarge," he commanded, and dutifully the image on the computer doubled in size.

Strange, he thought.

"Cursor down . . . stop."

Leaning forward again, straining, studying the screen.

Sand, Lincoln Rhyme reflected, is a criminalist's delight: bits of rock, sometimes mixed with other material, ranging from .05 to 2 millimeters (larger than that is gravel, smaller is silt). It adheres to a perp's clothing like sticky paint and conveniently leaps off at crime scenes and hideouts to link murderer and murdered. It also can tell a great deal about where a suspect has been. Opaque sand means he's been in the desert. Clear means beaches. Hornblende means Canada. Obsidian, Hawaii. Quartz and opaque igneous rock, New England. Smooth gray magnetite, the western Great Lakes.

But where this particular sand had come from, Rhyme didn't have a clue. Most of the sand in the New York area was quartz and feldspar. Rocky on Long Island Sound, dusty on the Atlantic, muddy on the Hudson. But this was white, glistening, ragged, mixed with tiny red spheres. And what are those rings? White stone rings like microscopic slices of calamari. He'd never seen anything like this.

The puzzle had kept Rhyme up till 4 A.M. He'd just sent a sample of the sand to a colleague at the FBI's crime lab in Washington. He'd had it shipped off with great reluctance – Lincoln Rhyme hated someone else's answering his own questions.

Motion at the window beside his bed. He glanced toward it. His neighbors – two compact peregrine falcons – were awake and about to go hunting. Pigeons beware, Rhyme thought. Then he cocked his head, muttering, "Damn," though he was referring not to his frustration at identifying this uncooperative evidence but at the impending interruption.

Urgent footsteps were on the stairs. Thom had let visitors in and Rhyme didn't want visitors. He glanced toward the hallway angrily. "Oh, not now, for God's sake."

But they didn't hear, of course, and wouldn't have paused even if they had.

Two of them . . .

One was heavy. One not.

A fast knock on the open door and they entered.

"Lincoln."

Rhyme grunted.

Lon Sellitto was a detective first grade, NYPD, and the one responsible for the giant steps. Padding along beside him was his slimmer, younger partner, Jerry Banks, spiffy in his pork gray suit of fine plaid. He'd doused his cowlick with spray – Rhyme could smell propane, isobutane, and vinyl acetate – but the charming spike still stuck up like Dagwood's.

The rotund man looked around the second-floor bedroom, which measured twenty by twenty. Not a picture on the wall. "What's different, Linc? About the place?"

"Nothing."

"Oh, hey, I know – it's clean," Banks said, then stopped abruptly as he ran into his faux pas.

"Clean, sure," said Thom, immaculate in ironed tan slacks, white shirt, and the flowery tie that Rhyme thought was pointlessly gaudy though he himself had bought it, mail order, for the young man. The aide had been with Rhyme for several years now – and though he'd been fired by Rhyme twice, and quit once, the criminalist had rehired the unflappable nurse/assistant an equal number of times. Thom knew enough about quadriplegia to be a doctor and had learned enough forensics from Lincoln Rhyme to be a detective. But he was content to be what the insurance company called a "caregiver," though both Rhyme and Thom disparaged the term. Rhyme called him, variously, his "mother hen" or "nemesis," both of which delighted the aide no end. He now maneuvered around the visitors. "He didn't like it but I hired Molly Maids and got the place scrubbed down. Practically needed to be fumigated. He wouldn't talk to me for a whole day afterwards."

"It didn't need to be cleaned. I can't find anything."

"But then he doesn't *have* to find anything, does he?" Thom countered. "That's what *I'm* for."

No mood for banter. "Well?" Rhyme cast his handsome face toward Sellitto. "What?"

"Got a case. Thought you might wanta help."

"I'm busy."

"What's all that?" Banks asked, motioning toward a new computer sitting beside Rhyme's bed.

"Oh," Thom said with infuriating cheer, "he's state-of-the-art now. Show them, Lincoln. Show them."

"I don't *want* to show them."

More thunder but not a drop of rain. Nature, as often, was teasing today.

Thom persisted. "Show them how it works."

"Don't want to."

"He's just embarrassed."

"Thom," Rhyme muttered.

But the young aide was as oblivious to threats as he was to recrimination. He tugged his hideous, or stylish, silk tie. "I don't know why he's behaving this way. He seemed very proud of the whole setup the other day."

"Did not."

Thom continued. "That box there" – he pointed to a beige contraption – "that goes to the computer."

"Whoa, two hundred megahertz?" Banks asked, nodding

at the computer. To escape Rhyme's scowl he'd grabbed the question like an owl snagging a frog.

"Yep," Thom said.

But Lincoln Rhyme was not interested in computers. At the moment Lincoln Rhyme was interested only in microscopic rings of sculpted calamari and the sand they nestled in.

Thom continued. "The microphone goes into the computer. Whatever he says, the computer recognizes. It took the thing a while to learn his voice. He mumbled a lot."

In truth Rhyme was quite pleased with the system – the lightning-fast computer, a specially made ECU box – environmental control unit – and voice-recognition software. Merely by speaking he could command the cursor to do whatever a person using a mouse and keyboard could do. And he could dictate too. Now, with words, he could turn the heat up or down and the lights on or off, play the stereo or TV, write on his word processor, make phone calls, and send faxes.

"He can even write music," Thom said to the visitors. "He tells the computer what notes to mark down on the staff."

"Now that's useful," Rhyme said sourly. "Music."

For a C4 quad – Rhyme's injury was at the fourth cervical vertebra – nodding was easy. He could also shrug, though not as dismissingly as he'd have liked. His other circus trick was moving his left ring finger a few millimeters in any direction he chose. That had been his entire physical repertoire for the past several years; composing a sonata for the violin was probably not in the offing.

"He can play games too," Thom said.

"I hate games. I don't play games."

Sellitto, who reminded Rhyme of a large unmade bed, gazed at the computer and seemed unimpressed. "Lincoln," he began gravely. "There's a task-forced case. Us 'n' the feds. Ran into a problem last night."

"Ran into a brick wall," Banks ventured to say.

"We thought . . . well, *I* thought you'd want to help us out on this one."

Want to help them out?

"I'm working on something now," Rhyme explained. "For

Perkins, in fact." Thomas Perkins, special agent in charge of the Manhattan office of the FBI. "One of Fred Dellray's boys is missing."

Special Agent Fred Dellray, a longtime veteran with the Bureau, was a handler for most of the Manhattan office's undercover agents. Dellray himself had been one of the Bureau's top undercover ops. He'd earned commendations from the director himself for infiltrating everything from Harlem drug lords' headquarters to black militant organizations. One of Dellray's agents, Tony Panelli, had gone missing a few days earlier.

"Perkins told us," Banks said. "Pretty weird."

Rhyme rolled his eyes at the unartful phrase. Though he couldn't dispute it. The agent had disappeared from his car across from the Federal Building in downtown Manhattan around 9 P.M. The streets weren't crowded but they weren't deserted either. The engine of the Bureau's Crown Victoria was running, the door open. There was no blood, no gunshot residue, no scuff marks indicating struggle. No witnesses – at least no witnesses willing to talk.

Pretty weird indeed.

Perkins had a fine crime scene unit at his disposal, including the Bureau's Physical Evidence Response Team. But it had been Rhyme who'd set up PERT and it was Rhyme whom Dellray had asked to work the scene of the disappearance. The crime scene officer who worked as Rhyme's partner had spent hours at Panelli's car and had come away with no unidentified fingerprints, ten bags of meaningless trace evidence, and – the only possible lead – a few dozen grains of this very odd sand.

The grains that now glowed on his computer screen, as smooth and huge as heavenly bodies.

Sellitto continued. "Perkins's gonna put other people on the Panelli case, Lincoln, if you'll help us. Anyway, I think you'll want this one."

That verb again – *want*. What was this all about?

Rhyme and Sellitto had worked together on major homicide investigations some years ago. Hard cases – and public cases. He knew Sellitto as well as he knew any cop. Rhyme generally distrusted his own ability to read people (his ex-wife, Blaine, had said – often, and heatedly – that Rhyme could spot a shell casing a mile away and miss a human being standing in front of him), but he could see now that Sellitto was holding back.

"Okay, Lon. What is it? Tell me."

Sellitto nodded toward Banks.

"Phillip Hansen," the young detective said significantly, lifting a puny eyebrow.

Rhyme knew the name only from newspaper articles. Hansen – a large, hard-living businessman originally from Tampa, Florida – owned a wholesale company in Armonk, New York. It was remarkably successful and he'd become a multimillionaire thanks to it. Hansen had a good deal for an entrepreneur. He never had to look for customers, never advertised, never had receivables problems. In fact, if there was any downside to PH Distributors, Inc., it was that the federal government and New York State were expending great energy to shut it down and throw its president in jail. Because the product Hansen's company sold was not, as he claimed, secondhand military surplus vehicles but weaponry, more often than not stolen from military bases or imported illegally. Earlier in the year two army privates had been killed when a truckload of small arms was hijacked near the George Washington Bridge on its way to New Jersey. Hansen was behind it – a fact the U.S. attorney and the New York attorney general knew but couldn't prove.

"Perkins and us're hammering together a case," Sellitto said. "Working with the army CID. But it's been a bitch."

"And nobody ever dimes him," said Banks. "Ever."

Rhyme supposed that, no, no one would dare snitch on a man like Hansen. The young detective continued. "But finally, last week, we got a break. See, Hansen's a pilot. His company's got warehouses at Mamaroneck Airport – that one near White Plains? A judge issued paper to check 'em out. Naturally we didn't find anything. But then last week, it's midnight? The airport's closed but there're some people there, working late. They see a guy fitting Hansen's description drive out to this private plane, load some big duffel bags into it, and take off. Unauthorized. No flight plan, just takes off. Comes back forty minutes later, lands, gets back into his car, and burns rubber out of there. No duffel bags. The witnesses give the registration number to the FAA. Turns out it's Hansen's private plane, not his company's."

Rhyme said, "So he knew you were getting close and he wanted to ditch something linking him to the killings." He was beginning to see why they wanted him. Some seeds of interest here. "Air Traffic Control track him?"

"LaGuardia had him for a while. Straight out over Long Island Sound. Then he dropped below radar for ten minutes or so."

"And you drew a line to see how far he could get over the Sound. There're divers out?"

"Right. Now, we knew that soon as Hansen heard we had the three witnesses he was gonna rabbit. So we managed to put him away till Monday. Federal Detention."

Rhyme laughed. "You got a judge to buy probable cause on that?"

"Yeah, with the risk of flight," Sellitto said. "And some bullshit FAA violations and reckless endangerment thrown in. No flight plan, flying below FAA minimums."

"What'd Mis-ter Han-sen say?"

"He knows the drill. Not a word to the arrestings, not a word to the prosecutors. Lawyer denies everything and's preparing suit for wrongful arrest, yadda, yadda, yadda . . . So if we find the fucking bags we go to the grand jury on Monday and, bang, he's away."

"Provided," Rhyme pointed out, "there's anything incriminating in the bags."

"Oh, there's something incriminating."

"How do you know?"

"Because Hansen's scared. He's hired somebody to kill the witnesses. He's already got one of 'em. Blew up his plane last night outside of Chicago."

And, Rhyme thought, they want me to find the duffel bags . . . Fascinating questions were now floating into his mind. Was it possible to place the plane at a particular location over the water because of a certain typc of precipitation or saline deposit or insect found crushed on the leading edge of the wing? Could one calculate the time of death of an insect? What about salt concentrations and pollutants in the water? Flying that low to the water, would the engines or wings pick up algae and deposit it on the fuselage or tail?

"I'll need some maps of the Sound," Rhyme began. "Engineering drawings of his plane—"

"Uhm, Lincoln, that's not why we're here," Sellitto said.

"Not to find the bags," Banks added.

"No? Then?" Rhyme tossed an irritating tickle of black hair off his forehead and frowned the young man down.

Sellitto's eyes again scanned the beige ECU box. The wires that sprouted from it were dull red and yellow and black and lay curled on the floor like sunning snakes.

"We want you to help us find the killer. The guy Hansen hired. Stop him before he gets the other two wits."

"And?" For Rhyme saw that Sellitto still had not mentioned what he was holding in reserve.

With a glance out the window the detective said, "Looks like it's the Dancer, Lincoln."

"The Coffin Dancer?"

Sellitto looked back and nodded.

"You're sure?"

"We heard he'd done a job in D.C. a few weeks ago. Killed a congressional aide mixed up in arms deals. We got pen registers and found calls from a pay phone outside Hansen's house to the hotel where the Dancer was staying. It's gotta be him, Lincoln."

On the screen the grains of sand, big as asteroids, smooth as a woman's shoulders, lost their grip on Rhyme's interest.

"Well," he said softly, "that's a problem now, isn't it?"

3

She remembered:

Last night, the cricket chrip of the phone intruding on the drizzle outside their bedroom window.

She'd looked at it contemptuously as if NYNEX were responsible for the nausea and the suffocating pain in her head, the strobe lights flashing behind her eyelids.

Finally she'd rolled to her feet and snagged the receiver on the fourth ring.

"Hello?"

Answered by the empty-pipe echo of a unicom radio-to-phone patch.

Then a voice. Perhaps.

A laugh. Perhaps.

A huge roar. A click. Silence.

No dial tone. Just silence, shrouded by the crashing waves in her ears.

Hello? Hello? . . .

She'd hung up the phone and returned to the couch, watched the evening rain, watched the dogwood bend and straighten in the spring storm's breeze. She'd fallen asleep again. Until the phone rang again a half hour later with the news about Lear Niner *Charlie Juliet* going down on approach and carrying her husband and young Tim Randolph to their deaths.

Now, on this gray morning, Percey Rachael Clay knew that the mysterious phone call last night had been from her husband. Ron Talbot – the one who'd courageously called to deliver the news of the crash – had explained he'd patched a call through to her at around the time the Lear had exploded.

Ed's laugh . . .

Hello? Hello?

Percey uncorked her flask, took a sip. She thought of the windy day years ago when she and Ed had flown a pontoon equipped Cessna 180 to Red Lake, Ontario, setting down with about six ounces of fuel left in the tank, and celebrated their arrival by downing a bottle of label-less Canadian whiskey, which turned out to give them both the most dire hangovers of their lives. The thought brought tears to her eyes now, as the pain had then.

"Come on, Perce, enough of that, okay?" said the man sitting on the living room couch. "Please." He pointed to the flask.

"Oh, right," her gravelly voice responded with controlled sarcasm. "Sure." And she took another sip. Felt like a cigarette but resisted. "What the hell was he doing calling me on final?" she asked.

"Maybe he was worried about you," Brit Hale suggested. "Your migraine."

Like Percey, Hale hadn't slept last night. Talbot had called him too with the news of the crash and he'd driven down from his Bronxville apartment to be with Percey. He'd stayed with her all night, helped her make the calls that had to be made. It was Hale, not Percey, who'd delivered the news to her own parents in Richmond.

"He had no business doing that, Brit. A call on final."

"That had nothing to do with what happened," Hale said gently.

"I know," she said.

They'd known each other for years. Hale had been one of Hudson Air's first pilots and had worked for free for the first four months until his savings ran out and he had to approach Percey reluctantly with a request for some salary. He never knew that she'd paid it out of her own savings, for the company didn't turn a profit for a year after incorporation. Hale resembled a lean, stern schoolteacher. In reality he was easygoing – the perfect antidote to Percey – and a droll practical joker who'd been known to roll a plane into inverted flight if his passengers were particularly rude and unruly and keep it there until they calmed down. Hale often took the right seat to Percey's left and was her favorite copilot in the world. "Privilege to fly with you, ma'am," he'd say, offering his imperfect Elvis Presley impersonation. "Thank you very much."

The pain behind her eyes was nearly gone now. Percey had lost friends – to crashes mostly – and she knew that psychic loss was an anesthetic to physical pain.

So was whiskey.

Another hit from the flask. "Hell, Brit." She slumped into the couch beside him. "Oh, hell."

Hale slipped his strong arm around her. She dropped her head, covered with dark curls, to his shoulder. "Be okay, babe," he said. "Promise. What can I do?"

She shook her head. It was an answerless question.

A sparse mouthful of bourbon, then she looked at the clock. Nine A.M. Ed's mother would be here any minute. Friends, relatives . . . There was the memorial service to plan . . .

So much to do.

"I've got to call Ron," she said. "We've got to do something. The Company . . ."

In airlines and charters the word "Company" didn't mean the same as in any other businesses. The Company, cap *C*, was an entity, a living thing. It was spoken of with reverence or frustration or pride. Sometimes with sorrow. Ed's death had inflicted a wound in many lives, the Company's included, and the injury could very well be lethal.

So much to do . . .

But Percey Clay, the woman who never panicked, the woman who'd calmly controlled deadly Dutch rolls, the nemesis of Lear 23s, who'd recovered from graveyard spirals that would have sent many seasoned pilots into spins, now sat paralyzed on the couch. Odd, she thought, as if from a different dimension, I can't move. She actually looked at her hands and feet to see if they were bone white and bloodless.

Oh, Ed . . .

And Tim Randolph too, of course. As good a copilot as you'd ever find, and good first officers were rare. She pictured his young, round face, like a younger Ed's. Grinning inexplicably. Alert and obedient but firm – giving no-nonsense orders, even to Percey herself, when he had command of the aircraft.

"You need some coffee," Hale announced, heading for the kitchen. "I'll getcha a whipped double mochaccino latte with steamed skim."

One of their private jokes was about sissy coffees. Real pilots, they both felt, drink only Maxwell House or Folgers.

Today, though, Hale, bless his heart, wasn't really talking about coffee. He meant: Lay off the booze. Percey took the hint. She corked the flask and dropped it on the table with a loud clink. "Okay, okay." She rose and paced through the living room. She caught sight of herself in the mirror. The pug face. Black hair in tight, stubborn curls. In her tormented adolescence, during a moment of despair, she'd given herself a crew cut. That'll show 'em. Though all this act of defiance did was to give the chamin' girls of the Lee School in Richmond even more ammunition against her. Percey had a slight figure and marbles of black eyes that her mother repeatedly said were her finest quality. Meaning her only quality. And a quality that men, of course, didn't give a shit about.

Dark lines under those eyes today and hopeless matte skin – smoker's skin, she remembered from the years she went through two packs of Marlboros a day. The earring holes in her lobes had long ago grown closed.

A look out the window, past the trees, into the street in front of the town house. She caught sight of the traffic and something tugged at her mind. Something unsettling.

What? What is it?

The feeling vanished, pushed away by the ringing of the doorbell.

Percey opened the door and found two burly police officers in the entryway.

"Mrs Clay?"

"Yes."

"NYPD." Showing IDs. "We're here to keep an eye on you until we get to the bottom of what happened to your husband."

"Come in," she said. "Brit Hale's here too."

"Mr Hale?" one of the cops said, nodding. "He's here? Good. We sent a couple of Westchester County troopers to his place too."

And it was then that she looked past one of the cops, into the street, and the elusive thought popped into her mind.

Stepping around the policemen onto the front stoop.

"We'd rather you stayed inside, Mrs Clay . . ."

Staring at the street. What was it?

Then she understood.

"There's something you should know," she said to the officers. "A black van."

"A . . . ?"

"A black van. There was this black van."

One of the officers took out a notebook. "You better tell me about it."

Wait," Rhyme said.

Lon Sellitto paused in his narration.

Rhyme now heard another set of footsteps approaching, neither heavy nor light. He knew whose they were. This was not deduction. He'd heard this particular pattern many times.

Amelia Sachs's beautiful face, surrounded by her long red hair, crested the stairs, and Rhyme saw her hesitate for a moment, then continue into the room. She was in full navy blue patrol uniform, minus only the cap and tie. She carried a Jefferson Market shopping bag.

Jerry Banks flashed her a smile. His crush was adoring and obvious and only moderately inappropriate – not many patrol officers have a history of a Madison Avenue modeling career behind them, as did tall Amelia Sachs. But the gaze, like the attraction, was not reciprocated, and the young man, a pretty boy himself despite the badly shaved face and cowlick, seemed resigned to carrying his torch a bit longer.

"Hi, Jerry," she said. To Sellitto she gave another nod and a deferential "sir." (He was a detective lieutenant and a legend in Homicide. Sachs had cop genes in her and had been taught over the dinner table as well as in the academy to respect elders.)

"You look tired," Sellitto commented.

"Didn't sleep," she said. "Looking for sand." She pulled a dozen Baggies out of the shopping bag. "I've been out collecting exemplars."

"Good," Rhyme said. "But that's old news. We've been reassigned."

"Reassigned?"

"Somebody's come to town. And we have to catch him."

"Who?"

"A killer," Sellitto said.

"Pro?" Sachs asked. "OC?"

"Professional, yes," Rhyme said. "No OC connection that we know about." Organized crime was the largest purveyor of for-hire killers in the country.

"He's freelance," Rhyme explained. "We call him the Coffin Dancer."

She lifted an eyebrow, red from worrying with a fingernail. "Why?"

"Only one victim's ever got close to him and lived long enough to give us any details. He's got – or had, at least – a tattoo on his upper arm: the Grim Reaper dancing with a woman in front of a coffin."

"Well, *that's* something to put in the 'Distinguishing Marks' box on an incident report," she said wryly. "What else you know about him?"

"White male, probably in his thirties. That's it."

"You traced the tattoo?" Sachs asked.

"Of course," Rhyme responded dryly. "To the ends of the earth." He meant this literally. No police department in any major city around the world could find any history of a tattoo like his.

"Excuse me, gentlemen and lady," Thom said. "Work to do." Conversation came to a halt while the young man went through the motions of rotating his boss. This helped clear his lungs. To quadriplegics certain parts of their body become personified; they develop special relationships with them. After his spine was shattered while searching a crime scene some years ago Rhyme's arms and legs had become his cruelest enemies and he'd spent desperate energy trying to force them to do what he wanted. But they'd won, no contest, and stayed as still as wood. Then he'd confronted the racking spasms that shook his body unmercifully. He'd tried to force them to stop. Eventually they had – on their own, it seemed. Rhyme couldn't exactly claim victory though he did accept their surrender. Then he'd turned to lesser challenges and had taken on his lungs. Finally, after a year of rehab, he weaned himself off the ventilator. Out came the trachea tube and he could breathe on his own. It was his only victory against his body and he harbored a dark superstition that the lungs were biding their time to get even. He figured he'd die of pneumonia or emphysema in a year or two.

Lincoln Rhyme didn't necessarily mind the idea of dying. But there were too many ways to die; he was determined not to go unpleasantly.

Sachs asked, "Any leads? LKA?"

"Last known was down in the D.C. area," Sellitto said in his Brooklyn drawl. "That's it. Nothin' else. Oh, we hear about him some. Dellray more'n us, with all his skels and CIs, you know. The Dancer, he's like he's ten different people. Ear jobs, facial implants, silicon. Adds scars, removes scars. Gains weight, loses weight. Once he skinned this corpse – took some guy's hands off and wore 'em like gloves to fool CS about the prints."

"Not me, though," Rhyme reminded. "I wasn't fooled."

Though I still didn't get him, he reflected bitterly.

"He plans everything," the detective continued. "Sets up diversions then moves in. Does the job. And he fucking cleans up afterwards real efficient." Sellitto stopped talking, looking strangely uneasy for a man who hunts killers for a living.

Eyes out the window, Rhyme didn't acknowledge his ex-partner's reticence. He merely continued the story. "That case – with the skinned hands – was the Dancer's most recent job in New York. Five, six years ago. He was hired by one Wall Street investment banker to kill his partner. Did the job nice and clean. My CS team got to the scene and started to walk the grid. One of them lifted a wad of paper out of the trash can. It set off a load of PETN. About eight ounces, gas enhanced. Both techs were killed and virtually every clue was destroyed."

"I'm sorry," Sachs said. There was an awkward silence between them. She'd been his apprentice and his partner for more than a year – and had become his friend too. Had even spent the night here sometimes, sleeping on the couch or even, as chaste as a sibling, in Rhyme's half-ton Clinitron bed. But the talk was mostly forensic, with Rhyme's lulling her to sleep with tales of stalking serial killers and brilliant cat burglars. They generally steered clear of personal issues. Now she offered nothing more than "It must have been hard."

Rhyme deflected the taut sympathy with a shake of his head. He stared at the empty wall. For a time there'd been art posters taped up around the room. They were long gone but his eyes played a game of connect-the-dots with the bits of tape still stuck there. A lopsided star was the shape they traced, while within him somewhere, deep, Rhyme felt an empty despair, replaying the horrid crime scene of the explosion, seeing the burnt, shattered bodies of his officers.

Sachs asked, "The guy who hired him, he was willing to dime the Dancer?"

"Was willing to, sure. But there wasn't much he could say. He delivered cash to a drop box with written instructions. No electronic transfers, no account numbers. They never met in person." Rhyme inhaled deeply. "But the worst part was that the banker who'd paid for the hit changed his mind. He lost his nerve. But he had no way to get in touch with the Dancer. It didn't matter anyway. The Dancer's told him right up front: 'Recall is not an option.'"

Sellitto briefed Sachs about the case against Phillip Hansen, the witnesses who'd seen his plane make its midnight run, and the bomb last night.

"Who are the other wits?" she asked.

"Percey Clay, the wife of this Carney guy killed last night in the plane. She's the president of their company, Hudson Air Charters. Her husband was VP. The other wit's Britton Hale. He's a pilot works for them. I sent baby-sitters to keep an eye on 'em both."

Rhyme said, "I've called Mel Cooper in. He'll be working the lab downstairs. The Hansen case is task-forced so we're getting Fred Dellray to represent the feds. He'll have agents for us if we need them and's clearing one of U.S. Marshal's wit-protection safe houses for the Clay woman and Hale."

Lincoln Rhyme's opulent memory intruded momentarily and he lost track of what Sellitto was saying. An image of the office where the Dancer had left the bomb five years ago came to mind again.

Remembering: The trash can, blown open like a black rose. The smell of the explosive – the choking chemical scent, nothing at all like wood-fire smoke. The silky alligatoring on the charred wood. The seared body of his techs, drawn into the pugilistic attitude by the flames.

He was saved from this horrid reverie by the buzz of the fax machine. Jerry Banks snagged the first sheet." Crime scene report from the crash," he announced.

Rhyme's head snapped toward the machine eagerly. "Time to go to work, boys and girls!"

Wash 'em. Wash 'em off.

Soldier, are those hands clean?

Sir, they're getting there, sir.

The solid man, in his mid-thirties, stood in the washroom of a coffee shop on Lexington Avenue, lost in his task.

Scrub, scrub, scrub . . .

He paused and looked out the men's room door. Nobody seemed interested that he'd been in here for nearly ten minutes.

Back to scrubbing.

Stephen Kall examined his cuticles and big red knuckles.

Lookin' clean, lookin' clean. No worms. Not a single one.

He'd been feeling fine as he moved the black van off the street and parked it deep in an underground garage. Stephen had taken what tools he needed from the back of the vehicle and climbed the ramp, slipping out onto the busy street. He'd worked in New York several times before but he could never get used to all the people, a thousand people on this block alone.

Makes me feel cringey.

Makes me feel *wormy*.

And so he stopped here in the men's room for a little scrub.

Soldier, aren't you through with that yet? You've got two targets left to eliminate.

Sir, almost, sir. Have to remove the risk of any trace evidence prior to proceeding with the operation, sir.

Oh, for the luva Christ . . .

The hot water pouring over his hands. Scrubbing with a brush he carried with him in a plastic Baggie. Squirting the pink soap from the dispenser. And scrubbing some more.

Finally he examined the ruddy hands and dried them under the hot air of the blower. No towels, no telltale fibers.

No worms either.

Stephen wore camouflage today, though not military olive drab or Desert Storm beige. He was in jeans, Reeboks, a work shirt, a gray windbreaker speckled with paint drips. On his belt was his cell phone and a large tape measure. He looked like any other contractor in Manhattan and was wearing this outfit today because no one would think twice about a workman wearing cloth gloves on a spring day.

Walking outside.

Still lots of people. But his hands were clean and he wasn't cringey anymore.

He paused at the corner and looked down the street at the building that had been the Husband's and Wife's town house but was the Wife's alone now because the Husband had been neatly blown into a million small pieces over the Land of Lincoln.

So, two witnesses were still alive and they both had to be dead before the grand jury convened on Monday. He glanced at his bulky stainless-steel watch. It was nine-thirty Saturday morning.

Solider, is that enough time to get them both?

Sir, I may not get them both now but I still have nearly forty-eight hours, sir. That is more than sufficient time to locate and neutralize both targets, sir.

But, Soldier, do you mind challenges?

Sir, I *live for* challenges, sir.

There was a single squad car in front of the town house. Which he'd expected.

All right, we have a known kill zone in front of the house, an unknown one inside . . .

He looked up and down the street, then started along the sidewalk, his scrubbed hands tingling. The backpack weighed close to sixty pounds but he hardly felt it. Crew-cut Stephen was mostly muscle.

As he walked he pictured himself as a local. Anonymous. He didn't think of himself as Stephen or as Mr Kall or Todd Johnson or Stan Bledsoe or any of the dozens of other aliases he'd used over the past ten years. His real name was like a rusty gym set in the backyard, something you were aware of but didn't really see.

He turned suddenly and stepped into the doorway of the building opposite the Wife's town house. Stephen pushed open the front door and looked out at the large glass windows across the street, partially obscured by a flowering dogwood tree. He put on a pair of expensive yellow-tinted shooting glasses and the glare from the window vanished. He could see figures moving around inside. One cop . . . no, two cops. A man with his back to the window. Maybe the Friend, the other witness he'd been hired to kill. And . . . yes! There was the Wife. Short. Homely. Boyish. She was wearing a white blouse. It made a good target.

She stepped out of view.

Stephen bent down and unzipped his backpack.

4

A sitting transfer into the Storm Arrow wheelchair.

Then Rhyme took over, gripping the plastic straw of the sip-and-puff controller in his mouth, and he drove into the tiny elevator, formerly a closet, that carried him unceremoniously down to the first floor of his town house.

In the 1890s, when the place had been built, the room into which Lincoln Rhyme now wheeled had been a parlor off the dining room. Plaster-and-lath construction, fleur-de-lis crown molding, domed icon recesses, and solid oak floorboards joined as tight as welded steel. An architect, though, would have been horrified to see that Rhyme had had the wall separating the two rooms demolished and large holes dug into the remaining walls to run additional electrical lines. The combined rooms were now a messy space filled not with Tiffany's stained glass or moody landscapes by George Innes but with very different objets d'art: density-gradient tubes, computers, compound microscopes, comparison 'scopes, a gas chromatograph/mass spectrometer, a PoliLight alternative light source, fuming frames for raising friction ridge prints. A very expensive scanning electron microscope hooked to an energy dispersive X-ray unit sat prominently in the corner. Here too were the mundane tools of the criminalist's trade: goggles, latex and cut-resistant gloves, beakers, screwdrivers and pliers, postmortem finger spoons, tongs, scalpels, tongue depressors, cotton swabs, jars, plastic bags, examining trays, probes. A dozen pairs of chopsticks (Rhyme ordered his assistants to lift evidence the way they picked up dim sum at Ming Wa's).

Rhyme steered the sleek, candy-apple red Storm Arrow into position beside the worktable. Thom placed the microphone over his head and booted up the computer.

A moment later Sellitto and Banks appeared in the doorway, joined by another man who'd just arrived. He was tall and rangy, with skin dark as tires. He was wearing a green suit and an unearthly yellow shirt.

"Hello, Fred."

"Lincoln."

"Hey." Sachs nodded to Fred Dellray as she entered the room. She'd forgiven him for arresting her not long ago – an interagency squabble – and they now had a curious affinity, this tall, beautiful cop and the tall, quirky agent. They were both, Rhyme had decisively concluded, *people* cops (he himself being an *evidence* cop). Dellray trusted forensics as little as Rhyme trusted the testimony of witnesses. As for former beat cop Sachs, well, there was nothing Rhyme could do about her natural proclivities but he was determined that she push those talents aside and become the best criminalist in New York, if not the country. A goal that was easily within her grasp, even if she herself didn't know it.

Dellray loped across the room, stationed himself beside the window, crossed his lanky arms. No one – Rhyme included – could peg the agent exactly. He lived alone in a small apartment in Brooklyn, loved to read literature and philosophy, and loved even more to play pool in tawdry bars. Once the jewel in the crown of the FBI's undercover agents, Fred Dellray was still referred to occasionally by the nickname he'd had when he was in the field: "the Chameleon". He'd been a renegade, everybody knew that, but his handlers in the Bureau gave him plenty of slack; Dellray had over a thousand arrests to his credit. But he'd spent too much time undercover and despite his considerable skill at being who he was not, he'd become "overextended," as the Bureau-ese went. It was only a matter of time before he'd be recognized and killed, so he'd reluctantly agreed to take an administrative job running other undercovers and CIs – confidential informants.

"So, mah boys tell me we got us the Dancer hisself," the agent muttered, the patois less Ebonics than, well . . . pure Dellray. His grammar and vocabulary, like his life, were largely improvised.

"Any word on Tony?" Rhyme asked.

"My boy gone missing?" Dellray asked, his face screwing up angrily. "Not. A. Thing."

Tony Panelli, the agent who'd disappeared from the Federal Building several days before, had left behind a wife at home, a gray Ford with a running engine, and a number of grains of infuriatingly mysterious sand – the sensuous asteroids that promised answers but had so far delivered none.

"When we catch the Dancer," Rhyme said, "we'll get back on it, Amelia and me. Full-time. Promise."

Dellray angrily tapped the unlit tip of a cigarette nestling behind his left ear. "The Dancer . . . Shit. Better nail his ass this time. Shit."

"What about the hit?" Sachs asked. "The one last night. Have any details?"

Sellitto read through the wad of faxes and some of his own handwritten notes. He looked up. "Ed Carney took off from Mamaroneck Airport around seven-fifteen last night. The company – Hudson Air – they're a private charterer. They fly cargo, corporate clients, you know. Lease out planes. They'd just gotten a new contract to fly – get this – body parts for transplants to hospitals around the Midwest and East Coast. Hear it's a real competitive business nowadays."

"Cutthroat," Banks offered and was the only one who smiled at his joke.

Sellitto continued. "The client was U.S. Medical and Healthcare. Based up in Somers. One of those for-profit hospital chains. Carney had a real tight schedule. Was supposed to fly to Chicago, Saint Louis, Memphis, Lexington, Cleveland, then lay over in Erie, Pennsylvania. Come back this morning."

"Any passengers?" Rhyme asked.

"Not whole ones," Sellitto muttered. "Just the cargo. Everything's routine about the flight. Then about ten minutes out of O'Hare, a bomb goes off. Blows the shit out of the plane. Killed both Carney and his copilot. Four injuries on the ground. His wife, by the way, was supposed to be flying with him but she got sick and had to cancel."

"There an NTSB report?" Rhyme asked. "No, of course not, there wouldn't be. Not yet."

"Report won't be ready for two, three days."

"Well, we can't *wait* two or three days!" Rhyme griped loudly. "I need it now!"

A pink scar from the ventilator hose was visible on his throat. But Rhyme had weaned himself off the fake lung and could breathe like nobody's business. Lincoln Rhyme was a C4 quad who could sigh, cough, and shout like a sailor. "I need to know everything about the bomb."

"I'll call a buddy in the Windy City," Dellray said. "He owes me major. Tell 'im what's what and have 'im ship us whatever they got pronto."

Rhyme nodded to the agent, then considered what Sellitto had told him. "Okay, we've got two scenes. The crash site in Chicago. That one's too late for you, Sachs. Contaminated as hell. We'll just have to hope the folks in Chicago do a halfway decent job. The other scene's the airport in Mamaroneck – where the Dancer got the bomb on board."

"How do we know he did it at the airport?" Sachs said. She was rolling her brilliant red hair in a twist, then pinning it on top of her head. Magnificent strands like these were a liability at crime scenes; they threatened to contaminate the evidence. Sachs went about her job armed with a Glock 9 and a dozen bobby pins.

"Good point, Sachs." He loved her outguessing him. "We *don't* know and we won't until we find the seat of the bomb. It might've been planted in the cargo, in a flight bag, a coffeepot."

Or a wastebasket, he thought grimly, again recalling the Wall Street bombing.

"I want every single bit of that bomb here as soon as possible. We have to have it," Rhyme said.

"Well, Linc," Sellitto said slowly, "the plane was a mile up when it blew. The wreckage's scattered over a whole fucking subdivision."

"I don't care," Rhyme said, neck muscles aching. "Are they still searching?"

Local rescue workers searched crash sites but investigations were federal so it was Fred Dellray who placed a call to the FBI special agent at the site.

"Tell him we need every piece of wreckage that tests positive for explosive. I'm talking nanograms. I want that bomb."

Dellray relayed this. Then he looked up, shook his head. "Scene's released."

"What?" Rhyme snapped. "After twelve hours? Ridiculous. Inexcusable!"

"They had to get the streets open. He said—"

"Fire trucks!" Rhyme called.

"What?"

"Every fire truck, ambulance, police car . . . every emergency vehicle that responded to the crash. I want the tires scraped."

Dellray's long, black face stared at him. "You wanna repeat that? For my ex–good friend here?" The agent pushed the phone at him.

Rhyme ignored the receiver and said to Dellray, "Emergency vehicle tires're one of the best sources for good evidence at contaminated crime scenes. They were first on the scene, they usually have new tires with deep tread grooves, and they probably didn't drive anywhere but to and from the site. I want all the tires scraped and the trace sent here."

Dellray managed to get a promise from Chicago that the tires of as many emergency vehicles as they could get to would be scraped.

"Not 'as many as,'" Rhyme called. "*All* of them."

Dellray rolled his eyes and relayed that information too, then hung up.

Suddenly Rhyme cried, "Thom! Thom, where are you?"

The belabored aide appeared at the door a moment later. "In the laundry room, that's where."

"Forget laundry. We need a time chart. Write, write . . ."

"Write *what*, Lincoln?"

"On that chalkboard, right there. The big one." Rhyme looked at Sellitto. "When's the grand jury convening?"

"Nine on Monday."

"The prosecutor'll want them there a couple hours early – the van'll pick 'em up between six and seven." He looked at the wall clock. It was now ten A.M. Saturday.

"We've got exactly forty-five hours. Thom, write, 'Hour 1 of 45.'"

The aide hesitated.

"Write!"

He did.

Rhyme glanced at the others in the room. He saw their eyes flickering uncertainly, a skeptical frown on Sachs's face. Her hand rose to her scalp and she scratched absently.

"Think I'm being melodramatic?" he asked. "Think we don't need a reminder?"

No one spoke for a moment. Finally Sellitto said, "Well, Linc, I mean, it's not like anything's going to happen by then."

"Oh, yes, something's going to happen," Rhyme said, eyes on the male falcon as the muscular bird launched himself effortlessly into the air over Central Park. "By seven o'clock on Monday morning, either we'll've nailed the Dancer, or both our witnesses'll be dead. There're no other options."

Thom hesitated then picked up the chalk and wrote.

The dense silence was broken by the chirp of Banks's cell phone. He listened for a minute, then looked up. "Here's something," he said.

"What?" Rhyme asked.

"Those uniforms guarding Mrs Clay and the other witness, Britton Hale?"

"What about them?"

"They're at her town house. One of 'em just called in. Seems Mrs Clay says there was a black van she'd never seen before parked on the block outside the house for the last couple days. Out-of-state plates."

"She get the tag? Or state?"

"No," Banks responded. "She said it was gone for a while last night after her husband left for the airport."

Sellitto stared at him.

Rhyme's head eased forward. "And?"

"She said it was back this morning for a little while. It's gone now. She was—"

"Oh, Jesus," Rhyme whispered.

"What?" Banks asked.

"Central!" the criminalist shouted. "Get on the horn to Central. Now!"

A taxi pulled up in front of the Wife's town house.

An elderly woman got out and walked unsteadily to the door.

Stephen watching, vigilant.

Soldier, is this an easy shot?

Sir, a shooter never thinks of a shot as easy. Every shot requires maximum concentration and effort. But, sir, I can make this shot and inflict lethal wounds, sir. I can turn my targets into jelly, sir.

The woman climbed up the stairs and disappeared into the lobby. A moment later Stephen saw her appear in the Wife's living room. There was a flash of white cloth – the Wife's blouse again. The two of them hugged. Another figure stepped into the room. A man. A cop? He turned around. No, it was the Friend.

Both targets, Stephen thought excitedly, only thirty yards away.

The older woman – mother or mother-in-law – remained in front of the Wife as they talked, heads down.

Stephen's beloved Model 40 was in the van. But he wouldn't need the sniper rifle for this shot, only the long-barrel Beretta. It was a wonderful gun. Old, battered, and functional. Unlike many mercenaries and pros, Stephen didn't make a fetish out of his weapons. If a rock was the best way to kill a particular victim, he'd use a rock.

He assessed his target, measuring angles of incidence, the window's potential distortion and deflection. The old woman stepped away from the Wife and stood directly in front of the glass.

Soldier, what is your strategy?

He'd shoot through the window and hit the elderly woman high. She'd fall. The Wife would instinctively step forward toward her and bend over her, presenting a fair target. The Friend would run into the room too and would profile just fine.

And what about the cops?

A slight risk. But uniformed patrolmen were modest shots at best and had probably never been fired on in the line of duty. They'd be sure to panic.

The lobby was still empty.

Stephen pulled back the slide to cock the weapon and give

himself the better control of squeezing the trigger in the gun's single-action mode. He pushed the door open and blocked it with his foot, looked up and down the street.

No one.

Breathe, soldier. Breathe, breathe, breathe . . .

He lowered the gun to his palm, the butt resting heavy in his gloved hand. He began applying imperceptible pressure to the trigger.

Breathe, breathe.

He stared at the old woman, and forgot completely about squeezing, forgot about aiming, forgot about the money he was making, forgot everything in the universe. He simply held the gun steady as a rock in his supple, relaxed hands and waited for the weapon to fire itself.

5

The elderly woman wiping tears, the Wife standing behind her, arms crossed.

They were dead, they were—

Soldier!

Stephen froze. Relaxed his trigger finger.

Lights!

Flashing lights, silently zooming along the street. The turret lights on a police cruiser. Then two more cars, then a dozen, and an Emergency Services van bounding over the potholes. Converging on the Wife's town house from both ends of the street.

Safety your weapon, Soldier.

Stephen lowered the gun, stepped back into the dim lobby.

Police ran from the cars like spilt water. They spread out along the sidewalk, gazing outward and up at the rooftops. They flung open the doors to the Wife's town house, shattering the glass and pushing inside.

The five ESU officers, in full tactical gear, deployed along the curb, covering exactly the spots that ought to be covered, eyes vigilant, fingers curled loosely on the black triggers of their black guns. Patrol officers might be glorified traffic cops but there were no better soldiers than New York's ESU. The Wife and the Friend had disappeared, probably flung to the floor. The old lady too.

More cars, filling the street and pulling up onto the sidewalks.

Stephen Kall, feeling cringey. Wormy. Sweat dotted his palms and he flexed his fist so the glove would soak it up.

Evacuate, Soldier . . .

With a screwdriver he pried open the lock to the main door and pushed inside, walking fast but not running, head down, making for the service entrance that led to the alley. No one saw him, and he slipped outside. Was soon on Lexington Avenue, walking south through the crowds toward the underground garage where he'd parked the van.

Looking ahead.

Sir, trouble here, sir.

More cops.

They'd closed down Lexington Avenue about three blocks south and were setting up a perimeter around the town house, stopping cars, looking over pedestrians, moving door to door, shining their long flashlights into parked cars. Stephen saw two cops, hands twitching on the butts of their Glocks, ask one man to step out of his car while they searched under a pile of blankets in the backseat. What troubled Stephen was that the man was white and about Stephen's age.

The building where he'd parked the van was within the search perimeter. He couldn't drive out without being stopped. The line of cops moved closer. He walked quickly back to the garage and pulled open the van door. Quickly he changed clothes – ditching the contractor outfit and dressing in blue jeans, work shoes (no telltale tread marks), a black T-shirt, a dark green windbreaker (no lettering of any kind), and a baseball cap (free of team insignia). The backpack contained his laptop, several cellular phones, his small-arms weapons, and ammunition from the van. He got more bullets, his binoculars, the night vision scope, tools, several packages of explosives, and various detonators. Stephen put the supplies in the large backpack.

The Model 40 was in a Fender bass guitar case. He lifted this out of the back of the van and set it with the backpack on the garage floor. He considered what to do about the van. Stephen had never touched any part of the vehicle without wearing gloves and there was nothing inside that would give away his identity. The Dodge itself was stolen and he'd removed both the dash VIN and the secret VINs. He'd made the license plates himself. He'd planned on abandoning it sooner or later and could finish the job without the vehicle.

He decided to leave it now. He covered the boxy Dodge with a blue Wolf car tarp, slipped his k-bar knife into the tires, flattening them, to make it look like the van had been there for months. He left the garage through the elevator to the building.

Outside, he slipped into the crowd. But there were police everywhere. His skin started to crawl. It felt wormy, moist. He stepped up to a phone booth and pretended to make a call, lowered his head to the metal plate of the phone, felt the sweat prickle on his forehead, under his arms. Thinking, They're *everywhere.* Looking for him, looking *at* him. From cars. From the street.

From *windows* . . .

The memory came back again . . .

The face in the window.

He took a deep breath.

The face in the window . . .

It had happened recently. Stephen'd been hired for a hit in Washington, D.C. The job was to kill a congressional aide selling classified military arms information to – Stephen assumed – a competitor of the man who'd hired Stephen. The aide had been understandably paranoid and kept a safe house in Alexandria, Virginia. Stephen had learned where it was and finally managed to get close enough for a pistol shot – although it would be a tricky one.

Once chance, one shot . . .

Stephen had waited for four hours, and when the victim arrived and darted toward his town house Stephen had managed to fire a single shot. Hit him, he believed, but the man had fallen out of sight in a courtyard.

Listen to me, boy. You listening?

Sir, yessir.

You track down every wounded target and finish the job. You follow the blood spoor to hell and back, you have to.

Well—

No well about it. You confirm *every* kill. You understand me? This's not an option.

Yessir.

Stephen had climbed over the brick wall into the man's courtyard. He found the aide's body sprawled on the cobblestones, beside a goat-head fountain. The shot had been fatal after all.

But something odd had happened. Something that sent a shiver through him and very few things in life had ever made him shiver. Maybe it was just a fluke, the way the aide had fallen or the way the bullet hit him. But it appeared that someone had carefully untucked the victim's bloody shirt and pulled it up to see the tiny entrance wound above the man's sternum.

Stephen had spun around, looking for whoever had done this. But, no, there was no one nearby.

Or so he thought at first.

Then Stephen happened to look across the courtyard. There was an old carriage house, its windows smeared and dirty, lit from behind with failing sunset light. In one of those windows he saw – or imagined he saw – a face looking out at him. He couldn't see the man – or woman – clearly. But whoever it was didn't seem particularly scared. They hadn't ducked or tried to run.

A witness, you left a witness, Soldier!

Sir, I will eliminate the possibility of identification immediately, sir.

But when he kicked in the door of the carriage house he found it was empty.

Evacuate, Soldier . . .

The face in the window . . .

Stephen had stood in the empty building, overlooking the courtyard of the aide's town house, lit with bold western sunlight, and turned around and around in slow, manic circles.

Who was it? What had he been doing? Or was it just Stephen's imagination? The way his stepfather used to see snipers in the hawk nests of West Virginia oak trees.

The face in the window had gazed at him the way his stepfather would look at him sometimes, studying him, inspecting. Stephen, remembering what young Stephen had often thought: Did I fuck up? Did I do good? What's he *thinking* about me?

Finally he couldn't wait any longer and he'd headed back to his hotel in Washington.

Stephen had been shot at and beaten and stabbed. But

nothing had shaken him as much as that incident in Alexandria. He'd never once been troubled by the faces of his victims, dead or alive. But the face in the window was like a worm crawling up his leg.

Cringey . . .

Which was exactly what he felt now, seeing the lines of officers moving toward him from both directions on Lexington. Cars were honking, drivers were angry. But the police paid no mind; they continued their dogged search. It was just a matter of minutes until they spotted him – an athletic white man by himself, carrying a guitar case that might easily contain the best sniper rifle God put on this earth.

His eyes went to the black, grimy windows overlooking the street.

He prayed he wouldn't see a face looking out.

Soldier, the fuck you talking about?

Sir, I—

Reconnoiter, Soldier.

Sir, yessir.

A burnt, bitter smell came to him.

He turned around and found he was standing outside a Starbucks. He walked in and while he pretended to read the menu in fact he surveyed the customers.

At a table by herself a large woman sat in one of the flimsy, uncomfortable chairs. She was reading a magazine and nursing a tall cup of tea. She was in her early thirties, dumpy, with a broad face and a thick nose. Starbucks, he free-associated . . . Seattle . . . dyke?

But, no, he didn't think so. She pored over the *Vogue* in her hands with envy, not lust.

Stephen bought a cup of Celestial Seasonings tea, chamomile. He picked up the container and started to walk toward a seat at the window. Stephen was just passing the woman's table when the cup slipped from his hand and dropped onto the chair opposite her, spraying the hot tea all over the floor. She slid back in surprise, looking up at the horrified expression on Stephen's face.

"Oh, my goodness," he whispered, "I am sooo sorry." He lunged for a handful of napkins. "Tell me I didn't get any on you. *Please!*"

Percey Clay pulled away from the young detective who held her pinned to the floor.

Ed's mother, Joan Carney, lay a few feet away, her face frozen in shock and bewilderment.

Brit Hale was up against the wall, covered by two strong cops. It looked as if they were arresting him.

"I'm sorry, ma'am, Mrs Clay," one cop said. "We—"

"What's going on?" Hale seemed mystified. Unlike Ed and Ron Talbot and Percey herself, Hale had never been military, never come close to combat. He was fearless – he always wore long sleeves instead of a pilots' traditional short-sleeve white shirt to hide the leathery burn scars on his arms from the time a few years ago he'd climbed into a flaming Cessna 150 to rescue a pilot and passenger. But the idea of crime – intentional harm – was wholly alien to him.

"We got a call from the task force," the detective explained. "They think the man who killed Mr Carney has been back. Probably to come after you two. Mr Rhyme thinks the killer was the one driving that black van you saw today."

"Well, we have *those* men to guard us," Percey snapped, tossing her head to the cops who'd arrived earlier.

"Jesus," Hale muttered, looked outside. "There must be twenty cops out there."

"Away from the window, please, sir," the detective said firmly. "He could be on a rooftop. The site's not secure yet."

Percey heard footsteps running up the stairs. "The roof?" she asked sourly. "Maybe he's tunneling into the basement." She put her arm around Mrs Carney. "You all right, Mother?"

"What's going on, what is all this?"

"They think you might be in danger," the officer said. "Not you, ma'am," he added to Ed's mother. "Mrs Clay and Mr Hale here. Because they're witnesses in that case. We were told to secure the premises and take them to the command post."

"They talk to him yet?" Hale asked.

"Don't know who that'd be, sir."

The lean man answered, "The guy we're witnesses *against*. Hansen." Hale's world was the world of logic. Of reasonable people. Of machines and numbers and hydraulics. His three marriages had failed because the only place where his heart poked out was in the science of flight and the irrefutable sense of the cockpit. He now swiped his hair off his forehead and said, "Just ask him. He'll tell you where the killer is. *He* hired him."

"Well, I don't think it's quite as easy as that."

Another officer appeared in the doorway. "Street's secure, sir."

"If you'll come with us, please. Both of you."

"What about Ed's mother?"

"Do you live in the area?" the officer asked.

"No. I'm staying with my sister," Mrs Carney answered. "In Saddle River."

"We'll drive you back there, have a New Jersey trooper stay outside the house. You're not involved in this, so I'm sure there's nothing to worry about."

"Oh, Percey."

The women hugged. "It'll be okay, Mother." Percey struggled to hold back the tears.

"No, it won't," the frail woman said. "It'll never be okay . . ."

An officer led her off to a squad car.

Percey watched the car drive off, then asked the cop beside her, "Where're we going?"

"To see Lincoln Rhyme."

Another officer said, "We're going to walk out together, an officer on either side of you. Keep your heads down and don't look up under any circumstance. We're going to walk fast to that second van there. See it? You jump in. Don't look out the windows, and get your belts on. We'll be driving fast. Any questions?"

Percey opened the flask and took a sip of bourbon. "Yeah, who the hell is Lincoln Rhyme?"

"You sewed that? Yourself?"

"I did," the woman said, tugging at the embroidered denim vest, which, like the plaid skirt she wore, was slightly too large, calculated to obscure her substantial figure. The stitching reminded him of the rings around a worm's body. He shivered, felt sick.

But he smiled and said, "That's amazing." He'd sopped up the tea and apologized like the gentleman his stepfather could sometimes be.

He asked if she minded if he sat down with her.

"Uhm . . . no," she said and hid the *Vogue* in her canvas bag as if it were porn.

"Oh, by the way," Stephen said, "I'm Sam Levine." Her eyes flickered at his surname and took in his Aryan features. "Well, it's Sammie mostly," he added. "To Mom I'm Samuel but only if I've done something wrong." A chuckle.

"I'll call you 'friend,'" she announced. "I'm Sheila Horowitz."

He glanced out the window to avoid having to shake her moist hand, tipped with five white, squooshy worms.

"Pleased to meet you," he said, turning back, sipping his new cup of tea, which he found disgusting. Sheila noticed that two of her stubby nails were dirty. She tried unobtrusively to dig the crud from under them.

"It's relaxing," she explained. "Sewing. I have an old Singer. One of those old black ones. Got it from my grams." She tried to straighten her shiny, short hair, wishing undoubtedly that today of all days she'd washed it.

"I don't know any girls who sew anymore," Stephen said. "Girl I dated in college did. Made most of her own clothes. Was *I* impressed."

"Uhm, in New York, like, nobody, and I mean nobody, sews." She sneered emphatically.

"My mother used to sew all the time, hours on end," Stephen said. "Every stitch had to be just perfect. I mean perfect. A thirty-second of an inch apart." This was true. "I still have some of the things she made. Stupid, but I kept 'em just 'cause she made them." This was not.

Stephen could still hear the start and stop of the Singer motor coming from his mother's tiny, hot room. Day and night. Get those stitches right. One thirty-second of an inch. Why? Because it's *important*! Here comes the ruler, here comes the belt, here comes the cock . . .

"Most men" – the stress she put on the word explained a

deal about Sheila Horowitz's life – "don't care doodles for sewing. They want girls to do sports or know movies." She added quickly, "And I do. I mean, I've been skiing. I'm not as good as you, I'll bet. And I like to go to the movies. Some movies."

Stephen said, "Oh, I don't ski. I don't like sports much." He looked outside and saw the cops everywhere. Looking in every car. A swarm of blue worms . . .

Sir, I don't understand why they're mounting this offensive, sir.

Soldier, your job is not to understand. Your job is to infiltrate, evaluate, delegate, isolate, and eliminate. That is your only job.

"Sorry?" he asked, missing what she'd said.

"I said, oh, don't give me that. I mean, I'd have to work out for, like, months to get in shape like you. I'm going to join the Health & Racquet Club. I've been planning to. Only, I've got back problems. But I really, really am going to join."

Stephen laughed. "Aw, I get so tired of – geez, all these girls look so sick. You know? All thin and pale. Take one of those skinny girls you see on TV and send her back to King Arthur's day and, bang, they'd call for the court surgeon and say, 'She must be dying, m'lord.'"

Sheila blinked, then roared with laughter, revealing unfortunate teeth. The joke gave her an excuse to rest her hand on his arm. He felt the five worms kneading his skin and fought down the nausea. "My daddy," she said, "he was a career army officer, traveled a lot. He told me in other countries they think American girls are way skinny."

"He was a soldier?" Sam Sammie Samuel Levine asked, smiling.

"Retired colonel."

"Well . . ."

Too much? he wondered. No. He said, "I'm service. Sergeant. Army."

"No! Where you stationed?"

"Special Operations. In New Jersey." She'd know enough not to ask any more about Special Ops activities. "I'm glad you've got a soldier in the family. I sometimes don't tell people what I do. It's not too cool. 'Specially around here. New York, I mean."

"Don't you worry about that. I think it's *very* cool, friend." She nodded at the Fender case. "And you're a musician, too?"

"Not really. I volunteer at a day care center. Teach kids music. It's something the base does."

Looking outside. Flashing lights. Blue white. A squad car streaked past.

She scooted her chair closer and he detected a repulsive scent. It made him go cringey again and the image came to mind of worms oozing through her greasy hair. He nearly vomited. He excused himself for a moment and spent three minutes scrubbing his hands. When he returned he noticed two things: that the top button of her blouse had been undone and that the back of her sweater contained about a thousand cat hairs. Cats, to Stephen, were just four-legged worms.

He looked outside and saw that the line of cops was getting closer. Stephen glanced at his watch and said, "Say, I've gotta pick up my cat. He's at the vet—"

"Oh, you have a cat? What's his name?" She leaned forward.

"Buddy."

Her eyes glowed. "Oh, cutey cutey cute. You have a picture?"

Of a fucking cat?

"Not on me," Stephen said, clicked his tongue regretfully.

"Is poor Buddy sicky-wicky?"

"Just a checkup."

"Oh, good for you. Watch out for those worms."

"How's that?" he asked, alarmed.

"You know, like heartworm."

"Oh. Right."

"Uhm, if you're good, friend," Sheila said, singsongy again, "maybe I'll introduce you to Garfield, Andrea, and Essie. Well, it's *really* Esmeralda but she'd never approve of that, of course."

"They sound so wonderful," he said, gazing at the pictures Sheila'd dug from her wallet. "I'd love to meet them."

"You know," she blurted, "I only live three blocks away. On Eighty-first."

"Hey, got an idea." He looked bright. "Maybe I could drop this stuff off and meet your babies. Then you could help me collect Buddy."

"Neat-o," Sheila said.

"Let's go."

Outside, she said, "Ooo, look at all the police. What's going on?"

"Wow. Dunno." Stephen slung the backpack over his shoulder. Something metal clinked. Maybe a flash grenade banged against his Beretta.

"What's in there?"

"Musical instruments. For the kids."

"Oh, like triangles?"

"Yeah, like triangles."

You want me to carry your guitar?"

"You mind?"

"Uhm, I think it'd be neat."

She took the Fender case and slipped her arm through his and they walked past a cluster of cops, who were blind to the loving couple, and continued down the street, laughing and talking about those crazy cats.

Hour 1 of 45

6

Thom appeared in Lincoln Rhyme's doorway and motioned someone inside.

A trim, crew-cut man in his fifties. Captain Bo Haumann, head of the NYPD's Emergency Services Unit – the police's SWAT team. Grizzled and tendony, Haumann looked like the drill sergeant he'd been in the service. He spoke slowly and reasonably, and he looked you dead in the eye, with a faint smile, when he talked. In tactical operations he was often suited up in flak jacket and Nomex hood and was usually one of the first officers through the door in a dynamic barricade entry.

"It's really him?" the captain asked. "The Dancer?"

"S'what we heard," Sellitto said.

The slight pause, which from the gray-haired cop was like a loud sigh from anyone else. Then he said, "I've got a couple of Thirty-two-E teams dedicated."

Thirty-two-E officers, nicknamed after their operations room at Police Plaza, were an unkept secret. Officially called Special Procedures Officers of the Emergency Services Unit, the men and women were mostly ex-military and had been relentlessly instructed in full S&S procedures – search and surveillance – as well as assault, sniping, and hostage rescue. There weren't many of them. The city's tough reputation notwithstanding, there were relatively few tactical operations in New York and the city's hostage negotiators – considered the best in the country – usually resolved standoffs before an assault was necessary. Haumann's committing two teams, which totaled ten officers, to the Dancer would have used up most of the 32-Es.

A moment later a slight, balding man wearing very unstylish glasses entered the room. Mel Cooper was the best lab man in IRD, the department's Investigation and Resources Division, which Rhyme used to head. He'd never searched a crime scene, never arrested a perp, had probably forgotten how to fire the slim pistol he grudgingly wore on the back of his old leather belt. Cooper had no desire to be anywhere in the world except sitting on a lab stool, peering into microscopes and analyzing friction ridge prints (well, there and on the ballroom dance floor, where he was an award-winning tango dancer).

"Detective," Cooper said, using the title that Rhyme had carried when he'd hired Cooper away from Albany PD some years ago, "thought I was going to be looking at sand. But I hear it's the Dancer." There's only one place the word travels faster than on the street, Rhyme reflected, and that's inside the Police Department itself. "We'll get him this time, Lincoln. We'll get him."

As Banks briefed the newcomers Rhyme happened to look up. He saw a woman in the doorway of the lab. Dark eyes scanning the room, taking it all in. Not cautious, not uneasy.

"Mrs Clay?" he asked.

She nodded. A lean man appeared in the doorway beside her. Britton Hale, Rhyme assumed.

"Please come in," the criminalist said.

She stepped into the middle of the room, glancing at Rhyme, then at the wall of forensic equipment near Mel Cooper.

"Percey," she said. "Call me Percey. You're Lincoln Rhyme?"

"That's right. I'm very sorry about your husband."

She nodded briskly, seemed uncomfortable with the sympathy.

Just like me, Rhyme thought.

He asked the man standing beside Percey, "And you're Mr Hale?"

The lanky pilot nodded and stepped forward to shake hands, then noticed Rhyme's arms were strapped to the wheelchair. "Oh," he muttered, then blushed. He stepped back.

Rhyme introduced them to the rest of the team, everyone except Amelia Sachs, who – at Rhyme's insistence – was changing out of her uniform and putting on the jeans and sweatshirt that happened to be hanging upstairs in Rhyme's closet. He'd explained that the Dancer often killed or wounded cops as a diversion; he wanted her to look as civilian as possible.

Percey pulled a flask from her slacks pocket, a silver flask, and took a short sip. She drank the liquor – Rhyme smelled expensive bourbon – as if it were medicine.

Betrayed by his own body, Rhyme rarely paid attention to the physical qualities in others, except victims and perps. But Percey Clay was hard to ignore. She wasn't much over five feet tall. Yet she radiated a distilled intensity. Her eyes, black as midnight, were captivating. Only after you managed to look away from them did you notice her face, which was unpretty – pug and tomboyish. She had a tangle of black curly hair, cropped short, though Rhyme thought that long tresses would soften the angular shape of her face. She didn't adopt the cloaking mannerisms of some short people – hands on hips, crossed arms, fingers stationed in front of the mouth. She offered as few gratuitous gestures as Rhyme did, he realized.

A sudden thought came to him: She's like a Gypsy.

He realized that she was studying him too. And hers seemed to be a curious reaction. Seeing him for the first time, most people slap a dumb grin on their faces, blush red as fruit, and force themselves to stare fixedly at Rhyme's forehead so their eyes won't drop accidentally to his damaged body. But Percey looked once at his face – handsome with its trim lips and Tom Cruise nose, a face younger than its forty-some years – and once at his motionless legs and arms and torso. But her attention focused immediately on the crip equipment – the glossy Storm Arrow wheelchair, the sip-and-puff controller, the headset, the computer.

Thom entered the room and walked up to Rhyme to take his blood pressure.

"Not now," his boss said.

"Yes now."

"No."

"Be quiet," Thom said and took the pressure reading anyway. He pulled off the stethoscope. "Not bad. But you're tired and you've been way too busy lately. You need some rest."

"Go away," Rhyme grumbled. He turned back to Percey Clay. Because he was a crip, a quad, because he was merely a portion of a human being, visitors often seemed to think he couldn't understand what they were saying; they spoke slowly or even addressed him through Thom. Percey now spoke to him directly and earned many points from him for doing this. "You think we're in danger, Brit and me?"

"Oh, you are. Serious danger."

Sachs walked into the room and glanced at Percey and Rhyme.

He introduced them.

"Amelia?" Percey asked. "Your name's *Amelia*?"

Sachs nodded.

A faint smile passed over Percey's face. She turned slightly and shared it with Rhyme.

"I wasn't named after her – the flier," Sachs said, recalling, Rhyme guessed, that Percey was a pilot. "One of my grandfather's sisters. Was Amelia Earhart a hero?"

"No," Percey said. "Not really. It's just kind of a coincidence."

Hale said, "You're going to have guards for her, aren't you? Full-time?" He nodded at Percey.

"Sure, you bet," Dellray said.

"Okay," Hale announced. "Good . . . One thing. I was thinking you really ought to have a talk with that guy. Phillip Hansen."

"A talk?" Rhyme queried.

"With Hansen?" Sellitto asked. "Sure. But he's denying everything and won't say a word more'n that." He looked at Rhyme. "Had the Twins on him for a while." Then back to Hale. "They're our best interrogators. And he stonewalled completely. No luck so far."

"Can't you threaten him . . . or something?"

"Uhm, no," the detective said. "Don't think so."

"Doesn't matter," Rhyme continued. "There's nothing

Hansen could tell us anyway. The Dancer never meets his clients face-to-face and he never tells them how he's going to do the job."

"The Dancer?" Percey asked.

"That's the name we have for the killer. The Coffin Dancer."

"*Coffin* Dancer?" Percey gave a faint laugh, as if the phrase meant something to her. But she didn't elaborate.

"Well, that's a little spooky," Hale said dubiously, as if cops shouldn't have eerie nicknames for their bad guys. Rhyme supposed he was right.

Percey looked into Rhyme's eyes, nearly as dark as hers. "So what happened to you? You get shot?"

Sachs – and Hale too – stirred at these blunt words but Rhyme didn't mind. He preferred people like himself – those with no use for pointless tact. He said equably, "I was searching a crime scene at a construction site. A beam collapsed. Broke my neck."

"Like that actor. Christopher Reeve."

"Yes."

Hale said, "That was tough. But, man, he's brave. I've seen him on TV. I think I would've killed myself if that'd happened."

Rhyme glanced at Sachs, who caught his eye. He turned back to Percey. "We need your help. We have to figure out how he got that bomb on board. Do you have any idea?"

"None," Percey said then looked at Hale, who shook his head.

"Did you see anyone you didn't recognize near the plane before the flight?"

"I was sick last night," Percey said. "I didn't even go to the airport."

Hale said, "I was upstate, fishing. I had the day off. Didn't get home till late."

"Where exactly was the plane before it took off?"

"It was in our hangar. We were outfitting it for the new charter. We had to take seats out, install special racks with heavy-duty power outlets. For the refrigeration units. You know what the cargo was, don't you?"

"Organs," Rhyme said. "Human organs. Do you share the hangar with any other company?"

"No, it's ours. Well, we lease it."

"How easy is it to get inside?" Sellitto asked.

"It's locked if nobody's around but the past couple days we've had crews working twenty-four hours to outfit the Lear."

"You know the crews?" Sellitto asked.

"They're like family," Hale said defensively.

Sellitto rolled his eyes at Banks. Rhyme supposed that the detective was thinking that family members were always the first suspects in a murder case.

"We'll take the names anyway, you don't mind. Check 'em out."

"Sally Anne, she's our office manager, 'll get you a list."

"You'll have to seal the hangar," Rhyme said. "Keep everybody out."

Percey was shaking her head. "We can't—"

"Seal it," he repeated. "Everybody out. Every . . . body."

"But—"

Rhyme said, "We have to."

"Whoa," Percey said, "hold up there." She looked at Hale. "*Foxtrot Bravo*?"

He shrugged. "Ron said it'll take another day at least."

Percey sighed. "The Learjet that Ed was flying was the only one outfitted for the charter. There's another flight scheduled for tomorrow night. We'll have to work nonstop to get the other plane ready for that flight. We can't close the hangar."

Rhyme said, "I'm sorry. This isn't an option."

Percey blinked. "Well, I don't know who you are to give me options . . ."

"I'm somebody trying to save your life," Rhyme snapped.

"I can't risk losing this contract."

"Hold up, miss," Dellray said. "You're not understandin' this bad guy . . ."

"He killed my husband," she responded in a flinty voice. "I understand him perfectly. But I'm not being bullied into losing this job."

Sachs's hands went to her hips. "Hey, hold up there. If

there's anybody who can save your skin, it's Lincoln Rhyme. I don't think we need an attitude here."

Rhyme's voice broke into the argument. He asked calmly, "Can you give us an hour for the search?"

"An hour?" Percey considered this.

Sachs gave a laugh and turned her surprised eyes on her boss. She asked, "Search a hangar in an hour? Come on, Rhyme." Her face said: Here I am defending you, and now you're pulling this? Whose side are you on?

Some criminalists assigned teams to search crime scenes. But Rhyme always insisted that Amelia Sachs search alone, just as he'd done. A single CS searcher had a focus that couldn't be achieved with other people on the scene. An hour was an extraordinarily brief time for a single person to cover a large scene. Rhyme knew this but he didn't respond to Sachs. He kept his eyes on Percey. She said, "An hour? All right. I can live with that."

"Rhyme," Sachs protested, "I'll need more time."

"Ah, but you're the best, Amelia," he joshed. Which meant the decision had already been made.

"Who can help us up there?" Rhyme asked Percey.

"Ron Talbot. He's a partner in the company and our operations manager."

Sachs jotted the name in her watch book. "Should I go now?" she asked.

"No," Rhyme responded, "I want you to wait until we have the bomb from the Chicago flight. I need you to help me analyze it."

"I only have an hour," she said testily. "Remember?"

"You'll have to wait," he grumbled, then asked Fred Dellray, "What about the safe house?"

"Oh, we got a place you'll like," the agent said to Percey. "In Manhattan. Your taxpayer dollars be working hard. Yep, yep. U.S. marshals use it for the crème de la crème in witness protection. Only thing is, we need somebody from NYPD for baby-sitting detail. Somebody knows and appreciates the Dancer."

And just then Jerry Banks looked up, wondering why everybody was staring at him. "What?" he asked. *"What?"* And tried in vain to pat down his persistent cowlick.

Stephen Kall, talker of soldier talk, shooter of soldier guns, had never in fact been a soldier.

But he now said to Sheila Horowitz, "I'm proud of my military heritage. And that's the truth."

"Some people don't—"

"No," he interrupted, "some people don't respect you for it. But that's their problem."

"It *is* their problem," Sheila echoed.

"You have a nice place here." He looked around the dump, filled with Conran's markdowns.

"Thank you, friend. Uhm, you, like, want something to drink? Oopsie, there I go using that old preposition the wrong way. Mom's always after me. Watching too much TV. Like, like, like. Shamie shamie."

What the fuck is she talking about?

"You live here alone?" he asked with a pleasant smile of curiosity.

"Yep, just me and the dynamic trio. I don't know why they're hiding. Those silly-billy scamps." Sheila nervously pinched the fine hem of her vest. And because he hadn't answered, she repeated, "So? Something to drink?"

"Sure."

He saw a single bottle of wine, dust encrusted, sitting on top of her refrigerator. Saved for that special occasion. Was this it?

Apparently not. She broke out the diet Dr Pepper.

He strolled to the window and looked out. No police on the street here. And only a half block to a subway stop. The apartment was on the second floor, and though she had grates on the back windows, they were unlocked. If he had to he could climb down the fire escape and disappear onto Lexington Avenue, which was always crowded . . .

She had a telephone and a PC. Good.

He glanced at a wall calendar – pictures of angels. There were a few notations but nothing for this weekend.

"Hey, Sheila, would you—" He caught himself and shook his head, fell silent.

"Uhm, what?"

"Well, it's . . . I know it's stupid to ask. I mean, it's such short notice and everything. I was just wondering if you had plans for the next couple of days."

Cautious here. "Oh, I, uhm, I was supposed to see my mother."

Stephen wrinkled his face in disappointment. "Too bad. See, I have this place in Cape May—"

"The Jersey shore!"

"Right. I'm going out there—"

"After you get Buddy?"

Who the fuck was Buddy?

Oh, the cat. "Right. If you weren't doing anything, I thought you might like to come out."

"You have . . . ?"

"My mom's going to be there, some of her girlfriends."

"Well, golly. I don't know."

"So, why don't you call your mother and tell her she'll have to live without you for the weekend?"

"Well . . . I don't really have to call. If I don't show up it's, like, no big deal. It was like, maybe I'll go, maybe I won't."

So she'd been lying. An empty weekend. Nobody'd miss her for the next few days.

A cat jumped up next to him, stuck her face into his. He pictured a thousand worms spraying over his body. He pictured the worms squirming through Sheila's hair. Her wormy fingers. Stephen began to detest this woman. He wanted to scream.

"Ooo, say hello to our new friend, Andrea. She likes you, Sam."

He stood up, looking around the apartment. Thinking:

Remember, boy, anything can kill.

Some things kill fast and some things kill slow. But anything can kill.

"Say," he asked, "you have any packing tape?"

"Uhm, for . . . ?" Her mind raced. "For . . . ?"

"The instruments I have in the bag? I need to tape one of the drums back together."

"Oh, sure, I've got some in here." She walked into the hallway. "I send my aunties packages every Christmas. I always buy a new roll of tape. I can never remember if I've bought one before so I end up with a ton of them. Aren't I a silly-billy?"

He didn't answer because he was surveying the kitchen and decided that was the best kill zone in the apartment.

"Here you go." She tossed him the roll of tape playfully. He instinctively caught it. He was angry because he hadn't had the chance to put his gloves on. He knew he'd left prints on the roll. He shivered in rage and when he saw Sheila grinning, saying, "Hey, good catch, friend," what he was really looking at was a huge worm moving closer and closer. He set the tape down and pulled on his gloves.

"Gloves? You cold? Say, friend, what're you . . . ?"

He ignored her and opened the refrigerator door, began removing the food.

She stepped farther into the room. Her giddy smile started to fade. "Uhm, you hungry?"

He began removing the shelves.

A look passed between them and suddenly, from deep within her throat, came a faint *"Eeeeeee."*

Stephen got the fat worm before she made it halfway to the front door.

Fast or slow?

He dragged her back into the kitchen. Toward the refrigerator.

7

Threes.

Percey Clay, honors engineering major, certified airframe and power plant mechanic, and holder of every license the Federal Aviation Agency could bestow on pilots, had no time for superstition.

Yet as she drove in a bulletproof van through Central Park on the way to the federal safe house in Midtown, she thought of the old adage that superstitious travelers repeat like a grim mantra. Crashes come in threes.

Tragedies too.

First, Ed. Now, the second sorrow: what she was hearing over the cell phone from Ron Talbot, who was in his office at Hudson Air.

She was sandwiched between Brit Hale and that young detective, Jerry Banks. Her head was down. Hale watched her, and Banks looked vigilantly out the window at traffic, passersby, and trees.

"U.S. Med agreed to give us one more shot." Talbot's breath wheezed in and out alarmingly. One of the best pilots she'd ever known, Talbot hadn't driven an aircraft for years – grounded because of his precarious health. Percey considered this a horrifyingly unjust punishment for his sins of liquor, cigarettes, and food (largely because she shared them). "I mean, they *can* cancel the contract. Bombs aren't force majeure. They don't excuse us from performance."

"But they're letting us make the flight tomorrow."

A pause.

"Yeah. They are."

"Come on, Ron," she snapped. "No bullshit between us." She heard him light another cigarette. Big and smokey – the man she'd bum Camels from when she was quitting smoking – Talbot was forgetful of fresh clothing and shaves. And inept at delivering bad news.

"It's *Foxtrot Bravo,*" he said reluctantly.

"What about her?"

N695FB was Percey Clay's Learjet 35A. Not that the paperwork indicated this. Legally the twin-engine jet was leased to Clay-Carney Holding Corporation Two, Inc., a wholly owned subsidiary of Hudson Air Charters, Ltd., by Morgan Air Leasing Inc., which in turn leased it from La Jolla Holding Two's wholly owned subsidiary Transport Solutions Incorporated, a Delaware company. This byzantine arrangement was legal and common, given the fact that both airplanes and airplane crashes are phenomenally expensive.

But everyone at Hudson Air Charters knew that November Six Nine Five *Foxtrot Bravo* was Percey's. She'd logged thousands of hours in the airplane. It was her pet. It was her children. And on the too-many nights Ed was gone just the thought of the aircraft would take the sting out of the loneliness. A sweet stick, the aircraft could cruise at forty-five thousand feet at speeds of 460 knots – over 500 miles per hour. She personally knew it could fly higher and faster, though that was a secret kept from Morgan Air Leasing, La Jolla Holding, Transport Solutions, and the FAA.

Talbot finally said, "Getting her outfitted – it's going to be trickier than I thought."

"Go on."

"All right," he said finally. "Stu quit." Stu Marquard, their chief mechanic.

"What?"

"The son of a bitch quit. Well, he hasn't yet," Talbot continued. "He called in sick but it sounded funny, so I made some calls. He's going over to Sikorsky. Already took the job."

Percey was stunned.

This was a major problem. Lear 35As came equipped as eight-seat passenger jets. To make the aircraft ready for the

U.S. Medical run, most of the seats had to be stripped out, shock-absorbed, refrigerated bays had to be installed, and extra power outlets had to be run from the engine's generators. This meant major electrical and airframe work.

There were no mechanics better than Stu Marquard and he'd outfitted Ed's Lear in record time. But without him Percey didn't know how they could finish in time for tomorrow's flight.

"What is it, Perce?" Hale asked, seeing her grimacing face.

"Stu quit," she whispered.

He shook his head, not understanding. "Quit what?"

"He left," she muttered. "Quit his job. Going to work on fucking choppers."

Hale gazed at her in shock. "Today?"

She nodded.

Talbot continued. "He's scared, Perce. They know it was a bomb. The cops aren't saying anything but everybody knows what happened. They're nervous. I was talking to John Ringle—"

"Johnny?" A young pilot they'd hired last year. "He's not leaving too?"

"He was just asking if we're closing down for a while. Until this all blows over."

"No, we're not closing down," she said firmly. "We're not canceling a single goddamn job. It's business as usual. And if anybody else calls in sick, fire them."

"Percey . . ."

Talbot was dour but everybody knew he was the company's soft touch.

"All right," she snapped, "*I'll* fire them."

"Look, about *Foxtrot Bravo,* I can do most of the work myself," said Talbot, a certified airframe mechanic himself.

"Do what you can. But see if you can find another mechanic," she told him. "We'll talk later."

She hung up.

"I can't believe it," Hale said. "He quit." The pilot was bewildered.

Percey was furious. People were bailing out – the worst sin

there was. The Company was dying. Yet she didn't have a clue how to save it.

Percey Clay had no monkey skills for running a business.

Monkey skills . . .

A phrase she'd heard when she was a fighter pilot. Coined by a navy flier, an admiral, it meant the esoteric, unteachable talents of a natural-born pilot.

Well, sure, Percey had monkey skills when it came to flying. Any type of aircraft, whether she'd flown it previously or not, under any weather conditions, VFR or IFR, day or night. She could drive the plane flawlessly and set it down on that magic spot pilots aimed for – exactly "a thousand past the numbers" – a thousand feet down the landing strip past the white runway designation. Sailplanes, biplanes, Hercs, seven three sevens, MiGs – she was at home in any cockpit.

But that was about as far as Percey Rachael Clay's monkey skills extended.

She had none at family relations, that was for sure. Her tobacco society father had refused to speak to her for years – had actually disinherited her – when she'd dropped out of his alma mater, UVA, to attend aviation school at Virginia Tech. (Even though she told him that the departure from Charlottesville was inevitable – six weeks into the first semester Percey'd KO'd a sorority president after the lanky blond commented in an overloud whisper that the troll girl might want to pledge at the ag school and not on Greek Row.)

Certainly no monkey skills at navy politics. Her awe-inspiring flight performance in the big Tomcats didn't quite tip the balance against her unfortunate habit of speaking her mind when everyone else was keeping mum about certain events.

And no skills at running the very charter company she was president of. It was mystifying to her how Hudson Air could be so busy yet continue to skirt bankruptcy. Like Ed and Brit Hale and the other staff pilots, Percey was constantly working (one reason she shunned scheduled airlines was the asinine FAA pronouncement that pilots fly no more than eighty hours a month). So why were they constantly broke? If it hadn't been for charming Ed's ability to get clients, and grumpy Ron Talbot's to cut costs and juggle creditors, they never would have survived for the past two years.

The Company had nearly gone under last month but Ed managed to snare the contract from U.S. Medical. The hospital chain made an astonishing amount of money doing transplants, which she learned was a business far bigger than just hearts and kidneys. The major problem was getting the donor organ to the appropriate recipient within hours of its availability. Organs were often flown on commercial flights (carried in coolers in the cockpit), but transporting them was dictated by commercial airline scheduling and routing. Hudson Air didn't have those restrictions. The Company agreed to dedicate one aircraft to U.S. Medical. It would fly a counterclockwise route throughout the East Coast and Midwest to six or eight of the company's locations, circulating organs wherever they were needed. Delivery was guaranteed. Rain, snow, wind shear, conditions at minimum – as long as the airport was open and it was legal to fly, Hudson Air would deliver the cargo on time.

The first month was to be a trial period. If it worked out they'd get an eighteen-month contract that would be the backbone for the Company's survival.

Apparently Ron had charmed the client into giving them another chance, but if *Foxtrot Bravo* wasn't ready for tomorrow's flight . . . Percey didn't even want to think about that possibility.

As she rode in the police car through Central Park Percey Clay looked over the early spring growth. Ed had loved the park and had run here frequently. He'd do two laps around the reservoir and return home looking bedraggled, his grayish hair hanging in strands around his face. And me? Percey laughed sadly to herself now. He'd find her sitting at home, poring over a nav log or an advanced turbofan repair manual, maybe smoking, maybe drinking a Wild Turkey. And, grinning, Ed would poke her in the ribs with a strong finger and ask if she could do anything *else* unhealthy at the same time. And while they laughed, he'd sneak a couple of swigs of the bourbon.

Remembering then how he'd bend down and kiss her shoulder. When they made love it was that juncture where he'd rest his face, bent forward, locked against her skin, and Percey Clay believed that there, where her neck flared onto her delicate shoulders, if only there, she was a beautiful woman.

Ed . . .

All the stars of evening . . .

Tears again filling her eyes, she glanced up into the gray sky. Ominous. She estimated the ceiling at one five hundred feet, winds 090 at fifteen knots. Wind shear conditions. She shifted in the seat. Brit Hale's strong fingers were encircling her forearm. Jerry Banks was chatting about something. She wasn't listening.

Percey Clay came to a decision. She unfolded the cell phone again.

8

The siren wailed.

Lincoln Rhyme expected to hear the Doppler effect as the emergency vehicle cruised past. But right outside his front door the siren gave a brief chirrup and went silent. A moment later Thom let a young man into the first-floor lab. Crowned with a spiffy crew cut, the Illinois state trooper wore a blue uniform, which had probably been immaculate when he put it on yesterday but was now wrinkled and streaked with soot and dirt. He'd run an electric razor over his face but had made only faint inroads into the dark beard that contrasted with his thin yellow hair. He was carrying two large canvas satchels and a brown folder, and Rhyme was happier to see him than he'd been to see anybody in the past week.

"The bomb!" he shouted. "Here's the bomb!"

The officer, surprised at the odd collection of law enforcers, must have wondered what hit him as Cooper scooped the bags away and Sellitto scrawled a signature on the receipt and chain-of-custody card and shoved them back into his hand. "Thanks so long see you," the detective exhaled, turning back to the evidence table.

Thom smiled politely to the trooper and let him out of the room.

Rhyme called, "Let's go, Sachs. You're just standing around! What've we got?"

She offered a cold smile and walked over to Cooper's table, where the tech was carefully laying out the contents of the bags.

What *was* her problem today? An hour was plenty of time

to search a scene, if that's what she was upset about. Well, he liked her feisty. He himself was always at his best that way. "Okay, Thom, help us out here. The blackboard. We need to list the evidence. Make us some charts. 'CS-One.' The first heading."

"C, uhm, S?"

"'Crime scene,'" the criminalist snapped. "What else would it be? 'CS-One, Chicago.'"

In a recent case, Rhyme had used the back of a limp Metropolitan Museum poster as an evidence profiling chart. He now was state-of-the-art – several large chalkboards were mounted to the wall, redolent with scents that took him back to humid spring school days in the Midwest, living for science class and despising spelling and English.

The aide, casting an exasperated glance toward his boss, picked up the chalk, brushed some dust from his perfect tie and knife-crease slacks, and wrote.

"What do we have, Mel? Sachs, help him."

They began unloading the plastic bags and plastic jars of ash and bits of metal and fiber and wads of plastic. They assembled contents in porcelain trays. The crash site searchers – if they were on a par with the men and women Rhyme had trained – would have used roller-mounted magnets, large vacuum cleaners, and a series of fine mesh screens to locate debris from the blast.

Rhyme, expert in most areas of forensics, was an authority on bombs. He'd had no particular interest in the subject until the Dancer left his tiny package in the wastebasket of the Wall Street office where Rhyme's two techs were killed. After that Rhyme had taken it on himself to learn everything he could about explosives. He'd studied with the FBI's Explosives Unit, one of the smallest – but most elite – in the federal lab, composed of fourteen agent-examiners and technicians. They didn't find IEDs – improvised explosive devices, the law enforcement term for bombs – and they didn't render them safe. Their job was to analyze bombs and bomb crime scenes and to trace and categorize the makers and their students (bomb manufacture was considered an art in certain circles and apprentices worked hard to learn the techniques of famous bomb makers).

Sachs was poking over the bags. "Doesn't a bomb destroy itself?"

"Nothing's ever completely destroyed, Sachs. Remember that." Though as he wheeled closer and examined the bags, he admitted, "This was a bad one. See those fragments? That pile of aluminum on the left? The metal's shattered, not bent. That means the device had a high brisance—"

"High . . . ?" Sellitto asked.

"Brisance." Rhyme explained: "Detonation rate. But even so, sixty to ninety percent of a bomb survives the blast. Well, not the explosive, of course. Though there's always enough residue to type it. Oh, we've got plenty to work with here."

"Plenty?" Dellray snorted a laugh. "Bad as puttin' Humpty-Dumpty together again."

"Ah, but that's not our job, Fred," Rhyme said briskly. "All we need to do is catch the son of a bitch who pushed him off the wall." He wheeled further down the table. "What's it look like, Mel? I see battery, I see wire, I see timer. What else? Maybe bits of the container or packing?"

Suitcases have convicted more bombers than timers and detonators. It's not talked about but unclaimed baggage is often donated to the FBI by airlines and blown up in an attempt to duplicate explosions and provide standards for criminalists. In the Pan Am flight 103 bombing, the FBI identified the bombers not through the explosive itself but through the Toshiba radio it had been hidden in, the Samsonite suitcase containing the radio, and the clothes packed around it. The clothing in the suitcase was traced back to a store in Sliema, Malta, whose owner identified a Libyan intelligence agent as the person who'd bought the garments.

But Cooper shook his head. "Nothing near the seat of detonation except bomb components."

"So it wasn't in a suitcase or flight bag," Rhyme mused. "Interesting. How the hell did he get it on board? Where'd he plant it? Lon, read me the report from Chicago."

"'Difficult to determine exact blast location,'" Sellitto read, "'because of extensive fire and destruction of aircraft. Site of device seems to be underneath and behind the cockpit.'"

"Underneath and behind. I wonder if a cargo bay's there.

Maybe . . ." Rhyme fell silent. His head swiveled back and forth, gazing at the evidence bags. "Wait, wait!" he shouted. "Mel, let me see those bits of metal there. Third bag from the left. The aluminum. Put it under a 'scope."

Cooper had connected the video output of his compound microscope to Rhyme's computer. What Cooper saw, Rhyme could see. The tech began mounting samples of the minuscule bits of debris on slides and running them under the 'scope.

A moment later Rhyme ordered, "Cursor down. Double click."

The image on his computer screen magnified.

"There, look! The skin of the plane was blown inward."

"Inward?" Sachs asked. "You mean the bomb was on the *outside*?"

"I think so, yes. What about it, Mel?"

"You're right. Those polished rivet heads are all bent inward. It was outside, definitely."

"A rocket maybe?" Dellray asked. "SAM?"

Reading from the report Sellitto said, "No radar blips consistent with missiles."

Rhyme shook his head. "No, everything points to a bomb."

"But on the *outside*?" Sellitto asked. "Never heard of that before."

"That explains this," Cooper called. The tech, wearing magnifying goggles and armed with a ceramic probe, was looking over bits of metal as fast as a cowboy counts heads in a herd. "Fragments of ferrous metal. Magnets. Wouldn't stick to the aluminum skin but there was steel under it. And I've got bits of epoxy resin. He stuck the bomb on the outside with the magnets to hold it until the glue hardened."

"And look at the shock waves in the epoxy," Rhyme pointed out. "The glue wasn't completely set, so he planted it not long before takeoff."

"Can we brand the epoxy?"

"Nope. Generic composition. Sold everywhere."

"Any hope of prints? Tell me true, Mel."

Cooper's answer was a faint, skeptical laugh. But he went through the motions anyway and scanned the fragments with the PoliLight wand. Nothing was evident except the blast residue. "Not a thing."

"I want to smell it," Rhyme announced.

"Smell it?" Sachs asked.

"With the brisance, we know it's high explosive. I want to know exactly what kind."

Many bombers used low explosives – substances that burn quickly but don't explode unless confined in, say, a pipe or box. Gunpowder was the most common of these. High explosives – like plastic or TNT – detonate in their natural state and don't need to be packed inside anything. They were expensive and hard to come by. The type and source of explosive could tell a lot about the bomber's identity.

Sachs brought a bag to Rhyme's chair and opened it. He inhaled.

"RDX," Rhyme said, recognizing it immediately.

"Consistent with the brisance," Cooper said. "You thinking C three or C four?" Cooper asked. RDX was the main component of these two plastic explosives, which were military; they were illegal for a civilian to possess.

"Not C three," Rhyme said, again smelling the explosive as if it were a vintage Bordeaux. "No sweet smell . . . Not sure. And strange . . . I smell something else . . . GC it, Mel."

The tech ran the sample through the gas chromatograph/mass spectrometer. This machine isolated elements in compounds and identified them. It could analyze samples as small as a millionth of a gram and, once it had determined what they were, could run the information through a database to determine, in many cases, brand names.

Cooper examined the results. "You're right, Lincoln. It's RDX. Also oil. And this is weird – starch . . ."

"Starch!" Rhyme cried. "That's what I smelled. It's guar flour . . ."

Cooper laughed as those very words popped up on the computer screen. "How'd you know?"

"Because it's military dynamite."

"But there's no nitroglycerine," Cooper protested. The active ingredient in dynamite.

"No, no, it's not real dynamite," Rhyme said. "It's a mixture of RDX, TNT, motor oil, and the guar flour. You don't see it very often."

"Military, huh?" Sellitto said. "Points to Hansen."

"That it does."

The tech mounted samples on his compound 'scope's stage.

The images appeared simultaneously on Rhyme's computer screen. Bits of fiber, wires, scraps, splinters, dust.

He was reminded of a similar image from years ago, though in circumstances very different. Looking through a heavy brass kaleidoscope he'd bought as a birthday present for a friend. Claire Trilling, beautiful and stylish. Rhyme had found the kaleidoscope in a store in SoHo. The two of them had spent an evening sharing a bottle of merlot and trying to guess what kind of exotic crystals or gemstones were making the astonishing images in the eyepiece. Finally, Claire, nearly as scientifically curious as Rhyme, had unscrewed the bottom of the tube and emptied the contents onto a table. They'd laughed. The objects were nothing more than scraps of metal, wood shavings, a broken paper clip, torn shreds from the Yellow Pages, thumbtacks.

Rhyme pushed those memories aside and concentrated on the objects he was seeing on the screen: A fragment of waxed manila paper – what the military dynamite had been wrapped in. Fibers – rayon and cotton – from the detonating cord the Dancer had tied around the dynamite, which would crumble too easily to mold around the cord. A fragment of aluminum and a tiny colored wire – from the electric blasting cap. More wire and an eraser-size piece of carbon from the battery.

"The timer," Rhyme called. "I want to see the timer."

Cooper lifted a small plastic bag from the table.

Inside was the still, cold heart of the bomb.

It was in nearly perfect shape, surprising Rhyme. Ah, your first slipup, he thought, speaking silently to the Dancer. Most bombers will pack explosives around the detonating system to destroy clues. But here the Dancer had accidentally placed the timer behind a thick steel lip in the metal housing that held the bomb. The lip had protected the timer from the blast.

Rhyme's neck stung as he strained forward, looking at the bent clock face.

Cooper scrutinized the device. "I've got the model number and manufacturer."

"Run everything through ERC."

The FBI's Explosives Reference Collection was the most extensive database on explosive devices in the world. It included information on all bombs reported in the United State. as well as actual physical evidence from many of them. Certain items in the collection were antiques, dating back to the 1920s.

Cooper typed on his computer keyboard. A moment later his modem whistled and crackled.

Two minutes later the results of the request came back.

"Not good," the bald man said, grimacing slightly, about as emotional as the technician ever got. "No specific profiles match this particular bomb."

Nearly all bombers fall into a pattern when they make their devices – they learn a technique and stick pretty close to it. (Given the nature of their product it's a good idea not to experiment too much.) If the parts of the Dancer's bomb matched an earlier IED in, say, Florida or California, the team might be able to pick up additional clues from those bomb sites that could lead them to the man's whereabouts. The rule of thumb is that if two bombs share at least four points of construction – soldered leads instead of taped, for instance, or analog versus digital timers – they were probably made by the same person or under his tutelage. The Dancer's bomb several years ago in Wall Street was different from this one. But, Rhyme knew, this was intended to serve a different purpose. That bomb was planted to hamper a crime scene investigation; this one, to blow a large airplane out of the sky. And if Rhyme knew anything about the Coffin Dancer, it was that he tailored his tools to the job.

"Gets worse?" Rhyme asked, reading Cooper's face as the tech stared at the computer screen.

"The timer."

Rhyme sighed. He understood. "How many billions and billions in production?"

"The Daiwana Corporation in Seoul sold a hundred and forty-two thousand of them last year. To retail stores, OEMs, and licensees. There's no coding on them to tell where they were shipped."

"Great. Just great."

Cooper continued to read the screen. "Hm. The folks at

ERC say they're very interested in the device and hope we'll add it to their database."

"Oh, our number one priority," Rhyme grumbled.

His shoulder muscles suddenly cramped and he had to lean back into the headrest of the wheelchair. He breathed deeply for a few minutes until the nearly unbearable pain subsided, then vanished. Sachs, the only one who noticed, stepped forward, but Rhyme shook his head toward her, said, "How many wires you make out, Mel?"

"Just two, it looks like."

"Multichannel or fiber optic?"

"Nope. Just average-ordinary bell wire."

"No shunts?"

"None."

A shunt is a separate wire, that completes the connection if a battery or timer wire is cut in an attempt to render the bomb safe. All sophisticated bombs have shunting mechanisms.

"Well," Sellitto said, "that's good news, isn't it? Means he's getting careless."

But Rhyme believed just the opposite. "Don't think so, Lon. The only point of a shunt is to make rendering safe tougher. Not having a shunt means he was confident enough the bomb wouldn't be found and would blow up just like he'd planned – in the air."

"This thing," Dellray asked contemptuously, looking over the bomb components. "What kind of people'd our boy have to rub shoulders with to make something like this? I got good CIs knowing 'bout bomb suppliers."

Fred Dellray too had learned more about bombs than he'd ever intended. His longtime partner and friend, Toby Doolittle, had been on the ground floor of the Oklahoma City federal building several years ago. He'd been killed instantly in the fertilizer bomb explosion.

But Rhyme shook his head. "It's all off-the-shelf stuff, Fred. Except for the explosives and the detonator cord. Hansen probably supplied them. Hell, the Dancer could've gotten everything he needed at Radio Shack."

"What?" Sachs asked, surprised.

"Oh, yeah," Cooper said, adding, "We call it the Bomber's Store."

Rhyme wheeled along the table over to a piece of steel housing twisted like crumpled paper, stared at it for a long moment.

Then he backed up and looked at the ceiling. "But why plant it outside?" he pondered. "Percey said there were always lots of people around. And doesn't the pilot walk around the plane before they take off, look at the wheels and things?"

"I think so," Sellitto said.

"Why didn't Ed Carney or his copilot see it?"

"Because," Sachs said suddenly, "the Dancer couldn't put the bomb on board until he knew for sure who was going to be in the plane."

Rhyme swiveled around to her. "That's it, Sachs! He was there watching. When he saw Carney get on board he knew he had at least one of the victims. He slipped it on somewhere after Carney got on board and before the plane took off. You've got to find out where, Sachs. And search it. Better get going."

"Only have an hour – well, less now," said cool-eyed Amelia Sachs as she started toward the door.

"One thing," Rhyme said.

She paused.

"The Dancer's a little different from everybody else you've ever been up against." How could he explain it? "With him, what you see isn't necessarily what is."

She cocked an eyebrow, meaning, Get to the point.

"He's probably not up there, at the airport. But if you see anyone make a move for you, well . . . shoot first."

"What?" She laughed.

"Worry about yourself first, the scene second."

"I'm just CS," she answered, walking through the door. "He's not going to care about me."

"Amelia, listen . . ."

But he heard her footsteps receding. The familiar pattern: the hollow thud on the oak, the mute steps as she crossed the Oriental carpet, then the tap on the marble entryway. Finally, the coda – as the front door closed with a snap.

9

The best soldiers are patient soldiers.

Sir, I'll remember that, sir.

Stephen Kall was sitting at Sheila's kitchen table, deciding how much he disliked Essie, the mangy cat, or whoever the fuck it was, and listening to a long conversation on his tape recorder. At first he'd decided to find the cats and kill them but he'd noticed that they occasionally gave an unearthly howl. If neighbors were used to the sound they might become suspicious if they heard only silence from Sheila Horowitz's apartment.

Patience . . . Watching the cassette roll. Listening.

It was twenty minutes later that he heard what he'd been hoping for on the tape. He smiled. Okay, good. He collected his Model 40 in the Fender guitar case, snug as a baby, and walked to the refrigerator. He cocked his head. The noises had stopped. It didn't shake any longer. He felt a bit of relief, less cringey, less *crawly,* thinking of the worm inside, now cold and still. It was safe to leave. He picked up his backpack and left the dim apartment with its pungent cat musk, dusty wine, and a million trails of disgusting worms.

Into the country.

Amelia Sachs sped though a tunnel of spring trees, rocks on one side, a modest cliff on another. A dusting of green, and everywhere the yellow starbursts of forsythia.

Sachs was a city girl, born in Brooklyn General Hospital, and was a lifetime resident of that borough. Nature, for her, was Prospect Park on Sundays or, on weekday evenings, Long Island forest preserves, where she'd hide her black sharklike Dodge Charger from the patrol cruisers prowling for her and her fellow racers.

Now, at the wheel of an Investigation and Resources Division rapid response vehicle – a crime scene station wagon – she punched the accelerator, swerved onto the shoulder, and passed a van that sported an upside-down Garfield cat suctioned to the rear window. She made the turnoff that took her deep into Westchester County.

Lifting her hand off the wheel she compulsively poked her finger into her hair and worried her scalp. Then she gripped the plastic wheel of the RRV once again and shoved the accelerator down until she burst into the suburban civilization of strip malls, sloppy commercial buildings, and fast food franchises.

She was thinking about bombs, about Percey Clay.

And about Lincoln Rhyme.

Something was different about him today. Something significant. They'd been working together for a year now, ever since he'd shanghaied her away from a coveted assignment with Public Affairs to help him catch a serial kidnapper. At the time Sachs had been at a low point in her life – an affair gone bad and a corruption scandal in the department that disillusioned her so much that she wanted out of Patrol altogether. But Rhyme wouldn't let her. Simple as that. Even though he was a civilian consultant he'd arranged for her transfer to Crime Scene. She protested some but soon gave up the pretense of reluctance; the fact was that she loved the work. And she loved working with Rhyme, whose brilliance was exhilarating and intimidating and – an admission she made to no one – goddamn sexy.

Which wasn't to say that she could read him perfectly. Lincoln Rhyme played life close to his chest and he wasn't revealing all to her.

Shoot first . . .

What was that all about? You *never* discharged a weapon at a crime scene if there was any way to avoid it. A single gunshot would contaminate a scene with carbon, sulfur, mercury, antimony, lead, copper, and arsenic, and the discharge and blowback could destroy vital trace evidence. Rhyme himself told her of the time he'd had to shoot a perp hiding at a scene, his biggest concern being that the shots had ruined much of the evidence. (And when Sachs, believing she'd at last outthought him, said, "But what did it matter, Rhyme? You got the perp, right?" he'd pointed out acerbically, "But what if he'd had *partners*, hm? What *then*?")

What was so different about the Coffin Dancer, other than the stupid name and the fact he seemed marginally smarter than the typical mafioso or Westie triggerman?

And working the scene at the hangar in an *hour*? It seemed to Sachs that he'd agreed to that as a favor for Percey. Which was completely unlike him. Rhyme would keep a scene sealed for days if he thought it was necessary.

These questions nagged and Amelia Sachs didn't like unanswered questions.

Though she had no more time for speculation. Sachs spun the wheel of the RRV and turned into the wide entrance to the Mamaroneck Regional Airport. It was a busy place, nestled into a woody area of Westchester County, north of Manhattan. The big airlines had affiliated companies with service here – United Express, American Eagle – but most of the planes parked here were corporate jets, all of them unmarked, for security reasons, she guessed.

At the entrance were several state troopers, checking IDs. They did a double take when she pulled up – seeing the beautiful redhead driving an NYPD crime scene RRV and wearing blue jeans, a windbreaker, and a Mets cap. They waved her through. She followed signs to Hudson Air Charters and found the small cinder-block building at the end of a row of commercial airline terminals.

She parked in front of the building and leapt out. She introduced herself to two officers who were standing guard over the hangar and the sleek, silver airplane that was inside. She was pleased that the local cops had run police tape around the hangar and the apron in front of it to secure the scene. But she was dismayed by the size of the area.

An hour to search? She could've spent an entire day here.

Thanks loads, Rhyme.

She hurried into the office.

A dozen men and women, some in business suits, some in overalls, stood in clusters. They were mostly in their twenties and thirties. Sachs supposed they'd been a young and enthusiastic group until last night. Now their faces revealed a collective sorrow that had aged them quickly.

"Is there someone named Ron Talbot here?" she asked, displaying her silver shield.

The oldest person in the room – a woman in her fifties, with spun and sprayed hair and wearing a frumpy suit – walked up to Sachs. "I'm Sally Anne McCay," she said. "I'm the office manager. Oh, how's Percey?"

"She's all right," Sachs said guardedly. "Where's Mr Talbot?"

A brunette in her thirties wearing a wrinkled blue dress stepped out of an office and put her arm around Sally Anne's shoulders. The older woman squeezed the younger's hand. "Lauren, you okay?"

Lauren, her puffy face a mask of shock, asked Sachs, "Do they know what happened yet?"

"We're just starting the investigation . . . Now, Mr Talbot?"

Sally Anne wiped tears then glanced toward an office in the corner. Sachs walked to the doorway. Inside was a bearish man with a stubbled chin and tangle of uncombed black-and-gray hair. He was poring over computer printouts, breathing heavily. He looked up, a dismal expression on his face. He'd been crying too, it seemed.

"I'm Officer Sachs," she said. "I'm with the NYPD."

He nodded. "You have him yet?" he asked, looking out the window as if he expected to see Ed Carney's ghost float past. He turned back to her. "The killer?"

"We're following up on several leads." Amelia Sachs, second-generation cop, had the art of evasion down cold.

Lauren appeared in Talbot's doorway. "I can't believe he's gone," she gasped, an edgy panic in her voice. "Who'd do something like that? *Who?*" As a patrol officer – a beat cop – Sachs had delivered her share of bad news to loved ones. She never got used to the despair she heard in the voices of surviving friends and family.

"Lauren." Sally Anne took her colleague's arm. "Lauren, go on home."

"No! I don't want to go home. I want to know who the hell did it? Oh, Ed . . ."

Stepping farther into Talbot's office, Sachs said, "I need your help. It looks like the killer mounted the bomb outside the plane underneath the cockpit. We have to find out where."

"Outside?" Talbot was frowning. "How?"

"Magnetized and glued. The glue wasn't completely set before the blast so it had to've been not long before takeoff."

Talbot nodded. "Whatever I can do. Sure."

She tapped the walkie-talkie on her hip. "I'm going to go on-line with my boss. He's in Manhattan. We're going to ask you some questions." Hooked up the Motorola, headset, and stalk mike.

"Okay, Rhyme, I'm here. Can you hear me?"

Though they were on an areawide Special Ops frequency and should have been ten-fiveing and K'ing, according to Communications Department procedures, Sachs and Rhyme rarely bothered with radioese. And they didn't now. His voice grumbled through the earphone, bouncing off who knew how many satellites. "Got it. Took you long enough."

Don't push it, Rhyme.

She asked Talbot, "Where was the plane before it took off? Say, an hour, hour and a quarter?"

"In the hangar," Talbot said.

"You think he could've gotten to the plane there? After the – what do you call it? When the pilot inspects the plane?"

"The walkaround. I suppose it's possible."

"But there were people around all the time," Lauren said. The crying fit was over and she'd wiped her face. She was calmer now and determination had replaced despair in her eyes.

"Who are you, please?"

"Lauren Simmons."

"Lauren's our assistant operations manager," Talbot said. "She works for me."

Lauren continued. "We'd been working with Stu – our chief mechanic, our *former* chief mechanic – to outfit the aircraft, working round the clock. We would've seen anybody near the plane."

"So," Sachs said, "he mounted the bomb after the plane left the hangar."

"Chronology!" Rhyme's voice crackled through the headset. "Where was it from the moment it left the hangar until takeoff?"

When she relayed this question Talbot and Lauren led her into a conference room. It was filled with charts and scheduling boards, hundreds of books and notebooks and stacks of papers. Lauren unrolled a large map of the airport. It contained a thousand numbers and symbols Sachs didn't understand, though the buildings and roadways were clearly outlined.

"No plane moves an inch," Talbot explained in a gruff baritone, "unless Ground Control gives the okay. *Charlie Juliet* was—"

"What? *Charlie . . .* ?"

"The number of the plane. We refer to planes by the last two letters on the registration number. CJ. So we called it *Charlie Juliet*." It was parked in the hangar here . . ." He tapped the map. "We finished loading—"

"When?" Rhyme called, so loud she wouldn't have been surprised if Talbot had heard. "We need times! Exact times."

The logbook in *Charlie Juliet*'d been burned to a cinder and the time-stamped FAA tape hadn't been transcribed yet. But Lauren examined the company's internal records. "Tower gave 'em push-back clearance at seven-sixteen. And they reported wheels up at seven-thirty."

Rhyme had heard. "Fourteen minutes. Ask them if the plane was ever both out of sight and stopped during that time."

Sachs did and Lauren answered, "Probably there." She pointed.

A narrow portion of taxiway about two hundred feet long. The row of hangars hid it from the rest of the airport. It ended at a T intersection.

Lauren said, "Oh, and it's an ATC No Vis area."

"That's right," Talbot said, as if this were significant.

"Translation!" Rhyme called.

"Meaning?" Sachs asked.

"Out of visibility from Air Traffic Control," Lauren answered. "A blind spot."

"Yes!" came the voice through her earphone. "Okay, Sachs. Seal and search. Release the hangar."

To Talbot she said, "We're not going to bother with the hangar. I'm releasing it. But I want to seal off that taxiway. Can you call the tower? Have them divert traffic?"

"I *can,*" he said doubtfully. "They aren't going to like it."

She said, "If there's any problem have them call Thomas Perkins. He's head of the FBI's Manhattan office. He'll clear it with FAA HQ."

"FAA? In Washington?" Lauren asked.

"That's the one."

Talbot gave a faint smile. "Well, okay."

Sachs started for the main door then paused, looking out at the busy airport. "Oh, I've got a car," she called to Talbot. "Is there anything special you do when you drive around an airport?"

"Yeah," he said, "try not to run into any airplanes."

II
THE KILL ZONE

A falconer's bird, however tame and affectionate, is as close to a wild animal in condition and habit as an animal that lives with man can be. Above all, it hunts.

A Rage for Falcons, Stephen Bodio

Hour 3 of 45

10

"I'm here, Rhyme," she announced.

Sachs climbed out of the RRV wagon and pulled latex gloves on her hands and wound rubber bands around her shoes – to make certain her footprints wouldn't be confused with the perp's, as Rhyme had taught her.

"And where, Sachs," he asked, "is *here*?"

"At the intersection of taxiways. Between a row of hangars. It's where Carney's plane would've stopped."

Sachs glanced uneasily at a line of trees in the distance. It was an overcast, dank day. Another storm was threatening. She felt exposed. The Dancer might be here now – maybe he'd returned to destroy evidence he'd left behind, maybe to kill a cop and slow down the investigation. Like the bomb in Wall Street a few years ago, the one that killed Rhyme's techs.

Shoot first . . .

Damn it, Rhyme, you're spooking me! Why're you acting like this guy walks through walls and spits poison?

Sachs took the PoliLight box and large suitcase from the back of the RRV. She opened the suitcase. Inside were a hundred tools of the trade: screwdrivers, wrenches, hammers, wire cutters, knives, friction ridge collection equipment, ninhydrin, tweezers, brushes, tongs, scissors, flex-claw pickups, a gunshot residue kit, pencils, plastic and paper bags, evidence collection tape . . .

One, establish the perimeter.

She ran yellow police line tape around the entire area.

Two, consider media and range of camera lenses and microphones.

No media. Not yet. Thank you, Lord.

"What's that, Sachs?"

"I'm thanking God there're no reporters."

"A fine prayer. But tell me what you're doing."

"Still securing the scene."

"Look for the—"

"Entrance and exit," she said.

Step three, determine the perpetrator's entrance and exit routes – they will be secondary crime scenes.

But she didn't have a clue as to where they might be. He could've come from anywhere. Snuck around the corners, driven here in a luggage cart, a gas truck . . .

Sachs donned goggles and began sweeping the PoliLight wand over the taxiway. It didn't work as well outside as in a dark room, but with the heavy overcast she could see flecks and streaks glowing under the eerie green-yellow light. There were, however, no footprints.

"Sprayed her down last night," the voice called behind her.

Sachs spun around, hand on her Glock, a half draw from the holster.

I'm *never* this edgy, Rhyme. It's all your fault.

Several men in coveralls were standing at the yellow tape. She walked up to them cautiously and checked their picture IDs. They matched the men's faces. Her hand slipped off the gun.

"They hose the place down every night. If you're looking for something. Thought you were."

"High-pressure hose," the second one added.

Great. Every bit of trace, every footprint, every fiber sloughed off the Dancer was gone.

"You see anybody here last night?"

"This have to do with the bomb?"

"Around seven-fifteen?" she persisted.

"Nope. Nobody comes up here. These hangars're deserted. Probably gonna tear 'em down someday."

"What're you doing here now?"

"Saw a cop. You are a cop, right? And just thought we'd have a look-see. This *is* about that bomb, right? Who did it? Arabs? Or them militia shits?"

She shooed them off. Into the microphone she said, "They cleaned the taxiway last night, Rhyme. High-pressure water, looks like."

"Oh, no."

"They—"

"Hey there."

She sighed, turning again, expecting to find the two workmen back. But the new visitor was a cocky county trooper, wearing a blocked Smokey the Bear hat and razor-creased gray slacks. He ducked under the tape.

"Excuse me," she protested. "This is a secure area."

He slowed but didn't stop. She checked his ID. It matched. The picture showed him looking off slightly, a cover boy on a men's fashion magazine.

"You're that officer from New York, right?" He laughed generously. "Nice uniforms they have down there." Eyeing her tight jeans.

"This area's sealed off."

"I can help. I took the forensics course. Mostly I'm highway detail but I've got major crimes experience. You have *some* hair. Bet you've heard that before."

"I really will have to ask you—"

"Jim Everts."

Don't go into first-name territory; it sticks like flypaper. "I'm Officer Sachs."

"Big hubbub, this. A bomb. Messy."

"See, Jim, this tape here's to keep people *out* of the scene. Now, you gonna be helpful and step back behind it?"

"Wait. You mean officers too?"

"That I do, yes."

"You mean me too?"

"Exactly."

There were five classic crime scene contaminators: weather, relatives of the victim, suspects, souvenir collectors, and – the all-time worst – fellow cops.

"I won't touch a thing. Cross my heart. Just be pleasure to watch you work, honey."

"Sachs," Rhyme whispered, "tell him to get the fuck out of your crime scene."

"Jim, get the fuck out of my crime scene."

"Or you'll report him."

"Or I'll report you."

"Oooo, gonna be *that* way, is it?" He held his hands up in surrender. The last of the flirt drained from his slick grin.

"Get *going,* Sachs."

The trooper ambled away slowly enough to drag some of his pride with him. He looked back once but a scathing retort eluded him.

Amelia Sachs began to walk the grid.

There were several different ways to search crime scenes. A strip search – walking in a serpentine pattern – was usually used for outdoor scenes because it covered the most ground quickly. But Rhyme wouldn't hear of that. He used the grid pattern – covering the entire area back and forth in one direction, walking one foot at a time, then turning perpendicular and walking back and forth the other way. When he was running IRD, "walking the grid" became synonymous with searching a crime scene, and heaven help any cops Rhyme caught taking shortcuts or daydreaming when they were on the grid.

Sachs now spent a half hour moving back and forth. While the spray truck might've eliminated prints and trace evidence, it wouldn't destroy anything larger that the Dancer might've dropped, nor would it ruin footprints or body impressions left in the mud beside the taxiway.

But she found nothing.

"Hell, Rhyme, not a thing."

"Ah, Sachs, I'll bet there is. I'll bet there's plenty. Just takes a little bit more effort than most scenes. The Dancer's not like other perps, remember."

Oh, *that* again.

"Sachs." His voice low and seductive. She felt a shiver. "Get into him," Rhyme whispered. "You know what I mean."

She knew exactly what he meant. Hated the thought. But, oh, yes, Sachs knew. The best criminalists were able to find a place in their minds where the line between hunter and hunted was virtually nonexistent. They moved through the crime scene not as cops tracking down clues but as the perp himself, feeling his desires, lusts, fears. Rhyme had this talent. And though she tried to deny it, Sachs did too. (She'd searched a scene a month ago – a father had murdered his wife and child – and managed to find the murder weapon when no one else had. After the case she hadn't been able to work for a week and had been plagued by flashbacks that *she'd* been the one who stabbed the victims to death. Saw their faces, heard their screams.)

Another pause. "Talk to me," he said. And finally the edginess in his voice was gone. "You're him. You're walking where he's walked, you're thinking the way he thinks . . ."

He'd said words like these to her before, of course. But now – as with everything else about the Dancer – it seemed to her that Rhyme had more in mind than just finding obscure evidence. No, she sensed that he was desperate to know about this perp. Who he was, what made him kill.

Another shiver. An image in her thoughts: Back to the other night. The lights of the airfield, the sound of airplane engines, the smell of jet exhaust.

"Come on, Amelia . . . You're him. You're the Coffin Dancer. You know Ed Carney's on the plane, you know you have to get the bomb on board. Just think about it for a minute or two."

And she did, summoning up from somewhere a need to kill.

He continued, speaking in an eerie, melodic voice. "You're brilliant," he said. "You have no morals whatsoever. You'll kill *anyone,* you'll do *anything* to get to your goal. You divert attention, you use people . . . Your deadliest weapon is deception."

I lay in wait.

My deadliest weapon . . .

She closed her eyes.

. . . *is deception.*

Sachs felt a dark hope, a vigilance, a hunt lust.

"I—"

He continued softly. "Is there any distraction, any diversion you can try?"

Eyes open now. "The whole area's empty. Nothing to distract the pilots with."

"Where are you hiding?"

"The hangars're all boarded up. The grass is too short

for cover. There're no trucks or oil drums. No alleys. No nooks."

In her gut: desperation. What'm I going to do? I've *got* to plant the bomb. I don't have any time. Lights . . . there're lights everywhere. What? What should I do?

She said, "I can't hide around the other side of the hangars. There're lots of workers. It's too exposed. They'll see me."

For a moment, Sachs herself floated back into her mind and she wondered, as she often did, why Lincoln Rhyme had the power to conjure her into someone else. Sometimes it angered her. Sometimes it thrilled.

Dropping into a crouch, ignoring the pain in her knees from the arthritis that had tormented her off and on for the past ten of her thirty-three years. "It's all too open here. I feel exposed."

"What're you thinking?"

There're people looking for me. I can't let them find me. I can't!

This is risky. Stay hidden. Stay down.

Nowhere to hide.

If I'm seen, everything's ruined. They'll find the bomb, they'll know I'm after all three witnesses. They'll put them in protective custody. I'll *never* get them then. I *can't* let that happen.

Feeling his panic she turned back to the only possible place to hide. The hangar beside the taxiway. In the wall facing her was a single broken window, about three by four feet. She'd ignored it because it was covered with a sheet of rotting plywood, nailed to the frame on the inside.

She approached it slowly. The ground in front was gravel; there were no footprints.

"There's a boarded-up window, Rhyme. Plywood on the inside. The glass is broken."

"Is it dirty, the glass that's still in the window?"

"Filthy."

"And the edges?"

"No, they're clean." She understood why he'd asked the question. "The glass was broken recently!"

"Right. Push the board. Hard."

It fell inward without any resistance and hit the floor with a huge bang.

"What was that?" Rhyme shouted. "Sachs, are you all right?"

"Just the plywood," she answered, once more spooked by his uneasiness.

She shone her halogen flashlight through the hangar. It was deserted.

"What do you see, Sachs?"

"It's empty. A few dusty boxes. There's gravel on the floor—"

"That was him!" Rhyme answered. "He broke in the window and threw gravel inside, so he could stand on the floor and not leave footprints. It's an old trick. Any footprints in front of the window? Bet it's more gravel," he added sourly.

"Is."

"Okay. Search the window. Then climb inside. But be sure to look for booby traps first. Remember the trash can a few years ago."

Stop it, Rhyme! Stop it.

Sachs shined the light around the space again. "It's clean, Rhyme. No traps. I'm examining the window frame."

The PoliLight showed nothing other than a faint mark left by a finger in a cotton glove. "No fiber, just the cotton pattern."

"Anything in the hangar? Anything worth stealing?"

"No. It's empty."

"Good," Rhyme said.

"Why good?" she asked. "I said there's no print."

"Ah, but it means it's *him,* Sachs. It's not logical for someone to break in wearing cotton gloves when there's nothing to steal."

She searched carefully. No footprints, no fingerprints, no visible evidence. She ran the Dustbuster and bagged the trace.

"The glass and gravel?" she asked. "Paper bag?"

"Yes."

Moisture often destroyed trace and though it looked unprofessional, certain evidence was best transported in brown paper bags rather than in plastic.

"Okay, Rhyme. I'll have it back to you in forty minutes."

They disconnected.

As she packed the bags carefully into the RRV, Sachs felt edgy, as she often did just after searching a scene where she'd found no obvious evidence – guns or knives or the perp's wallet. The trace she'd collected *might* have a clue as to who the Dancer was and where he was hiding. But the whole effort could have been a bust too. She was anxious to get back to Rhyme's lab and see what he could find.

Sachs climbed into the station wagon and sped back to the Hudson Air office. She hurried into Ron Talbot's office. He was talking to a tall man whose back was to the door. Sachs said, "I found where he was, Mr Talbot. The scene's released. You can have the tower—"

The man turned around. It was Brit Hale. He frowned, trying to think of her name, remembered it. "Oh. Officer Sachs. Hey. How you doing?"

She started to nod an automatic greeting, then stopped.

What was he doing here? He was supposed to be in the safe house.

She heard a soft crying and looked into the conference room. There was Percey Clay sitting next to Lauren, the pretty brunette who Sachs remembered was Ron Talbot's assistant. Lauren was crying and Percey, resolute in her own sorrow, was trying to comfort her. She glanced up, saw Sachs, and nodded to her.

No, no, no . . .

Then the third shock.

"Hi, Amelia," Jerry Banks said cheerfully, sipping coffee and standing by a window, where he'd been admiring the Learjet parked in the hangar. "That plane's something, isn't it?"

"What're they doing here?" Sachs snapped, pointing at Hale and Percey, forgetting that Banks outranked her.

"They had some problem or other about a mechanic," Banks said. "Percey wanted to stop by here. Try to find—"

"Rhyme," Sachs shouted into the microphone. "She's here."

"Who?" he asked acerbically. "And *where* is there?"

"Percey. And Hale too. At the airport."

"No! They're supposed to be at the safe house."

"Well, they're not. They're right here in front of me."

"No, no, no!" Rhyme raged. A moment passed. Then he asked, "Ask Banks if they followed evasive driving procedures."

Banks, uncomfortable, responded that they hadn't. "She was real insistent that they stop here first. I tried to talk her—"

"Jesus, Sachs. He's there someplace. The Dancer. I know he's there."

"How could he be?" Sachs's eyes strayed to the window.

"Keep 'em down," Rhyme said. "I'll have Dellray get an armored van from the Bureau's White Plains field office."

Percey heard the commotion. "I'll go to the safe house in an hour or so. I have to find a mechanic to work on—"

Sachs waved her silent, then said, "Jerry, keep them here." She ran to the door and looked out over the gray expanse of the airfield as a noisy prop plane charged down the runway. She pulled the stalk mike closer to her mouth. "How, Rhyme?" she asked. "How'll he come at us?"

"I don't have a clue. He could do anything."

Sachs tried to reenter the Dancer's mind, but couldn't. All she thought was, *Deception . . .*

"How secure is the area?" Rhyme asked.

"Pretty tight. Chain-link fence. Troopers at a roadblock at the entrance, checking tickets and IDs."

Rhyme asked, "But they're not checking IDs of police, right?"

Sachs looked at the uniformed officers, recalling how casually they'd waved her through. "Oh, hell, Rhyme, there're a dozen marked cars here. A couple unmarkeds too. I don't know the troopers or detectives . . . He could be any one of them."

"Okay, Sachs. Listen, find out if any local cops're missing. In the past two or three hours. The Dancer might've killed one and stolen their ID and uniform."

Sachs called a state trooper up to the door, examined him and his ID closely, and decided he was the real article. She said, "We think the killer may be nearby, maybe impersonating an officer. I need you to check out everybody here. If you don't recognize 'em, let me know. Also, find out from your dispatcher if any cops from around the area've gone missing in the past few hours."

"I'm on it, Officer."

She returned to the office. There were no blinds on the windows and Banks had moved Percey and Hale into an interior office.

"What's going on?" Percey asked.

"You're out of here in five minutes," Sachs said, glancing out the window, trying to guess how the Dancer would attack. She had no idea.

"Why?" the flier asked, frowning.

"We think the man who killed your husband's here. Or on his way here."

"Oh, come on. There're cops all over the field. It's perfectly safe. I need to—"

Sachs snapped to her, "No arguments."

But argue she did. "We can't leave. I've just had my chief mechanic quit. I have to—"

"Perce," Hale said uneasily, "maybe we ought to listen to her."

"We've got to get that aircraft—"

"Get back. In there. And be quiet."

Percey's mouth opened wide in shock. "You can't talk to me that way. I'm not a prisoner."

"Officer Sachs? Hellooo?" The trooper she'd spoken to outside stepped into the doorway. "I've done a fast visual of everybody here in uniform and the detectives too. No unknowns. And no reports of any state or Westchester officers missing. But our Central Dispatch told me something maybe you oughta know about. Might be nothing, but—"

"Tell me."

Percey Clay said, "Officer, I have to talk to you . . ."

Sachs ignored her and nodded to the trooper. "Go on."

"Traffic Patrol in White Plains, about two miles away. They found a body in a Dumpster. Think he was killed about an hour ago, maybe less."

"Rhyme, you hear?"

"Yes."

Sachs asked the cop, "Why d'you think that's important?"

"It's the way he was killed. Was a hell of a mess."

"Ask him if the hands and face were missing," Rhyme asked.

"What?"

"Ask him!"

She did, and everyone in the office stopped talking and stared at Sachs.

The trooper blinked in surprise and said, "Yes, ma'am, Officer. Well, the hands at least. The dispatcher didn't say anything about the face. How'd you know . . . ?"

Rhyme blurted, "Where's it now? The body?"

She relayed the question.

"In a coroner's bus. They're taking it to the county morgue."

"No," Rhyme said. "Have them get it to you, Sachs. I want you to examine it."

"The—"

"Body," he said. "It's got the answer to how he's going to come at you. I don't want Percey and Hale moved until we know what we're up against."

She told the cop Rhyme's request.

"Okay," he said. "I'll get on it. That's . . . You mean you want the body *here*."

"Yes. Now."

"Tell 'em to get it there fast, Sachs," Rhyme said. He sighed. "Oh, this is bad. Bad."

And Sachs had the uneasy thought that Rhyme's urgent grief was not only for the man who had just died so violently, whoever he was, but for those who, maybe, were about to.

People believe that the rifle is the important tool for a sniper, but that's wrong. It's the telescope.

What do we call it, Soldier? Do we call it a *telescopic sight*? Do we call it a '*scope*?"

Sir, we do not. It's a *telescope*. This one is a Redfield, three-by-nine variable, with crosshair reticles. There is none better, sir.

The telescope Stephen was mounting on top of the Model 40 was twelve and three-quarters inches long and weighed just over twelve ounces. It had been matched to this particular rifle with corresponding serial numbers and had been painstakingly adjusted for focus. The parallax had been fixed by the optical engineer in the factory so that the crosshairs resting on the lip of a man's heart five hundred yards away would not move perceptibly when the sniper's head eased from left to right. The eye relief was so accurate that the recoil would knock the eyepiece back to within one millimeter of Stephen's eyebrow and yet never touch a hair.

The Redfield telescope was black and sleek, and Stephen kept it draped in velvet and nestled in a Styrofoam block in his guitar case.

Now, hidden in a nest of grass some three hundred yards from the Hudson Air hangar and office, Stephen fitted the black tube of the telescope into its mount, perpendicular to the gun (he always thought of his stepfather's crucifix when he mounted it), then he swung the heavy tube into position with a satisfying click. He screwed down the lug nuts.

Soldier, are you a competent sniper?

Sir, I am the best, sir.

What are your qualifications?

Sir, I am in excellent physical shape, I am fastidious, I am right-handed, I have 20/20 vision, I do not smoke or drink or take any kind of drugs, I can lie still for hours at a time, and I live to send bullets up the ass of my enemy.

He nestled further into the pile of leaves and grass.

There might be worms here, he thought. But he wasn't feeling cringey at the moment. He had his mission and that was occupying his mind completely.

Stephen cradled the gun, smelling the machine oil from the bolt-action receiver and the neat's-foot oil from the sling, so worn and soft it was like angora. The Model 40 was a 7.62 millimeter NATO rifle and weighed eight pounds, ten ounces. The trigger pull generally ranged from three to five pounds, but Stephen set it a bit higher because his fingers were very strong. The weapon had a rated effective range of a thousand yards, though he had made kills at more than thirteen hundred.

Stephen knew this gun intimately. In sniper teams, his stepfather had told him, the snipers themselves have no disassemble authority, and the old man wouldn't let him strip the weapon himself. But that was one rule of the man's that hadn't seemed right to Stephen and so, in a moment of uncharacteristic defiance, he'd secretly taught himself how to dismantle the rifle, clean it, repair it, and even machine parts that needed adjustment or replacement.

Through the telescope he scanned Hudson Air. He couldn't see the Wife, though he knew she was there or soon would be. Listening to the tape of the phone tap on the Hudson Air office lines, Stephen had heard her tell someone named Ron that they were changing their plans; rather than going to the safe house they were driving to the airport to find some mechanics who could work on the airplane.

Using the low crawl technique, Stephen now moved forward until he was on a slight ridge, still hidden by trees and grass but with a better view of the hangar, the office, and the parking lot in front of it, separated from him by flat grass fields and two runways.

It was a glorious kill zone. Wide. Very little cover. All entrances and exits easily targeted from here.

Two people stood outside at the front door. One was a county or state trooper. The other was a woman – red hair dipping beneath a baseball cap. Very pretty. She was a cop, plainclothes. He could see the boxy outline of a Glock or Sig-Sauer high on her hip. He lifted his range finder and put the split image on the woman's red hair. He twisted a ring until the images moved together seamlessly.

Three hundred and sixteen yards.

He replaced the range finder, lifted the rifle, and sighted on the woman, centering the reticles on her hair once more. He glanced at her beautiful face. It troubled him, her attractiveness. He didn't like it. Didn't like *her*. He wondered why.

The grass rustled around him. He thought: Worms.

Was starting to feel cringey.

The face in the window . . .

He put the crosshairs on her chest.

The cringey feeling went away.

Soldier, what is the sniper's motto?

Sir, it is "One chance, one shot, one kill."

The conditions were excellent. There was a slight right-to-left crosswind, which he guessed was four miles an hour. The air was humid, which would buoy the slug. He was shooting over unvaried terrain with only moderate thermals.

He slid back down the knoll and ran a cleaning rod, tipped with a soft cotton cloth, through the Model 40. You always cleaned your weapon before firing. The slightest bit of moisture or oil could put a shot off by an inch or so. Then he made a loop sling and lay down in his nest.

Stephen loaded five rounds into the chamber. They were M-118 match-quality rounds, manufactured at the renowned Lake City arsenal. The bullet itself was a 173-grain boattail and it struck its target at a speed of a half mile a second. Stephen had altered the slugs somewhat, however. He'd drilled into the core and filled them with a small explosive charge and replaced the standard jacket with a ceramic nose that would pierce most kinds of body armor.

He unfolded a thin dish towel and spread it out on the ground to catch the ejected cartridges. Then he doubled the sling around his left biceps and planted that elbow firmly on the ground, keeping the forearm absolutely perpendicular to the ground – a bone support. He "spot-welded" his cheek and right thumb to the stock above the trigger.

Then slowly he began scanning the kill zone.

It was hard to see inside the offices but Stephen thought he caught a glimpse of the Wife.

Yes! It was her.

She was standing behind a big curly-haired man in a wrinkled white shirt. He held a cigarette. A young blond man in a suit, a badge on his belt, ushered them back out of sight.

Patience . . . she'll present again. They don't have a clue that you're here. You can wait all day. As long as the worms—

Flashing lights again.

Into the parking lot sped a county ambulance. The red-haired cop saw it. Her eyes grew excited. She ran toward the vehicle.

Stephen breathed deeply.

One chance . . .

Zero your weapon, Soldier.

Normal come-up elevation at 316 yards is three minutes, sir. He clicked the sight so that the barrel would be pointed upward slightly to take gravity into account.

One shot . . .

Calculate the crosswind, Soldier.

Sir, the formula is range in hundreds of yards times velocity divided by fifteen. Stephen's mind thought instantly: Slightly less than one minute of windage. He adjusted the telescope accordingly.

Sir, I am ready, sir.

One kill . . .

A shaft of light streamed from behind a cloud and lit the front of the office. Stephen began to breathe slowly and evenly.

He was lucky; the worms stayed away. And there were no faces watching him from the windows.

Hour 4 of 45

11

The medic rolled out of the ambulance.

She nodded to him. "I'm Officer Sachs."

He aimed his rotund belly her way and, straight-faced, said, "So. You ordered the pizza?" Then giggled.

She sighed. "What happened?" Sachs said.

"What happened? T'him? He got himself dead's what happened." He looked her over, shook his head. "What kinda cop are you? I never seen you up here."

"I'm from the city."

"Oh, the city. She's from the city. Well, better ask," he added gravely. "You ever see a body before?"

Sometimes you bend just a little. Learning how and how far takes some doing but it's a valuable lesson. Sometimes more than valuable, sometimes necessary. She smiled. "You know, we've got a real critical situation here. I'd sure appreciate your help. Could you tell me where you found him?"

He studied her chest for a moment. "Reason I ask about seeing bodies is this one's gonna bother you. I could do what needs to be done, searching it or whatever."

"Thanks. We'll get to that. Now, again, where'd you find him?"

"Dumpster in a parking lot 'bout two clicks—"

"That's miles," another voice added.

"Hey, Jim," the medic said.

Sachs turned. Oh, great. It was the *GQ* cop. The one who'd been flirting with her on the taxiway. He strode up to the ambulance.

"Hi, honey. Me again. How's your police tape holdin' up? Whatcha got, Earl?"

"One body, no hands." Earl yanked the door open, reached in, and unzipped the body bag. Blood flowed out onto the floor of the ambulance.

"Ooops." Earl winked. "Say, Jim, after you're through here, wanna get some spaghetti?"

"Mebbe pig's knuckles."

"There's a thought."

Rhyme interrupted. "Sachs, what's going on there? You got the body?"

"I've got it. Trying to figure out the story." To the medic she said, "We've gotta *move* on this. Anybody have any idea who he is?"

"Wasn't anything around to ID him. No missing persons reported. Nobody saw nothing."

"Any chance he's a cop?"

"Naw. Nobody I know," Jim said. "You, Earl?"

"Nup. Why?"

Sachs didn't answer. She said, "I need to examine him."

"Okay, miss," Earl said. "How 'bout I give you a hand?"

"Hell," the trooper said, "sounds like *he's* the one needs a hand." He chuckled; the medic gave another of his piggy giggles.

She climbed up in the back of the ambulance and unzipped the body bag completely.

And because she wasn't going to tug off her jeans and have intercourse with them or at the very least flirt back, they had no choice but to torment her further.

"The thing is, this isn't the kind of traffic detail you're probably used to," Earl said to her. "Hey, Jim, this as bad as the one you saw last week?"

"That head we found?" The cop mused, "Hell, I'd rather have a fresh head any day than a month-er. You ever seen a month-er, honey? Now, they're about as unpleasant as can be. Give a body three, four months in the water, hey, not a problem – mostly just bones. But you get one's been simmering for a month . . ."

"Nasty," Earl said. "Uck-o."

"You ever seen a month-er, honey?"

"'Preciate your not saying that, Jim," she said absently to the cop.

"'Month-er'?"

"'Honey.'"

"Sure, sorry."

"Sachs," Rhyme snapped, "what the hell is going on?"

"No ID, Rhyme. Nobody's got a clue as to who it is. Hands removed with a fine-bladed razor saw."

"Is Percey safe? Hale?"

"They're in the office. Banks's with them. Away from the windows. What's the word on the van?"

"Should be there in ten minutes. You've got to find out about that body."

"You talking to yourself, hon – Officer?"

Sachs studied the poor man's body. She guessed the hands had been removed just after he'd died, or as he was dying, because of the copious amount of blood. She pulled on her latex examining gloves.

"It's strange, Rhyme. Why's he only partially ID-proofed?"

If killers don't have time to dispose of a body completely they ID-proof it by removing the main points of identification: the hands and the teeth.

"I don't know," the criminalist responded. "It's not like the Dancer to be careless, even if he was in a hurry. What's he wearing?"

"Just skivvies. No clothes or other ID found at the scene."

"Why," Rhyme mused, "did the Dancer pick him?"

"*If* it was the Dancer did this."

"How many bodies turn up like that in Westchester?"

"To hear the locals tell it," she said ruefully, "every other day."

"Tell me about the corpse. COD?"

"You determine the cause of death?" she called to chubby Earl.

"Strangled," the tech said.

But Sachs noticed right away there were no petechial hemorrhages on the inner surface of the eyelids. No damage to the tongue either. Most strangulation victims bite their tongue at some point during the attack.

"I don't think so."

Earl cast another glance at Jim and snorted. "Sure, he was. Lookit that red line on his neck. We call that a ligature mark, honey. You know, we can't keep him here forever. They start going ripe, days like this. Now, *that's* a smell you haven't lived till you smelt."

Sachs frowned. "He wasn't strangled."

They double-teamed her. "Hon – Officer, that's a ligature mark," Jim, the trooper, said. "I seen hundreds of 'em."

"No, no," she said. "The perp just ripped a chain off him."

Rhyme broke in. "That's probably it, Sachs. First thing you do when you're ID-proofing a corpse, get rid of the jewelry. It was probably a Saint Christopher, maybe inscribed. Who's there with you?"

"A pair of cretins," she said.

"Oh. Well, what *is* the COD?"

After a brief search she found the wound. "Ice pick or narrow-bladed knife in the back of the skull."

The medic's round form eased into the doorway. "We woulda found that," he said defensively. "I mean, we were in such an all-fire hurry to get here, thanks to you folks."

Rhyme said to Sachs, "Describe him."

"He's overweight, big gut. Lotta flab."

"Tan or sunburn?"

"On his arms and torso only. Not legs. He's got untrimmed toenails and a cheap earring – steel posts, not gold. His briefs are Sears and they've got holes in them."

"Okay, he's looking blue collar," Rhyme said. "Workman, deliveryman. We're closing in. Check his throat."

"What?"

"For his wallet or papers. If you want to keep a corpse anonymous for a few hours you shove their IDs down their throat. It doesn't get spotted till the autopsy."

A chortle of laughter from outside.

Which Sachs ended quickly when she grabbed the man's jaws, pulled wide, and started reaching inside.

"Jesus," Earl muttered. "What're you doing?"

"Nothing there, Rhyme."

"You better cut. The throat. Go deeper."

Sachs had bridled at some of Rhyme's more macabre requests in the past. But today she glanced at the grinning boys behind her and lifted her illegal but cherished switchblade from her jeans pocket, clicked it open.

Took the grins off both faces.

"Say, honey, what're you doing?"

"Little surgery. Gotta look inside." Like she did this every day.

"I mean, I can't deliver no corpse to the coroner cut up by some New York City cop."

"Then *you* do it."

She offered him the handle of the knife.

"Aw, she's shitting us, Jim."

She lifted an eyebrow and slipped the knife into the man's Adams' apple like a fisherman gutting a trout.

"Oh, Jesus, Jim, lookit what she's doing. Stop her."

"I'm outa here, Earl. I didn't see that." The trooper walked off.

She finished the tidy incision and gazed inside, sighed. "Nothing."

"What the hell is he up to?" Rhyme asked. "Let's think . . . What if he isn't ID-proofing the body? If he'd wanted to he would've taken the teeth. What if there's something else he's trying to hide from us?"

"Something on the vic's hands?" Sachs suggested.

"Maybe," Rhyme responded. "Something that he couldn't wash off the corpse easily. And something that'd tell us what he was up to."

"Oil? Grease?"

"Maybe he was delivering jet fuel," Rhyme said. "Or maybe he was a caterer – maybe his hands smelled of garlic."

Sachs looked around the airport. There were dozens of gasoline deliverymen, ground crews, repairmen, construction workers building a new wing on one of the terminals.

Rhyme continued, "He's a big guy?"

"Yep."

"He was probably sweating today. Maybe he wiped his head. Or scratched it."

I've been doing that all day myself, Sachs thought, and felt an urge to dig into her hair, hurt her skin as she always did when she felt frustrated and tense.

"Check his scalp, Sachs. Behind the hairline."

She did.

And there she found it.

"I see streaks of color. Blue. Bits of white too. On the hair and skin. Oh, hell, Rhyme. It's paint! He's a painting contractor. And there're about twenty construction workers on the grounds."

"The line on the neck," Rhyme continued. "The Dancer pulled off his necklace ID."

"But the picture'd be different."

"Hell, the ID's probably covered with paint or he faked it somehow. He's on the field somewhere, Sachs. Get Percey and Hale down on the floor. Put a guard on 'em and get everybody else out, looking for the Dancer. SWAT's on its way."

Problems.

He was watching the red-haired cop in the back of the ambulance. Through the Redfield telescope he couldn't see clearly what she was doing. But he suddenly felt uneasy.

He felt she was doing something to *him.* Something to expose him, to tie him down.

The worms were getting closer. The face at the window, the wormy face, was looking for him.

Stephen shuddered.

She jumped out of the ambulance, looking around the field.

Something's happening, Soldier.

Sir, I am aware of that, sir.

The redhead began shouting orders to other cops. Most of them looked at her, took her news grimly, then looked around. One ran to his car, then a second.

He saw the redhead's pretty face and her wormy eyes scanning the airport grounds. He rested the reticles on her perfect chin. What had she found? What was she looking for?

She paused and he saw her talking to herself.

No, not herself. She was talking into a headset. The way she'd listen, then nod, it seemed that she was taking orders from someone.

Who? he wondered.

Someone who'd figured out that I'm here, Stephen thought.

Someone looking for me.

Someone who can watch me through windows and disappear instantly. Who can move through walls and holes and tiny cracks to sneak up and find me.

A chill down his back – he actually shivered – and for a moment the reticles of the telescope danced away from the redheaded cop and he lost acquisition of a target completely.

What the fuck was that, Soldier?

Sir, I don't know, sir.

When he reacquired the redhead he saw how bad things were. She was pointing right at the painting contractor's van he'd just stolen. It was parked about two hundred feet from him, in a small parking lot reserved for construction trucks.

Whoever the redhead was talking to had found the painter's body and discovered how he'd gotten onto the airport grounds.

The worm moved closer. He felt its shadow, its cold slime.

The cringey feeling. Worms crawling up his legs . . . worms crawling down his neck . . .

What should I do? he wondered

One chance . . . one shot . . .

They're so close, the Wife and the Friend. He could finish everything right now. Five seconds was all it would take. Maybe those were their outlines he could see in the window. That shadowy form. Or *that* one . . . But Stephen knew that if he fired through the glass, everyone would drop to the floor. If he didn't kill the Wife with the first shot, he'd ruin the chance.

I need her outside. I need to draw them out of cover into the kill zone. I can't miss there.

He had no time. No time! Think!

If you want a doe, endanger the calf.

Stephen began breathing slowly. In, out, in, out. He drew his target. Began applying pressure, imperceptible, to the trigger. The Model 40 fired.

The *ka-boom* rolled over the field and all the cops hit the ground, drawing their weapons.

Another shot, and a second puff of smoke flew from the tail-mounted engine of the silver jet in the hangar.

The redheaded cop, her own gun in hand, was crouching, scanning for location. She glanced at the two smoking holes in the skin of the plane, then looked out over the field once more, pointing a stubby Glock out in front of her.

Take her out?

Yes? No?

Negative, Soldier. Stay fixed on your target.

He fired again. The puff of explosion tore another tiny chunk out of the side of the airplane.

Calm. Another shot. The kick in the shoulder, the sweet smell of the burnt powder. A windshield in the cockpit exploded.

This was the shot that did it.

Sudden there she was – the Wife – forcing her way through the office door, grappling with the young blond cop who tried to hold her back.

No target yet. Keep her coming.

Squeeze. Another bullet tore through the engine.

The Wife, her face horrified, broke free and ran down the stairs toward the hangar to close the doors, to protect her child.

Reload.

He laid the reticles on her chest as she stepped to the ground and started to run.

Full target lead of four inches, Stephen calculated automatically. He moved the gun ahead of her and squeezed the trigger. It fired just as the blond cop tackled her and they went down below a slight dip in the earth. A miss. And they had just enough cover to keep him from skimming slugs into their backs.

They're moving in, Soldier. They're flanking you.

Yessir, understood.

Stephen glanced over the runways. Other police had appeared. They were crawling toward their cars. One car was speeding directly toward him, only fifty yards away. Stephen used one shot to take out the engine block. Steam spraying from the front end, the car eased to a stop.

Stay calm, he told himself.

We're prepared to evacuate. We just need one clear shot.

He heard several fast pistol shots. He looked back at the

redhead. She was in a competition combat stance, pointing the stubby pistol in his direction, looking for his muzzle flash. The sound of the shot wouldn't do her any good, of course; it was why he never bothered with silencers. Loud noises are as hard to pinpoint as soft ones.

The redheaded cop was standing tall, squinting as she gazed.

Stephen closed the bolt of the Model 40.

Amelia Sachs saw a faint glimmer and she knew where the Coffin Dancer was.

In a small grove of trees about three hundred yards away. His telescopic sight caught the reflected glint of the pale clouds overhead.

"Over there," she cried, pointing, to two county cops huddling in their cruiser.

The troopers rolled into their car and took off, skidding behind a nearby hangar to flank him.

"Sachs," Rhyme called through her headset. "What's—"

"Jesus, Rhyme, he's on the field, shooting at the plane."

"What?"

"Percey's trying to get to the hangar. He's shooting explosive slugs. He's shooting to draw her out."

"You stay down, Sachs. If Percey's going to kill herself, let her. But you stay down!"

She was sweating furiously, hands shaking, heart pounding. She felt the quiver of panic run down her back.

"Percey!" Sachs cried.

The woman had broken free from Jerry Banks and rolled to her feet. She was speeding toward the hangar door.

"No!"

Oh, hell.

Sachs's eyes were on the spot where she'd seen the flare of the Dancer's scope.

Too far, it's too far, she thought. I can't hit anything at that distance.

If you stay calm, you can. You've got eleven rounds left. There's no wind. Trajectory's the only problem. Aim high and work down.

She saw several leaves fly outward as the Dancer fired again.

An instant later a bullet passed within inches of her face. She felt the shock wave and heard the snap as the slug, traveling twice the speed of sound, burned the air around her.

She uttered a faint whimper and dropped to her stomach, cowering.

No! You had a chance to shoot. Before he rechambered. But it's too late now. He's locked and loaded again.

She looked up fast, lifted her gun, then lost her nerve. Head down, the Glock pointed generally in the direction of the trees, she fired five fast shots.

But she might as well have been shooting blanks.

Come on, girl. Get up. Aim and shoot. You got six left and two clips on your belt.

But the thought of the near miss kept her pinned to the ground.

Do it! she raged at herself.

But she couldn't.

All Sachs had the courage for was to raise her head a few inches – just far enough to see Percey Clay, sprinting, race to the hangar door just as Jerry Banks caught up with her. The young detective shoved her down to the ground behind a generator cart. Almost simultaneously with the rolling boom of the Coffin Dancer's rifle there came the sickening crack of the bullet striking Banks, who spun about like a drunk as blood puffed into a cloud around him.

And on his face, first a look of surprise, then of bewilderment, then of nothing whatsoever as he spiraled down to the damp concrete.

Hour 5 of 45

12

"Well?" Rhyme asked.

Lon Sellitto folded up his phone. "They still don't know." Eyes out the window of Rhyme's town house, tapping the glass compulsively. The falcons had returned to the ledge but kept their eyes vigilantly on Central Park, uncharacteristically oblivious to the noise.

Rhyme had never seen the detective this upset. His doughy, sweat-dotted face was pale. A legendary homicide investigator, Sellitto was usually unflappable. Whether he was reassuring victims' families or relentlessly punching holes in a suspect's alibi, he always concentrated on the job before him. But at the moment his thoughts seemed miles away, with Jerry Banks, in surgery – maybe dying – in a Westchester hospital. It was now three on Saturday afternoon and Banks had been in the operating room for an hour.

Sellitto, Sachs, Rhyme, and Cooper were on the ground floor of Rhyme's town house, in the lab. Dellray had left to make sure the safe house was ready and to check out the new baby-sitter the NYPD was providing to replace Banks.

At the airport they'd loaded the wounded young detective into the ambulance – the same one containing the dead, handless painting-contractor. Earl, the medic, had stopped being an asshole long enough to work feverishly to stop Banks's torrential bleeding. Then he'd sped the pale, unconscious detective to the emergency room several miles away.

FBI agents from White Plains got Percey and Hale into an armored van and started south to Manhattan, using evasive driving techniques. Sachs worked the new crime scenes: the sniper nest, the painter's van, and the Dancer's getaway wheels – a catering van. It was found not far from where he'd killed the contractor and where, they guessed, he'd have hidden the car he'd driven to Westchester in.

Then she'd sped back to Manhattan with the evidence.

"What've we got?" Rhyme now asked her and Cooper. "Any rifle slugs?"

Worrying a tattered bloody nail, Sachs explained, "Nothing left of them. They were explosive rounds." She seemed very spooked, eyes flitting like birds'.

"That's the Dancer. Not only deadly but his evidence self-destructs."

Sachs prodded a plastic bag. "Here's what's left of one. I scraped it off a wall."

Cooper spilled the contents into a porcelain examining tray. He stirred them. "Ceramic tipped too. Vests're pointless."

"Grade-A asshole," Sellitto offered.

"Oh, the Dancer knows his tools," Rhyme said.

There was a bustle of activity at the doorway and Thom let two suited FBI agents into the room. Behind them were Percey Clay and Brit Hale.

Percey asked Sellitto, "How's he doing?" Her dark eyes looked around the room, saw the coolness that greeted her. Didn't seem fazed. "Jerry, I mean."

Sellitto didn't answer.

Rhyme said, "He's still in surgery."

Her face was fretted, hair more tangled than this morning. "I hope he'll be all right."

Amelia Sachs turned to Percey and said coldly, "You what?"

"I said, I hope he'll be all right."

"You *hope*?" The policewoman towered over her, stepped closer. The squat woman stood her ground as Sachs continued. "Little late for that, isn't it?"

"What's your problem?"

"That's what I oughta be asking you. You got him shot."

"Hey, Officer," Sellitto said.

Composed, Percey said, "I didn't ask him to run after me."

"You'd be dead if it wasn't for him."

"Maybe. We don't know that. I'm sorry he was hurt. I—"

"And how sorry are you?"

"Amelia," Rhyme said sharply.

"No, I want to know *how* sorry. Are you sorry enough to give blood? To wheel him around if he can't walk? Give his eulogy if he dies?"

Rhyme snapped, "Sachs, take it easy. It's not her fault."

Sachs slapped her hands, tipped in chewed nails, against her thighs. "It's not?"

"The Dancer outthought us."

Sachs continued, gazing down into Percey's dark eyes. "Jerry was baby-sitting you. When you ran into the line of fire, what'd you think he was going to do?"

"Well, I didn't think, okay? I just reacted."

"Jesus."

"Hey, Officer," Hale said, "maybe you act a lot cooler under pressure than some of us. But we're not used to getting shot at."

"Then she should've stayed down. In the office. Where I told her to stay."

There seemed to be a slight drawl in Percey's voice when she continued. "I saw my aircraft endangered. I reacted. Maybe for you it's like seeing your partner wounded."

Hale said, "She just did what any pilot would've done."

"Exactly," Rhyme announced. "That's what I'm saying, Sachs. That's the way the Dancer works."

But Amelia Sachs wasn't letting go. "You should've been in the safe house in the first place. You never should have gone to the airport."

"That was Jerry's fault," said Rhyme, growing angrier. "He had no authority to change the route."

Sachs glanced at Sellitto, who'd been Banks's partner for two years. But apparently he wasn't about to stand up for the young man.

"This's been real pleasure," Percey Clay said dryly, turning toward the door. "But I've got to get back to the airport."

"What?" Sachs almost gasped. "Are you crazy?"

"That's impossible," Sellitto said, emerging from his gloom.

"It was bad enough just trying to get my aircraft outfitted

for the flight tomorrow. Now we've got to repair the damage too. And since it looks like every certified mechanic in Westchester's a damn coward I'm going to have to do the work myself."

"Mrs Clay," Sellitto began, "not a good idea. You'll be okay in the safe house but there's no way we can guarantee your safety anywhere else. You stay there until Monday, you'll be—"

"Monday," she blurted. "Oh, no. You don't understand. I'm driving that aircraft tomorrow night – the charter for U.S. Medical."

"You can't—"

"A question," asked the icy voice of Amelia Sachs. "Could you tell me exactly who else you want to kill?"

Percey stepped forward. She snapped, "Goddamn it, I lost my husband and one of my best employees last night. I'm not losing my company too. You can't tell me where I'm going or not. Not unless I'm under arrest."

"Okay," Sachs said, and in a flash the cuffs were ratcheted onto the woman's narrow wrists. "You're under arrest."

"Sachs," Rhyme called, enraged. "What are you doing? Uncuff her. Now!"

Sachs swung to face him, snapped back, "You're a civilian. You can't order me to do a *thing*!"

"*I* can," Sellitto said.

"Uh-un," she said adamantly. "I'm the arresting, Detective. You can't stop me from making a collar. Only the DA can throw a case out."

"What is this bullshit?" Percey spat out, the vestigial drawl returning full force. "What're you arresting me for? Being a witness?"

"The charge is reckless endangerment, and if Jerry dies then it'll be criminally negligent homicide. Or maybe manslaughter."

Hale worked up some courage and said, "Look now. I don't really like the way you've been talking to her all day. If you arrest her, you're going to have to arrest me . . ."

"Not a problem," Sachs said, then asked Sellitto, "Lieutenant, I need your cuffs."

"Officer, enougha this crap," he grumbled.

"Sachs," Rhyme called, "we don't have time for this! The Dancer's out there, planning another attack right now."

"You arrest me," Percey said, "I'll be out in two hours."

"Then you'll be dead in two hours and ten minutes. Which would be your business—"

"Officer," Sellitto snapped, "you're on real thin ice here."

"—if you didn't have this habit of taking other people with you."

"Amelia," Rhyme said coldly.

She swung to face him. He called her "Sachs" most of the time; using her first name now was like a slap in the face.

The chains on Percey's bony wrists clinked. In the window the falcon fluttered its wings. No one said a word.

Finally, in a reasonable voice, Rhyme asked, "Please take the cuffs off and let me have a few minutes alone with Percey."

Sachs hesitated. Her face was an expressionless mask.

"Please, Amelia," Rhyme said, struggling to be patient.

Without a word she unhooked the cuffs.

Everyone filed out.

Percey rubbed her wrists then pulled her flask from her pocket and took a sip.

"Would you mind closing the door?" Rhyme asked Sachs.

But she merely glanced toward him and then continued into the corridor. It was Hale who swung the heavy oak door shut.

Outside in the hallway Lon Sellitto called again about Banks. He was still in surgery and the floor nurse would say nothing else about him.

Sachs took this news with a faint nod. She walked to the window overlooking the alley behind Rhyme's town house. The oblique light fell onto her hands and she looked at her torn nails. She'd put bandages on two of the most damaged fingers. Habits, she thought. Bad habits . . . Why can't I stop?

The detective walked up beside her, looked up at the gray sky. More spring storms were promised.

"Officer," he said, speaking softly so none of the others could hear. "She fucked up, that lady did, okay. But you gotta understand – she's not a pro. Our mistake was *letting* her fuck up and, yeah, Jerry should've known better. It hurts me more than I can even think about to say it. But he blew it."

"No," she said through clenched teeth. "You don't understand."

"Whatsat?"

Could she say it? The words were so hard.

"*I* blew it. It's not Jerry's fault." She tossed her head toward Rhyme's room. "Or Percey's. It's mine."

"You? Fuck, you 'n' Rhyme're the ones figured out he was at the airport. He mighta nailed everybody, it wasn't for you."

She was shaking her head. "I saw . . . I saw the Dancer's position before he capped Jerry."

"And?"

"I knew exactly where he was. I drew a target. I . . ."

Oh, hell. This was hard.

"What're you sayin', Officer?"

"He let off a round at me . . . Oh, Christ. I clenched. I hit the ground." Her finger disappeared into her scalp and she scratched until she felt slick blood. Stop it. Shit.

"So?" Sellitto didn't get it. "Everybody hit the deck, right? I mean, who wouldn't?"

Staring out the window, face burning with shame. "After he fired and missed, I'd've had at least three seconds to fire – I knew he was shooting bolt action. I could've lost a whole clip at him. But I tongued dirt. Then I didn't have the balls to get up again because I knew he'd rechambered."

Sellitto scoffed. "What? You're worried 'cause you didn't stand up, without cover, and give a sniper a nice fat target? Come on, Officer . . . And, hey, wait a minute, you had your service weapon?"

"Yeah, I—"

"Three hundred yards with a Glock nine? In your dreams."

"I might not have hit him but I could've parked enough nearby to keep him pinned down. So he wouldn't've got that last shot in and hit Jerry. Oh, hell." She clenched her hands, looked at her index-finger nail again. It was dark with blood. She scratched again.

The brilliant red reminded her of the dust cloud of blood rising around Jerry Banks and so she scratched harder still.

"Officer, I wouldn't lose any sleep over that one."

How could she explain? What was eating at her now was more complex than the detective knew. Rhyme was the best criminalist in New York, maybe in the country. Sachs aspired, but she'd never match him at that. But shooting – like driving fast – was one of *her* gifts. She could outshoot most of the men and women on thc force, either-handed. She'd prop dimes up on the fifty-yard range and shoot for the glare, making presents of the bent coins for her goddaughter and her friends. She *could* have saved Jerry. Hell, she might even have hit the son of a bitch.

She was furious with herself, furious with Percey for putting her in this position.

And furious with Rhyme too.

The door swung open and Percey appeared in the door. With a cold look at Sachs she asked Hale to join them. He disappeared into the room and a few minutes later it was Hale who opened the door and said, "He'd like everyone back inside."

Sachs found them this way: Percey was sitting next to Rhyme in a battered old armchair. She had this ridiculous image of them as a married couple.

"We're compromising," Rhyme announced. "Brit and Percey'll go to Dellray's safe house. They'll have somebody else do the repairs on the plane. Whether we find the Dancer or not, though, I've agreed to let her make the flight tomorrow night."

"And if I just arrest her?" Sachs said heatedly. "Take her to detention?"

She'd thought Rhyme would explode at this – she was ready for it – but he said reasonably, "I thought about that, Sachs. And I don't belive it's a good idea. There'd be more exposure – court, detention, transport. The Dancer'd have more of a chance to get them."

Amelia Sachs hesitated then gave in, nodded. He was right; he usually was. But right or not, he'd have things his way. She was his assistant, nothing more. An employee. That's all she was to him.

Rhyme continued. "Here's what I've got in mind. We're going to set a trap. I'll need your help, Lon."

"Talk to me."

"Percey and Hale'll go to the safe house. But I want to make it look like they're going someplace else. We'll make a big deal out of it. Very visible. I'd pick one of the precincts, pretend they're going into the lockup there for security. We'll put out a transmission or two on citywide, unscrambled, that we're closing the street in front of the station house for security and transporting all booked suspects down to detention to keep the facility clear. If we're lucky the Dancer'll be listening on a scanner. If not, the media'll pick it up and he might hear about it that way."

"How 'bout the Twentieth?" Sellitto suggested.

The Twentieth Precinct, on the Upper West Side, was only a few blocks from Lincoln Rhyme's town house. He knew many of the officers there.

"Okay, good."

Sachs then noticed some uneasiness in Sellitto's eyes. He leaned forward toward Rhyme's chair, sweat dripping down his broad, creased forehead. In a voice only Rhyme and Sachs could hear, he whispered, "You're sure about this, Lincoln. I mean, you thought about it?"

Rhyme's eyes swiveled toward Percey. A look passed between the two of them. Sachs didn't know what it meant. She knew only that she didn't like it.

"Yes," Rhyme said. "I'm sure."

Though to Sachs he didn't seem very sure at all.

Hour 6 of 45

13

"Lots of trace, I see."

Rhyme looked approvingly at the plastic bags Sachs had brought back from the airport crime scenes.

Trace evidence was Rhyme's favorite – the bits and pieces, sometimes microscopic, left by perps at crime scenes, or picked up there by them unwittingly. It was trace evidence that even the cleverest of perps didn't think to alter or plant and it was trace that even the most industrious couldn't dispose of altogether.

"The first bag, Sachs? Where did it come from?"

She flipped angrily through her notes.

What was eating at her? he wondered. Something was wrong, Rhyme could see. Maybe it had to do with her anger at Percey Clay, maybe her concern for Jerry Banks. But maybe not. He could tell from the cool glances that she didn't want to talk about it. Which was fine with him. The Dancer had to be caught. It was their only priority at the moment.

"This's from the hangar where the Dancer waited for the plane." She held up two of the bags. She nodded at three others. "This's from the sniper's nest. This's from the painting van. This's from the catering van."

"Thom . . . Thom!" Rhyme shouted, startling everyone in the room.

The aide appeared in the doorway. He asked a belabored "Yes? I'm trying to fix some food here, Lincoln."

"Food?" Rhyme asked, exasperated. "We don't need to eat. We need more charts. Write: 'CS-Two, Hangar.' Yes, 'CS-Two, Hangar.' That's good. Then another one. 'CS-Three.' That's where he fired from. His grassy knoll."

"I should write that? 'Grassy Knoll'?"

"Of course not. It's a joke. I *do* have a sense of humor, you know. Write: 'CS-Three, Sniper's Nest.' Now, let's look at the hangar first. What do you have?"

"Bits of glass," Cooper said, spilling the contents out on a porcelain tray like a diamond merchant. Sachs added, "And some vacuumed trace, a few fibers from the windowsill. No FR."

Friction ridge prints, he meant. Finger or palm.

"He's too careful with prints," Sellitto said glumly.

"No, that's *encouraging,*" Rhyme said, irritated – as he often was – that no one else drew conclusions as quickly as he could.

"Why?" the detective asked.

"He's careful because he's on file somewhere! So when we *do* find a print we'll stand a good chance of ID'ing him. Okay, okay, cotton glove prints, they're no help . . . No boot prints because he scattered gravel on the hangar floor. He's a smart one. But if he were stupid, nobody'd need us, right? Now, what does the glass tell us?"

"What could it tell us," Sachs asked shortly, "except he broke in the window to get into the hangar?"

"I wonder," Rhyme said. "Let's look at it."

Mel Cooper mounted several shards on a slide and placed it under the lens of the compound 'scope at low magnification. He clicked the video camera on to send the image to Rhyme's computer.

Rhyme motored back to it. He instructed, "Command mode." Hearing his voice, the computer dutifully slipped a menu onto the glowing screen. He couldn't control the microscope itself but he could capture the image on the computer screen and manipulate it – magnify or shrink it, for instance. "Cursor left. Double click."

Rhyme strained forward, lost in the rainbow auras of refraction. "Looks like standard PPG single-strength window glass."

"Agreed," Cooper said, then observed, "No chipping. It was broken by a blunt object. His elbow maybe."

"Uh-huh, uh-huh. Look at the conchoidal, Mel."

When someone breaks a window the glass shatters in a

series of conchoidal breaks – curved fracture lines. You can tell from the way they curve which direction the blow came from.

"I see it," the tech said. "Standard fractures."

"Look at the dirt," Rhyme said abruptly. "On the glass."

"See it. Rainwater deposits, mud, fuel residue."

"What *side* of the glass is the dirt on?" Rhyme asked impatiently. When he was running IRD, one of the complaints of the officers under him was that he acted like a schoolmarm. Rhyme considered it a compliment.

"It's . . . oh." Cooper caught on. "How can that be?"

"What?" Sachs asked.

Rhyme explained. The conchoidal fractures began on the clean side of the glass and ended on the dirty side. "He was *inside* when he broke the window."

"But he couldn't've been," Sachs protested. "The glass was inside the hangar. He—" She stopped and nodded. "You mean he broke it out, then scooped the glass up and threw it inside with the gravel. But why?"

"The gravel wasn't to prevent shoe prints. It was to fool us into thinking he broke *in*. But he was already *inside* the hangar and broke *out*. Interesting." The criminalist considered this for a moment, then shouted, "Check that trace. There any brass in it? Any brass with *graphite* on it?"

"A key," Sachs said. "You're thinking somebody gave him a key to get into the hangar."

"That's exactly what I'm thinking. Let's find out who owns or leases the hangar."

"I'll call," Sellitto said and flipped open his cell phone.

Cooper looked through the eyepiece of another microscope. He had it on high magnification. "Here we go," he said. "Lot of graphite and brass. What I'd guess is some 3-In-One oil too. So it was an old lock. He had to fiddle with it."

"Or?" Rhyme prompted. "Come on, think!"

"Or a new-made key!" Sachs blurted.

"Right! A sticky one. Good. Thom, the chart, please! Write: 'Access by key.'"

In his precise handwriting the aide wrote the words.

"Now, what else do we have?" Rhyme sipped and

puffed and swung closer to the computer. He misjudged and slammed into it, nearly knocking over his monitor.

"Goddamn," he muttered.

"You all right?" Sellitto asked.

"Fine, I'm fine," he snapped. "Anything *else*? I was asking – anything else?"

Cooper and Sachs brushed the rest of the trace onto a large sheet of clean newsprint. They put on magnifying goggles and went over it. Cooper lifted several flecks with a probe and placed them on a slide.

"Okay," Cooper said. "We've got fibers."

A moment later Rhyme was looking at the tiny strands on his computer screen.

"What do you think, Mel? Paper, right?"

"Yep."

Speaking into his headset, Rhyme ordered his computer to scroll through the microscopic images of the fibers. "Looks like two different kinds. One's white or buff. The other's got a green tint."

"Green? Money?" Sellitto suggested.

"Possibly."

"You have enough to gas a few?" Rhyme asked. The chromatograph would destroy the fibers.

Cooper said they had and proceeded to test several of them.

He read the computer screen. "No cotton and no soda, sulfite, or sulfate."

These were chemicals added to the pulping process in making high-quality paper.

"It's cheap paper. And the dye's water soluble. There's no oil-based ink."

"So," Rhyme announced, "it's not money."

"Probably recycled," Cooper said.

Rhyme magnified the screen again. The matrix was large now and the detail lost. He was momentarily frustrated and wished that he was looking through a real compound 'scope eyepiece. There was nothing like the clarity of fine optics.

Then he saw something.

"Those yellow blotches, Mel? Glue?"

The tech looked through the microscope's eyepiece and announced, "Yes. Envelope glue, looks like."

So possibly the key had been delivered to the Dancer in an envelope. But what did the green paper signify? Rhyme had no idea.

Sellitto folded up his phone. "I talked to Ron Talbot at Hudson Air. He made a few calls. Guess who leases that hangar where the Dancer waited."

"Phillip Hansen," Rhyme said.

"Yep."

"We're making a good case," Sachs said.

True, Rhyme thought, though his goal was not to hand the Dancer over to the AG with a watertight case. No, he wanted the man's head on a pike.

"Anything else there?"

"Nothing."

"Okay, let's movc on to the other scene. The sniper's nest. He was under a lot of pressure there. Maybe he got careless."

But, of course, he hadn't been careless.

There were no shell casings.

"Here's why," Cooper said, examining the trace through the scope. "Cotton fibers. He used a dish towel to catch the casings."

Rhyme nodded. "Footprints?"

"Nope." She explained that the Dancer'd worked his way around the patches of exposed mud, staying on the grass even when he was racing to the catering van to escape.

"How many FRs you find?"

"None at the sniper's nest," Sachs explained. "Close to two hundred in the two vans."

Using AFIS – the automated fingerprint identification system that linked digitalized criminal, military, and civil service fingerprint databases around the country – a cold search of this many prints would be possible (though very time consuming). But as obsessed as Rhyme was with finding the Dancer, he didn't bother with an AFIS request. Sachs reported that she'd found his glove prints in the vans too; the friction ridges prints inside the vehicles wouldn't be the Dancer's.

Cooper emptied the plastic bag onto an examining tray. He and Sachs looked over it. “Dirt, grass, pebbles . . . Here were go. Can you see this, Lincoln?” Cooper mounted another slide.

“Hairs,” Cooper said, bent over his own ’scope. “Three, four, six, nine . . . a dozen of ’em. It looks like a continuous medulla.”

The medulla is a canal running through the middle of a strand of some types of hair. In humans, the medulla is either nonexistent or fragmented. A continuous medulla meant the hair was animal. “What do you think, Mel?”

“I’ll run them through the SEM.” The scanning electron microscope. Cooper ran the scale up to fifteen-hundred-times magnification and adjusted dials until one of the hairs was centered in the screen. It was a whitish stalk with sharp-edged scales resembling a pineapple’s skin.

“Cat,” Rhyme announced.

“Cats, plural,” Cooper corrected, looking into the compound ’scope again. “Looks like we’ve got a black and a calico. Both shorthairs. Then a tawny, long and fine. Persian, something like that.”

Rhyme snorted. “Don’t think the Dancer’s profile’s that he’s an animal lover. He’s either passing for somebody with cats or’s staying with somebody who’s got ’em.”

“More hair,” Cooper announced and mounted a slide on the compound ’scope. “Human. It’s . . . wait, two strands about six inches long.”

“He’s shedding, huh?” Sellitto asked.

“Who knows?” Rhyme said skeptically. Without the bulb attached, it’s impossible to determine the sex of the person who lost the strand. Age, except with an infant’s hair, was also impossible to tell. Rhyme suggested, “Maybe it’s the paint truck driver’s. Sachs? He have long hair?”

“No. Crew cut. And it was blond.”

“What do you think, Mel?”

The tech scanned the length of the hair. “It’s been colored.”

“The Dancer’s known for changing his appearance,” Rhyme said.

“Don’t know, Lincoln,” Cooper said. “The dye’s similar to the natural shade. You’d think he’d go for something real different if he wanted to change his identity. Wait, I see two colors of dye. The natural shade is black. It's had some auburn added, and then more recently a dark purple wash. About two to three months apart."

"I'm also picking up a lot of residue here, Lincoln. I ought to gas one of the hairs."

"Do it."

A moment later Cooper was reading the chart on the computer connected to the GC/MS. "Okay, we've got some kind of cosmetic."

Makeup was very helpful to the criminalist; cosmetic manufacturers were notorious for changing the formulation of their products to take advantage of new trends. Different compositions could often be pinpointed to different dates of manufacture and distribution locations.

"What do we have?"

"Hold on." Cooper was sending the formula to the brand name database. A moment later he had an answer. "Slim-U-Lite. Swiss made, imported by Jencon, outside of Boston. It's a regular detergent-based soap with oils and amino acids added. It was in the news – the FTC's on their case for claiming that it takes off fat and cellulite."

"Let's profile," he announced. "Sachs, what do you think?"

"About him?"

"About *her*. The one aiding and abetting him. Or the one he killed to hide out in her apartment. And maybe steal her car."

"You're sure it's a woman?" wondered Lon Sellitto.

"No. But we don't have time to be timid in our speculations. More women are worried about cellulite than men. More women color their hair than men. Bold propositions! Come on!"

"Well, overweight," Sachs said. "Self-image problem."

"Maybe punky, New Wave, or whatever the fuck the weirdos call 'emselves nowadays," Sellitto suggested. "My daughter turned her hair purple. Pierced some stuff too, which I don't want to talk about. How 'bout the East Village?"

"I don't think she's going for a rebel image," Sachs said. "Not with those colors. They're not different enough. She's trying to be stylish and nothing she's doing is working. I say she's fat, with short hair, in her thirties, professional. Goes home alone to her cats at night."

Rhyme nodded, staring at the chart. "Lonely. Just the sort to get suckered in by somebody with a glib tongue. Let's check veterinarians. We know she's got three cats, three different colors."

"But where?" Sellitto asked. "Westchester? Manhattan?"

"Let's first ask," Rhyme mulled, "why would he hook up with this woman in the first place?"

Sachs snapped her fingers. "Because he *had* to! Because we nearly trapped him." Her face had lit up. Some of the old Amelia was back.

"Yes!" Rhyme said. "This morning, near Percey's town house. When ESU moved in."

Sachs continued. "He ditched the van and hid out in her apartment until it was safe to move."

Rhyme said to Sellitto, "Get some people calling vets. For ten blocks around the town house. No, make it the whole Upper East Side. Call, Lon, call!"

As the detective punched numbers into his phone, Sachs asked gravely, "You think she's all right? The woman?"

Rhyme answered from his heart though not with what he believed to be the truth. "We can hope, Sachs. We can hope."

Hour 7 of 45

14

To Percey Clay the safe house didn't appear particularly safe.

It was a three-story brownstone structure like many others along this block near the Morgan Library.

"This's it," an agent said to her and Brit Hale, nodding out the window of the van. They parked in the alley and she and Hale were hustled through a basement entrance. The steel door slammed shut. They found themselves staring at an affable man in his late thirties, lean and with thinning brown hair. He grinned.

"Howdy," he said, showing his NYPD identification and gold shield. "Roland Bell. From now on you meet anybody, even somebody charming as me, ask 'em for an ID and make sure it's got an i-dentical picture on it."

Percey listened to his relentless drawl and asked, "Don't tell me . . . you're a Tarheel?"

"That I am." He laughed. "Lived in Hoggston – not a joke, no – until I escaped to Chapel Hill for four years. Understand you're a Richmond gal."

"Was. Long time ago."

"And you, Mr Hale?" Bell asked. "You flying the Stars and Bars too?"

"Michigan," Hale said, shaking the detective's vigorous hand. "Via Ohio."

"Don't you worry, I'll forgive you for that little mistake of yours in the eighteen sixties."

"I myself would've surrendered," Hale joked. "Nobody asked me."

"Hah. Now, I'm a Homicide detective but I keep drawing this witness protection detail 'cause I have this knack of keeping people alive. So my dear friend Lon Sellitto asked me to help him out. I'll be baby-sitting y'all for a spell."

Percey asked, "How's that other detective?"

"Jerry? What I hear, he's still in the operating room. No news yet."

His speech may have been slow but his eyes were very fast, scooting over their bodies. Looking for what? Percey wondered. To see if they were armed? Had microphones hidden on them? Then he'd scan the corridor. Then the windows.

"Now," Bell said, "I'm a nice fellow but I can be a bit muley when it comes to looking after who I'm s'posed to." He gave Percey a faint smile. "You look a bit muley yourself, but just remember that everything I tell you t'do's for your own good. All right? All right. Hey, I think we're going to get along just fine. Now lemme show you our grade-A accommodations."

As they walked upstairs he said, "Y'all're probably dead to know how safe this place is . . ."

Hale asked uncertainly, "What was that again? 'Dead to know'?"

"Means, uhm, eager. I guess I talk a bit South still. Boys down in the Big Building – that's headquarters – fool with me some. Leave messages saying they've collared themselves a redneck and want me to translate for 'em. Anyway, this place is good 'n' safe. Our friends in Justice, oh, they know what they're doing. Bigger'n it looks from the outside, right?"

"Bigger than a cockpit, smaller than an open road," Hale said.

Bell chuckled. "Those front windows? Didn't look too secure when you were driving up?"

"That *was* one thing . . .," Percey began.

"Well, here's the front room. Take a peek." He pushed open a door.

There *were* no windows. Sheets of steel had been bolted over them. "Curtains're on the other side," Bell explained. "From the street it looks just like dark rooms. All the other windows're bulletproof glass. But you stay away from 'em all the same. And keep the shades drawn. The fire escape and roof're loaded with sensors and we've got tons of video cameras hidden around the place. Anybody comes near we check 'em clip and clean 'fore they get to the front door. It'd take a ghost with anorexia to get in here." He walked down a wide corridor. "Follow me down this dogtrot here . . . Okay, that's your room there, Mrs Clay."

"Long as we're living together, you may's well call me Percey."

"Done deal. And you're over here . . ."

"Brit."

The rooms were small and dark and very still – very different from Percey's office in the corner of the hangar at Hudson Air. She thought of Ed, who preferred to have an office in the main building, his desk organized, pictures of B17s and P-51s on the wall, Lucite paperweights on every stack of documents. Percey liked the smell of jet fuel, and for a sound track to her workday the buzz saw of pneumatic wrenches. She thought of them together, him perched on her desk, sharing coffee. She managed to push the thought away before the tears started again.

Bell called onto his walkie-talkie. "Principals in position." A moment later two uniformed policemen appeared in the corridor. They nodded and one of them said, "We'll be out here. Full-time." Curiously, their New York twang didn't seem that different from Bell's resonant drawl.

"That was good," Bell said to Percey.

She raised an eyebrow.

"You checked his ID. Nobody's gonna get the bulge on you."

She smiled wanly.

Bell said to Percey, "Now, we've got two men with your mother-in-law in New Jersey. Any other family needs watching?"

Percey said she didn't, not in the area.

He repeated the question to Hale, who answered, with a rueful grin, "Not unless an ex-wife's considered family. Well, wives."

"Okay. Cats'r dogs need watering?"

"Nope," Percey said. Hale shook his head.

"Then we may's well just ree-lax. No phone calls from cell

phones if you've got one. Only use that line there. Remember the windows and curtains. Over there, that's a panic button. Worse comes to worst, and it won't, you hit it and drop to the ground. Now, you need anything, just give me a holler."

"As a matter of fact, I do," Percey said. She held up the silver flask.

"Well, now," Bell drawled, "you want me to help you empty it, I'm afraid I'm still on duty. But 'preciate the offer. You want me to help you *fill* it, why, that's a done deal."

Their scam didn't make the five o'clock news.

But three transmissions went out unscrambled on a citywide police channel, informing the precincts about a 10–66 secure operation at the Twentieth Precinct and broadcasting a 10–67 traffic advisory about street closures on the Upper West Side. All suspects apprehended within the borders of the Twentieth were to be taken directly to Central Booking and the Men's or Women's Detention Center downtown. No one would be allowed in or out of the precinct without a special okay from the FBI. Or the FAA – Dellray's touch.

As this was being broadcast, Bo Haumann's 32-E teams went into position around the station house.

Haumann was now in charge of that portion of the operation. Fred Dellray was putting together a federal hostage rescue team in case they discovered the cat lady's identity and her apartment. Rhyme, along with Sachs and Cooper, continued to work the evidence from the crime scenes.

There were no new clues, but Rhyme wanted Sachs and Cooper to reexamine what they'd already found. This was criminalistics – you looked and looked and looked, and then, when you couldn't find anything, you looked some more. And when you hit another brick wall, you kept right on looking.

Rhyme had wheeled up close to his computer and was ordering it to magnify images of the timer found in the wreckage of Ed Carney's plane. The timer itself might have been useless, because it was so generic, but Rhyme wondered if it might not contain a little trace or even a partial latent print. Bombers often believe that fingerprints are destroyed in the detonation and will shun gloves when working with the tinier components of the devices. But the blast itself will not necessarily destroy prints. Rhyme now ordered Cooper to fume the timer in the SuperGlue frame and, when that revealed nothing, to dust it with the Magna-Brush, a technique for raising prints that uses fine magnetic powder. Once again he found nothing.

Finally he ordered that the sample be bombarded by the nit-yag, slang for a garnet laser that was state-of-the-art in raising otherwise invisible prints. Cooper was looking at the image under the 'scope while Rhyme examined it on his computer screen.

Rhyme gave a short laugh, squinted, then looked again, wondering if his eyes were playing tricks on him.

"Is that? . . . Look. Lower right-hand corner!" Rhyme called.

But Cooper and Sachs could see nothing.

His computer-enhanced image had found something that Cooper's optical 'scope had missed. On the lip of metal that had protected the timer from being blown to smithereens was a faint crescent of ridge endings, crossings and bifurcations. It was no more than a sixteenth of an inch wide and maybe a half inch long.

"It's a print," Rhyme said.

"Not enough to compare," Cooper said, gazing at Rhyme's screen.

There are a total of about 150 individual ridge characteristics in a single fingerprint but an expert can determine a match with only eight to sixteen ridge matches. Unfortunately this sample didn't even provide half that.

Still, Rhyme was excited. The criminalist who couldn't twist the focus knob of a compound 'scope had found something that the others hadn't. Something he probably would have missed if he'd been "normal."

He ordered the computer to load a screen capture program and he saved the print as a .bmp file, not compressing it to .jpg, to avoid any risk of corrupting the image. He printed out a hard copy on his laser printer and had Thom tape it up next to the crash-site-scene evidence board.

The phone rang and, with his new system, Rhyme tidily answered the call and turned on the speakerphone.

It was the Twins.

Also known by the affectionate handle "the Hardy Boys," this pair of Homicide detectives worked out of the Big Building, One Police Plaza. They were interrogators and canvassers – the cops who interview residents, bystanders, and witnesses after a crime – and these two, who bore a vague resemblance to each other, were considered the best in the city. Even Lincoln Rhyme, with his distrust of the powers of human observation and recall, respected them.

Despite their delivery.

"Hey, Detective. Hey, Lincoln," said one of them. Their names were Bedding and Saul. In person, you could hardly tell them apart. Over the phone, Rhyme didn't even try.

"What've you got?" he asked. "Find the cat lady?"

"This one was easy. Seven veterinarians, two boarding services—"

"Made sense to hit them too. And—"

"We did three pet walking companies too. Even though—"

"Who walks cats, right? But they also feed and water and change the litter when you're away. Figured it couldn't hurt."

"Three of the vets had a maybe, but they weren't sure. They were pretty big operations."

"Lotsa animals on the Upper East Side. You'd be surprised. Maybe you wouldn't."

"And so we had to call employees at home. You know, doctors, assistants, washers—"

"That's a job. Pet washer. Anyway, a receptionist at a vet on Eighty-second was thinking it might be this customer, Sheila Horowitz. She's mid-thirties, short dark hair, heavyset. Has three cats. One black and the other blond. They don't know the color on the third one. She lives on Lexington between Seventy-eighth and Seventy-ninth."

Five blocks from Percey's town house.

Rhyme thanked them and told them to stay on call, then barked, "Get Dellray's teams over there now! You too, Sachs. Whether he's there or not, we'll have a scene to search. I think we're getting close. Can you feel it, everybody? We're getting close!"

Percey Clay was telling Roland Bell about her first solo flight.

Which didn't go quite as she planned.

She'd taken off from the small grass strip four miles outside of Richmond, feeling the familiar *ka-thunk ka-thunk* as the Cessna's gear bounded over the rough spots just before she hit V1 speed. Then back on the yoke and the crisp little 150 took to the air. A humid spring afternoon, just like this one.

"Must've been exciting," Bell offered, with a curiously dubious look.

"Got more so," Percey said, then took a hit from the flask.

Twenty minutes later the engine quit over the Wilderness in eastern Virginia, a nightmare of brambles and loblolly pine. She set the staunch plane down on a dirt road, cleared the fuel line herself, and took off once again, returning home without incident.

There was no damage to the little Cessna – so the owner never found out about the joyride. In fact the only fallout from the incident was the whipping she got from her mother because the principal at the Lee School had reported Percey'd been in yet another fight and had punched Susan Beth Halworth in the nose and fled after fifth period.

"I had to get away," Percey explained to Bell. "They were picking on me. I think they were calling me 'troll'. I got called that a lot."

"Kids can be cruel," Bell said. "I'd tan my boys' hide, they ever did anything like – Wait, how old were you?"

"Thirteen."

"Can you do that? I mean, don't you need to be eighteen to fly?"

"Sixteen."

"Oh. Then . . . how'd it work that you were flyin'?"

"They never caught me," Percey said. "That's how it worked."

"Oh."

She and Roland Bell were sitting in her room in the safe house. He'd refilled her flask with Wild Turkey – a bread-and-butter present from a mob informant who'd lived here for five weeks – and they were sitting on a green couch, the squelch mercifully turned down on his walkie-talkie. Percey sat back, Bell forward – his posture due not to the uncomfortable furniture but to his extraordinary mindfulness. His eye would catch the motion of a fly zipping past the door, a breath of air pushing a curtain, and his hand would stray to one of the two large guns he carried.

At his prompting she continued the story of her flying career. She got her student pilot certificate at age sixteen, her private pilot certificate a year later, and at eighteen she had her commercial ticket.

To her parents' horror, she fled the tobacco business circuit (Father didn't work for a "company" but for a "grower," though it was a $6 billion corporation to everyone else) and went for her engineering degree. ("Dropping out of UVA was the first sensible thing she's done," her mother pointed out to Percey's father, the only time the girl could remember her mother taking her side. The woman had added, "It'll be easier to find a husband at Virginia Tech." Meaning the boys won't have such high standards.)

But it wasn't parties or boys or sororities she was interested in. It was one thing and one thing only. Aircraft. Every day that it was physically and financially possible, she flew. She got her flight instructor's cert and started teaching. She didn't like the job particularly, but she persisted for a very savvy reason: the hours you spent flight-instructing went in your logbook as pilot-in-command time. Which would look good on the résumé when she went knocking on airline doors.

After graduation she began the life of an unemployed pilot. Lessons, air shows, joyrides, an occasional left-hand seat assignment for a delivery service or small charter company. Air taxis, seaplanes, crop dusting, even stunts, flying old Stearman and Curtis Jenny biplanes on Sunday afternoons at roadside carnivals.

"It was tough, real tough," she said to Roland Bell. "Maybe like getting started in law enforcement."

"Not a world of difference, I'd guess. I was running speed traps and overseeing crossing guard detail as sheriff of Hoggston. We had three consecutive years with no homicides, even accidental. Then I started moving up – got a job as a deputy with the county, working Highway Patrol. But that was mostly picking folk outa moonshine wrecks. So I went back to UNC for a criminology/sociology degree. Then I moved to Winston-Salem and got myself a gold shield."

"A what?"

"Detective. Course, I got beat up twice and shot at three times before my first review . . . Hey, be careful what you ask for; you may get it. You ever hear that?"

"But you were doing what you wanted."

"I was that. You know, my aunt who raised me'd always say, 'You walk the direction God points you.' Think there's something to that. I'm keen to know, how'd you start your own company?"

"Ed – my husband – and Ron Talbot and I did that. About seven, eight years ago. But I had a stopover first."

"How's that?"

"I enlisted."

"No fooling?"

"Yep. I was desperate to fly and nobody was hiring. See, before you can get a job with a big charter or an airline you have to be rated on the kind of planes they fly. And in order to get rated you've got to pay for training and simulator time – out of your own pocket. Can cost you ten thousand bucks to get a ticket to fly a big jet. I was stuck flying props 'cause I couldn't afford any training. Then it occurred to me: I could enlist and get paid to fly the sexiest aircraft on earth. So I signed up. Navy."

"Why them?"

"Carriers. Thought it'd be fun to land on a moving runway."

Bell winced. She cocked her eyebrow and he explained. "In case you didn't guess, I'm not a huge fan of your business."

"You don't like pilots?"

"Oh, no, don't mean that. It's flying I don't like."

"You'd rather be shot at than go flying?"

Without consideration, he nodded emphatically, then asked, "You see combat?"

"Sure did. Las Vegas."

He frowned.

"Nineteen ninety-one. The Hilton Hotel. Third floor."

"Combat? I don't get it."

Percey asked, "You ever hear about Tailhook?"

"Oh, wasn't that the navy convention or something? Where a bunch of male pilots got all drunk and attacked some women? You were *there*?"

"Got groped and pinched with the best of 'em. Decked one lieutenant and broke the finger of another, though I'm sorry to say he was too drunk to feel the pain till the next day." She sipped some more bourbon.

"Was it as bad as they said?"

After a moment she said, "You're used to expecting some North Korean or some Iranian in a MiG to drop out of the sun and lock on. But when the people supposed to be on your side do it, well, it really throws you. Makes you feel dirty, betrayed."

"What happened?"

"Aw, kind of a mess," she muttered. "I wouldn't roll over. I named names and put some folks out of business. Some pilots, but some high-up folks too. That didn't sit well in the briefing room. As you can imagine."

Monkey skills or no monkey skills, you don't fly with wingmen you don't trust. "So I left. It was all right. I'd had fun with the 'Cats, fun flying sorties. But it was time to leave. I'd met Ed – my husband – and we'd decided to open up this charter. I kissed and made up with Daddy – sort of – and he lent me most of the money for the Company." She shrugged. "Which I paid back at prime plus three, never late a day on a payment. The son of a gun . . ."

This brought back a dozen memories of Ed. Helping her negotiate the loan. Shopping together for aircraft at the skeptical leasing companies. Renting hangar space. Arguing as they struggled to fix a nav-com panel at three in the morning, trying to get ready for a 6 A.M. flight. The images hurt as bad as her ferocious migraines. Trying to deflect her thoughts, she asked, "So what brings you to parts north?"

"Wife's family's up here. On Long Island."

"You gave up North Carolina for in-laws?" Percey nearly made a comment about how'd his wife lasso him into that but was glad she hadn't. Bell's hazel eyes easily held hers as he said, "Beth was pretty sick. Passed away nineteen months ago."

"Oh, I'm so sorry."

"Thank you. They had Sloan-Kettering up here and her folks and sister too. The fact is I needed some help with the kids. I'm fine pitching the football and making chili but they need other stuff than that. Like, I shrunk most of their sweaters first time I dried 'em. That sort of thing. I wasn't averse to a move anyway. Wanted to show the kids there's more to life than silos and harvesters."

"You got pictures?" Percey asked, tipping back the flask. The hot liquor burned for a brief exquisite moment. She decided she'd quit drinking. Then decided not to.

"'Deed I do." He fished a wallet from his baggy slacks and displayed the children. Two blond boys, around five and seven. "Benjamin and Kevin," Bell announced.

Percey also caught a glimpse of another photo – a pretty, blond woman, short hair in bangs.

"They're adorable."

"You have any kids?"

"No," she answered, thinking, I always had my reasons. There was always next year or the next. When the company was doing better. When we'd leased that 737. After I got my DC-9 rating . . . She gave him a stoic smile. "Yours? They want to be cops when they grow up?"

"Soccer players's what they want to be. Not much of a market for that in New York. Unless the Mets keep playing the way they've been."

Before the silence grew too thick, Percey asked, "Is it okay if I call the Company? I've got to see how my aircraft's coming."

"You bet. I'll leave you be. Just make sure you don't give our number or address to a soul. It's the one thing I'm gonna be real muley about."

15

"Ron. It's Percey. How is everyone?"

"Shook up," he answered. "I sent Sally home. She couldn't—"

"How is she?"

"Just couldn't deal with it. Carol too. And Lauren. Lauren was out of control. I've never seen anybody that upset. How're you and Brit?"

"Brit's mad. I'm mad. What a mess this is. Oh, Ron . . ."

"And that detective, the cop who got shot?"

"I don't think they know yet. How's *Foxtrot Bravo*?"

"It's not as bad as it could be. I've already replaced the cockpit window. No breaches in the fuselage. Number two engine . . . that's a problem. We've got to replace a lot of the skin. We're trying to find a new fire extinguisher cartridge. I don't think it'll be a problem . . ."

"But?"

"But the annular has to be replaced."

"The combustor? Replace it? Oh, Jesus."

"I've already called the Garrett distributor in Connecticut. They agreed to deliver one tomorrow, even though it's Sunday. I can have it installed in a couple, three hours."

"Hell," she muttered, "I should be there . . . I told them I'd stay put but, damn it, I should be there."

"Where are you, Percey?"

And Stephen Kall, listening to this conversation as he sat in Sheila Horowitz's dim apartment, was ready to write. He pressed the receiver closer to his ear.

But the Wife said only, "In Manhattan. About a thousand cops around us. I feel like the pope or the president."

Stephen had heard on his police scanner reports of some curious activity around the Twentieth Precinct, which was on the Upper West Side. The station house was being closed and suspects were being relocated. He wondered if that was where the Wife was right now – at the precinct house.

Ron asked, "Are they going to stop this guy? Do they have any leads?"

Yes, do they? Stephen wondered.

"I don't know," she said.

"Those gunshots," Ron said. "Jesus, they were scary. Reminded me of the service. You know, that sound of the guns."

Stephen wondered again about this Ron fellow. Could he be useful?

Infiltrate, evaluate . . . *interrogate*.

Stephen considered tracking him down and torturing him to get him to call Percey back and ask where the safe house was . . .

But although he probably could get through the airport security again it would be a risk. And it would take too much time.

As he listened to their conversation Stephen gazed at the laptop computer in front of him. A message saying, *Please wait,* kept flashing. The remote tap was connected to a NYNEX relay box near the airport and had been transmitting their conversations to Stephen's tape recorder for the past week. He was surprised the police hadn't found it yet.

A cat – Esmeralda, *Essie,* the worm sack – climbed onto the table and arched her back. Stephen could hear the irritating purring.

He began to feel cringey.

He elbowed the cat roughly to the floor and enjoyed her pained bleat.

"I've been looking for more pilots," Ron said uncomfortably. "I've got—"

"We just need one. Right-hand seat."

A pause. "What?" Ron asked.

"I'm taking the flight tomorrow. All I need is an FO."

"You? I don't think that's a good idea, Perce."

"You have anybody?" she asked shortly.

"Well, the thing is—"

"Do you *have* anyone?"

"Brad Torgeson's on the call list. He said he had no problem helping us out. He knows about the situation."

"Good. A pilot with balls. How's his Lear time?"

"Plenty . . . Percey, I thought you were hiding out until the grand jury."

"Lincoln agreed to let me take the flight. If I stayed here until then."

"Who's Lincoln?"

Yes, Stephen thought. Who *is* Lincoln?

"Well, he's this weird man . . ." The Wife hesitated, as if she wanted to talk about him but wasn't sure what to say. Stephen was disappointed when she said only, "He's working with the police, trying to find the killer. I told him I'd stay here until tomorrow but I was definitely making the flight. He agreed."

"Percey, we can delay it. I'll talk to U.S. Medical. They know we're going through some—"

"No," she said firmly. "They don't want excuses. They want wheels-up on schedule. And if we can't do it they'll find somebody else. When are they delivering the cargo?"

"Six or seven."

"I'll be there late afternoon. I'll help you finish with the annular."

"Percey," he wheezed, "everything's going to be fine."

"We get that engine fixed on time, everything'll be *great*."

"You must be going through hell," Ron said.

"Not really," she said.

Not yet, Stephen corrected silently.

Sachs skidded the RRV station wagon around the corner at forty miles per hour. She saw a dozen tactical agents trotting along the street.

Fred Dellray's teams were surrounding the building where Sheila Horowitz lived. A typical Upper East Side brownstone, next door to a Korean deli, in front of which an employee squatted on a milk crate, peeling carrots for the salad bar and staring with no particular curiosity at the machine-gun-armed men and women surrounding the building.

Sachs found Dellray, weapon unholstered, in the foyer, examining the directory.

S.Horowitz. 204.

He tapped his radio. "We're on four eight three point four."

The secure federal tactical operations frequency. Sachs adjusted her radio as Dellray peered into the Horowitz woman's mailbox with a small black flashlight. "Nothin' picked up today. Got a feeling that girl's gone." He then said, "We got our folk on the fire escape and floor above and below with a SWAT cam and some mikes. Haven't seen anybody inside. But we're pickin' up some scratching and purring. Nothing sounds human, though. She got cats, remember. That was a feather in his cap, thinking of the vets. Our man Rhyme, I mean."

I know who you mean, she thought.

Outside, the wind was howling and another line of black clouds was trooping over the city. Big slabs of bruise-colored cloud.

Dellray snarled into his radio. "All teams. Status?"

"Red Team. We're on the fire escape."

"Blue Team. First floor."

"Roger," Dellray muttered. "Search and Surveillance. Report."

"Still not sure. We're getting faint infrared readings. Whoever or whatever's in there isn't moving. Could be a sleeping cat. Or a wounded victim. Or might be a pilot light or lamp that's been burning for a while. Could be the subject, though. In an interior part of the apartment."

"Well, what do you *think*?" Sachs asked.

"Who's that?" the agent asked over the radio.

"NYPD, Portable Five Eight Eight Five," Sachs responded, giving her badge number. "I want to know what your opinion is. Do you think the suspect is inside?"

"Why you askin'?" Dellray wanted to know.

"I want an uncontaminated scene. I'd like to go in alone if they think he's not there." A dynamic entry by a dozen tactical officers was probably the most efficient way to utterly decimate a crime scene.

Dellray looked at her for a moment, his dark face creased, then said into his stalk mike, "What's your opinion, S&S?"

"We just can't say for sure, sir," the disembodied agent reported.

"Know you can't, Billy. Just gimme what your gut's telling you."

A pause, then: "I *think* he's rabbited. Think it's clean."

"Hokay." To Sachs he said, "But you take one officer with you. That's an order."

"I go in first, though. He can cover me from the door. Look, this guy just isn't leaving *any* evidence anywhere. We need a break."

"All right, Officer." Dellray nodded to several of the federal SWAT agents. "Entry approved," he muttered, slipping out of hipster as he spoke words of law enforcement art.

One of the tactical agents had the lobby door lock disassembled in thirty seconds.

"Hold up," Dellray said, cocking his head. "It's a call from Central." He spoke into the radio. "Give 'em the frequency." He looked at Sachs. "Lincoln's calling you."

A moment later the criminalist's voice intruded. "Sachs," he said, "what're you doing?"

"I'm just—"

"Listen," he said urgently. "Don't go in alone. Let them secure the scene first. You know the rule."

"I've got backup—"

"No, let SWAT secure it first."

"They're sure he's not there," she lied.

"That's not good enough," he shot back. "Not with the Dancer. Nobody's ever sure with him."

This again. I don't need it, Rhyme. Exasperated, she said, "This's the sort of scene he's not expecting us to find. He probably hasn't hosed it. We could find a fingerprint, a shell casing. Hell, we could find his credit card."

No response. It wasn't often that Lincoln Rhyme was rendered silent.

"Quit spooking me, Rhyme. Okay?"

He didn't respond and she had a strange feeling that he wanted her to be spooked. "Sachs . . . ?"

"What?"

"Just be careful" was his only advice and the words were offered tentatively.

Then suddenly five tactical agents appeared, wearing Nomex gloves and hoods, blue flak jackets, and holding black H&K's.

"I'll call you from inside," she said.

She started up the stairs after them, her thoughts more on the heavy crime scene suitcase she held in her weak hand, her left, than on the black pistol in her right.

In the old days, in the Before days, Lincoln Rhyme had been a walker.

There was something about motion that soothed him. A stroll through Central or Washington Square Park, a brisk walk through the Fashion District. Oh, he'd pause often – maybe to collect a bit of evidence for the databases at the IRD lab – but once the bits of dirt or the plants or the samples of building materials were safely stowed and their sources jotted in his notebook, he'd continue on his way again. Miles and miles he'd walk.

One of the most frustrating things about his present condition was the inability to let off tension. He now had his eyes closed and he rubbed the back of his head into the headrest of the Storm Arrow, grinding his teeth together.

He asked Thom for some scotch.

"Don't you need to be clearheaded?"

"No."

"I think you do."

Go to hell, Rhyme thought, and ground his teeth harder. Thom would have to clean off a bloody gum, have to arrange for the dentist to come over. And I'll be a prick with *him* too.

Thunder rolled in the distance and the lights dimmed.

He pictured Sachs at the front of the tactical force. She was right, of course: an ESU team doing a full secure of the apartment would contaminate it badly. Still, he was worried sick for her. She was too reckless. He'd seen her scratching her skin, pulling eyebrows, chewing nails. Rhyme, ever skeptical of the psychologist's black arts, nonetheless knew self-destructive behavior when he saw it. He'd also been for a drive with her – in her souped-up sports car. They'd hit speeds over 150 miles per hour and she seemed frustrated that the rough roads on Long Island wouldn't let her do twice that.

He was startled to hear her whispering voice. "Rhyme, you there?"

"Go ahead, Amelia."

A pause. "No first names, Rhyme. It's bad luck."

He tried to laugh. Wished he hadn't used the name, wondered why he had.

"Go ahead."

"I'm at the front door. They're going to take it down with a battering ram. The other team reported in. They really don't think he's there."

"You wearing your armor?"

"Stole a feebie's flak jacket. Looks like I'm wearing black cereal boxes for a bra."

"On three," Rhyme heard Dellray's voice, "all teams, take out door and windows, cover all areas, but hold short of entry. One . . ."

Rhyme was so torn. How badly he wanted the Dancer – he could taste it. But, oh, how frightened he was for her.

"Two . . ."

Sachs, damn it, he thought. I don't want to worry about you . . .

"Three . . ."

He heard a soft snap, like a teenager cracking his knuckles, and found himself leaning forward. His neck quivered with a huge cramp and he leaned back. Thom appeared and began to massage it.

"It's all right," he muttered. "Thank you. Could you just get the sweat? Please."

Thom looked at him suspiciously – at the word "please" – then wiped his forehead.

What're you doing, Sachs?

He wanted to ask but wouldn't think of distracting her just now.

Then he heard a gasp. The hairs on the back of his neck stirred. "Jesus, Rhyme."

"What? Tell me."

"The woman . . . the Horowitz woman. The refrigerator door's open. She's inside. She's dead but it looks like . . . Oh, God, her eyes."

"Sachs . . ."

"It looks like he put her inside when she was still alive. Why the hell would he—"

"Think past it, Sachs. Come on. You can do it."

"Jesus."

Rhyme knew Sachs was claustrophobic. He imagined the terror she'd be feeling, looking at the terrible mode of death.

"Did he tape her or tie her?"

"Tape. Some kind of clear packing tape on her mouth. Her eyes, Rhyme. Her eyes . . ."

"Don't get shook, Sachs. The tape'll be a good surface for prints. What're the floor surfaces?"

"Carpet in the living room. And linoleum in the kitchen. And—" A scream. "Oh God!"

"What?"

"Just one of the cats. It jumped in front of me. Little shit . . . Rhyme?"

"What?"

"I'm smelling something. Something funny."

"Good." He'd taught her always to smell the air at a crime scene. It was the first fact a CS officer should note. "But what does 'funny' mean?"

"A sour smell. Chemical. Can't place it."

Then he realized that something didn't make sense.

"Sachs," he asked abruptly. "Did *you* open the refrigerator door?"

"No. I found it that way. It's propped open with a chair, looks like."

Why? Rhyme wondered. *Why'd* he do that? He thought furiously.

"That smell, it's stronger. Smokey."

The woman's a distraction! Rhyme thought suddenly. He left the door open to make sure the entry team would focus on it!

Oh, no, not again!

"Sachs! That's fuse you're smelling. A time-delay fuse.

There's another bomb! Get out now! He left the refrigerator door open to lure us inside."

"What?"

"It's a fuse! He's set a bomb. You've got seconds. Get out! Run!"

"I can get the tape. On her mouth."

"Get the fuck out!"

"I can get it . . ."

Rhyme heard a rustle, a faint gasp, and seconds later, the ringing bang of the explosion, like a sledgehammer on a boiler.

It stunned his ear.

"No!" he cried. "Oh, no!"

He glanced at Sellitto, who was staring at Rhyme's horrified face. "What happened, what happened?" the detective was calling.

A moment later Rhyme could hear through the earpiece a man's voice, panicky, shouting, "We've got a fire. Second floor. The walls're gone. They're gone . . . We got injuries . . . Oh, God. What happened to her? Look at the blood. All the blood! We need help. Second floor! Second floor . . ."

Stephen Kall walked a circle around the Twentieth Precinct on the Upper West Side.

The station house wasn't far from Central Park and he caught a glimpse of the trees.

The cross street the precinct house was located on was guarded, but security wasn't too bad. There were three cops in front of the low building, looking around nervously. But there were.none on the east side of the station house, where a thick steel grille covered the windows. He guessed that this was the lockup.

Stephen continued around the corner and then walked south to the next cross street. There were no blue sawhorses closing off this street, but there were guards – two more cops. They eyed every car and pedestrian that passed. He studied the building briefly then continued yet another block south and circled around the west side of the precinct. He slipped through a deserted alley, took his binoculars from his backpack, and gazed at the station house.

Can you *use* this, Soldier?

Sir, yes, I can, sir.

In a parking lot beside the station house was a gas pump. An officer was filling his squad car with gas. It never occurred to Stephen that police cars wouldn't buy their gas at Amoco or Shell stations.

For a long moment he gazed at the pumps through his small, heavy Leica binoculars, then put them back into the bag and hurried west, conscious, as always, of people on the lookout for him.

Hour 12 of 45

16

"Sachs!" Rhyme cried again.

Damnit, what was she *thinking* of? How could she be so careless?

"What happened?" Sellitto asked again. "What's going on?"

What happened to her?

"A bomb in the Horowitz apartment," Rhyme said hopelessly. "Sachs was inside when it went off. Call them. Find out what happened. On the speakerphone."

All the blood . . .

An interminable three minutes later Sellitto was patched through to Dellray.

"Fred," Rhyme shouted, "how is she?"

A harrowing pause before he answered.

"Ain't good, Lincoln. We're just gettin' the fire out now. It was an AP of some kind. Shit. We shoulda looked first. Fuck."

Antipersonnel booby traps were usually plastic explosive or TNT and often contained shrapnel or ball bearings – to inflict the most damage they could.

Dellray continued. "Took a coupla walls down and burned mosta the place out." A pause. "I have to tell you, Lincoln. We . . . found . . ." Dellray's voice – usually so steady – now waffled uneasily.

"What?" Rhyme demanded.

"Some body parts . . . A hand. Part of an arm."

Rhyme closed his eyes and felt a horror he hadn't felt in years. An icy stab through his insentient body. His breath came out in a low hiss.

"Lincoln—," Sellitto began.

"We're still searching," Dellray continued. "She might not be dead. We'll find her. Get her to the hospital. We'll do everything we can. You know we will."

Sachs, why the hell did you do it? Why did I let you?

I should never—

Then a crackle sounded in his ear. A pop loud as a firecracker. "Could somebody . . . I mean, Jesus, could somebody get this off me?"

"Sachs?" Rhyme called into the microphone. He was sure the voice was hers. Then it sounded like she was choking and retching.

"Uck," she said. "Oh, boy . . . This's gross."

"Are you all right?" He turned to the speakerphone. "Fred, where is she?"

"Is that you, Rhyme?" she asked. "I can't hear anything. Somebody talk to me!"

"Lincoln," Dellray called. "We got her! She's A-okay. She's all right."

"Amelia?"

He heard Dellray shouting for medics. Rhyme, whose body hadn't shivered for some years, noted that his left ring finger was trembling fiercely.

Dellray came back on. "She can't hear too good, Lincoln. What happened was . . . looks like what happened was it was the *woman's* body we saw. Horowitz. Sachs pulled it out of the fridge just 'fore the bang. The corpse took mosta the blast."

Sellitto said, "I see that look, Lincoln. Give her a break."

But he didn't.

In a fierce growl he said, "What the hell were you thinking of, Sachs? I told you it was a bomb. You should've *known* it was a bomb and bailed out."

"Rhyme, is that you?"

She was faking. He knew she was.

"Sachs—"

"I had to get the tape, Rhyme. Are you there? I can't hear you. It was plastic packing tape. We need to get one of his prints. You said so yourself."

"Honestly," he snapped, "you're impossible."

"Hello? Hello-o? Can't hear a word you're saying."

"Sachs, don't give me any crap."

"I'm going to check something, Rhyme."

There was silence for a moment.

"Sachs? . . . Sachs, you there? What the hell . . . ?"

"Rhyme, listen – I just hit the tape with the PoliLight. And guess what? There's a partial on it! I've got one of the Dancer's prints!"

That stopped him for a moment, but he soon resumed his tirade again. He was well into his lecture before he realized that he was reading the riot act to an empty line.

She was sooty and had a stunned look about her.

"No dressing-down, Rhyme. It was stupid but I didn't think about it. I just moved."

"What happened?" he asked. His stern visage had fallen away momentarily, he was so happy to see her alive.

"I was halfway inside. I saw the AP charge behind the door and didn't think I could make it out in time. I grabbed the woman's body out of the fridge. I was going to pull her to the kitchen window. It blew before I got halfway there."

Mel Cooper looked over the bag of evidence Sachs handed him. He examined the soot and fragments from the bomb. "M forty-five charge. TNT, with a rocker switch and forty-five-second fuse delay. The entry team knocked it over when they rammed the door; that ignited the fuse. There's graphite, so it's newer-formulation TNT. Very powerful, very bad."

"Fucker," Sellitto spat out. "Time delay . . . He wanted to make sure as many people got into the room as possible 'fore it blew."

Rhyme asked, "Anything traceable?"

"Off-the-shelf military. Won't lead us anywhere except—"

"To the asshole gave it to him," Sellitto muttered. "Phillip Hansen." The detective's phone rang and he took the call, lowered his head as he listened, nodding.

"Thank you," he said finally, shut off the phone.

"What?" Sachs asked.

The detective's eyes were closed.

Rhyme knew it was about Jerry Banks.

"Lon?"

"It's Jerry." The detective looked up. Sighed. "He'll live. But he lost his arm. They couldn't save it. Too much damage."

"Oh, no," Rhyme whispered. "Can I talk to him?"

"No," the detective said. "He's asleep."

Rhyme thought of the young man, pictured him saying the wrong thing at the wrong time, poking at his cowlick, rubbing a razor cut on his smooth, pink chin. "I'm sorry, Lon."

The detective shook his head, much the same way Rhyme deflected bouquets of sympathy. "We got other things to worry about."

Yes, they did.

Rhyme noticed the plastic packing tape – the gag the Dancer had used. He could see, as could Sachs, a faint lipstick mark on the adhesive side.

Sachs was staring at the evidence, but it wasn't a clinical look. Not a *scientist's* gaze. She was troubled.

"Sachs?" he asked.

"Why'd he do that?"

"The bomb?"

She shook her head. "Why'd he put her in the refrigerator?" She lifted a finger to her mouth and chewed a nail. Of her ten fingers, only one nail – the little finger of her left hand – was long and shapely. The others were chewed. Some were brown with dried blood.

The criminalist answered, "I think it was because he wanted to distract us so we wouldn't focus on the bomb. A body in a refrigerator – that got our attention."

"I don't mean that," she answered. "COD was suffocation. He put her in there *alive*. Why? Is he a sadist or something?"

Rhyme answered, "No, the Dancer's not a sadist. He can't afford to be. His only urge is to complete the job, and he's got enough willpower to keep his other lusts under control. Why'd he suffocate her when he could have used a knife or rope? . . . I'm not exactly sure, but it could be good for us."

"How's that?"

"Maybe there was something about her that he hated, and he wanted to kill her in the most unpleasant way he could."

"Yeah, but why's that good for us?" Sellitto asked.

"Because" – it was Sachs who answered – "it means maybe he's losing his cool. He's getting careless."

"Exactly," Rhyme called, proud of Sachs for making the connection. But she didn't notice his smile of approval. Her eyes dipped closed momentarily and she shook her head, probably replaying the image of the dead woman's horrified eyes. People thought criminalists were cold (how often had Rhyme's wife leveled that charge at him?), but in fact the best ones had a heartbreaking empathy for the victims of the scenes they searched. Sachs was one of these.

"Sachs," Rhyme whispered gently, "the print?"

She looked at him.

"You found a print, you said. We have to move fast."

Sachs nodded. "It's a partial." She held up the plastic bag.

"Could it be hers?"

"No, I printed her. Took a while to find her hands. But the print definitely isn't hers."

"Mel," Rhyme said.

The tech put the bit of packing tape in a SuperGlue frame and heated some glue. Immediately a tiny portion of the print became evident.

Cooper shook his head. "I don't believe it," he muttered.

"What?"

"He wiped the tape, the Dancer. He must've known he touched it without a glove on. There's only a bit of one partial left."

Like Rhyme, Cooper was a member of the International Association for Identification. They were experts at identifying people from fingerprints, DNA, and odontology – dental remains. But this particular print – like the one on the metal lip of the bomb – was beyond their power. If any experts could find and classify a print, it would be the two of them. But not this print.

"Shoot it and mount it," Rhyme muttered. "Up on the wall." They'd go through the motions because it was what you had to do in this business. But he was very frustrated. Sachs had nearly died for nothing.

Edmond Locard, the famous French criminalist, developed a principle named after him. He said that in every encounter between criminal and victim there is an exchange of evidence.

It might be microscopic, but a transfer takes place. Yet it seemed to Rhyme that if anyone could disprove Locard's Principle, it was the ghost they called the Coffin Dancer.

Sellitto, seeing the frustration on Rhyme's face, said, "We've got the trap at the station house. If we're lucky we'll get him."

"Let's hope. We could use some goddamn luck."

He closed his eyes, rested his head in the pillow. A moment later he heard Thom saying, "It's nearly eleven. Time for bed."

At times it's easy to neglect the body, to forget we even *have* bodies – times like these, when lives are at stake and we have to step out of our physical beings and keep working, working, working. We have to go far beyond our normal limitations. But Lincoln Rhyme had a body that wouldn't tolerate neglect. Bedsores could lead to sepsis and blood poisoning. Fluid in the lungs, to pneumonia. Didn't catheterize the bladder? Didn't massage the bowels to encourage a movement? Spenco boots too tight? Dysreflexia was the consequence and that could mean a stroke. Exhaustion alone could bring on an attack.

Too many ways to die . . .

"You're going to bed," Thom said.

"I have to—"

"Sleep. You have to sleep."

Rhyme acquiesced; he was tired, very tired.

"All right, Thom. All right." He wheeled toward the elevator. "One thing." He looked back. "Could you come up in a few minutes, Sachs?"

She nodded, watching the tiny elevator door swing shut.

She found him in the Clinitron.

Sachs had waited ten minutes to give him time to take care of bedtime functions – Thom had applied the catheter and brushed his boss's teeth. She knew Rhyme talked tough – he had a crip's disregard for modesty. But she knew too that there were personal routines he didn't want her to witness.

She used the time to take a shower in the downstairs bathroom, dressed in clean clothes – hers – which Thom happened to have in the laundry room in the basement.

The lights were dim. Rhyme was rubbing his head against the pillow like a bear scratching his back on a tree. The Clinitron was the most comfortable bed in the world. Weighing a half ton, it was a massive slab containing glass beads through which flowed heated air.

"Ah, Sachs, you did good today. You outthought him."

Except thanks to me Jerry Banks lost his arm.

And I let the Dancer get away.

She walked to his bar and poured a glass of Macallan, lifted an eyebrow.

"Sure," he said. "Mother's milk, the dew of nepenthe . . ."

She kicked her issue shoes off, pulled up her blouse to look at the bruise.

"Ouch," Rhyme said.

The bruise was the shape of Missouri and dark as an eggplant.

"I don't like bombs," she said. "Never been that close to one. And I don't like them."

Sachs opened her purse, found and swallowed three aspirin dry (a trick arthritics learn early). She walked to the window. There were the peregrines. Beautiful birds. They weren't large. Fourteen, sixteen inches. Tiny for a dog. But for a bird . . . utterly intimidating. Their beaks were like the claws on a creature from one of those *Alien* movies.

"You all right, Sachs? Tell me true?"

"I'm okay."

She returned to the chair, sipped more of the smokey liquor.

"You want to stay tonight?" he asked.

On occasion she'd spend the night here. Sometimes on the couch, sometimes in bed next to him. Maybe it was the fluidized air of the Clinitron, maybe it was the simple act of lying next to another human being – she didn't know the reason – but she never slept better than when she slept here. She hadn't enjoyed being close to another man since her most recent boyfriend, Nick. She and Rhyme would lie together and talk. She'd tell him about cars, about her pistol matches, about her mother and her goddaughter. About her father's full life and sad, protracted death. She'd ante up far more personal information than he. But that was all right. She loved listening to him say whatever he wanted to. His mind was astonishing. He'd tell her about old New York, about Mafia hits the rest of the world had never heard about, about crime scenes so clean they seemed hopeless until the searchers found the single bit of dust, the fingernail, the dot of spit, the hair or fiber that revealed who the perp was or where he lived – well, revealed these facts to *Rhyme*, not necessarily anyone else. No, his mind never stopped. She knew that before the injury he'd roam the streets of New York looking for samples of soil or glass or plants or rocks – anything that might help him solve cases. It was as if that restlessness had moved from his useless legs into his mind, which roamed the city – in his imagination – well into the night.

But tonight was different. Rhyme was distracted. She didn't mind him ornery – which was good because he was ornery a lot. But she didn't like him being elsewhere. She sat on the edge of the bed.

He began to say what he'd apparently asked her here for. "Sachs . . . Lon told me. About what happened at the airport."

She shrugged.

"There's nothing you could've done except gotten yourself killed. You did the right thing, going for cover. He fired one for range and would've gotten you with the second shot."

"I had two, three seconds. I could've hit him. I *know* I could've."

"Don't be reckless, Sachs. That bomb—"

The fervent look in her eyes silenced him. "I want to get him, whatever it takes. And I have a feeling you want to get him just as much. I think you'd take chances too." She added with cryptic significance, "Maybe you *are* taking chances."

This had a greater reaction than she'd expected. He blinked, looked away. But he said nothing else, sipped his scotch.

On impulse she asked, "Can I ask something? If you don't want me to, you can tell me to clam up."

"Come on, Sachs. We've got secrets, you and me? I don't think so."

Eyes on the floor, she said, "I remember once I was telling you about Nick. How I felt about him and so on. How what happened between us was so hard."

He nodded.

"And I asked you if you'd felt that way about anyone, maybe your wife. And you said yes, but not Blaine." She looked up at him.

He recovered fast, though not fast enough. And she realized she'd blown cold air on an exposed nerve.

"I remember," he answered.

"Who was she? Look, if you don't want to talk about it . . ."

"I don't mind. Her name was Claire. Claire Trilling. How's that for a last name?"

"Probably put up with the same crap in school I had to. Amelia Sex. Amelia Sucks . . . How'd you meet her?"

"Well . . ." He laughed at his own reluctance to continue. "In the department."

"She was a cop?" Sachs was surprised.

"Yep."

"What happened?"

"It was a . . . difficult relationship." Rhyme shook his head ruefully. "I was married, she was married. Just not to each other."

"Kids?"

"She had a daughter."

"So you broke up?"

"It wouldn't have worked, Sachs. Oh, Blaine and I were destined to get divorced – or kill each other. It was only a matter of time. But Claire . . . she was worried about her daughter – about her husband taking the little girl if she got divorced. She didn't love him, but he was a good man. Loved the girl a lot."

"You meet her?"

"The daughter? Yes."

"You ever see her now? Claire?"

"No. That was the past. She's not on the force anymore."

"You broke up after your accident?"

"No, no, before."

"She knows you were hurt, though, right?"

"No," Rhyme said after another hesitation.

"Why didn't you tell her?"

A pause. "There were reasons . . . Funny you bring her up. Haven't thought about her for years."

He offered a casual smile, and Sachs felt the pain course through her – actual pain like the blow that left the bruise in the shape of the Show Me State. Because what he was saying was a lie. Oh, he'd been thinking about this woman. Sachs didn't believe in woman's intuition, but she did believe in cop's intuition; she'd walked a beat for far too long to discount insights like these. She *knew* Rhyme'd been thinking about Ms Trilling.

Her feelings were ridiculous, of course. She had no patience for jealousy. Hadn't been jealous of Nick's job – he was undercover and spent weeks on the street. Hadn't been jealous of the hookers and blond ornaments he'd drink with on assignments.

And beyond jealousy, what could she possibly hope for with Rhyme? She'd talked about him to her mother many times. And the cagey old woman would usually say something like "It's good to be nice to a cripple like that."

Which just about summed up all that their relationship should be. All that it *could* be.

It was *more* than ridiculous.

But jealous she was. And it wasn't of Claire.

It was of Percey Clay.

Sachs couldn't forget how they'd looked together when she'd seen them sitting next to each other in his room, earlier today.

More scotch. Thinking of the nights she and Rhyme had spent here, talking about cases, drinking this very good liquor.

Oh, great. Now I'm maudlin. That's a mature feeling. I'm gonna group a cluster right in its chest and kill it dead.

But instead she offered the sentiment a little more liquor.

Percey wasn't an attractive woman, but that meant nothing; it had taken Sachs all of one week at Chantelle, the modeling agency on Madison Avenue where she'd worked for several years, to understand the fallacy of the beautiful. Men love to look at gorgeous women, but nothing intimidates them more.

"You want another hit?" she asked.

"No," he said.

Without thinking now, she reclined, laid her head on his pillow. It was funny how we adjust to things, she thought. Rhyme couldn't, of course, pull her to his chest and slip his arm around her. But the comparable gesture was his tilting his head to hers. In this way they'd fallen asleep a number of times.

Tonight, though, she sensed a stiffness, a caution.

She felt she was losing him. And all she could think about was trying to be closer. As close as possible.

Sachs had once confided with her friend Amy, her goddaughter's mother, about Rhyme, about her feelings for him. The woman had wondered what the attraction was and speculated, "Maybe it's that, you know, he can't move. He's a man but he doesn't have any control over you. Maybe that's a turn-on."

But Sachs knew it was just the opposite. The turn-on was that he was a man who had complete control, *despite* the fact he couldn't move.

Fragments of his words floated past as he spoke about Claire, then about the Dancer. She tilted her head back and looked at his thin lips.

Her hands started roving.

He couldn't feel, of course, but he could see her perfect fingers with their damaged nails slide over his chest, down his smooth body. Thom exercised him daily with a passive range of motion exercises and though Rhyme wasn't muscular he had a body of a young man. It was as if the aging process had stopped the day of the accident.

"Sachs?"

Her hand moved lower.

Her breathing was coming faster now. She tugged the blanket down. Thom had dressed Rhyme in a T-shirt. She tugged it up, moved her hands over his chest. Then she pulled her own shirt off, unhooked her bra, pressed her flushed skin against his pallid. She expected it to be cold but it wasn't. It was hotter than hers. She rubbed harder.

She kissed him once on the cheek, then the corner of the mouth, then squarely on the mouth.

"Sachs, no . . . Listen to me. No."

But she didn't listen.

She'd never told Rhyme, but some months ago she'd bought a book called *The Disabled Lover*. Sachs was surprised to learn that even quadriplegics can make love and father children. A man's perplexing organ literally has a mind of its own, and severing the spinal cord eliminates only one type of stimulus. Handicapped men were capable of perfectly normal erections. True, he'd have no sensation, but – for her – the physical thrill was only a part of the event, often a minor part. It was the closeness that counted; that was a high that a million phony movie orgasms would never approach. She suspected that Rhyme might feel the same way.

She kissed him again. Harder.

After a moment's hesitation he kissed her back. She was not surprised that he was good at it. After his dark eyes, his perfect lips were the first thing she'd noticed about him.

Then he pulled his face away.

"No, Sachs, don't . . ."

"Shhh, quiet . . ." She worked her hand under the blankets, began rubbing, touching.

"It's just that . . ."

It was *what*? she wondered. That things might not work out?

But things were working out fine. She felt him growing hard under her hand, more responsive than some of the most macho lovers she'd had.

She slid on top of him, kicked the sheets and blanket back, bent down and kissed him again. Oh, how she wanted to be here, face-to-face – as close as they could be. To make him understand that she saw he was her perfect man. He was whole as he was.

She unpinned her hair, let it fall over him. Leaned down, kissed him again.

Rhyme kissed back. They pressed their lips together for what seemed like a full minute.

Then suddenly he shook his head, so violently that she thought he might have been having an attack of dysreflexia.

"No!" he whispered.

She'd expected playful, she'd expected passionate, at worst a flirtatious *Oh-oh, not a good idea* . . . But he sounded weak. The hollow sound of his voice cut into her soul. She rolled off, clutching a pillow to her breasts.

"No, Amelia. I'm sorry. No."

Her face burned with shame. All she could think was how many times she'd been out with a man who was a friend or a casual date and suddenly been horrified to feel him start to grope her like a teenager. Her voice had registered the same dismay that she now heard in Rhyme's.

So this was all that she was to him, she understood at last. A partner. A colleague. A capital *F* Friend.

"I'm sorry, Sachs . . . I can't. There're complications."

Complications? None that she could see, except, of course, for the fact that he didn't love her.

"No, *I'm* sorry," she said brusquely. "Stupid. Too much of that damn single-malt. I never could hold the stuff. You know that."

"Sachs."

She kept a terse smile on her face as she dressed.

"Sachs, let me say something."

"No." She didn't want to hear another word.

"Sachs . . ."

"I should go. I'll be back early."

"I want to say something."

But Rhyme never got a chance to say anything, whether it was an explanation or apology or a confession. Or a lecture.

They were interrupted by a huge pounding on the door. Before Rhyme could ask who it was, Lon Sellitto burst into the room.

He glanced at Sachs without judgment, then back to Rhyme and announced, "Just heard from Bo's guys over at the Twentieth. The Dancer was there, staking out the place. The son of a bitch's taken the bait! We're gonna get him, Lincoln. This time we're gonna get him."

"Couple hours ago," the detective continued his story, "some of the S&S boys saw a white male taking a stroll around the

Twentieth Precinct house. He ducked into an alley and it looked like he was checking out guards. And then they saw him scoping out the gas pump next to the station house."

"Gas pump? For the RMPs?" Radio mobile patrols – Squad cars.

"Right."

"They follow him?"

"Tried. But he vanished 'fore they got close."

Rhyme was aware of Sachs's discreetly fixing the top button of her blouse . . . He had to have a talk with her about what had happened. He *had* to make her understand. But considering what Sellitto was now saying, it would have to wait.

"Gets better. Half hour ago, we got a report of a truck hijacking. Rollins Distributing. Upper West Side near the river. They deliver gas to independent service stations. Some guy cuts through the chain-link. The guard hears and goes to investigate. He gets blindsided. Gets the absolute crap beat out of him. And the guy gets away with one of the trucks."

"Is Rollins the company the department uses for gas?"

"Naw, but who'd know? The Dancer pulls up to the Twentieth in a tanker, the guards there don't think anything of it, they wave him through, next thing—"

Sachs interrupted. "The truck blows."

This brought Sellitto up short. "I was just thinking he'd use it as a way to get inside. You're thinking a bomb?"

Rhyme nodded gravely. Angry with himself. Sachs was right. "Outsmarted ourselves here. Never occurred to me he'd try anything like this. Jesus, a tanker truck goes up in that neighborhood . . ."

"A fertilizer bomb?"

"No," Rhyme said. "I don't think he'd have time to put that together. But all he needs is an AP charge on the side of a small tanker and he's got a super gas-enhanced device. Burn the precinct to the ground. We've got to evacuate everyone. Quietly."

"Quietly," Sellitto muttered. "That'll be easy."

"How's the guard from the gas distributor? Can he talk?"

"Can, but he got hit from behind. Didn't see a thing."

"Well, I want his clothes at least. Sachs" – she caught his eye – "could you get over to the hospital and bring them back? You'll know how to pack them to save the trace. And then work the scene where he stole the truck."

He wondered what her response would be. He wouldn't have been surprised if she'd quit cold and walked out the door. But he saw in her still, beautiful face that she was feeling exactly what he was: ironically, relief that the Dancer had intervened to change the disastrous course of their evening.

Finally, finally, some of the luck Rhyme had hoped for.

An hour later Amelia Sachs was back. She held up a plastic bag containing a pair of wire cutters.

"Found them near the chain-link. The guard must've surprised the Dancer and he dropped them."

"Yes!" Rhyme shouted. "I've never known him to make a mistake like that. Maybe he *is* getting careless . . . I wonder what's spooking him."

Rhyme glanced at the cutters. Please, he prayed silently, let there be a print.

But a groggy Mel Cooper – he'd been sleeping in one of the smaller bedrooms upstairs – went over every square millimeter of the tool. Not a print to be found.

"Does it tell us *anything*?" Rhyme asked.

"It's a Craftsman model, top of the line, sold in every Sears around the country. And you can pick them up in garage sales and junkyards for a couple bucks."

Rhyme wheezed in disgust. He gazed at the clippers for a moment then asked, "Tool marks?"

Cooper looked at him curiously. Tool marks are distinctive impressions left at crime scenes by the tools criminals used – screwdrivers, pliers, lock picks, crowbars, slim jims, and the like. Rhyme had once linked a burglar to a crime scene solely on the basis of a tiny V notch on a brass lock plate. The notch matched an imperfection in a chisel found on the man's workbench. Here, though, they had the *tool,* not any marks it might have made. Cooper didn't understand what tool marks Rhyme might be referring to.

"I'm talking about marks *on* the blade," he said impatiently.

"Maybe the Dancer's been cutting something distinctive, something that might tell us where he's holing up."

"Oh." Cooper examined it closely. "It's nicked, but take a look . . . Do you see anything unusual?"

Rhyme didn't. "Scrape the blade and handle. See if there's any residue."

Cooper ran the scrapings through the gas-chromatograph.

"Phew," he muttered as he read the results. "Listen to this. Residue of RDX, asphalt, and rayon."

"Detonating cord," Rhyme said.

"He cut it with clippers?" Sachs asked. "You can do that?"

"Oh, it's stable as clothesline," Rhyme said absently, picturing what a thousand gallons of flaming gasoline would do to the neighborhood around the Twentieth Precinct.

I should've made them leave, he was thinking, Percey and Brit Hale. Put them into protective custody and sent them to Montana until the grand jury. This is damn nuts what I'm doing, this trap idea.

"Lincoln?" Sellitto asked. "We've got to find that truck."

"We've got a little time," Rhyme said. "He's not going to try to get in until the morning. He needs the cover story of a delivery. Anything else, Mel? Anything in the trace?"

Cooper scanned the vacuum filter. "Dirt and brick. Wait . . . here're some fibers. Should I GC them?"

"Yes."

The tech hunched over the screen as the results came up. "Okay, okay, it's vegetable fiber. Consistent with paper. And I'm reading a compound . . . NH four OH."

"Ammonium hydroxide," Rhyme said.

"Ammonia?" Sellitto asked. "Maybe you're wrong about the fertilizer bomb."

"Any oil?" Rhyme asked.

"None."

Rhyme asked, "The fiber with the ammonia – was it from the handle of the clipper?"

"No. It was on the clothes of the guard he beat up."

Ammonia? Rhyme wondered. He asked Cooper to look at one of the fibers through the scanning electron microscope. "High magnification. How's the ammonia attached?"

The screen clicked on. The strand of fiber appeared like a tree trunk.

"Heat fused, I'd guess."

Another mystery. Paper and ammonia . . .

Rhyme looked at the clock. It was 2:40 A.M.

Suddenly he realized Sellitto had asked him a question. He cocked his head.

"I said," the detective repeated, "should we start evacuating everybody around the precinct? I mean, better now than wait till it's closer to the time he might attack."

For a long moment Rhyme gazed at the bluish tree trunk of fiber on the screen of the SEM. Then he said abruptly, "Yes. We have to get everybody out. Evacuate the buildings around the station house. Let's think – the four apartments on either side and across the street."

"That many?" Sellitto asked, giving a faint laugh. "You think we really gotta do that?"

Rhyme looked up at the detective and said, "No, I've changed my mind. The whole block. We've got to evacuate the whole block. Immediately. And get Haumann and Dellray over here. I don't care where they are. I want them now."

17

Some of them had slept.

Sellitto in an armchair, waking more rumpled than ever, his hair askew. Cooper downstairs.

Sachs had apparently spent the night on a couch downstairs or in the other bedroom on the first floor. No interest in the Clinitron anymore.

Thom, himself bleary, was hovering, a dear busybody, taking Rhyme's blood pressure. The smell of coffee filled the town house.

It was just after dawn and Rhyme was staring at the evidence charts. They'd been up till four, planning their strategy for snagging the Dancer – and responding to the legion of complaints about the evacuation.

Would this work? Would the Dancer step into their trap? Rhyme believed so. But there was another question, one that Rhyme didn't like to think about but couldn't avoid. How bad would springing the trap be? The Dancer was deadly enough on his own territory. What would he be like when he was cornered?

Thom brought coffee around and they looked over Dellray's tactical map. Rhyme, back in the Storm Arrow, rolled into position and studied it too.

"Everybody in place?" he asked Sellitto and Dellray.

Both Haumann's 32-E teams and Dellray's federal pickup band of Southern and Eastern District FBI SWAT officers were ready. They'd moved in under cover of night, through sewers and basements and over rooftops, in full urban camouflage; Rhyme was convinced that the Dancer was maintaining surveillance of his target.

"He won't be sleeping tonight," Rhyme had said.

"You sure he's going in this way, Linc?" Sellitto'd asked uncertainly.

Sure? he thought testily. Who can be sure about anything with the Coffin Dancer?

His deadliest weapon is deception . . .

Rhyme said wryly, "Ninety-two point seven percent sure."

Sellitto snorted a sour laugh.

It was then that the doorbell rang. A moment later a stocky, middle-aged man Rhyme didn't recognize appeared in the doorway of the living room.

The sigh from Dellray suggested trouble brewing. Sellitto knew the man too, it seemed, and nodded cautiously.

He identified himself as Reginald Eliopolos, assistant U.S. attorney in the Southern District. Rhyme recalled he was the prosecutor handling the Phillip Hansen case.

"You're Lincoln Rhyme? Hear good things about you. Uh-huh. Uh-huh." He started forward, automatically offering his hand. Then he realized that the extended arm was wasted on Rhyme, so he simply pointed it toward Dellray, who shook it reluctantly. Eliopolos's cheerful "Fred, good to see you" meant just the opposite and Rhyme wondered what was the source of the cold fusion between them.

The attorney ignored Sellitto and Mel Cooper. Thom instinctively sensed what was what and didn't offer the visitor coffee.

"Uh-huh, uh-huh. Hear you've got quite an operation together. Not checking too much with the boys upstairs, but, hell, I know all about improvising. Sometimes you just can't spend time waiting for signatures in triplicate." Eliopolos walked up to a compound 'scope, peered through the eyepiece. "Uh-huh," he said, though what he might be seeing was a mystery to Rhyme since the stage light was off.

"Maybe—" Rhyme began.

"The chase? Cut to the chase?" Eliopolos swung around. "Sure. Here it is. There's an armored van at the Federal Building downtown. I want the witnesses in the Hansen case in it within the hour. Percey Clay and Brit Hale. They'll be taken to the Shoreham federal protective reserve, on Long Island. They'll be kept there until their grand jury testimony late on Monday. Period. End of chase. How's that?"

"You think that's a wise idea?"

"Uh-huh, we do. We think it's wiser than using them as bait for some kind of personal vendetta by the NYPD."

Sellitto sighed.

Dellray said, "Open your eyes little bit here, Reggie. You're not exactly out of the loop. Do I see a joint operation? Do I see *task-forced* operation?"

"And a good thing too," Eliopolos said absently. His full attention was on Rhyme. "Tell me, did you really think that nobody downtown would remember that this was the perp who killed your techs five years ago?"

Well, *uh-huh,* Rhyme *had* hoped that nobody would remember. And now that somebody had, he and the team were swimming in the soup pot.

"But, hey, hey," the attorney said with jolly cheer, "I don't want a turf war. Do I want that? Why would I want that? What I want is Phillip Hansen. What *everybody* wants is Hansen. Remember? He's the big fish."

As a matter of fact Rhyme had largely forgotten about Phillip Hansen, and now that he'd been reminded he understood exactly what Eliopolos was doing. And the insight troubled him a great deal.

Rhyme snuck around Eliopolos like a coyote. "You've got yourself some good agents out there, do you," he asked innocently, "who'll protect the witnesses?"

"At Shoreham?" the attorney responded uncertainly. "Well, you bet we do. Uh-huh."

"You've briefed them about security? About how dangerous the Dancer is?" Innocent as a babe.

A pause. "I've briefed them."

"And what exactly are their orders?"

"Orders?" Eliopolos asked lamely. He wasn't a stupid man. He knew that he'd been caught.

Rhyme laughed. He glanced at Sellitto and Dellray. "See, our U.S. attorney friend here has *three* witnesses he hopes can nail Hansen."

"Three?"

"Percey, Hale . . . and the Dancer himself." Rhyme

scoffed. "He wants to capture him so he'll turn evidence." He looked at Eliopolos. "So *you're* using Percey as bait too."

"Only," Dellray chuckled, "he's putting her in a Havaheart trap. Got it, got it."

"You're thinking," Rhyme said, "that your case against Hansen's not so good, whatever Percey and Hale saw."

Mr Uh-huh tried sincerity. "They saw him ditch some goddamn evidence. Hell, they didn't even actually *see* him do that. If we find the duffel bags and it links him to the killings of those two soldiers last spring, fine, we've got a case. Maybe. But, A, we might not find the bags, and, B, the evidence inside them might be damaged."

Then, C, call *me,* Rhyme thought. I can find evidence in the clear night wind.

Sellitto said, "But you get Hansen's hit man alive, he can dime his boss."

"Exactly." Eliopolos crossed his arms the way he must have done in court, when he was delivering closing statements.

Sachs had been listening from the doorway. She asked the question Rhyme had just been about to. "And what would you plea the Dancer out to?"

Eliopolos asked, "Who're you?"

"Officer Sachs. IRD."

"It's not really a crime scene tech's place to question—"

"Then *I'm* asking the fuckin' question," Sellitto barked, "and if I don't get an answer, the mayor's gonna be asking it too."

Eliopolos had a political career ahead of him, Rhyme supposed. And a successful one, most likely. Eliopolos said, "It's important that we successfully prosecute Hansen. He's the greater of the two evils. The more potential for harm."

"That's a pretty answer," Dellray said, scrunching up his face. "But it don't do a thing for the question. What're you gonna agree to give the Dancer if he snitches on Hansen?"

"I don't know," the attorney said evasively. "That hasn't been discussed."

"Ten years in medium security?" Sachs muttered.

"It hasn't been *discussed.*"

Rhyme was thinking about the trap that they'd planned so

carefully until 4 A.M. If Percey and Hale were moved now, the Dancer would learn of it. He'd regroup. He'd find out they were at Shoreham and, against guards with orders to take him alive, he'd waltz in, kill Percey and Hale – and a half dozen U.S. marshals – and leave.

The attorney began, "We don't have much time—"

Rhyme interrupted with, "You have paper?"

"I was hoping you'd be willing to cooperate."

"We aren't."

"You're a civilian."

"*I'm* not," echoed Sellitto.

"Uh-huh. I see." He looked at Dellray but didn't even bother asking the agent whose side he was on. The attorney said, "I can get an order to show cause for protective custody in three or four hours."

On Sunday morning? Rhyme thought. *Uh-uh.* "We're not releasing them," he said. "Do what you have to do."

Eliopolos smiled a smile in his round bureaucratic face. "I should tell you that if this perp dies in any attempt to collar him I will personally be reviewing the shooting committee report, and it is a distinct possibility that I'll conclude that proper orders on the use of deadly force in an arrest situation were not given by supervisory personnel." He looked at Rhyme. "There could also be issues of interference by civilians with federal law enforcement activity. That could lead to major civil litigation. I just want you to be forewarned."

"Thanks," Rhyme said breezily. "Appreciate it."

When he was gone, Sellitto crossed himself. "Jesus, Linc, you hear him. He said *major* civil litigation."

"My my my . . . Speaking for myself, *minor* litigation woulda scared this boy plenty," Dellray chimed in.

They laughed.

Then Dellray stretched and said, "A pisser what's going round. You hear 'bout it, Lincoln? That bug?"

"What's that?"

"Been infecting a lotta folk lately. My SWAT boys and me're out on some operation or other and what happens but they come down with this nasty twitch in their trigger fingers."

Sellitto, a much worse actor than the agent, said broadly, "You too? I thought it was just our folks at ESU."

"But listen," said Fred Dellray, the Alec Guinness of street cops. "I got a cure. All you gotta do is kill yourself a mean asshole, like this Dancer fella, he so much as looks cross-eyed at you. That always works." He flipped open his phone. "Think I'll call in and make sure my boys and girls remember 'bout that medicine. I'm gonna do that right now."

Hour 22 of 45

18

Waking in the gloomy safe house at dawn, Percey Clay rose from her bed and walked to the window. She drew aside the curtain and looked out at the gray monotonous sky. A slight mist was in the air.

Close to minimums, she estimated. Wind 090 at five knots. Quarter mile visibility. She hoped the weather cleared for the flight tonight. Oh, she could fly in any weather – and had. Anyone with an IFR ticket – instrument flight rules rating – could take off, fly, and land in dense overcast. (In fact, with their computers, transponders, radar, and collision avoidance systems, most commercial airliners could fly themselves – even setting down for a perfect, hands-free landing.) But Percey liked to fly in clear weather. She liked to see the ground pass by beneath her. The lights at night. The clouds. And above her the stars.

All the stars of evening . . .

She thought again of Ed and her call to his mother in New Jersey last night. They'd made plans for his memorial service. She wanted to think some more about it, work on the guest list, plan the reception.

But she couldn't. Her mind was preoccupied with Lincoln Rhyme.

Recalling the conversation they'd had yesterday behind closed doors in his bedroom – after the fight with that officer, Amelia Sachs.

She'd sat next to Rhyme in an old armchair. He'd studied her for a moment, looking her up and down. A curious sensation came over her. It wasn't personal perusal – not the way men looked over some women (not her, of course) in bars or on the street. It was the way a senior pilot might study her before their first flight together. Checking her authority, her demeanor, her quickness of thought. Her courage.

She'd pulled her flask from her pocket but Rhyme had shaken his head and suggested eighteen-year-old scotch. "Thom thinks I drink too much," he'd said. "Which I do. But what's life without vices, right?"

She gave a wan laugh. "My father's a purveyor."

"Of booze? Or vice in general?"

"Cigarettes. Executive with U.S. Tobacco in Richmond. Excuse me. They're not called that anymore. It's U.S. Consumer Products or something like that."

There was a flutter of wings outside the window.

"Oh." She'd laughed. "It's a tiercel."

Rhyme had followed her gaze out the window. "A what?"

"A male peregrine. Why's his aerie down here? They nest higher in the city."

"I don't know. I woke up one morning and there they were. You know falcons?"

"Sure."

"Hunt with them?" he asked.

"I used to. I had a tiercel I used for hunting partridge. I got him as an eyas."

"What's that?"

"A young bird in the nest. They're easier to train." She'd examined the nest carefully, a faint smile on her face. "But my best hunter was a haggard – a mature goshawk. Female. They're bigger than the males, better killers. Hard to work with. But she'd take anything – rabbit, hare, pheasant."

"You still have her?"

"Oh, no. One day, she was waiting on – that means hovering, looking for prey. Then she just changed her mind. Let a big fat pheasant get away. Flew into a thermal that took her hundreds of feet up. Disappeared into the sun. I staked bait for a month but she never came back."

"She just vanished?"

"Happens with haggards," she'd said, shrugging unsentimentally. "Hey, they're wild animals. But we had a good six months together." It was this Falcon that had been the inspiration for the Hudson Air logo. Nodding toward the window. "You're lucky for the company. Have you named them?"

Rhyme'd given a scornful laugh. "Not the kind of thing I'd do. Thom tried. I laughed him out of the room."

"Is that officer Sachs really going to arrest me?"

"Oh, I think I can persuade her not to. Say, I have to tell you something."

"Go ahead."

"You have a choice to make, you and Hale. That's what I wanted to talk to you about."

"Choice?"

"We can get you out of town. To a witness protection facility. With the right evasive maneuvers I'm pretty sure we can lose the Dancer and keep you safe for the grand jury."

"But?" she'd asked.

"But he'll keep after you. And even after the grand jury you'll still be a threat to Phillip Hansen because you'll have to testify at trial. That could be months away."

"The grand jury might not indict him, no matter what we say," Percey'd pointed out. "Then there's no point in killing us."

"It doesn't matter. Once the Dancer's been hired to kill someone he doesn't stop until they're dead. Besides, the prosecutors'll go after Hansen for killing your husband and you'll be a witness in that case too. Hansen needs you gone."

"I think I see where you're heading."

He'd cocked an eyebrow.

"Worm on a hook," she'd said.

His eyes had crinkled and he'd laughed. "Well, I'm not going to parade you around in public, just put you into a safe house here in town. Fully guarded. State-of-the-art security. But we'll dig in and keep you there. The Dancer'll surface and we'll stop him, once and for all. It's a crazy idea, but I don't think we have much choice."

Another tipple of the scotch. It wasn't bad. For a product not bottled in Kentucky. "Crazy?" she'd repeated. "Let me ask you a question. You have your role models, Detective? Somebody you admire?"

"Sure. Criminalists. August Vollmer, Edmond Locard."

"Do you know Beryl Markham?"

"No."

"Aviatrix in the thirties and forties. She – not Amelia Earhart – was an idol of mine. She led a very dashing life. British upper class. The *Out of Africa* crowd. She was the first person – not first *woman,* the first person – to fly solo across the Atlantic the hard way, east to west. Lindbergh used tailwinds." She laughed. "Everybody thought *she* was crazy. Newspapers were running editorials begging her not to try the flight. She did, of course."

"And made it?"

"Crash-landed short of the airport, but, yeah, she made it. Well, I don't know if that was brave or crazy. Sometimes I don't think there's any difference."

Rhyme continued. "You'll be pretty safe, but you won't be completely safe."

"Let me tell you something. You know that spooky name? That you call the killer?"

"The Dancer."

"The *Coffin* Dancer. Well, there's a phrase we use in flying jets. The 'coffin corner.' "

"What's that?"

"It's the margin between the speed your plane stalls at and the speed it starts to break apart from Mach turbulence – when you approach the speed of sound. At sea level you've got a couple hundred miles per hour to play with, but at fifty or sixty thousand feet, your stall speed's maybe five hundred knots per hour and your Mach buffet's about five forty. You don't stay within that forty-knots-per-hour margin, you turn the coffin corner and you've had it. Any planes that fly that high have to have autopilots to keep the speed inside the margin. Well, I'll just say that I fly that high all the time and I hardly ever use an autopilot. Completely safe isn't a concept I'm familiar with."

"Then you'll do it."

But Percey didn't answer right away. She scrutinized him for a moment. "There's more to this, isn't there?"

"More?" Rhyme had asked, but the innocence in his voice had been a thin patina.

"I read the *Times* Metro section. You cops don't go all

out like this for just any murderer. What'd Hansen do? He killed a couple of soldiers, and my husband, but you're after him like he's Al Capone."

"I don't give a damn about Hansen," quiet Lincoln Rhyme had said, sitting in his motorized throne, with a body that didn't move and eyes that flickered like dark flames, exactly like the eyes of her hawk. She hadn't told Rhyme that she, like him, would never name a hunting bird, that she'd called the haggard merely, "the falcon."

Rhyme had continued. "I want to get the Dancer. He's killed cops, including two who worked for me. I'm *going* to get him."

Still, she'd sensed there was more. But she hadn't pushed it. "You'll have to ask Brit too."

"Of course."

Finally, she'd said, "All right, I'll do it."

"Thank you. I—"

"But," she interrupted.

"What?"

"There's a condition."

"What's that?" Rhyme lifted an eyebrow, and Percey had been struck by this thought: once you overlooked his damaged body you saw what a handsome man he was. And, yes, yes, realizing that, she felt her old enemy – the familiar cringe of being in the presence of a good-looking man. Hey, Troll Face, Pug Face, Troll, Trollie, Frog Girl, gotta date for Saturday night? Betcha don't . . .

Percey'd said, "That I fly the U.S. Medical charter tomorrow night."

"Oh, I don't think that would be a very good idea."

"It's a deal breaker," she'd said, recalling a phrase Ron and Ed used occasionally.

"Why do *you* have to fly?"

"Hudson Air needs this contract. Desperately. It's a narrow-margin flight and we need the best pilot in the company. That's me."

"What do you mean, narrow margin?"

"Everything's planned out to the nth degree. We're going with minimum fuel. I can't have a pilot wasting time making go-arounds because he's blown the approach or declaring alternates because of minimum conditions." She'd paused, then added, "I am *not* letting my company go down the tubes."

Percey'd said this with an intensity that matched his, but she'd been surprised when he nodded without any protest. "All right," Rhyme said. "I'll agree."

"Then we have a deal." She instinctively reached forward to shake his hand but caught herself.

He'd laughed. "I stick to solely verbal agreements these days." They sipped the scotch to seal the bargain.

Now, early on Sunday morning, she rested her head against the glass of the safe house. There was so much to do. Getting *Foxtrot Bravo* repaired. Preparing the nav log and the flight plan – which alone would take hours. But still, despite her uneasiness, despite her sorrow about Ed, she felt that indescribable sense of pleasure; she'd be flying tonight.

"Hey," a friendly voice drawled.

She turned to see Roland Bell in the doorway.

"Morning," she said.

He walked forward quickly. "You have those curtains open you better be keepin' low as a bedbaby." He tugged the drapes shut.

"Oh. I heard Detective Rhyme was springing some trap. Guaranteed to catch him."

"Well, word is Lincoln Rhyme is all the time right. But I wouldn't trust this particular killer behind a dime. You sleep decent?"

"No," she said. "You?"

"I dozed a couple hours aback," Bell said, peering with sharp eyes out through the curtain. "But I don't need much sleep. Wake up full of git most days. Havin' youngsters does that to you. Now, just you keep that curtain closed. Remember, this *is* New York City, and think what'd happen to my career if you got yourself winged by some gansta shootin' stray bullets in the air. I'd have the dry grins for a week, that happened. Now how about some coffee?"

Here were a dozen punchy clouds reflected in the windows of the old town house this Sunday morning.

Here was a hint of rain.

Here was the Wife standing in a bathrobe at the window, her white face surrounded by dark curly hair mussed from just waking.

And here was Stephen Kall, one block away from the Justice Department's safe house on Thirty-fifth Street, blending into the shadows beneath a water tower on the top of an old apartment building, watching her through his Leica binoculars, the reflection of the clouds swimming across her thin body.

He knew that the glass would be bulletproof and would certainly deflect the first shot. He could place another round within four seconds, but she'd stumble backward in reaction to the shattering glass even if she didn't realize she was being fired at. The odds were he couldn't inflict a mortal wound.

Sir, I will stick to my original plan, sir.

A man appeared beside her and the curtain fell back. Then his face peered through the crack, eyes scanning the rooftops where a sniper would logically be positioned. He looked efficient and dangerous. Stephen memorized his appearance.

Then he ducked behind the facade of the building before he was seen.

The police trick – he guessed it was Lincoln the Worm's idea – about moving the Wife and the Friend into the police precinct building on the West Side hadn't fooled him for more than ten minutes. After listening to the Wife and Ron over the tapped line, he'd simply run a renegade software program – a remote star-69 – he'd downloaded from the warez newsgroup on the Internet. It returned a 212 phone number. Manhattan.

What he'd done next was a long shot.

But how are victories won, Soldier?

By considering every possibility, however improbable, sir.

He logged on to the Net and a moment later was typing the phone number into a reverse phone book, which gave you the address and name of the subscriber. It didn't work with unlisted numbers and Stephen was certain that no one in the federal government would be so stupid as to use a listed number for a safe house.

He was wrong.

The name *James L. Johnson, 258 East 35th Street* popped onto the screen.

Impossible . . .

He then called the Manhattan Federal Building and asked to speak to Mr Johnson. "That'd be James Johnson."

"Hold please, I'll put you through."

"Excuse me," Stephen interrupted. "What department is he in again?"

"That'd be the Justice Department. Facilities Management Office."

Stephen hung up as the call was being transferred.

Once he knew the Wife and Friend were in a safe house on Thirty-fifth Street, he'd stolen some official city maps of the block to plan his assault. Then he'd taken his stroll around the Twentieth Precinct building on the West Side and let himself be seen gazing at the gas pump. After that he'd boosted a gas delivery truck and left plenty of evidence behind so that they'd think he'd be using the truck as a giant gas bomb to take out the witnesses.

And so here was Stephen Kall now, within small-arms range of the Wife and the Friend.

Thinking of the job, trying not to think about the obvious parallel: the face in the window, looking for him.

A little cringey, not too bad. A little wormy.

The curtain closed. Stephen now examined the safe house again.

It was a three-story building unattached to adjacent buildings, the alley like a dark mote around the structure. The walls were brownstone – the hardest building material other than granite or marble to tunnel or blast through – and the windows were blocked with bars that looked like old iron but that Stephen knew were really case-hardened steel and would be wired with motion or decibel sensors or both.

The fire escape was real, but if you looked closely you could see that behind the curtained windows was darkness. Probably sheet steel bolted to the inside frame. He'd found the real fire door – behind a large theatrical poster pasted to the brick. (Why would anyone put up an ad in an alley unless it was to disguise a door?) The alley itself looked like any other in midtown, cobblestone and asphalt, but he could see the glass eyes of security cameras recessed into the walls. Still, there were trash bags and several Dumpsters in the alley that would provide pretty good cover. He could climb into the alley from a window in the office building next door and use the Dumpsters for cover to get to the fire door.

In fact, there was an open window on the first floor of the office building, a curtain blowing in and out. Whoever was monitoring the security screens would have seen the motion and become used to it. Stephen could drop through the window, six feet to the ground, and then move behind the Dumpster and crawl to the fire door.

He also knew they wouldn't be expecting him here – he'd heard the reports of an evacuation of all the buildings near the Twentieth Precinct, so they'd really believed that he'd try to get a gas truck bomb close to the station house.

Evaluate, Soldier.

Sir, my evaluation is that the enemy is relying on both physical structure and anonymity of the premises for defense. I note the absence of large numbers of tactical personnel and I have concluded that a single-person assault on the premises has a good likelihood of success in eliminating one or both of the targets, sir.

Despite the confidence, though, he felt momentarily cringey.

Picturing Lincoln searching for him. Lincoln the Worm. A big lumpy thing, a larva, moist with worm moisture, looking everywhere, seeing through walls, oozing up through cracks.

Looking through windows . . .

Crawling up his leg.

Chewing on his flesh.

Wash 'em off. Wash them off!

Wash what off, Soldier? You still harping on those fucking worms?

Sir, I am . . . Sir, no, sir.

Are you going soft on me, Soldier? Are you feeling like a little pussy *schoolgirl*?

Sir, no sir. I am a knife blade, sir. I am pure death. I have a hard-on to kill, sir!

Breathed deeply. Slowly calmed.

He hid the guitar case containing the Model 40 on the roof, under a wooden water tower. The rest of the equipment he transferred to a large book bag, and then pulled on the Columbia University windbreaker and his baseball cap.

He climbed down the fire escape and disappeared into the alley, feeling ashamed, even scared – not of his enemy's bullets but of the piercing hot gaze of Lincoln the Worm, moving closer, easing slowly but relentlessly through the city, looking for him.

Stephen had planned on an invasive entry, but he didn't have to kill a soul. The office building next to the safe house was empty.

The lobby was deserted and there were no security cameras inside. The main door was wedged partly open with a rubber doorstop and he saw dollies and furniture pads stacked beside it. It was tempting, but he didn't want to run into any movers or tenants, so he stepped outside again and slipped around the corner, away from the safe house. He eased behind a potted pine tree, which hid him from the sidewalk. With his elbow he broke the narrow window leading into a darkened office – of a psychiatrist, it turned out – and climbed in. He stood completely still for five minutes, pistol in hand. Nothing. He then eased silently out the door and into the first-floor corridor of the building.

He paused outside the office he believed was the one with the window opening onto the alley – the one with the blowing curtain. Stephen reached for the doorknob.

But instinct told him to change his plans. He decided to try the basement. He found the stairs and descended into the musty warren of basement rooms.

Stephen worked his way silently toward the side of the building closest to the safe house and pushed open a steel door. He walked into a dimly lit twenty-by-twenty room filled with boxes and old appliances. He found a head-high window that opened onto the alley.

It'd be a tight fit. He'd have to remove the glass and the frame. But once he was out he could slip directly behind a pile of trash bags and in a sniper's low crawl make his way to the fire door of the safe house. Much safer than the window upstairs.

Stephen thought: I've done it.

He'd fooled them all.

Fooled Lincoln the Worm! This gave him as much pleasure as killing the two victims would.

He took a screwdriver from his book bag and began to work the glazier's putty out of the window. The gray wads came away slowly and he was so absorbed in his task that by the time he dropped the screwdriver and got his hand on the butt of his Beretta, the man was on top of him, shoving a pistol into Stephen's neck and telling him in a whisper, "You move an inch and you're dead."

III
CRAFTSMANSHIP

[The falcon] began to fly. To fly: the horrible aerial toad, the silent-feathered owl, the hump-backed aviating Richard III, he made toward me close to the ground. His wings beat with a measured purpose, the two eyes of his low-held head fixed me with a ghoulish concentration.

The Goshawk, T. H. White

19

Short-barrel, probably Colt or Smittie or Dago knockoff, not fired recently. Or oiled.

I smell rust.

And what does a rusty gun tell us, Soldier?

Plenty, sir.

Stephen Kall lifted his hands.

The high, unsteady voice said, "Drop your gun over there. And your walkie-talkie."

Walkie-talkie?

"Come on, do it. I'll blow your brains out." The voice crackled with desperation. He sniffled wetly.

Soldier, do professionals threaten?

Sir, they do not. This man is an amateur. Should we immobilize him?

Not yet. He still represents a threat.

Sir, yessir.

Stephen dropped his gun on a cardboard box.

"Where . . . ? Come on, where's your radio?"

"I don't have a radio," Stephen said.

"Turn around. And don't try anything."

Stephen eased around and found himself looking at a skinny man with darting eyes. He was filthy and looked sick. His nose ran and his eyes were an alarming red. His thick brown hair was matted. And he stank. Homeless, probably. A wino, his stepfather would have called him. Or a hophead.

The old battered snub-nose Colt was thrust forward at Stephen's belly and the hammer was back. It wouldn't take much for the cams to slip, especially if it was old. Stephen smiled a benign smile. He didn't move a muscle. "Look," he said, "I don't want any trouble."

"Where's your radio?!" the man blurted.

"I don't *have* a radio."

The man nervously patted his captive's chest. Stephen could have killed him easily – the man's attention kept wandering. He felt the skittering fingers glide over his body, probing. Finally the man stepped back. "Where's your partner?"

"Who?"

"Don't give me any shit. You know."

Suddenly cringey again. Wormy . . . Something was wrong. "I really don't know what you mean."

"The cop who was just here."

"Cop?" Stephen whispered. "In *this* building?"

The man's rheumy eyes flickered with uncertainty. "Yeah. Aren't you his partner?"

Stephen walked to the window and looked out.

"Hold it. I'll shoot."

"Point that someplace else," Stephen commanded, glancing over his shoulder. No longer worried about slipping cams. He was beginning to see the extent of his mistake. He felt sick to his stomach.

The man's voice cracked as he threatened, "Stop. Right there. I fucking mean it."

"Are they in the alley too?" Stephen asked calmly.

A moment of confused silence. "You really aren't a cop?"

"Are they in the alley too?" Stephen repeated firmly.

The man looked uneasily around the room. "A bunch of them were a while ago. They're the ones put those trash bags there. I don't know 'bout now."

Stephen stared into the alley. The trash bags . . . They'd been left there to lure me out. False cover.

"If you signal anybody, I swear—"

"Oh, be quiet." Stephen scanned the alley slowly, patient as a boa, and finally he saw a faint shadow on the cobblestones – behind a Dumpster. It moved an inch or two.

And on top of the building behind the safe house – on the elevator tower – he saw a ripple of shadow. They were too good to let their gun muzzles show but not good enough to think about blocking the light reflecting upward from the standing water that covered the roof of the building.

Jesus, Lord . . . Somehow Lincoln the Fucking Worm had known that Stephen wouldn't buy the setup about the Twentieth Precinct. They'd been expecting him *here* all along. Lincoln had even figured out his strategy – that Stephen would try to get through the alley from *this* very building.

The face in the window . . .

Stephen suddenly had the absurd idea that it had been Lincoln the Worm in Alexandria, Virginia, standing in the window, lit with rosy light, looking at him. He couldn't have been the one, of course. Still, that impossibility didn't stop the cringey, pukey nausea from unfurling in Stephen's gut.

The chocked door, the open window, and the fluttering curtain . . . a fucking welcome mat. And the alley: a perfect kill zone.

The only thing that had saved him was his instinct.

Lincoln the Worm had set him up.

Who the hell *is* he?

Rage boiled in him. A wave of heat swept over his body. If they were expecting him they'd be following S&S procedures – search and surveillance. Which meant the cop this little shit had seen would be coming back soon to check this room. Stephen spun around to the thin man. "When was the last time the cop checked in here?"

The man's apprehensive eyes flickered, then blossomed with fear.

"Answer me," Stephen snapped, despite the black bore of the Colt pointed at him.

"Ten minutes ago."

"What kind of weapon does he have?"

"I don't know. I guess one of those fancy ones. Like a machine gun."

"Who *are* you?" Stephen asked.

"I don't have to answer your fucking questions," the man said defiantly. He wiped his runny nose on his sleeve. And made the mistake of doing this with his gun hand. In a flash Stephen lifted the gun away from him and shoved the little man to the floor.

"No! Don't hurt me."

"Shut up," Stephen barked. Instinctively he opened the little Colt to see how many rounds were in the cylinder. There were none. "It's empty?" he asked, incredulous.

The man shrugged. "I—"

"You were threatening me with an unloaded weapon?"

"Well . . . See, if they catch you and it's not loaded, they don't put you away for as long."

Stephen didn't understand the point. He thought he might just kill the man for the stupidity of carrying an unloaded gun. "What're you doing here?"

"Just go away and leave me alone," the man whimpered, struggling to climb to his feet.

Stephen dropped the Colt into his pocket then snagged his Beretta and trained it at the man's head. "What are you doing here?"

He wiped his face again. "There're doctors' offices upstairs. And nobody's here on Sunday so I hit 'em for, you know, samples."

"Samples?"

"Doctors get all these free samples of drugs and shit and there's no record, so you can steal as much as you want and nobody knows. Percodan, Fiorinol, diet pills, stuff like that."

But Stephen wasn't listening. He felt the chill of the Worm again. Lincoln was very close.

"Hey, you all right?" the man asked, looking at Stephen's face.

Oddly, the worms went away.

"What's your name?" Stephen asked.

"Jodie. Well, Joe D'Oforio. But everybody, like, calls me Jodie. What's yours?"

Stephen didn't answer. Staring out the window. Another shadow moved on top of the building behind the safe house.

"Okay, Jodie. Listen up. You want to make some money?"

"Well?" Rhyme asked impatiently. "What's going *on*?"

"He's still in the building to the east of the safe house. He hasn't gone into the alley yet." Sellitto reported.

"Why not? He *has* to. There's no reason for him not to. What's the problem?"

"They're checking every floor. He's not in the office we thought he'd go for."

The one with the open window. Damn! Rhyme had debated about leaving the window open, letting the curtain blow in and out, tempting him. But it was too obvious. The Dancer'd become suspicious.

"Everybody's loaded and locked?" Rhyme asked.

"Of course. Relax."

But he couldn't relax. Rhyme hadn't known exactly how the Dancer would try his assault on the safe house. He'd been sure, though, it would be through the alley. He'd hoped that the trash bags and Dumpsters would lull him into thinking there was enough cover to make his approach from that direction. Dellray's agents and Haumann's 32-E teams were surrounding the alley, in the office building itself, and on the buildings around the safe house. Sachs was with Haumann, Sellitto, and Dellray in a fake UPS van parked up the block from the house.

Rhyme had been temporarily fooled by the feint with the supposed gas truck bomb. That the Dancer would drop a tool at a crime scene was improbable but somewhat credible. But then Rhyme grew suspicious about the quantity of detonating cord residue on the clippers. It suggested that Dancer had smeared the blade with explosive to make sure the police thought he'd try an assault on the precinct house with a bomb. He decided that, no, the Dancer hadn't been losing his touch – as he and Sachs had originally thought. Being spotted surveying his intended route of attack and then leaving a guard alive so that the man could call the police and tell them about the theft of the truck – those were intentional.

The final gram tipping the scales, though, was physical evidence. Ammonia bound to a paper fiber. There are only two sources for that combination – old architectural blueprints and land plat maps, which were reproduced by large-sheet ammonia printers. Rhyme had had Sellitto call Police Plaza and ask about break-ins at architectural firms or the county deeds office. A report came back that the recorder's office had been broken into. Rhyme asked them to check East

Thirty-fifth Street, amazing the city guards, who reported that, yes, those plats were missing.

Though how the Dancer'd found out that Percey and Brit were at the safe house and what its address was remained a mystery.

Five minutes ago two ESU officers had found a broken window on the first floor of the office building. The Dancer'd shunned the open front door but had still moved in for the assault on the safe house through the alley just as Rhyme had predicted. But something had spooked him. He was loose in the building and they had no idea where. A poisonous snake in a dark room. Where was he, what was he planning?

Too many ways to die . . .

"He wouldn't wait," Rhyme muttered. "It's too risky." He was growing frantic.

An agent called in, "Nothing on the first floor. We're still making our rounds."

Five minutes passed. Guards checked in with negative reports but all Rhyme really heard was the static rustling in his headset.

Jodie answered, "Who doesn't wanna make money? But I don't know doing what."

"Help me get out of here."

"I mean, what're you doing here? Are they looking for *you*?"

Stephen looked the sad little man up and down. A loser, but not crazy or stupid. Stephen decided it was best tactically to be honest. Besides, the man'd be dead in a few hours anyway.

He said, "I've come here to kill somebody."

"Whoa. Like, are you in the Mafia or something? Who're you gonna kill?"

"Jodie, be quiet. We're in a tough situation here."

"*We?* I didn't do anything,"

"Except you're at the wrong place at the wrong time," Stephen said. "And that's too bad, but you're in the same situation I am because they want me and they aren't going to believe you're not with me. Now, you gonna help me or not? All I've got time for is yes or no."

Jodie tried not to look scared, but his eyes betrayed him.

"Yes. Or. No."

"I don't want to get hurt."

"If you're on my side you'll never get hurt. One thing I'm good at is making sure who gets hurt and who doesn't."

"And you'll pay me? Money? Not a check."

Stephen had to laugh. "Not a check. No. Cash."

The jelly beans of eyes were considering something. "How much?"

The little crud was negotiating.

"Five thousand."

The fear remained in the eyes but it was pushed aside by shock. "For real? You're not shitting me?"

"No."

"What if I get you out and you kill me so you don't have to pay?"

Stephen laughed again. "I'm getting paid a lot more than that. Five's nothing to me. Anyway, if we get out of here I could use your help again."

"I—"

A sound in the distance. Footsteps coming closer.

It was the S&S cop, looking for him.

Just one, Stephen could tell, listening to the steps. Made sense. They'd be expecting him to go for the first floor office with the open window, where Lincoln the Worm would've stationed most of the troopers.

Stephen replaced the pistol in his book bag and pulled out his knife. "You going to help me?"

A no-brainer, of course. If Jodie didn't help he'd be dead in sixty seconds. And he knew it.

"Okay." He extended his hand.

Stephen ignored it and asked, "How do we get out?"

"See those cinder blocks there. You can pull 'em out. See, there? It leads to an old tunnel. There're these delivery tunnels going underneath the city. Nobody knows about them."

"There are?" Stephen wished he'd known it before.

"I can get us to the subway. That's where I live. This old subway station."

It was two years since Stephen had worked with a partner. Sometimes he wished he hadn't killed the man.

Jodie started toward the concrete blocks.

"No," Stephen whispered. "Here's what I want you to do. You stand against that wall. There." He pointed to a wall opposite the doorway.

"But he'll see me. He checks in here with his flashlight and I'll be the first thing he'll see!"

"Just stand there and put your hands up."

"He'll shoot me," Jodie whimpered.

"No, he won't. You've got to trust me."

"But . . ." His eyes darted toward the door. He wiped his face.

Is this man going to buckle, Soldier?

That is a risk, sir, but I've considered the odds and I think he won't. This is a man who wants money badly.

"You'll have to trust me."

Jodie sighed. "Okay, okay . . ."

"Make sure your hands are up or he *will* shoot."

"Like this?" He lifted his arms.

"Step back so your face is in the shadows. Yeah, like that. I don't want him to see your face . . . Good. Perfect."

The footsteps were coming closer now. Walking softly. Hesitating.

Stephen touched his fingers to his lips and went prone, disappearing into the floor.

The footsteps grew soft and then paused. The figure appeared in the doorway. He was in body armor and wore an FBI windbreaker.

He pushed into the room, scanning with the flashlight attached to the end of his H&K. When the beam caught Jodie's midriff he did something that astonished Stephen.

He started to pull the trigger.

It was very subtle. But Stephen had shot so many animals and so many people that he knew the ripple of muscles, the tension of stance, just before you fired your weapon.

Stephen moved fast. He leapt up, lifting the machine gun away and breaking off the agent's stalk microphone. Then he drove his k-bar knife up under the agent's triceps, paralyzing his right arm. The man cried out in pain.

They're green-lighted to kill! Stephen thought. No surrender pitch. They see me, they shoot. Armed or not.

Jodie cried, "Oh, my God!" He stepped forward uncertainly, hands still airborne – almost comically.

Stephen knocked the agent to his knees and pulled his Kevlar helmet over his eyes, gagged him with a rag.

"Oh, God, you stabbed him," Jodie said, lowering his arms and walking forward.

"Shut up," Stephen said. "What we talked about. The exit."

"But—"

"Now."

Jodie just stared.

"Now!" Stephen raged.

Jodie ran to the hole in the wall as Stephen pulled the agent to his feet and led him into the the corridor.

Green-lighted to kill . . .

Lincoln the Worm had decided he'd die. Stephen was furious.

"Wait there," he ordered Jodie.

Stephen plugged the headset back into the man's transceiver and listened. They were on the Special Operations channel and there must have been a dozen or so cops and agents, calling in as they searched different parts of the building.

He didn't have much time, but he had to slow them up.

Stephen led the dazed agent out into the yellow hallway.

He pulled out his knife again.

20

"Damn. *Damn!*" Rhyme snapped, flecking his chin with spittle. Thom stepped up to the chair and wiped it, but Rhyme angrily shook him away.

"Bo?" he called into his microphone.

"Go ahead," Haumann said from the command van.

"I think somehow he made us and's going to fight his way out. Tell your agents to form defensive teams. I don't want anybody alone. Move everybody into the building. I think—"

"Hold on . . . Hold on. Oh, no . . ."

"Bo? Sachs? . . . Anybody?"

But nobody answered.

Rhyme heard shouting voices through the radio. The transmission was cut off. Then staccato bursts: ". . . assistance. We've got a blood trail . . . In the office building. Right, right . . . no . . . downstairs . . . Basement. Innelman's not reporting in. He was . . . basement. All units move, move. Come on, *move!* . . ."

Rhyme called, "Bell, you hear me? Double up on the principals. Do not, repeat, do not leave them unguarded. The Dancer's loose and we don't know where he is."

Roland Bell's calm voice came over the line. "Got 'em under our wing. Nobody's getting in here."

An infuriating wait. Unbearable. Rhyme wanted to scream with frustration.

Where was he?

A snake in a dark room . . .

Then one by one the troopers and agents called in, telling

Haumann and Dellray that they'd secured one floor after another.

Finally, Rhyme heard: "Basement's secure. But Jesus Lord there's a lot of blood down here. And Innelman's gone. We can't find him! Jesus, all this blood!"

"Rhyme, can you hear me?"

"Go ahead."

"I'm in the basement of the office building," Amelia Sachs said into her stalk mike, looking around her.

The walls were filthy yellow concrete and the floors were painted battleship gray. But you hardly noticed the decor of the dank place; blood spatter was everywhere, like a horrific Jackson Pollock painting.

The poor agent, she thought. Innelman. Better find him fast. Someone bleeding this much couldn't last more than fifteen minutes.

"You have the kit?" Rhyme asked her.

"We don't have time! All the blood, we've got to find him!"

"Steady, Sachs. The kit. Open the kit."

She sighed. "All right! Got it."

The crime scene blood kit contained a ruler, protractor with string attached, tape measure, the Kastle-Meyer Reagent presumptive field test. Luminol too – which detects iron oxide residue of blood even when a perp scrubs away all visual trace.

"It's just a mess, Rhyme," she said. "I'm not going to be able to figure out anything."

"Oh, the scene'll tell us more than you think, Sachs. It'll tell us plenty."

Well, if anybody could make sense of this macabre setting, it would be Rhyme; she knew that he and Mel Cooper were long-standing members of the International Association of Blood Pattern Analysts. (She didn't know which was more disturbing – the gruesome blood spatter at crime scenes or the fact that there was a group of people who specialized in the subject.) But this seemed hopeless.

"We've got to *find* him . . ."

"Sachs, calm down . . . You with me?"

After a moment she said, "Okay."

"All you need for now is the ruler," he said. "First, tell me what you see."

"There're drips all over the place here."

"Blood spatter's very revealing. But it's meaningless unless the surface it's on is uniform. What's the floor like?"

"Smooth concrete."

"Good. How big are the drops? Measure them."

"He's *dying,* Rhyme."

"How *big*?" he snapped.

"All different sizes. There're hundreds of them about three-quarters of an inch. Some are bigger. About an inch and a quarter. Thousands of very little ones. Like a spray."

"Forget the little ones. They're 'overcast' drops, satellites of the others. Describe the biggest ones. Shape?"

"Mostly round."

"Scalloped edges?"

"Yes,' she muttered. "But there are some that just have smooth edges. Here're some in front of me. They're a little smaller, though."

Where *is* he? she wondered. Innelman. A man she'd never met. Missing and bleeding like a fountain.

"Sachs?"

"What?" she snapped.

"What about the smaller drops? Tell me about them."

"We don't have time to do this!"

"We don't have time *not* to," he said calmly.

God damn you, Rhyme, she thought, then said, "All right." She measured. "They're about a half inch. Perfectly round. No scalloped edges . . ."

"Where are those?" he asked urgently. "At one end of the corridor, or the other?"

"Mostly in the middle. There's a storeroom at the end of the hall. Inside there and near it they're bigger and have ragged or scalloped edges. At the other end of the corridor, they're smaller."

"Okay, okay," Rhyme said absently, then he announced, "Here's the story . . . What's the agent's name?"

"Innelman. John Innelman. He's a friend of Dellray's."

"The Dancer got Innelman in the storeroom, stabbed him once, high. Debilitated him, probably arm or neck. Those are the big, uneven drops. Then he led him down the corridor, stabbing him again, lower. Those are the smaller, rounder ones. The shorter the distance blood falls, the more even the edges."

"Why'd he do that?" she gasped.

"To slow us down. He knows we'll look for a wounded agent before we start after him."

He's right, she thought, but we're not looking *fast* enough!

"How long's the corridor?"

She sighed, looked down it. "About fifty feet, give or take, and the blood trail covers the whole thing."

"Any footprints in the blood?"

"Dozens. They go everywhere. Wait . . . There's a service elevator. I didn't see it at first. That's where the trail leads! He must be inside. We have to—"

"No, Sachs, wait. That's too obvious."

"We have to get the elevator door open. I'm calling the Fire Department for somebody with a Halligan tool or an elevator key. They can—"

Calmly Rhyme said, "Listen to me. Do the drops leading to the elevator look like teardrops? With the tails pointing in different directions?"

"He's got to be in the elevator! There's smears on the door. He's dying, Rhyme! Will you listen to me!"

"Teardrops, Sachs?" he asked soothingly. "Do they look like tadpoles?"

She looked down. They did. Perfect tadpoles, with the tails pointing in a dozen different directions.

"Yeah, Rhyme. They do."

"Backtrack until those stop."

This was crazy. Innelman was bleeding out in the elevator shaft. She gazed at the metal door for a moment, thought about ignoring Rhyme, but then trotted back down the corridor.

To the place where they stopped.

"Here, Rhyme. They stop here."

"It's at a closet or door?"

"Yes, how'd you know?"

"And it's bolted from the outside?"

"That's right."

How the hell does he *do* it?

"So the search team'd see the bolt and pass it by – the Dancer couldn't very well bolt himself inside. Well, Innelman's in there. Open the door, Sachs. Use the pliers on the handle, not the knob itself. There's a chance we can lift a print. And Sachs?"

"Yes?"

"I don't think he left a bomb. He hardly had time. But whatever shape the agent's in, and it won't be good, ignore him for a minute and look for any traps first."

"Okay."

"Promise?"

"Yes."

Pliers out . . . unbolt the latch . . . twist the knob.

Glock up. Apply poundage. Now!

The door flew outward.

But there was no bomb or other trap. Just the pale, blood-slicked body of John Innelman, unconscious, tumbling to her feet.

She barked a soft scream. "He's here. Need medics! He's cut bad."

Sachs bent over him. Two EMS techs and more agents ran up, Dellray with them, grim faced.

"What'd he do to you, John? Oh, man." The lanky agent stood back while the medics went to work. They cut off much of his clothing and examined the stab wounds. Innelman's eyes were half open, glazed.

"Is he . . . ?" Dellray asked.

"Alive, just barely."

The medics slapped pads on the slashes, put a tourniquet on his leg and arm, and then ran a plasma line. "Get him in the bus. We gotta move. I mean, move!"

They placed the agent on a gurney and hurried down the corridor, Dellray with him, head down, muttering to himself and squeezing his dead cigarette between his fingers.

"Could he talk?" Rhyme asked. "Any clue where the Dancer went?"

"No. He was unconscious. I don't know if they can save him. Jesus."

"Don't get rattled, Sachs. We've got a crime scene to analyze. We *have* to find out where the Dancer is, if he's still around. Go back to the storeroom. See if there are exterior doors or windows."

As she walked to it she asked, "How'd you know about the closet?"

"Because of the direction of the drops. He shoved Innelman inside and soaked a rag in the cop's blood. He walked to the elevator, swinging the rag. The drops were moving in different directions when they fell. So they had a teardrop appearance. And since he tried leading us to the elevator, we should look in the opposite direction for his escape route. The storeroom. Are you there?"

"Yes."

"Describe it."

"There's a window looking out on the alley. Looks like he started to open it. But it's puttied shut. No doors." She looked out the window. "I can't see any of the trooper's positions, though. I don't know what tipped him."

"*You* can't see any of the troopers," Rhyme said cynically. "He could. Now, walk the grid and let's see what we find."

She searched the scene carefully, walking the grid, then vacuumed for trace and carefully bagged the filters.

"What do you see? Anything?"

She shone her light on the walls and she found two mismatched blocks. A tight squeeze, but someone limber could have fit through there.

"Got his exit route, Rhyme. He went through the wall. Some loose concrete blocks."

"Don't open it. Get SWAT there."

She called several agents down to the room and they pulled the blocks out, sweeping the inner chamber with flashlights mounted on the barrels of their H&K submachine guns.

"Clear," one agent called. Sachs drew her weapon and slipped into the cool, dank space.

It was a narrow declining ramp filled with rubble, leading through a hole in the foundation. Water dripped. She was careful to step on large chunks of concrete and leave the damp earth untouched.

"What do you see, Sachs? Tell me!"

She waved the PoliLight wand over the places where the Dancer would logically have gripped with his hands and stepped with his feet. "Whoa, Rhyme."

"What?"

"Fingerprints. Fresh latents . . . Wait. But here're the glove prints too. In blood. From holding the rag. I don't get it. It's like a cave . . . Maybe he took the gloves off for some reason. Maybe he thought he was safe in the tunnel."

Then she looked down and shone the eerie glow of yellow-green light at her feet. "Oh."

"What?"

"They're not his prints. He's with somebody else."

"Somebody else? How do you know?"

"There's another set of footprints too. They're both fresh. One bigger than the other. They go off in the same direction, running. Jesus, Rhyme."

"What's the matter?"

"It means he's got a partner."

"Come on, Sachs. The glass is half full." Rhyme added cheerfully, "It means we'll have twice as much evidence to help us track him down."

"I was thinking," she said darkly, "that it meant he'd be twice as dangerous."

"What've you got?" Lincoln Rhyme asked.

Sachs had returned to his town house and she and Mel Cooper were looking over the evidence collected at the scene. Sachs and SWAT had followed the footsteps into a Con Ed access tunnel, where they lost track of both the Dancer and his companion. It looked as if the men had climbed to the street and escaped through a manhole.

She gave Cooper the print she'd found in the entrance to the tunnel. He scanned it into the computer and sent it off to the feds for an AFIS search.

Then she held up two electrostatic prints for Rhyme to examine. "These're the footprints in the tunnel. This one's the Dancer's." She lifted one of the prints – transparent, like an X ray. "It matches a print in the shrink's office he broke into on the first floor."

"Wearing average ordinary factory shoes," Rhyme said.

"You'd think he'd be in combat boots," Sellitto muttered.

"No, those'd be too obvious. Work shoes have rubber soles for gripping and steel caps in the toes. They're as good as boots if you don't need ankle support. Hold the other one closer, Sachs."

The smaller shoes were very worn at the heel and the ball of the foot. There was a large hole in the right shoe and through it you could see a lattice of skin wrinkles.

"No socks. Could be his friend's homeless."

"Why's he got somebody with him?" Cooper asked.

"Don't know," Sellitto said. "Word is he always works alone. He uses people but he doesn't trust them."

Just what I've been accused of, Rhyme thought. He said, "And leaving fingerprints at the scene? This guy's no pro. He must have something the Dancer needs."

"A way out of the building, for one thing," Sachs suggested.

"That could be it."

"And's probably dead now," she suggested.

Probably, Rhyme agreed silently.

"The prints," Cooper said. "They're pretty small. I'd guess size eight male."

The size of the sole doesn't necessarily correspond to shoe size and provides even less insight into the stature of the person wearing them, but it was reasonable to conclude the Dancer's partner had a slight build.

Turning to the trace evidence, Cooper mounted samples onto a slide and slipped it under the compound 'scope. He patched the image through to Rhyme's computer.

"Command mode, cursor left," Rhyme ordered into his microphone. "Stop. Double click." He examined the computer monitor. "More of the mortar from the cinder block. Dirt and dust . . . Where'd you get this, Sachs?"

"I scraped it from around the cinder blocks and vacuumed the floor of the tunnel. I also found a nest behind some boxes where it looked like somebody'd been hiding."

"Good. Okay, Mel, gas it. There's a lot of stuff here I don't recognize."

The chromatograph rumbled, separating the compounds, and sent the resulting vapors to the spectrometer for identification. Cooper examined the screen.

He exhaled a surprised breath. "I'm surprised his friend's able to walk at all."

"Little more specific there, Mel."

"He's a drug store, Lincoln. We've got secobarbital, phenobarbital, Dexedrine, amobarbital, meprobamate, chlordiazepoxide, diazepam."

"Jesus," Sellitto muttered. "Reds, dexies, blue devils . . ."

Cooper continued, "Lactose and sucrose too. Calcium, vitamins, enzymes consistent with dairy products."

"Baby formula," Rhyme muttered. "Dealers use it to cut drugs."

"So the Dancer's got himself a cluckhead for a sidekick. Go figure."

Sachs said, "All those doctors' offices there . . . This guy must've been boosting pills."

"Log onto FINEST," Rhyme said. "Get a list of every drugstore cowboy they've got."

Sellitto laughed. "It's gonna be big as the White Pages, Lincoln."

"Nobody says it's easy, Lon."

But before he could make the call, Cooper received an E-mail. "Don't bother."

"Huh?"

"The AFIS report on the fingerprints?" The tech tapped the screen. "Whoever the guy is, he doesn't have a record in New York City or State or NCIC."

"Hell!" Rhyme snapped. He felt cursed. Couldn't it be just a little easier? He muttered, "Any other trace?"

"Something here," Cooper said. "A bit of blue tile, grouted on the back, attached to what looks like concrete."

"Let's see it."

Cooper mounted the specimen onto the 'scope's stage.

His neck quivering, almost breaking into a spasm, Rhyme leaned forward and studied it carefully. "Okay. Old mosaic tile. Porcelain, crackle finish, lead based. Sixty, seventy years old, I'd guess." But he could make no cunning deductions from the sample. "Anything else?" he muttered.

"Some hairs." Cooper mounted them to do a visual. He bent over the 'scope.

Rhyme too examined the thin shafts.

"Animal," he announced.

"More cats?" Sachs asked.

"Let's see," Cooper said, head down.

But these hairs weren't feline. They were rodent. "Rat," Rhyme announced. "*Rattus norvegicus*. Your basic sewer rat."

"Keep going. What's in that bag, Sachs?" Rhyme asked like a hungry boy looking over chocolates in a candy store display case. "No, no. There. Yes, that one."

Inside the evidence bag was a square of paper towel smeared with a faint brown stain.

"I found that on the cinder block, the one he moved. I think it was on his hands. There were no prints but the pattern could've been made by a palm."

"Why do you think that?"

"Because I rubbed my hand in some dirt and pushed on another cinder block. The mark was the same."

That's my Amelia, he thought. For an instant his thoughts returned to last night – the two of them lying in bed together. He pushed the thought away.

"What is it, Mel?"

"Looks like it's grease. Impregnated with dust, dirt, fragments of wood, bits of organic material. Animal flesh, I think. All very old. And look there in the upper corner."

Rhyme examined some silvery flecks on his computer screen. "Metal. Ground or shaved off of something. Gas it. Let's find out for certain."

Cooper did.

"Petrochemical," he answered. "Crudely refined, no additives . . . There's iron with traces of manganese, silicon, and carbon."

"Wait," Rhyme called. "Any other elements – chromium, cobalt, copper, nickel, tungsten?"

"No."

Rhyme gazed at the ceiling. "The metal? It's old steel, made from pig iron in a Bessemer furnace. If it were modern it'd have some of those other materials in it."

"And here's something else. Coal tar."

"Creosote!" Rhyme cried. "I've got it. The Dancer's first big mistake. His partner's a walking road map."

"To where?" Sachs asked.

"To the subway. That grease is old, the steel's from old fixtures and tie spikes, the creosote's from the ties. Oh, and the fragment of tile is from a mosaic. A lot of the old stations were tiled – they had pictures of something that related to the neighborhood."

Sachs said, "Sure – the Astor Place station's got mosaics of the animals that John Jacob Astor traded."

"Grouted porcelain tile. So that's what the Dancer wanted him for. A place to hide out. The Dancer's friend's probably a homeless druggie living in an abandoned siding or tunnel or station somewhere."

Rhyme realized that everyone was looking at a man's shadow in the doorway. He stopped speaking.

"Dellray?" Sellitto said uncertainly.

The dark, somber face of Fred Dellray was focused out the window.

"What is it?" Rhyme asked.

"Innelman's what it is. They stitched him up. Three hundred stitches they gave him. But it was too late. Lost too much blood. He just died."

"I'm sorry," Sachs said.

The agent lifted his hands, long sticklike fingers raised like spikes.

Everyone in the room knew about Dellray's longtime partner – the one killed in the Oklahoma City federal building bombing. And Rhyme thought too of Tony Panelli – 'napped downtown a few days ago. Probably dead by now, the only clue to his whereabouts the grains of curious sand.

And now another of Dellray's friends was gone.

The agent paced in a threatening lope.

"You know why he got cut, don't you – Innelman?"

Everyone knew; no one answered.

"A diversion. That's the only reason in the world. To keep us off the scent. Can you believe that? A fuckin' di-version." He stopped pacing abruptly. He looked at Rhyme with his frightening black eyes. "You got any leads at all, Lincoln?"

"Not much." He explained about the Dancer's homeless friend, the drugs, the hidey-hole in the subway. Somewhere.

"That's it?"

"Afraid so. But we still have some more evidence to look at."

"Evidence," Dellray whispered contemptuously. He walked to the door, paused. "A distraction. That's no fucking reason for a good man to die. No reason at all."

"Fred, wait . . . we need you."

But the agent didn't hear, or he ignored Rhyme if he did. He stalked out of the room.

A moment later the door downstairs closed with a sharp click.

21

"Home, sweet home," Jodie said.

A mattress and two boxes of old clothes, canned food. Magazines – *Playboy* and *Penthouse* and some cheap hard-core porn, which Stephen glanced at distastefully. A book or two. The fetid subway station where Jodie lived, somewhere downtown, had been closed decades ago and replaced by one up the street.

A good place for worms, Stephen thought grimly, then pried the image from his mind.

They'd entered the small station from the platform below. They'd made their way here – probably two or three miles from the safe house – completely underground, moving through the basements of buildings, tunnels, huge sewer pipes, and small sewer pipes. Leaving a false lead – an open manhole cover. Finally they'd entered the subway tunnel and made good time, though Jodie was pathetically out of shape and gasped for breath trying to keep up with Stephen's frantic pace.

There was a door leading out to the street, barred from the inside. Slanting lines of dusty light fell through the slats in the boards. Stephen peered outside into the grim spring overcast. It was a poor part of town. Derelicts sat on street corners, bottles of Thunderbird and Colt 44 were strewn on the sidewalk, and the polka dots of crack vial caps were everywhere. A huge rat chewed something gray in the alley.

Stephen heard a clatter behind him and turned to see Jodie dropping a handful of stolen pills into coffee cans.

He was hunched over, carefully organizing them. Stephen dug through his book bag and found his cell phone. He made a call to Sheila's apartment. He was expecting to hear her answering machine, but a recording came on that said the line was out of order.

Oh, no . . .

He was stunned.

It meant that the antipersonnel satchel had gone off in Sheila's apartment. And *that* meant they'd found out he'd been there. How the hell had they done that?

"You all right?" Jodie asked.

How?

Lincoln, King of the Worms. That's how!

Lincoln, the white, wormy face peering out the window . . .

Stephen's palms began to sweat.

"Hey?"

Stephen looked up.

"You seem—"

"I'm fine," Stephen answered shortly.

Stop worrying, he told himself. If it blew, the explosion was big enough to hose the apartment and destroy any trace of him. It's all right. You're safe. They'll never find you, never tie you down. The worms won't get you . . .

He looked at Jodie's easy smile of curiosity. The cringe went away. "Nothing," he said. "Just a change of plans." He hung up.

Stephen opened his book bag again, counted out $5,000. "Here's the money."

Jodie was transfixed by the cash. His eyes flipped back and forth between the bills and Stephen's face. The thin hand reached out, shaking, and took the five thousand carefully, as if it might crumble if he held it too hard.

As he gripped the bills Jodie's hand touched Stephen's. Even through the glove the killer felt a huge jolt – like the time he'd been stabbed in the gut with a razor knife – stunning but painless. Stephen let go of the money and, looking away, said, "If you'll help me again I'll pay you another ten."

The man's red, puffy face broke into a cautious smile. He took a deep breath, and poked through one of his coffee cans.

"I get . . . I don't know . . . nervous, sort of." He found a pill, swallowed it. "It's a blue devil. Makes you feel nice. Makes you feel all comfy. Want one?"

"Uhm . . ."

Soldier, do men take a drink occasionally?

Sir, I don't know, sir.

Well, they do. Here, have one.

"I don't think I—"

Take a drink, Soldier. That's an order.

Well, sir—

You're not a pussy girl, are you, Soldier? You have titties?

I . . . Sir, I do not, sir.

Then drink, Soldier.

Sir, yessir.

Jodie repeated, "You want one?"

"No," Stephen whispered.

Jodie closed his eyes and lay back. "Ten . . . thousand . . ." After a moment he asked, "You killed him, didn't you?"

"Who?" Stephen asked.

"Back there, that cop? Hey, you want some orange juice?"

"That agent in the basement? *Maybe* I killed him. I don't know. That wasn't the point."

"Was it hard to do? Like, I don't mean anything, I'm just curious. Orange juice? I drink a lot of it. Pills make you thirsty. Your mouth gets all dry."

"No." The can looked dirty. Maybe worms had crawled on it. Maybe crawled *inside*. You could drink a worm and never know it . . . He shivered. "Do you have running water here?"

"No. But I have some bottles. Poland Spring. I stole a case from A&P."

Cringey.

"I need to wash my hands."

"You do?"

"To get the blood off them. It soaked through the gloves."

"Oh. It's right there. Why do you wear gloves all the time? Fingerprints?"

"That's right."

"You were in the army, right? I knew it."

Stephen was about to lie, changed his mind suddenly. He said, "No. I was almost in the army. Well, the marines. I was going to join. My stepfather was a marine and I was going in like him."

"Semper Fi."

"Right."

There was silence and Jodie was looking at him expectantly. "What happened?"

"I tried to enlist but they wouldn't let me in."

"That's stupid. Wouldn't *let* you? You'd make a great soldier." Jodie was looking Stephen up and down, nodding. "You're strong. Great muscles. I" – he laughed – "I don't hardly get any exercise, 'cept running from niggers or kids want to mug me. And they always catch me anyway. You're handsome too. Like soldiers ought to be. Like the soldiers in movies."

Stephen felt the wormy feeling going away and, my God, he started blushing. He stared at the floor. "Well, I don't know about that."

"Come on. Your girlfriend thinks you're handsome, bet."

Little cringey here. Worms starting to move.

"Well, I—"

"Don't you have a girlfriend?"

Stephen asked, "You got that water?"

Jodie pointed to the box of Poland Spring. Stephen opened two bottles and began washing his hands. Normally he hated people watching him do this. When people watched him wash he kept being cringey and the worms never went away. But for some reason he didn't mind Jodie watching.

"No girlfriend, huh?"

"Not right now," Stephen explained carefully. "It's not like I'm a homo or anything, if you were wondering."

"I wasn't."

"I don't believe in that cult. Now, I don't think my stepfather was right – that AIDS is God's way of getting rid of homosexual people. Because if that's what God wanted to do he'd be smart and just get rid of them, the faggots, I mean. Not make there be a risk that normal people might get sick too."

"That makes sense," Jodie said from his hazy plateau.

"I don't have one either, a girlfriend." He laughed bitterly. "Well, how could I? Right? What've I got? I'm not good-looking like you, I don't have any money . . . I'm just a fucking junkie is all."

Stephen felt his face burn hot and he washed harder.

Scrub that skin, yes, yes, yes . . .

Worms, worms, go away . . .

Looking at his hands Stephen continued. "The fact is I've been in a situation lately where I haven't really . . . where I haven't been as interested in women as most men are. But it's just a temporary condition."

"Temporary," Jodie repeated.

Eyes watching the bar of soap, as if it were a prisoner trying to escape.

"Temporary. Owing to my necessary vigilance. In my work, I mean."

"Sure. Your vigilance."

Scrub, scrub, the soap lathered like thunderheads.

"Have you ever killed a faggot?" Jodie asked, curious.

"I don't know. I'll tell you I've never killed anybody *because* he's a homosexual. That would make no sense." Stephen's hands tingled and buzzed. He scrubbed harder, not looking at Jodie. He suddenly felt swollen with an odd feeling – of talking to someone who might just understand him. "See, I don't kill people just to kill them."

"Okay," Jodie said. "But what if some drunk came up to you on the street and pushed you around and called you, I don't know, a motherfucking faggot? You'd kill him, right? Say you could get away with it."

"But . . . well, a faggot wouldn't want to have sex with his mother now, would he?"

Jodie blinked then laughed. "That's pretty good."

Did I just make a joke? Stephen wondered. He smiled, pleased that Jodie'd been impressed.

Jodie continued, "Okay, let's say he just called you a motherfucker."

"Of course I wouldn't kill him. And I'll tell you this, if you're talking about faggots let's talk about Negroes and Jewish people too. I wouldn't kill a Negro unless I'd been hired to kill somebody who happened to be a Negro. There are probably reasons why Negroes shouldn't live, or at least shouldn't live here in this country. My stepfather had a lot of reasons for that. I'm pretty much in accord with him. He felt the same about Jewish people, but there I disagree. Jewish people make very good soldiers. I respect them."

He continued. "See, killing's a business, that's all it is. Look at Kent State. I was just a kid then, but my stepfather told me about it. You know Kent State? Those students got shot by the National Guard?"

"Sure. I know."

"Now, come on, nobody really cared that those students died, right? But to me it was stupid shooting them. Because what purpose did it serve? None. If you wanted to stop the movement, or whatever it was, you should've targeted the leaders and taken them out. It would've been so easy. Infiltrate, evaluate, delegate, isolate, eliminate."

"That's how you kill people?"

"You infiltrate the area. Evaluate the difficulty of the kill and the defenses. You delegate the job of diverting everyone's attention from the victim – make it look like you're coming at them from one way but it turns out that it's just a delivery boy or shoe shine boy or something, and meanwhile you've come up behind the victim. Then you isolate him, and eliminate him."

Jodie sipped his orange juice. There were dozens of empty orange juice cans piled in the corner. It seemed to be all he lived on. "You know," he said, wiping his mouth on his sleeve, "you think professional killers'd be crazy. But you don't seem crazy."

"I don't think I'm crazy," Stephen said matter-of-factly.

"The people you kill, are they bad? Like crooks and Mafia people and things?"

"Well, they've done something bad to people who pay me to kill them."

"Which means they're bad?"

"Sure."

Jodie laughed dopily, eyelids half closed. "Well, some people'd say that's not exactly how you, you know, figure out what's good or bad."

"Okay, what *is* good and bad?" Stephen responded. "I

don't do anything different than God does. Good people die and bad people die in a train wreck and nobody gets on God's case because of it. Some professional killers call their victims 'targets' or 'subjects.' One guy I heard about calls them 'corpses.' Even before he kills them. Like, 'The corpse is leaving his car. I'm targeting him.' It's easier for him to think of the victims that way, I guess. Me, I don't care. I call 'em what they are. Who I'm after now are the Wife and the Friend. I already killed the Husband. That's how I think of them. They're people I kill, is all. No big deal."

Jodie considered what he'd heard and said, "You know something? I don't think you're evil. You know why?"

"Why's that?"

"Because evil is something that looks innocent but turns out to be bad. The thing about you is you're exactly what you are. I think that's good."

Stephen flicked his scrubbed fingernails with a click. He felt himself blushing again. Hadn't done that for years. Finally, he asked, "I scare you, don't I?"

"No," Jodie said. "I wouldn't want to have you against me. No sir, I wouldn't want that. But I feel like we're friends. I don't think you'd hurt me."

"No," Stephen said. "We're partners."

"You talked about your stepfather. He still alive?"

"No, he died."

"I'm sorry. When you mentioned him I was thinking about my father – he's dead too. He said the thing he respected most in the world was craftsmanship. He liked watching a talented man do what he did best. That's kind of like you."

"Craftsmanship," Stephen repeated, feeling swollen with inexplicable feelings. He watched Jodie hide the cash in a slit in his filthy mattress. "What're you going to do with the money?"

Jodie sat up and looked at Stephen with dumb but earnest eyes. "Can I show you something?" The drugs made his voice slurred.

"Sure."

He lifted a book out of his pocket. The title was *Dependent No More.*

"I stole it from this bookstore on Saint Marks Place. It's for people who don't want to be, you know, alcoholics or drug addicts anymore. It's pretty good. It mentions these clinics you can go to. I found this place in New Jersey. You go in there and you spend a month – a whole month – but you come out and you're clean. They say it really works."

"That's good of you," Stephen said. "I approve of that."

"Yeah, well," Jodie curled up his face. "It costs fourteen thousand."

"No shit."

"For *one* month. Can you believe that?"

"Somebody's making some bucks there." Stephen made $150,000 for a hit, but he didn't share this information with Jodie, his newfound friend and partner.

Jodie sighed, wiped his eyes. The drugs had made him weepy, it seemed. Like Stephen's stepfather when he drank. "My whole life's been so messed up," he said. "I went to college. Oh, yeah. Didn't do too bad either. I taught for a while. Worked for a company. Then I lost my job. Everything went bad. Lost my apartment . . . I'd always had a pill problem. Started stealing . . . Oh, hell . . ."

Stephen sat down next to him. "You'll get your money and go into that clinic there. Get your life turned around."

Jodie smiled blearily at him. "My father had this thing he said, you know? When there was something you had to do that was hard. He said don't think about the hard part as a problem, just think about it as a factor. Like something to consider. He'd look me in the eye and say, 'It's not a problem, it's just a factor.' I keep trying to remember that."

"Not a problem, just a factor," Stephen repeated. "I like that."

Stephen put his hand on Jodie's leg to prove that he really did like it.

Soldier, what the fuck are you doing?

Sir, busy at the moment, sir. Will report in later.

Soldier—

Later, *sir*!

"Here's to you," Jodie said.

"No, to you," Stephen said.

And they toasted, mineral water and orange juice, to their strange alliance.

22

A labyrinth.

The New York City subway system extends for over 250 miles and incorporates more than a dozen separate tunnels that crisscross four of the five boroughs (Staten Island only being excluded, though the islanders, of course, have a famous ferry of their very own).

A satellite could find a sailboat adrift in the North Atlantic quicker than Lincoln Rhyme's team could locate two men hiding in the New York subway.

The criminalist, Sellitto, Sachs, and Cooper were poring over a map of the system taped inelegantly to Lincoln Rhyme's wall. Rhyme's eyes scanned the different-colored lines representing the various routes, blue for Eighth Avenue, green for Lex, red for Broadway.

Rhyme had a special relationship with the cantankerous system. It was in the pit of a subway construction site that an oak beam had split and crushed Rhyme's spine – just as he'd said, "Ah," and leaned forward to lift a fiber, golden as an angel's hair, from the body of a murder victim.

Yet even before the accident, subways played an important role in NYPD forensics. Rhyme'd studied them diligently when he was running IRD: because they covered so much terrain and incorporated so many different kinds of building materials over the years, you could often link a perp to a particular subway line, if not his neighborhood and station, on the basis of good trace evidence alone. Rhyme had collected subway exemplars for years – some of the samples dating to the prior century. (It had been in the 1860s that Alfred

Beach, the publisher of the *New York Sun* and *Scientific American,* decided to adapt his idea of transmitting mail via small pneumatic tubes to moving people in large ones.)

Rhyme now ordered his computer to dial a number and in a few moments was connected with Sam Hoddleston, chief of the Transit Authority Police. Like the Housing Police, they were regular New York City cops, no different from NYPD, merely assigned to the transportation system. Hoddleston knew Rhyme from the old days and the criminalist could hear in the silence after he identified himself some fast mental tap-dancing; Hoddleston, like many of Rhyme's former colleagues, didn't know that Rhyme had returned from the near dead.

"Should we power-off any of the lines?" Hoddleston asked after Rhyme briefed him about the Dancer and his partner. "Do a field search?"

Sellitto heard the question on the speakerphone and shook his head.

Rhyme agreed. "No, we don't want to tip our hand. Anyway, I think he's in an abandoned area."

"There aren't many empty stations," Hoddleston said. "But there're a hundred deserted spurs and yards, work areas. Say, Lincoln, how're you doing? I—"

"Fine, Sam. I'm fine," Rhyme said briskly, deflecting the question as he always did. Then added, "We were talking – we think they're probably going to stick to foot. Stay off the trains themselves. So we're guessing they're in Manhattan. We've got a map here and we're going to need your help in narrowing it down some."

"Whatever I can do," the chief said. Rhyme couldn't remember what he looked like. From his voice he sounded fit and athletic, but then Rhyme supposed he himself might seem like an Olympian to someone who couldn't see his destroyed body.

Rhyme now considered the rest of the evidence that Sachs had found in the building next to the safe house – the evidence left by the Dancer's partner.

He said to Hoddleston, "The dirt has a high moisture content and's loaded with feldspar and quartz sand."

"I remember you always like your dirt, Lincoln."

"Useful, soil is," he said, then continued. "Very little rock and none of it blasted or chipped, no limestone or Manhattan mica schist. So we're looking at downtown. And from the amount of old wood particles, probably closer to Canal Street."

North of Twenty-seventh Street the bedrock lies close to the surface of Manhattan. South of that, the ground is dirt, sand, and clay, and it's very damp. When the sandhogs were digging the subways years ago the soupy ground around Canal Street would flood the shaft. Twice a day all work had to cease while the tunnel was pumped out and the walls shored up with timber, which over the years had rotted away into the soil.

Hoddleston wasn't optimistic. Although Rhyme's information limited the geographic area, he explained, there were dozens of connecting tunnels, transfer platforms, and portions of stations themselves that had been closed off over the years. Some of them were as sealed and forgotten as Egyptian tombs. Years after Alfred Beach died workmen building another subway line broke through a wall and discovered his original tunnel, long abandoned, with its opulent waiting room, which had included murals, a grand piano, and a goldfish tank.

"Any chance he's just sleeping in active stations or between stations in a cutout?" Hoddleston asked.

Sellitto shook his head. "Not his profile. He's a druggie. He'd be worried about his stash."

Rhyme then told Hoddleston about the turquoise mosaic.

"Impossible to say where that came from, Lincoln. We've done so much work retiling, there's tile dust and grout everywhere. Who knows where he could've picked it up."

"So give me a number, chief," Rhyme said. "How many spots we looking at?"

"I'd guess twenty locations," Hoddleston's athletic voice said. "Maybe a few less."

"Ouch," Rhyme muttered. "Well, fax us a list of the most likely ones."

"Sure. When do you need it?" But before Rhyme could answer, Hoddleston said, "Never mind. I remember you from the old days, Lincoln. You want it yesterday."

"Last week," Rhyme joked, impatient the chief was bantering and not writing.

Five minutes later the fax machine buzzed. Thom set the piece of paper in front of Rhyme. It listed fifteen locations in the subway system. "Okay, Sachs, get going."

She nodded as Sellitto called Haumann and Dellray to have the S&S teams get started. Rhyme added emphatically, "Amelia, you stay in the rear now, okay? You're Crime Scene, remember? Only Crime Scene."

On a curb in downtown Manhattan sat Leon the Shill. Beside him was the Bear Man – so named because he wheeled around a shopping cart filled with dozens of stuffed animals, supposedly for sale, though only the most psychotic of parents would buy one of the tattered, licey little toys for their child.

Leon and the Bear Man lived together – that is, they shared an alley near Chinatown – and survived on bottle deposits and handouts and a little harmless petty larceny.

"He dying, man," Leon said.

"Naw, bad dream's what it is," Bear Man responded, rocking his shopping cart as if trying to put the bears to sleep.

"Oughta spenda dime, get a ambulance here."

Leon and the Bear Man were looking across the street, into an alley. There lay another homeless man, black and sick looking, with a twitchy and mean – though currently unconscious – face. His clothes were in tatters.

"Oughta call somebody."

"Les take a look."

They crossed the street, skittish as mice.

The man was skinny – AIDS, probably, which told them he probably used smack – and filthy. Even Leon and Bear Man bathed occasionally in the Washington Square Park fountain or the lagoon in Central Park, despite the turtles. He wore ragged jeans, caked socks, no shoes, and a torn, filthy jacket that said, *Cats . . . The Musical,* on it.

They stared at him for a moment. When Leon tentatively touched Cats's leg the man jerked awake and sat up, freezing them with a weird glare. "The fuck're you? The fuck're you?"

"Hey, man, you okay?" They backed away a few feet.

Cats shivered, clutching his abdomen. He coughed long and Leon whispered, "Looks too fucking mean to be sick, you know?"

"He's scary. Les go." Bear Man wanted to get back to his A&P baby carriage.

"I need help," Cats muttered. "I hurt, man."

"There's a clinic over on—"

"Can't go to no *clinic,*" Cats snapped, as if they'd insulted him.

So he had a record, and on the street refusing to go to a clinic when you were this sick meant you had a *serious* record. Felony warrants outstanding. Yeah, this mutt was trouble.

"I need medicine. You got some? I pay you. I got money."

Which they normally wouldn't've believed except that Cats was a can picker. And fucking good at it, they could see. Beside him was a huge bag of soda and beer cans he'd culled from the trash. Leon eyed it enviously. Must've taken two days to get that many. Worth thirty bucks, forty.

"We don't got nothing. We don't do that. Stuff, I mean."

"Pills, he means."

"You wanna bottle? T-bird. I got some nice T-bird, yessir. Trade you a bottle fo' them cans . . ."

Cats struggled up on one arm. "I don't want no fuckin' bottle. I got beat up. Some kids, they beat me up. They busted something in me. It don't feel right. I need medicine. Not crack or smack or fucking T-bird. I need something stop me hurtin'. I need pills!" He climbed to his feet and teetered, swaying toward Bear Man.

"Nothing, man. We don't got nothing."

"I'ma ask you a las' time, you gonna give me somethin'?" He groaned and held his side. They knew how crazy strong some crackheads were. And this guy was *big.* He could easily break both of them in half.

Leon whispered to Bear Man, "That guy, th'other day?"

Bear Man was nodding avidly, though it was a fear reflex. He didn't know who the hell Leon was talking about.

Leon continued, "There's this guy, okay? Was trying to sell us some shit yesterday. Pills. Pleased as could be."

"Yeah, pleased as could be," Bear Man said quickly, as if confirming the story might calm Cats down.

"Didn't care who saw him. Just selling pills. No crack, no smack, no Jane. But uppers, downers, you name it."

"Yeah, you name it."

"I got money." Cats fumbled in his filthy pocket and pulled out two or three crumpled twenties. "See? So where this motherfucker be?"

"Over near City Hall. Old subway station . . ."

"I'm sick, man. I got beat up. Why somebody beat me up? What I do? I's pickin' some cans's all. And look what happen. Fuck. What his name?"

"I don't know," Bear Man said quickly, squiggling up his forehead as if he were thinking fiercely. "No, wait. He said something."

"I don't remember."

"You remember . . . He was looking at your bears."

"An' he said something. Yeah, yeah. Said his name was Joe or something. Maybe Jodie."

"Yeah, that was it. I'm sure."

"Jodie," Cats repeated, then wiped his forehead. "I'ma see him. Man, I need somethin'. I'm sick, man. Fuck you. I'm sick. Fuck you too."

When Cats had staggered off, moaning and muttering to himself, dragging his bag of cans behind him, Leon and Bear Man returned to the curb and sat down. Leon cracked a Voodoo ale and they started drinking.

"Shouldn'ta done that to that fella," he said.

"Who?"

"Jodie or whatever his name was."

"You want that motherfucker round here?" Bear Man asked. "He dangerous. He scare me. You want him to hang round here?"

"Course I don't. But, man, you know."

"Yeah, but—"

"You know, man."

"Yeah, I know. Gimme the bottle."

Hour 25 of 45

23

Sitting next to Jodie on the mattress, Stephen was listening through the tap box to the Hudson Air phone line.

He was listening to Ron's phone. Talbot was his last name, Stephen had learned. He wasn't exactly sure what Ron's job was but he seemed to be an executive with the charter company and Stephen believed he'd get the most information about the Wife and Friend by listening to this line.

He heard the man arguing with someone from the distributor who handled parts for Garrett turbines. Because it was Sunday they were having trouble getting the final items for the repairs – a fire extinguisher cartridge and something called the annular.

"You promised it by three," Ron grumbled. "I want it by three."

After some bargaining – and bitching – the company agreed to fly the parts into their Connecticut office from Boston. They'd be trucked to the Hudson Air office and arrive by three or four. They hung up.

Stephen listened for a few minutes longer but there were no other calls.

He clicked the phone off, frustrated.

He didn't have a clue as to where the Wife and Friend were. Still in the safe house? Had they been moved?

What was wormy Lincoln thinking now? How clever was he?

And *who* was he? Stephen tried to picture him, tried to picture him as a target through the Redfield telescope. He couldn't. All he saw was a mass of worms and a face looking at him calmly through a greasy window.

He realized that Jodie'd said something to him.

"What?"

"What'd he do? Your stepfather?"

"Just odd jobs mostly. Hunted and fished a lot. He was a hero in Vietnam. He went behind enemy lines and killed fifty-four people. Politicians and people like that, not just soldiers."

"He taught you all this, about . . . what you do?" The drugs had worn off and Jodie's green eyes were brighter now.

"I got most of my practice in Africa and South America, but he started me. I called him 'WGS.' The World's Greatest Soldier. He laughed at that."

At ages eight and nine and ten Stephen would walk behind Lou as they trooped through the hills of West Virginia, hot drops of sweat falling down their noses and into the crooks of their index fingers, which curled around the ribbed triggers of their Winchesters or Rugers. They'd lie in the grass for hours and be quiet, be still. The sweat glistened on Lou's scalp just below the bristly crew cut, both eyes open as they sighted on their targets.

Don't you squint that left eye, Soldier.

Sir, never, sir.

Squirrels, wild turkeys, deer in season or out, bear when they could find them, dogs on slow days.

"Make 'em dead, Soldier. Watch me."

Ka-rack. The thud against the shoulder, the bewildered eyes of an animal dying.

Or on steaming August Sundays they'd slip the CO_2 cartridges into their paint-ball guns and strip down to their shorts, stalking each other and raising molehills of welts on their chests and thighs with the marble-sized balls that hissed through the air at three hundred feet per second, young Stephen struggling to keep from crying at the awful sting. The paint balls came in every color, but Lou insisted on loading with red. Like blood.

And at night, sitting in front of a fire in the backyard as the smoke curled toward the sky and into the open window where his mother stood cleaning the supper dishes with a toothbrush, the taut little man – Stephen at fifteen was as tall as Lou – would sip from the newly opened bottle of Jack Daniel's and talk and talk and talk, whether Stephen was listening or not, as they watched the sparks flying into the sky like orange lightning bugs.

"Tomorrow I want you to bring down a deer with just a knife."

"Well . . ."

"Can you do that, Soldier?"

"Yessir, I can."

"Now look here." He'd take another sip. "Where d'you think the neck vein is?"

"I—"

"Don't be afraid to say you don't know. A good soldier admits his ignorance. But then he does something to correct it."

"I don't know where the vein is, sir."

"I'll show it on you. It's right here. Feel that? Right there. Feel it?"

"Yessir. I feel it."

"Now, what you do is you find a family – doe and calves. You come up close. That's the hard part, getting up close. To kill the doe, you endanger the calf. You move for her baby. You threaten the calf and then the mother won't run off. She'll come after you. Then, swick! Cut through her neck. Not sideways, but at an angle. Okay? A V-shape. You feel that? Good, good. Hey, boy, aren't we having a high old time!"

Then Lou would go inside to inspect the plates and bowls and make sure they were lined up on the checkered tablecloth, four squares from the edge, and sometimes when they were only three and a half squares from the edge or there was still a dot of grease on the rim of a melamine plate Stephen would listen to the slaps and the whimpers from inside the house as he lay on his back beside the fire and watched the sparks fly toward the dead moon.

"You gotta be good at something," the man would say later, his wife in bed and he outside again with his bottle. "Otherwise there's no point in being alive."

Craftsmanship. He was talking about *craftsmanship.*

Jodie now asked, "How come you couldn't be in the marines? You never told me."

"Well, it was stupid," Stephen said, then paused and added, "I got into some trouble when I was a kid. D'you ever do that?"

"Get into trouble? Not much. I was scared to. I didn't want to upset my mother, stealing and shit. What'd you do?"

"Something that wasn't real bright. There was this man lived up the road in our town. He was, you know, a bully. I saw him twisting this woman's arm. She was sick, and what was he doing hurting her? So I went up to him and said if he didn't stop I'd kill him."

"You said that?"

"Oh, and another thing my stepfather taught me. You don't threaten. You either kill someone or let them be, but you don't threaten. Well, he kept on hassling this woman and I had to teach him a lesson. I started hitting him. It got out of hand. I grabbed a rock and hit him. I wasn't thinking. I did a couple years for manslaughter. I was just a kid. Fifteen. But it was a criminal record. And that was enough to keep me out of the marines."

"I thought I read somewhere that even if you've got a record you can go into the service. If you go to some special boot camp."

"I guess maybe 'cause it was manslaughter."

Jodie's hand pressed Stephen's shoulder. "That's not fair. Not one *bit* fair."

"I didn't think so."

"I'm real sorry," Jodie said.

Stephen, who never had any trouble looking any man in the eye, glanced at Jodie once then down immediately. And from somewhere, totally weird, this image came to mind. Jodie and Stephen living together in the cabin, going hunting and fishing. Cooking dinner over a campfire.

"What happened to him? Your stepfather?"

"Died in an accident. He was hunting and fell off a cliff."

Jodie said, "Sounds like it was probably the way he'd've wanted to go."

After a moment Stephen said, "Maybe it was."

He felt Jodie's leg brush his. Another electric jolt. Stephen stood quickly and looked out the window again. A police car cruised past but the cops inside were drinking soda and talking.

The street was deserted except for a clutch of homeless men, four or five whites and one Negro.

Stephen squinted. The Negro, lugging a big garbage bag full of soda and beer cans, was arguing, looking around, gesturing, offering the bag to one of the white guys, who kept shaking his head. He had a crazy look in his eyes and the whites were scared. Stephen watched them argue for a few minutes, then he returned to the mattress, sat down next to Jodie.

Stephen put his hand on Jodie's shoulder.

"I want to talk to you about what we're going to do."

"Okay, all right. I'm listening, partner."

"There's somebody out there looking for me."

Jodie laughed. He said, "Seems to me after what happened back at that building there's a buncha people looking for you."

Stephen didn't smile. "But there's one person in particular. His name's Lincoln."

Jodie nodded. "That's his first name?"

Stephen shrugged. "I don't know . . . I've never met anyone like him."

"Who is he?"

A worm . . .

"Maybe a cop. FBI. A consultant or something. I don't know exactly." Stephen remembered the Wife describing him to Ron – the way somebody'd talk about a guru, or a ghost. He felt cringey again. He slid his hand down Jodie's back. It rested at the base of his spine. The bad feeling went away.

"This is the second time he's stopped me. And he almost got me caught. I'm trying to figure him out and I can't."

"What do you have to figure out?"

"What he's going to do next. So I can stay ahead of him."

Another squeeze to the spine. Jodie didn't seem to mind. He didn't look away either. He wasn't timid anymore. And the look he gave Stephen was odd. Was it a look of . . . ? Well, he didn't know. Admiration maybe . . .

Stephen realized that it was the way Sheila had looked at him in Starbucks when he was saying all the right things. Except that, with her, he hadn't been Stephen, he was somebody else. Somebody who didn't exist. Jodie was now looking at him this way even though he knew exactly who Stephen was, that he was a killer.

Leaving his hand on the man's back, Stephen said, "What I can't figure out is if he's going to move them out of their safe house. The one next to the building where I met you."

"Move who? The people you're trying to kill?"

"Yeah. He's going to try to outguess me. He's thinking . . ." Stephen's voice faded.

Thinking . . .

And what *was* Lincoln the Worm thinking? Would he move the Wife and the Friend, guessing I'll try the safe house again? Or would he leave them, thinking I'll wait and try for them at a new location? And even if he thinks I'll try the safe house again, will he leave them there as bait, trying to sucker me back for another ambush? Will he move two decoys to a new safe house? And try to take me when I follow them?

The thin man said, almost whispering, "You seem, I don't know, shook up or something."

"I can't *see* him . . . I can't see what he's going to do. Everybody else's ever been after me I can see. I can figure them out. Him, I can't."

"What do you want me to do?" Jodie asked, swaying against Stephen. Their shoulders brushed.

Stephen Kall, craftsman extraordinaire, stepson of a man who never had a moment's hesitation in anything he did – killing deer or inspecting plates cleaned with a toothbrush – was now confounded, staring at the floor, then looking up into Jodie's eyes.

Hand on the man's back. Shoulders touching too.

Stephen made up his mind.

He bent forward and rummaged through his backpack. He found a black cell phone, looked at it for a moment, then handed it to Jodie.

"Whatsis?" the man asked.

"A phone. For you to use."

"A cell phone! Cool." He examined it as if he'd never seen one, flipped it open, studying all the buttons.

Stephen asked, "You know what a spotter is?"

"No."

"The best snipers don't work alone. They always have a spotter with them. He locates the target and figures out how far away it is, looks for defensive troops, things like that."

"You want me to do that for you?"

"Yep. See, I think Lincoln's going to move them."

"Why, you figure?" Jodie asked.

"I can't explain it. I just have this feeling." He looked at his watch. "Okay, here's the thing. At twelve-thirty this afternoon, what I want you to do is walk down the street like a . . . homeless person."

"You can say 'bum', you want."

"And watch the safe house. Maybe you could look through trash cans or something."

"For bottles. I do that. All the time."

"You find out what kind of car they get into, then call and tell me. I'll be on the street around the corner, in a car, waiting. But you'll have to watch out for decoys."

An image of the red-haired woman cop came to mind. She could hardly be a decoy for the Wife. Too tall, too pretty. He wondered why he disliked her so much . . . He regretted not judging that shot at her better.

"Okay. I can do that. You'll shoot them in the street?"

"It depends. I might follow them to the new safe house and do it there. I'll be ready to improvise."

Jodie studied the phone like a kid at Christmas. "I don't know how it works."

Stephen showed him. "You call me on it when you're in position."

"'In position.' That sounds professional." Then Jodie looked up from the phone. "You know, after this's over and I go through the rehab thing, why don't we get together sometime? We could have some juice or coffee or something. Huh? You wanta do that?"

"Sure," Stephen said. "We could—"

But suddenly a huge pounding shook the door. Spinning

around like a dervish, whipping his gun from his pocket, Stephen dropped into a two-handed shooting position.

"Open the fuckin' door," a voice from outside shouted. "Now!"

"Quiet," Stephen whispered to Jodie. Heart racing.

"You in there, booger?" the voice persisted. "Jo-die. Where the fuck're you?"

Stephen stepped to the boarded-over window and looked out again. The Negro homeless guy from across the street. He wore a tattered jacket that read, *Cats . . . The Musical.* The Negro didn't see him.

"Where'sa little man?" the Negro said. "I needa little man. I gotta have some pills! Jodie Joe? Where you be?"

Stephen said, "You know him?"

Jodie looked out, shrugged, and whispered, "I don't know. Maybe. Looks like a lota people on the street."

Stephen studied the man for a long moment, thumbing the plastic grip of his pistol.

The homeless man called, "I know you here, man." His voice dissolved into a gargle of disgusting cough. "Jo-die. Jo-die! It cos' me, man. As' wha' it cos' me. Cos' me a fuckin' weeka pickin' cans's what it cos' me. They *tole* me you here. Ever-bod-y told me. Jodie, Jodie!"

"He'll just go away," Jodie said.

Stephen said, "Wait. Maybe we can use him."

"How?"

"Remember what I told you? *Delegate.* This is good . . ." Stephen was nodding. "He looks scary. They'll focus on him, not you."

"You mean take him along with me? To that safe house place?"

"Yes," Stephen said.

"I need some *stuff,* man," the Negro moaned. "Come on. I'm fucked-up, man. Please. I got the wobblies. You *fuck*!" He kicked the door hard. "Please, man. You in there, Jodie? The fuck you at? You booger! Help me." It sounded like he was crying.

"Go on out," Stephen said. "Tell him you'll give him

something if he goes along with you. Just have him go through the trash or something across the street from the safe house, while you're watching the traffic. It'll be perfect."

Jodie looked at him. "You mean now. Just go talk to him?"

"Yeah. Now. Tell him."

"You want him to come in?"

"No, I don't want him to see me. Just go talk to him."

"Well . . . Okay." Jodie pried the front door open. "What if he stabs me or something?"

"Look at him. He's almost dead. You could beat the crap out of him with one hand."

"Looks like he has AIDS."

"Go on."

"What if he touches—"

"Go!"

Jodie took a deep breath then stepped outside. "Hey, keep it down," he said to the man. "What the hell you want?"

Stephen watched the Negro look over Jodie with his crazed eyes. "Word up you selling shit, man. I got money. I got sixty bucks. I need pills. Look, I'm sick."

"Whatta you want?"

"Whatchu got, man?"

"Reds, bennies, dexies, yellow jackets, demmies."

"Yeah, demmies're good shit, man. I pay you. Fuck. I got money. I'm hurting inside. Got beat up. Where my money?" He slapped his pockets several times before realizing he was clutching the precious twenties in his left hand.

"But," Jodie said, "you gotta do something for me first."

"Yeah, whatta I gotta do that? You wanna blow job?"

"No," Jodie snapped, horrified. "I want you to help me go through some trash."

"Why I gotta do that shit?"

"Picking some cans."

"Cans?" the man roared, scratching his nose compulsively. "The fuck you need a nickel for? I just give away a hunnerd cans find out where yo' ass be. Fuck cans. I pay you money, man."

"I give you the demmies for free, only you gotta help me get some bottles."

"Free?" The man didn't seem to understand this. "You mean, free like I don't gotta pay?"

"Yeah."

The Negro looked around as if he was trying to find somebody to explain this.

"Wait here," Jodie said.

"Where I gotta look for bottles?"

"Just wait . . ."

"Where?" he demanded.

Jodie stepped back inside. He said to Stephen, "He's gonna do it."

"Good job." Stephen smiled.

Jodie grinned back. He started to turn back to the door but Stephen said, "Hey."

The little man paused.

Stephen blurted suddenly, "It's good I met you."

"I'm glad I met you too." Jodie hesitated for a minute. "Partner." He stuck his hand out.

"Partner," Stephen echoed. He had a fierce urge to take his glove off, so he could feel Jodie's skin on his. But he didn't.

Craftsmanship had to come first.

Hour 25 of 45

24

The debate was feverish.

"I think you're wrong, Lincoln," Lon Sellitto said. "We gotta move 'em. He'll hit the safe house again, we leave 'em there."

They weren't the only ones considering the dilemma. Prosecutor Reg Eliopolos hadn't checked in – not yet – but Thomas Perkins, the FBI special agent in charge of the Manhattan office, was here in person, representing the federal side of the debate. Rhyme wished Dellray were here – and Sachs too, though she was with the joint city/federal tactical force searching abandoned subway locations. So far they hadn't found any trace of the Dancer or his compatriot.

"I'm being completely proactive in my take on the situation," said earnest Perkins. "We have other facilities." He was appalled that it had taken the Dancer only eight hours to find out where the witnesses were being held and to get within five yards of the disguised fire door of the safe house. "*Better* facilities," he added quickly. "I think we should expedite immediate transferal. I've gotten a heads-up from high levels. Washington itself. They want the witnesses immunized."

Meaning, Rhyme assumed, move 'em and move 'em now.

"No," the criminalist said adamantly. "We have to leave them where they are."

"Prioritizing the variables," Perkins said, "I think the answer's pretty clear. Move them."

But Rhyme said, "He'll come after them wherever they are, a new safe house or the existing one. We know the turf there, we know something about his approach. We've got good ambush coverage."

"That's a good point," Sellitto conceded.

"It'll also throw him off stride."

"How so?" Perkins asked.

"He's debating right now too, you know."

"He is?"

"Oh, you bet," Rhyme said. "He's trying to figure out what *we're* going to do. If we decide to keep them where they are, he'll do one thing. If we move them – which I think is what he's guessing we'll do – he'll try for a transport hit. And however good security is on the road, it's always worse than fixed premises. No, we have to keep them where they are and be prepared for the next attempt. Anticipate it and be ready to move in. The last time—"

"The last time, an agent got killed."

Rhyme snapped back to the SAC, "If Innelman had had a backup, it would've gone different."

Perkins of the perfect suit was a self-protecting bureaucrat, but he was reasonable. He nodded his concession.

But *am* I right? Rhyme wondered.

What *is* the Dancer thinking? Do I really know?

Oh, I can look over a silent bedroom or filthy alleyway and read perfectly the story that turned them into crime scenes. I can see, in the Rorschach of blood pasted to carpet and tile, how close the victim came to escaping or how little chance he had and what kind of death he died. I can look at the dust the killer leaves behind and know immediately where he comes from.

I can answer who, I can answer why.

But what's the Dancer *going* to do?

That I can guess at but I can't say for certain.

A figure appeared in the doorway, one of the officers from the front door. He handed Thom an envelope and stepped back to his guard post.

"What's that?" Rhyme eyed it carefully. He wasn't expecting any lab reports and he was all too conscious of the Dancer's predilection for bombs. The package was no more than a sheet of paper thick, however, and was from the FBI.

Thom opened it and read.

"It's from PERT. They tracked down a sand expert."

Rhyme explained to Perkins, "It's not for this case. It's about that agent who disappeared the other night."

"Tony?" the SAC asked. "We haven't had a single lead so far."

Rhyme glanced at the report.

Substance submitted for analysis is not technically sand. It is coral rubble from reef formations and contains spicules, cross sections of marine worm tubes, gastropod shells and foraminifers. Most likely source is the northern Caribbean: Cuba, the Bahamas.

Caribbean . . . Interesting. Well, he'd have to put the evidence on hold for the time being. After the Dancer was bagged and tagged he and Sachs would get back—

His headset crinkled.

"Rhyme, you there?" Sachs's voice snapped.

"Yes! Where are you, Sachs? What do you have?"

"We're outside an old subway station near City Hall. All boarded up. S&S says there's somebody inside. At least one, maybe two."

"Okay, Sachs," he said, heart racing at the thought they might be close to the Dancer. "Report back." Then he looked up at Sellitto and Perkins. "Looks like we may not have to decide about moving them from the safe house after all."

"They found him?" the detective asked.

But the criminalist – a scientist foremost – refused to give voice to his hopes. Afraid he might jinx the operation – well, jinx *Sachs,* he was thinking. He muttered, "Let's keep our fingers crossed."

Silently the ESU troops surrounded the subway station.

This was probably the place where the Dancer's new partner lived, Amelia Sachs concluded. S&S had found several locals who'd reported a druggie selling pills out of the place. He was a slightly built man – in line with a size-eight shoe.

The station was, almost literally, a hole in the wall, supplanted years ago by the fancier City Hall stop a few blocks away.

The 32-E team went into position, while S&S began to set up their microphones and infrareds, and other officers cleared the street of traffic and the homeless men sitting on curbs or in doorways.

The commander moved Sachs away from the main entrance, out of the line of fire. They gave her the demeaning job of guarding a subway exit that had been barred and padlocked for years. She actually wondered if Rhyme had cut a deal with Haumann to keep her safe. Her anger from last night, in abeyance in their search for the Dancer, now bubbled up again.

Sachs nodded toward the rusty lock. "Hmm. He probably won't be getting out this way," she'd offered brightly.

"Gotta guard all entrances," the masked ESU officer muttered, missing or ignoring her sarcasm, and returned to his comrades.

Rain fell around her, a chill rain, dropping straight down from a dirty gray sky, tapping loudly on the refuse banked in front of the iron bars.

Was the Dancer inside? If so, there'd be a firefight. Absolutely. She couldn't imagine he'd give it up without a violent struggle.

And it infuriated her that she wouldn't be part of it.

You're a slick dick when you've got a rifle and a quarter mile of protection, she thought to the killer. But tell me, asshole, how're you with a handgun at close range? How'd you like to face me down? On her mantel at home were a dozen trophies of gold-plated shooters aiming pistols. (The gilt figures were all men, which for some reason tickled Amelia Sachs immensely.)

She stepped farther down the stairs, to the bars, then flattened against the wall.

Sachs, the criminalist, examined the squalid spot carefully, smelling garbage, rot, urine, the salty smell of the subway. She examined the bars and the chain and padlock. She peered inside the dim tunnel and could see nothing, hear nothing.

Where is he?

And what are the cops and agents doing? What's the delay?

She heard the answer a moment later in her earphone: they were waiting for backup. Haumann had decided to call in another twenty ESU officers and the second 32-E team.

No, no, no, she thought. That was all wrong! All the Dancer has to do is take one peek outside and see that not a single car or taxi or pedestrian is going by and he'll know instantly there's a tactical operation under way. There'll be a bloodbath . . . Don't they get it?

Sachs left the crime scene kit at the foot of the stairs and climbed back to street level. A few doors away was a drugstore. She went inside. She bought two large cans of butane and borrowed the storekeeper's awning rod – a five-foot-long piece of steel.

Back at the gated subway exit, Sachs slipped the awning rod through one of the chain links that was partially sawn through, and twisted until the chain was taut. She pulled on a Nomex glove and emptied the contents of butane cans on the metal, watching it grow frosty from the freezing gas. (Amelia Sachs hadn't walked a beat along the Deuce in Times Square – Forty-second Street – for nothing; she knew enough about breaking and entering to take up a second line of work.)

When the second can was empty she gripped the rod in both hands and began to twist. The icy gas had made the metal very brittle. With a soft *snap* the link cracked in half. She caught the chain before it fell to the ground and set it quietly in a pile of leaves.

The hinges were wet with rainwater but she spit on them for good measure to keep them from squeaking and pushed inside, sweeping her Glock from its holster, thinking: I missed you at three hundred yards. I won't at thirty.

Rhyme wouldn't have approved of this, of course, but Rhyme didn't know. She thought momentarily about him, about last night, lying in his bed. But the image of his face vanished quickly. Like driving at a hundred and fifty miles an hour, her mission now left no time for ruing the disaster of her personal life.

She disappeared into the dim corridor, leapt over the ancient wooden turnstile, and started along the platform toward the station.

She heard the voices before she got more than twenty feet.

"I have to leave . . . understand . . . I'm saying? Go away."

White, male.

Was it the Dancer?

Heart slamming in her chest.

Breathe slow, she told herself. Shooting is breathing.

(But she hadn't been breathing slow at the airport. She'd been gasping in fear.)

"Yo, whatchu sayin'?" Another voice. Black male. Something about it scared her. Something dangerous. "I can get money, I can. I can get a shitload a money. I got sixty, I tell you that? But I can get mo'. I can get as much's you want. I ha' me a good job. Fuckers took it away. I knew too much."

The weapon is merely an extension of your arm. Aim yourself, not the weapon.

(But she hadn't been aiming at all when she'd been at the airport. She'd been on her belly like a scared rabbit, shooting blind – the most pointless and dangerous of practices with a firearm.)

"You understand me? I changed my mind, okay? Let me . . . and just leave. I'll give . . . demmies."

"You ain' tole me where we goin'. Where this place we gotta look through? You tell me that first. Where? Tell me!"

"You're not going anywhere. I want you to go away."

Sachs started up the stairs slowly.

Thinking: Draw your target, check your background, squeeze three. Return to cover. Draw, squeeze three more if you have to. Cover. Don't get rattled.

(But she had been rattled at the airport. That terrible bullet snapping past her face . . .)

Forget it. Concentrate.

Up a few more stairs.

"An' now you sayin' I don't get 'em fo' free, right? Now you sayin' I gotta pay. You motherfuck!"

Stairs were the worst. Knees, her weak spot. Fucking arthritis . . .

"Here. Here's a dozen demmies. Take 'em and go!"

"A dozen. And I ain' gotta pay you?" He brayed a laugh. "A dozen?"

Approaching the top of the stairs.

She could almost peer into the station itself. She was ready to shoot. He moves any direction more than six inches, girl, take him out. Forget the rules. Three head shots. Pop, pop, pop. Forget the chest. Forget—

Suddenly the stairs vanished.

"Ugh." A grunt from deep in her throat as she fell.

The step she'd placed her foot on was a trap. The riser had been removed and the step rested only on two shoe boxes. They collapsed under her weight and the concrete slab pitched downward, sending her backward down the stairs. The Glock flew from her hand and as she started to shout, "Ten-thirteen!" she realized that the cord linking her headset to her Motorola had been yanked out of the radio.

Sachs fell with a thud onto the concrete-and-steel landing. Her head slammed into a pole supporting the handrail. She rolled onto her stomach, stunned.

"Oh, great," the white guy's voice muttered from the top of the stairs.

"Who the fuck that?" the black voice asked.

She lifted her head and caught a glimpse of two men standing at the top of the stairs, gazing down at her.

"Shit," the black man muttered. "Fuck. What the fuck goin' on here?"

The white guy snagged a baseball bat and started down the stairs.

I'm dead, she thought. I'm dead.

The switchblade rested in her pocket. It took every ounce of energy to get her right arm out from underneath her. She rolled onto her back, fishing for the knife. But it was too late. He stepped on her arm, pinning it to the ground, and he gazed down at her.

Oh, man, Rhyme, blew it bad. Wish we'd had a better farewell night . . . I'm sorry . . . I'm sorry . . .

She lifted her hands defensively to deflect the blow to her head, glanced for her Glock. It was too far away.

With a tendony hand tough as a bird claw, the small man pulled the knife from her pocket. He tossed it away.

Then he stood and gripped the club.

Pop, she spoke to her deceased father, how bad d'I blow this one? How many rules d'I break? Recalling that he'd told her all it took to get killed on the street was a one-second lapse.

"Now, you're gonna tell me what you're doing here," he muttered, swinging the club absently, as if he couldn't decide what to break first. "Who the hell're you?"

"Her name's Mizz Amelia Sachs," said the homeless guy, suddenly sounding a lot less homeless. He stepped off the bottom stair and moved up to the white guy quickly, pulling the bat away. "And unless I'm most mistaken, she's come here to bust your little ass, my friend. Just like me." Sachs squinted to see the homeless guy straighten up and turn into Fred Dellray. He was pointing a very large Sig-Sauer automatic pistol at the astonished man.

"You're a cop?" he sputtered.

"FBI."

"Shit!" he spat out, closing his eyes in disgust. "This is just my fucking luck."

"Nup," Dellray said. "Luck didn't have a bitsy thing to do with it. Now, I'm gonna cuff you and you're gonna let me. You don't, you gonna hurt for months and months. We all together on that?"

"How'd you do it, Fred?"

"'Seasy," the lanky FBI agent said to Sachs as they stood in front of the deserted subway station. He still was dressed homeless and was filthy with the mud he'd smeared on his face and hands to simulate weeks of living on the street. "Rhyme was tellin' me 'bout the Dancer's friend being a junkie and living downtown in the subways, knew just where I hadta come. Bought a bag of empties and talked to who I knew I oughta talk to. Just 'bout got di-rections t'his livin' room." He nodded toward the subway. They glanced at a squad car, where Jodie sat, cuffed and miserable, in the backseat.

"Why didn't you tell us what you were doing?"

Dellray's answer was a laugh and Sachs knew the question was pointless; undercover cops rarely told anyone – fellow cops included, and especially supervisors – what they were doing. Nick, her ex, had been undercover too and there'd been a hell of a lot he hadn't told her.

She massaged her side where she'd fallen. It hurt like a son of a bitch, and the medics said she ought to have X rays. Sachs reached up and squeezed Dellray's biceps. She felt uneasy *receiving* gratitude – she was truly Lincoln Rhyme's protégée there – but she now had no problem saying, "You saved my life. My ass'd be capped now if it wasn't for you. What can I say?"

Dellray shrugged, deflecting the thanks, and bummed a cigarette from one of the uniformed cops standing in front of the station. He sniffed the Marlboro and slipped it behind his ear. He looked toward a blacked-out window in the station. "Please," he said to no one, sighing. "'Bout time we had some luck here."

When they'd arrested Joe D'Oforio and flung him into the back of a car, he'd told them that the Dancer had left only ten minutes before, climbing down the stairs and vanishing along a spur line. Jodie – the mutt's nickname – didn't know which direction he'd gone, only that he'd disappeared suddenly with his gun and his backpack. Haumann and Dellray sent their troopers to scour the station, the tracks, and the nearby City Hall station. They were now waiting for the results of the sweep.

"Come on . . ."

Ten minutes later a SWAT officer pushed through the doorway. Sachs and Dellray both looked at him hopefully. But he shook his head. "Lost his prints a hundred feet down the tracks. Don't have a clue where he went."

Sachs sighed and reluctantly relayed the message to Rhyme and asked if she should do a search of the tracks and the nearby station.

He took the news as acerbically as she'd guessed he would. "Damnit," the criminalist muttered. "No, just the station itself. Pointless to grid the others. Shit, how does he *do* it? It's like he's got some kind of fucking second sight."

"Well," she said, "at least we've got a witness."

And regretted immediately that she'd said that.

"Witness?" Rhyme spat out. "A witness? I don't *need* witnesses. I need evidence! Well, get him down here anyway. Let's hear what he has to say. But, Sachs, I want that station swept like you've never swept a scene before. You hear me? Are you there, Sachs? Do you hear me?"

25

"And what do we have here?" Rhyme asked, giving a soft puff into the Storm Arrow control straw to scoot forward.

"An itsy piece of garbage," offered Fred Dellray, cleaned up and back in uniform – if you could call an Irish green suit a uniform. "Uh, uh, uh. Don't say a word. Not till we ask fo' it." He turned his alarming stare on Jodie.

"You fooled me!"

"Quiet, you little skel."

Rhyme wasn't pleased that Dellray had gone out on his own, but that was the nature of undercover work, and even if the criminalist didn't understand it exactly, he couldn't dispute that – as the agent's skills just proved – it could get results.

Besides, he'd saved Amelia Sachs's hide.

She'd be here soon. The medics had taken her to the emergency room for a rib X ray. She was bruised from the fall down the stairs, but nothing was broken. He'd been dismayed to learn that his talk the other night had had no effect; she'd gone into the subway after the Dancer alone.

Damn it, he thought, she's as pigheaded as me.

"I wasn't going to hurt anybody," Jodie protested.

"Hard o' hearing? I said don't say a word."

"I didn't know who she was!"

"No," Dellray said, "that pretty silver badge of hers didn't give nuthin' away." Then remembered he didn't want to hear from the man.

Sellitto walked up close and bent over Jodie. "Tell us some more about your friend."

"I'm not his friend. He kidnaped me. I was in that building on Thirty-fifth because—"

"Because you were boosting pills. We know, we know."

Jodie blinked. "How'd you—"

"But we don't care about that. Not yet, at least. Keep going."

"I thought he was a cop but then he said he was there to kill some people. I thought he was going to kill me too. He needed to escape so he told me to stand still and I did, and this cop or somebody came to the door and he stabbed him—"

"And killed him," Dellray spat out.

Jodie sighed and looked miserable. "I didn't know he was going to kill him. I thought he was just going to knock him out or something."

"Well, asshole," Dellray spat out, "he *did* kill him. Killed him dead as a rock."

Sellitto looked over the evidence bags from the subway, containing scuzzy porn magazines, hundreds of pills, clothes. A new cellular phone. A stack of money. He turned his attention back to Jodie. "Keep going."

"He said he'd pay me to get him out of there and I led him through this tunnel to the subway. How'd you *find* me, man?" He looked at Dellray.

"'Cause you were skipping 'long the street hawking your be-bops to everybody you came across. I even knew your *name.* Jee-sus, you *are* a mutt. I oughta squeeze your neck till you're blue."

"You can't hurt me," he said, struggling to be defiant. "I have rights."

"Who hired him?" Sellitto asked Jodie. "He mention the name Hansen?"

"He didn't say." Jodie's voice quavered. "Look, I only agreed to help him 'cause I knew he'd kill me if I didn't. I wasn't going to do it." He turned to Dellray. "He wanted me to get you to help. But soon as he left I wanted you to leave. I was going to the police and telling them. I *was.* He's a scary guy. I'm afraid of him!"

"Fred?" Rhyme asked.

"Yeah, yeah," the agent conceded, "he did have a change of tune. Wanted me gone. Didn't say anything about going to the police, though."

"Where's he going? What were you supposed to do?"

"I was supposed to go through the trash bins in front of that town house and watch the cars. He told me to look for a man and a woman getting into a car and leaving. I was supposed to tell him what kind of car. I was going to call on that phone there. Then he was going to follow."

"You were right, Lincoln," Sellitto said. "About keeping them in the safe house. He's going for a transport hit."

Jodie continued, "I was going to come to you—"

"Man, you're useless when you lie. Don't you have any dignity?"

"Look, I was *going* to," he said, calmer now. He smiled. "I figured there was a reward."

Rhyme glanced at the greedy eyes and tended to believe him. He looked at Sellitto, who nodded in agreement.

"You cooperate now," Sellitto grumbled, "and we might just keep your ass out of jail. I don't know about money. Maybe."

"I've never hurt anybody. I wouldn't. I—"

"Cool that tongue," Dellray said. "We all together on that?"

Jodie rolled his eyes.

"Together?" the agent whispered maliciously.

"Yeah, yeah, yeah."

Sellitto said, "We've got to move fast here. When were you supposed to be at the town house?"

"At twelve-thirty."

They had fifty minutes left.

"What kind of car's he driving?"

"I don't know."

"What's he look like?"

"In his early, mid-thirties, I guess. Not tall. But he was strong. Man, he had muscles. Crew-cut black hair. Round face. Look, I'll do one of those drawings . . . The police sketch thing."

"Did he give you a name? Anything? Where he's from?"

"I don't know. He has kind of a Southern accent. Oh, and one thing – he said he wears gloves all the time because he's got a record."

Rhyme asked, "Where and for what?"

"I don't know where. But it's for manslaughter. He said he killed this guy in his town. When he was a teenager."

"What else?" Dellray barked.

"Look," Jodie said, crossing his arms and looking up at the agent, "I've done some bad shit but I've never hurt anybody in my life. This guy kidnaps me and he's got all these guns and is one crazy fucked-up guy and I was scared to death. I think you woulda done the same thing I did. So I'm not putting up with this crap anymore. You want to arrest me, do it and, like, take me to detention. But I'm not gonna say anything else. Okay?"

Dellray's gangly face suddenly broke into a grin. "Well, the rock cracks."

Amelia Sachs appeared in the doorway and she walked in, glancing at Jodie.

"Tell them!" he said. "I didn't hurt you. Tell 'em."

She looked at him the way you'd look at a wad of used chewing gum. "He was going to brain me with a Louisville Slugger."

"Not so, not so!"

"You okay, Sachs?"

"Another bruise is all. On my back. Bookends."

Sellitto, Sachs, and Dellray huddled with Rhyme, who told Sachs what Jodie'd reported.

The detective asked Rhyme in a whisper, "We believe him?"

"Little skel," Dellray muttered. "But I gotta say I think he's telling the God-ugly truth."

Sachs nodded too. "I guess. But I think we have to keep him on a tight leash, whatever we do."

Sellitto agreed. "Oh, we'll keep him close."

Rhyme reluctantly agreed too. It seemed impossible to get ahead of the Dancer without this man's help. He'd been adamant about keeping Percey and Hale in the safe house but in fact he hadn't *known* that the Dancer was going for a transport hit. He was only leaning toward that conclusion. He might easily have decided to move Percey and Hale and they might have been killed as they drove to the new safe house.

The tension gripped his jaw.

"How do you think we should handle it, Lincoln?" Sellitto asked.

This was tactical, not evidentiary. Rhyme looked at Dellray, who tugged his unlit cigarette out from behind his ear and smelled it for a moment. He finally said, "Have the mutt make the call and try to get whatever dope he can from the Dancer. We'll set up a decoy car, send the Dancer after it. Have it full of our folks. Stop it fast, sandwich him in with a couple unmarkeds, and take him down."

Rhyme nodded reluctantly. He knew how dangerous a tactical assault on a city street would be. "Can we get him out of midtown?"

"We could lead him over to the East River," Sellitto suggested. "There's plenty of room there for a takedown. Some of those old parking lots. We could make it look like we're transferring them to another van. Doin' a round-robin."

They agreed this would be the least dangerous approach.

Sellitto nodded toward Jodie, whispered, "He's diming the Coffin Dancer . . . what're we gonna give him? Gotta be good to make it worth his while."

"Waive conspiracy and aiding and abetting," Rhyme said. "Give him some money."

"Fuck," said Dellray, though he was generally known for his generosity with the undercover CIs who worked for him. But finally he nodded. "Hokay, hokay. We'll split the bill. Depending on how greedy the rodent is."

Sellitto called him over.

"All right, here's the deal. You help us, you make the call like he wanted *and* we get him, then we'll drop all charges and get you some reward money."

"How much?" Jodie asked.

"Yo, mutt, you're not in any way, shape, or form to negotiate here."

"I need money for a drug rehab program. I need another ten thousand. Is there any way?"

Sellitto looked at Dellray. "What's your snitch fund look like?"

"We could go there," the agent said, "if you do halvsies. Yeah."

"Really?" Jodie repressed a smile. "Then I'll do whatever you want."

Rhyme, Sellitto, and Dellray hashed out a plan. They'd set up a command post on the top floor of the safe house, where Jodie would be with the phone. Percey and Brit would be on the main floor, with troopers protecting them. Jodie would call the Dancer and tell him that the couple had just gotten into a van and were leaving. The van would move slowly through traffic to a deserted parking lot on the East Side. The Dancer'd follow. They'd take him in the lot.

"All right, let's put it together," Sellitto said.

"Wait," Rhyme ordered. They stopped and looked at him. "We're forgetting the most important part of all."

"Which is?"

"Amelia searched the scene at the subway. I want to analyze what she found. It might tell us how he's coming at us."

"We *know* how he's coming at us, Linc," Sellitto said, nodding at Jodie.

"Humor an old crip, will you? Now, Sachs, let's see what we've got."

The Worm.

Stephen was moving through alleys, riding on buses, dodging the cops he saw and the Worm he couldn't see.

The Worm, watching him through every window on every street. The Worm, getting closer and closer.

He thought about the Wife and the Friend, he thought about the job, about how many bullets he had left, about whether the targets would be wearing body armor, what range he would shoot from, whether this time he should use a suppressor or not.

But these were automatic thoughts. He didn't control them any more than he controlled his breathing or heartbeat or the speed of the blood coursing through his body.

What his conscious thoughts were consumed with was Jodie.

What was there about him that was so fascinating?

Stephen couldn't say for certain. Maybe it was the way he lived by himself and didn't seem to be lonely. Maybe the way he carried that little self-help book around with him and truly wanted to crawl out of the hole he was in. Or the way he hadn't balked when Stephen told him to stand in the doorway and risk getting shot.

Stephen felt funny. He—

You feel what, Soldier?

Sir, I—

Funny, Soldier? What the fuck does 'funny' mean? You going soft on me?

No, sir, I am not.

It wasn't too late to change the plans. There were still alternatives. Plenty of alternatives.

Thinking about Jodie. About what he'd said to Stephen. Hell, maybe they *could* get coffee after the job was over.

They could go to Starbucks. It would be like when he was talking to Sheila, only this would be real. And he wouldn't have to drink that pissy little tea but he'd have real coffee, double strong like the kind Stephen's mother made in the morning for his stepfather, water at a rolling boil for exactly sixty seconds, exactly two and three-quarters level tablespoons per cup, not a single black ground spilled *anywhere*.

And was fishing or hunting totally out of the question? Or the campfire . . .

He could tell Jodie to abort the mission. He could take the Wife and the Friend on his own.

Abort, Soldier? What're you *talking* about?

Sir, nothing, sir. I am considering all eventualities regarding the assault, as I have been instructed, sir.

Stephen climbed off the bus and slipped into the alley behind the fire station on Lexington. He rested the book bag behind a Dumpster, slipped his knife from the sheath under his jacket.

Jodie. Joe D. . . .

He pictured the thin arms again, the way the man had looked at him.

I'm glad I met you too, partner.

Then Stephen shivered suddenly. Like the time in Bosnia when he'd had to jump into a stream to avoid being caught by guerrillas. The month was March and the water just above freezing.

He closed his eyes and pressed up against the brick wall, smelled the wet stone.

Jodie was—

Soldier, what the fuck is going on there?

Sir, I—

What?

Sir, uhm . . .

Spit it out. Now, Soldier!

Sir, I have ascertained that the enemy was trying psychological warfare. His attempts have proved unsuccessful, sir. I am ready to proceed as planned.

Very good, Soldier. But watch your fucking step.

And Stephen realized, as he opened the back door to the firehouse and slipped inside, that there'd be no changing the plans now. This was a perfect setup and he couldn't waste it, particularly when there was a chance not only of killing the Wife and the Friend but of killing Lincoln the Worm and the redheaded woman cop too.

Stephen glanced at his watch. Jodie would be in position in fifteen minutes. He'd call Stephen's phone. Stephen would answer and hear the man's high-pitched voice one last time.

And he'd push the transmit button that would detonate the twelve ounces of RDX in Jodie's cell phone.

Delegate . . . isolate . . . eliminate.

He really had no choice.

Besides, he thought, what would we ever have to talk about? What would we ever have to do after we'd finished our coffee?

IV
MONKEY SKILLS

[Falcons'] capacity for aerial acrobatics and foolery is matched only by the clowning of ravens, and they seem to fly for the pure hell of it.

A Rage for Falcons, Stephen Bodio

26

Waiting.

Rhyme was now alone in his bed upstairs, listening in to the Special Ops frequency. He was dead tired. It was noon on Sunday and he'd had virtually no sleep. And he was exhausted from the most arduous effort of all – of trying to outthink the Dancer. It was taking its toll on his body.

Cooper was downstairs in the lab, running tests to confirm Rhyme's conclusions about the Dancer's latest tactic. Everyone else was at the safe house, Amelia Sachs too. Once Rhyme, Sellitto, and Dellray had decided how to counter what they believed would be the Dancer's next effort to kill Percey Clay and Brit Hale, Thom had checked Rhyme's blood pressure and asserted his virtual parental authority and ordered his boss into bed, no arguments, reasonable or otherwise, accepted. They'd ridden up in the elevator, Rhyme oddly silent, uneasy, wondering if he'd guessed right again.

"What's the matter?" Thom asked.

"Nothing. Why?"

"You're not complaining about anything. No grousing means something's wrong."

"Ha. Very funny," Rhyme grumbled.

After a sitting transfer to get him in bed, some bodily functions taken care of, Rhyme was now leaning back into his luxurious down pillow. Thom had slipped the voice recognition headset over his head and, despite his fatigue, Rhyme himself had gone through the steps of talking to the computer and having it patch into the Special Ops frequency.

This system *was* an amazing invention. Yes, he'd downplayed it to Sellitto and Banks. Yes, he'd *groused.* But the device, more than any other of his aids, made him feel differently about himself. For years he'd been resigned to never leading a life that approached normal. Yet with this machine and software he *did* feel normal.

He rolled his head in a circle and let it ease back into the pillow.

Waiting. Trying not to think of the debacle with Sachs last night.

Motion nearby. The falcon strutted into view. Rhyme saw a flash of white breast, then the bird turned his blue-gray back to Rhyme and looked out over Central Park. It was the male. The tiercel, he remembered Percey Clay telling him. Smaller and less ruthless than the female. He remembered something else about peregrines. They'd come back from the dead. Not too many years ago the entire population in eastern North America grew sterile from chemical pesticides and the birds nearly became extinct. Only through captive breeding efforts and control of pesticides had the creatures thrived

Back from the dead . . .

The radio clattered. It was Amelia Sachs calling in. She sounded tense as she told him that everything was set up at the safe house.

"We're all on the top floor with Jodie," she said. "Wait . . . Here's the truck."

An armored 4×4 with mirrored windows, filled with four officers from the tactical team, was being used as the bait. It would be followed by a single unmarked van, containing – apparently – two plumbing supply contractors. In fact they were 32-E troopers in street clothes. In the back of the van were four others.

"The decoys're downstairs. Okay . . . okay."

They were using two officers from Haumann's unit for decoys.

Sachs said, "Here they go."

Rhyme was pretty sure that given the Dancer's new plans, he wouldn't try a sniper shot from the street. Still, he found himself holding his breath.

"On the run . . ."

A click as the radio went dead.

Another click. Static. Sellitto broadcast, "They made it. Looks good. Starting to drive. The tail cars're ready."

"All right," Rhyme said. "Jodie's there?"

"Right here. In the safe house with us."

"Tell him to make the call."

"Okay, Linc. Here we go."

The radio clicked off.

Waiting.

To see if this time the Dancer had faltered. To see if this time Rhyme had outthought the cold brilliance of the man's mind.

Waiting.

Stephen's cell phone brayed. He flipped it open.

"'Lo."

"Hi. It's me. It's—"

"I know," Stephen said. "Don't use names."

"Right, sure." Jodie sounded nervous as a cornered 'coon. A pause, then the little man said, "Well, I'm here."

"Good. You got that Negro to help you?"

"Uhm, yeah. He's here."

"And where are you? Exactly?"

"Across the street from that town house. Man, there're a lot of cops. But nobody's paying any attention to me. There's a van just pulled up a minute ago. One of those four-by-fours. A big one. A Yukon. It's blue and it's easy to spot." In his discomfort he was rambling. "It's really, really neat. It has mirrored windows."

"That means they're bulletproof."

"Oh. Really. It's neat how you know all this stuff."

You're going to die, Stephen said to him silently.

"This man and a woman just ran out of the alley with, like, ten cops. I'm sure it's them."

"Not decoys?"

"Well, they didn't look like cops and they were looking pretty freaked out. Are you on Lexington?"

"Yeah."

"In a car?" Jodie asked.

"Of course in a car," Stephen said. "I stole some little shit Jap thing. I'm going to follow them. Then wait 'till they get to some deserted areas and do it."

"How?"

"How what?"

"How're you going to do it? Like a grenade or a machine gun?"

Stephen thought, Wouldn't you like to know?

He said, "I'm not sure. It depends."

"You see 'em?" Jodie asked, sounding uncomfortable.

"I see them," Stephen said. "I'm behind them. I'm pulling into traffic now."

"A Jap car, huh?" Jodie said. "Like a Toyota or something?"

Why, you little asshole traitor, Stephen thought bitterly, stung deeply by the betrayal even though he'd known it was probably inevitable.

Stephen was in fact watching the Yukon and backup vans speed past him. He wasn't, however, in any Japanese cars, shitty or otherwise. He wasn't in any car at all. Wearing the fireman's uniform he'd just stolen, he was standing on the street corner exactly one hundred feet from the safe house, watching the real version of the events Jodie was fictionalizing. He knew they were decoys in the Yukon. He knew the Wife and the Friend were still in the safe house.

Stephen picked up the gray remote-det transmitter. It looked like a walkie-talkie but had no speaker or microphone. He set the frequency to the bomb in Jodie's phone and armed the device.

"Stand by," he said to Jodie.

"Heh," Jodie laughed. "Will do, sir."

Lincoln Rhyme, just a spectator now, a voyeur.

Listening through his headset. Praying that he was right.

"Where's the van?" Rhyme heard Sellitto ask.

Two blocks away," Haumann said. "We're on it. It's moving slowly up Lex. Getting near traffic. He . . . wait." A long pause.

"What?"

"We've got a couple cars, a Nissan, a Subaru. An Accord too, but that's got three people in it. The Nissan's getting close to the van. That might be it. Can't see inside."

Lincoln Rhyme closed his eyes. He felt his left ring finger, his only extant digit, flick nervously on the comforter covering the bed.

"Hello?" Stephen said into the phone.

"Yeah," Jodie responded. "I'm still here."

"Directly across from the safe house?"

"That's right."

Stephen was looking at the building directly across from the safe house. No Jodie, no Negro.

"I want to say something to you."

"What's that?" the little man asked.

Stephen remembered the electric sizzle as his knee touched the man's.

I can't do it . . .

Soldier . . .

Stephen gripped the remote-det box in his left hand. He said, "Listen carefully."

"I'm listening. I—"

Stephen pushed the transmit button.

The explosion was astonishingly loud. Louder than even Stephen expected. It rattled panes and sent a million pigeons reeling into the sky. Stephen saw the glass and wood from the top floor of the safe house go spraying into the alley beside the building.

Which was even better than he hoped. He'd expected Jodie to be *near* the safe house. Maybe in a police van in front. Maybe in the alley. But he couldn't believe his good fortune that Jodie'd actually been inside. It was perfect!

He wondered who else had died in the blast.

Lincoln the Worm, he prayed.

The redheaded cop?

He looked over at the safe house and saw the smoke curling from the top window.

Now, just a few more minutes, until the rest of his team joined him.

The telephone rang and Rhyme ordered the computer to shut off the radio and answer the phone.

"Yes," he said.

"Lincoln." It was Lon Sellitto. "I'm landline," he said, referring to the phone. "Want to keep Special Ops free for the chase."

"Okay. Go ahead."

"He blew the bomb."

"I know." Rhyme had heard it; the safe house was a mile or two from his bedroom, but his windows had rattled and the peregrines outside his window had taken off and flown a slow circle, angry at the disturbance.

"Everybody okay?"

"The mutt's freaking out, Jodie. But 'side from that everything's okay. 'Cept for the feds're looking at more damage to the safe house than they'd planned on. Already bitching about it."

"Tell 'em we'll pay our taxes early this year."

What had tipped Rhyme to the cell phone bomb had been tiny fingernails of polystyrene that Sachs had found in the trace at the subway station. That and more residue of plastic explosive, a slightly different formula from that of the AP bomb in Sheila Horowitz's apartment. Rhyme had simply matched the polystyrene fragments to the phone the Dancer'd given to Jodie and realized that somebody had unscrewed the casing.

Why? Rhyme had wondered. There was only one logical reason that he could see and so he'd called the bomb squad down at the Sixth Precinct. Two detectives had rendered the phone safe, removed the large wad of plastic explosive and the firing circuit from the phone, then mounted a much smaller bit of explosive and the same circuit in an oil drum near one of the windows, pointed into the alley like a mortar. They'd filled the room with bomb blankets and stepped into the corridor, handing the harmless phone back to Jodie, who held it with shaking hands, demanding that they prove to him all the explosive had been taken out.

Rhyme had guessed that the Dancer's tactic was to use the bomb to divert attention away from the van and give him a better chance to assault it. The killer had also probably guessed that Jodie would turn and, when he made the call, that the little man would be close to the cops who were mounting the operation. If he took out the leaders the Dancer would have an even better chance of success.

Deception . . .

There was no perp Rhyme hated more than the Coffin Dancer, no one he wanted more to run to ground and skewer through his hot heart. Still, Rhyme was a criminalist before anything else and he had a secret admiration for the man's brilliance.

Sellitto explained, "We've got two tail cars behind the Nissan. We're going to—"

There was a long pause.

"Stupid," Sellitto, muttered.

"What?"

"Oh, nothing. It's just nobody called Central. We've got fire trucks coming in. Nobody called to tell 'em to ignore the reports of the blast."

Rhyme had forgotten about that too.

Sellitto continued. "Just got word. The decoy van's turning east, Linc. The Nissan's following. Maybe forty yards behind the van. It's about four blocks to the parking lot by the FDR."

"Okay, Lon. Is Amelia there? I want to talk to her."

"Jesus," he heard someone call in the background. Bo Haumann, Rhyme thought. "We got fire trucks all over the place here."

"Didn't somebody . . . ?" another voice began to ask, then faded.

No, somebody didn't, Rhyme thought. You can't think of—

"Have to call you back, Lincoln," Sellitto said. "We gotta do something. There're fire trucks up on the goddamn sidewalks."

"I'll call Amelia myself," Rhyme said.

Sellitto hung up.

The room darkened, curtains drawn.

Percey Clay was afraid.

Thinking of her haggard, the *falcon,* captured by the snare, flapping her muscular wings. The talons and beaks slicing the air like honed blades, the mad screech. But the most horrifying of all to Percey, the bird's frightened eyes. Denied her sky, the bird was lost in terror. Vulnerable.

Percey felt the same. She detested it here in the safe house. Closed in. Looking at – hating – the foolish pictures on the wall. Crap from Woolworth or J. C. Penney. The limp rug. The cheap water basin and pitcher. A ratty pink chenille bedspread, a dozen threads pulled out in long hoops from a particular corner; maybe a mob informant had sat there, tugging compulsively on the white knobby cloth.

Another sip from the flask. Rhyme had told her about the trap. That the Dancer would be following the van he believed Percey and Hale were in. They'd stop his car and arrest or kill him. Her sacrifice was now going to pay off. In ten minutes they'd have him, the man who killed Ed. The man who'd changed her life forever.

She trusted Lincoln Rhyme, and believed him. But she believed him the same way she believed Air Traffic Control when they reported no wind shear and you suddenly found your aircraft dropping at three thousand feet a minute when you were only two thousand feet in the air.

Percey tossed her flask on the bed, stood up and paced. She wanted to be flying, where it was safe, where she had control. Roland Bell had ordered her lights out, had ordered her to stay locked in her room. Everyone was upstairs on the top floor. She'd heard the bang of the explosion. She'd been expecting it. But she hadn't been expecting the fear that it brought. Unbearable. She'd have given anything to look out the window.

She walked to the door, unlocked it, stepped into the corridor.

It too was dark. Like the night . . . *All the stars of evening.*

She smelled a pungent chemical scent. From whatever had made the bang, she guessed. The hallway was deserted. There was slight motion at the end of the hall. A shadow from the stairwell. She looked at it. It wasn't repeated.

Brit Hale's room was only ten feet away. She wanted badly to talk to him, but she didn't want him to see her this way, pale, hands shaking. Eyes watering in fear . . . My God, she'd pulled a seven three seven out of a wing-ice nosedive more calmly than this: looking into that dark corridor.

She stepped back into her room.

Did she hear footsteps?

She closed the door, returned to the bed.

More footsteps.

"Command mode," Lincoln Rhyme instructed. The box dutifully came up on-screen.

He heard a faint siren in the distance.

And it was then that Rhyme realized his mistake.

Fire trucks . . .

No! I didn't think about that.

But the Dancer did. Of course! He'd have stolen a fireman's or medic's uniform and was strolling into the safe house at this moment!

"Oh, no," he muttered. "No! How could I be so far off?"

And the computer heard the last word of Rhyme's sentence and dutifully shut off his communications program.

"No!" Rhyme cried. "No!"

But the system couldn't understand his loud, frantic voice and with a silent flash the message came up, *Do you really want to shut off your computer?*

"No," he whispered desperately.

For a moment nothing happened, but the system didn't shut down. A message popped up. *What would you like to do now?*

"Thom!" he shouted. "Somebody . . . please. Mel!"

But the door was closed; there was no response from downstairs.

Rhyme's left ring finger twitched dramatically. At one time he'd had a mechanical ECU controller and he could use his one working finger to dial the phone. The computer system had replaced that and he now *had* to use the dictation program to call the safe house and tell them that the Dancer was on his way there, dressed as a fireman or rescue worker.

"Command mode," he said into the microphone. Fighting to stay calm.

I did not understand what you just said. Please try again.

Where was the Dancer now? Was he inside already? Was he just about to shoot Percey Clay or Brit Hale?

Or Amelia Sachs?

"Thom! Mel!"

I did not understand . . .

Why wasn't I thinking better?

"Command mode," he said breathlessly, trying to master the panic.

The command mode message box popped up. The cursor arrow sat at the top of the screen and, a continent away, at the bottom, was the communications program icon.

"Cursor down," he gasped.

Nothing happened.

"Cursor down," he called, louder.

The message came back: *I did not understand what you just said. Please try again.*

"Oh, goddamn . . ."

I did not understand . . .

Softer, forcing himself to speak in a normal tone, he said, "Cursor down."

The glowing white arrow began its leisurely trip down the screen.

We've still got time, he told himself. And it wasn't as though the people in the safe house were unprotected or unarmed.

"Cursor left," he gasped.

I did not understand . . .

"Oh, come on!"

I did not understand . . .

"Cursor up . . . cursor left."

The cursor moved like a snail over the screen until it came to the icon.

Calm, calm . . .

"Cursor stop. Double click."

Dutifully, an icon of a walkie-talkie popped up on the screen.

He pictured the faceless Dancer moving up behind Percey Clay with a knife or garrote.

In as calm a voice as he could muster he ordered the cursor to the set-frequency box.

It seated itself perfectly.

"Four," Rhyme said, pronouncing the word so very carefully.

A *4* popped up into the box. Then he said, "Eight."

The letter *A* appeared in the second box.

Lord in heaven!

"Delete left."

I did not understand . . .

No, no!

He thought he heard footsteps. "Hello?" he cried. "Is someone there? Thom? Mel?"

No answer except from his friend the computer, which placidly offered its contrarian response once again.

"Eight," he said slowly.

The number appeared. His next attempt, "Three," popped into the box without a problem.

"Point."

The word *point* appeared.

Goddamn!

"Delete left." Then, "Decimal."

The period popped up.

"Four."

One space left. Remember, it's *zero* not *oh*. Sweat streaming down his face, he added the final number of the Secure Ops frequency without a glitch.

The radio clicked on.

Yes!

But before he could transmit, static clattered harshly and, with a frozen heart, he heard a man's frantic voice crying, "Ten-thirteen, need assistance, federal protection location six."

The safe house.

He recognized the voice as Roland Bell's. "Two down

and . . . Oh, Jesus, he's still here. He's got us, he's hit us! We need—"

There were two gunshots. Then others. A dozen. A huge firefight. It sounded like Macy's fireworks on the fourth of July.

"We need—"

The transmission ended.

"Percey!" Rhyme cried. "Percey . . ."

On the screen came the message in simple type: *I did not understand what you just said. Please try again.*

A nightmare.

Stephen Kall, in ski mask and wearing the bulky fireman's coat, lay pinned down in the corridor of the safe house, behind the body of one of the two U.S. marshals he'd just killed.

Another shot, closer, digging a piece out of the floor near his head. Fired by the detective with the thinning brown hair – the one he'd seen in the window of the safe house that morning. He crouched in a doorway, presenting a fair target, but Stephen couldn't get a clean shot at him. The detective held automatic pistols in both his hands and was an excellent shot.

Stephen crawled forward another yard, toward one of the open doorways.

Panicked, cringey, coated with worms . . .

He fired again and the brown-haired detective ducked back into the room, called something on his radio, but came right back, firing coolly.

Wearing a fireman's long, black coat – the same as thirty or forty other men and women in front of the safe house – Stephen had blown open the alley door with a cutting charge and run inside, expecting to find the interior a fiery shambles and the Wife and Friend – as well as half the other people inside – blown to pieces or badly wounded. But Lincoln the Worm had fooled him again. He'd figured out that the phone was booby-trapped. The only thing they hadn't expected was that he'd hit the safe house again; they believed he was going for a transport hit. Still, when he burst inside he was met by the frantic fire from the two marshals. But they'd been stunned by the cutting charge and he'd managed to kill them.

Then the brown-haired detective charged around the corner firing both-handed, skimming two off Stephen's vest, while Stephen himself danced one round off the detective's and they fell backward simultaneously. More shooting, more near misses. The cop was almost as good a shot as he was.

A minute at the most. He had no more time than that.

He felt so wormy he wanted to cry . . . He'd thought his plan out as best he could. He couldn't get any smarter than he'd been and Lincoln the Worm had *still* outthought him. Was this him? The balding detective with the two guns?

Another volley from Stephen's gun. And . . . damn . . . the brown-haired detective dove right into it, kept coming forward. Every other cop in the world would've run for cover. But not him. He struggled another two feet forward, then three. Stephen reloaded, fired again, crawling about the same distance toward the door of his target's room.

You disappear into the ground, boy. You can make yourself invisible, you want to.

I want to, sir. I want to be invisible . . .

Another yard, almost to the doorway.

"This's Roland Bell again!" the cop shouted into his microphone. "We need backup immediately!"

Bell, Stephen noted the name So he's not Lincoln the Worm.

The cop reloaded and continued to fire. A dozen shots, two dozen . . . Stephen could only admire his technique. This Bell would keep track of how many shots he'd fired from each gun and alternate reloading so he was never without a loaded weapon.

The cop parked a slug in the wall an inch from Stephen's face, and Stephen returned a shot that landed just as close.

Crawling forward another two feet.

Bell glanced up and saw that Stephen had finally made it to the doorway of the darkened bedroom. Their eyes locked and, mock soldier though he was, Stephen Kall had seen enough combat to know that the string of rationality within this cop had snapped and he'd become the most dangerous thing there was – a skillful soldier with no regard for his own safety. Bell rose to his feet and started forward, firing from both guns.

That's why they used .45s in the Pacific Theater, boy. Big slugs to stop those crazy little Japs. When they came at you they didn't care about getting killed; they just didn't want to get stopped.

Stephen lowered his head, tossed the one-second-delay flash bang at Bell and closed his eyes. The grenade detonated with an astonishingly loud explosion. He heard the cop cry out and saw him stumble to his knees, hands over his face.

Stephen had guessed that because of the guards and Bell's furious effort to stop him, either the Wife or the Friend was in this room. Stephen had also guessed that whoever it was would be hiding in the closet or under the bed.

He was wrong.

As he glanced into the doorway he saw the figure come charging at him, holding a lamp as a weapon and uttering a wail of fear and anger.

Five fast shots from Stephen's gun. Head and chest hits, well grouped. The body spun around fast and flew backward to the floor

Good job, Soldier.

Then more footsteps on the floor coming down the stairs. A woman's voice. And more voices too. No time to finish Bell, no time to look for the other target.

Evacuate . . .

He ran to the back door and stuck his head outside, shouting for more firemen.

A half dozen of them ran up cautiously.

Stephen nodded them inside. "Gas line just blew. I'd get everybody out. Now!"

And he disappeared into the alley, then stepped into the street, dodging the Mack and Seagrave fire trucks, the ambulances, the police cars.

Shaken, yes.

But satisfied. His job was now two-thirds finished.

Amelia Sachs was the first to respond to the bang of the entry charge and the shouts.

Then Roland Bell's voice from the first floor: "Backup! Backup! Officer down!"

And gunfire. A dozen sharp cracks, a dozen more.

She didn't know how the Dancer'd done it and she didn't care. She wanted only a fair glimpse of target and two seconds to sink half a clip of nine-millimeter hollow-points into him.

The light Glock in her hand, she pushed into the second floor corridor. Behind her were Sellitto and Dellray and a young uniform, whose credentials under fire she wished she'd taken the time to learn. Jodie cowered on the floor, painfully aware he'd betrayed a very dangerous man who was armed and no more than thirty feet away.

Sachs's knees screamed as she took the stairs fast, the arthritis again, and she winced as she leapt down the last three steps to the first floor.

In her headset she heard Bell's repeated request for assistance.

Down the dark corridor, pistol close to the body, where it couldn't be knocked aside (only TV cops and movie gangsters stick a gun out in front of them phallically before turning corners, or tilt a weapon on its side). Fast glance into each of the rooms she passed, crouching, below chest height, where a muzzle would be pointed.

"I'll take the front," Dellray called and vanished down the hallway behind her, his big Sig-Sauer in hand.

"Watch our backs," Sachs ordered Sellitto and the uniform, caring not a bit about rank.

"Yes'm," the young man answered. "I'm watching. Our backs."

Puffing Sellitto was too, his head swiveling back and forth.

Static crinkled in her ear but she heard no voices. She tugged the headset off – no distractions – and continued cautiously down the corridor.

At her feet two U.S. marshals lay dead on the floor.

The smell of chemical explosive was strong and she

glanced toward the back door of the safe house. It was steel but he'd blown it open with a powerful cutting charge as if it had been paper.

"Jesus," Sellitto said, too professional to bend down over the fallen marshals but too human not to glance in horror at their riddled bodies.

Sachs came to one room, paused at the door. Two of Haumann's troops entered from the destroyed doorway.

"Cover," she called and before anyone had a chance to stop her she leapt through the doorway fast.

Glock up, scanning the room.

Nothing.

No cordite smell either. There'd been no shooting here.

Back into the corridor. Heading toward the next doorway.

She pointed to herself and then into the room. The 32-E officers nodded.

Sachs spun around the doorway, ready to fire, the troopers right behind. She froze at the sight of the gun muzzle aimed at her chest.

"Lord," Roland Bell muttered and lowered his weapon. His hair was mussed and his face was sooty. Two bullets had torn his shirt and streaked over his body armor.

Then her eyes took in the terrible sight on the floor.

"Oh, no . . ."

"Building's clear," a patrolman called from the corridor. "They saw him leave. He was wearing a fireman's uniform. He's gone. Lost in the crowd out front."

Amelia Sachs, once again a criminalist and not a tactical officer, observed the blood spatter, the astringent scent of gunshot residue, the fallen chair, which might indicate a struggle and therefore would be a logical transfer point for trace evidence. The bullet casings, which she immediately noticed were from a 7.62 millimeter automatic.

She observed too the way the body had fallen, which told her that the victim had been attacking the attacker, apparently with a lamp. There were other stories the crime scene would tell and, for that reason, she knew she should help Percey Clay to her feet and lead her away from the body of her slain friend. But Sachs couldn't do that. All she could do was watch the small woman with the squat unpretty face cradle Brit Hale's bloody head, muttering, "Oh, no, oh, no . . ."

Her face was a mask, unmoving, untouched by tears.

Finally Sachs nodded to Roland Bell, who slipped his arms around Percey and led her out into the corridor, still vigilant, still clutching his own weapon.

Two hundred and thirty yards from the safe house.

Red and blue lights from the dozens of emergency vehicles flashed and tried to blind him but he was sighting through the Redfield telescope and was oblivious to anything but the reticles. He scanned back and forth over the kill zone.

Stephen had stripped off the fireman's uniform and was dressed again as a late-blooming college student. He'd recovered the Model 40 from under the water tank, where he'd hidden it that morning. The weapon was loaded and locked. The sling was around his arm and he was ready to murder.

At the moment it wasn't the Wife he was after.

And it wasn't Jodie, the little faggot Judas.

He was looking for Lincoln the Worm. The man who'd outthought him once again.

Who was he? Which of them?

Cringey.

Lincoln . . . Prince of Worms.

Where are you? Are you right in front of me now? In that crowd standing around the smoking building?

Was he that large lump of a cop, sweating like a hog?

The tall, thin Negro in the green suit? He looked familiar. Where had Stephen seen him before?

An unmarked car streaked up and several men in suits climbed out.

Maybe Lincoln was one of *them*.

The red-haired policewoman stepped outside. She was wearing latex gloves. Crime Scene, are you? Well, I treat my casings and slugs, darling, he said to her silently as the reticles of the telescope picked out a pretty target on her neck. And you'll have to fly to Singapore before you pick up a lead to my gun.

He figured he had time to fire just one shot and then be driven into the alley by the fusillade that would follow.

Who are you?

Lincoln? Lincoln?

But he had no clue.

Then the front door swung open and Jodie appeared, stepping out the door uneasily. He looked around, squinted, shrank back against the building.

You . . .

The electric sizzle again. Even at this distance.

Stephen easily moved the reticles onto his chest.

Go ahead, Soldier, fire your weapon. He's a logical target; he can identify you.

Sir, I am adjusting for tracking and windage.

Stephen upped the poundage on his trigger.

Jodie . . .

He betrayed you, Soldier. Take . . . him . . . out.

Sir, yessir. He is ice cold. He is dead meat. Sir, vultures are already hovering.

Soldier, the USMC sniper's manual dictates that you increase poundage on the trigger of your Model 40 imperceptibly so that you are not aware of the exact moment your weapon will discharge. Is that correct, Soldier?

Sir, yessir.

Then why the fuck aren't you doing it?

He squeezed harder.

Slowly, slowly . . .

But the gun wasn't firing. He lifted the sights to Jodie's head. And as it happened, Jodie's eyes, which had been scanning the rooftops, saw him.

He'd waited too long.

Shoot, Soldier. Shoot!

A whisper of a pause . . .

Then he jerked the trigger like a boy on the .22 rifle range at summer camp.

Just as Jodie leapt out of the way, pushing the cops with him aside.

How the fuck d'you miss that shot, Soldier? Repeat fire!

Sir, yessir.

He got off two more rounds but Jodie and everyone else was under cover or crawling fast along the sidewalk and street.

And then the return fire began. First a dozen guns, then a dozen more. Mostly pistols but some H&Ks too, spewing the bullets so fast they sounded like unmuffled car engines.

Bullets were striking the elevator tower behind him, showering him with bits of brick and concrete and lead and sharp, craggy copper jackets from the slugs, cutting his forearms and the backs of his hands.

Stephen fell backward, covering his face with his hands. He felt the cuts and saw tiny drops of his blood fall on the tar paper roof.

Why did I wait? Why? I could have shot him and been gone.

Why?

The sound of a helicopter speeding toward the building. More sirens.

Evacuate, Soldier! Evacuate!

He glanced down to see Jodie scrambling to safety behind a car. Stephen threw the Model 40 into the case, slung the backpack over his shoulder, and slid down the fire escape into the alley.

The second tragedy.

Percey Clay had changed her clothes and stepped into the corridor, slumped against the strong figure of Roland Bell. He put his arm around her.

The second of three. It hadn't been their mechanic quitting or problems with the charter. It had been the death of her dear friend.

Oh, Brit . . .

Imagining him, eyes wide, mouth open in a soundless shout, charge toward the terrible man. Trying to stop him, appalled that someone would actually be trying to kill him, to kill Percey. More indignant and betrayed than scared. Your life was so precise, she thought to him. Even your risks were calculated. The inverted flight at fifty feet, the tailspins, the skydiving. To spectators, it looked impossible.

But you knew what you were doing and if you thought about the chance of an early death, you believed it would be from a bum linkage or a clogged fuel line or some careless student who intruded into your airspace.

The great aviation writer Ernest K. Gann wrote that fate was a hunter. Percey'd always thought he meant nature or circumstance – the fickle elements, the faulty mechanisms that conspire to send airplanes hurtling into the ground. But fate was more complicated than that. Fate was as complicated as the human mind. As complicated as evil.

Tragedies came in threes . . . And what would the last one be? Her death? The Company's? Someone else's?

Huddling against Roland Bell, she shivered with anger at the coincidence of it all. Thinking back: she and Ed and Hale, groggy from lack of sleep, standing in the glare of the hangar lights around Learjet *Charlie Juliet,* hoping desperately they'd win the U.S. Medical contract, shivering in the damp night as they tried to figure out how best to outfit the jet for the job.

Late, a misty night. The airport deserted and dark. Like the final scene in *Casablanca.*

Hearing the squeal of brakes and glancing outside.

The man lugging the huge duffle bags out of the car on the tarmac, flinging them inside, and firing up the Beachcraft. The distinctive whine of a piston engine starting.

She remembered Ed saying, incredulous, "What's he doing? The airport's closed."

Fate.

That they happened to be there that night.

That Phillip Hansen had chosen that exact moment to get rid of his damaging evidence.

That Hansen was a man who would kill to keep that flight a secret.

Fate . . .

Then she jumped – at a knocking on the door of the safe house.

Two men stood there. Bell recognized them. They were from the NYPD Witness Protection Division. "We're here to transport you to the Shoreham facility on Long Island, Mrs Clay."

"No, no," she said. "There's a mistake. I have to go to Mamaroneck Airport."

"Percey," Roland Bell said.

"I *have* to."

"I don't know about that, ma'am," one of the officers said. "We've got orders to take you to Shoreham and keep you in protective confinement until a grand jury appearance on Monday."

"No, no, no. Call Lincoln Rhyme. He knows about it."

"Well . . ." One of the officers looked to the other.

"Please," she said, "call him. He'll tell you."

"Actually, Mrs Clay, it was Lincoln Rhyme who ordered you moved. If you'll come with us, please. Don't you worry. We'll take good care of you, ma'am."

Hour 28 of 45

27

"It's not pleasant," Thom told Amelia Sachs.

From behind the bedroom door she heard, "I want that bottle and I want it now."

"What's going on?"

The handsome young man grimaced. "Oh, he can be such a prick sometimes. He got one of the patrol officers to pour him some scotch. For the pain, he said. He said he's got a prescription for single-malt. Can you believe it? Oh, he's insufferable when he drinks."

A howl of rage from his room.

Sachs knew the only reason he wasn't throwing things was that he couldn't.

She reached for the doorknob.

"You might want to wait a little," Thom warned.

"We can't wait."

"*Goddamnit!*" Rhyme snarled. "I want that fucking bottle!"

She opened the door. Thom whispered, "Don't say I didn't warn you."

Inside, Sachs paused in the doorway. Rhyme was a sight. His hair was disheveled, there was spittle on his chin, and his eyes were red.

The Macallan bottle was on the floor. He must have tried to grab it with his teeth and knocked it over.

He noticed Sachs but all he said was a brisk "Pick it up."

"We've got work to do, Rhyme."

"Pick. Up. That. Bottle."

She did. And placed it on the shelf.

He raged, "You know what I mean. I want a drink."

"You've had more than enough, sounds like."

"Pour some whiskey in my goddamn glass. Thom! Get the hell in here . . . Coward."

"Rhyme," she snapped, "we've got evidence to look at."

"Hell with the evidence."

"How much did you drink?"

"The Dancer got inside, didn't he? Fox in the henhouse. Fox in the henhouse."

"I've got a vacuum filter full of trace, I've got a slug, I've got samples of his blood . . ."

"Blood? Well, that's fair. He's got plenty of ours."

She snapped back, "You oughta be like a kid on his birthday, all the evidence I've got. Quit feeling sorry for yourself, and let's get to work."

He didn't respond. As she looked at him she saw his bleary eyes focused past her on the doorway. She turned. There was Percey Clay.

Immediately, Rhyme's eyes dropped to the floor. He fell silent.

Sure, Sachs thought. Doesn't want to misbehave in front of his new love.

She walked into the room, looked at the mess that was Lincoln Rhyme.

"Lincoln, what's going on?" Sellitto had accompanied Percey here, she guessed. He stepped into the room.

"Three dead, Lon. He got three more. Fox in the henhouse."

"Lincoln," Sachs blurted. "Stop it. You're embarrassing yourself."

Wrong thing to say. Rhyme slapped a bewildered gaze on his face. "I'm not embarrassed. Do I look embarrassed? Anyone? Am I embarrassed? *Am I fucking embarrassed?*"

"We've got—"

"No, we've got zip! It's over with. It's done. It's finished. Duck 'n' cover. We're heading for the hills. Are you going to join us, Amelia? Suggest you do."

He finally looked at Percey. "What are you doing here? You're supposed to be on Long Island."

"I want to talk to you."

He said nothing at first, then, "Give me a drink, at least."

Percey glanced at Sachs and stepped forward to the shelf, poured herself and Rhyme both glasses. Sachs glared at her and she noticed, didn't respond.

"Here's a classy lady," Rhyme said. "I kill her partner and she still shares a drink with me. *You* didn't do that, Sachs."

"Oh, Rhyme, you can be such an asshole," Sachs spat out. "Where's Mel?"

"Sent him home. Nothing more to do . . . We're bundling her up and shipping her off to Long Island, where she'll be safe."

"What?" Sachs asked.

"Doing what we should've done at the beginning. Hit me again."

Percey began to. Sachs said, "He's had enough."

"Don't listen to her," Rhyme blurted. "She's mad at me. I don't do what she wants and so she gets mad."

Oh, thank you, Rhyme. Let's air linen in public, why don't we? She turned her beautiful, cold eyes on him. He didn't even notice; he was gazing at Percey Clay.

Who said, "You made a deal with me. The next thing I know there're two agents about to take me off to Long Island. I thought I could trust you."

"But if you *trust* me, you'll die."

"It was a risk," Percey said. "You told us there was a chance he'd get into the safe house."

"Sure, but you didn't know that I figured it out."

"You . . . what?"

Sachs frowned, listened.

Rhyme continued, "I figured out he was going to hit the safe house. I figured out he was in a fireman's uniform. I fucking figured out he'd use a cutting charge on the back door. I'll bet it was an Accuracy Systems Five Twenty-one or Five Twenty-two with an Instadet firing system. Am I right?"

"I—"

"Am I right?"

"A Five Twenty-one," Sachs said.

"See? I figured all that out. I knew it five minutes before he got in. It's just that I couldn't fucking call anyone and tell them! I couldn't . . . pick up . . . the fucking phone and tell anybody what was going to happen. And your friend died. Because of me."

Sachs felt pity for him and it was sour. She was torn apart by his pain, yet she didn't have a clue what she might say to comfort him.

There was moisture on his chin. Thom stepped forward with a tissue, but he waved the aide away with a furious nod of his handsome jaw. He nodded toward the computer. "Oh, I got cocky. I got to thinking I was pretty normal. Driving around like a race car driver in the Storm Arrow, flipping on lights and changing CDs . . . What bullshit!" He closed his eyes and pressed his head back in the pillow.

A sharp laugh, surprising everyone, filled the room.

Percey Clay poured some more scotch into her glass. Then a little more for Rhyme too. "There's bullshit here, that's for sure. But it's only what I'm hearing from you."

Rhyme opened his eyes, glaring.

Percey laughed again.

"Don't," Rhyme warned ambiguously.

"Oh, please," she muttered dismissingly. "Don't what?"

Sachs watched Percey's eyes narrow. "What're you saying?" Percey began. "That somebody's dead because of . . . technical failure?"

Sachs realized that Rhyme had been expecting her to say something else. He was caught off guard. After a moment he said, "Yes. That's exactly what I'm saying. If I'd been able to pick up the phone—"

She cut him off. "And, what? That gives you the right to have a goddamn tantrum? To renege on your promises?" She tossed back her liquor and gave an exasperated sigh. "Oh, for God's sake . . . Do your have any idea what I do for a living?"

To her astonishment Sachs saw that Rhyme was calm now. He started to speak, but Percey cut him off. "Think about this." Her drawl was back. "I sit in a little aluminum tube going four hundred knots an hour, six miles above the ground. It's sixty below zero outside and the winds are a hundred miles an hour. I'm not even talking about lightning, wind sheer, and ice. Jesus Christ, I'm only alive *because* of machines." Another laugh. "How's that different from you?"

"You don't understand," he said snippily.

"You're not answering my question. How?" she demanded, unrelenting. "How's it different?"

"You can walk around, you can pick up the phone—"

"I can walk around? I'm at fifty thousand feet. I open that door and my blood boils in seconds."

For the first time she'd known him, Sachs thought, Rhyme's met his match. He's speechless.

Percey continued, "I'm sorry, Detective, but I don't see a lick of difference between us. We're products of twentieth-century science. Goddamn it, if I had wings I'd be flying on my own. But I don't and never will. To do what we have to do, both of us . . . we *rely*."

"Okay . . ." He grinned devilishly.

Come on, Rhyme, Sachs thought. Let her have it! How badly Sachs wanted him to win, to boot this woman off to Long Island, have done with her forever.

The criminalist said, "But if *I* screw up, people die."

"Oh? And what happens if my deicer fails? What happens if my yaw damper goes? What if a pigeon flies into my pitot tube on an ILS approach? I . . . am . . . dead. Flameouts, hydraulic failures, mechanics who forget to replace bum circuit breakers . . . Redundant systems fail. In *your* case they might get a chance to recover from their gunshots. But my aircraft hits the ground at three hundred miles an hour, there ain't nothing left."

Rhyme seemed completely sober now. His eyes were swiveling around the room as if looking for an infallible bit of evidence to refute Percey's argument.

"Now," Percey said evenly, "I understand Amelia here has some evidence she found back at the safe house. My suggestion is you start looking at it and stop this asshole once and for all. Because I am on my way to Mamaroneck right now to finish repairing my aircraft and then I'm flying that job tonight. Now, I'll ask you point-blank: You going to let me go to the airport, like you agreed? Or do I have to call my lawyer?"

He was still speechless.

A moment passed.

Sachs jumped when Rhyme called in his booming baritone, "Thom! *Thom!* Get in here."

The aide peered around the doorway suspiciously.

"I've made a mess here. Look, I knocked my glass over. And my hair's mussed. Would you mind straightening up a little? Please?"

"Are you fooling with us, Lincoln?" he asked dubiously.

"And Mel Cooper? Could you call him, Lon? He must have taken me seriously. I was kidding. He's such a goddamn scientist. No sense of humor. We'll need him back here."

Amelia Sachs wanted to flee. To bolt out of here, get into her car, and tear up the roads in New Jersey or Nassau County at 120 miles an hour. She couldn't stand to be in the same room with this woman a moment longer.

"All right, Percey," Rhyme said, "take Detective Bell with you and we'll make sure plenty of Bo's troopers are with you too. Get up to your airport. Do what you have to do."

"Thank you, Lincoln." She nodded, and offered a smile.

Just enough of one to make Amelia Sachs wonder if part of Percey Clay's speech wasn't meant for Sachs's benefit too, to make clear who the undisputed winner in this contest was. Well, some sports Sachs believed she was doomed to lose. Champion shooter, decorated cop, a demon of a driver, and pretty good criminalist, Sachs nonetheless possessed an unjacketed heart. Her father had sensed this about her; he'd been a romantic too. After she'd gone through a bad affair some years ago he'd said to her, "They oughta make body armor for the soul, Amie. They oughta do that."

Good-bye, Rhyme, she thought. Good-bye.

And his response to this tacit farewell? A minuscule glance and the gruff words "Let's look at that evidence, Sachs. Time's a-wasting."

Hour 29 of 45

28

Individuation is the goal of the criminalist.

It's the process of tracing a piece of evidence back to a single source, to the exclusion of all other sources.

Lincoln Rhyme now gazed at the most individuated evidence there was: blood from the Dancer's body. A restriction fragment length polymorphism DNA test could eliminate virtually any possibility that the blood had come from anyone else.

Yet there was little that this evidence could tell him. CODIS – the Computer-Based DNA Information System – contained profiles of some convicted felons, but it was a small database, made up primarily of sex offenders and a limited number of violent criminals. Rhyme wasn't surprised when the search of the Dancer's blood came back negative.

Still, Rhyme harbored a faint pleasure that they now had a piece of the killer himself, swabbed and stuck into a test tube. For most criminalists, the perps were usually "out there"; he rarely met them face-to-face, often never saw them at all unless it was at trial. So he felt a deep stirring to be in the presence of the man who'd caused so many people, himself included, so much pain.

"What else did you find?" he asked Sachs.

She'd vacuumed Brit Hale's room for trace but she and Cooper, donning magnifiers, had been through it all and found nothing except gunshot residue and fragments of bullets and brick and plaster from the shoot-outs.

She'd found casings from the semiautomatic pistol he'd

used. His weapon was a 7.62-millimeter Beretta. It was probably old; it showed breach spread. The casings, all of which Sachs had recovered, had been dipped in cleansers to eliminate even the prints of the employees of the ammunition company – so no one could trace the purchase back to a certain shift at one of the Remington plants and then forward to a shipment that ended up in a particular location. And the Dancer had apparently loaded them with his knuckles to avoid prints. An old trick.

"Keep going," Rhyme said to Sachs.

"Pistol slugs."

Cooper looked over the bullets. Three flattened. And one in pretty good shape. Two were covered with Brit Hale's black, cauterized blood.

"Scan them for prints," Rhyme ordered.

"I did," she said, her voice clipped.

"Try the laser."

Cooper did.

"Nothing, Lincoln." The tech looked at a piece of cotton in a plastic bag. He asked, "What's that?"

Sachs said, "Oh, I got one of his rifle slugs too."

"What?"

"He took a couple shots at Jodie. Two of them hit the wall and exploded. This one hit dirt – a bed of flowers – and didn't go off. I found a hole in one of the geraniums and—"

"Wait." Cooper blinked. "That's one of the *explosive* rounds?"

Sachs said, "Right, but it didn't go off."

He gingerly set the bag on the table and stepped back, pulling Sachs – two inches taller than he was – along with him.

"What's the matter?"

"Explosive bullets're very unstable. Powder grains could be smouldering right now . . . It could go off at any minute. A piece of shrapnel could kill you."

"You saw the fragments of the other ones, Mel," Rhyme said. "How's it made?"

"It's nasty, Lincoln," the tech said uneasily, his bald crown dotted with sweat. "A PETN filling, smokeless powder as the primary. That makes it unstable."

Sachs asked, "Why didn't it go off?"

"The dirt'd be soft impact. And he makes them himself. Maybe his quality control wasn't so good for that one."

"He makes them himself?" Rhyme asked. "How?"

Eye fixed on the plastic bag, the tech said, "Well, the usual way is to tap a hole from the point almost through the base. Drop in a BB and some black or smokeless powder. You roll a thread of plastic and feed it inside. Then seal it up again – in his case with a ceramic nose cone. When it hits, the BB slams into the powder. That sets off the PETN."

"Rolls the plastic?" Rhyme asked. "Between his fingers?"

"Usually."

Rhyme looked at Sachs and for a moment the rift between them vanished. They smiled and said simultaneously, "Fingerprints!"

Mel Cooper said, "Maybe. But how're you going to find out? You'd have to take it apart."

"Then," Sachs said, "we'll take it apart."

"No, no, no, Sachs," Rhyme said curtly. "Not you. We'll wait for the bomb squad."

"We don't have time."

She bent over the bag, started to open it.

"Sachs, what the hell're you trying to prove?"

"Not trying to prove anything," she responded coolly. "I'm trying to catch the killer."

Cooper stood by helplessly.

"Are you trying to save Jerry Banks? Well, it's too late for that. Give him up. Get on with your job."

"This *is* my job."

"Sachs, it wasn't your fault!" Rhyme shouted. "Forget it. Give up the dead. I've told you that a dozen times."

Calmly she said, "I'll put my vest on top of it, work from behind it." She stripped her blouse off and ripped the Velcro straps of her American Body Armor. She set this up like a tent over the plastic bag containing the bullet.

Cooper said, "You're behind the armor but your hands won't be."

"Bombs suits don't have hand protection either," she pointed out, and pulled her shooting earplugs from her pocket, screwed them into her ears. "You'll have to shout," she said to Cooper. "What do I do?"

No, Sachs, no, Rhyme thought.

"If you don't tell me I'll just cut it apart." She picked up a forensic razor saw. The blade hovered over the bag. She paused.

Rhyme sighed, nodded to Cooper. "Tell her what to do."

The tech swallowed. "All right. Unwrap it. But carefully. Here, put it on this towel. Don't jar it. That's the worst thing you can do."

She exposed the bullet, a surprisingly tiny piece of metal with an off-white tip.

"That cone?" Cooper continued. "If the bullet goes off the cone'll go right through the body armor and at least one or two walls. It's Teflon-coated."

"Okay." She turned it aside, toward the wall.

"Sachs," Rhyme said soothingly. "Use forceps, not your fingers."

"It won't make any difference if it blows, Rhyme. And I need the control."

"Please."

She hesitated and took the hemostat that Cooper offered her. She gripped the base of the slug.

"How do I open it up? Cut it?"

"You can't cut through the lead," Cooper called. "The heat from the friction'll set off the black powder. You'll have to work the cone off and pull the wad of plastic out."

Sweat was rolling down her face. "Okay. With pliers?"

Cooper picked up a pair of needle-nose pliers from the worktable and walked to her side. He put them in her right hand, then retreated.

"You'll have to grip it and twist hard. He glued it on with epoxy. That doesn't bond well with lead, so it should just pop off. But don't squeeze too hard. If it fractures you'll never get it off without drilling. And that'll set it off."

"Hard but not too hard," she muttered.

"Think of all those cars you worked on, Sachs," Rhyme said.

"What?"

"Trying to get those old spark plugs out. Hard enough to unseat them, not so hard you broke the ceramic."

She nodded absently and he didn't know if she'd heard him. Sachs lowered her head behind the tepee of her body armor.

Rhyme saw her eyes squinting shut.

Oh, Sachs . . .

He never saw any motion. He just heard a very faint snap. She froze for a moment, then looked over the armor. "It came off. It's open."

Cooper said, "Do you see the explosive?"

She looked inside. "Yes."

He handed her a can of light machine oil. "Drip some of this inside then tilt it. The plastic should fall out. We can't pull it or the fingerprints'll be ruined."

She added the oil, then tilted the slug, open end down, toward the towel.

Nothing happened.

"Damn," she muttered.

"Don't—"

She shook it. Hard.

"—shake it!" Cooper shouted.

"Sachs!" Rhyme gasped.

She shook harder. "Damn it."

"No!"

A tiny white thread fell out, followed by some grains of black powder.

"Okay," Cooper said, exhaling. "It's safe."

He walked over and, using a needle probe, rolled the plastic onto a glass slide. He walked in the smooth gait of criminalists around the world – back straight, hand buoyed and carrying the sample rock steady – to the microscope. He mounted the explosive.

"Magna-Brush?" Cooper asked, referring to a fine gray fingerprint powder.

"No," Rhyme responded. "Use gentian violet. It's a plastic print. We just need a little contrast."

Cooper sprayed it, then mounted the slide in the 'scope.

The image popped onto the screen of Rhyme's computer simultaneously.

"Yes!" he shouted. "There it is."

The whorls and bifurcations were very visible.

"You nailed it, Sachs. Good job."

As Cooper slowly rotated the plug of explosive, Rhyme made progressive screen captures – bitmap images – and saved them on the hard drive. He then assembled them and printed out a single, two-dimensional sliver of print.

But when the tech examined it he sighed.

"What?" Rhyme asked.

"Still not enough for a match. Only a quarter inch by a five eighths. No AFIS in the world could pick up anything from this."

"Jesus," Rhyme spat out. All that effort . . . wasted.

A sudden laugh.

From Amelia Sachs. She was staring at the wall, the evidence charts. CS-1, CS-2 . . .

"Put them together," she said.

"What?"

"We've got three partials," she explained. "They're probably all from his index finger. Can't you fit them together?"

Cooper looked at Rhyme. "I've never heard of doing that."

Neither had Rhyme. The bulk of forensic work was analyzing evidence for presentation at trial – "forensic" *means* "relating to legal proceedings" – and a defense lawyer'd go to town if cops started assembling fragments of perps' fingerprints.

But their priority was *finding* the Dancer, not making a case against him.

"Sure," Rhyme said. "Do it!"

Cooper grabbed the other pictures of the Dancer's prints from the wall and rested them on the table in front of him.

They started to work, Sachs and the tech. Cooper made photocopies of the prints, reducing two so they were all the same size. Then he and Sachs began fitting them together like a jigsaw puzzle. They were like children, trying variations, rearranging, arguing playfully. Sachs went so far as to take out a pen and connect several lines over a gap in the print.

"Cheating," Cooper joked.

"But it fits," she said triumphantly.

Finally they cut and pasted a print together. It represented about three-quarters of a friction ridge print, probably the right index finger.

Cooper held it up. "I have my doubts about this, Lincoln."

But Rhyme said, "It's art, Mel. It's beautiful!"

"Don't tell anyone at the identification association or they'll drum us out."

"Put it through AFIS. Authorize a priority search. All states."

"Oooo," Cooper said. "That'll cost my annual salary."

He scanned the print into the computer.

"It could take a half hour," said Cooper, more realistic than pessimistic.

But it didn't take that long at all. Five minutes later – long enough only for Rhyme to speculate who'd be more willing to pour him a drink, Sachs or Cooper – the screen fluttered and a new image came up.

Your request has found . . . 1 match. 14 points of comparison. Statistical probability of identity: 97%.

"Oh, my God," Sachs muttered. "We've got him."

"Who is he, Mel?" Rhyme asked softly, as if he were afraid the words would blow the fragile electrons off the computer screen.

"He's not the Dancer anymore," Cooper said. "He's Stephen Robert Kall. Thirty-six. Present whereabouts unknown. LKA, fifteen years ago, an RFD number in Cumberland, West Virginia."

Such a mundane name. Rhyme found himself experiencing an unreasonable tug of disappointment. Kall.

"Why was he on file?"

Cooper read. "What he was telling Jodie . . . He did twenty months for manslaughter when he was fifteen." A faint laugh. "Apparently the Dancer *didn't* bother to tell him that the victim was his stepfather."

"Stepfather, hm?"

"Tough reading," Cooper said, poring over the screen. "Man."

"What?" Sachs asked.

"Notes from the police reports. Here's what happened. Seems like there'd been a history of domestic disputes. The boy's mother was dying of cancer and her husband – Kall's stepfather – hit her for doing something or another. She fell and broke her arm. She died a few months later and Kall got it into his head her death was Lou's fault."

Cooper continued to read and he actually seemed to shiver. "Want to hear what happened?"

"Go ahead."

"A couple months after she died Stephen and his stepfather were out hunting. The kid knocked him out, stripped him naked, and tied him to a tree in the woods. Left him there for a few days. Just wanted to scare him, his lawyer said. By the time the police got to him, well, let's just say the infestation was pretty bad. Maggots, mostly. Lived for two days after that. Delirious."

"Man," Sachs whispered.

"When they found him, the boy was there, just sitting next to him, watching." Cooper read, " 'The suspect surrendered without resistance. Appeared in a disoriented state. Kept repeating, "Anything can kill, anything can kill . . ." Taken to Cumberland Regional Mental Health Center for evaluation.' "

The psychological makeup didn't interest Rhyme very much. He trusted his forensic profiling techniques far more than the behavioral law enforcers'. He knew the Dancer was a sociopath – all professional killers were – and the sorrows and traumas that made him who he was weren't much help at the moment. He asked, "Picture?"

"No pictures in juvie."

"Right. Hell. How 'bout military?"

"Nope. But there's another conviction," Cooper said. "He tried to enlist in the marines but the psych profile got him rejected. He hounded the recruiting officers in D.C. for a couple months and finally assaulted a sergeant. Pled a suspended."

Sellitto said, "We'll run the name through FINEST, the alias list, and NCIC."

"Have Dellray get some people to Cumberland and start tracing him," Rhyme ordered.

"Will do."

Stephen Kall . . .

After all these years. It was like finally visiting a shrine you'd read about all your life but never seen in person.

There was a startling knock on the door. Sachs and Sellitto's hands both twitched impulsively toward their weapons.

But the visitor was just one of the cops from downstairs. He had a large satchel. "Delivery."

"What is it?" Rhyme asked.

"A trooper from Illinois. Said this was from Du Page County Fire and Rescue."

"What is it?"

The cop shrugged. "He *said* it was shit from some truck treads. But that's nuts. Must've been kidding."

"No," Rhyme said, "that's exactly what it is." He glanced at Cooper. "Tire scrapings from the crash site."

The cop blinked. "You wanted that? Flown in from Chicago?"

"We've been waiting with bated breath."

"Well. Life's funny sometimes, ain't it?"

And Lincoln Rhyme could only agree.

Professional flying is only partly about flying.

Flying is also about paperwork.

Littering the back of the van transporting Percey Clay to Mamaroneck Airport was a huge stack of books and charts and documents: NOS's *Airport/Facility Directory,* the *Airman's Information Manual*, the FAA's NOTAMs – "Notices to Airmen" – and advisory circulars, and the Jeppesen "J-Aids," the *Airport and Information Directory.* Thousands of pages. Mountains of information. Percey, like most pilots, knew much of it by heart. But she also wouldn't think about driving an aircraft without going back to the original materials and studying them, literally, from the ground up.

With this information and her calculator she was filling out the two basic pre-flight documents: the navigation log and the flight plan. On the log she'd mark their attitude, calculate the course variations due to wind and the variance between true course and magnetic course, determine their ETE – estimated time en route – and come up with the Godhead number: the amount of fuel they'd need for the flight. Six cities, six different logs, dozens of checkpoints in between . . .

Then there was the FAA flight plan itself, on the reverse side of the navigation log. Once airborne, the copilot would activate the plan by calling the Flight Service Station at Mamaroneck, which would in turn call ahead to Chicago with *Foxtrot Bravo*'s estimated time of arrival. If the aircraft didn't arrive at its destination within a half hour after ETA, it would be declared overdue and search-and-rescue procedures would start.

These were complicated documents and had to be calculated perfectly. If aircraft had unlimited fuel supplies they could rely on radio navigation and spend as much time as they wanted cruising from destination to destination at whatever altitudes they wanted. But not only was fuel expensive to begin with (and the twin Garrett turbofans burned an astonishing amount of it); it was also extremely heavy and cost a lot – in extra fuel charges – just to carry. On a long flight, especially with a number of fuel-hungry take-offs, carrying too much gas could drastically erode the profit the Company was making on the flight. The FAA dictated that each flight have enough fuel to make it to the point of destination, plus a reserve, in the case of a night flight, of forty-five minutes' flying time.

Fingers tapping over the calculators, Percey Clay filled in the forms in her precise handwriting. Careless about so much else in her life, she was meticulous about flying. The merest act of filling in ATIS frequencies or the magnetic heading variations gave her pleasure. She never scrimped, never estimated when accurate calculations were called for. Today, she submerged herself in the work.

Roland Bell was beside her. He was haggard and sullen. The good ole boy was long gone. She grieved for him, as much as for herself; it seemed that Brit Hale was the first witness he'd lost. She felt an unreasonable urge to touch his arm, to reassure him, as he'd done for her. But he seemed to be one of those men who, when faced with loss, disappear into themselves; any sympathy would jar. He was much like herself, she believed. Bell gazed out the window of the van, his hand frequently touching the checkered black grip of the pistol in his shoulder holster.

Just as she finished the last flight plan card, the van turned the corner and entered the airport, stopping for the armed guards, who examined their IDs and waved them through.

Percey directed them to the hangar but she noticed that the lights were still on in the office. She told the cars to stop and she climbed out, as Bell and her other bodyguards walked with her, vigilant and tense, into the main part of the office.

Ron Talbot, grease-stained and exhausted, sat in the office, wiping his sweating forehead. His face was an alarming red.

"Ron . . ." She hurried forward. "Are you all right?"

They embraced.

"Brit," he said, shaking his head, gasping. "He got Brit too. Percey, you shouldn't be here. Go someplace safe. Forget about the flight. It isn't worth it."

She stepped back. "What's wrong? You sick?"

"Just tired."

She took the cigarette out of his hand and stubbed it out. "You did the work yourself? On *Foxtrot Bravo*?"

"I—"

"Ron?"

"Most of it. It's almost finished. The guy from Northeast delivered the fire extinguisher cartridge and the annular about an hour ago. I started to mount them. Just got a little tired."

"Chest pains?"

"No, not really."

"Ron, go home."

"I can—"

"Ron," she snapped, "I've lost two dear people in the last two days. I'm not going to lose a third . . . I can mount an annular. It's a piece of cake."

Talbot looked like he couldn't even lift a wrench, much less a heavy combustor.

Percey asked, "Where's Brad?" The FO for the flight.

"On his way. Be here in an hour."

She kissed his sweaty forehead. "You get home. And lay off the weeds, for God's sake. You crazy?"

He hugged her. "Percey, about Brit . . ."

She hushed him with a finger to her lips. "Home. Get some sleep. When you wake up I'll be in Erie and we'll have ourselves that contract. Signed, sealed, and delivered."

He struggled to his feet, stood for a moment looking out the window at *Foxtrot Bravo.* His face revealed an acrid bitterness. It was the same look she'd remembered in his milky eyes when he'd told her that he'd flunked his physical and could no longer fly for a living. Talbot headed out the door.

It was time to get to work. She rolled up her sleeves, motioned Bell over to her. He lowered his head to her in a way she found charming. The same pose Ed fell into when she was speaking softly. She said, "I'm going to need a few hours in the hangar. Can you keep that son of a bitch off me until then?"

No down-home aphorisms, no done deals. Roland Bell, the man with two guns, nodded solemnly, his eyes moving quickly from shadow to shadow.

They had a mystery on their hands.

Cooper and Sachs had examined all the trace found in the treads of the Chicago fire trucks and police cars that had been at the scene of the Ed Carney crash. There was the useless dirt, dog shit, grass, oil, and garbage that Rhyme had expected to find. But they made one discovery that he felt was important.

He just didn't have a clue what it meant.

The only batch of trace exhibiting indications of bomb residue were tiny fragments of a pliable beige substance. The gas chromatograph/mass spectrometer reported it was C_5H_8.

"Isoprene," Cooper reflected.

"What's that?" Sachs had asked.

"Rubber," Rhyme answered.

Cooper continued. "I'm also reading fatty acids. Dyes, talcum."

"Any hardening agents?" Rhyme asked. "Clay? Magnesium carbonate? Zinc oxide?"

"None."

"It's soft rubber. Like latex."

"And little fragments of rubber cement too," Cooper added, peering at a sample in the compound microscope. "Bingo," he said.

"Don't tease, Mel," Rhyme grumbled.

"Bits of soldering and tiny pieces of plastic embedded in the rubber. Circuit boards."

"Part of the timer?" Sachs wondered aloud.

"No, that was intact," Rhyme reminded.

He felt they were onto something here. If this was another part of the bomb, it might give them a clue as to the source of the explosive or another component.

"We have to know for sure whether this's from the bomb or from the plane itself. Sachs, I want you to go up to the airport."

"The—"

"Mamaroneck. Find Percey and have her give you samples of anything with latex, rubber, or circuit boards that would be in the belly of a plane like the one Carney was flying. Near the seat of the explosion. And, Mel, send the info off to the Bureau's Explosives Reference Collection and check army CID – maybe there's a latex waterproof coating of some kind the army uses for explosives. Maybe we can trace it that way."

Cooper began typing the request on his computer, but Rhyme noticed Sachs wasn't pleased with her assignment.

"You want me to go talk to her?" she asked. "To Percey?"

"Yes. That's what I'm saying."

"Okay." She sighed. "All right."

"And don't give her any crap like you've been doing. We need her cooperation."

Rhyme didn't have a clue why she pulled on her vest so angrily and stalked out the door without saying good-bye.

Hour 31 of 45

29

At Mamaroneck Airport Amelia Sachs saw Roland Bell lurking outside the hangar. Another six officers stood guard around the huge building. She supposed there were snipers nearby too.

Her eye caught the hillock where she'd dropped to the ground under fire. She remembered, with a disgusted twist in her belly, the smell of the dirt mingling with the sweet cordite scent from her own impotent pistol shots.

Turned to Bell. "Detective."

His eyes glanced at her once. "Hey." Then he returned to scanning the airport. His easy Southern demeanor was gone. He'd changed. Sachs realized that they shared something notorious now. They'd both had a shot at the Coffin Dancer and missed.

They both had also been in his kill zone and survived. Bell, though, with more glory than she. *His* body armor, she noticed, bore stigmata: the streaks from the two slugs that had glanced off him during the safe house attack. He'd stood *his* ground.

"Where's Percey?" Sachs asked.

"Inside. Finishing up the repairs."

"By herself?"

"Think so. She's something, she is. You wouldn't think a woman that wasn't so, well, attractive'd have quite the draw she does. You know?"

Ugh. Don't get me started.

"Anybody else here? From the Company?" She nodded toward the Hudson Air office. There was a light on inside.

"Percey sent 'most everybody home. Fellow's going to be her copilot's due here anytime. And somebody from Operations's inside. Needs to be on duty when there's a flight going on, I guess. I checked him out. He's okay."

"So she's really going to fly?" Sachs asked.

"Looks that way."

"The plane's been guarded the whole time?"

"Yep, since yesterday. What're you doing here?"

"Need some samples for analysis."

"That Rhyme, he's something too."

"Uh-huh."

"All two of you go back a ways?"

"We've worked a few cases," she said dismissingly. "He saved me from Public Affairs."

"That's his good deed. Say, I hear you can really drive a nail."

"I can . . . ?"

"Shoot. Sidearms. You're on a team."

And here I am at the site of my latest competition, she thought bitterly. "Just weekend sport," she muttered.

"I do some pistol work myself, but I'll tell you, even on a good day, with a nice, long barrel and firing single-action, fifty, sixty yards is all the far I can shoot."

She appreciated his comments but recognized that they were just an attempt to reassure her about yesterday's fiasco; the words meant nothing to her.

"Better talk to Percey now."

"Right through there, Officer."

Sachs pushed into the huge hangar. She walked slowly, looking at all the places the Dancer could hide. Sachs paused behind a tall row of boxes; Percey didn't see her.

The woman was standing on a small scaffolding, hands on her hips, as she gazed at the complicated network of pipes and tubes of the open engine. She'd rolled her sleeves up and her hands were covered with grease. She nodded to herself then reached forward into the compartment.

Sachs was fascinated, watching the woman's hands fly over the machinery, adjusting, probing, seating metal to metal, and tightening the fixtures down with judicious swipes of her thin arms. She mounted a large red cylinder, a fire extinguisher, Sachs guessed, in about ten seconds flat.

But one part – it looked like a big metal inner tube – wouldn't fit correctly.

Percey climbed off the scaffolding, selected a socket wrench, and climbed up again. She loosened bolts, removed another part to give her more room to maneuver, and tried again to push the big ring into place.

Wouldn't budge.

She shouldered it. Didn't move an inch. She removed yet another part, meticulously setting each screw and bolt in a plastic tray at her feet. Percey's face turned bright red as she struggled to mount the metal ring. Her chest heaved as she fought the part. Suddenly it slipped, dropping completely out of position, and knocked her backward off the scaffolding. She landed on her hands and knees. The tools and bolts that she'd arranged so carefully in the tray spilled to the floor beneath the plane's tail.

"No!" Percey cried. "No!"

Sachs stepped forward to see if she was hurt, but noticed immediately that the outburst had nothing to do with pain – Percey grabbed a large wrench and slammed it furiously into the floor of the hangar. The policewoman stopped, stepped into the shadow beside a large carton.

"No, no, no . . .," Percey cried, hammering the smooth concrete.

Sachs remained where she was.

"Oh, Ed . . ." She dropped the wrench. "I can't do it alone." Gasping for breath, she rolled into a ball. "Ed . . . oh, Ed . . . I miss you so much!" She lay, curled like a frail leaf, on the shiny floor and wept.

Then, suddenly, the attack was over. Percey rolled upright, took a deep breath, and climbed to her feet, wiped the tears from her face. The aviatrix within her took charge once again and she picked up the bolts and tools and climbed back up onto the scaffolding. She stared at the troublesome ring for a moment. She examined the fittings carefully but couldn't see where the metal pieces were binding.

Sachs retreated to the door, slammed it hard, and then started back into the hangar, walking with loud steps.

Percey swung around, saw her, then turned back to the engine. She gave a few swipes to her face with her sleeve and continued to work.

Sachs walked up to the base of the scaffolding and watched as Percey struggled with the ring.

Neither woman said anything for a long moment.

Finally Sachs said, "Try a jack."

Percey glanced back at her, said nothing.

"It's just that the tolerance is close," Sachs continued. "All you need is more muscle. The old coercion technique. They don't teach it in mechanics school."

Percey looked carefully at the mounting brackets on the pieces of metal. "I don't know."

"I do. You're talking to an expert."

The flier asked, "You've mounted a combustor in a Lear?"

"Nope. Spark plugs in a Chevy Monza. You have to jack up the engine to reach them. Well, only in the V-eight. But who'd buy a four-cylinder car? I mean, what's the point?"

Percey looked back at the engine.

"So?" Sachs persisted. "A jack?"

"It'll bend the outer housing."

"Not if you put it there." Sachs pointed to a structural member connecting the engine to the support that went to the fuselage.

Percey studied the fitting. "I don't have a jack. Not one small enough to fit."

"I do. I'll get it."

Sachs stepped outside to the RRV and returned with the accordion jack. She climbed up on the scaffolding, her knees protesting the effort.

"Try right there." She touched the base of the engine. "That's I-beam steel."

As Percey positioned the jack, Sachs admired the intricacies of the engine. "How much horsepower?"

Percey laughed. "We don't rate in horsepower. We rate in pounds of thrust. These're Garrett TFE Seven Three Ones. They give up about thirty-five hundred pounds each."

"Incredible." Sachs laughed. "Brother." She hooked the handle into the jack, then felt the familiar resistance as she started turning the crank. "I've never been this close to a turbine engine," she said. "Was always a dream of mine to take a jet car out to the salt flats."

"This isn't a pure turbine. There aren't many of those left anymore. Just the Concorde. Military jets, of course. These're turbofans. Like the airliners. Look in the front – see those blades? That's nothing more than a fixed-pitch propeller. Pure jets are inefficient at low altitudes. These're about forty percent more fuel efficient."

Sachs breathed hard as she struggled to turn the jack handle. Percey put her shoulder against the ring again and shoved. The part didn't seem large but it was very heavy.

"You know cars, huh?" Percey asked, also gasping.

"My father. He loved them. We'd spend the afternoon taking 'em apart and putting 'em back together. When he wasn't walking a beat."

"A beat?"

"He was a cop too."

"And you got the mechanic bug?" Percey asked.

"Naw, I got the *speed* bug. And when you get that you better get the suspension bug and the transmission bug and the engine bug or you ain't going anywhere fast."

Percey asked, "You ever driven an aircraft?"

" 'Driven'?" Sachs smiled at the word. "No. But maybe I'll think about it, knowing you've got that much oomph under the hood."

She cranked some more, her muscles aching. The ring groaned slightly and scraped as it rose into its fittings.

"I don't know," Percey said uncertainly.

"Almost there!"

With a loud metallic clang the ring popped onto the mounts perfectly. Percey's squat face broke into a faint smile.

"You torque 'em?" Sachs asked, fitting bolts into the slots on the ring and looking for a wrench.

"Yeah," Percey said. "The poundage I use is 'Till there's no way in hell they'll come loose.' "

Sachs tightened the bolts down with a ratcheting socket.

The clicking of the tool took her back to high school, cool Saturday afternoons with her father. The smells of gasoline, of fall air, of meaty casseroles cooking in the kitchen of their Brooklyn attached house.

Percey checked Sachs's handiwork then said, "I'll do the rest." She started reconnecting wires and electronic components. Sachs was mystified but fascinated. Percey paused. She added a soft "Thanks." A few moments later: "What're you doing here?"

"We found some other materials we think might be from the bomb, but Lincoln didn't know if it was part of the plane or not. Bits of beige latex, circuit board? Sound familiar?"

Percey shrugged. "There're thousands of gaskets in a Lear. They could be latex, I don't have any idea. And circuit boards? There're probably another thousand of them." She nodded to a corner, toward a closet and workbench. "The boards are special orders, depending on the component. But there should be a good stock of gaskets over there. Take samples of whatever you need."

Sachs walked over to the bench, began slipping all the beige-colored bits of rubber she could find into an evidence bag.

Without glancing at Sachs, Percey said, "I thought you were here to arrest me. Haul me back to jail."

I ought to, the policewoman thought. But she said, "Just collecting exemplars." Then, after a moment: "What other work needs to be done? On the plane?"

"Just recalibration. Then a run-up to check the power settings. I have to take a look at the window too, the one Ron replaced. You don't want to lose a window at four hundred miles an hour. Could you hand me that hex set? No, the metric one."

"I lost one at a hundred once," Sachs said, passing over the tools.

"A what?"

"A window. A perp I was chasing had a shotgun. Double-ought buckshot. I ducked in time. But it blew the windshield clean out . . . I'll tell you, I caught a few bugs in my teeth before I collared him."

"And I thought *I* lived an adventurous life," Percey said.

"Most of it's dull. They pay you for the five percent that's adrenaline."

"I hear that," Percey said. She hooked up a laptop computer to components in the engine itself. She typed on the keyboard, read the screen. Without looking down she asked, "So, what is it?"

Eyes on the computer, the numbers flicking past, Sachs asked, "What do you mean?"

"This, uhm, tension. Between us. You and me."

"You nearly got a friend of mine killed."

Percey shook her head. She said reasonably, "That's not it. There're risks in your job. You decide if you're going to assume them or not. Jerry Banks wasn't a rookie. It's something else – I felt it before Jerry got shot. When I first saw you, in Lincoln Rhyme's room."

Sachs said nothing. She lifted the jack out of the engine compartment and set it on a table, absently wound it closed.

Three pieces of metal slipped into place around the engine and Percey applied her screwdriver like a conductor's baton. Her hands were truly magic. Finally she said, "It's about him, isn't it?"

"Who?"

"You know who I mean. Lincoln Rhyme."

"You think I'm jealous?" Sachs laughed.

"Yes, I do."

"Ridiculous."

"It's more than just work between you. I think you're in love with him."

"Of course I'm not. That's crazy."

Percey offered a telling glance and then carefully twined excess wire into a bundle and nestled it into a cutout in the engine compartment. "Whatever you saw is just respect for his talent, that's all." She lifted a grease-stained hand toward herself. "Come on, Amelia, look at me. I'd make a lousy lover. I'm short, I'm bossy, I'm not good looking."

"You're—" Sachs began.

Percey interrupted. "The ugly duckling story? You know, the bird that everybody thought was ugly until it turned out to be a swan? I read that a million times when I was little. But I never turned into a swan. Maybe I learned to fly like one," she said with a cool smile, "but it isn't the same. Besides," Percey continued, "I'm a widow. I just lost my husband. I'm not the least interested in anyone else."

"I'm sorry," Sachs began slowly, feeling unwillingly drawn into this conversation, "but I've got to say . . . well, you don't really seem to be in mourning."

"Why? Because I'm trying my hardest to keep my company going?"

"No, there's more than that," Sachs replied cautiously. "Isn't there?"

Percey examined Sachs's face. "Ed and I were incredibly close. We were husband and wife and friends and business partners . . . And yes, he was seeing someone else."

Sachs's eyes swiveled toward the Hudson Air office.

"That's right," Percey said. "It's Lauren. You met her yesterday."

The brunette who'd been crying so hard.

"It tore me apart. Hell, it tore Ed apart too. He loved me but he needed his beautiful lovers. Always did. And, you know, I think it was harder on them. Because he always came home to me." She paused for a moment and fought the tears. "That's what love is, I think. Who you come home to."

"And you?"

"Was I faithful?" Percey asked. She gave another of her wry laughs – the laugh of someone who has keen self-awareness but who doesn't like all the insights. "I didn't have a lot of opportunities. I'm hardly the kind of girl gets picked up walking down the street." She examined a socket wrench absently. "But, yeah, after I found out about Ed and his girlfriends, a few years ago, I was mad. It hurt a lot. I saw some other men. Ron and I – Ron Talbot – spent some time together, a few months." She smiled. "He even proposed to me. Said I deserved better than Ed. And I supposed I did. But even with those other women in his life, Ed was the man I had to be with. That never changed."

Percey's eyes grew distant for a moment. "We met in the navy, Ed and I. Both fighter pilots. When he proposed . . . See, the traditional way to propose in the military is you say, 'You want to become my dependent?' Sort of a joke. But we were both lieutenants j.g., so Ed said, 'Let's you and me become each other's dependents.' He wanted to get me a ring but my father'd disowned me—"

"For real?"

"Yep. Real soap opera, which I won't go into now. Anyway, Ed and I were saving every penny to open our own charter company after we were discharged and we were completely broke. But one night he said, 'Let's go up.' So we borrowed this old Norseman they had on the field. Tough plane. Big air-cooled rotary engine . . . You could do anything with that aircraft. Well, I was in the left-hand seat. I'd taken off and'd got us up to about six thousand feet. Suddenly he kissed me and wobbled the yoke, which meant he was taking over. I let him. He said, 'I got you a diamond after all, Perce.'"

"He did?" Sachs asked.

Percey smiled. "He throttled up, all the way to the fire wall, and pulled the yoke back. The nose went straight up in the air." Tears were coming fast now to Percey Clay's eyes. "For a moment, before he kicked rudder and we started down out of the stall, we were looking straight up into the night sky. He leaned over and said, 'Take your pick. All the stars of evening – you can have any one you want.'" Percey lowered her head, caught her breath. All the stars of evening . . .

After a moment she wiped her eyes with her sleeve, then turned back to the engine. "Believe me, you don't have anything to worry about. Lincoln's a fascinating man, but Ed was all I ever wanted."

"There's more to it than you know." Sachs sighed. "You remind him of someone. Someone he was in love with. You show up and all of a sudden it's like he's with her again."

Percey shrugged. "We have some things in common. We understand each other. But so what? That doesn't mean anything. Take a look, Amelia. Rhyme loves you."

Sachs laughed. "Oh, I don't think so."

Percey gave her another look that said, *Whatever* . . ., and began replacing the equipment in boxes as meticulously as she'd worked with the tools and computers.

Roland Bell ambled inside, checking windows and scanning the shadows.

"All quiet?" he asked.

"Not a peep."

"Got a message to pass on. The folk from U.S. Medical just left Westchester Hospital. The shipment'll be here in an hour. I've got a car of my people behind them just to be on the safe side. But don't worry that it'll spook 'em and be bad for business – my guys're top-notch. The driver'll never know he's being followed."

Percey looked at her watch. "Okay." She glanced at Bell, who was looking uncertainly at the open engine compartment, like a snake at a mongoose. She asked, "We don't need baby-sitters on the flight, do we?"

Bell's sigh was loud. "After what happened at the safe house," he said in a low, solemn voice, "I'm not letting you outa my sight." He shook his head and, already looking airsick, he walked back to the front door and disappeared into the cool late afternoon air.

Her head in the engine compartment, studying her work carefully, Percey said in a reverberating voice, "Looking at Rhyme and looking at you, I wouldn't give it much more than fifty-fifty, I've got to say." She turned and looked down at Sachs. "But you know, I had this flight instructor a long time ago."

"And?"

"When we'd fly multi-engine he had this game of throttling back one engine to idle and feathering the prop, then telling us to land. Lot of instructors'll cut power for a few minutes, with altitude, just to see how you can handle it. But they always throttled up again before landing. This instructor, though – uh-uh. He'd make us land on one engine. Students'd always be asking him, 'Isn't that risky?' His answer was, 'God don't give out certain. Sometimes you just gotta play the odds.'"

Percey lowered the flap of the engine cowl and clamped it into place. "All right, this's done. Damn aircraft may actually fly." She swatted the glossy skin like a cowgirl patting a rodeo rider's butt.

Hour 32 of 45

30

At 6 P.M. on Sunday they summoned Jodie from Rhyme's downstairs bedroom, where he'd been under lock and key.

He trotted up the stairs reluctantly, clutching his silly book, *Dependent No More,* like a Bible. Rhyme remembered the title. It had been on the *Times* best-seller list for months. In a black mood at the time, he'd noticed the book and thought cynically, about himself, dependent forever.

A team of federal agents was flying from Quantico to Cumberland, West Virginia, Stephen Kall's old residence, to pick up whatever leads they could, hoping they might track him to his present whereabouts from there. But Rhyme had seen how carefully he'd scoured his crime scenes and he had no reason to think the man would have been any less careful in covering his other tracks.

"You told us some things about him," Rhyme said to Jodie. "Some *facts,* some *nutritional* information. I want to know more."

"I—"

"Think hard."

Jodie squinted. Rhyme supposed he was considering what he could say to mollify them, superficial impressions. But he was surprised when Jodie said, "Well, for one thing, he's afraid of you."

"Us?" Rhyme asked.

"No. Just you."

"Me?" he asked, astonished. "He knows about me?"

"He knows your name's Lincoln. And that you're out to get him."

"How?"

"I don't know," the man said, then added, "You know, he made a couple of calls on that cell phone. And he listened for a long time. I was thinking—"

"Oh, hellfire," Dellray sang out. "He's tapping somebody's line."

"Of course!" Rhyme cried. "Probably the Hudson Air office. That's how he found out about the safe house. Why didn't we think about that?"

Dellray said, "We gotta sweep the office. But the bug might be in a relay box somewheres. We'll find it. We'll find it." He placed a call to the Bureau's tech services.

To Jodie, Rhyme said, "Go on. What else does he know about me?"

"He knows you're a detective. I don't think he knows where you live, or your last name. But you scare the hell out of him."

If Rhyme's belly had been able to register the lub-dub of excitement – and pride – he'd have felt that now.

Let's see, Stephen Kall, if we can't give you a little more to be afraid of.

"You helped us once, Jodie. I need you to help us again."

"Are you crazy?"

"Shut the fuck up," Dellray barked. "And listen t'what the man's sayin', hokay? *Hokay*?"

"I did what I said I would. I'm not doing anything more." The whine really was too much. Rhyme glanced at Sellitto. This called for people skills.

"It's in your interest," Sellitto said reasonably, "to help us."

"Gettin' shot in the *back*'s in my interest? Gettin' shot in the *head*'s in my interest? Uh-huh. I see. You wanna explain that?"

"Sure, I'll fucking explain it," Sellitto grumbled. "The Dancer knows you dimed him. He didn't *have* to target you back there at the safe house, right? Am I right?"

Always get the mutts to talk. To *participate*. Sellitto

had often explained the ways of interrogation to Lincoln Rhyme.

"Yeah. I guess."

Sellitto motioned Jodie closer with a crooked finger. "It woulda been the smart thing for him just to take off. But he went to the trouble to take up a sniper position and try to cap your ass. Now, what's that tell us?"

"I—"

"It tells us that he ain't gonna rest till he clips you."

Dellray, happy to play straight man for a change, said, "And he's the sort I don't think you wanna have knocking on yo' door at three in the morning – this week, next month, or next year. We all together on that?"

"So," Sellitto resumed snappily, "agreed that it's in your *interest* to help us?"

"But you'll give me, like, witness protection?"

Sellitto shrugged. "Yes and no."

"Huh?"

"If you help us, yes. If you don't, no."

Jodie's eyes were red and watery. He seemed so afraid. In the years since his accident Rhyme had been fearful for others – Amelia and Thom and Lon Sellitto. But he himself didn't believe he'd ever been afraid to die, certainly not since the accident. He wondered what it must be like to live so timidly. A mouse's life.

Too many ways to die . . .

Sellitto, slipping into his good-cop persona, offered a faint smile to Jodie. "You were there when he killed that agent, in the basement, right?"

"I was there, yeah."

"That man could be alive now. And Brit Hale could be alive now. A lot of other people could too . . . *if* somebody'd helped us stop this asshole a coupla years ago. Well, you can help us stop him now. You can keep Percey alive, maybe dozens of others. *You* can do that."

This was Sellitto's genius at work. Rhyme would have bullied and coerced and, in a pinch, bribed the little man. But it never occurred to him to appeal to the splinter of decency that the detective, at least, could see within him.

Jodie absently riffled the pages in his book with a filthy

thumb. Finally he looked up and – with surprising sobriety – said, "When I was taking him to my place, in the subway, a couple times I thought I'd maybe push him into a sewer interceptor pipe. The water goes real fast there. Wash him right down to the Hudson. Or I know where they have these piles of tie spikes in the subway. I could grab one and hit him over the head when he wasn't looking. I really, really thought about doing that. But I got scared." He held up the book. "'Chapter Three. Confronting your Demons.' I've always run, you know. I never stood up to anything. I thought maybe I could stand up to him, but I couldn't."

"Hey, now's your chance to," Sellitto said.

Flipping through the tattered pages again. Sighing. "Whatta I gotta do?"

Dellray pointed an alarmingly long thumb toward the ceiling. His mark of approval.

"We'll get to that in a minute," Rhyme said, looking around the room. Suddenly he shouted, "Thom! Thom! Come *here*. I need you."

The handsome, exasperated face of the aide poked around the corner. "Yessss?"

"I'm feeling vain," Rhyme announced dramatically.

"What?"

"I'm feeling vain. I need a mirror."

"You want a mirror?"

"A big one. And would you please comb my hair. I keep asking you and you keep forgetting."

The U.S. Medical and Healthcare van pulled onto the tarmac. If the two white-jacketed employees, carting a quarter million dollars' worth of human organs, were concerned about the machine-gun-armed cops ringing the field, they gave no indication of it.

The only time they flinched was when King, the bomb squad German shepherd, sniffed the cargo cases for explosives.

"Uhm, I'd watch that dog there," one of the deliverymen said uneasily. "I imagine to them liver's liver and heart's heart."

But King behaved like a thorough professional and signed off on the cargo without sampling any. The men carried the containers on board, loaded them into the refrigeration units. Percey returned to the cockpit where Brad Torgeson, a sandy-haired young pilot who flew occasional freelance jobs for Hudson Air, was going through the pre-flight check.

They'd both already done the walkaround, accompanied by Bell, three troopers, and King. There was no way the Dancer could have gotten to the plane in the first place, but the killer now had a reputation of materializing out of thin air; this was the most meticulous pre-flight visual in the history of aviation.

Looking back into the passenger compartment, Percey could see the lights of the refrigeration units. She felt that tug of satisfaction she always felt when inanimate machinery, built and honed by humans, came to life. The proof of God, for Percey Clay, could be found in the hum of servomotors and the buoyancy of a sleek metal wing at that instant when the airfoil creates negative top pressure and you become weightless.

Continuing with the pre-flight checklist, Percey was startled by the sound of heavy breathing next to her.

"Whoa," Brad said as King decided there were no explosives in his crotch and continued his examination of the inside of the plane.

Rhyme had spoken to Percey not long ago and told her that he and Amelia Sachs had examined the gaskets and tubing and found no match for the latex discovered at the crash site in Chicago. Rhyme got the idea that he might have used the rubber to seal the explosives so that the dogs couldn't smell it. So he had Percey and Brad stand down for a few minutes while Tech Services went through the entire plane, inside and out, with hypersensitive microphones, listening for a detonator timer.

Clean.

When the plane rolled out, the taxiway would be guarded by uniformed patrolmen. Fred Dellray had contacted the FAA to arrange that the flight plan be sealed so that the Dancer couldn't learn where the plane was going – if he even knew that Percey was at the helm. The agent had also contacted the FBI field offices in each of the arrival cities and arranged for tactical agents to be on the tarmac when the shipments were delivered.

Now, engines started, Brad in the right-hand seat and Roland Bell shifting uneasily in one of the two remaining passenger seats, Percey Clay spoke to the tower, "Lear Six Niner Five *Foxtrot Bravo* at Hudson Air. Ready for taxi."

"Roger, Niner Five *Foxtrot Bravo*. Cleared onto taxiway zero nine right."

"Zero nine right, Niner Five *Foxtrot Bravo.*"

A touch to the smooth throttles and the spritely plane turned onto the taxiway and proceeded through the gray, early spring evening. Percey was driving. Copilots have flight authority but only the pilot can steer the plane on the ground.

"You having fun, Officer?" she called back to Bell.

"I'm just tickled," he said, looking sourly out the large round window. "You know, you can see straight down. I mean, the windows go so far round. Why'd they make it that way?"

Percey laughed. She called out, "On airliners, they try to keep you from realizing you're flying. Movies, food, small windows. Where's the fun? What's the point?"

"I can see a point or two," he said, chewing his Wrigley's with energetic teeth. He closed the curtain.

Percey's eyes were on the taxiway, checking left and right, always vigilant. To Brad she said, "I'll do the briefing now. Okay?"

"Yes'm."

"This'll be a rolling takeoff with flaps set to 15 degrees," Percey said. "I'll advance the throttles. You call airspeed, eighty knots, cross-check, V one, rotate, V two, and positive rate. I'll command gear up and you raise it. Got that?"

"Airspeed, eighty, V one, rotate, V two, positive rate. Gear."

"Good. You'll monitor all instruments and the annunciator panel. Now, if we get a red panel light or there's an engine malfunction before V one, sing out 'Abort' loud and clear and I'll make a go/no-go decision. If there's a malfunction at or after V one, we will continue the takeoff and we'll treat the situation as an in-flight emergency. We will continue on heading and you'll request VFR clearance for an immediate return to the airport. Understood?"

"Understood."

"Good. Let's do some flying . . . You ready, Roland?"

"*I'm* ready. Hope you are. Don't drop your candy."

Percey laughed again. Their housekeeper in Richmond had used that expression. It meant, don't screw up.

She wobbled the throttles a little closer to the firewall. The engines gave a grinding sound and the Learjet sped forward. They continued to the hold position, where the killer had placed the bomb on Ed's plane. She looked out the window and saw two cops standing guard.

"Lear Niner Five *Foxtrot Bravo*," Ground Control called through the radio, "proceed to and hold short of runway five left."

"*Foxtrot Bravo*. Hold short of zero five left."

She steered onto the taxiway.

The Lear was a ground hugger, yet whenever Percey Clay sat in left-hand seat, whether in the air or on the ground, she felt that she was a mile high. It was a powerful place to be. All the decisions would be hers, followed unquestioningly. All the responsibility was on her shoulders. She was the captain.

Eyes scanning the instruments.

"Flaps fifteen, fifteen, green," she said, repeating the degree setting.

Doubling the redundancy, Brad said, "Flaps fifteen, fifteen, green."

ATC called, "Lear Niner Five *Foxtrot Bravo*, turn into position. Cleared for takeoff, runway five left."

"Five left, *Foxtrot Bravo*. Cleared for takeoff."

Brad concluded the takeoff checklist. "Pressurization, normal. Temperature select is in auto. Transponder and exterior lights on. Ignition, pitot heat, and strobes, your side."

Percey checked those controls, said, "Ignition, pitot heat, and strobes on."

She turned the Lear onto the runway, straightened the nosewheel, and lined up with centerline. She glanced at the compass. "All heading indicators check zero five. Runway five L. I'm setting power."

She pushed the throttles forward. They began racing down the middle of the concrete strip. She felt his hand grip the throttles just below hers.

"Power set." Then Brad called, "Airspeed alive," as the airspeed indicators jumped off the peg and started to move upward, twenty knots, forty knots . . .

The throttles nearly to the fire wall, the plane shot forward. She heard a "wayl . . ." from Roland Bell and repressed a smile.

Fifty knots, sixty knots, seventy . . .

"Eighty knots," Brad called out, "cross-check."

"Check," she called after a glance at the airspeed indicator.

"V one," Brad sang out. "Rotate."

Percey removed her right hand from the throttles and took the yoke. Wobbly until now, the plastic control suddenly grew firm with air resistance. She eased back, rotating the Lear upward to the standard seven-and-a-half-degree incline. The engines continued to roar smoothly and so she pulled back slightly more, increasing the climb to ten degrees.

"Positive rate," Brad called.

"Gear up. Flaps up. Yaw damp on."

Through the headphone came the voice of ATC. "Lear Niner Five *Foxtrot Bravo,* turn left heading two eight oh. Contact departure control."

"Two eight oh, Niner Five *Foxtrot Bravo.* Thank you, sir."

"Good evening."

Tugging the yoke a bit more, eleven degrees, twelve, fourteen . . . Leaving the power settings at takeoff level, higher than normal, for a few minutes. Hearing the sweet grind of the turbofans behind her, the slipstream.

And in this sleek silver needle, Percey Clay felt herself flying into the heart of the sky, leaving behind the cumbersome, the heavy, the painful. Leaving behind Ed's death and Brit's, leaving behind even that terrible man, the devil, the Coffin Dancer. All of the hurt, all of the uncertainty, all of the ugliness were trapped far below her, and she was free. It seemed unfair that she should escape these stifling burdens so easily but that was the fact of it. For the Percey Clay who sat in the left-hand seat of Lear N695FB was not Percey Clay the short girl with the squat face, or Percey Clay the girl whose only sex appeal was the lure of Daddy's chopped-tobacco money. It wasn't Per-ceee Pug, Percey the Mug, Percey the Troll, the awkward brunette struggling with the ill-fitting gloves at her cotillion, on the arm of her mortified cousin, surrounded by willowy blonds who nodded at her with pleasant smiles and stored up the sight for a gossip fest later.

That wasn't the real Percey Clay.

This was.

Another gasp from Roland Bell. He must have peeked through the window curtain during their alarming bank.

"Mamaroneck Departure, Lear Niner Five *Foxtrot Bravo* with you out of two thousand."

"Evening, Five *Foxtrot Bravo.* Climb and maintain six thousand."

And then they began the mundane tasks of setting nav com for the VOR frequencies that would guide them to Chicago as straight as a samurai's arrow.

At six thousand feet they broke through the cloud cover into a sky that was as spectacular as any sunset Percey had ever seen. Not really an outdoor person, she never grew tired of the sight of beautiful skies. Percey allowed herself a single sentimental thought – that it would have been a very good thing if Ed's last sight had been as beautiful as this.

At twenty-one thousand feet she said, "Your aircraft."

Brad responded, "Got it."

"Coffee?"

"Love some."

She stepped into the back of the plane, poured three cups, took one to Brad, and then sat down next to Roland Bell, who took the cup in shaking hands.

"How you doing?" she asked.

"It's not like I get airsick. It's just I get" – his face folded – "well, nervous as a . . ." There were probably a thousand good Tarheel similes to choose from, but for once his Southern talk failed him. "Just nervous," he concluded.

"Take a look," she said, pointing out the cockpit window.

He eased forward in the seat and looked out the windshield. She watched his craggy face blossom in surprise as they stared into the maw of the sunset.

Bell whistled. "Well, now. Lookit that . . . Say, that was a real rush, takeoff."

"She's a sweet bird. You ever hear of Brooke Knapp?"

"Don't believe so."

"Businesswoman in California. Set an around-the-world speed record in a Lear thirty-five A – what we're in right now. Took her a hair over fifty hours. I'm going to break that someday."

"I don't doubt you are." Calmer now. Eyes on the controls. "Looks awful complicated."

She sipped the coffee. "There's a trick to flying we don't tell people. Sort of a trade secret. It's a lot simpler than you'd think."

"What's that?" he asked eagerly. "The trick?"

"Well, look outside. You see those colored lights on the wing tips?"

He didn't want to look, but he did. "Okay, got it."

"There's one on the tail too."

"Uh-huh. Remember seeing that, I think."

"All we have to do is make sure we keep the plane in between those lights and everything'll go fine."

"In between . . ." It took a moment for the joke to register. He gazed at her deadpan face for a minute, then smiled. "You get a lotta people with that one?"

"A few."

But the joke didn't really amuse him. His eyes were still on the carpet. After a long moment of silence she said, "Brit Hale could've said no, Roland. He knew the risks."

"No, he didn't," Bell answered. "Nope. He went along with what we had in mind, not knowing much of anything. I should've thought better. I should've guessed about the fire trucks. Should've guessed that the killer'd know where your rooms were. I could've put you in the basement, or someplace. And I could've shot better too."

Bell seemed so despondent that Percey could think of nothing to say. She rested her veiny hand on his forearm. He seemed thin, but he was really quite strong.

He gave a soft laugh. "You wanta know something?"

"What?"

"This is the first time I've seen you looking halfway comfortable since I met you."

"Only place I feel really at home," she said.

"We're going two hundred miles an hour a mile up in the air and you feel safe." Bell sighed.

"No, we're going four hundred miles an hour, four miles up."

"Uh. Thanks for sharing that."

"There's an old pilot's saying," Percey said. "'Saint Peter doesn't count the time spent flying, and he doubles the hours you spend on the ground.'"

"Funny," Bell said. "My uncle said something like that too. Only he used it talking about fishing. I'd vote for his version over yours any day. Nothing personal."

31

Worms . . .

Stephen Kall, sweating, stood in a filthy bathroom in the back of a Cuban Chinese restaurant.

Scrubbing to save his soul.

Worms gnawing, worms eating, worms swarming . . .

Clean 'em away . . . Clean them away!!!

Soldier—

Sir, I'm busy, sir.

Sol—

Scrub, scrub, scrub, scrub.

Lincoln the Worm is looking for me.

Everywhere Lincoln the Worm looks, worms appear.

Go away!!!

The brush moved whisk, whisk, back and forth until his cuticles bled.

Soldier, that blood is evidence. You can't—

Go away!!!!

He dried his hands then grabbed the Fender guitar case and the book bag, pushed into the restaurant.

Soldier, your gloves—

The alarmed patrons stared at his bloody hands, his crazed expression. "Worms," he muttered in explanation to the entire restaurant, "fucking worms," then burst outside onto the street.

Hurrying down the sidewalk, calming. He was thinking about what he had to do. He *had* to kill Jodie, of course. Have to kill him have to kill him have to . . . Not because he was a traitor, but because he'd given away so much information—

And why the fuck d'you do that, Soldier?

—about himself to the man. And he had to kill Lincoln the Worm because . . . because the worms would get him if he didn't.

Have to kill have to have to have . . .

Are you *listening* to me, Soldier? Are you?

That was all there was left to do.

Then he'd leave this city. Head back to West Virginia. Back to the hills.

Lincoln, dead.

Jodie, dead.

Have to kill have to have to have to . . .

Nothing more to keep him here.

As for the Wife – he looked at his watch. Just after 7 P.M. Well, she was probably dead already.

"'Sbulletproof."

"Against *those* bullets?" Jodie asked. "You said they blow up!"

Dellray assured him it was effective. The vest was thick Kevlar on top of a steel sheet. It weighed forty-two pounds and Rhyme didn't know a cop in the city who wore a vest like this, or ever would.

"But what if he shoots my head?"

"He wants me a lot more than he wants *you*," Rhyme said.

"And how's he gonna know I'm staying here?"

"How d'ya think, mutt?" Dellray snapped. "I'ma tell him."

The agent cinched up the little man tight in the vest and tossed him a windbreaker. He'd showered – after protesting – and had been given a set of clean clothes. The large navy blue jacket, covering the bulletproof vest, was a little lopsided but actually gave him a muscular physique. He caught sight of himself in the mirror – his scrubbed and newly attired self – and smiled for the first time since he'd been here.

"Okay," Sellitto said to two undercover officers, "take him downtown."

The officers ushered him out the door.

After he'd left, Dellray looked at Rhyme, who nodded. The lanky agent sighed and flicked open his cell phone, placed a call to Hudson Air Charters, where another agent was waiting to pick up the phone. The fed's tech group had found a remote tap on a relay box near the airport, clipped into the Hudson Air phone lines. The agents hadn't removed it, though; in fact at Rhyme's insistence they checked to make sure it was working and had replaced the weak batteries. The criminalist was relying on the device for the new trap.

On the speakerphone, several rings then a click.

"Agent Mondale," came the deep voice. Mondale wasn't Mondale and he was speaking according to a prewritten script.

"Mondale," Dellray said, sounding lily white, to a Connecticut manor born. "Agent Wilson here, we're at Lincoln's now." (Not "Rhyme"; the Dancer knew him as "Lincoln".)

"How's the airport?"

"Still secure."

"Good. Listen, got a question. We've got a CI working for us, Joe D'Oforio."

"He was the one—"

"Right."

"—turned. You're working with him?"

"Yeah," said Wilson, AKA Fred Dellray. "Bit of a mutt, but he's cooperating. We're going to run him down to his hidey-hole and back here."

"Where's 'here'? You mean, back to Lincoln's?"

"Right. He wants his stuff."

"Fuck you doing that for?"

"He cut a deal. He dimes this killer and Lincoln agreed he could have some stuff from his place. This old subway station . . . Anyway, we're not doing a convoy. Just one car. Reason I called, we need a good driver. You worked with somebody you liked, right?"

"Driver?"

"On the Gambino thing?"

"Oh, yeah . . . Lemme think."

They stretched it out. Rhyme was, as always, impressed

with Dellray's performance. Whoever he wanted to be, he was.

The phony agent Mondale – who deserved a best-supporting award himself – said, "I remember. Tony Glidden. No, Tommy. The blond guy, right?"

"That's him. I want to use him. He around?"

"Naw. He's in Phillie. That carjacking sting."

"Phillie. Too bad. We're going in about twenty minutes. Can't wait any longer than that. Well, I'll just do it myself then. But that Tommy. He—"

"Fucker could drive a car! He could lose a tail in two blocks. Man was amazing."

"Sure could use him now. Listen, thanks, Mondale."

"Later."

Rhyme winked, a quad's equivalent of applause. Dellray hung up, exhaled long and slow. "We'll see. We'll see."

Sellitto uttered an optimistic "The third time we're baiting him. This should be it."

Lincoln Rhyme didn't believe that was a rule of law enforcement, but he said, "Let's hope."

Sitting in a stolen car not far from Jodie's subway station, Stephen Kall watched a government-issue sedan pull up.

Jodie and two uniformed cops climbed out, scanning the rooftops. Jodie ran inside and, five minutes later, escaped back to the car with two bundles under his arm.

Stephen could see no backup, no tail cars. What he'd heard on the tap was accurate. They pulled into traffic and he started after them, thinking there was no place in the world like Manhattan for following and not being seen. He couldn't be doing this in Iowa or Virginia.

The unmarked car drove fast, but Stephen was a good driver too and he stayed with it as they made their way uptown. The sedan slowed when they got to Central Park West and drove past a town house in the Seventies. There were two men in front of it, wearing street clothes, but they were obviously cops. A signal – probably "All clear" – passed between them and the driver of the unmarked sedan.

So that's it. That's Lincoln the Worm's house.

The car continued north. Stephen did too for a little ways, then parked suddenly and climbed out, hurrying into the trees with the guitar case. He knew there'd be some surveillance around the apartment and he moved quietly.

Like a deer, Soldier.

Yessir.

He vanished into a stand of brush and crawled back toward the town house, finding a good nest on a stony ledge under a budding lilac tree. He opened the case. The car containing Jodie, now going south, screeched up to the town house. Standard evasive practice, Stephen recognized – it had made an abrupt U-turn in heavy traffic and sped back here.

He was watching the two cops climb out of the sedan, look around, and escort a very scared Jodie along the sidewalk.

Stephen flipped the covers off the telescope and took careful aim on the traitor's back.

Suddenly a black car drove past and Jodie spooked. His eyes went wide and he pulled away from the cops, running into the alley beside the town house.

His escorts spun around, hands on their weapons, staring at the car that had startled him. They looked at the quartet of Latino girls inside and realized it was just a false alarm. The cops laughed. One of them called to Jodie.

But Stephen wasn't interested in the little man right now. He couldn't get both the Worm and Jodie, and Lincoln was the one he had to kill now. He could taste it. It was a hunger, a need as great as scrubbing his hands.

To shoot the face in the window, to kill the worm.

Have to have to have to have to . . .

He was looking through the telescope, scanning the building's windows. And there he was. Lincoln the Worm.

A shiver rippled through Stephen's entire body.

Like the electricity he felt when his leg rubbed against Jodie's . . . only a thousand times greater. He actually gasped in excitement.

For some reason Stephen wasn't the least surprised to see that the Worm was crippled. In fact, this was how he knew the handsome man in a fancy motorized wheelchair *was* Lincoln. Because Stephen believed it would take an extraordinary man to catch him. Someone who wasn't distracted by everyday life. Someone whose essence was his mind.

Worms could crawl over Lincoln all day long and he'd never even feel them. They could crawl into his skin and he'd never know. He was immune. And Stephen hated him all the more for his invulnerability.

So the face in the window during the Washington, D.C., hit . . . it hadn't been Lincoln.

Or had it?

Stop thinking about it! Stop! The worms'll get you if you don't.

The explosive rounds were in the clip. He chambered one, and scanned the room again.

Lincoln the Worm was speaking to someone Stephen couldn't see. The room, on the first floor, seemed to be a laboratory. He saw a computer screen and some other equipment.

Stephen wrapped the sling around him, spot-welded the rifle butt to his cheek. It was a cool, damp evening. The air was heavy; it would sustain the explosive bullet easily. There was no need to correct; the target was only eighty yards away. Safety off, breathe, breathe . . .

Go for a head shot. It would be easy from here.

Breathe . . .

In, out, in, out.

He looked through the reticles, centered them on Lincoln the Worm's ear as he stared at the computer screen.

The pressure on the trigger began to build.

Breathe. Like sex, like coming, like touching firm skin . . .

Harder.

Harder . . .

Then Stephen saw it.

Very faint – a slight unevenness on Lincoln the Worm's sleeve. But not a wrinkle. It was a distortion.

He relaxed his trigger finger and studied the image through the telescope for a moment. Stephen clicked to a higher resolution on the Redfield telescope. He looked at the type on the computer screen. The letters were backwards.

A mirror! He was sighting on a mirror.

It was *another* trap!

Stephen closed his eyes. He'd almost given his position away. Cringey now. Smothering in worms, choking on worms. He looked around him. He knew there must be a dozen search-and-surveillance troopers in the park with Big Ears microphones just waiting to pinpoint the gunshot. They'd sight on him with M-16s mounted with Starlight scopes and nail him in a cross fire.

Green-lighted to kill. No surrender pitch.

Quickly but in absolute silence he removed the telescope with shaking hands and replaced it and the gun in the guitar case. Fighting down the nausea, the cringe.

Soldier . . .

Sir, go away, sir.

Soldier, what are you—

Sir, fuck you, sir!

Stephen slipped through the trees to a path and walked casually around the meadow, heading east.

Oh, yes, he was now even more certain than before that he had to kill Lincoln. A new plan. He needed an hour or two, to think, to consider what he was going to do.

He turned suddenly off the path, paused in the bushes for a long moment, listening, looking around him. They'd been so worried he'd be suspicious if he noticed that the park was deserted, so they hadn't closed the entrances.

That was their mistake.

Stephen saw a group of men about his age – yuppies, from the look of them, dressed in sweats or jogging outfits. They were carrying racquetball cases and backpacks and headed for the Upper East Side, talking loudly as they walked. Their hair glistened from the showers they'd just had at a nearby athletic club.

Stephen waited until they were just past, then fell in behind them, as if he were a part of the group. Offered one of them a big smile. Walking briskly, swinging the guitar case jauntily, he followed them toward the tunnel that led to the East Side.

32

Dusk surrounded them.

Percey Clay, once again in the left-hand seat of the Learjet, saw the cusp of light that was Chicago in front of them.

Chicago Center cleared them down to twelve thousand feet.

"Starting descent," she announced, easing back on the throttles. "ATIS."

Brad clicked his radio to the automated airport information system and repeated out loud what the recorded voice told him. "Chicago information, Whiskey. Clear and forever. Wind two five oh at three. Temperature fifty-nine degrees. Altimeter thirty point one one."

Brad set the altimeter as Percey said into her microphone, "Chicago Approach, this is Lear Niner Five *Foxtrot Bravo.* With you inbound at twelve thousand. Heading two eight zero."

"Evening, *Foxtrot Bravo.* Descend and maintain one zero thousand. Expect vectors runway twenty-seven right."

"Roger. Descend and maintain ten. Vectors, two seven right. Niner Five *Foxtrot Bravo.*"

Percey refused to look down. Somewhere below and ahead of them was the grave of her husband and his aircraft. She didn't know if he'd been cleared to land on O'Hare's runway 27 right, but it was likely that he had and, if so, ATC would've vectored Ed through exactly the same airspace she was now sailing through.

Maybe he'd started to call her right about here . . .

No! Don't think about it, she ordered herself. Fly the aircraft.

In a low, calm voice she said, "Brad, this will be a visual approach to runway twenty-seven right. Monitor the approach and call all assigned altitudes. When we turn on final please monitor airspeed, altitude, and rate of descent. Warn me of a sink rate greater than one thousand fpm. Go-around will be at ninety-two percent."

"Roger."

"Flaps ten degrees."

"Flaps, ten, ten, green."

The radio crackled, "Lear Niner Five *Foxtrot Bravo*, turn left heading two four zero, descend, and maintain four thousand."

"Five *Foxtrot Bravo*, out of ten for four. Heading two four zero."

She eased back on the throttle and the plane settled slightly, the grinding sound of the engines diminished, and she could hear the woosh of the air like a whisper of wind over bedsheets beside an open window at night.

Percey yelled back to Bell, "You're about to have your first landing in a Lear. Let's see if I can set her down without rippling your coffee."

"In one piece's all I'm asking for," Bell said and cinched his seat belt tight as a bungee cord harness.

"Nothing, Rhyme."

The criminalist closed his eyes in disgust. "I don't believe it. I just don't believe it."

"He's gone. He was there, they're pretty sure. But the mikes didn't pick up a sound."

Rhyme glanced up at the big mirror he'd ordered Thom to prop up across the room. They'd been waiting for the explosive rounds to crash into it. Central Park was peppered with Haumann's and Dellray's tactical officers, just waiting for a gunshot.

"Where's Jodie?" Rhyme asked.

Dellray snickered. "Hiding in the alley. Saw some car go by and spooked."

"What car?" Rhyme asked.

The agent laughed. "If it *was* the Dancer, then he turned hisself into four fat Puerto Rican girls. Little shit said he won't come out till somebody shuts off the streetlight in front of your building."

"Leave him. He'll come back when he gets cold."

"Or to get his money," Sachs reminded.

Rhyme scowled. He was bitterly disappointed that this trick too hadn't worked.

Was it his failing? Or was there some uncanny instinct that the Dancer had? A sixth sense? The idea was repugnant to Lincoln Rhyme, the scientist, but he couldn't discount it completely. After all, even the NYPD used psychics from time to time.

Sachs started toward the window.

"No," Rhyme said to her. "We still don't know for certain he's gone." Sellitto stood away from the glass as he drew the drapes shut.

Oddly, it was scarier not knowing exactly where the Dancer was than thinking he was pointing a large rifle through a window twenty feet away.

It was then that Cooper's phone rang. He took the call.

"Lincoln, it's the Bureau's bomb people. They've checked the Explosives Reference Collection. They say they've got a possible match on those bits of latex."

"What do they say?"

Cooper listened to the agent for a moment.

"No leads on the specific type of rubber, but they say its not inconsistent with a material used in altimeter detonators. There's a latex balloon filled with air. It expands when the plane goes up because of the low pressure at higher altitudes, and at a certain height the balloon presses into a switch on the side of the bomb wall. Contact's completed. The bomb goes off."

"But this bomb was detonated by a timer."

"They're just telling me about the latex."

Rhyme looked at the plastic bags containing components of the bomb. His eyes fell to the timer, and he thought: Why's it in such perfect shape?

Because it had been mounted behind the overhanging lip of steel.

But the Dancer could have mounted it anywhere, pressed it into the plastic explosive itself, which would have reduced it to microscopic pieces. Leaving the timer intact had seemed careless at first. But now he wondered.

"Tell him that the plane exploded as it was *descending*," Sachs said.

Cooper relayed the comment, then listened. The tech reported, "He says it could just be a point-of-construction variation. As the plane climbs, the expanding balloon trips a switch that arms the bomb; when the plane descends the balloon shrinks and closes the circuit. That detonates it."

Rhyme whispered, "The timer's a fake! He mounted it behind the piece of metal so it wouldn't be destroyed. So we'd *think* it was a time bomb, not an altitude bomb. How high was Carney's plane when it exploded?"

Sellitto raced through the NTSB report. "It was just descending through five thousand feet."

"So it armed when they climbed through five thousand outside of Mamaroneck and detonated when he went below it near Chicago," Rhyme said.

"Why on descent?" the detective asked.

"So the plane would be farther away?" Sachs suggested.

"Right," Rhyme said. "It'd give the Dancer a better chance to get away from the airport before it blew."

"But," Cooper asked, "why go to all the trouble to fool us into thinking it was one kind of bomb and not another?"

Rhyme saw that Sachs figured it out just as fast as he did. "Oh, no!" she cried.

Sellitto still didn't get it. "What?"

"Because," she said, "the bomb squad was looking for a *time* bomb when they searched Percey's plane tonight. Listening for the timer."

"Which means," Rhyme spat out, "Percey and Bell've got an altitude bomb on board too."

"Sink rate twelve hundred feet per minute," Brad sang out.

Percey gentled the yoke of the Lear back slightly, slowing the descent. They passed through fifty-five hundred feet.

Then she heard it.

A strange chirping sound. She'd never heard any sound like it, not in a Lear 35A. It sounded like a warning buzzer of some kind, but distant. Percey scanned the panels but could see no red lights. It chirped again.

"Five three hundred feet," Brad called. "What's that noise?"

It stopped abruptly.

Percey shrugged.

An instant later, she heard a voice shouting beside her, "Pull up! Go higher! Now!"

Roland Bell's hot breath was on her cheek. He was beside her, in a crouch, brandishing his cell phone.

"What?"

"There's a bomb on! Altitude bomb. It goes off when we hit five thousand feet."

"But we're above—"

"I know! Pull up! Up!"

Percey shouted, "Set power, ninety-eight percent. Call out altitude."

Without a second's hesitation, Brad shoved the throttles forward. Percey pulled the Lear into a ten-degree rotation. Bell stumbled backward and landed with a crash on the floor.

Brad said, "Five thousand two, five one five . . . five two, five thousand three, five four . . . Five eight. Six thousand feet."

Percey Clay had never declared an emergency in all her years flying. Once, she'd declared a "pan-pan" – indicating an urgency situation – when an unfortunate flock of pelicans decided to commit suicide in her number two engine and clog up her pitot tube to boot. But now, for the first time in her career, she said, "May-day, may-day, Lear Six Niner Five *Foxtrot Bravo*."

"Go ahead, *Foxtrot Bravo*."

"Be advised, Chicago Approach. We have reports of a bomb on board. Need immediate clearance to one zero thousand feet and a heading for holding pattern over unpopulated area."

"Roger, Niner Five *Foxtrot Bravo,*" the ATC controller said calmly. "Uhm, maintain present heading of two four zero. Cleared to ten thousand feet. We are vectoring all aircraft around you . . . Change transponder code to seven seven zero zero and squawk."

Brad glanced uneasily at Percey as he changed the transponder setting – to the code that automatically sent a warning signal to all radar facilities in the area that *Foxtrot Bravo* was in trouble. Squawking meant sending out a signal from the transponder to let everyone at ATC and other aircraft know exactly which blip was the Lear.

She heard Bell say into his phone, "Th'only person got close to the plane, 'cept for me and Percey, was the business manager, Ron Talbot – and, nothing personal to him, but my boys or I watched him like a hawk while he was doing the work, stood over his shoulder the whole time. Oh, and that guy delivered some of the engine parts came by too. From Northeast Aircraft Distributors in Greenwich. But I checked him out good. Even got his home phone and called his wife, had them talk – to make sure he was legit." Bell listened for a moment more then hung up. "They'll call us back."

Percey looked at Brad and at Bell, then returned to the task of piloting her aircraft.

"Fuel?" she asked her copilot. "How much time?"

"We're under our estimated. Headwinds've been good." He did the calculations. "A hundred and five minutes."

She thanked God, or fate, or her own intuition, for deciding not to refuel at Chicago, but to load enough to get them to Saint Louis, plus the FAA requirement for an additional forty-five minutes' flying time.

Bell's phone chirped again.

He listened, sighed, then asked Percey, "Did that Northeast company deliver a fire extinguisher cartridge?"

"Shit, did he put it in *there?*" she asked bitterly.

"Looks like it. The delivery truck had a flat tire just after it left the warehouse on the way to make that delivery to you. Driver was busy for about twenty minutes. Connecticut trooper just found a mess of what looks like carbon dioxide foam in the bushes right near where it happened."

"God*damn!*" Percey glanced involuntarily toward the engine. "And I installed the fucker myself."

Bell asked, "Rhyme wants to know about heat. Wouldn't it blow the bomb?"

"Some parts are hot, some aren't. It's not that hot by the cartridge."

Bell told this to Rhyme, then he said, "He's going to call you directly."

A moment later, through the radio, Percey heard the patch of a unicom call.

It was Lincoln Rhyme.

"Percey, can you hear me?"

"Loud and clear. That prick pulled a fast one, hm?"

"Looks like it. How much flying time do you have?"

"Hour forty-five minutes. About."

"Okay, okay," the criminalist said. A pause. "All right . . . Can you get to the engine from the inside?"

"No."

Another pause. "Could you somehow disconnect the whole engine? Unbolt it or something? Let it drop off?"

"Not from the inside."

"Is there any way you could refuel in midair?"

"Refuel? Not with this plane."

Rhyme asked, "Could you fly high enough to freeze the bomb mechanism?"

She was amazed at how fast his mind worked. These were things that wouldn't have occurred to her. "Maybe. But even at emergency descent rate – I'm talking nosedive – it'd still take eight, nine minutes to get down. I don't think any bomb parts'd stay very frozen for that long. And the Mach buffet would probably tear us apart."

Rhyme continued, "Okay, what about getting a plane in front of you and tethering some parachutes back?"

Her initial thought was that she would never abandon her aircraft. But the realistic answer – the one she gave him – was that given the stall speed of a Lear 35A and the configur-ation of door, wings, and engines, it was unlikely that anyone could leap from the aircraft without being struck and killed.

Rhyme was again silent for a moment. Brad swallowed and wiped his hands on his razor-creased slacks. "Brother."

Roland Bell rocked back and forth.

Hopeless, she thought, staring down at the murky blue dusk.

"Lincoln?" Percey asked. "Are you there?"

She heard his voice. He was calling to someone in his lab – or bedroom. In a testy tone he was demanding, "Not *that* map. You know which one I mean. Well, why would I want that one? No, no . . ."

Silence.

Oh, Ed, Percey thought. Our lives have always followed parallel paths. Maybe our deaths will too. She was most upset about Roland Bell, though. The thought of leaving his children orphans was unbearable.

Then she heard Rhyme asking, "On the fuel you've got left, how far can you fly?"

"At the most efficient power settings . . ." She looked at Brad, who was punching in the figures.

He said, "If we got some altitude, say, eight hundred miles."

"Got an idea," Rhyme said. "Can you make it to Denver?"

33

"Airport elevation's fifty-one eighty feet," Brad said, reviewing the *Airman's Guide of Denver International.* "We were about that outside of Chicago and the thing didn't blow."

"How far?" Percey asked.

"From present location, nine oh two miles."

Percey debated for no more than a few seconds, nodded. "We go for it. Give me a dead-reckoning heading, just something to play with till we get VORs." Then into the radio: "We're going to try it, Lincoln. The gas'll be real close. We've got a lot to do. I'll get back to you."

"We'll be here."

Brad eyeballed the map and referred to the flight log. "Turn left heading two six six."

"Two six six," she repeated, then called ATC. "Chicago Center, Niner Five *Foxtrot Bravo.* We're heading for Denver International. Apparently it's a . . . we've got an altitude-sensitive bomb on board. We need to get on the ground at five thousand feet or higher. Request immediate VORs for vectoring to Denver."

"Roger, *Foxtrot Bravo.* We'll have those in a minute."

Brad asked, "Please advise the weather en route, Chicago Center."

"High pressure front moving through Denver right now. Headwinds vary from fifteen to forty at ten thousand, increasing to sixty, seventy knots at twenty-five."

"Ouch," Brad muttered then returned to his calculations. After a moment he said, "Fuel depletion about fifty-five miles short of Denver."

Bell asked, "Can you set down on the highway?"

"In a big ball of flames we can," Percey said.

ATC asked, "*Foxtrot Bravo*, ready to copy VOR frequencies?"

While Brad took down the information, Percey stretched, pressed her head into the back of her seat. The gesture seemed familiar and she remembered she'd seen Lincoln Rhyme do the same in his elaborate bed. She thought about her little speech to him. She'd meant it, of course, but hadn't realized how true the words were. How dependent they were on fragile bits of metal and plastic.

And maybe about to die because of them.

Fate is the hunter . . .

Fifty-five miles short. What could they do?

Why wasn't her mind as far-ranging as Rhyme's? Wasn't there anything she could think of to conserve fuel?

Flying higher was more fuel efficient.

Flying lighter was too. Could they throw anything out of the aircraft?

The cargo? The U.S. Medical shipment weighed exactly 478 pounds. That would buy them some miles.

But even as she considered this, she knew she'd never do it. If there was any chance she could salvage the flight, salvage the Company, she would.

Come on, Lincoln Rhyme, she thought, give me an idea. Give me . . . Picturing his room, picturing sitting beside him, she remembered the tiercel – the male falcon – lording about on the window ledge.

"Brad," she asked abruptly, "what's our glide ratio?"

"A Lear thirty-five A? No idea."

Percey had flown a Schweizer 2–32 sailplane. The first prototype was built in 1962 and it had set the standard for glider performance ever since. Its sink rate was a miraculous 120 feet per minute. It weighed about thirteen hundred pounds. The Lear she was flying was fourteen thousand pounds. Still, aircraft will glide, any aircraft. She remembered the incident of the Air Canada 767 a few years ago – pilots still talked about it. The jumbo jet ran out of fuel due to a combination of computer and human error. Both engines flamed out at forty-one thousand feet and the aircraft became a 143-ton glider. It crash-landed without a single death.

"Well, let's think. What'd the sink rate be at idle?"

"We could keep it twenty-three hundred, I think."

Which meant a vertical drop of about thirty miles per hour.

"Now. Calculate if we burned fuel to take us to fifty-five thousand feet, when would we deplete?"

"Fifty-five?" Brad asked with some surprise.

"Roger."

He punched in numbers. "Maximum climb is forty-three hundred fpm; we'd burn a lot down here, but after thirty-five thousand the efficiency goes way up. We could power back . . ."

"Go to one engine?"

"Sure. We could do that."

He tapped in more numbers. "That scenario, we'd deplete about eighty-three miles short. But, of course, then we'd have altitude."

Percey Clay, who got A's in math and physics and could dead reckon without a calculator, saw the numbers stream past in her head. Flame out at fifty-five thousand, sink rate of twenty-three . . . They could cover a little over eighty miles before they touched down. Maybe more if the headwinds were kind.

Brad, with the help of a calculator and fast fingers, came up with the same conclusion. "Be close, though."

God don't give out certain.

She said, "Chicago Center. Lear *Foxtrot Bravo* requesting immediate clearance to five five thousand feet."

Sometimes you play the odds.

"Uh, say again, *Foxtrot Bravo*."

"We need to go high. Five five thousand feet."

The ATC controller's voice intruded: "*Foxtrot Bravo*, you're a Lear three five, is that correct?"

"Roger."

"Maximum operating ceiling is forty-five thousand feet."

"That's affirmative, but we need to go higher."

"Your seals've been checked lately?"

Pressure seals. Doors and windows. What kept the aircraft from exploding.

"They're fine," she said, neglecting to mention that *Foxtrot Bravo* had been shot full of holes and jerry-rigged back together just that afternoon.

ATC answered, "Roger, you're cleared to five five thousand feet, *Foxtrot Bravo*."

And Percey said something that few, if any, Lear pilots had ever said, "Roger, out of ten for fifty-five thousand."

Percey commanded, "Power to eighty-eight percent. Call out rate of climb and altitude at forty, fifty, and fifty-five thousand."

"Roger," Brad said placidly.

She rotated the plane and it began to rise.

They sailed upward.

All the stars of evening . . .

Ten minutes later Brad called out, "Five five thousand."

They leveled off. It seemed to Percey that she could actually hear the groaning of the aircraft's seams. She recalled her high-altitude physiology. If the window Ron had replaced were to blow out or any pressure seal burst – if it didn't tear the aircraft apart – hypoxia would knock them out in about five seconds. Even if they were wearing masks, the pressure difference would make their blood boil.

"Increase cabin pressure to ten thousand feet."

"Pressure to ten thousand," he said. This at least would relieve some of the terrible pressure on the fragile hull.

"Good idea," Brad said. "How'd you think of that?"

Monkey skills . . .

"Dunno," she responded. "Let's cut power in number two. Throttle closed, autothrottle disengaged."

"Closed, disengaged," Brad echoed.

"Fuel pumps off, ignition off."

"Pumps off, ignition off."

She felt the slight swerve as their right side thrust vanished. Percey compensated for the yaw with a slight adjustment to the rudder trim tabs. It didn't take much. Because the jets were mounted on the rear of the fuselage and not on the wings, losing one power plant didn't affect the stability of the aircraft much.

Brad asked, "What do we do now?"

"I'm having a cup of coffee," Percey said, climbing out of her seat like a tomboy jumping from a tree house. "Hey, Roland, how d'you like yours again?"

For a tortuous forty minutes there was silence in Rhyme's room. No one's phone rang. No faxes came in. No computer voices reported, "You've got mail."

Then, at last, Dellray's phone brayed. He nodded as he spoke, but Rhyme could see the news wasn't good. He clicked the phone off.

"Cumberland?"

Dellray nodded. "But it's a bust. Kall hasn't been there for years. Oh, the locals're still talking about the time the boy tied his stepdaddy up 'n' let the worms get him. Sorta a legend. But no family left in the area. And nobody knows nuthin'. Or's willing to say."

It was then that Sellitto's phone chirped. The detective unfolded it and said, "Yeah?"

A lead, Rhyme prayed, please let it be a lead. He looked at the cop's doughy, stoic face. He flipped the phone closed.

"That was Roland Bell," he said. "He just wanted us to know. They're outa gas."

Hour 38 of 45

34

Three different warning buzzers went off simultaneously.

Low fuel, low oil pressure, low engine temperature.

Percey tried adjusting the attitude of the aircraft slightly to see if she could trick some fuel into the lines, but the tanks were bone dry.

With a faint clatter, number one engine quit coughing and went silent.

And the cockpit went completely dark. Black as a closet.

Oh, no . . .

She couldn't see a single instrument, a single control lever or knob. The only thing that kept her from slipping into blind-flight vertigo was the faint band of light that was Denver – in the far distance in front of them.

"What's this?" Brad asked.

"Jesus. I forgot the generators."

The generators are run by the engines. No engines, no electricity.

"Drop the RAT," she ordered.

Brad groped in the dark for the control and found it. He pulled the lever and the ram air turbine dropped out beneath the aircraft. It was a small propeller connected to a generator. The slipstream turned the prop, which powered the generator. It provided basic power for the controls and lights. But not the flaps, gear, speed brakes.

A moment later some of the lights returned.

Percey was staring at the vertical speed indicator. It showed a decent rate of thirty-five hundred feet per minute.

Far faster than they'd planned on. They were dropping at close to fifty miles an hour.

Why? she wondered. Why was the calculation so far off?

Because of the rarified air here! She was calculating sink rate based on denser atmosphere. And now that she considered this she remembered that the air around Denver would be rarified too. She'd never flown a sailplane more than a mile up.

She pulled back on the yoke to arrest the descent. It dropped to twenty-one hundred feet per minute. But the airspeed dropped too, fast. In this thin air the stall speed was about three hundred knots. The shaker stick began to vibrate and the controls went mushy. There'd be no recovery from a powerless stall in an aircraft like this.

The coffin corner . . .

Forward with the yoke. They dropped faster, but the airspeed picked up. For nearly fifty miles she played this game. Air Traffic Control told them where the headwinds were strongest and Percey tried to find the perfect combination of altitude and route – winds that were powerful enough to give the Lear optimal lift but not so fast that they slowed their ground speed too much.

Finally, Percey – her muscles aching from controlling the aircraft with brute force – wiped sweat from her face and said, "Give 'em a call, Brad."

"Denver Center, this is Lear Six Niner Five *Foxtrot Bravo,* with you out of one nine thousand feet. We are twenty-one miles from the airport. Airspeed two hundred twenty knots. We're in a no-power situation here and requesting vectoring to longest available runway consistent with our present heading of two five zero."

"Roger, *Foxtrot Bravo*. We've been expecting you. Altimeter thirty point nine five. Turn left heading two four zero. We're vectoring you to runway two eight left. You'll have eleven thousand feet to play with."

"Roger, Denver Center."

Something was nagging at her. That ping in the gut again. Like she'd felt recalling the black van.

What was it? Just superstition?

Tragedies come in threes . . .

Brad said, "Nineteen miles from touchdown. One six thousand feet."

"*Foxtrot Bravo,* contact Denver Approach." He gave them the radio frequency, then added, "They've been apprised of your situation. Good luck, ma'am. We're all thinking of you."

"Goodnight, Denver. Thanks."

Brad clicked the radio to the new frequency.

What's wrong? she wondered again. There's something I haven't thought of.

"Denver Approach, this is Lear Six Niner Five *Foxtrot Bravo*. With you at one three thousand feet, thirteen miles from touchdown."

"We have you, *Foxtrot Bravo.* Come right heading two five zero. Understand you are power-free, is that correct?"

"We're the biggest damn glider you ever saw, Denver."

"You have flaps and gear?"

"No flaps. We'll crank the gear down manually."

"Roger. You want trucks?"

Meaning emergency vehicles.

"We think we've got a bomb on board. We want everything you've got."

"Roger that."

Then, with a shudder of horror, it occurred to her: the air pressure!

"Denver Approach," she asked, "what's the altimeter?"

"Uhm, we have three oh point nine six, *Foxtrot Bravo*."

It had gone up a hundredth of an inch of mercury in the last minute.

"It's rising?"

"That's affirmative, *Foxtrot Bravo.* Major high-pressure front moving in."

No! That would increase the ambient pressure around the bomb, which would shrink the balloon, as if they were lower than they actually were.

"Shit on the street," she muttered.

Brad looked at her.

She said to him, "What was the mercury at Mamaroneck?"

He looked it up in the log. "Twenty-nine point six."

"Calculate five thousand feet altitude at that pressure reading compared with thirty-one point oh."

"Thirty-one? That's awful high."

"That's what we're moving into."

He stared at her. "But the bomb . . ."

Percey nodded. "Calculate it."

The young man punched numbers with a steady hand.

He sighed, his first visible display of emotion. "Five thousand feet at Mamaroneck translates to forty-eight five here."

She called Bell forward again. "Here's the situation. There's a pressure front coming in. By the time we get to the runway, the bomb may be reading the atmosphere as below five thousand feet. It may blow when were're fifty to a hundred feet above the ground."

"Okay." He nodded calmly. "Okay."

"We don't have flaps, so we're going to be landing fast, close to two hundred miles an hour. If it blows we'll lose control and crash. There won't be much fire 'cause the tanks are dry. And depending on what's in front of us, if we're low enough we may skid a ways before we start tumbling. There's nothing to do but keep the seat belts tight and keep your head down."

"All right," he said, nodding, looking out the window.

She glanced at his face. "Can I ask you something, Roland?"

"You bet."

"This isn't your first airplane flight, is it?"

He sighed. "You know, you live mosta your born days in North Carolina, you just don't have much of a chance to travel. And coming to New York, well, those Amtraks're nice and comfy." He paused. "Fact is, I've never been higher than an elevator'll take me."

"They're not all like this," she said.

He squeezed her on the shoulder, whispered, "Don't drop your candy." He returned to his seat.

"Okay," Percey said, looking over the *Airman's Guide* information on Denver International. "Brad, this'll be a nighttime visual approach to runway two eight left. I'll have command of the aircraft. You'll lower the gear manually and call out rate of descent, distance to runway, and altitude – give me true altitude above ground, not sea level – and airspeed." She tried to think of something else. No power, no flaps, no speed brakes. There was nothing else to say; it was the shortest pre-landing briefing in the history of her flying career. She added, "One last thing. When we stop, just get the fuck out as fast as you can."

"Ten miles to runway," he called. "Speed two hundred knots. Altitude nine thousand feet. We need to slow descent."

She pulled up on the yoke slightly and the speed dropped dramatically. The shaker stick vibrated again. Stall now and they died.

Forward again.

Nine miles . . . Eight . . .

Sweating like a rainstorm. She wiped her face. Blisters on the soft skin between her thumbs and index fingers.

Seven . . . Six . . .

"Five miles from touchdown, forty-five hundred feet. Airspeed two hundred ten knots."

"Gear down," Percey commanded.

Brad spun the wheel that manually lowered the heavy gear. He had gravity helping him, but it was nonetheless a major effort. Still, he kept his eyes glued to the instruments and recited, calm as an accountant reading a balance sheet, "Four miles from touchdown, thirty-nine hundred feet . . ."

She fought the buffeting of the lower altitude and the harsh winds.

"Gear down," Brad called, panting, "three green."

The airspeed dropped to one hundred eighty knots – about two hundred miles an hour. It was too fast. Way too fast. Without their reverse thrusters they'd burn up even the longest runway in a streak.

"Denver Approach, what's the altimeter?"

"Three oh nine eight," the unflappable ATC controller said.

Rising. Higher and higher.

She took a deep breath. According to the bomb, the runway was slightly less than five thousand feet above sea level. How accurate had the Coffin Dancer been when he'd made the detonator?

"The gear's dragging. Sink rate's twenty-six hundred."

Which meant a vertical speed of about thirty-eight miles per hour. "We're dropping too fast, Percey," Brad called. "We'll hit in front of the approach lights. A hundred yards short. Two, maybe."

ATC's voice had noticed this too: "*Foxtrot Bravo,* you have to get some altitude. You're coming in too low."

Back on the stick. The speed dropped. Stall warning. Forward on the stick.

"Two and a half miles from touchdown, altitude nineteen hundred feet."

"Too low, *Foxtrot Bravo*!" the ATC controller warned again.

She looked out over the silver nose. There were all the lights – the strobes of the approach lights beckoning them forward, the blue dots of the taxiway, the orange-red of the runway . . . And lights that Percey'd never seen before on approach. Hundreds of flashing lights. White and red. All the emergency vehicles.

Lights everywhere.

All the stars of evening . . .

"Still low," Brad called. "We're going to impact two hundred yards short."

Hands sweating, straining forward, Percey thought again of Lincoln Rhyme, strapped to his seat, himself leaning forward, examining something in the computer screen.

"Too low, *Foxtrot Bravo,*" ATC repeated. "I'm moving emergency vehicles to the field in front of the runway."

"Negative that," Percey said adamantly.

Brad called, "Altitude thirteen hundred feet. One and a half miles from touchdown."

We've got thirty seconds! What do I do?

Ed? Tell me? Brit? Somebody . . .

Come on, monkey skills . . . What the hell do I do?

She looked out the cockpit window. In the light of the moon she could see suburbs and towns and some farmland but also, to the left, large patches of desert.

Colorado's a desert state . . . Of course!

Suddenly she banked sharply to the left.

Brad, without a clue as to what she was doing, called out, "Rate of descent thirty-two hundred, altitude one thousand feet, nine hundred feet, eight five . . ."

Banking a powerless aircraft sheds altitude in a hurry.

ATC called, "*Foxtrot Bravo,* do *not* turn. Repeat, do not turn! You don't have enough altitude as is."

She leveled out over the patch of desert.

Brad gave a fast laugh. "Altitude steady . . . Altitude rising, we're at nine hundred feet, one thousand feet, twelve hundred feet. Thirteen hundred feet . . . I don't get it."

"A thermal," she said. "Desert soaks up heat during the day and releases it all night."

ATC had figured it out too. "Good, *Foxtrot Bravo*! Good. You just bought yourself about three hundred yards. Come right two nine oh . . . good, now left two eight oh. Good. On course. Listen, *Foxtrot Bravo*, you want to take out those approach lights, you go right ahead."

"Thanks for the offer, Denver, but I think I'll set her down a thousand past the numbers."

"That's all right too, ma'am."

They had another problem now. They could reach the runway, but the airspeed was way too high. Flaps were what decreased the stall speed of an aircraft so it could land more slowly. The Lear 35A's normal stall speed was about 110 miles an hour. Without flaps it was closer to 180. At that speed even a two-mile-long runway vanishes in an instant.

So Percey sideslipped.

This is a simple maneuver in a private plane, used in crosswind landings. You bank to the left and hit the right rudder pedal. It slows the aircraft considerably. Percey didn't know if anyone had ever used this technique in a seven-ton jet, but she couldn't think of anything else to do. "Need your help here," she called to Brad, gasping at the effort and the pain shooting through her raw hands. He gripped the yoke and shoved on the pedal too. This had the effect of slowing the aircraft, though it dropped the left wing precipitously.

She'd straighten it out just before contact with the runway.

She hoped.

"Airspeed?" she called.

"One fifty knots."

"Looking good, *Foxtrot Bravo*."

"Two hundred yards from runway, altitude two hundred eighty feet," Brad called. "Approach lights, twelve o'clock."

"Sink rate?" she asked.

"Twenty-six hundred."

Too fast. Landing at that sink rate could destroy the undercarriage. And might very well set off the bomb too.

There were the approach strobes right in front of her – guiding them forward . . .

Down, down, down . . .

Just as they hurtled toward the scaffolding of the lights, Percey shouted, "My aircraft!"

Brad released the yoke.

Percey straightened from the sideslip and brought the nose up. The plane flared beautifully and grabbed air, halting the precipitous descent right over the numbers at the end of the runway.

Grabbed air so well, in fact, that it wouldn't land.

In the thicker air of the relatively lower atmosphere the speeding plane – lighter without fuel – refused to touch down.

She glimpsed the yellow-green of the emergency vehicles scattered along the side of the runway.

A thousand feet past the numbers, still thirty feet above the concrete.

Then two thousand feet past. Then three thousand.

Hell, fly her into the ground.

Percey eased the stick forward. The plane dipped dramatically and Percey yanked all the way back on the yoke. The silver bird shuddered then settled gently on the concrete. It was the smoothest landing she'd ever made.

"Full brakes!"

She and Brad jammed their feet down on the rudder pedals and they heard the squealing of the pads, the fierce vibrations. Smoke filled the cabin.

They'd used well over half the runway already and were still speeding at a hundred miles an hour.

Grass, she thought, I'll veer into it if I have to. Wreck the undercarriage but I'll still save the cargo . . .

Seventy, sixty . . .

"Fire light, right wheel," Brad called. Then: "Fire light, nosewheel."

Fuck it, she thought, and pressed down on the brakes with all her weight.

The Lear began to skid and shudder. She compensated with the nosewheel. More smoke filling the cabin.

Sixty miles per hour, fifty, forty . . .

"The door," she called to Bell.

In an instant the detective was up, pushing the door outward; it became a staircase.

The fire trucks were converging on the aircraft.

With a wild groan of the smoking brakes, Lear N695FB skidded to a stop ten feet from the end of the runway.

The first voice to fill the cabin was Bell's. "Okay, Percey, out! Move."

"I have to—"

"I'm taking over now!" the detective shouted. "I have to drag you outa here, I'll do it. Now move!"

Bell hustled her and Brad out the door, then leapt to the concrete himself, led them away from the aircraft. He called to the rescue workers, who'd started shooting foam at the wheel wells, "There's a bomb on board, could go any minute. In the engine. Don't get close." One of his guns was in his hand and he surveyed the crowd of rescue workers circling the plane. At one time Percey would have thought he was being paranoid. No longer.

They paused about a hundred feet from the plane. The Denver Police Bomb Squad truck pulled up. Bell waved it over.

A lanky cowboy of a cop got out of the truck and walked up to Bell. They flashed ID at each other and Bell explained about the bomb, where they thought it was.

"So," the Denver cop said, "you're not sure it's on board."

"Nope. Not a hundred percent."

Though as Percey happened to glance at *Foxtrot Bravo* – her beautiful silver skin flecked with foam and glistening under the fierce spotlights – there was a deafening bang. Everyone except Bell and Percey hit the ground fast as the rear half of the aircraft disintegrated in a huge flash of orange flame, strewing bits of metal into the air.

"Oh," Percey gasped, her hand rising to her mouth.

There was no fuel left in the tanks, of course, but the interior of the aircraft – the seats, the wiring, the carpet, the plastic fittings, and the precious cargo – burned furiously as the fire trucks waited a prudent moment then streamed forward, pointlessly shooting more snowy foam on the ruined metallic corpse.

V
DANCE MACABRE

I looked up to see a dot dropping, becoming an inverted heart, a diving bird. The wind screamed through her bells, making a sound like nothing else on earth as she fell a half mile through the clear autumn air. At the last moment she turned parallel to the chukar's line of flight and hit it from behind with the solid "thwack" of a large-caliber bullet striking flesh.

A Rage for Falcons, Stephen Bodio

Hour 42 of 45

35

It was after 3 A.M., Rhyme noted. Percey Clay was flying back to the East Coast on an FBI jet and in just a few hours she'd be on her way to the courthouse to get ready for her grand jury appearance.

And he still had no idea where the Coffin Dancer was, what he was planning, what identity he was now assuming.

Sellitto's phone brayed. He listened. His face screwed up. "Jesus. The Dancer just got somebody else. They found another body – ID-proofed – in a tunnel in Central Park. Near Fifth Avenue."

"Completely ID-proofed?"

"Did it up right, sounds like. Removed the hands, teeth, jaw, and clothes. White male. Youngish. Late twenties, early thirties." The detective listened again. "Not a bum," he reported. "He's clean, in good shape. Athletic. Haumann thinks he's some yuppie from the East Side."

"Okay," Rhyme said. "Bring him here. I want to go over it myself."

"The body?"

"Right."

"Well, okay."

"So the Dancer's got a new identity," Rhyme mused angrily. "What the hell is it? How's he going to come at us next?"

Rhyme sighed, looked on the window. He said to Dellray, "What safe house're you going to put them in?"

"I been thinking 'bout that," the lanky agent said. "Seems to me—"

"Ours," a new voice said.

They looked at the heavyset man in the doorway.

"*Our* safe house," Reggie Eliopolos said. "We're taking custody."

"Not unless you've got—" Rhyme began.

The prosecutor waved the paper too fast for Rhyme to read it, but they all knew the protective custody order would be legit.

"That's not a good idea," Rhyme said.

"It's better than *your* idea of trying to get our last witness killed any way you can."

Sachs stepped forward, angrily, but Rhyme shook his head.

"Believe me," Rhyme said, "the Dancer'll figure out that you're going to take them into custody. He's probably *already* figured it out. In fact," he added ominously, "he may be banking on it."

"He'd have to be a mind reader."

Rhyme tipped his head. "You're catching on."

Eliopolos snickered. He looked around the room, spotted Jodie. "You're Joseph D'Oforio?"

The little man stared back. "I – yes."

"You're coming too."

"Hey, hold on a minute, they said I'd get my money and I could—"

"This doesn't have anything to do with rewards. If you're entitled to it you'll get it. We're just going to make sure you're safe until the grand jury."

"Grand jury! Nobody said anything about testifying!"

"Well," Eliopolos said, "you're a material witness." A nod toward Rhyme. "*He* may have been intent on murdering some hit man. *We're* making a case against the man who hired him. Which is what most law enforcers do."

"I'm not going to testify."

"Then you're going to do time for contempt. In general population. And I'll bet you know how safe you'll be there."

The little man tried to be angry but was just too scared. His face shriveled. "Oh, Jesus."

"You're not going to have enough protection," Rhyme said to Eliopolos. "We know him. Let *us* protect them."

"Oh, and Rhyme?" Eliopolos turned to him. "Because of the incident with the plane, I'm charging you with interference with criminal investigation."

"The fuck you are," Sellitto said.

"The fuck I am," the round man snapped back. "He could've ruined the case, letting her make that flight. I'm having the warrant served Monday. And I'm going to supervise the prosecution myself. He—"

Rhyme said softly, "He's been here, you know."

The assistant U.S. attorney stopped speaking. After a moment he asked, "Who?"

Though he knew who.

"He was right outside that window not an hour ago, pointing a sniper rifle, loaded with explosive shells, into this room." Rhyme's eyes dipped to the floor. "Probably the very spot where you're standing."

Eliopolos wouldn't have stepped back for the world. But his eyes flickered to the windows to make certain the shades were closed.

"Why . . . ?"

Rhyme finished the sentence. "Didn't he shoot? Because he had a better idea."

"What's that?"

"Ah," Rhyme said. "That's the million-dollar question. All we know is he's killed somebody else – some young man in Central Park – and stripped him. He's ID-proofed the body and taken over his identity. I don't doubt for one minute that he knows the bomb didn't kill Percey and that he's on his way to finish the job. And he'll make you a co-conspirator."

"He doesn't even know I exist."

"If that's what you want to believe."

"Jesus, Reggie Boy," Dellray said. "Get with the picture!"

"Don't call me that."

Sachs joined in. "Aren't you figuring it out? You've never been up against anybody like him."

Eyes on her, Eliopolos spoke to Sellitto. "Guess you do things different on the city level. Federal, our people know their places."

Rhyme snapped, "You're a fool if you treat him like a gansta or some has-been mafioso. Nobody can hide from him. The only way is to stop him."

"Yeah, Rhyme, that's been your war cry all along. Well, we're not sacrificing any more troops because you've got a hard-on for a guy killed two of your techs five years ago. Assuming you can get a hard-on—"

Eliopolos was a large man and so he was surprised to find himself slammed so lithely to the floor, gasping for breath and staring up into Sellitto's purple face, the lieutenant's fist drawn back.

"Do that, Officer," the attorney wheezed, "and you'll be arraigned within a half hour."

"Lon," Rhyme said, "let it go, let it go . . ."

The detective calmed, glared at the man, walked away. Eliopolos climbed to his feet.

The insult in fact meant nothing. He wasn't even thinking of Eliopolos. Or the Dancer for that matter. For he'd happened to glance at Amelia Sachs, at the hollowness in her eyes, the despair. And he knew what she was feeling: the desperation at losing her prey. Eliopolos was stealing away her chance to get the Dancer. As with Lincoln Rhyme, the killer had come to be the dark focus of her life.

All because of a single misstep – the incident at the airport, her going for cover. A small thing, minuscule to everyone but her. But what was the expression? A fool can throw a stone into a pond that a dozen wise men can't recover. And what was Rhyme's life now but the result of a piece of wood breaking a piece of bone? Sachs's life had been snapped in that single moment of what she saw as cowardice. But unlike Rhyme's case, there was – he believed – a chance for her to mend.

Oh, Sachs, how it hurts to do this, but I have no choice. He said to Eliopolos, "All right, but you have to do one thing in exchange."

"Or you'll what?" Eliopolos snickered.

"Or I won't tell you where Percey is," Rhyme said simply. "We're the only ones who know."

Eliopolos's face, no longer flushed from his World Wrestling pin, gazed icily at Rhyme. "What do you want?"

Rhyme inhaled deeply. "The Dancer's shown an interest in targeting the people looking for him. If you're going to protect Percey, I want you to protect the chief forensic investigator in the case too."

"You?" the lawyer asked.

"No, Amelia Sachs," Rhyme replied.

"Rhyme, no," she said, frowning.

Reckless Amelia Sachs . . . And I'm putting her square in the kill zone.

He motioned her over to him.

"I want to stay here," she said. "I want to find him."

He whispered, "Oh, don't worry about that, Sachs. He'll find *you.* We'll try to figure out his new identity, Mel and me. But if he makes a move out on Long Island, I want you there. I want you with Percey. You're the only one who understands him. Well, you and me. And I won't be doing any shooting in the near future."

"He could come back here—"

"I don't think so. There's a chance this is the first fish of his that's going to get away and he doesn't like that one bit. He's going after Percey. He's desperate to. I know it."

She debated for a moment, then nodded.

"Okay," Eliopolos said, "you'll come with us. We've got a van waiting."

Rhyme said, "Sachs?"

She paused.

Eliopolos said, "We really should move."

"I'll be down in a minute."

"We're under some time pressure here, Officer."

"I said, a minute." She handily won the staring contest and Eliopolos and his trooper escort led Jodie down the stairs. "Wait," the little man shouted from the hallway. He returned, grabbed his self-help book, and trotted down the stairs.

"Sachs . . ."

He thought of saying something about avoiding heroics, about Jerry Banks, about being too hard on herself.

About giving up the dead . . .

But he knew that any words of caution or encouragement would ring like lead.

And so he settled for "Shoot first."

She placed her right hand on his left. He closed his eyes and tried so very hard to feel the pressure of her skin on his. He believed he did, if just in his ring finger.

He looked up at her. She said, "And you keep a minder handy, okay?" Nodding at Sellitto and Dellray.

Then an EMS medic appeared in the door, looking around the room at Rhyme, at the equipment, at the beautiful lady cop, trying to fathom why on earth he was doing what he'd been instructed to. "Somebody wanted a body?" he asked uncertainly.

"In here!" Rhyme shouted. "Now! We need it now!"

The van drove through a gate and then down a one-lane driveway. It extended for what seemed like miles.

"If this's the driveway," Roland Bell muttered, "can't wait to see the house."

He and Amelia Sachs flanked Jodie, who irritated everybody to no end as he fidgeted nervously, his bulky bulletproof vest banging into them as he'd examined shadows and dark doorways and passing cars on the Long Island Expressway. In the back were two 32-E officers, armed with machine guns. Percey Clay was in the front passenger seat. When they'd picked up her and Bell at the Marine Air Terminal at LaGuardia on their way to Suffolk County, Sachs had been shocked at the sight of the woman.

Not exhaustion – though she was clearly tired. Not fear. No, it was Percey's complete resignation that troubled Sachs. As a Patrol officer, she'd seen plenty of tragedy on the street. She'd delivered her share of bad news, but she'd never seen someone who'd given up so completely as Percey Clay.

Percey was on the phone with Ron Talbot. Sachs deduced from the conversation that U.S. Medical hadn't even waited for the cinders of her airplane to cool before canceling the contract. When she hung up she stared at the passing scenery for a moment. She said absently to Bell, "The insurance company isn't even going to pay for the cargo. They're saying I assumed a known risk. So, that's it. That's it." She added briskly, "We're bankrupt."

Pine trees swept past, scrub oaks, patches of sand. Sachs, a city girl, had come to Nassau and Suffolk Counties when she was a teenager not for the beaches or the shopping malls but to pop the clutch of her Charger and goose the maroon car up to sixty within five point nine seconds in the renegade drag races that made Long Island famous. She appreciated trees and grass and cows but enjoyed nature best when she was streaking past it at 110 miles per hour.

Jodie crossed and uncrossed his arms and burrowed into the center seat, playing with the seat belt, knocking into Sachs again.

"Sorry," he muttered.

She wanted to slug him.

The house didn't live up to the driveway.

It was a rambling split-level, a combination of logs and clapboard. A ramshackle place, added on to over the years with plenty of federal money and no inspiration.

The night was overcast, filled with dense patches of mist, but Sachs could see enough to note that the house was set in a tight ring of trees. The grounds around it had been cleared for two hundred yards. Good cover for the residents of the house and good groomed open areas to pick off anyone trying an assault. A grayish band in the distance suggested the resumption of the forest. There was a large, still lake behind the house.

Reggie Eliopolos climbed out of the lead van and motioned everyone out. He led them into the main entryway of the building. He handed them off to a round man, who seemed cheerful even though he never once smiled.

"Welcome," he said. "I'm U.S. Marshal David Franks. Want to tell you a little about your home away from home here. The most secure witness protection enclave in the country. We have weight and motion sensors built into the entire perimeter of the place. Can't be broken through without setting off all sorts of other alarms. The computer's programmed to sense human motion patterns, correlated to weight, so the alarm doesn't go off if a deer or dog happens to wander over the perimeter. Somebody – some *human* – steps where he shouldn't, this whole place lights up like Times Square on Christmas Eve. What if somebody tries to ride a horse into the perimeter? We thought of that. The computer pick-ups a weight anomaly correlated to the distance between the animal's hooves, the alarm goes off. And any motion at all – racoon or squirrel – starts the infrared videos going.

"Oh, and we're covered by radar from the Hampton Regional Airport, so any aerial assault gets picked up plenty early. Anything happens, you'll hear a siren and maybe see the lights. Just stay where you are. Don't go outside."

"What kind of guards do you have?" Sachs asked.

"We've got four marshals inside. Two outside at the front guard station, two in the back by the lake. And hit that panic button there and there'll be a Huey full of SWAT boys here in twenty minutes."

Jodie's face said twenty minutes seemed like a very long time. Sachs had to agree with him.

Eliopolos looked at his watch. He said, "We're going to have an armored van here at six to take you to the grand jury. Sorry you won't get much sleep." He glanced at Percey. "But if I'd had my way, you'd've been here all night, safe and sound."

No one said a word of farewell as he walked out the door.

Franks continued, "Few other things need mentioning. Don't look out windows. Don't go outside without an escort. That phone there" – he pointed to a beige phone in the corner of the living room – "is secure. It's the only one you should use. Shut off your cell phones and don't use them under any circumstances. So. That's it. Any questions?"

Percey asked, "Yeah, you got any booze?"

Franks bent to the cabinet beside him and pulled out a bottle of vodka and one of bourbon. "We like to keep our guests happy."

He set the bottles on the table, then walked to the front door, slipping his windbreaker on. "I'm headed home. 'Night, Tom," he said to the marshal at the door and nodded to the quartet of guardees, standing incongruously in the middle of the varnished wood hunting lodge, two bottles of liquor between them and a dozen deer and elk heads staring down.

The phone rang, startling them all. One of the marshals got it on the third ring. "Hello? . . ."

He glanced at the two women. "Amelia Sachs?"

She nodded and took the receiver.

It was Rhyme. "Sachs, how safe is it?"

"Pretty good," she said. "High tech. Any luck with the body?"

"Nothing so far. Four missing males reported in Manhattan in the last four hours. We're checking them all out. Is Jodie there?"

"Yes."

"Ask him if the Dancer ever mentioned assuming a particular identity."

She relayed the question.

Jodie thought back. "Well, I remember him saying something once . . . I mean, nothing specific. He said if you're going to kill somebody you have to infiltrate, evaluate, delegate, then eliminate. Or something like that. I don't remember exactly. He meant delegate somebody else to do something, then when everybody's distracted, he'd move in. I think he mentioned like a delivery guy or shoeshine boy."

Your deadliest weapon is deception . . .

After she relayed this to Rhyme he said, "We're thinking the body's a young businessman. Could be a lawyer. Ask Jodie if he ever mentioned trying to get into the courthouse for the grand jury."

Jodie didn't think so.

Sachs told Rhyme this.

"Okay. Thanks." She heard him calling something to Mel Cooper. "I'll check in later, Sachs."

After they hung up, Percey asked them, "You want a nightcap?"

Sachs couldn't decide if she did or not. The memory of the scotch preceding her fiasco in Lincoln Rhyme's bed made her cringe. But on impulse she said, "Sure."

Roland Bell decided he could be off duty for a half hour.

Jodie opted for a fast, medicinal shot of whiskey, then headed off to bed, toting his self-help book under his arm and staring with a city boy's fascination at a mounted moose head.

Outside, in the thick spring air, cicada chirped and bullfrogs belched their peculiar, unsettling calls.

As he looked out the window into the early morning darkness Jodie could see the starbursts of searchlights radiating through the fog. Shadows danced sideways – the mist moving through the trees.

He stepped away from his window and walked to the door of his room, looked out.

Two marshals guarded this corridor, sitting in a small security room twenty feet away. They seemed bored and only moderately vigilant.

He listened and heard nothing other than the snaps and ticks of an old house late in the evening.

Jodie returned to his bed and sat on the sagging mattress. He picked up his battered, stained copy of *Dependent No More*.

Let's get to work, he thought.

He opened the book wide, the glue cracking, and tore a small patch of tape off the bottom of the spine. A long knife slid onto the bed. It looked like black metal though it was made of ceramic-impregnated polymer and wouldn't register on a metal detector. It was stained and dull, sharp as a razor on one edge, serrated like a surgical saw on the other. The handle was taped. He'd designed and constructed it himself. Like most serious weapons it wasn't glitzy and it wasn't sexy and it did only one thing: it killed. And it did this very, very well.

He had no qualms about picking up the weapon – or touching doorknobs or windows – because he was the owner of new fingerprints. The skin on the pads of eight fingers and two thumbs had been burned away chemically last month by a surgeon in Berne, Switzerland, and a new set of prints etched into the scar tissue by a laser used for microsurgery. His own prints would regenerate, but not for some months.

Sitting on the edge of the bed, eyes closed, he pictured

the common room and took a mental stroll through it, remembering the location of every door, every window, every piece of furniture, the bad landscapes on the walls, the elk antlers above the fireplace, ashtrays, weapons, and potential weapons. Jodie had such a good memory he would have been able to walk through the room blindfolded, never brushing a single chair or table.

Lost in this meditation, he steered his imaginary self to the telephone in the corner and spent a moment considering the safe house's communications system. He was completely familiar with how it worked (he spent much of his free time reading operating manuals of security and communications systems) and he knew that if he cut the line the drop in voltage would send a signal to the marshals' panel here and probably to a field office as well. So he'd have to leave it intact.

Not a problem, just a factor.

On with his mental stroll. Examining the common-room video cameras – which the marshal had "forgotten" to tell them about. They were in the Y configuration that a budget-conscious security designer would use for a government safe house. He knew this system too and that it harbored a serious design flaw – all you had to do was tap the middle of the lens hard. This misaligned all the optics; the image in the security monitor would go black but there'd be no alarm, which would happen if the coaxial cable were cut.

Thinking about the lighting . . . He could shut out six – no, five – of eight lights he'd seen in the safe house but no more than that. Not until all the marshals were dead. He noted the location of each lamp and light switch, then moved on, more phantom walking. The TV room, the kitchen, the bedrooms. Thinking of distances, angles of view from outside.

Not a problem . . .

Noting the location of each of his victims. Considering the possibility that they might have moved in the past fifteen minutes.

. . . just a factor.

Now his eyes opened. He nodded to himself, slipped the knife in his pocket, and stepped to the door.

Silently he eased into the kitchen, stole a slotted spoon

from a rack over the sink. Walked to the refrigerator and poured himself a glass of milk. Then he walked into the common room and meandered from bookshelf to bookshelf, pretending to look for something to read. As he passed each of the video surveillance cameras he reached up with the spoon and slapped the lenses. Then he set the milk and spoon on a table and headed into the security room.

"Hey, check out the monitors," one marshal muttered, turning a knob on the TV screen in front of him.

"Yeah?" the other asked, not really interested.

Jodie walked past the first marshal, who looked up and started to ask, "Hey, sir, how you doing?" when *swish, swish,* Jodie tidily opened the man's throat in a V, spraying his copious velvet blood in a high arc. His partner's eyes flashed wide and he reached for his gun, but Jodie pulled it from his hand and stabbed him once in the throat and once in the chest. He dropped to the floor and thrashed for a moment. It was a noisy death – as Jodie'd known it would be. But he couldn't do more knife work on the man; he needed the uniform and had to kill him with a minimum of blood.

As the marshal lay on the floor, shaking and dying, he gazed up at Jodie, who was stripping off his own blood-soaked clothes. The marshal's eyes flickered to Jodie's biceps. They focused on the tattoo.

As Jodie bent down and began to undress the marshal he noticed the man's gaze and said, "It's called 'Dance Macabre.' See? Death's dancing with his next victim. That's her coffin behind them. Do you like it?"

He asked this with genuine curiosity, though he expected no answer. And received none.

36

Mel Cooper, clad in latex gloves, was standing over the body of the young man they'd found in Central Park.

"I could try the plantars," he suggested, discouraged.

The friction ridge prints on the feet were as unique as fingerprints but they were of marginal value until you had samples from a suspect; plantars weren't cataloged in AFIS databases.

"Don't bother," Rhyme muttered.

Who the hell *is* this? Rhyme wondered, looking at the savaged body in front of him. He's the key to the Dancer's next move. Oh, this was the worst feeling in the world: an unreachable itch. To have a piece of evidence in front of you, to *know* it was the key to the case, and yet to be unable to decipher it.

Rhyme's eyes strayed to the evidence chart on the wall. The body was like the green fibers they'd found at the hangar – significant, Rhyme felt, but its meaning unknown.

"Anything else?" Rhyme asked the tour doctor from the medical examiner's office. He'd accompanied the body here. He was a young man, balding, with dots of sweat in constellations on his crown. The doctor said, "He's gay or, to be accurate, he'd lived a gay lifestyle when he was young. He's had repeated anal intercourse though not for some years."

Rhyme continued, "What does that scar tell you? Surgery?"

"Well, it's a precise incision. But I don't know of any

reason to operate there. Maybe some intestinal blockage. But even then I've never heard of a procedure in that quadrant of the abdomen."

Rhyme regretted Sachs was not here. He wanted to throw around ideas with her. She'd think of *something* he'd overlooked.

Who could he be? Rhyme racked his brain. Identification was a complex science. He'd established a man's identity once with nothing more that a single tooth. But the procedure took time – usually weeks or months.

"Run blood type and DNA profile," Rhyme said.

"Already ordered," the tour doctor said. "I sent the samples downtown already."

If he were HIV positive that might help them ID him through doctors or clinics. But without anything else to go on, the blood work wouldn't be very helpful.

Fingerprint . . .

I'd give *anything* for a nice friction ridge print, Rhyme thought. Maybe—

"Wait!" Rhyme laughed out loud. "His dick!"

"What?" Sellitto blurted.

Dellray lifted an arching brow.

"He doesn't have any hands. But what's the one part of his anatomy he'd be sure to touch?"

"Penis," Cooper called out. "If he peed in the last couple of hours we can probably get a print."

"Who wants to do the honors?"

"No job too disgusting," the tech said, donning a double layer of latex gloves. He went to work with Kromekote skin-printing cards. He lifted two excellent prints – a thumb from the top of the corpse's penis and an index finger from the bottom.

"Perfect, Mel."

"Don't tell my girlfriend," he said coyly. He fed the prints through the AFIS system.

The message came up on the screen: *Please Wait . . . Please Wait . . .*

Be on file, Rhyme thought desperately. Please be on file.

He was.

But when the results came back, Sellitto and Dellray, closest to Cooper's computer, stared at the screen in disbelief.

"What the hell?" the detective said.

"What?" Rhyme cried. "Who is it?"

"It's Kall."

"What?"

"It's Stephen Kall," Cooper repeated. "It's a twenty-point match. There's no doubt." Cooper found the composite print they'd constructed earlier to find the Dancer's identity. He dropped it on the table next to the Kromekote. "It's identical."

How? Rhyme was wondering. How on earth?

"What if," Sellitto said, "it's Kall's prints on this guy's dick? What if Kall's a bone smoker?"

"We've got genetic markers from Kall's blood, right? From the water tower?"

"Right," Cooper called.

"Compare them," Rhyme called out. "I want a profile of the corpse's markers. And I want it now."

Poetry was not lost on him.

The "Coffin Dancer" . . . I like that, he thought. Much better than "Jodie" – the name he'd picked for this job because it was so unthreatening. A silly name, a diminutive name.

The Dancer . . .

Names were important, he knew. He read philosophy. The act of naming – of designating – is unique to humans. The Dancer now spoke silently to the late, dismembered, Stephen Kall: It was me you heard about. *I'm* the one who calls my victims "corpses." You call them Wives, Husbands, Friends, whatever you like.

But once I'm hired, they're corpses. That's all they are.

Wearing a U.S. marshal's uniform, he started down the dim hallway from the bodies of the two officers. He hadn't avoided the blood completely, of course, but in the murkiness of the enclave you couldn't see that the navy blue uniform had patches of red on it.

On his way to find Corpse three.

The Wife, if you will, Stephen. What a mixed-up, nervous creature you were. With your scrubbed hands and your confused dick. The Husband, the Wife, the Friend . . .

Infiltrate, Evaluate, Delegate, Eliminate . . .

Ah, Stephen . . . I could have taught you there's only one rule in this business: You stay one step ahead of every living soul.

He now had two pistols but wouldn't use them yet. He wouldn't think of acting prematurely. If he stumbled now he'd never have another chance to kill Percey Clay before the grand jury met later that morning.

Moving silently into a parlor where two more U.S. marshals sat, one reading a paper, one watching TV.

The first one glanced up at the Dancer, saw the uniform, and returned to the paper. Then looked up again.

"Wait," the marshal said, suddenly realizing he didn't recognize the face.

But the Dancer didn't wait.

He answered with *swish, swish* to both carotid arteries. The man slid forward to die on page 6 of the *Daily News* so quietly that his partner never turned from the TV, where a blond woman wearing excessive gold jewelry was explaining how she met her boyfriend through a psychic.

"Wait? For what?" the second marshal asked, not looking away from the screen.

He died slightly more noisily than his partner, but no one in the compound seemed to notice. The Dancer dragged the bodies flat, stowed them under a table.

At the back door he made certain there were no sensors on the doorframe and then slipped outside. The two marshals in the front were vigilant, but their eyes were turned away from the house. One quickly glanced toward the Dancer, nodded a greeting, then turned back to their reconnaissance. The light of dawn was in the sky, but it was still dim enough so that the man didn't recognize him. They both died almost silently.

As for the two in the back, at the guard station overlooking the lake, the Dancer came up behind them. He tickled the heart of one marshal with a stab in the back and then, *swish, swish,* sliced apart the throat of the second guard. Lying on the ground, the first marshal gave a plaintive scream as he died. But once again no one seemed to notice; the sound, the Dancer decided, was very much like the call of a loon, waking to the beautiful pink and gray dawn.

Rhyme and Sellitto were deep in bureaucratic debt by the time the fax of the DNA profile arrived. The test had been the fast version, the polymerase chain reaction test, but it was still virtually conclusive; the odds were about six thousand to one that the body in front of them was Stephen Kall.

"Somebody killed *him*?" Sellitto muttered. His shirt was so wrinkled it looked like a fiber sample under five hundred times magnification. "Why?"

But why was not a criminalist's question.

Evidence . . . Rhyme thought. Evidence was his only concern.

He glanced at the crime scene charts on his wall, scanning all the clues of the case. The fibers, the bullets, the broken glass . . .

Analyze! Think!

You know the procedure. You've done it a million times.

You identify the facts. You quantify and categorize them. You state your assumptions. And your draw your conclusions. Then you test—

Assumptions, Rhyme thought.

There was one glaring assumption that had been present in this case from the beginning. They'd based their entire investigation on the belief that Kall *was* the Coffin Dancer. But what if he weren't? What if *he* were the pawn and the Dancer'd been using him as a weapon?

Deception . . .

If so, there'd be some evidence that didn't fit. Something that pointed to the real Dancer.

He pored over the charts carefully.

But there was nothing unaccounted for except the green fiber. And that told him nothing.

"We don't have any of Kall's clothes, right?"

"No, he was buck naked when we found him," the tour doctor said.

"We have anything he came in contact with?"

Sellitto shrugged. "Well, Jodie."

Rhyme asked, "He changed clothes here, didn't he?"

"Right," Sellitto said.

"Bring 'em here. Jodie's clothes. I want to look at them."

"Uck," Dellray said. "They're excessively unpleasant."

Cooper found and produced them. He brushed them out over sheets of clean newsprint. He mounted samples of the trace on slides and set them in the compound scope.

"What do we have?" Rhyme asked, looking over the computer screen, a copycat image of what Cooper was seeing in his microscope.

"What's that white stuff?" Cooper asked. "Those grains. There's a lot of it. It was in the seams of his pants."

Rhyme felt his face flush. Some of it was his erratic blood pressure from exhaustion, some of it was the phantom pain that still plagued him every now and then. But mostly it was the heat of the chase.

"Oh, my God," he whispered.

"What, Lincoln?"

"It's oolite," he announced.

"The fuck's that?" Sellitto asked.

"Eggstone. It's a wind-borne sand. You find it in the Bahamas."

"Bahamas?" Cooper asked, frowning. "What else did we just hear about the Bahamas?" He looked around the lab. "I don't remember."

But Rhyme did. His eyes were fixed on the bulletin board, where was pinned the FBI analyst's report on the sand Amelia Sachs had found last week in Tony Panelli's car, the missing agent downtown.

He read:

"Substance submitted for analysis is not technically sand. It is coral rubble from reef formations and contains spicules, cross sections of marine worm tubes, gastropod shells and foraminifers. Most likely source is the northern Caribbean: Cuba, the Bahamas."

Dellray's agent, Rhyme reflected . . . A man who'd know

where the most secure federal safe house in Manhattan was. Who'd tell whoever was torturing him the address.

So that the Dancer could wait there, wait for Stephen Kall to show up, befriend him, and then arrange to get captured and get close to the victims.

"The drugs!" Rhyme cried.

"What?" Sellitto asked.

"What was I thinking of? Dealers don't cut prescription drugs! It's too much trouble. Only street drugs!"

Cooper nodded. "Jodie wasn't cutting them with the baby formula. He just dumped out the drugs. He was popping placebos, so we'd think he was a druggie."

"Jodie's the Dancer," Rhyme called. "Get on the phone! Call the safe house now!"

Sellitto picked up the phone and dialed.

Was it too late?

Oh, Amelia, what've I done? Have I killed you?

The sky was turning a metallic rosy color.

A siren sounded far away.

The peregrine falcon – the *tiercel*, he reminded – was awake and about to go hunting.

Lon Sellitto looked up desperately from the phone. "There's no answer," he said.

Hour 44 of 45

37

They'd talked for a while, the three of them, in Percey's room.

Talked about airplanes and cars and police work.

Then Bell went off to bed and Percey and Sachs had talked about men.

Finally Percey'd lain back on the bed, closed her eyes. Sachs lifted the bourbon glass from the sleeping woman's hand and shut out the lights. Decided to try to sleep herself.

She now paused in the corridor to look out at the dim dawn sky – pink and orange – when she realized that the phone in the compound's main hallway had been ringing for a long time.

Why wasn't anybody answering it?

She continued down the corridor.

She couldn't see the two guards nearby. The enclave seemed darker than before. Most of the lights had been shut off. A gloomy place, she thought. Spooky. Smelling of pine and mold. Something else? Another smell that was very familiar to her. What?

Something from crime scenes. In her exhaustion she couldn't place it.

The phone continued to chirp.

She passed Roland Bell's room. The door was partly open and she looked in. His back was to the door. He was sitting in an armchair that faced a curtained window, his head forward on his chest, arms crossed.

"Detective?" she asked.

He didn't answer.

Sound asleep. Just what *she* wanted to be. She closed his door softly and continued down the corridor, toward her room.

She thought about Rhyme. She hoped *he* was getting some sleep too. She'd seen one of his dysreflexia attacks. It had been terrifying and she didn't want him to go through another one.

The phone went quiet, cut off in the middle of a ring. She glanced toward where she'd heard it, wondering if it was for her. She couldn't hear whoever'd answered. She waited a moment, but no one summoned her.

Silence. Then a tap, a faint scrape. More silence.

She stepped into her room. It was dark. She turned to grope for the switch and found herself staring at two eyes that caught a sliver of reflected light from outside.

Right hand on the butt of her Glock, she swept her left up to the light switch. The eight-point buck stared at her with his shiny, false eyes.

"Dead animals," she muttered. "Great idea in a safe house . . ."

She pulled her blouse off and removed the bulky American Body Armor suit. Not as bulky as Jodie's of course. What a kick he was. The little . . . what was Dellray's street word? Skel. Short for skeleton. Scrawny little loser. What a mutt.

She reached under her mesh undershirt and scratched frantically. Her boobs, her back under the bra, her sides.

Ooooo, feels good.

Exhausted, sure, but could she sleep?

The bed looked pretty damn nice.

She pulled on her blouse again, buttoned it, and lay down on the comforter. Closed her eyes. Did she hear footsteps?

One of the guards making coffee, she supposed.

Sleep? Breathe deep . . .

No sleep.

Her eyes opened and she stared at the webby ceiling.

The Coffin Dancer, she mused. How would he come at them? What would his weapon be?

His deadliest weapon is deception . . .

Glancing out a crack in the curtain, she saw the beautiful

fish-gray dawn. A haze of mist bleached the color from the distant trees.

Somewhere inside the compound she heard a thud. A footstep.

Sachs swung her feet around to the floor and sat up. May as well just give up and get some coffee. I'll sleep tonight.

She had a sudden urge to talk to Rhyme, to see if he'd found anything. She could hear him saying, *"If I'd found something I would've called you, wouldn't I? I* said *I'd check in"*

No, she didn't want to wake him, but she doubted he was asleep. She pulled her cell phone out of her pocket and clicked it on before she remembered Marshal Franks's warning to use only the secure line in the living room.

As she was about to shut the phone off, it chirped loudly.

She shivered – not at the jarring sound, but at the thought that the Dancer had somehow found her number and wanted to confirm she was in the compound. For an instant she wondered if somehow he'd slipped explosives into her phone too.

Damnit, Rhyme, look how spooked I am!

Don't answer it, she told herself.

But instinct told her to, and while criminalists may shun instinct, Patrol cops, *street* cops, always listen to those inner voices. She pulled the antenna out of the phone.

"'Lo?"

"Thank God . . ." The panicked tone of Lincoln Rhyme chilled her.

"Hey, Rhyme. What's—"

"Listen very carefully. Are you alone?"

"Yeah. What's going on?"

"Jodie's the Dancer."

"What?"

"Stephen Kall was the diversion. Jodie killed him. It was his body in the park we found. Where's Percey?"

"In her room. Up the hall. But how—"

"No time. He's going for the kill right now. If the marshals're still alive, tell them to get into a defensive position in one of the rooms. If they're dead find Percey and Bell and get out. Dellray's scrambled SWAT but it'll be twenty or thirty minutes before they're there."

"But there're eight guards. He can't've taken them all out . . ."

"Sachs," he said sternly, "remember who he is. Move! Call me when you're safe."

Bell! she thought suddenly, recalling the detective's still posture, his head slumped forward.

She raced to her door, threw it open, drew her gun. The black living room and corridor gaped. Dark. Only faint dawn light filtering into the rooms. She listened. A shuffle. A clink of metal. But where were the sounds coming from?

Sachs turned toward Bell's room and trotted as quietly as she could.

He got her just before she got to his room.

As the figure stepped from the doorway she dropped into a crouch and swung the Glock toward him. He grunted and slapped the pistol from her hand. Without thinking, she shoved him forward, slamming his back into the wall.

Groping for her switchblade.

Roland Bell gasped, "Hold up there. Hey, now . . ."

Sachs let go of his shirt.

"It's you!"

"You scared the everlivin' you-know-what outa me. What's—?

"You're all right!" she said.

"Just dozed off for a minute. What's going on?"

"Jodie's the Dancer. Rhyme just called."

"What? How?"

"I don't know." She looked around, shivering in panic. "Where're the guards?"

The hall was empty.

Then she recognized the smell she'd wondered about. It was blood! Like hot copper. And she knew then that all the guards were dead. Sachs went to retrieve her weapon, which was lying on the floor. She frowned, looking at the end of the grip. Where the clip should have been was an empty hole. She picked up the gun.

"No!"

"What?" Bell asked.

"My clip. It's gone." She slapped her utility belt. The two clips in the keepers were gone too.

Bell drew his weapons – the Glock and the Browning. They too were clipless. The chambers of the guns were empty too.

"In the car!" she stammered. "I'll bet he did it in the car. He was sitting between us. Fidgeting all the time. Bumping into us."

Bell said, "I saw a gun case in the living room. A couple of hunting rifles."

Sachs remembered it. She pointed. "There." They could just make it out in the dim light of dawn. Bell looked around him and hurried to it, crouching, while Sachs ran to Percey's room and looked in. The woman was asleep on the bed.

Sachs stepped back to the corridor, flicked her knife open, and crouched, squinting. Bell returned a moment later. "It's been broken into. All the rifles're gone. And no ammo for the sidearms."

"Let's get Percey and get out of here."

A footstep not far away. A click of a bolt-action rifle's safety going off.

She grabbed Bell's collar and pulled him to the floor.

The gunshot was deafening and the bullet broke the sound barrier directly over them. She smelled her own burning hair. Jodie must have had a sizable arsenal by now – all the sidearms of the marshals – but he was using the hunting rifle.

They sprinted for Percey's door. It opened just as they got there and she stepped out, saying, "My God, what's—"

The full body tackle from Roland Bell shoved Percey back into her room. Sachs tumbled in on top of them. She slammed the door shut, locked it, and ran to the window, flung it open. "Go, go, go, go . . ."

Bell lifted a stunned Percey Clay off the ground and dragged her toward the window as several high-powered deer slugs tore through the door around the lock.

None of them looked to see how successful the Coffin Dancer'd been. They rolled through the window into the dawn and ran and ran and ran through the dewy grass.

38

Sachs stopped beside the lake. Mist, tinted red and pink, wafted in ghostly tatters over the still, gray water.

"Go on," she shouted to Bell and Percey. "Those trees."

She was pointing to the nearest cover – a wide band of trees at the end of a field on the other side of the lake. It was more than a hundred yards away but was the closest cover.

Sachs glanced back at the cabin. There was no sign of Jodie. She dropped into a crouch over the body of one of the marshals. His holster was empty of course, his clip cases too. She'd known Jodie had taken those weapons, but she hoped there was one thing he hadn't thought of.

He *is* human, Rhyme . . .

And frisking the cool body she found what she was looking for. Tugging up the marshal's pants cuff she pulled his backup weapon out of his ankle holster. A silly gun. A tiny five-shot Colt revolver with a two-inch barrel.

She glanced at the cabin just as Jodie's face appeared in the window. He lifted the hunting rifle. Sachs spun and squeezed off a round. Glass broke inches from his face and he stumbled backward into the room.

Sachs sprinted around the lake after Bell and Percey. They ran fast, weaving sideways, through the dewy grass.

They got nearly a hundred yards from the house before they heard the first shot. It was a rolling sound, echoing off the trees. It kicked up dirt near Percey's leg.

"Down," Sachs cried. "There." Pointing to a dip in the earth.

They rolled to the ground just as he fired again. If Bell had been upright the shot would have hit him directly between the shoulder blades.

They were still fifty feet from the nearest clump of trees that would give them protection. But to try for it now would be suicide. Jodie was apparently every bit the marksman that Stephen Kall had been.

Sachs lifted her head briefly.

She saw nothing but heard an explosion. An instant later the slug snapped through the air beside her. She felt the same draining terror as at the airport. She pressed her face into the cool spring grass, slick with dew and her sweat. Her hands shook.

Bell looked up fast and then down again.

Another shot. Dirt kicked up inches from his face.

"I think I saw him," the detective drawled. "There're some bushes to the right of the house. On that hill."

Sachs breathed a trio of fast breaths. Then she rolled five feet to the right, poked her head up fast, ducked again.

Jodie chose not to shoot this time and she'd gotten a good look. Bell was right: The killer was on the side of a hill, targeting them with the telescopic deer rifle; she'd seen the faint glint from the scope. He couldn't quite hit them where they were if they stayed prone. But all he had to do was move up the hill. From its crest he could shoot down into the pit they were hiding in now – a perfect kill zone.

Five minutes passed without a shot. He'd be working his way up the hill, though cautiously – he knew Sachs was armed and he'd seen she was a good shot. Could they wait him out? When would the SWAT chopper get here?

Sachs squeezed her eyes closed, smelled the dirt, the grass.

She thought of Lincoln Rhyme.

You know him better than anybody, Sachs . . . .

You never really know a perp until you've walked where he's walked, until you've cleaned up after his evil . . .

But, Rhyme, she thought, this isn't Stephen Kall. Jodie *isn't* the killer I know. It wasn't *his* crime scenes I walked through. It wasn't *his* mind I peered into . . .

She looked for a low spot in the ground that might lead

them safely to the trees but there was nothing. If they moved five feet in either direction he'd have a clean shot.

Well, he'd have a clean shot at them any minute now, when he got to the crest of the hill.

Then something occurred to her. That the crime scenes she'd worked really *were* the Dancer's scenes. He may not have been the one who fired the bullet that killed Brit Hale or planted the bomb that blew up Ed Carney's plane or swung the knife that killed John Innelman in the basement of the office building.

But Jodie *was* a perpetrator.

Get into his mind, Sachs, she heard Lincoln Rhyme say.

His deadliest – *my* deadliest weapon is deception.

"Both of you," Sachs called, looking around. "There." She pointed toward a slight ravine.

Bell glanced at her. She saw how badly he wanted the Dancer too. But the look in her eyes told him that the killer was her prey and hers alone. No debate and no argument. Rhyme had given this chance to her and nothing in the world could stop her from doing what she was about to.

The detective nodded solemnly and he pulled Percey after him into the shallow notch in the earth.

Sachs checked the pistol. Four rounds left.

Plenty.

More than enough . . .

If I'm right.

Am I? she wondered, face against the wet, fragrant earth. And she decided that, yes, she was right . . . A frontal assault wasn't the Dancer's way. *Deception.*

And that's just what I'm going to give him.

"Stay down. Whatever happens, stay down." She rose to her hands and knees, looking over the ridge. Getting ready, preparing herself. Breathing slowly.

"That's a hundred-yard shot, Amelia," Bell whispered. "With a snub-nose?"

She ignored him.

"Amelia," Percey said. The flier held her eyes for a moment and the women shared a smile. "Head down," Sachs ordered and Percey complied, nestling into the grass.

Amelia Sachs stood up.

She didn't crouch, didn't turn sideways to present a more narrow target. She just slipped into the familiar two-hand target pistol stance. Facing the house, the lake, facing the prone figure halfway up the hill, who pointed the telescopic sight directly at her. The stubby pistol felt as light as a scotch glass in her hand.

She aimed at the glare of the telescopic sight, a football field away.

Sweat and mist forming on her face.

Breathe, breathe.

Take your time.

Wait . . .

A ripple passed through her back and arms and hands. She forced the panic away.

Breathe . . .

Listen, listen.

Breathe . . .

Now!

She spun around and dropped to her knees as the rifle jutting from the grove of trees behind her, fifty feet away, fired. The bullet split the air just over her head.

Sachs found herself staring at Jodie's astonished face, the hunting rifle still at his cheek. He realized that he hadn't fooled her after all. That she'd figured out his tactic. How he'd fired a few shots from the lake, then dragged one of the guards up the hill and propped him there with one of the hunting rifles to keep them pinned down while he jogged up the road and circled behind.

Deception . . .

For a moment neither of them moved.

The air was completely still. No tatters of mist floating past, no trees or grass bending in the wind.

A faint smile crossed Sachs's face as she lifted the pistol in both hands.

Frantic, he ejected the shell from the deer rifle and chambered another round. As he lifted the gun to his cheek again Sachs fired. Two shots.

Both clean hits. Saw him fly backward, the rifle sailing through the air like a majorette's baton.

"Stay with her, Detective!" Sachs called to Bell and sprinted toward Jodie.

She found him in the grass, lying on his back.

One of her bullets had shattered his left shoulder. The other had hit the telescopic sight straight on and blown metal and glass into the man's right eye. His face was a bloody mess.

She cocked her tiny gun, put a good ration of pressure on the trigger and pressed the muzzle against his temple. She frisked him. Lifted a single Glock and a long carbide knife out of his pocket. She found no other weapons.

"Clear," she called.

As she stood, pulling her cuffs out of the case, the Dancer coughed and spit, wiped blood out of his good eye. Then he lifted his head and looked out over the field. He spotted Percey Clay as she slowly rose from the grass, staring at her attacker.

Jodie seemed to shiver as he gazed at her. Another cough then a deep moan. He startled Sachs by pushing against her leg with his uninjured arm. He was badly hurt— maybe mortally – and had little strength. It was a curious gesture, the way you'd push an irritating Pekinese out of your way.

She stepped back, keeping the gun trained squarely on his chest.

Amelia Sachs was no longer of any interest to the Coffin Dancer. Neither were his wounds or the terrible pain they must be radiating. There was only one thing on his mind. With superhuman effort he rolled onto his belly and, moaning and clawing dirt, he began muscling his way toward Percey Clay, toward the woman he'd been hired to kill.

Bell joined Sachs. She handed him the Glock and together they kept their weapons on the Dancer. They could easily have stopped him – or killed him. But they remained transfixed, watching this pitiable man so desperately absorbed in his task that he didn't even seem to know his face and shoulder had been destroyed.

He moved another few feet, pausing only to grab a sharp rock about the size of a grapefruit. And he continued on toward his prey. Never saying a word, drenched in blood and sweat, his face a knot of agony. Even Percey, who had every reason to hate this man, to sweep Sachs's pistol from her hand and end the killer's life right here, even she was mesmerized, watching this hopeless effort to finish what he'd started.

"That's enough," Sachs said finally. She bent down and lifted the rock away.

"No," he gasped. "No . . ."

She cuffed him.

The Coffin Dancer gave a horrifying moan – which might have been from his pain but seemed to arise more out of unbearable loss and failure – and dropped his head to the ground.

He lay still. The trio stood around him, watching his blood soak the grass and innocent crocuses. Soon the heartrending call of the loons was lost in the *whup whup whup* of a helicopter skimming over the trees. Sachs noticed that Percey Clay's attention slipped immediately away from the man who'd caused her so much sorrow, and the flier watched in rapt attention as the cumbersome aircraft eased through the misty air and touched down lithely on the grass.

39

"Ain't kosher, Lincoln. Can't do it."

Lon Sellitto was insistent.

But so was Lincoln Rhyme. "Give me a half hour with him."

"They're not comfy with it." Which really meant what the detective added: "They shit when I suggested it. You're civilian."

It was nearly ten on Monday morning. Percey's appearance before the grand jury had been postponed until tomorrow. The navy divers had found the duffle bags that Phillip Hansen had sunk deep in Long Island sound. They were being raced to an FBI PERT team in the Federal Building downtown for analysis. Eliopolos had delayed the grand jury to be able to present as much damning evidence against Hansen as possible.

"What're they worried about?" Rhyme asked petulantly. "It's not as if I can beat him up."

He thought about lowering his offer to twenty minutes. But that was a sign of weakness. And Lincoln Rhyme did not believe in showing weakness. So he said, "*I* caught him. I deserve a chance to talk to him."

And fell silent.

Blaine, his ex-wife, had told him in a moment of very uncharacteristic perception that Rhyme's eyes, dark as night, argued better than his words did. And so he stared at Sellitto until the detective sighed, then glanced at Dellray.

"Aw, give him a little time," the agent said. "What's it gonna hurt? Bring the billy-boy up here. And if he tries to run, hell, gimme a golden excuse for some target practice."

Sellitto said, "Oh, all right. I'll make the call. Only, don't fuck up this case."

The criminalist barely heard the words. His eyes turned toward the doorway, as if the Coffin Dancer were about to materialize magically.

He wouldn't have been surprised if that had happened.

"What's your real name? Is it really Joe or Jodie?"

"Ah, what's it matter? You caught me. You can call me what you want."

"How 'bout a first name?" Rhyme asked.

"How 'bout what *you* call me? The Dancer. I like that."

The small man examined Rhyme carefully with his good eye. If he was in pain from the wounds, or groggy from medication, he didn't show it. His left arm was in a shoulder cast but he still wore thick cuffs attached to a waist shackle. His feet were chained too.

"Whatever you like," Rhyme said pleasantly. And continued to study the man as if he were an unusual pollen spore picked up at a crime scene.

The Dancer smiled. Because of the damaged facial nerves and the bandages, his expression was grotesque. Tremors occasionally shook his body and his fingers twitched, his broken shoulder rose and fell involuntarily. Rhyme had a curious feeling – that he himself was healthy and it was the prisoner who was the cripple.

In the valley of the blind, the one-eyed man is king.

The Dancer smiled at him. "You're just dying to know, aren't you?" he asked Rhyme.

"Know what?"

"To know all . . . That's why you brought me here. You were lucky – catching me, I mean – but you don't really have a clue as to how I did it."

Rhyme clucked his tongue. "Oh, but I know exactly how you did it."

"Do you now?"

"I just asked you here to talk to you," Rhyme replied. "That's all. To talk to the man who almost outthought me."

"'Almost.'" The Dancer laughed. Another twisted smile. It was really quite eerie. "Okay, then tell me."

Rhyme sipped from his straw. It was fruit juice. He'd astonished Thom by asking him to dump out the scotch and replace it with Hawaiian Punch. Rhyme now said agreeably, "All right. You were hired to kill Ed Carney, Brit Hale, and Percey Clay. You were paid a lot, I'd guess. Six figures."

"Seven," the Dancer said proudly.

Rhyme lifted an eyebrow. "Lucrative line of work."

"If you're good."

"You deposited the money in the Bahamas. You'd gotten Stephen Kall's name from somewhere – I don't know where exactly. Probably a mercenary network—" the Dancer nodded "—and you hired him as a subcontractor. Anonymously, maybe by E-mail, maybe fax, using references he'd trust. You'd never meet him face-to-face of course. And I assume you tried him out?"

"Of course. A hit outside of Washington, D.C. I was hired to kill a congressional aide sneaking secrets out of Armed Services Committee files. It was an easy job, so I subcontracted it to Stephen. Gave me a good chance to check him out. I watched him every step of the way. I checked the entrance wound on the body myself. Very professional. I think he saw me watching him and he came after me to take care of witnesses. That was good too."

Rhyme continued. "You left him his cash and the key to Phillip Hansen's hangar – where he waited to plant the bomb on Carney's plane. You knew he was good but you weren't sure he was good enough to kill all three of them. You probably thought he could get one at the most but would provide enough diversion for you to get close to the other two."

The Dancer nodded, reluctantly impressed. "Him killing Brit Hale surprised me. Oh, yes. And it surprised me even more that he got away afterward and got the second bomb onto Percey Clay's plane."

"You guessed that you'd have to kill at least one of the victims yourself so last week you became Jodie, started hawking your drugs everywhere so that people on the street'd know about you. You kidnaped the agent in front of the federal building, found out which safe house they'd be in. You waited in the most logical place for Stephen to make his attack and let him kidnap you. You left plenty of clues to your subway hideout so we'd be sure to find you . . . and use you to get to Kall. We all trusted you. Sure, we did – Stephen didn't have a clue *you'd* hired him. All he knew was that you betrayed him and he wanted to kill you. Perfect cover for you. But risky."

"But what's life without risk?" the Dancer asked playfully. "Makes it all worthwhile, don't you think? Besides, when we were together I built in a few . . . let's call them countermeasures, so that he'd hesitate to shoot me. Latent homosexuality is *always* helpful."

"But," Rhyme added, piqued that his narrative had been interrupted, "when Kall was in the park, you slipped out of the alley where you were hiding, found him, and killed him . . . You disposed of the hands, teeth, and clothes – and his guns – in the sewer interceptor pipes. And then we invited you out to Long Island . . . Fox in the henhouse." Rhyme added flippantly, "That's the schematic . . . That's the bare bones. But I think it tells the story."

The man's good eye closed momentarily, then opened again. Red and wet, it stared at Rhyme. He gave a faint nod of concession, or perhaps admiration. "What was it?" the Dancer finally asked. "What tipped you?"

"Sand," Rhyme answered. "From the Bahamas."

He nodded, winced at the pain. "I turned my pockets out. I vacuumed."

"In the folds of the seams. The drugs too. Residue and the baby formula."

"Yes. Sure." After a moment the Dancer added, "He was right to be scared of you. Stephen, I mean." The eye was still scanning Rhyme. Like a doctor looking for a tumor. He added, "Poor man. What a sad creature. Who buggered him, d'you think? Stepdad or the boys in reform? Or all of the above?"

"I wouldn't know," Rhyme said. On the windowsill the male falcon landed and folded his wings.

"Stephen got scared," the Dancer mused. "And when you get scared it's all over. He thought the worm was looking for him. Lincoln the Worm. I heard him whisper that a few times. He was scared of you."

"But you weren't scared."

"No," the Dancer said. "I don't get scared." Suddenly he nodded, as if he'd finally noticed something that had been nagging him. "Ah, listening carefully, are you? Trying to peg the accent?"

Rhyme had been.

"But, see, it changes. Mountain . . . Connecticut . . . Plains Southern and swamp Southern . . . Mizzura. Kayntuckeh. Why're you interrogating me? You're Crime Scene. I'm caught. Time for beddy-bye. End of story. Say, I like chess. I *love* chess. You ever play, Lincoln?"

He'd used to like it. He and Claire Trilling had played quite a bit. Thom had been after him to play on the computer and had bought him a good chess program, installed it. Rhyme had never loaded it. "I haven't played for a long time."

"You and I'll have to play a game of chess sometime. You'd be a good man to play against . . . You want to know a mistake some players make?"

"What's that?" Rhyme felt the man's hot gaze. He was suddenly uneasy.

"They get curious about their opponents. They try to learn things about their personal life. Things that aren't *useful.* Where they're from, where they were born, who their siblings are."

"Is that right?"

"That may satisfy an itch. But it confuses them. It can be dangerous. See, the game is all on the board, Lincoln. It's all on the board." A lopsided smile. "You can't accept not knowing anything about me, can you?"

No, Rhyme thought, I can't.

The Dancer continued, "Well, what exactly do you want? An address? A high school yearbook? How about a clue? 'Rosebud.' How's that? I'm surprised at you, Lincoln. You're a criminalist – the best I've ever seen. And here you are right now on some kind of pathetic sentimental journey. Well, who am I? The headless horseman. Beelzebub. I'm Queen Mab. I'm 'them' as in 'Look out for them; they're after you.' I'm not your proverbial worst nightmare because nightmares aren't real and I am more real than anybody wants to admit. I'm a craftsman. I'm a businessman. You won't get my name, rank or serial number. I don't play according to the Geneva convention."

Rhyme could say nothing.

There was a knock on the door.

The transport had arrived.

"Can you take the shackles off my feet?" the Dancer asked the two officers in a pathetic voice, his good eye blinking and tearful. "Oh, please. I hurt so much. And it's *so* hard to walk."

One of the guards looked at him sympathetically then at Rhyme, who said matter-of-factly, "You loosen so much as one restraint and you'll lose your job and never work in this city again."

The trooper stared at Rhyme for a moment, then nodded at his partner. The Dancer laughed. "Not a problem," he said, eyes on Rhyme. "Just a factor."

The guards gripped him by his good arm and lifted him to his feet. He was dwarfed by the two tall men as they led him to the door. He looked back.

"Lincoln?"

"Yes?"

"You're going to miss me. Without me, you'll be bored." His single eye burned into Rhyme's. "Without me, you're going to die."

An hour later the heavy footsteps announced the arrival of Lon Sellitto. He was accompanied by Sachs and Dellray.

Rhyme knew immediately there was trouble. For a moment he wondered if the Dancer had escaped.

But that wasn't the problem.

Sachs sighed.

Sellitto gave Dellray a look. The agent's lean face grimaced.

"Okay, tell me," Rhyme snapped.

Sachs delivered the news. "The duffle bags. PERT's been through 'em."

"Guess what was inside," Sellitto said.

Rhyme sighed, exhausted, and not in the mood for games. "Detonators, plutonium, and Jimmy Hoffa's body."

Sachs said, "A bunch of Westchester County Yellow Pages and five pounds of rocks."

"What?"

"There's nothing, Lincoln. Zip."

"You're sure they were phone books, not encrypted business records?"

"Bureau cryptology looked 'em over good," Dellray said. "Fuckin' off-the-shelf Yellow Pages. And the rocks're nothin'. Just added 'em to make it sink."

"They're gonna release Hansen's fat ass," Sellitto muttered darkly. "They're doin' the paperwork right now. They're not even presenting it to the grand jury. All those people died for nothing."

"Tell him the rest," Sachs added.

"Eliopolos is on his way here now," Sellitto said. "He's got paper."

"A warrant?" Rhyme asked shortly. "For what?"

"Oh. Like he said. To arrest you."

40

Reginald Eliopolos appeared at the doorway, backed up by two large agents.

Rhyme had thought of the attorney as middle aged. But in the daylight he seemed to be in his early thirties. The agents were young too and dressed as well as he was, but they reminded Rhyme of pissed-off longshoremen.

What exactly did he need them for? Against a man flat on his back?

"Well, Lincoln, I guess you didn't believe me when I said there'd be repercussions. Uh-huh. You didn't believe me."

"What the fuck're you bitchin' about, Reggie?" Sellitto asked. "We caught him."

"Uh-huh . . . uh-huh. I'll tell you what I'm—" he lifted his hands and made imaginary quotation marks in the air "—bitchin' for. The case against Hansen is kaput. No evidence in the duffle bags."

"That's not our fault," Sachs said. "We kept your witness alive. And caught Hansen's hired killer."

"Ah," Rhyme said, "but there's more to it than that, right, Reggie?"

The assistant U.S. attorney gazed at him coldly.

Rhyme continued, "See, Jodie – I mean, the Dancer – is the only chance they have to make a case against Hansen now. Or that's what he thinks. But Dancer'll never dime a client."

"Oh, that a fact? Well, you don't know him as well as you think you do. I just had a long talk with him. He was more than willing to implicate Hansen. Except now he's stonewalling. Thanks to you."

"Me?" Rhyme asked.

"He said you threatened him. During that little unauthorized meeting you had a few hours ago. Uh-huh. Heads are going to roll because of *that.* Rest assured."

"Oh, for God's sake," Rhyme spat out, laughing bitterly. "Don't you see what he's doing? Let me guess . . . you told him that you'd arrest me, right? And he'd agree to testify if you did."

The pendulum swing of Eliopolos's eyes told Rhyme that this was exactly what happened.

"Don't you get it?"

But Eliopolos didn't get a thing.

Rhyme said, "Don't you think he'd like to get me in detention, maybe fifty, sixty feet from where he is?"

"Rhyme," Sachs said, frowning with concern.

"What're you talking about?" the attorney said.

"He wants to *kill* me, Reggie. That's his point. I'm the only man who's ever stopped him. He can't very well go back to work knowing I'm out there."

"But he's not going anywhere. Ever."

Uh-huh.

Rhyme said, "After I'm dead he'll recant. He'll never testify against Hansen. And what're you going to pressure him with? Threaten him with the needle? He won't care. He's not afraid of anything. Not a single thing."

What was nagging? Rhyme wondered. Something seemed wrong here. Very wrong.

He decided it was the phone books . . .

Phone books and rocks.

Rhyme was lost in thought, staring at the evidence chart on the wall. He heard a jingle, glanced up. One of the agents with Eliopolos actually pulled out his handcuffs and was proceeding toward the Clinitron. Rhyme laughed to himself. Better shackle the old feet. Might run away.

"Come on, Reggie," Sellitto said.

The green fiber, phone books, and rocks.

He remembered something the Dancer had told him. Sitting in the very chair Eliopolos stood beside now.

A million dollars . . .

Rhyme was vaguely aware of the agent trying to figure

out how to best subdue a crip. And he was vaguely aware of Sachs stepping forward trying to figure out how to subdue the *agent.* Suddenly he barked, "Wait," in a voice commanding enough to freeze everyone in the room.

The green fiber . . .

He stared at it on the chart.

People were talking to him. The agent was still eyeing Rhyme's hands, brandishing the tinkling cuffs. But Rhyme ignored them all. He said to Eliopolos, "Give me a half hour."

"Why should I?"

"Come on, what's it going to hurt? It's not like I'm going anywhere?" And before the attorney could agree, or disagree, Rhyme was shouting, "Thom! *Thom,* I need to make a phone call. Are you going to help me, or not? I don't know where he gets to sometimes. Lon, will you call for me?"

Percey Clay had just returned from burying her husband when Lon Sellitto tracked her down. Wearing black she sat in the crinkly wicker chair beside Lincoln Rhyme's bed. Standing nearby was Roland Bell, in a tan suit, badly cut – thanks to the size of the two guns he wore. He pushed his thinning brown hair straight back over the crown of his head.

Eliopolos was gone, though his two goons were outside, guarding the hallway. Apparently they actually *did* believe that, given a chance, Thom try would to wheel Rhyme out the door and he'd make a getaway in the Storm Arrow, top speed 7.5 mph.

Percey's outfit chafed at collar and waist, and Rhyme bet that it was the only dress she owned. She began to lift ankle to knee as she sat back, realized a skirt was wrong for this pose and sat up formally, knees together.

She eyed him with impatient curiosity and Rhyme realized that no one else – Sellitto and Sachs had fetched her – had delivered the news.

Cowards, he thought grumpily.

"Percey . . . They won't be presenting the case against Hansen to the grand jury."

For an instant there was a flash of relief. Then she understood the implication. "No!" she gasped.

"That flight Hansen made? To dump those duffle bags? The bags were fake. There was nothing in them."

Her face grew pallid. "They're letting him go?"

"They can't find any connection between the Dancer and Hansen. Until we do, he's free."

Her hands rose to her face. "It was all a waste then? Ed . . . And Brit? They died for nothing."

He asked her, "What's happening to your company now?"

Percey wasn't expecting the question. She wasn't sure she heard him. "I'm sorry?"

"Your company? What's going to happen to Hudson Air now?"

"We'll sell it probably. We've had an offer from another company. They can carry the debt. We can't. Or maybe we'll just liquidate." It was the first time he'd heard resignation in her voice. A Gypsy in defeat.

"What other company?"

"I frankly don't remember. Ron's been talking to them."

"That's Ron Talbot, right?"

"Yes."

"Would he know about the financial condition of the company?"

"Sure. As much as the lawyers and accountants. More than me."

"Could you call him, ask him to come down here as soon as possible?"

"I suppose I could. He was at the cemetery. He's probably home by now. I'll call him."

"And, Sachs?" he said, turning to her, "we've got another crime scene. I need you to search it. As fast as possible."

Rhyme looked over the big man coming through the doorway, wearing a dark blue suit. It was shiny and had the color and cut of a uniform about it. Rhyme supposed it was what he'd worn when he flew.

Percey introduced them.

"So you got that son of a bitch," Talbot grumbled. "Think he'll get the chair?"

"I collect the trash," Rhyme said, pleased as always when he could think up a melodramatic line. "What the DA does with it is up to him. Did Percey tell you we've had trouble with the evidence implicating Hansen?"

"Yeah, she said something about that. The evidence he dumped was fake? Why'd he do that?"

"I think I can answer that, but I need some more information. Percey tells me you know the Company pretty well. You're a partner, right?"

Talbot nodded, took out a pack of cigarettes, saw no one else was smoking, replaced them in his pocket. He was even more rumpled than Sellitto and it looked as if it had been a long time since he'd been able to button his jacket around his ample belly.

"Let me try this out on you," Rhyme said. "What if Hansen didn't want to kill Ed and Percey because they were witnesses?"

"But then why?" Percey blurted.

Talbot asked, "You mean, he had another motive? Like what?"

Rhyme didn't respond directly. "Percey tells me the Company hasn't been doing well for a while."

Talbot shrugged. "Been a tough couple years. Deregulation, lots of small carriers. Fighting UPS and FedEx. Postal Service too. Margins've shrunk."

"But you still have good – What is that, Fred. You did some white-collar crime work, right? Money that comes in. What's the word for it?"

Dellray snorted a laugh. "Revy-nue, Lincoln."

"You had good revenue."

Talbot nodded. "Oh, cash flow's never been a problem. It's just that more goes out than comes in."

"What do you think about the theory that the Dancer was hired to murder Percey and Ed so that the killer could buy the Company at a discount?"

"What company? Ours?" Percey asked, frowning.

"Why would Hansen do that?" Talbot said, wheezing again.

Percey added, "And why not just come to us with a big check? He never even approached us."

"I didn't actually say Hansen," Rhyme pointed out. "The question I asked before was what if *Hansen* didn't want to kill Ed and Percey? What if it was somebody else?"

"Who?" Percey asked.

"I'm not sure. It's just . . . well, that green fiber."

"Green fiber?" Talbot followed Rhyme's eyes to the evidence chart.

"Everyone seems to've forgotten about it. Except me."

"Man never forgets a single thing. Do you, Lincoln?"

"Not too often, Fred. Not too often. That fiber. Sachs – my partner—"

"I remember you," Talbot said, nodding toward her.

"She found it in the hangar that Hansen leased. It was in some trace materials near the window where Stephen Kall waited before he planted the bomb on Ed Carney's plane. She also found bits of brass and some white fibers and envelope glue. Which tells us that somebody left a key to the hangar in an envelope somewhere for Kall. But then I got to thinking – why did Kall need a key to break into an empty hangar? He was a pro. He could've broken into the place in his sleep. The only reason for the key was to make it look like Hansen had left it. To implicate him."

"But the hijacking," Talbot said, "when he killed those soldiers and stole the guns. Everybody knows he's a murderer."

"Oh, he probably is," Rhyme agreed. "But he didn't fly his airplane over Long Island sound and play bombardier with those phone books. Somebody else did."

Percey stirred uneasily.

Rhyme continued, "Somebody who never thought we'd find the duffle bags."

"Who?" Talbot demanded.

"Sachs?"

She pulled three large evidence envelopes out of a canvas bag and rested them on the table.

Inside two of them were accounting books. The third contained a stack of white envelopes.

"Those came from your office, Talbot."

He gave a weak laugh. "I don't think you can just take those without a warrant."

Percey Clay frowned. "I gave them permission. I'm still head of the Company, Ron. But what're you saying, Lincoln?"

Rhyme regretted not sharing his suspicions with Percey before this; it was coming as a terrible shock. But he couldn't risk that she might tip their hand to Talbot. He'd covered his tracks so well until now.

Rhyme glanced at Mel Cooper, who said, "The green fiber that we found with the particles of key came from a ledger sheet. The white ones from an envelope. There's no doubt they match."

Rhyme continued, "And all from your office, Talbot."

"What do you mean, Lincoln?" Percey gasped.

Rhyme said to Talbot, "Everybody at the airport knew Hansen was under investigation. You thought you'd use that fact. So you waited until one night when Percey and Ed and Brit Hale were working late. You stole Hansen's plane for the flight, you dumped the fake duffle bags. You hired the Dancer. I assume you'd heard about him on your jobs in Africa or the Far East. I made a few calls. You worked for the Botswana air force and the Burmese government advising them in buying used military airplanes. The Dancer told me he was paid a million for the hit." Rhyme shook his head. "That should have tipped me right there. Hansen could have had all three witnesses killed for a couple hundred thousand. Professional killing's definitely a buyer's market nowadays. A million told me that the man ordering the hit was an amateur. And that he had a lot of money at his disposal."

The scream rose from Percey Clay's mouth and she leapt for him. Talbot stood, backed up. "How could you?" she screamed. "Why?"

Dellray said, "My boys from financial crimes're looking over your books now. What we think we're gonna be finding is lots and lots of money that ain't where it oughta be."

Rhyme continued, "Hudson Air's a lot more successful than you were thinking, Percey. Only most of it was going into Talbot's pocket. He knew he was going to get caught some day and he needed to get you and Ed out of the way and buy the company himself."

"The stock purchase option," she said. "As a partner he had a right to buy our interest from our estates at a discount if we die."

"This's bullshit. That guy was shooting at me too, remember."

"But you didn't hire Kall," Rhyme reminded. "You hired Jodie – the Coffin Dancer – and he subcontracted the work with Kall. Who didn't know you from beans."

"How could you?" Percey repeated in a hollow voice. "Why? *Why*?"

Talbot raged, "Because I loved you!"

"What?" Percey gasped.

Talbot continued. "You laughed when I said I wanted to marry you."

"Ron, no. I—"

"And you went back to him." He sneered. "Ed Carney, the handsome fighter pilot. Top gun . . . He treated you like shit and you still wanted him. Then . . ." His face was purple with fury. "Then . . . then I lost the last thing I had – I was grounded. I couldn't fly anymore. I watched the two of you logging hundreds of hours a month while all I could do was sit at a desk and push papers. You had each other, you had flying . . . You don't have a clue what it's like to lose everything you love. You just don't have a clue!"

Sachs and Sellitto saw him tense. They anticipated his trying something but they hadn't guessed Talbot's strength. As Sachs stepped forward, unholstering her weapon, Talbot scooped the tall woman completely off her feet and flung her into the evidence table, scattering microscopes and equipment, knocking Mel Cooper back into the wall. Talbot pulled the Glock from her hand.

He swung it toward Bell, Sellitto and Dellray. "All right, throw your guns on the floor. Do it now. Now!"

"Come on, man," Dellray said, rolling his eyes. "What're you gonna do? Climb out the window? You ain't going nowhere."

He shoved the gun toward Dellray's face. "I'm not going to say it again."

His eyes were desperate. He reminded Rhyme of a cornered bear. The agent and the cops tossed their guns onto the ground. Bell dropped both of his.

"Where does that door lead?" He nodded to the wall. He'd have seen Eliopolos's guards outside and knew there was no escape that way.

"That's a closet," Rhyme said quickly.

He opened it, eyed the tiny elevator.

"Fuck you," Talbot whispered, pointing the gun at Rhyme.

"No," Sachs shouted.

Talbot swung the weapon her way.

"Ron," Percey cried, "think about it. Please . . ."

Sachs, embarrassed but unhurt, was on her feet, looking at the pistols that lay on the floor ten feet away.

No, Sachs, Rhyme thought. Don't!

She'd survived the coolest professional killer in the country and now was about to get shot by a panicked amateur.

Talbot's eyes were flicking back and forth from Dellray and Sellitto to the elevator, trying to figure out the switchpad.

No, Sachs, don't do it.

Rhyme was trying to catch her attention but her eyes were judging distances and angles. She'd never make it in time.

Sellitto said, "Let's just talk, Talbot. Come on, put the gun down."

Please, Sachs, don't do it . . . He'll see you. He'll go for a head shot – amateurs always do – and you'll die.

She tensed, eyes on Dellray's Sig-Sauer.

No . . .

The instant Talbot looked back at the elevator Sachs leapt for the floor and snagged Dellray's weapon as she rolled. But Talbot saw her. Before she could lift the large automatic he shoved the Glock at her face, squinting as he started to pull the trigger in panic.

"No!" Rhyme shouted.

The gunshot was deafening. Windows rattled and the falcons took off into the sky.

Sellitto scrambled for his weapon. The door burst open and Eliopolos's officers ran into the room, their own pistols drawn.

Ron Talbot, the tiny red hole in his temple, stood perfectly still for an instant, then dropped in a spiral to the ground.

"Oh, brother," said Mel Cooper, frozen in position, holding an evidence bag and staring down at his skinny, little .38 Smith & Wesson, held in Roland Bell's steady hand, pointing out from beside the tech's elbow. "Oh, my." The detective had eased up behind Cooper and slipped the weapon off the narrow belt holster on the back of the tech's belt. Bell had fired from the hip – well, from Cooper's hip.

Sachs rose to her feet and lifted her Glock out of Talbot's hand. She felt for a pulse, shook her head.

The wailing filled the room as Percey Clay dropped to her knees over the body and, sobbing, pounded her fist into Talbot's dense shoulder again and again. No one moved for a long moment. Then both Amelia Sachs and Roland Bell started toward her. They paused and it was Sachs who backed away and let the lanky detective put his arm around the petite woman and lead her from the body of her friend and enemy.

41

A little thunder, a sprinkling of spring rain late at night. The window was open wide – not the falcon window of course; Rhyme didn't like them disturbed – and the room was filled with cool evening air.

Amelia Sachs popped the cork and poured Cakebread chardonnay into Rhyme's tumbler and her glass.

She looked down and gave a faint laugh.

"I don't believe it."

On the computer beside the Clinitron was a chess program.

"You don't play games," she said. "I mean, I've *never* seen you play games."

"Hold on," he said to her.

On the screen: "*I did not understand what you said. Please say it again.*"

In a clear voice he said, "Rook to queen's bishop four. Checkmate."

A pause. The computer said, "*Congratulations.*" Followed by a digitized version of Sousa's *Washington Post* march.

"It's not for entertainment," he said churlishly. "Keeps the mind sharp. It's my Nautilus machine. You want to play sometime, Sachs?"

"I don't play chess," she said after a swallow of the fine wine. "Some damn knight goes for my king I'd rather blow him away than figure out how to outsmart him. How much did they find?"

"Money? That Talbot had hidden? Over five million."

After the auditors had gone through the second set of books, the real books, they found that Hudson Air was an extremely profitable company. Losing the aircraft and the U.S. Medical contract would sting but there was plenty of cash to keep the company, as Percey told him, "aloft."

"Where's the Dancer?"

"In SD."

Special Detention was a little known facility in the criminal courts building. Rhyme had never seen the place – few cops had – but in thirty-five years no one had ever broken out of it.

"Coped his talons pretty good," Percey Clay had said when Rhyme told her this. Which meant, she explained, the filing down of a hunting falcon's claws.

Rhyme – given his special interest in the case – insisted on being informed about the Dancer's tenure in SP. He'd heard from the guards that he'd been asking about windows in the facility, what floor they were on, what part of town the facility was located in.

"Do I smell a service station nearby?" he'd asked cryptically.

When he'd heard this, Rhyme had immediately called Lon Sellitto and asked him to call the head of the detention center and double the guard.

Amelia Sachs took another fortifying sip of wine and whatever was coming was coming now.

She inhaled deeply then blurted, "Rhyme, you should go for it." Another sip. "I wasn't sure I was going to say that."

"Beg pardon?"

"She's right for you. It could be real good."

They rarely had trouble looking at each other's eyes. But, rough water ahead, Sachs looked down at the floor.

What *was* this all about?

When she glanced up and saw her words weren't registering she said, "I know how you feel about her. And she doesn't admit it but I know how she feels about you."

"Who?"

"You know who. Percey Clay. You're thinking she's a widow, she's not going to want someone in her life right now. But . . . you heard what Talbot said – Carney had a girlfriend. A woman in the office. Percey knew about it. They stayed together because they were friends. And because of the company."

"I never—"

"Go for it, Rhyme. Come on. I really mean that. You think it'd never work. But she doesn't care about your situation. Hell, look at what she said the other day. She was right – you're both real similar."

There were times when you just needed to lift your hands and let them flop into your lap in frustration. Rhyme settled for nestling his head in his luxurious down pillow. "Sachs, where on earth did you get this idea?"

"Oh, please. It's so obvious. I've seen how you've been since she showed up. How you look at her. How obsessed you've been to save her. I know what's going on."

"What *is* going on?"

"She's like Claire Trilling, the woman who left you a few years ago. That's who you want."

Oh . . . He nodded. So that's it.

He smiled. Said, "Sure, Sachs, I have been thinking about Claire a lot the past few days. I lied when I said I hadn't been."

"Whenever you mentioned her I could tell you were still in love with her. I know that after the accident she never saw you again. I figured it was still an open book for you. Like me and Nick after he left me. You met Percey and she reminded you of Claire all over again. You realized that you could be with someone again. With her, I mean. Not . . . not with me. Hey, that's life."

"Sachs," he began, "it's not Percey you should've been jealous of. She's not the one that booted you out of bed the other night."

"No?"

"It was the Dancer."

Another splash of wine in her glass. She swirled it and looked down at the pale liquid. "I don't understand."

"The other night?" He sighed. "I had to draw the line between us, Sachs. I'm already too close to you for my own good. If we're going to keep working together, I had to keep that barrier up. Don't you see? I can't be close to you, not *that* close, and still send you in harm's way. I can't let it happen again."

"*Again?*" She was frowning, then her face flooded with understanding.

Ah, that's my Amelia, he thought. A fine criminalist. A good shot. And she's quick as a fox.

"Oh, no, Lincoln, Claire was . . ."

He was nodding. "She was the tech I assigned to search the crime scene in Wall Street after the Dancer's hit five years ago. She was the one who rcached into the wastebasket and pulled out the paper that set off the bomb."

Which is why he'd been so obsessed with the man. Why he'd wanted, so uncharacteristically, to debrief the killer. He wanted to catch the man who'd killed his lover. Wanted to know all about him.

It was revenge, undiluted revenge. When Lon Sellitto – who'd known about Claire – had wondered if it might not be better for Percey and Hale to leave town, he was asking if Rhyme's personal feelings weren't intruding into the case.

Well, yes, they were. But Lincoln Rhyme, for all the overwhelming stasis of his present life, was as much a hunter as the falcons on his window ledge. Every criminalist is. And when he scented his prey he wouldn't be stopped.

"So, that's it, Sachs. It has nothing to do with Percey. And as much as I wanted you to spend the night – to spend every night – I can't risk loving you any more than I do."

It was so astonishing – bewildering – to Lincoln Rhyme to be having this conversation. After the accident he'd come to believe that the oak beam that had snapped his spine actually did its worst damage to his heart, killing all sensation within it. And his ability to love and be loved were as crushed as the thin fiber of his spinal cord. But the other night, Sachs close to him, he'd realized how wrong he was.

"You understand, don't you, Amelia?" Rhyme whispered.

"Last names only," she said, smiling, walking close to the bed.

She bent down and kissed him on the mouth. He pressed back into his pillow for a moment then returned the kiss.

"No, no," he persisted. But he kissed her hard once again.

Her purse dropped to the floor. Her jacket and watch went on the bedside table. Followed by the last of the fashion accessories to come off – her Glock 9.

They kissed again.

But he pulled away. "Sachs . . . It's too risky!"

"God don't give out certain," she said, their eyes locked on each other's. Then she stood and walked across the room to the light switch.

"Wait," he said.

She paused, looked back. Her red hair fell over her face, obscuring one eye.

Into the microphone hanging on the bed frame Rhyme commanded, "Lights out."

The room went dark.